THE FALL OF GONDOLIN

Works by J.R.R. Tolkien

THE HOBBIT
LEAF BY NIGGLE
ON FAIRY-STORIES
FARMER GILES OF HAM
THE HOMECOMING OF BEORHTNOTH
THE LORD OF THE RINGS
THE ADVENTURES OF TOM BOMBADIL
THE ROAD GOES EVER ON (WITH DONALD SWANN)
SMITH OF WOOTTON MAJOR

Works published posthumously

SIR GAWAIN AND THE GREEN KNIGHT, PEARL AND SIR ORFEO*
THE FATHER CHRISTMAS LETTERS
THE SILMARILLION*
PICTURES BY J.R.R. TOLKIEN*
UNFINISHED TALES*
THE LETTERS OF J.R.R. TOLKIEN*
FINN AND HENGEST
MR BLISS
THE MONSTERS AND THE CRITICS & OTHER ESSAYS*
ROVERANDOM
THE CHILDREN OF HÚRIN*
THE LEGEND OF SIGURD AND GUDRÚN*
THE FALL OF ARTHUR*
BEOWULF: A TRANSLATION AND COMMENTARY*
THE STORY OF KULLERVO
BEREN AND LÚTHIEN*

The History of Middle-earth – by Christopher Tolkien

I THE BOOK OF LOST TALES, PART ONE
II THE BOOK OF LOST TALES, PART TWO
III THE LAYS OF BELERIAND
IV THE SHAPING OF MIDDLE-EARTH
V THE LOST ROAD AND OTHER WRITINGS
VI THE RETURN OF THE SHADOW
VII THE TREASON OF ISENGARD
VIII THE WAR OF THE RING
IX SAURON DEFEATED
X MORGOTH'S RING
XI THE WAR OF THE JEWELS
XII THE PEOPLES OF MIDDLE-EARTH

* Edited by Christopher Tolkien

THE FALL OF GONDOLIN

BY

J.R.R. Tolkien

Edited by Christopher Tolkien

With illustrations by Alan Lee

HOUGHTON MIFFLIN HARCOURT
BOSTON   NEW YORK

First U.S. edition

For information about permission to reproduce selections from this book, write
to trade.permissions@hmhco.com or to Permissions, Houghton Mifflin Harcourt
Publishing Company, 3 Park Avenue, 19th Floor, New York, New York 10016.

hmhco.com

® and "Tolkien,"® "The Fall of Gondolin"® are registered trademarks of
The Tolkien Estate Limited

First published by HarperCollins*Publishers* 2018

Library of Congress Cataloging-in-Publication Data is available.
ISBN 978-1-328-61304-2

Printed in the United States of America
22 23 24 25 26 LSB 9 8 7 6 5

To my family

CONTENTS

PLATES

8

PREFACE

In my preface to *Beren and Lúthien* I remarked that 'in my ninety-third year this is (presumptively) the last book in the long series of editions of my father's writings'. I used the word 'presumptively' because at that time I thought hazily of treating in the same way as *Beren and Lúthien* the third of my father's 'Great Tales', *The Fall of Gondolin*. But I thought this very improbable, and I 'presumed' therefore that *Beren and Lúthien* would be my last. The presumption proved wrong, however, and I must now say that 'in my ninety-fourth year *The Fall of Gondolin* is (indubitably) the last'.

In this book one sees, from the complex narrative of many strands in various texts, how Middle-earth moved towards the end of the First Age, and how my father's perception of this history that he had conceived unfolded through long years until at last, in what was to be its finest form, it foundered.

The story of Middle-earth in the Elder Days was always a

shifting structure. My *History* of that age, so long and complex as it is, owes its length and complexity to this endless welling up: a new portrayal, a new motive, a new name, above all new associations. My father, as the Maker, ponders the large history, and as he writes he becomes aware of a new element that has entered the story. I will illustrate this by a very brief but notable example, which may stand for many.

An essential feature of the story of the Fall of Gondolin was the journey that the Man, Tuor, undertook with his companion Voronwë to find the Hidden Elvish City of Gondolin. My father told of this very briefly in the original Tale, without any noteworthy event, indeed no event at all; but in the final version, in which the journey was much elaborated, one morning out in the wilderness they heard a cry in the woods. We might almost say, 'he' heard a cry in the woods, sudden and unexpected.* A tall man clothed in black and holding a long black sword then appeared and came towards them, calling out a name as if he were searching for one who was lost. But without any speech he passed them by.

Tuor and Voronwë knew nothing to explain this extraordinary sight; but the Maker of the history knows very well who he was. He was none other than the far-famed Túrin Turambar, who was the first cousin of Tuor, and he was fleeing from the ruin – unknown to Tuor and Voronwë

---

* To show that this is not fanciful, in his letter to me of 6 May 1944 my father wrote: 'A new character has come on the scene (I am sure I did not invent him, I did not even want him, though I like him, but there he came walking into the woods of Ithilien): Faramir, the brother of Boromir.'

– of the city of Nargothrond. Here is a breath of one of the great stories of Middle-earth. Túrin's flight from Nargothrond is told in *The Children of Húrin* (my edition, pp.180–1), but with no mention of this meeting, unknown to either of those kinsmen, and never repeated.

To illustrate the transformations that took place as time passed nothing is more striking than the portrayal of the god Ulmo as originally seen, sitting among the reeds and making music at twilight by the river Sirion, but many years later the lord of all the waters of the world rises out of the great storm of the sea at Vinyamar. Ulmo does indeed stand at the centre of the great myth. With Valinor largely opposed to him, the great God nonetheless mysteriously achieves his end.

Looking back over my work, now concluded after some forty years, I believe that my underlying purpose was at least in part to try to give more prominence to the nature of 'The Silmarillion' and its vital existence in relation to *The Lord of the Rings* – thinking of it rather as the *First Age* of my father's world of Middle-earth and Valinor.

There was indeed *The Silmarillion* that I published in 1977, but this was composed, one might even say 'contrived' to produce narrative coherence, many years after *The Lord of the Rings*. It could seem 'isolated', as it were, this large work in a lofty style, supposedly descending from a very remote past, with little of the power and immediacy of *The Lord of the Rings*. This was no doubt inescapable, in the form in which I undertook it, for the narrative of the First Age was of a radically different literary and imaginative nature. Nevertheless, I knew that long before, when *The Lord of the Rings* was finished but well before its publication, my father had expressed a deep wish and conviction that the First Age and the Third Age (the world of *The Lord of the Rings*) should be treated, *and published*, as elements, or parts, *of the same work*.

In the chapter of this book, *The Evolution of the Story*, I have printed parts of a long and very revealing letter that he wrote to his publisher, Sir Stanley Unwin, in February 1950, very soon after the actual writing of *The Lord of the Rings* had reached its end, in which he unburdened his mind on this matter. At that time he portrayed himself self-mockingly as horrified when he contemplated 'this impracticable monster of some six hundred thousand words' – the more especially when the publishers were expecting what they had demanded, a sequel to *The Hobbit*, while this new book (he said) was 'really a sequel to *The Silmarillion*'.

He never modified his opinion. He even wrote of *The Silmarillion* and *The Lord of the Rings* as 'one long Saga of the Jewels and the Rings'. He held out against the separate publication *of either work* on those grounds. But in the end he was defeated, as will be seen in *The Evolution of the Story*, recognizing that there was no hope that his wish would be granted: and he consented to the publication of *The Lord of the Rings* alone.

After the publication of *The Silmarillion* I turned to an investigation, lasting many years, of the entire collection of manuscripts that he had left to me. In *The History of Middle-earth* I restricted myself as a general principle to 'drive the horses abreast', so to speak: not story by story through the years in their own paths, but rather the whole narrative movement as it evolved through the years. As I observed in the foreword to the first volume of the *History*,

> the author's vision of his own vision underwent a continual slow shifting, shedding and enlarging: only in *The Hobbit* and *The Lord of the Rings* did parts of it emerge to become fixed in print, in his own lifetime. The study of Middle-earth and Valinor is thus complex; for the object of the study was not stable, but existed, as it were, 'longitudinally' in time (the author's lifetime), and not only 'transversely' in time, as a printed book that undergoes no essential further change.

Thus it comes about that from the nature of the work the *History* is often difficult to follow. When the time had come, as I supposed, to end at last this long series of editions it occurred to me to try out, as best as I could, a different mode: to follow, using previously published texts, one single particular narrative from its earliest existing form and throughout its later development: hence *Beren and Lúthien*. In my edition of *The Children of Húrin* (2007) I did indeed describe in an appendix the chief alterations to the narrative in successive versions; but in *Beren and Lúthien* I actually cited earlier texts in full, beginning with the earliest form in the *Lost Tales*. Now that it is certain that the present book is the last, I have adopted the same curious form in *The Fall of Gondolin*.

In this mode there come to light passages, or even full-fledged conceptions, that were later abandoned; thus in *Beren and Lúthien* the commanding if brief entrance of Tevildo, Prince of Cats. *The Fall of Gondolin* is unique in this respect. In the original version of the Tale the overwhelming attack on Gondolin with its unimagined new weapons is seen with such clarity and in such detail that the very names are given of the places in the city where the buildings were burnt down or where celebrated warriors died. In the later versions the destruction and fighting is reduced to a paragraph.

That the Ages of Middle-earth are conjoint can be brought home most immediately by the reappearance – in their persons, and not merely as memories – of the figures of the Elder Days in *The Lord of the Rings*. Very old indeed was the Ent, Treebeard; the Ents were the most ancient people surviving in the Third Age. As he carried Meriadoc and Peregrin through the forest of Fangorn he chanted to them:

> In the willow-meads of Tasarinan I walked in the Spring.
> Ah! the sight and the smell of the Spring in Nan-tasarion!

It was very long indeed before Treebeard sang to the hobbits in Fangorn that Ulmo Lord of Waters came to Middle-earth to speak to Tuor in Tasarinan, the Land of Willows. Or again, at the end of the story we read of Elrond and Elros, sons of Eärendel, in a later age the master of Rivendell and the first king of Númenor: here they are very young, taken into protection by a son of Fëanor.

*

14

But here I will introduce, as an emblem of the Ages, the figure of Círdan, the Shipwright. He was the bearer of Narya, the Ring of Fire, one of the Three Rings of the Elves, until he surrendered it to Gandalf; of him it was said that 'he saw further and deeper than any other in Middle-earth'. In the First Age he was the lord of the havens of Brithombar and Eglarest on the coasts of Beleriand, and when they were destroyed by Morgoth after the Battle of Unnumbered Tears he escaped with a remnant of his people to the Isle of Balar. There and at the mouths of Sirion he turned again to the building of ships, and at the request of King Turgon of Gondolin he built seven. These ships sailed into the West, but no message from any one of them ever came back until the last. In that ship was Voronwë, sent out from Gondolin, who survived shipwreck and became the guide and companion of Tuor on their great journey to the Hidden City.

To Gandalf Círdan declared long after, when he gave him the Ring of Fire: 'But as for me, my heart is with the Sea, and I will dwell by the grey shores, guarding the Havens until the last ship sails.' So Círdan appears for the last time on the last day of the Third Age. When Elrond and Galadriel, with Bilbo and Frodo, rode up to the gates of the Grey Havens, where Gandalf was awaiting them,

Círdan the Shipwright came forth to greet them. Very tall he was, and his beard was long, and he was grey and old, save that his eyes were keen as stars; and he looked at them and bowed, and said: 'All is now ready.' Then Círdan led them to the Havens, and there was a white ship lying . . .

After farewells were spoken those who were departing went aboard:

> and the sails were drawn up, and the wind blew, and slowly the ship slipped away down the long grey firth; and the light of the glass of Galadriel that Frodo bore glimmered and was lost. And the ship went out into the High Sea and passed on into the West . . .

thus following the path of Tuor and Idril as the end of the First Age approached, who 'set sail into the sunset and the West, and came no more into any tale or song.'

*

The tale of *The Fall of Gondolin* gathers as it proceeds many glancing references to other stories, other places, and other times: to events in the past that govern actions and presumptions in the present time of the tale. The impulse, in such cases, to offer explanation, or at least some enlightenment, is strong; but keeping in mind the purpose of the book I have not peppered the texts with small superimposed numbers leading to notes. What I have aimed at is to provide some assistance of this nature in forms that can be readily neglected if desired.

In the first place, I have in the 'Prologue' introduced a citation from my father's *Sketch of the Mythology* of 1926, in order to provide a picture, in his words, of the World from its beginning to the events leading finally to the foundation of Gondolin. Further, I have used the List of Names in many cases for statements a good deal fuller than the name implies; and I have also introduced, after the List of Names, a number of separate notes on very varied topics, ranging from the creation of the World to the significance of the name Eärendel and the Prophecy of Mandos.

Very intractable of course is the treatment of the changing of names, or of the forms of names. This is the more complex since a particular form is by no means necessarily an indication of the relative date of the composition in which it occurs. My father would make the same change in a text at quite different times, when he noticed the need for it. I have not aimed at consistency throughout the book: that is to say, neither settling for one form throughout, nor in every case following that in the manuscript, but allowing such variation as seems best. Thus I retain *Ylmir* when it occurs for *Ulmo*, since it is a regular occurrence of a linguistic nature, but give always *Thorondor* for *Thorndor*, 'King of Eagles', since my father was clearly intending to change it throughout.

Lastly, I have arranged the content of the book in a manner distinct from that in *Beren and Lúthien*. The texts of the Tale appear first, in succession and with little or no commentary. An account of the evolution of the story then follows, with a discussion of my father's profoundly saddening abandonment of the last version of the *Tale* at the moment when Tuor passed through the Last Gate of Gondolin.

I will end by repeating what I wrote nearly forty years ago.

It is the remarkable fact that the only full account that my father ever wrote of the story of Tuor's sojourn in Gondolin, his union with Idril Celebrindal, the birth of Eärendel, the treachery of Maeglin, the sack of the city, and the escape of the fugitives – a story that was a central element in his imagination of the First Age – was the narrative composed in his youth.

Gondolin and Nargothrond were each made once, and not remade. They remained powerful sources and images – the more powerful, perhaps, because never remade, and never remade, perhaps, because so powerful.

Though he set out to remake Gondolin he never reached the city again: after climbing the endless slope of the Orfalch Echor and passing through the long line of heraldic gates he paused with Tuor at the vision of Gondolin amid the plain, and never recrossed Tumladen.

The publication 'in its own history' of the third and last of the Great Tales is the occasion for me to write a few words in honour of the work of Alan Lee, who has illustrated each Tale in turn. He has brought to this task a deep perception of the inner nature of scene and event that he has chosen from the great range of the Elder Days.

Thus, he has seen, and shown, in *The Children of Húrin*, the captive Húrin, chained to a stone chair on Thangorodrim, listening to Morgoth's terrible curse. He has seen, and shown, in *Beren and Lúthien*, the last of Fëanor's sons seated motionless on their horses and gazing at the new star in the western sky, which is the Silmaril, for which so many lives had been taken. And in *The Fall of Gondolin* he has stood beside Tuor and with him marvelled at the sight of the Hidden City, for which he has journeyed so far.

Finally, I am very grateful to Chris Smith of Harper-Collins for the exceptional help that he has given to me in the preparation of the detail of the book, especially in his assiduous accuracy, drawing on his knowledge both of the demands of publication and the nature of the book. To my wife Baillie also: without her unwavering support during the long time the book has been in the making it would never have been made. I would also thank all those who generously wrote to me when it appeared that *Beren and Lúthien* was to be my last book.

ILLUSTRATIONS

At the end of the book there will be found a map, and genealogies of the House of Bëor and the princes of the Noldor. These are taken from *The Children of Húrin*, with some minor alterations.

PROLOGUE

I will begin this book by returning to the quotation that I used to open *Beren and Lúthien*: a letter written by my father in 1964, in which he said that 'out of my head' he wrote *The Fall of Gondolin* 'during sick-leave from the army in 1917', and the original version of *Beren and Lúthien* in the same year.

There is some doubt about the year, arising from other references made by my father. In a letter of June 1955 he wrote '*The Fall of Gondolin* (and the birth of Eärendil) was written in hospital and on leave after surviving the Battle of the Somme in 1916'; and in a letter to W.H. Auden of the same year he dated it to 'sick-leave at the end of 1916'. The earliest reference of his that I know of was in a letter to me of 30 April 1944, commiserating with me on my experiences of that time. 'I first began' (he said) 'to write The History of the Gnomes* in army huts, crowded, filled with the noise of

---

* For the use of *Gnomes* for the people of the Elves named the Noldor (earlier Noldoli) see *Beren and Lúthien* pp.32–3.

gramophones'. This does not sound like sick-leave: but it may be that he began the writing before he went on leave.

Very important, however, in the context of this book, was what he said of *The Fall of Gondolin* in his letter to W.H. Auden of 1955: it was 'the first real story of this imaginary world.'

My father's treatment of the original text of *The Fall of Gondolin* was unlike that of *The Tale of Tinúviel*, where he erased the first, pencilled manuscript and wrote a new version in its place. In this case he did indeed extensively revise the first draft of the Tale, but rather than erase it he wrote a revised text in ink on the pencilled original, increasing the multiplicity of change as he progressed. It can be seen from passages where the underlying text is legible that he was following the first version fairly closely.

On this basis my mother made a fair copy, notably exact in view of the difficulties now presented by the text. Subsequently my father made many changes to this copy, by no means all at the same time. Since it is not my purpose in this book to enter into the textual complexities that all but invariably accompany the study of his works, the text that I give here is my mother's, including the changes made to it.

It must however be mentioned in this connection that many of the changes to the original text had been made before my father, in the spring of 1920, read the Tale to the Essay Club of Exeter College at Oxford. In his introductory and apologetic words, explaining his choice of this work in place of an 'Essay', he said of it: 'It has of course never seen the light before. A complete cycle of events in an Elfinesse of my own imagining has for some time past grown up (rather, has been constructed) in my mind. Some of the episodes have been scribbled down. This tale is not the best of them, but it is the only one that has so far been revised at all and that, insufficient as that revision has been, I dare read aloud.'

The original title of the tale was *Tuor and the Exiles of Gondolin*, but my father always later called it *The Fall of Gondolin*, and I have done the same. In the manuscript the title is followed by the words 'which bringeth in the Great Tale of Eärendel'. The teller of the tale in the Lonely Isle, on which see *Beren and Lúthien* pp.30–31, was Littleheart (Ilfiniol), son of that Bronweg (Voronwë) who plays an important part in the Tale.

It is in the nature of this, the third of the 'Great Tales' of the Elder Days, that the massive change in the world of Gods and Elves that had taken place should bear upon the immediate narrative of the Fall of Gondolin – and is indeed a part of it. A brief account of those events is needed; and rather than write one myself I think it far better to use my father's own condensed, and characteristic, work. This is found in the 'Original *Silmarillion*' (also '*A Sketch of the Mythology*'), as he himself called it, which can be dated to 1926, and subsequently revised. I used this work in *Beren and Lúthien*, and again in this book as an element in the evolution of the tale of *The Fall of Gondolin*; but I use it here for the purpose of providing a concise account of the history before

Gondolin came into being: it also has the advantage of itself deriving from a very early period.

In view of the purpose of its inclusion I have omitted passages that are not here relevant, and here and there made other minor modifications and additions for the sake of clarity. My text opens at the point where the original *'Sketch'* begins.

After the despatch of the Nine Valar for the governance of the world Morgoth (Demon of Dark) rebels against the overlordship of Manwë, overthrows the lamps set up to illumine the world, and floods the isle of Almaren where the Valar (or Gods) dwelt. He fortifies a palace of dungeons in the North. The Valar remove to the uttermost West, bordered by the Outer Seas and the final Wall, and eastward by the towering Mountains of Valinor which the Gods built. In Valinor they gather all light and beautiful things, and build their mansions, gardens, and city, but Manwë and his wife Varda have halls upon the highest mountain (Taniquetil) whence they can see across the world to the dark East. Yavanna Palúrien plants the Two Trees in the middle of the plain of Valinor outside the gates of the city of Valmar. They grow under her songs, and one has dark green leaves with shining silver beneath, and white blossoms like the cherry from which a dew of silver light falls; the other has gold-en-edged leaves of young green like the beech and yellow blossom like the hanging blossoms of laburnum which give out heat and blazing light. Each tree waxes for seven hours to full glory and then wanes for seven; twice a day therefore comes a time of softer light when each tree is faint and their light is mingled.

The Outer Lands [Middle-earth] are in darkness. The growth of things was checked when Morgoth quenched the lamps. There are forests of darkness, of yew and fir and ivy. There Oromë sometimes hunts, but in the North Morgoth and his demonic broods (Balrogs) and the Orcs (Goblins, also called *Glamhoth* or people of hate) hold sway. Varda looks on the darkness and is moved, and taking all the hoarded light of Silpion, the White Tree, she makes and strews the stars.

At the making of the stars the children of Earth awake – the Eldar (or Elves). They are found by Oromë dwelling by the star-lit pool, Cuiviénen, Water of Awakening, in the East. He rides home to Valinor filled with their beauty and tells the Valar, who are reminded of their duty to the Earth, since they came thither knowing that their office was to govern it for the two races of Earth who should after come each in appointed time. There follows an expedition to the fortress of the North (Angband, Iron-hell), but this is now too strong for them to destroy. Morgoth is nonetheless taken captive, and consigned to the halls of Mandos who dwelt in the North of Valinor.

The Eldalië (people of the Elves) are invited to Valinor for fear of the evil things of Morgoth that still wandered in the dark. A great march is made by the Eldar from the East led by Oromë on his white horse. The Eldar are divided into three hosts, one under Ingwë after called the Quendi

(Light-elves), one after called the Noldoli (Gnomes or Deep-elves), one after called the Teleri (Sea-elves). Many of them are lost upon the march and wander in the woods of the world; becoming the various hosts of the Ilkorindi (Elves who never dwelt in Kôr in Valinor). The chief of these was Thingol, who heard Melian and her nightingales singing and was enchanted and fell asleep for an age. Melian was one of the divine maidens of the Vala Lórien who sometimes wandered into the outer world. Melian and Thingol became Queen and King of woodland Elves in Doriath, living in a hall called the Thousand Caves.

The other Elves came to the ultimate shores of the West. In the North these in those days sloped westward in the North until only a narrow sea divided them from the land of the Gods, and this narrow sea was filled with grinding ice. But at the point to which the Elf-hosts came a wide dark sea stretched west.

There were two Valar of the Sea. Ulmo (Ylmir), the mightiest of all Valar next to Manwë, was lord of all waters, but dwelt often in Valinor, or in the Outer Seas. Ossë and the lady Uinen, whose tresses lay through all the sea, loved rather the seas of the world that washed the shores beneath the Mountains of Valinor. Ulmo uprooted the half-sunk island of Almaren where the Valar had first dwelt, and embarking on it the Noldoli and Quendi, who arrived first, bore them to Valinor. The Teleri dwelt some time by the shores of the sea awaiting him, and hence their love of it. While they were being also transported by Ulmo, Ossë in jealousy and out of love for their singing chained the island to the sea-bottom far out in the bay of Faërie whence the Mountains of Valinor could dimly be seen. No other land was near it, and it was called the Lonely Isle. There the Teleri dwelt a long age becoming different in tongue, and learning strange music from Ossë, who made the sea-birds for their delight.

The Gods gave a home in Valinor to the other Eldar. Because they longed even among the Tree-lit gardens of Valinor for a glimpse of the stars, a gap was made in the encircling mountains, and there in a deep valley a green hill, Kôr, was built. This was lit from the West by the Trees, to the East it looked out onto the Bay of Faërie and the Lonely Isle, and beyond to the Shadowy Seas. Thus some of the blessed light of Valinor filtered into the Outer Lands [Middle-earth], and falling on the Lonely Isle caused its western shores to grow green and fair.

On the top of Kôr the city of the Elves was built and was called Tûn. The Quendi became most beloved by Manwë and Varda, the Noldoli by Aulë (the Smith) and Mandos the Wise. The Noldoli invented gems and made them in count-less numbers, filling all Tûn with them, and all the halls of the Gods.

The greatest in skill and magic of the Noldoli was Finwë's elder son Fëanor.* He contrived three jewels (Silmarils)

---

* Finwë was the leader of the Noldoli on the great journey from Cuiviénen. His eldest son was Fëanor; his second son Fingolfin, father of Fingon and Turgon; his third son Finarfin, father of Finrod Felagund.

wherein a living fire combined of the light of the Two Trees was set, they shone of their own light, impure hands were burned by them.

The Teleri seeing afar the light of Valinor were torn between desire to rejoin their kindred and to dwell by the sea. Ulmo taught them craft of boat-building. Ossë yielding gave them swans, and harnessing many swans to their boats they sailed to Valinor, and dwelt there on the shores where they could see the light of the Trees, and go to Valmar if they wished, but could sail and dance in the waters touched to light by the radiance that came out past Kôr. The other Eldar gave them many gems, especially opals and diamonds and other pale crystals which were strewn upon the beaches of the Bay of Faërie. They themselves invented pearls. Their chief town was Swanhaven upon the shores northward of the pass of Kôr.

The Gods were now beguiled by Morgoth, who having passed seven ages in the prisons of Mandos in gradually lightened pain came before the conclave of the Gods in due course. He looks with greed and malice upon the Eldar, who also sit there about the knees of the Gods, and lusts especially after the jewels. He dissembles his hatred and desire for revenge. He is allowed a humble dwelling in Valinor, and after a while goes freely about, only Ulmo foreboding ill, while Tulkas the strong, who first captured him, watches him. Morgoth helps the Eldar in many deeds, but slowly poisons their peace with lies.

He suggests that the Gods brought them to Valinor out

of jealousy, for fear their marvellous skill, and magic, and beauty, should grow too strong for them outside in the world. The Quendi and Teleri are little moved, but the Noldoli, the wisest of the Elves, become affected. They begin at whiles to murmur against the Gods and their kindred; they are filled with vanity of their skill.

Most of all does Morgoth fan the flames of the heart of Fëanor, but all the while he lusts for the immortal Silmarils, although Fëanor has cursed for ever anyone, God or Elf or mortal that shall come hereafter, who touches them. Morgoth lying tells Fëanor that Fingolfin and his son Fingon are plotting to usurp the leadership of the Gnomes from Fëanor and his sons, and to gain the Silmarils. A quarrel breaks out between the sons of Finwë. Fëanor is summoned before the Gods, and the lies of Morgoth laid bare. Fëanor is banished from Tûn, and with him goes Finwë who loves Fëanor best of his sons, and many of the Gnomes. They build a Treasury northward in Valinor in the hills near Mandos' halls. Fingolfin rules the Gnomes that are left in Tûn. Thus Morgoth's words seem justified and the bitterness he sowed goes on after his words are disproved.

Tulkas is sent to put Morgoth in chains once more, but he escapes through the pass of Kôr into the dark region beneath the feet of Taniquetil called Arvalin, where the shadow is thickest in all the world. There he finds Ungoliant, Gloomweaver, who dwells in a cleft in the mountains, and sucks up light or shining things to spin them out again in webs of black and choking darkness, fog, and gloom. With Ungoliant he plots revenge. Only a terrible reward will bring her to dare the dangers of Valinor or the sight of the Gods. She weaves a dense gloom about her to protect her and swings on cords from pinnacle to pinnacle till she has scaled the highest peak of the mountains in the south of Valinor (little guarded because of their height and their distance from the old fortress of Morgoth). She makes a ladder that Morgoth can scale. They creep into Valinor. Morgoth stabs the Trees and Ungoliant sucks up their juices, belching forth clouds of blackness. The Trees succumb slowly to the poisoned sword, and to the venomous lips of Ungoliant.

The Gods are dismayed by a twilight at midday, and vapours of black float in about the ways of the city. They are too late. The Trees die while they wail about them. But Tulkas and Oromë and many others hunt on horseback in the gathering gloom for Morgoth. Wherever Morgoth goes there the confusing darkness is greatest owing to the webs of Ungoliant. Gnomes from the Treasury of Finwë come in and report that Morgoth is assisted by a spider of darkness. They had seen them making for the North. Morgoth had stayed his flight at the Treasury, slain Finwë and many of his men, and carried off the Silmarils and a vast hoard of the most splendid jewels of the Elves.

In the meanwhile Morgoth escapes by Ungoliant's aid northward and crosses the Grinding Ice. When he has re-gained the northern regions of the world Ungoliant summons him to pay the other half of her reward. The first half was the sap of the Trees of Light. Now she claims one half of the jewels. Morgoth yields them up and she devours them. She is now become monstrous, but he will not give her any share in the Silmarils. She enmeshes him in a black web, but he is rescued by the Balrogs with whips of flame, and the hosts of the Orcs; and Ungoliant goes away into the uttermost South.

Morgoth returns to Angband, and his power and the numbers of his demons and Orcs becomes countless. He forges an iron crown and sets therein the Silmarils, though his hands are burned black by them, and he is never again free from the pain of the burning. The crown he never leaves off for a moment, and he never leaves the deep dungeons of his fortress, governing his vast armies from his deep throne.

When it became clear that Morgoth had escaped the Gods assemble about the dead Trees and sit in the darkness stricken and dumb for a long while, caring about nothing. The day which Morgoth chose for his attack was a day of festival throughout Valinor. Upon this day it was the custom of the chief Valar and many of the Elves, especially the Quendi, to climb the long winding paths in endless procession to Manwë's halls upon Taniquetil. All the Quendi and some of the Noldoli (who under Fingolfin dwelt still in Tûn) had gone to Taniquetil, and were singing upon its topmost height when the watchers from afar descried the fading of the Trees. Most of the Noldoli were in the plain, and the Teleri upon the shore. The fogs and darkness drift in now off the seas through the pass of Kôr as the Trees die. Fëanor summons the Gnomes to Tûn (rebelling against his banishment).

There is a vast concourse on the square on the summit
of Kôr about the tower of Ing, lit by torches. Fëanor makes
a violent speech, and though his wrath is for Morgoth his
words are in part the fruit of Morgoth's lies. He bids the
Gnomes fly in the darkness while the Gods are wrapped in
mourning, to seek freedom in the world and to seek out
Morgoth, now Valinor is no more blissful than the world
outside. Fingolfin and Fingon speak against him. The assembled Gnomes vote for flight, and Fingolfin and Fingon yield;
they will not desert their people, but they retain command
over a half of the Noldoli of Tûn.

The flight begins. The Teleri will not join. The Gnomes
cannot escape without boats, and do not dare to cross the
Grinding Ice. They attempt to seize the swan-ships in Swanhaven, and a fight ensues (the first between the races of
the Earth) in which many Teleri are slain, and their ships
carried off. A curse is pronounced upon the Gnomes, that
they shall after suffer often from treachery and the fear of
treachery among their own kindred in punishment for the
blood spilled at Swanhaven. They sail North along the coast
of Valinor. Mandos sends an emissary, who speaking from
a high cliff hails them as they sail by, and warns them
to return, and when they will not, speaks the 'Prophecy of
Mandos' concerning the fate of after days.

The Gnomes come to the narrowing of the seas, and
prepare to sail. While they are encamped upon the shore
Fëanor and his sons and people sail off taking with them all
the boats, and leave Fingolfin on the far shore treacherously,
thus beginning the curse of Swanhaven. They burn the boats

as soon as they land in the East of the world, and Fingolfin's people see the light in the sky. The same light also tells the Orcs of the landing.

Fingolfin's people wander miserably. Some under Fingolfin return to Valinor to seek the Gods' pardon. Fingon leads the main host North, and over the Grinding Ice. Many are lost.

Among the poems that my father embarked on during his years at the University of Leeds (most notably the *Lay of the Children of Húrin* in alliterative verse) was *The Flight of the Noldoli from Valinor*. This poem, also in alliterative verse, was abandoned after 150 lines. It is certain that it was written at Leeds, in (I think it extremely probable) 1925, the year in which he took up his appointment to the professorship of Anglo-Saxon at Oxford. From this poetic fragment I will cite a part, beginning at the 'vast concourse on the square on the summit of Kôr' where Fëanor 'made a violent speech', described in a passage of the *Sketch of the Mythology* p.32. The name *Finn* at lines 4 and 16 is the Gnomish form of Finwë, the father of Fëanor; *Bredhil* at line 49 the Gnomish name of Varda.

> But the Gnomes were numbered   by name and kin,
> marshalled and ordered   in the mighty square
> upon the crown of Kôr.   There cried aloud
> the fierce son of Finn.   Flaming torches
> he held and whirled   in his hands aloft,   5
> those hands whose craft   the hidden secret

knew, that none   Gnome or mortal
hath matched or mastered   in magic or in skill.
'Lo! slain is my sire   by the sword of fiends,
his death he has drunk   at the doors of his hall   10
and deep fastness,   where darkly hidden
the Three were guarded,   the things unmatched
that Gnome and Elf   and the Nine Valar
can never remake   or renew on earth,
recarve or rekindle   by craft or magic,   15
not Fëanor Finn's son   who fashioned them of yore –
the light is lost   whence he lit them first,
the fate of Faërie   hath found its hour.

Thus the witless wisdom   its reward hath earned
of the Gods' jealousy,   who guard us here   20
to serve them, sing to them   in our sweet cages,
to contrive them gems   and jewelled trinkets,
their leisure to please   with our loveliness,
while they waste and squander   work of ages,
nor can Morgoth master   in their mansions sitting   25
at countless councils.   Now come ye all,
who have courage and hope!   My call harken
to flight, to freedom   in far places!
The woods of the world   whose wide mansions
yet in darkness dream   drowned in slumber,   30
the pathless plains   and perilous shores
no moon yet shines on   nor mounting dawn
in dew and daylight   hath drenched for ever,
far better were these   for bold footsteps

than gardens of the Gods   gloom-encircled   35
with idleness filled   and empty days.
Yea! though the light lit them   and the loveliness
beyond heart's desire   that hath held us slaves
here long and long.   But that light is dead.
Our gems are gone,   our jewels ravished;   40
and the Three, my Three,   thrice-enchanted
globes of crystal   by gleam undying
illumined, lit   by living splendour
and all hues' essence,   their eager flame –
Morgoth has them   in his monstrous hold,   45
my Silmarils.   I swear here oaths
unbreakable bonds   to bind me ever,
by Timbrenting   and the timeless halls
of Bredhil the Blessed   that abides thereon –
may she hear and heed –   to hunt endlessly   50
unwearying unwavering   through world and sea,
through leaguered lands,   lonely mountains,
over fens and forest   and the fearful snows,
till I find those fair ones,   where the fate is hid
of the folk of Elfland   and their fortune locked,   55
where alone now lies   the light divine.'

Then his sons beside him,   the seven kinsmen,
crafty Curufin,   Celegorm the fair,
Damrod and Díriel   and dark Cranthir,
Maglor the mighty,   and Maidros tall   60
(the eldest, whose ardour   yet more eager burnt
than his father's flame,   than Fëanor's wrath;

35

him fate awaited   with fell purpose),
these leapt with laughter   their lord beside,
with linkéd hands   there lightly took   65
the oath unbreakable;   blood thereafter
it spilled like a sea   and spent the swords
of endless armies,   nor hath ended yet.

*

The Tale of

THE FALL OF GONDOLIN

Then said Littleheart son of Bronweg: 'Know then that Tuor was a man who dwelt in very ancient days in that land of the North called Dor-lómin or the Land of Shadows, and of the Eldar the Noldoli know it best.

Now the folk whence Tuor came wandered the forests and fells and knew not and sang not of the sea; but Tuor dwelt not with them, and lived alone about that lake called Mithrim, now hunting in its woods, now making music beside its shores on his rugged harp of wood and the sinews of bears. Now many hearing of the power of his rough songs came from near and far to hearken to his harping, but Tuor left his singing and departed to lonely places. Here he learnt many strange things and got knowledge of the wandering Noldoli, who taught him much of their speech and lore; but he was not fated to dwell for ever in those woods.

Thereafter it is said that magic and destiny led him on a day to a cavernous opening down which a hidden river flowed from Mithrim. And Tuor entered that cavern seeking to learn its secret, but the waters of Mithrim drove him forward into the heart of the rock and he might not win back into the light. And this, it is said, was the will of Ulmo Lord of Waters at whose prompting the Noldoli had made that hidden way.

Then came the Noldoli to Tuor and guided him along dark passages amid the mountains until he came out in the light once more, and saw that the river flowed swiftly in a ravine of great depth with sides unscalable. Now Tuor desired no more to return but went ever forward, and the river led him always toward the west.

The sun rose behind his back and set before his face, and where the water foamed among many boulders or fell over falls there were at times rainbows woven across the ravine, but at evening its smooth sides would glow in the setting sun, and for these reasons Tuor called it Golden Cleft or the Gully of the Rainbow Roof, which is in the speech of the Gnomes Glorfalc or Cris Ilbranteloth.

Now Tuor journeyed here for three days, drinking the waters of the secret river and feeding on its fish; and these were of gold and blue and silver and of many wondrous shapes. At length the ravine widened, and ever as it opened its sides became lower and more rough, and the bed of the river more impeded with boulders against which the waters foamed and spouted. Long times would Tuor sit and gaze at the splashing water and listen to its voice, and then he would rise and leap onward from stone to stone singing as he went; or as the stars came out in the narrow strip of heaven above the gully he would raise echoes to answer the fierce twanging of his harp.

One day after a great journey of weary going Tuor at deep evening heard a cry, and he might not decide of what creature it came. Now he said: 'It is a fay-creature', now, 'Nay, 'tis but some small beast that waileth among the rocks'; or again it seemed to him that an unknown bird piped with a voice new to his ears and strangely sad – and because he had not heard the voice of any bird in all his wandering down Golden Cleft he was glad of the sound although it was mournful. On the next day at an hour of the morning he heard the same cry above his head, and looking up beheld three great white birds beating back up the gully on strong wing, and uttering cries like to the ones he had heard amid the dusk. Now these were the gulls, the birds of Ossë.

In this part of that riverway there were islets of rock amid the currents, and fallen rocks fringed with white sand at the gullyside, so that it was ill-going, and seeking a while Tuor found a spot where he might with labour scale the cliffs at last. Then came a fresh wind against his face, and he said: 'This is very good and like the drinking of wine,' but he knew not that he was near the confines of the Great Sea.

As he went along above the waters that ravine again drew together and the walls towered up, so that he fared on a high cliff-top, and there came a narrow neck, and this was full of noise. Then Tuor looking downward saw the greatest of marvels, for it seemed that a flood of angry water would come up the narrows and flow back against the river to its source, but that water which had come down from distant

Mithrim would still press on, and a wall of water rose nigh to the cliff-top, and it was crowned with foam and twisted by the winds. Then the waters of Mithrim were overthrown and the incoming flood swept roaring up the channel and whelmed the rocky islets and churned the white sand – so that Tuor fled and was afraid, who did not know the ways of the Sea; but the Ainur put it into his heart to climb from the gully when he did, or had he been whelmed in the incoming tide, and that was a fierce one by reason of a wind from the west. Then Tuor found himself in a rugged country bare of trees, and swept by a wind coming from the set of the sun, and all the shrubs and bushes leaned to the dawn because of the prevalence of that wind. And here for a while he wandered till he came to the black cliffs by the sea and saw the ocean and its waves for the first time, and at that hour the sun sank beyond the rim of Earth far out to sea, and he stood on the cliff-top with outspread arms, and his heart was filled with a longing very great indeed. Now some say that he was the first of Men to reach the Sea and look upon it and know the desire it brings; but I know not if they say well.

In those regions he set up his abode, dwelling in a cove sheltered by great sable rocks, whose floor was of white sand, save when the high flood partly overspread it with blue water; nor did foam or froth come there save at times of the direst tempest. There long he sojourned alone and roamed about the shore or fared over the rocks at the ebb, marvelling at the pools and the great weeds, the dripping caverns and the strange sea-fowl that he saw and came to know; but the rise and fall of the water and the voice of the waves was ever to him the greatest wonder and ever did it seem a new and unimaginable thing.

Now on the quiet waters of Mithrim over which the voice of the duck or moorhen would carry far he had fared much in a small boat with a prow fashioned like to the neck of a swan, and this he had lost on the day of his finding the hidden river. On the sea he adventured not as yet, though his heart was ever egging him with a strange longing thereto, and on quiet evenings when the sun went down beyond the edge of the sea it grew to a fierce desire.

Timber he had that came down the hidden river; a goodly wood it was, for the Noldoli hewed it in the forests of Dor-lómin and floated it to him of a purpose. But he built not as yet aught save a dwelling in a sheltered place of his cove, which tales among the Eldar since name Falasquil. This by slow labour he adorned with fair carvings of the beasts and trees and flowers and birds that he knew about the waters of Mithrim, and ever among them was the Swan the chief, for Tuor loved this emblem and it became the sign of himself, his kindred and folk thereafter. There he passed a very great while until the loneliness of the empty sea got into his heart, and even Tuor the solitary longed for the voice of men. Herewith the Ainur had something to do: for Ulmo loved Tuor.

One morning while casting his eye along the shore – and it was then the latest days of summer – Tuor saw three swans flying high and strong from the northward. Now these birds he had not before seen in these regions, and he took them for a sign, and said; 'Long has my heart been set on a journey far from here; lo! now at length I will follow these swans.' Behold, the swans dropped into the water of his cove and there swimming thrice about rose again and winged slowly south along the coast, and Tuor bearing his harp and spear followed them.

It was a great day's journey that Tuor put behind him that day; and he came ere evening to a region where trees again appeared, and the manner of the land through which he now fared differed greatly from those shores about Falasquil. There had Tuor known mighty cliffs beset with caverns and great spoutholes, and deep-walled coves, but from the cliff-tops a rugged land and flat ran bleakly back to where a blue rim far to the east spoke of distant hills. Now however did he see a long and sloping shore and stretches of sand, while the distant hills marched ever nearer to the margin of the sea, and their dark slopes were clad with pine or fir and about their feet sprang birches and ancient oaks. From the feet of the hills fresh torrents rushed down narrow chasms and so found the shores and the salt waves. Now some of these clefts Tuor might not overleap, and often was it ill-going in these places, but still he laboured on, for the swans fared ever before him, now circling suddenly, now speeding forward, but never coming to earth, and the rush of their strong-beating wings encouraged him.

It is told that in this manner Tuor fared onward for a great number of days, and that winter marched from the North somewhat speedier than he for all his tirelessness. Nevertheless came he without scathe of beast or weather at a time of

first spring to a river mouth. Now here was the land less
northerly and more kindly than about the issuing of Golden
Cleft, and moreover by a trend of the coast was the sea now
rather to the south of him than to the west, as he could mark
by the sun and stars; but he had kept his right hand always
to the sea.

The river flowed down a goodly channel and on its banks
were rich lands: grasses and moist meadow to the one side
and tree-grown slopes of the other; its waters met the sea
sluggishly and fought not as the waters of Mithrim in the
north. Long tongues of land lay islanded in its course covered
with reeds and bushy thicket, until further to seaward sandy
spits ran out; and these were places beloved by such a multitude of birds as Tuor had nowhere yet encountered. Their
piping and wailing and whistling filled the air; and here amid
their white wings Tuor lost sight of the three swans, nor saw
he them again.

Then did Tuor grow for a season weary of the sea, for the
buffeting of his travel had been sore. Nor was this without
Ulmo's devising, and that night the Noldoli came to him
and he arose from sleep. Guided by their blue lanterns he
found a way beside the river border, and strode so mightily
inland that when dawn filled the sky to his right hand lo!
the sea and its voice were far behind him, and the wind
came from before him so that its odour was not even in the
air. Thus came he soon to that region that has been called
Arlisgion 'the place of reeds', and this is in those lands that
are to the south of Dor-lómin and separated therefrom by
the Shadowy Mountains whose spurs run even to the sea.

From these mountains came this river, and of a great clearness and marvellous chill were its waters even at this place. Now this is a river most famous in the histories of Eldar and Noldoli and in all tongues is it named Sirion. Here Tuor rested a while until driven by desire he arose once more to journey further and further by many days' marches along the river borders. Full spring had not yet brought summer when he came to a region yet more lovely. Here the song of small birds shrilled about him with a music of loveliness, for there are no birds that sing like the songbirds of the Land of Willows; and to this region of wonder he had now come. Here the river wound in wide curves with low banks through a great plain of the sweetest grass and very long and green; willows of untold age were about its borders, and its wide bosom was strewn with water-lily leaves, whose flowers were not yet in the earliness of the year, but beneath the willows the green swords of the flaglilies were drawn, and sedges stood, and reeds in embattled array. Now there dwelt in these dark places a spirit of whispers, and it whispered to Tuor at dusk and he was loath to depart; and at morn for the glory of the unnumbered buttercups he was yet more loath, and he tarried.

Here saw he the first butterflies and was glad at the sight; and it is said that all butterflies and their kindred were born in the valley of the Land of Willows. Then came the summer and the time of moths and the warm evenings, and Tuor wondered at the multitude of flies, at their buzzing and the droning of the beetles and the hum of bees; and to all these things he gave names of his own, and wove the names into new songs on his old harp; and these songs were softer than his singing of old.

Then Ulmo grew in dread lest Tuor dwell for ever here and the great things of his design come not to fulfilment. Therefore he feared longer to trust Tuor's guidance to the Noldoli alone, who did service to him in secret, and out of fear of Melko wavered much. Nor were they strong against the magic of that place of willows, for very great was its enchantment.

Behold now Ulmo leapt upon his car before the doorway of his palace below the still waters of the Outer Sea; and his car was drawn by narwhal and sealion and was in fashion like a whale; and amidst the sounding of great conches he sped from Ulmonan. So great was the speed of his going that in days, and not in years without count as might be thought, he reached the mouth of the river. Up this his car might not fare without hurt to its water and its banks; therefore Ulmo, loving all rivers and this one more than most, went thence on foot, robed to the middle in mail like the scales of blue and silver fishes; but his hair was a bluish silver and his beard to his feet was of the same hue, and he bore neither helm nor crown. Beneath his mail fell the skirts of his kirtle of shimmering greens, and of what substance these were woven is not known, but whoso looked into the depths of their subtle colours seemed to behold the faint movements of deep waters shot with the stealthy lights of phosphorescent fish that live in the abyss. Girt was he with a rope of mighty pearls, and he was shod with mighty shoes of stone.

Thither he bore too his great instrument of music; and

this was of strange design, for it was made of many long twisted shells pierced with holes. Blowing therein and playing with his long fingers he made deep melodies of a magic greater than any other among musicians hath ever compassed on harp or lute, on lyre or pipe, or instruments of the bow. Then coming along the river he sat among the reeds at twilight and played upon his thing of shells; and it was nigh to those places where Tuor tarried. And Tuor hearkened and was stricken dumb. There he stood knee-deep in the grass and heard no more the hum of insects, nor the murmur of the river borders, and the odour of flowers entered not into his nostrils; but he heard the sound of waves and the wail of sea-birds, and his soul leapt for rocky places and the ledges that reek of fish, for the splash of the diving cormorant and those places where the sea bores into the black cliffs and yells aloud.

Then Ulmo arose and spoke to him and for dread he came near to death, for the depth of the voice of Ulmo is of the uttermost depth: even as deep as his eyes which are the deepest of all things. And Ulmo said: 'O Tuor of the lonely heart, I will not that thou dwell for ever in fair places of birds and flowers; nor would I lead thee through this pleasant land, but that so it must be. But fare now on thy destined journey and tarry not, for far from hence is thy weird set. Now must thou seek through the lands for the city of the folk called Gondothlim or the dwellers in stone, and the Noldoli shall escort thee thither in secret for fear of the spies of Melko. Words I will set to your mouth there, and there you shall abide awhile. Yet maybe thy life shall turn again to the mighty waters; and of a surety a child shall come of thee than whom no man shall know more of the uttermost deeps, be it of the sea or of the firmament of heaven.'

Then spoke Ulmo also to Tuor some of his design and desire, but thereof Tuor understood little at that time and feared greatly. Then Ulmo was wrapped in a mist as it were of sea-air in those inland places, and Tuor, with that music in his ears, would fain return to the regions of the Great Sea; yet remembering his bidding turned and went inland along the river, and so fared till day. Yet he that has heard the conches of Ulmo hears them call him till death, and so did Tuor find.

When day came he was weary and slept till it was nigh dusk again, and the Noldoli came to him and guided him. So fared he many days by dusk and dark and slept by day, and because of this it came afterwards that he remembered not over well the paths that he traversed in those times. Now Tuor and his guides held on untiring, and the land became one of rolling hills and the river wound about their feet, and there were many dales of exceeding pleasantness; but here the Noldoli became ill at ease. 'These,' said they, 'are the confines of those regions which Melko infesteth with his Goblins, the people of hate. Far to the north – yet alas not far enough, would they were ten thousand leagues – lie the Mountains of Iron where sits the power and terror of Melko, whose thralls we are. Indeed in this guiding of thee we do in secret from him, and did he know all our purposes the torment of the Balrogs would be ours.'

Falling then into such fear the Noldoli soon after left him and he fared alone amid the hills, and their going proved ill afterwards, for 'Melko has many eyes', it is said, and while Tuor fared with the Gnomes they took him twilight ways and by many secret tunnels through the hills. But now he became lost, and climbed often to the tops of knolls and hills scanning the lands about. Yet he might not see signs of any dwelling of folk, and indeed the city of the Gondothlim was not found with ease, seeing that Melko and his spies had not even yet discovered it. It is said nonetheless that at this time those spies got wind thus that the strange foot of Man had been set in those lands, and that for that Melko doubled his craft and watchfulness.

Now when the Gnomes out of fear deserted Tuor, one Voronwë or Bronweg followed afar off despite his fear, when chiding availed not to enhearten the others. Now Tuor had fallen into a great weariness and was sitting beside the rushing stream, and the sea-longing was about his heart, and he was minded once more to follow this river back to the wide waters and the roaring waves. But this Voronwë the faithful came up with him again, and standing by his ear said: 'O Tuor, think not that but thou shalt again one day see thy desire; arise now, and behold, I will not leave thee. I am not of the road-learned of the Noldoli, being a craftsman and maker of things made by hand of wood and of metal, and I joined not the band of escort till late. Yet of old have I heard whispers and sayings said in secret amid the weariness of thraldom, concerning a city where Noldoli might be free could they find the hidden way thereto; and we twain may without a doubt find a road to the City of Stone, where is that freedom of the Gondothlim.'

Know then that the Gondothlim were that kin of the Noldoli who alone escaped Melko's power when at the Battle of Unnumbered Tears he slew and enslaved their folk and wove spells about them and caused them to dwell in the Hells of Iron, faring thence at his will and bidding only.

Long time did Tuor and Voronwë seek for the city of that folk, until after many days they came upon a deep dale amid the hills. Here went the river over a very stony bed with much rush and noise, and it was curtained with a heavy growth of alders; but the walls of the dale were sheer, for they were nigh to some mountains which Voronwë knew not. There in the green wall that Gnome found an opening like a great door with sloping sides, and this was cloaked with thick bushes and long-tangled undergrowth; yet Voronwë's piercing sight might not be deceived. Nonetheless it is said that such a magic had its builders set about it (by aid of Ulmo whose power ran in that river even if the dread of Melko fared upon its banks) that none save of the blood of the Noldoli might light on it thus by chance; nor would Tuor have found it ever but for the steadfastness of that Gnome Voronwë. Now the Gondothlim made their abode thus secret out of dread of Melko; yet even so no few of the braver Noldoli would slip down the river Sirion from those mountains, and if many perished so by Melko's evil, many finding this magic passage came at last to the City of Stone and swelled its people.

Greatly did Tuor and Voronwë rejoice to find this gate,

yet entering they found there a way dark, rough-going, and circuitous; and long time they travelled faltering within its tunnels. It was full of fearsome echoes, and there a countless stepping of feet would come behind them, so that Voronwë became adread, and said: 'It is Melko's goblins, the Orcs of the hills.' Then would they run, falling over stones in the blackness, till they perceived it was but the deceit of the place. Thus did they come, after it seemed a measureless time of fearful groping, to a place where a far light glimmered, and making for this gleam they came to a gate like that by which they had entered, but in no way overgrown. Then they passed into the sunlight and could for a while see nought, but instantly a great gong sounded and there was a clash of armour, and behold, they were surrounded by warriors in steel. Then they looked up and could see, and lo! they were at the foot of steep hills, and these hills made a great circle wherein lay a wide plain, and set therein, not rightly at the midmost but rather nearer to that place where they stood, was a great hill with a level top, and upon that summit rose a city in the new light of the morning.

Then Voronwë spoke to the guard of the Gondothlim, and his speech they comprehended, for it was the sweet tongue of the Gnomes. Then spoke Tuor also and questioned where they might be, and who might be the folk in arms who stood about, for he was in amaze and wondered much at the goodly fashion of their weapons. Then it was said to him by one of that company: 'We are the guardians of the issue of the Way of Escape. Rejoice that ye have found it, for behold before you the City of Seven Names where all who war with Melko may find hope.'

Then said Tuor: 'What be those names?' And the chief of the guard made answer: 'It is said and it is sung: "Gondobar am I called and Gondothlimbar, City of Stone and City of the Dwellers in Stone; Gondolin the Stone of Song and Gwarestrin am I named, the Tower of Guard, Gar Thurion or the Secret Place, for I am hidden from the eyes of Melko; but they who love me most greatly call me Loth, for like a flower am I, even Lothengriol the flower that blooms on the plain." Yet,' said he, 'in our daily speech we speak and we name it mostly Gondolin.' Then said Voronwë: 'Bring us thither, for we fain would enter,' and Tuor said that his heart desired much to tread the ways of that fair city.

Then said the chief of the guard that they themselves must abide here, for there were yet many days of their moon of watch to pass, but that Voronwë and Tuor might pass on to Gondolin; and moreover that they would need thereto no guide, for 'Lo, it stands fair to see and very clear, and its towers prick the heavens above the Hill of Watch in the midmost plain.' Then Tuor and his companion fared over the plain that was of a marvellous level, broken but here and there by boulders round and smooth which lay amid a sward, and by pools in rocky beds. Many fair pathways lay across that plain, and they came after a day's light march to the foot of the Hill of Watch (which is in the tongue of the Noldoli Amon Gwareth). Then did they begin to ascend the winding stairways which climbed up to the city gate; nor might any one reach that city save on foot and espied from the walls. As the westward gate was golden in the last sun-light did they come to the long stair's head, and many eyes gazed upon them from the battlements and towers.

But Tuor looked upon the walls of stone, and the uplifted towers, upon the glistering pinnacles of the town, and he looked upon the stairs of stone and marble, bordered by slender balustrades and cooled by the leap of threadlike waterfalls seeking the plain from the fountains of Amon Gwareth, and he fared as one in some dream of the Gods, for he deemed not such things were seen by men in the visions of their sleep, so great was his amaze at the glory of Gondolin.

Even so came they to the gates, Tuor in wonder and Voronwë in great joy that daring much he had both brought Tuor hither in the will of Ulmo and had himself thrown off the yoke of Melko for ever. Though he hated him no wise less, no longer did he dread that Evil One with a binding terror (and of a sooth that spell which Melko held over the Noldoli was one of bottomless dread, so that he seemed ever nigh them even were they far from the Hells of Iron, and their hearts quaked and they fled not even when they could; and to this Melko trusted often).

Now is there a sally from the gates of Gondolin and a throng comes about these twain in wonder, rejoicing that yet another of the Noldoli has fled hither from Melko, and marvelling at the stature and the great limbs of Tuor, his heavy spear barbed with fish bone and his great harp. Rugged was his aspect, and his locks were unkempt, and he was clad in the skins of bears. It is written that in those days the fathers of the fathers of men were of less stature than men now are, and the children of Elfinesse of greater growth, yet was Tuor taller than any that stood there. Indeed the Gondothlim were not bent of back as some of their unhappy kin became, labouring without rest at delving and hammering for Melko, but small were they and slender and very lithe. They were swift of foot and surpassing fair; sweet and sad were their mouths, and their eyes had ever a joy within quivering to tears; for in those times the Gnomes were exiles at heart, haunted with a desire for their ancient homes that faded not. But fate and unconquerable eagerness after knowledge had driven them into far places, and now were they hemmed by Melko and must make their abiding as fair as they might by labour and by love.

How it came ever that among men the Noldoli have been confused with the Orcs who are Melko's goblins, I know not, unless it be that certain of the Noldoli were twisted to the evil of Melko and mingled among these Orcs, for all that race were bred by Melko of the subterranean heats and slime. Their hearts were of granite and their bodies deformed; foul their faces which smiled not, but their laugh that of the clash of metal, and to nothing were they more fain than to aid in the basest of the purposes of Melko. The greatest hatred was between them and the Noldoli, who named them *Glamhoth*, or folk of dreadful hate.

Behold, the armed guardians of the gate pressed back the thronging folk that gathered about the wanderers, and one among them spoke saying: 'This is a city of watch and ward, Gondolin on Amon Gwareth, where all may be free who are of true heart, but none may be free to enter unknown. Tell me then your names.' But Voronwë named himself Bronweg of the Gnomes, come hither by the will of Ulmo as guide to this son of Men; and Tuor said: 'I am Tuor son of Peleg son of Indor of the house of the Swan of the sons of the Men of the North who live far hence, and I fare hither by the will of Ulmo of the Outer Oceans.'

Then all who listened grew silent, and his deep and rolling voice held them in amaze, for their own voices were fair as the plash of fountains. Then a saying arose among them: 'Lead him before the king.'

Then did the throng return within the gates and the wanderers with them, and Tuor saw they were of iron and of great height and strength. Now the streets of Gondolin were paved with stone and wide, kerbed with marble, and fair houses and courts amid gardens of bright flowers were set about the ways, and many towers of great slenderness and beauty builded of white marble and carved most marvellously rose to the heaven. Squares there were lit with fountains and the home of birds that sang amid the branches of their aged trees, but of all these the greatest was that place where stood the king's palace, and the tower thereof was the loftiest in the city, and the fountains that played before the doors shot twenty fathoms and seven in the air and fell in a singing rain of crystal: therein did the sun glitter splendidly by day, and the moon most magically shimmered by night. The birds that dwelt there were of the whiteness of snow and their voices sweeter than a lullaby of music.

On either side of the doors of the palace were two trees,

one that bore blossom of gold and the other of silver, nor did they ever fade, for they were shoots of old from the glorious trees of Valinor that lit those places before Melko and Gloomweaver withered them: and those trees the Gondothlim named Glingol and Bansil.

Then Turgon king of Gondolin robed in white with a belt of gold, and a coronet of garnets was upon his head, stood before his doors and spoke from the head of the white stairs that led thereto. 'Welcome, O Man of the Land of Shadows. Lo! thy coming was set in our books of wisdom, and it has been written that there would come to pass many great things in the homes of the Gondothlim whenso thou faredst hither.'

Then spoke Tuor, and Ulmo set power in his heart and majesty in his voice. 'Behold, O father of the City of Stone, I am bidden by him who maketh deep music in the Abyss, and who knoweth the mind of Elves and Men, to say unto thee that the days of Release draw nigh. There have come to the ears of Ulmo whispers of your dwelling and your hill of vigilance against the evil of Melko, and he is glad: but his heart is wroth and the hearts of the Valar are angered who sit in the mountains of Valinor and look upon the world from the peak of Taniquetil, seeing the sorrow of the thraldom of the Noldoli and the wanderings of Men; for Melko ringeth them in the Land of Shadows beyond the hills of iron. Therefore have I been brought by a secret way to bid you number your hosts and prepare for battle, for the time is ripe.'

Then spoke Turgon: 'That will I not do, though it be the words of Ulmo and all the Valar. I will not adventure this my people against the terror of the Orcs, nor emperil my city against the fire of Melko.'

Then spoke Tuor: 'Nay, if thou dost not now dare greatly then will the Orcs dwell for ever and possess in the end most of the mountains of the Earth, and cease not to trouble both Elves and Men, even though by other means the Valar contrive hereafter to release the Noldoli; but if thou trust now to the Valar, though terrible the encounter, then shall the Orcs fall, and Melko's power be minished to a little thing.'

But Turgon said that he was king of Gondolin and no will should force him against his counsel to emperil the dear labour of long ages gone; but Tuor said, for thus was he bidden by Ulmo who had feared the reluctance of Turgon: 'Then am I bidden to say that men of the Gondothlim repair swiftly and secretly down the river Sirion to the sea, and there build them boats and go seek back to Valinor: lo! the paths thereto are forgotten and the highways faded from the world, and the seas and mountains are about it, yet still dwell there the Elves on the hill of Kôr and the Gods sit in Valinor, though their mirth is minished for sorrow and fear of Melko, and they hide their land and weave about it inaccessible magic that no evil come to its shores. Yet still might thy messengers win there and turn their hearts that they rise in wrath and smite Melko, and destroy the Hells of Iron that he has wrought beneath the Mountains of Darkness.'

Then said Turgon: 'Every year at the lifting of winter have messengers repaired swiftly and by stealth down the river that is called Sirion to the coasts of the Great Sea, and there builded them boats whereto have swans and gulls been harnessed or the strong wings of the wind, and these have sought back beyond the moon and sun to Valinor; but the paths thereto are forgotten and the highways faded from the world, and the seas and mountains are about it, and they that sit within in mirth reck little of the dread of Melko or the sorrow of the world, but hide their land and weave about it inaccessible magic, that no tidings of evil come ever to their ears. Nay, enough of my people have for years untold gone out to the wide waters never to return, but have perished in the deep places or wander now lost in the shadows that have no paths; and at the coming of next year no more shall fare to the sea, but rather will we trust to ourselves and our city for the warding off of Melko; and thereto have the Valar been of scant help aforetime.'

Then Tuor's heart was heavy, and Voronwë wept; and Tuor sat by the great fountain of the king and its splashing recalled the music of the waves, and his soul was troubled by the conches of Ulmo and he would return down the waters of Sirion to the sea. But Turgon, who knew that Tuor, mortal as he was, had the favour of the Valar, marking his stout glance and the power of his voice sent to him and bade him dwell in Gondolin and be in his favour, and abide even in the royal halls if he would.

Then Tuor, for he was weary, and that place was fair, said yea; and hence cometh the abiding of Tuor in Gondolin. Of all Tuor's deeds among the Gondothlim the tales tell not, but it is said that many a time would he have stolen thence, growing weary of the concourses of folk, and thinking of empty forest and fell or hearing afar the sea-music of Ulmo, had not his heart been filled with love for a woman of the Gondothlim, and she was a daughter of the king.

Now Tuor learnt many things in those realms taught by Voronwë whom he loved, and who loved him exceeding greatly in return; or else was he instructed by the skilled men of the city and the wise men of the king. Wherefore he became a man far mightier than aforetime and wisdom was in his counsel; and many things became clear to him that were unclear before, and many things known that are still unknown to mortal men. There he heard concerning that city of Gondolin and how unstaying labour through ages of years had not sufficed to its building and adornment whereat folk travailed yet; of the delving of that hidden tunnel he heard, which the folk named the Way of Escape, and how there had been divided counsels in that matter, yet pity for the enthralled Noldoli had prevailed in the end to its making; of the guard without ceasing he was told, that was held there in arms and likewise at certain low places in the encircling mountains, and how watchers dwelt ever vigilant on the highest peaks of that range beside builded beacons ready for the fire; for never did that folk cease to look for an onslaught of the Orcs did their stronghold become known.

Now however was the guard of the hills maintained rather by custom than necessity, for the Gondothlim had long ago with unimagined toil levelled and cleared and delved all that plain about Amon Gwareth, so that scarce Gnome or bird or beast or snake could approach but was espied from many leagues off, for among the Gondothlim were many whose eyes were keener than the very hawks of Manwë Súlimo

Lord of Gods and Elves who dwells upon Taniquetil; and for this reason did they call that vale Tumladen or the valley of smoothness. Now this great work was finished to their mind, and folk were the busier about the quarrying of metals and the forging of all manner of swords and axes, spears and bills, and the fashioning of coats of mail, byrnies and hauberks, greaves and vambraces, helms and shields. Now it was said to Tuor that already the whole folk of Gondolin shooting with bows without stay day or night might not expend their hoarded arrows in many years, and that yearly their fear of the Orcs grew the less for this.

There learnt Tuor of building with stone, of masonry and the hewing of rock and marble; crafts of weaving and spinning, broidure and painting, did he fathom, and cunning in metals. Musics most delicate he there heard; and in these were they who dwelt in the southern city the most deeply skilled, for there played a profusion of murmuring founts and springs. Many of these subtleties Tuor mastered and learned to entwine with his songs to the wonder and heart's joy of all who heard. Strange stories of the Sun and Moon and Stars, of the manner of the Earth and its elements, and of the depths of heaven, were told to him; and the secret characters of the Elves he learnt, and their speeches and old tongues, and heard tell of Ilúvatar, the Lord for Always, who dwelleth beyond the world, of the great music of the Ainur about Ilúvatar's feet in the uttermost deeps of time, whence came the making of the world and the manner of it, and all therein and their governance.

Now for his skill and his great mastery over all lore and

craft whatsoever, and his great courage of heart and body, did Tuor become a comfort and stay to the king who had no son; and he was beloved by the folk of Gondolin. Upon a time the king caused his most cunning artficers to fashion a suit of armour for Tuor as a great gift, and it was made of Gnome-steel overlaid with silver; but his helm was adorned with a device of metals and jewels like to two swan-wings, one on either side, and a swan's wing was wrought on his shield; but he carried an axe rather than a sword, and this in the speech of the Gondothlim he named Dramborleg, for its buffet stunned and its edge clove all armour.

A house was built for him upon the southern walls, for he loved the free airs and liked not the close neighbourhood of other dwellings. There it was his delight often to stand on the battlements at dawn, and folk rejoiced to see the new light catch the wings of his helm – and many murmured and would fain have backed him into battle with the Orcs, seeing that the speeches of those two, Tuor and Turgon, before the palace were known to many; but the matter went not further for reverence of Turgon, and because at this time in Tuor's heart the thought of the words of Ulmo seemed to have grown dim and far off.

Now came days when Tuor had dwelt among the Gondothlim many years. Long had he known and cherished a love for the king's daughter, and now was his heart full of that love. Great love too had Idril for Tuor, and the strands of her fate were woven with his even from that day when first she gazed upon him from a high window as he stood a way-worn suppliant before the palace of the king. Little cause had Turgon to withstand their love, for he saw in Tuor a kinsman of comfort and great hope. Thus was first wed a child of Men with a daughter of Elfinesse, nor was Tuor the last. Less bliss have many had than they, and their sorrow in the end was great. Yet great was the mirth of those days when Idril and Tuor were wed before the folk in Gar Ainion, the Place of the Gods, nigh to the king's halls. A day of merriment was that wedding to the city of Gondolin, and of the greatest happiness to Tuor and Idril. Thereafter dwelt they in joy in that house upon the walls that looked out south over Tumladen, and this was good to the hearts of all in the city save Meglin alone. Now that Gnome was come of an ancient house, though now were its numbers less than others, but he himself was nephew to the king by his mother the king's sister Isfin; and that tale may not here be told.

Now the sign of Meglin was a sable Mole, and he was great among quarrymen and a chief of the delvers after ore; and many of these belonged to his house. Less fair was he than most of this goodly folk, swart and of none too kindly mood, so that he won small love, and whispers there were that he had Orc's blood in his veins, but I know not how this could be true. Now he had bid often with the king for the hand of Idril, yet Turgon finding her very loath had as often said nay, for him seemed Meglin's suit was caused as much by the desire of standing in high power beside the royal throne as by love of that fair maid. Fair indeed was she and brave thereto; and the people called her Idril of the Silver Feet in that she went ever barefoot and bareheaded, king's daughter as she was, save only at pomps of the Ainur; and Meglin gnawed his anger seeing Tuor thrust him out.

In these days came to pass the fulfilment of the time of the desire of the Valar and the hope of the Eldalië, for in great love Idril bore to Tuor a son and he was called Eärendel. Now thereto there are many interpretations both among Elves and Men, but belike it was a name wrought of some secret tongue among the Gondothlim and that has perished with them from the dwellings of the Earth.

Now this babe was of greatest beauty; his skin of a shining white and his eyes of a blue surpassing that of the sky in southern lands – bluer than the sapphires of the raiment of Manwë; and the envy of Meglin was deep at his birth, but the joy of Turgon and all the people very great indeed.

Behold now many years have gone since Tuor was lost amid the foothills and deserted by those Noldoli; yet many years too have gone since to Melko's ears came first those strange tidings – faint were they and various in form – of a man wandering amid the dales of the waters of Sirion. Now Melko was not much afraid of the race of Men in those days of his great power, and for this reason did Ulmo work through one of this kindred for the better deceiving of Melko, seeing that no Valar and scarce any of the Eldar or Noldoli might stir unmarked of his vigilance. Yet nonetheless foreboding smote that ill heart at the tidings, and he got together a mighty army of spies: sons of the Orcs were there with eyes of yellow and green like cats that could pierce all glooms and see through mist or fog or night; snakes that could go everywhither and search all crannies or the deepest pits or the highest peaks, listen to every whisper that ran in the grass or echoed in the hills; wolves there were and ravening dogs and great weasels full of the thirst of blood whose nostrils could take scent moons old through running water, or whose eyes find among shingle footsteps that had passed a lifetime since; owls came and falcons whose keen glances might descry by day or night the fluttering of small birds in all the woods of the world, and the movement of every mouse or vole or rat that crept or dwelt throughout the Earth. All these he summoned to his Hall of Iron, and they came in multitudes. Thence he sent them over the Earth to seek this man who had escaped from the Land of Shadows, but yet far more curiously and more intently to search out the dwelling of the Noldoli that had escaped his thraldom; for these his heart burnt to destroy or to enslave.

Now while Tuor dwelt in happiness and in great increase of knowledge and might in Gondolin, these creatures through the years untiring nosed among the stones and rocks, hunted the forests and the heaths, espied the airs and lofty places, tracked all the paths about the dales and plains, and neither let nor stayed. From this hunt they brought a wealth of tidings to Melko – indeed among many hidden things that they dragged to light they discovered that 'Way of Escape' whereby Tuor and Voronwë entered aforetime. Nor had they done so save by constraining some of the less stout of the Noldoli with dire threats of torment to join in that great ransacking; for because of the magic about that gate no folk of Melko unaided by the Gnomes could come to it. Yet now they had pried of late far into its tunnels and captured within many of the Noldoli creeping there to flee from thraldom. They had scaled too the Encircling Hills at certain places and gazed upon the beauty of the city of Gondolin and the strength of Amon Gwareth from afar; but into the plain they could not win for the vigilance of its guardians and the difficulty of those mountains. Indeed the Gondothlim were mighty archers, and bows they made of a marvel of power. Therewith they might shoot an arrow into heaven seven times as far as could the best bowman among Men shoot at a mark upon the ground; and they would have suffered no falcon to hover long over their plain or snake to crawl therein; for they liked not creatures of blood, broodlings of Melko.

Now in those days was Eärendel one year old when these ill tidings came to that city of the spies of Melko and how they encompassed the vale of Tumladen around. Then Turgon's heart was saddened, remembering the words of Tuor in past years before the palace doors; and he caused the watch and ward to be thrice strengthened at all points, and engines of war to be devised by his artificers and set upon the hill. Poisonous fires and hot liquids, arrows and great rocks, was he prepared to shoot down on any who would assail those gleaming walls; and then he abode as well content as might be, but Tuor's heart was heavier than the king's, for now the words of Ulmo came ever to his mind, and their purport and gravity he understood more deeply than of old; nor did he find any great comfort in Idril, for her heart boded more darkly even than his own.

Know then that Idril had a great power of piercing with her thought the darkness of the hearts of Elves and Men, and

the glooms of the future thereto – further even than is the common power of the kindreds of the Eldalië; therefore she spoke thus on a day to Tuor: 'Know, my husband, that my heart misgives me for doubt of Meglin, and I fear that he will bring an ill on this fair realm, though by no means may I see how or when – yet I dread lest all that he knows of our doings and preparations become in some manner known to the Foe, so that he devise a new means of whelming us, against which we have thought of no defence. Lo! I dreamed on a night that Meglin builded a furnace, and coming at us unawares flung therein Eärendel our babe, and would after thrust in thee and me; but that for sorrow at the death of our fair child I would not resist.'

And Tuor answered: 'There is reason in thy fear, for neither is my heart good towards Meglin; yet is he the nephew of the king and thine own cousin, nor is there charge against him, and I see nought to do but to abide and watch.'

But Idril said: 'This is my rede thereto: gather thou in deep secret those delvers and quarrymen who by careful trial are found to hold least love for Meglin by reason of the pride and arrogance of his dealings among them. From these thou must choose trusty men to keep watch upon Meglin whenso he fares to the outer hills, yet I counsel thee to set the greater part of those in whose secrecy thou canst confide at a hidden delving, and to devise with their aid – howsoever cautious and slow that labour be – a secret way from thy house here beneath the rocks of this hill unto the vale below. Now this way must not lead toward the Way of Escape, for my heart bids me trust it not, but even to that far distant pass, the Cleft of the Eagles in the southern mountains; and the further this delving reach thitherward beneath the plain so much the better would I esteem it – yet let all this labour be kept dark save from a few.'

Now there are none such delvers of earth or rock as the Noldoli (and this Melko knows), but in those places is the earth of a great hardness; and Tuor said: 'The rocks of the hill of Amon Gwareth are as iron, and only with much travail may they be cloven; yet if this be done in secret then must great time and patience be added; but the stone of the floor of the Vale of Tumladen is as forgéd steel, nor may it be hewn without the knowledge of the Gondothlim save in moons and years.'

Idril said then: 'Sooth this may be, but such is my rede, and there is yet time to spare.' Then Tuor said that he might not see all its purport, 'but "better is any plan than a lack of counsel", and I will do even as thou sayest.'

Now it so chanced that not long after Meglin went to the hills for the getting of ore, and straying in the mountains alone was taken by some of the Orcs prowling there, and they would do him evil and terrible hurt, knowing him to be a man of the Gondothlim. This was however unknown of Tuor's watchers. But evil came into the heart of Meglin, and he said to his captors: 'Know then that I am Meglin son of Eöl, who had to wife Isfin sister of Turgon king of the Gondothlim.' But they said: 'What is that to us?' And Meglin answered: 'Much is that to you; for if you slay me, be it speedy or slow, ye will lose great tidings concerning the city of Gondolin that your master would rejoice to hear.'

Then the Orcs stayed their hands, and said they would give him life if the matters he opened to them seemed to merit that; and Meglin told them of all the fashion of that plain and city, of its walls and their height and thickness, and the valour of its gates; of the host of men at arms who now obeyed Turgon he spoke, and the countless hoard of weapons gathered for their equipment, of the engines of war and the venomous fires.

Then the Orcs were wroth, and having heard these matters were yet for slaying him there and then as one who impudently enlarged the power of his miserable folk to the mockery of the great might and puissance of Melko; but Meglin catching at a straw said: 'Think ye not that ye would rather pleasure your master if ye bore to his feet so noble a captive, that he might hear my tidings of himself and judge of their verity?'

Now this seemed good to the Orcs, and they returned from the mountains about Gondolin to the Hills of Iron and the dark halls of Melko; thither they haled Meglin with them, and now was he in a sore dread. But when he knelt before the black throne of Melko in terror of the grimness of the shapes about him, of the wolves that sat beneath that chair and of the adders that twined about its legs, Melko bade him speak. Then told he those tidings, and Melko hearkening spoke very fair to him, that the insolence of his heart in great measure returned.

Now the end of this was that Melko aided by the cunning of Meglin devised a plan for the overthrow of Gondolin. For this Meglin's reward was to be a great captaincy among the

Orcs – yet Melko purposed not in his heart to fulfil such a promise – but Tuor and Eärendel should Melko burn, and Idril be given to Meglin's arms – and such promises was that evil one fain to redeem. Yet as meed of treachery did Melko threaten Meglin with the torment of the Balrogs. Now these were demons with whips of flame and claws of steel by whom he tormented those of the Noldoli who durst withstand him in anything – and the Eldar have called them Malkarauki. But the rede that Meglin gave to Melko was that not all the host of the Orcs nor the Balrogs in their fierceness might by assault or siege hope ever to overthrow the walls and gates of Gondolin even if they availed to win unto the plain without. Therefore he counselled Melko to devise out of his sorceries a succour for his warriors in their endeavour. From the greatness of his wealth of metals and his powers of fire he bid him make beasts like snakes and dragons of irresistible might that should overcreep the Encircling Hills and lap that plain and its fair city in flame and death.

Then Meglin was bidden fare home lest at his absence men suspect somewhat; but Melko wove about him the spell of bottomless dread, and he had thereafter neither joy nor quiet in his heart. Nonetheless he wore a fair mask of good liking and gaiety, so that men said: 'Meglin is softened', and he was held in less disfavour; yet Idril feared him the more. Now Meglin said: 'I have laboured much and am minded to rest, and to join in the dance and the song and the merrymakings of the folk', and he went no more quarrying stone or ore in the hills: yet in sooth he sought herein to drown his fear and disquiet. A dread possessed him that Melko was ever at hand,

and this came of the spell; and he durst never again wander amid the mines lest he again fall in with the Orcs and be bidden once more to the terrors of the halls of darkness.

Now the years fare by, and egged by Idril Tuor keepeth ever at his secret delving; but seeing that the leaguer of spies hath grown thinner Turgon dwelleth more at ease and in less fear. Yet these years are filled by Melko in the utmost ferment of labour, and all the thrall-folk of the Noldoli must dig unceasingly for metals while Melko sitteth and deviseth fires and calleth flames and smokes to come from the lower heats, nor doth he suffer any of the Noldoli to stray ever a foot from their places of bondage. Then on a time Melko assembled all his most cunning smiths and sorcerers, and of iron and flame they wrought a host of monsters such as have only at that time been seen and shall not again be till the Great End. Some were all of iron so cunningly linked that they might flow like slow rivers of metal or coil themselves around and above all obstacles before them, and these were filled in their innermost depths with the grimmest of the Orcs with scimitars and spears; others of bronze and copper were given hearts and spirits of blazing fire, and they blasted all that stood before them with the terror of their snorting or trampled whatso escaped the ardour of their breath; yet others were creatures of pure flame that writhed like ropes of molten metal, and they brought to ruin whatever fabric they came nigh, and iron and stone melted before them and became as water, and upon them rode the Balrogs in hundreds; and these were the most dire of all those monsters which Melko devised against Gondolin.

Now when the seventh summer had gone since the treason of Meglin, and Eärendel was yet of very tender years though a valorous child, Melko withdrew all his spies, for every path and corner of the mountains was now known to him; yet the Gondothlim thought in their unwariness that Melko would no longer seek against them, perceiving their might and the impregnable strength of their dwelling.

But Idril fell into a dark mood and the light of her face was clouded, and many wondered thereat; yet Turgon reduced the watch and ward to its ancient numbers, and to somewhat less, and as autumn came and the gathering of fruits was over folk turned with glad hearts to the feasts of winter: but Tuor stood upon the battlements and gazed upon the Encircling Hills.

Now behold, Idril stood beside him, and the wind was in her hair, and Tuor thought that she was exceeding beautiful, and stooped to kiss her; but her face was sad, and she said: 'Now come the days when thou must make choice,' and Tuor knew not what she said. Then drawing him within their halls she said to him how her heart misgave her for fear concerning Eärendel their son, and for boding that some great evil was nigh, and that Melko would be at the bottom of it. Then Tuor would comfort her, but might not, and she questioned him concerning the secret delving, and he said how it now led a league into the plain, and at that was her heart somewhat lightened. But still she counselled that the delving be pressed on, and that henceforth should speed weigh more than secrecy, 'because now is the time very near.' And another rede she gave him, and this he took also, that

certain of the bravest and most true among the lords and
warriors of the Gondothlim be chosen with care and told
of that secret way and its issue. These she counselled him
to make into a stout guard and to give them his emblem to
wear that they become his folk, and to do this under pretext
of the right and dignity of a great lord, kinsman to the king.
'Moreover,' said she, 'I will get my father's favour to that.'
In secret too she whispered to folk that if the city came to
its last stand or Turgon be slain that they rally about Tuor
and her son, and to this they laughed a yea, saying however
that Gondolin would stand as long as Taniquetil or the
Mountains of Valinor.

Yet to Turgon she spoke not openly, nor suffered Tuor
to do so, as he desired, despite their love and reverence for
him – a great and a noble and a glorious king he was – seeing
that he trusted in Meglin and held with blind obstinacy his
belief in the impregnable might of the city and that Melko
sought no more against it, perceiving no hope therein. Now
in this he was ever strengthened by the cunning sayings
of Meglin. Behold, the guile of that Gnome was very great,
for he wrought much in the dark, so that folk said: 'He doth
well to bear the sign of a sable mole'; and by reason of the
folly of certain of the quarrymen, and yet more by reason
of the loose words of certain among his kin to whom word
was somewhat unwarily spoken by Tuor, he gathered a
knowledge of the secret work and laid against that a plan of
his own.

So winter deepened, and it was very cold for those regions,
so that frost fared about the plain of Tumladen and ice lay on

its pools; yet the fountains played ever on Amon Gwareth and the two trees blossomed, and folk made merry till the day of terror that was hidden in the heart of Melko.

In these ways that bitter winter passed, and the snows lay deeper than ever before on the Encircling Hills; yet in its time a spring of wondrous glory melted the skirts of those white mantles and the valley drank the waters and burst into flowers. So came and passed with revelry of children the festival of Nost-na-Lothion or the Birth of Flowers, and the hearts of the Gondothlim were uplifted for the good promise of the year, and now at length is that great feast Tarnin Austa or the Gates of Summer near at hand. For know that on a night it was their custom to begin a solemn ceremony at midnight, continuing it even till the dawn of Tarnin Austa broke, and no voice was uttered in the city from midnight till the break of day, but the dawn they hailed with ancient songs. For years uncounted had the coming of summer thus been greeted with music of choirs, standing upon their gleaming eastern wall; and now comes even the night of vigil and the city is filled with silver lamps, while in the groves upon the new-leaved trees lights of jewelled colours swing, and low musics go along the ways, but no voice sings until the dawn.

The sun has sunk beyond the hills and folk array them for the festival very gladly and eagerly – glancing in expectation to the East. Lo! even when she had gone and all was dark, a new light suddenly began, and a glow there was, but it was beyond the northward heights, and men marvelled, and there was a thronging of the walls and battlements. Then wonder grew to doubt as the light waxed and became yet redder, and doubt to dread as men saw the snow upon the mountains dyed as it were with blood. And thus it was that the fire-serpents of Melko came upon Gondolin.

Then came over the plain riders who bore breathless tidings from those who kept vigil on the peaks; and they told of the fiery hosts and the shapes like dragons, and said: 'Melko is upon us.' Great was the fear and anguish within that beauteous city, and the streets and byways were filled with the weeping of women and the wailing of children, and the squares with the mustering of soldiers and the ring of arms. There were the gleaming banners of all the great houses and kindreds of the Gondothlim. Mighty was the array of the house of the king and their colours were white and gold and red, and their emblems the moon and the sun and the scarlet heart. Now in the midmost of these stood Tuor above all heads, and his mail of silver gleamed; and about him was a press of the stoutest of the folk. Lo! all these wore wings as it were of swans or gulls upon their helms, and the emblem of the White Wing was upon their shields. But the folk of Meglin were drawn up in the same place, and sable was their harness, and they bore no sign or emblem, but their round caps of steel were covered with moleskin, and they fought with axes two-headed like mattocks. There Meglin prince of Gondobar gathered many warriors of dark countenance and lowering gaze about him, and a ruddy glow shone upon their faces and gleamed about the polished surfaces of their accoutrement. Behold, all the hills to the north were ablaze, and it was as if rivers of fire ran down the slopes that led to the plain of Tumladen, and folk might already feel the heat thereof.

And many other kindreds were there, the folk of the Swallow and the Heavenly Arch, and from these folk came the greatest number and the best of the bowmen, and they were arrayed upon the broad places of the walls. Now the folk of the Swallow bore a fan of feathers on their helms, and they were arrayed in white and dark blue and in purple and black and showed an arrowhead on their shields. Their lord was Duilin, swiftest of all men to run and leap and surest of archers at a mark. But they of the Heavenly Arch being a folk of uncounted wealth were arrayed in a glory of colours, and their arms were set with jewels that flamed in the light now over the sky. Every shield of that battalion was of the blue of the heavens and its boss a jewel built of seven gems, rubies and amethysts and sapphires, emeralds, chrysoprase, topaz, and amber, but an opal of great size was set in their helms. Egalmoth was their chieftain, and wore a blue mantle upon which the stars were broidered in crystal, and his sword was bent – now none else of the Noldoli bore curved swords – yet he trusted rather to the bow, and shot therewith further than any among that host.

There too were the folk of the Pillar and of the Tower of Snow, and both these kindreds were marshalled by Penlod, tallest of Gnomes. There were those of the Tree, and they were a great house, and their raiment was green. They fought with iron-studded clubs or with slings, and their lord Galdor was held the most valiant of all the Gondothlim save Turgon alone. There stood the house of the Golden Flower who bore

74

THE FALL OF GONDOLIN

a rayed sun upon their shield, and their chief <u>Glorfindel</u>
bore a mantle so broidered in threads of gold that it was diapered with celandine as a field in spring; and his arms were
damascened with cunning gold.

Then came there from the south of the city <u>the people of
the Fountain</u>, and <u>Ecthelion</u> was their lord, and silver and
diamonds were their delight; and swords very long and
bright and pale did they wield, and they went into battle to
the music of flutes. Behind them came the <u>host of the Harp</u>,
and this was a <u>battalion of brave warriors</u>; but their leader
<u>Salgant</u> was a craven, and <u>he fawned upon Meglin</u>. They
were dight with tassels of silver and tassels of gold, and a
harp of silver shone in their blazonry upon a field of black;
but Salgant bore one of gold, and he alone rode into battle of
all the sons of the Gondothlim, and he was heavy and squat.

Now the last of the battalions was furnished by the folk
of the <u>Hammer of Wrath</u>, and of these came many of the
best smiths and craftsmen, and all that kindred reverenced
Aulë the Smith more than all other Ainur. They fought with
great maces like hammers, and their shields were heavy, for
their arms were very strong. In older days they had been
much recruited by Noldoli who escaped from the mines of
Melko, and the hatred of this house for the works of that evil
one and the Balrogs his demons was exceeding great. Now
their leader was <u>Rog,</u> strongest of the Gnomes, scarce second
in valour to that Galdor of the Tree. The sign of this people
was the Stricken Anvil, and a hammer that smiteth sparks
about it was set on their shields, and red gold and black iron
was their delight. Very numerous was that battalion, nor had

any amongst them a faint heart, and they won the greatest
glory of all those fair houses in that struggle against doom;
yet were they ill-fated, and none ever fared away from that
field, but fell about Rog and vanished from the Earth; and
with them much craftsmanship and skill has vanished for
ever.

This was the fashion and the array of the eleven houses
of the Gondothlim with their signs and emblems, and the
bodyguard of Tuor, the folk of the Wing, was accounted
the twelfth. Now is the face of that chieftain grim and he
looks not to live long – and there in his house upon the walls
Idril arrays herself in mail, and seeks Eärendel. And that
child was in tears for the strange lights of red that played
about the walls of the chamber where he slept; and tales that
his nurse Meleth had woven him concerning fiery Melko at
times of his waywardness came to him and troubled him.
But his mother coming set about him a tiny coat of mail
that she had let fashion in secret, and at that he was glad
and exceeding proud, and he shouted for pleasure. Yet Idril
wept, for much had she cherished in her heart the fair city
and her goodly house, and the love of Tuor and herself that
had dwelt therein; but now she saw its destroying nigh at
hand, and feared that her contriving would fail against this
overwhelming might of the terror of the serpents.

It was now four hours still from the middle night, and the
sky was red in the north and in the east and west; and those
serpents of iron had reached the levels of Tumladen, and
those fiery ones were among the lowest slopes of the hills, so
that the guards were taken and set in evil torment by the

Balrogs that scoured all about, saving only to the furthest south where was Cristhorn the Cleft of Eagles.

Then did King Turgon call a council, and thither fared Tuor and Meglin, as royal princes; and Duilin came with Egalmoth and Penlod the tall, and Rog strode thither with Galdor of the Tree and golden Glorfindel and Ecthelion of the voice of music. Thither too fared Salgant atremble at the tidings, and other nobles beside of less blood but better heart.

Then spoke Tuor and this was his rede, that a mighty sally be made forthwith, ere the light and heat grew too great in the plain; and many backed him, being but of different minds as to whether the sally should be made by the entire host with the maids and wives and children amidmost, or by diverse bands seeking out in many directions; and to this last Tuor leaned.

But Meglin and Salgant alone held other counsel and were for holding to the city and seeking to guard those treasures that lay within. Out of guile did Meglin speak thus, fearing lest any of the Noldoli escape the doom that he had brought upon them, and he dreaded lest his treason become known and somehow vengeance find him in after days. But Salgant spoke both echoing Meglin and being grievously afraid of issuing from the city, for he was fain rather to do battle from an impregnable fortress than to risk hard blows upon the field.

Then the lord of the house of the Mole played upon the one weakness of Turgon, saying: 'Lo! O King, the city of Gondolin contains a wealth of jewels and metals and stuffs

and of things wrought by the hands of the Gnomes to surpassing beauty, and all these thy lords – more brave meseems
than wise – would abandon to the Foe. Even should victory
be thine upon the plain thy city will be sacked and the
Balrogs get hence with a measureless booty'; and Turgon
groaned, for Meglin had known his great love for the wealth
and loveliness of that burg upon Amon Gwareth. Again said
Meglin, putting fire in his voice: 'Lo! Hast thou for nought
laboured through years uncounted at the building of walls of
impregnable thickness and in the making of gates whose
valour may not be overthrown; is the power of the hill Amon
Gwareth become as lowly as the deep vale, or the hoard of
weapons that lie upon it and its unnumbered arrows of so
little worth that in the hour of peril thou wouldst cast all
aside and go naked into the open against enemies of steel and
fire, whose trampling shakes the earth and the Encircling
Mountains ring with the clamour of their footsteps?'

And Salgant quailed to think of it and spoke noisily,
saying: 'Meglin speaks well, O King, hear thou him.' Then
the king took the counsel of those twain though all the lords
said otherwise, nay rather the more for that: therefore at his
bidding does all that folk abide now the assault upon their
walls. But Tuor wept and left the king's hall, and gathering
the men of the Wing went through the streets seeking his
home; and by that hour was the light great and lurid and
there was stifling heat and a black smoke and stench arose
about the pathways to the city.

And now came the Monsters across the valley and the
white towers of Gondolin reddened before them; but the

stoutest were in dread seeing those dragons of fire and those serpents of bronze and iron that fare already about the hill of the city; and they shot unavailing arrows at them. Then is there a cry of hope, for behold, the snakes of fire may not climb the hill for its steepness and for its glassiness, and by reason of the quenching waters that fall upon its sides; yet they lie about its feet and a vast steam arises where the streams of Amon Gwareth and the flames of the serpents drive together. <u>Then grew there such a heat</u> that women became faint and men sweated to weariness beneath their mail, and all the springs of the city, save only the fountain of the king, grew hot and smoked.

But now <u>Gothmog lord of Balrogs</u>, captain of the hosts of Melko, took counsel and gathered all his things of iron that could coil themselves around and above all obstacles before them. These he bade pile themselves before the northern gate; and behold, their great spires reached even to its threshold and thrust at the towers and bastions about it, and by reason of the exceeding heaviness of their bodies those gates fell, and great was the noise thereof: yet the most of the walls around them still stood firm. Then the engines and the catapults of the king poured darts and boulders and molten metals on those ruthless beasts, and their hollow bellies clanged beneath the buffeting, yet it availed not for they might not be broken, and the fires rolled off them. Then were the topmost opened about their middles, and an innumerable host of the Orcs, the goblins of hatred, poured therefrom into the breach; and who shall tell of their scimitars or the flash of their broad-bladed spears with which they stabbed?

Then did Rog shout in a mighty voice, and all the people of the Hammer of Wrath and the kindred of the Tree with Galdor the valiant leapt at the foe. There the blows of their great hammers and the dint of their clubs rang to the Encircling Mountains and the Orcs fell like leaves; and those of the Swallow and the Arch poured arrows like the dark rains of autumn upon them, and both Orcs and Gondothlim fell thereunder for the smoke and the confusion. Great was that battle, yet for all their valour the Gondothlim by reason of the might of ever increasing numbers were borne slowly backwards till the goblins held part of the northernmost city.

At this time is Tuor at the head of the folk of the Wing struggling in the turmoil of the streets, and now he wins through to his house and finds that Meglin is before him. Trusting in the battle now begun about the northern gate and in the uproar in the city, Meglin had looked to this hour for the consummation of his designs. Learning much of the secret delving of Tuor (yet only at the last moment had he got this knowledge and he could not discover all) he said nought to the king or any other, for it was his thought that of a surety that tunnel would go in the end toward the Way of Escape, this being the most nigh to the city, and he had a mind to use this to his good, and to the ill of the Noldoli. Messengers by great stealth he despatched to Melko to set a guard about the outer issue of that Way when the assault was made; but he himself thought now to take Eärendel and cast him into the fire beneath the walls, and seizing Idril he would constrain her to guide him to the secrets of the passage, that he might win out of this terror of fire and slaughter and drag her withal along with him to the lands of Melko. Now Meglin was afeared that even the secret token which Melko had given him would fail in that direful sack, and was minded to help that Ainu to the fulfilment of his promises of safety. No doubt had he however of the death of Tuor in that great burning, for to Salgant he had confided the task of delaying him in the king's halls and egging him straight thence into the deadliest of the fight – but lo! Salgant fell into a terror unto death, and he rode home and lay there now aquake on his bed; but Tuor fared home with the folk of the Wing.

Now Tuor did this, though his valour leapt to the noise of war, that he might take farewell of Idril and Eärendel, and speed them with a bodyguard down the secret way ere he returned himself to the battle throng to die if must be: but he found a press of the Mole-folk about his door, and these were the grimmest and least good-hearted of folk that Meglin might get in that city. Yet were they free Noldoli and under no spell of Melko's like their master, wherefore though for the lordship of Meglin they aided not Idril, no more would they touch of his purpose despite all his curses.

Now then Meglin had Idril by the hair and sought to drag her to the battlements out of cruelty of heart, that she might see the fall of Eärendel to the flames; but he was cumbered by that child, and she fought, alone as she was, like a tigress for all her beauty and slenderness. There he now struggles and delays amid oaths while that folk of the Wing draws nigh – and lo! Tuor gives a shout so great that the Orcs hear it afar and waver at the sound of it. Like a crash of tempest the guard of the Wing were amid the men of the Mole, and these were stricken asunder. When Meglin saw this he would stab Eärendel with a short knife he had; but that child bit his left hand, that his teeth sank in, and he staggered, and stabbed weakly, and the mail of the small coat turned the blade aside; and thereupon Tuor was upon him and his wrath was terrible to see. He seized Meglin by that hand that held the knife and broke the arm with the wrench, and then taking him by the middle leapt with him upon the walls, and flung him far out. Great was the fall of his body, and it smote Amon Gwareth three times ere it pitched in the midmost of the flames; and the name of Meglin has gone out in shame from among Eldar and Noldoli.

Then the warriors of the Mole being more numerous than those few of the Wing, and loyal to their lord, came at Tuor, and there were great blows, but no man might stand before the wrath of Tuor, and they were smitten and driven to fly into what dark holes they might, or flung from the walls. Then Tuor and his men must get them to the battle of the Gate, for the noise of it has grown very great, and Tuor has it still in his heart that the city may stand; yet with Idril he left there Voronwë against his will and some other swordsmen to be guard for her till he returned or might send tidings from the fray.

Now was the battle at that gate very evil indeed, and Duilin of the Swallow as he shot from the walls was smitten by a fiery bolt of the Balrogs who leapt about the base of Amon Gwareth; and he fell from the battlements and perished. Then the Balrogs continued to shoot darts of fire and flaming arrows like small snakes into the sky, and these fell upon the roofs and gardens of Gondolin till all the trees were scorched, and the flowers and grass burned up, and the whiteness of those walls and colonnades was blackened and seared: yet a worse matter was it that a company of those demons climbed upon the coils of the serpents of iron and thence loosed unceasingly from their bows and slings till a fire began to burn in the city to the back of the main army of the defenders.

Then said Rog in a great voice: 'Who now shall fear the Balrogs for all their terror? See before us the accursed ones who for ages have tormented the children of the Noldoli, and who now set a fire at our backs with their shooting. Come ye of the Hammer of Wrath and we will smite them for their evil.' Thereupon he lifted his mace, and its handle was long; and he made a way before him by the wrath of his onset even unto the fallen gate: but all the people of the Stricken Anvil ran behind like a wedge, and sparks came from their eyes for the fury of their rage. A great deed was that sally, as the Noldoli sing yet, and many of the Orcs were borne backward into the fires below; but the men of Rog leapt even upon the coils of the serpents and came at those Balrogs and smote them grievously, for all they had whips of flame and claws of steel, and were in stature very great. They battered them into nought, or catching at their whips wielded these against them, that they tore them even as they had aforetime torn the Gnomes; and the number of Balrogs that perished was a marvel and dread to the hosts of Melko, for ere that day never had any of the Balrogs been slain by the hand of Elves or Men.

Then Gothmog Lord of Balrogs gathered all his demons that were about the city and ordered them thus: a number made for the folk of the Hammer and gave before them, but the greater company rushing upon the flank contrived to get to their backs, higher upon the coils of the drakes and nearer to the gates, so that Rog might not win back save with great slaughter among his folk. But Rog seeing this essayed not to win back, as was hoped, but with all his folk fell on those whose part was to give before him; and they fled before him now of dire need rather than of craft. Down into the plain were they harried, and their shrieks rent the airs of Tumladen. Then that house of the Hammer fared about smiting and hewing the astonied bands of Melko till they were hemmed at the last by an overwhelming force of the Orcs and the Balrogs, and a fire-drake was loosed upon them. There did they perish about Rog hewing to the last till iron and flame overcame them, and it is yet sung that each man of the Hammer of Wrath took the lives of seven foemen to pay for his own. Then did dread fall more heavily still upon the Gondothlim at the death of Rog and the loss of his battalion, and they gave back further yet into the city, and Penlod perished there in a lane with his back to the wall, and about him many of the men of the Pillar and many of the Tower of Snow.

Now therefore Melko's goblins held all the gate and a great part of the walls on either side, whence numbers of the Swallow and those of the Rainbow were thrust to doom; but within the city they had won a great space reaching nigh to the centre, even to the Place of the Well that adjoined the

Square of the Palace. Yet about those ways and around the gate their dead were piled in uncounted heaps, and they halted therefore and took counsel, seeing that for the valour of the Gondothlim they had lost many more than they had hoped and far more than those defenders. Fearful too they were for that slaughter Rog had done amid the Balrogs, because of those demons they had great courage and confidence of heart.

Now then the plan that they made was to hold what they had won, while those serpents of bronze and with great feet for trampling climbed slowly over those of iron, and reaching the walls there opened a breach wherethrough the Balrogs might ride upon the dragons of flame: yet they knew this must be done with speed, for the heats of those drakes lasted not for ever, and might only be plenished from the wells of fire that Melko had made in the fastness of his own land.

But even as their messengers were sped they heard a sweet music that was played amid the host of the Gondothlim and they feared what it might mean: and lo! there came Ecthelion and the people of the Fountain whom Turgon till now had held in reserve, for he watched the most of that affray from the heights of his tower. Now marched these folk to a great playing of their flutes, and the crystal and silver of their array was most lovely to see amid the red light of the fires and the blackness of the ruins.

Then on a sudden their music ceased and Ecthelion of the fair voice shouted for the drawing of swords, and before the Orcs might foresee his onslaught the flashing of those pale blades was amongst them. It is said that Ecthelion's folk there slew more of the goblins than fell ever in all the battles of the Eldalië with that race, and that his name is a terror among them to this latest day, and a warcry to the Eldar.

Now it is that Tuor and the men of the Wing fare into the fight and range themselves beside Ecthelion and those of the Fountain, and the twain strike mighty blows and ward each many a thrust from the other, and harry the Orcs so that they win back almost to the gate. But there behold a quaking and a trampling, for the dragons labour mightily at beating a path up Amon Gwareth and at casting down the walls of the city; and already there is a gap therein and a confusion of masonry where the ward-towers have fallen in ruin. Bands of the Swallow and of the Arch of Heaven there fight bitterly amid the wreck or contest the walls to east and west with the foe; but even as Tuor comes nigh driving the Orcs, one of those brazen snakes heaves against the western wall and a great mass of it shakes and falls, and behind comes a creature of fire and Balrogs upon it. Flames gust from the jaws of that worm and folk wither before it, and the wings of the helm of Tuor are blackened, but he stands and gathers about him his guard and all of the Arch and Swallow he can find, whereas on his right Ecthelion rallies the men of the Fountain of the South.

Now the Orcs again take heart from the coming of the drakes, and they mingle with the Balrogs that pour about the breach, and they assail the Gondothlim grievously. There Tuor slew Othrod a lord of the Orcs cleaving his helm, and Balcmeg he hewed asunder, and Lug he smote with his axe that his limbs were cut from beneath him at the knee, but Ecthelion shore through two captains of the goblins at a sweep and cleft the head of Orcobal their chiefest champion to his teeth; and by reason of the great doughtiness of those two lords they came even unto the Balrogs. Of those demons of power Ecthelion slew three, for the brightness of his sword cleft the iron of them and did hurt to their fire, and they writhed; yet of the leap of that axe Dramborleg that was swung by the hand of Tuor were they still more afraid, for it sang like the rush of eagle's wings in the air and took death as it fell, and five of them went down before it.

But so it is that few cannot fight always against the many, and Ecthelion's left arm got a sore rent from a whip of the Balrog's and his shield fell to earth even as that dragon of fire drew nigh amid the ruin of the walls. Then Ecthelion must lean on Tuor, and Tuor might not leave him, though the very feet of the trampling beast were upon them, and they were like to be overborne: but Tuor hewed at a foot of the creature so that flame spouted forth, and that serpent screamed, lashing with its tail; and many of both Orcs and Noldoli got their death therefrom. Now Tuor gathered his might and lifted Ecthelion, and amid a remnant of the folk got thereunder and escaped the drake; yet dire was the killing of men that beast had wrought, and the Gondothlim were sorely shaken.

Thus it was that Tuor son of Peleg gave before the foe, fighting as he yielded ground, and bore from that battle Ecthelion of the Fountain, but the drakes and the foemen held half the city and all the north of it. Thence marauding bands fared about the streets and did much ransacking, or slew in the dark men and women and children, and many, if occasion let, they bound and led back and flung in the iron chambers amid the dragons of iron, that they might drag them afterward to be thralls of Melko.

Now Tuor reached the Square of the Folkwell by a way entering from the north, and found there Galdor denying the western entry by the Arch of Inwë to a horde of the goblins, but about him was now but a few of those men of the Tree. There did Galdor become the salvation of Tuor, for he fell behind his men stumbling beneath Ecthelion over a body that lay in the dark, and the Orcs had taken them both but for the sudden rush of that champion and the dint of his club.

There were the scatterlings of the guard of the Wing and of the houses of the Tree and the Fountain, and of the Swallow and the Arch, welded to a good battalion, and by the counsel of Tuor they gave way out of that Place of the Well, seeing that the Square of the King that lay next was the more defensible. Now that place had aforetime contained many beautiful trees, both oak and poplar, around a great well of vast depth and great purity of water; yet at that hour it was full of the riot and ugliness of those hideous people of Melko, and those waters were polluted with their carcases.

Thus comes the last stout gathering of those defenders in the Square of the Palace of Turgon. Among them are many wounded and fainting, and Tuor is weary for the labours of the night and the weight of Ecthelion who is in a deadly swoon. Even as he led that battalion in by the Road of

Arches from the north-west (and they had much ado to prevent any foe getting behind their backs) a noise arose at the eastward of the square, and lo! Glorfindel is driven in with the last of the men of the Golden Flower.

Now these had sustained a terrible conflict in the Great Market to the east of the city, where a force of Orcs led by Balrogs came on them at unawares as they marched by a circuitous way to the fight about the gate. This they did to surprise the foe upon his left flank, but were themselves ambuscaded; there fought they bitterly for hours till a firedrake new-come from the breach overwhelmed them, and Glorfindel cut his way out very hardly and with few men; but that place with its stores and its goodly things of fine workmanship was a waste of flames.

The story tells that Turgon had sent the men of the Harp to their aid because of the urgency of messengers from Glorfindel, but Salgant concealed this bidding from them, saying they were to garrison the square of the Lesser Market to the south where he dwelt, and they fretted thereat. Now however they brake from Salgant and were come before the king's hall; and that was very timely, for a triumphant press of foemen was at Glorfindel's heels. On these the men of the Harp unbidden fell with great eagerness and utterly redeemed the cravenhood of their lord, driving the enemy back into the market, and being leaderless fared even over wrathfully, so that many of them were trapped in the flames or sank before the breath of the serpent that revelled there.

Tuor now drank of the great fountain and was refreshed, and loosening Ecthelion's helm gave him to drink, splashing his face that his swoon left him. Now those lords Tuor and Glorfindel clear the square and withdraw all the men they may from the entrances and bar them with barriers, save as yet on the south. Even from that region comes now Egalmoth. He had had charge of the engines on the wall; but long since deeming matters to call rather for handstrokes about the streets than shooting upon the battlements he gathered some of the Arch and of the Swallow about him and cast away his bow. Then did they fare about the city dealing good blows whenever they fell in with bands of the enemy. Thereby he rescued many bands of captives and gathered no few wandering and driven men, and so got to the King's Square with hard fighting; and men were fain to greet him for they had feared him dead. Now are all the women and children that had gathered there or been brought in by Egalmoth stowed in the king's halls, and the ranks of the houses made ready for the last. In that host of survivors are some, be it however few, of all the kindreds save of the Hammer of Wrath alone; and the king's house is as yet untouched. Nor is this any shame, for their part was ever to bide fresh to the last and defend the king.

But now the men of Melko have assembled their forces, and seven dragons of fire have come with Orcs about them, and Balrogs upon them down all the ways from north, east, and west seeking the Square of the King. Then there was carnage at the barriers, and Egalmoth and Tuor went from place to place of the defence, but Ecthelion lay by the fountain; and that stand was the most stubborn-valiant that is remembered in all the songs or in any tale. Yet at long last a drake bursts the barrier to the north – and there had once been the issue of the Alley of Roses and a fair place to see or to walk in, but now there is but a lane of blackness and it is filled with noise.

Tuor stood then in the way of that beast, but was sundered from Egalmoth, and they pressed him backward even to the centre of the square nigh the fountain. There he became weary from the strangling heat and was beaten down by a great demon, even Gothmog lord of Balrogs, son of Melko. But lo! Ecthelion, whose face was of the pallor of grey steel and whose shield-arm hung limp at his side, strode above him as he fell, and that Gnome drove at the demon, yet did not give him his death, getting rather a wound to his sword-arm that his weapon left his grasp. Then leapt Ecthelion lord of the Fountain, fairest of the Noldoli, full at Gothmog even as he raised his whip, and his helm that had a spike upon it he drove into that evil breast, and he twined his legs about his foeman's thighs; and the Balrog yelled and fell forward; but those two dropped into the basin of the king's fountain which was very deep. There found that creature his bane; and Ecthelion sank steel-laden into the depths, and so perished the lord of the Fountain after fiery battle in cool waters.

Now Tuor had arisen when the assault of Ecthelion gave him space, and seeing that great deed he wept for his love of that fair Gnome of the Fountain, but being wrapped in battle he scarce cut his way to the folk about the palace. There seeing the wavering of the enemy by reason of the dread of the fall of Gothmog the marshal of the hosts, the royal house laid on and the king came down in splendour among them and hewed with them, that they swept again much of the square, and of the Balrogs slew even two score, which is a very great prowess indeed: but greater still did they do, for they hemmed in one of the fire-drakes for all his flaming, and forced him into the very waters of the fountain that he perished therein. Now this was the end of that fair water; and its pools turned to steam and its spring was dried up, and it shot no more into the heaven, but rather a vast column of vapour arose to the sky and the cloud therefrom floated over all the land.

Then dread fell on all for the doom of the fountain, and the square was filled with mists of scalding heat and blinding fogs, and the people of the royal house were killed therein by heat and by the foe and by the serpents and by one another; but a body of them saved the king, and there was a rally of men beneath Glingol and Bansil.

Then said the king: 'Great is the fall of Gondolin', and men shuddered, for such were the words of Amnon the prophet of old; but Tuor speaking wildly for ruth and love of the king cried: 'Gondolin stands yet, and Ulmo will not suffer it to perish!' Now they were at that time standing, Tuor by the Trees and the King upon the Stairs, as they had stood aforetime when Tuor spoke the embassy of Ulmo. But Turgon said: 'Evil have I brought upon the Flower of the Plain in despite of Ulmo, and now he leaveth it to wither in the fire. Lo! hope is no more in my heart for my city of loveliness, but the children of the Noldoli shall not be worsted for ever.'

Then did the Gondothlim clash their weapons, for many stood nigh, but Turgon said: 'Fight not against doom, O my children! Seek ye who may safety in flight, if perhaps there be time yet: but let Tuor have your lealty.' But Tuor said: 'Thou art king', and Turgon made answer: 'Yet no blow will I strike more', and he cast his crown at the roots of Glingol. Then did Galdor who stood there pick it up, but Turgon accepted it not, and bare of head climbed to the topmost pinnacle of that white tower that stood nigh his palace. There he shouted in a voice like a horn blown among the mountains, and all that were gathered beneath the Trees and the foemen in the mists of the square heard him: 'Great is the victory of the Noldoli!' And it is said that it was then middle night, and that the Orcs yelled in derision.

Then did men speak of a sally, and were of two minds. Many held that it were impossible to burst through, nor might they even so get over the plain or through the hills, and that it were better therefore to die about the king. But Tuor might not think well of the death of so many fair women and children, were it at the hands of their own folk in the last resort, or by the weapons of the enemy, and he spoke of the delving and of the secret way. Therefore did he counsel that they beg Turgon to have other mind, and coming among them lead that remnant southward to the walls and the entry of that passage; but he himself burnt with desire to fare thither and know how Idril and Eärendel might be, or to get tidings hence to them and bid them be gone speedily, for Gondolin was taken. Now Tuor's plan seemed to the lords desperate indeed – seeing the narrowness of the tunnel and the greatness of the company that must pass it – yet would they fain take this rede in their straits. But Turgon hearkened not, and bid them fare now ere it was too late, and 'Let Tuor,' said he, 'be your guide and your chieftain. But I Turgon will not leave my city, and will burn with it.' Then sped they messengers again to the tower, saying: 'Sire, who are the Gondothlim if thou perish? Lead us!' But he said: 'Lo! I abide here'; and a third time, and he said: 'If I am king, obey my behests, and dare not to parley further with my commands.' After that they sent no more and made ready for the forlorn attempt. But the folk of the royal house that yet lived would not budge a foot, but gathered thickly about the base of the king's tower. 'Here,' said they, 'we will stay if Turgon goes not forth'; and they might not be persuaded.

Now was Tuor torn sorely between his reverence for the king and the love for Idril and his child, wherewith his heart was sick; yet already serpents fare about the square trampling upon dead and dying, and the foe gathers in the mists for the last onslaught; and the choice must be made. Then because of the wailing of the women in the halls of the palace and the greatness of his pity for that sad remainder of the peoples of Gondolin, he gathered all that rueful company, maids, children, and mothers, and setting them amidmost marshalled as well as he might his men around them. Deepest he set them at flank and at rear, for he purposed falling back southward fighting as best he might with the rearguard as he went; and thus if it might so be to win down the Road of Pomps to the Place of the Gods ere any great force be sent to circumvent him. Thence was it his thought to go by the Way of Running Waters past the Fountains of the South to the walls and to his home; but the passage of the secret tunnel he doubted much. Thereupon espying his movement the foe made forthwith a great onslaught upon his left flank and his rear – from east and north – even as he began to withdraw; but his right was covered by the king's hall and the head of that column drew already into the Road of Pomps.

Then some hugest of the drakes came on and glared in the fog, and he must perforce bid the company to go at a run, fighting on the left at haphazard; but Glorfindel held the rear manfully and many more of the Golden Flower fell there. So it was that they passed the Road of Pomps and reached Gar Ainion, the Place of the Gods; and this was very open and at its middle the highest ground of all the city. Here Tuor looks for an evil stand and it is scarce in his hope to get much further; but behold, the foe seems already to slacken and scarce any follow them, and this is a wonder. Now comes Tuor at their head to the Place of Wedding, and lo! there stands Idril before him with her hair unbraided as on that day of their marriage before; and great is his amaze. By her stood Voronwë and none other, but Idril saw not even Tuor, for her gaze was set back upon the Place of the King that now lay somewhat below them. Then all that host halted and looked back whither her eyes gazed and their hearts stood still; for now they saw why the foe pressed them so little and the reason of their salvation. Lo! a drake was coiled even on the very steps of the palace and defiled their whiteness; but swarms of the Orcs ransacked therein and dragged

95

forth forgotten women and children or slew men that fought alone. Glingol was withered to the stock and Bansil was blackened utterly, and the king's tower was beset. High up they could descry the form of the king, but about the base a serpent of iron spouting flame lashed and rowed with his tail, and Balrogs were round him; and there was the king's house in great anguish, and dread cries carried up to the watchers. So was it that the sack of the halls of Turgon and that most valiant stand of the royal house held the mind of the foe, so that Tuor got thence with his company, and stood now in tears upon the Place of the Gods.

Then said Idril: 'Woe is me whose father awaiteth doom even upon his topmost pinnacle; but seven times woe whose lord hath gone down before Melko and will stride home no more' – for she was distraught with the agony of that night.

Then said Tuor: 'Lo! Idril, it is I, and I live; yet now will I get thy father hence, be it from the Hells of Melko!' With that he would make down the hill alone, maddened by the grief of his wife; but she coming to her wits in a storm of weeping clasped his knees saying: 'My lord! My lord!' and delayed him. Yet even as they spoke a great noise and a yelling rose from that place of anguish. Behold, the tower leapt into a flame and in a stab of fire it fell, for the dragons crushed the base of it and all who stood there. Great was the clangour of that terrible fall, and therein passed Turgon King of the Gondothlim, and for that hour the victory was to Melko.

Then said Idril heavily: 'Sad is the blindness of the wise'; but Tuor said: 'Sad too is the stubbornness of those we love – yet it was a valiant fault,' then stooping he lifted and kissed

her, for she was more to him than all the Gondothlim; but she wept bitterly for her father. Then turned Tuor to the captains, saying: 'Lo, we must get hence with all speed, lest we be surrounded'; and forthwith they moved onward as swiftly as they might and got them far from thence ere the Orcs tired of sacking the palace and rejoicing at the fall of the tower of Turgon.

Now are they in the southward city and meet but scattered bands of plunderers who fly before them; yet do they find fire and burning everywhere for the ruthlessness of that enemy. Women do they meet, some with babes and some laden with chattels, but Tuor would not let them bear away aught save a little food. Coming now at length to a greater quiet Tuor asked Voronwë for tidings, in that Idril spoke not and was well-nigh in a swoon; and Voronwë told him of how she and he had waited before the doors of the house while the noise of those battles grew and shook their hearts; and Idril wept for lack of tidings from Tuor. At length she had sped the most part of her guard down the secret way with Eärendel, constraining them to depart with imperious words, yet was her grief great at that sundering. She herself would bide, said she, nor seek to live after her lord; and then she fared about gathering womenfolk and wanderers and speeding them down the tunnel, and smiting marauders with her small band; nor might they dissuade her from bearing a sword.

At length they had fallen in with a band somewhat too numerous, and Voronwë had dragged her thence but by the luck of the Gods, for all else with them perished, and their foe burned Tuor's house; yet found not the secret way. 'Therewith,' said Voronwë, 'thy lady became distraught of weariness and grief, and fared into the city wildly to my great fear – nor might I get her to sally from the burning.'

About the saying of these words were they come to the southern walls and nigh to Tuor's house, and lo! it was cast down and the wreckage was asmoke; and thereat was Tuor bitterly wroth. But there was a noise that boded the approach of Orcs, and Tuor despatched that company as swiftly as might be down that secret way.

Now is there great sorrow upon that staircase as those exiles bid farewell to Gondolin; yet are they without much hope of further life beyond the hills, for how shall any slip from the hand of Melko?

Glad is Tuor when all have passed the entrance and his fear lightens; indeed by the luck of the Valar only can all the folk have got therein unspied of the Orcs. Some now are left who casting aside their arms labour with picks from within and block up the entry of the passage, faring then after the host as they might; but when that folk had descended the stairway to a level with the valley the heat grew to a torment for the fire of the dragons that were about the city; and they were indeed nigh, for the delving there was at no great depth in the earth. Boulders were loosened by the tremors of the ground and falling crushed many, and fumes were in the air so that their torches and lanterns went out. Here they fell over bodies of some that had gone before and perished, and Tuor was in fear for Eärendel; and they pressed on in great darkness and anguish. Nigh two hours were they in that tunnel of the earth, and towards its end it was scarce finished, but rugged at the sides and low.

Then came they at the last lessened by wellnigh a tithe to the tunnel's opening, and it debouched cunningly in a large basin where once water had lain, but it was now full of thick bushes. Here were gathered no small press of mingled folk whom Idril and Voronwë had sped down the hidden way before them, and they were weeping softly in weariness and sorrow, but Eärendel was not there. Thereat were Tuor and Idril in anguish of heart. Lamentation was there too among all those others, for amidmost of the plain about them loomed afar the hill of Amon Gwareth crowned with flames, where had stood the gleaming city of their home. Fire-drakes are about it and monsters of iron fare in and out of its gates, and great is that sack of the Balrogs and Orcs. Somewhat of comfort has this nonetheless for the leaders, for they judge the plain to be nigh empty of Melko's folk save hard by the city, for thither have fared all his evil ones to revel in that destruction.

'Now,' therefore said Galdor, 'we must get as far hence toward the Encircling Mountains as may be ere dawn come upon us, and that giveth no great space of time, for summer is at hand.' Thereat rose a dissension, for a number said that it were folly to make for Cristhorn as Tuor purposed. 'The sun,' say they, 'will be up long ere we win the foothills, and we shall be whelmed in the plain by those drakes and those demons. Let us fare to Bad Uthwen, the Way of Escape, for that is but half the journeying, and our weary and our wounded may hope to win so far if no further.'

Yet Idril spoke against this, and persuaded the lords that they trust not to the magic of that way that had aforetime shielded it from discovery: 'for what magic stands if Gondolin be fallen?' Nonetheless a large body of men and women sundered from Tuor and fared to Bad Uthwen, and there into the jaws of a monster who by the guile of Melko at Meglin's rede sat at the outer issue that none came through. But the others, led by Legolas Greenleaf of the house of the Tree, who knew all that plain by day or by dark, and was night-sighted, made much speed over the vale for all their weariness, and halted only after a great march. Then was all the Earth spread with the grey light of that sad dawn which looked no more on the beauty of Gondolin; but the plain was full of mists – and that was a marvel, for no mist or fog came there ever before, and this perchance had to do with the doom of the fountain of the king. Again they rose, and covered by the vapours fared long past dawn in safety, till they were already too far away for any to descry them in those misty airs from the hill or from the ruined walls.

Now the Mountains or rather their lowest hills were on that side seven leagues save a mile from Gondolin, and Cristhorn the Cleft of Eagles two leagues of upward going from the beginning of the Mountains, for it was at a great height; wherefore they had yet two leagues and part of a third to traverse amid the spurs and foothills, and they were very weary. By now the sun hung well above a saddle in the eastern hills, and she was very red and great; and the mists nigh them were lifted, but the ruins of Gondolin were utterly hidden as in a cloud. Behold then at the clearing of the airs they saw, but a few furlongs off, a knot of men that fled on foot, and these were pursued by a strange cavalry, for on great wolves rode Orcs, as they thought, brandishing spears. Then said Tuor: 'Lo! there is Eärendel my son; behold, his face shineth as a star in the waste, and my men of the Wing are about him, and they are in sore straits.' Forthwith he chose fifty of the men that were least weary, and leaving the main company to follow he fared over the plain with that troop as swiftly as they had strength left. Coming now to carry of voice Tuor shouted to the men about Eärendel to stand and flee not, for the wolfriders were scattering them and slaying them piecemeal, and the child was upon the shoulders of one Hendor, a house-carle of Idril's, and he seemed like to be left with his burden. Then they stood back to back and Hendor and Eärendel amidmost; but Tuor soon came up, though all his troop were breathless.

Of the wolfriders there were a score, and of the men that were about Eärendel but six living; therefore had Tuor opened his men into a crescent of but one rank, and hoped so to envelop the riders, lest any escaping bring tidings to the main foe and draw ruin upon the exiles. In this he suc-ceeded, so that only two escaped, and therewithal wounded and without their beasts, wherefore were their tidings brought too late to the city.

Glad was Eärendel to greet Tuor, and Tuor most fain of his child; but said Eärendel: 'I am thirsty, father, for I have run far – nor had Hendor need to bear me.' Thereto his father said nought, having no water, and thinking of the need of all that company that he guided; but Eärendel said again: 'It was good to see Meglin die so, for he would set arms about my mother – and I liked him not; but I would travel in no tunnels for all Melko's wolfriders.' Then Tuor smiled and set him upon his shoulders. Soon after this the main company came up, and Tuor gave Eärendel to his mother who was in great joy; but Eärendel would not be borne in her arms, for he said: 'Mother Idril, thou art weary, and warriors in mail ride not among the Gondothlim, save it be old Salgant!' – and his mother laughed amid her sorrow; but Eärendel said: 'Nay, where is Salgant?' – for Salgant had told him quaint tales or played drolleries with him at times, and Eärendel had much laughter of the old Gnome in those days when he came many a day to the house of Tuor, loving the good wine and fair repast he there received. But none could say where Salgant was, nor can they now. Mayhap he was whelmed by fire upon his bed; yet some have it that he was taken captive to the halls of Melko and made his buffoon – and this is an ill fate for a noble of the good race of the Gnomes. Then was Eärendel sad at that, and walked beside his mother in silence.

Now came they to the foothills and it was full morning but still grey, and there nigh to the beginning of the upward road folk stretched them and rested in a little dale fringed with trees and with hazel-bushes, and many slept despite their peril, for they were utterly spent. Yet Tuor set a strict watch, and himself slept not. Here they made one meal of scanty food and broken meats; and Eärendel quenched his thirst and played beside a little brook. Then said he to his mother: 'Mother Idril, I would we had good Ecthelion of the Fountain here to play to me on his flute, or make me willow-whistles! Perchance he has gone on ahead?' But Idril said nay, and told what she had heard of his end. Then said Eärendel that he cared not ever to see the streets of Gondolin again, and he wept bitterly; but Tuor said that he would not again see those streets, 'for Gondolin is no more.'

Thereafter nigh to the hour of sundown behind the hills Tuor bade the company arise, and they pressed on by rugged paths. Soon now the grass faded and gave way to mossy stones, and trees fell away, and even the pines and firs grew sparse. About the set of the sun the way so wound behind a shoulder of the hills that they might not again look towards Gondolin. There all that company turned, and lo! the plain is clear and smiling in the last light as of old; but afar off as they gazed a great flare shot up against the darkened north – and that was the fall of the last tower of Gondolin, even that which had stood hard by the southern gate, and whose shadow fell oft across the walls of Tuor's house. Then sank the sun, and they saw Gondolin no more.

Now the pass of Cristhorn, that is the Eagles' Cleft, is one of dangerous going, and that host had not ventured it by dark, lanternless and without torches, and very weary and cumbered with women and children and sick and stricken men, had it not been for their great fear of Melko's scouts, for it was a great company and might not fare very secretly. Darkness gathered rapidly as they approached that high place, and they must string out into a long and straggling line. Galdor and a band of men spear-armed went ahead, and Legolas was with them, whose eyes were like cats' for the dark, yet could they see further. Thereafter followed the least weary of the women supporting the sick and the wounded that could go on foot. Idril was with these, and Eärendel who bore up well, but Tuor was in the midmost behind them with all his men of the Wing, and they bare some who were grievously hurt, and Egalmoth was with him, but he had got a hurt in that sally from the square. Behind again came many women with babes, and girls, and lamed men, yet was the going slow enough for them. At the rearmost went the largest band of men battle-whole, and there was Glorfindel of the golden hair.

Thus were they come to Cristhorn, which is an ill place by reason of its height, for this is so great that spring nor summer come ever there, and it is very cold. Indeed while the valley dances in the sun, there all the year snow dwells in those bleak places, and even as they came there the wind howled, coming from the north behind them, and it bit sorely. Snow fell and whirled in wind-eddies and got into their eyes, and this was not good, for there the path is narrow, and of the right or westerly hand a sheer wall rises nigh seven chains from the way, ere it bursts atop into jagged pinnacles where are many eyries. There dwells Thorondor King of Eagles, Lord of the Thornhoth, whom the Eldar named Sorontur. But of the other hand is a fall not right sheer yet dreadly steep, and it has long teeth of rock up-pointing so that one may climb down – or fall maybe – but by no means up. And from that deep is no escape at either end any more than by the sides, and Thorn Sir runs at bottom. He falls therein from the south over a great

precipice but with a slender water, for he is a thin stream in those heights, and he issues to the north after flowing but a rocky mile above ground down a narrow passage that goes into the mountain, and scarce a fish could squeeze through with him.

Galdor and his men were come now to the end nigh to where Thorn Sir falls into the abyss, and the others straggled, for all Tuor's efforts, back over most of the mile of the perilous way between chasm and cliff, so that Glorfindel's folk were scarce come to its beginning, when there was a yell in the night that echoed in that grim region. Behold, Galdor's men were beset in the dark suddenly by shapes leaping from behind rocks where they had lain hidden even from the glance of Legolas. It was Tuor's thought that they had fallen in with one of Melko's ranging companies, and he feared no more than a sharp brush in the dark, yet he sent the women and sick around him rearward and joined his men to Galdor's, and there was an affray upon the perilous path. But now rocks fell from above, and things looked ill, for they did grievous hurt; but matters seemed to Tuor yet worse when the noise of arms came from the rear, and tidings were said to him by a man of the Swallow that Glorfindel was ill bested by men from behind, and that a Balrog was with them.

Then was he sore afraid of a trap, and this was even what had in truth befallen, for watchers had been set by Melko all about the encircling hills. Yet so many did the valour of the Gondothlim draw off to the assault ere the city could be taken that these were but thinly spread, and were at the least here in the south. Nonetheless one of these had espied the

company as they started the upward going from the dale of
hazels, and as many bands were got together against them as
might be, and devised to fall upon the exiles to front and rear
even upon the perilous way of Cristhorn. Now Galdor and
Glorfindel held their own despite the surprise of assault, and
many of the Orcs were struck into the abyss; but the falling
of the rocks was like to end all their valour, and the flight
from Gondolin to come to ruin. The moon about that hour
rose above the pass, and the gloom somewhat lifted, for his
pale light filtered into dark places; yet it lit not the path for
the height of the walls. Then arose Thorondor, King of
Eagles, and he loved not Melko; for Melko had caught many
of his kindred and chained them against sharp rocks to
squeeze from them the magic words whereby he might learn
to fly (for he dreamed of contending even against Manwë in
the air); and when they would not tell he cut off their wings
and sought to fashion therefrom a mighty pair for his use,
but it availed not.

Now when the clamour from the pass rose to his great
eyrie he said: 'Wherefore are these foul things, these Orcs of
the hills, climbed near to my throne; and why do the sons of
the Noldoli cry out in the low places for fear of the children
of Melko the accursed? Arise O Thornhoth, whose beaks
are of steel and whose talons swords!'

Thereupon there was a rushing like a great wind in rocky
places, and the Thornhoth, the people of the Eagles, fell on
those Orcs who had scaled above the path, and tore their
faces and their hands and flung them to the rocks of Thorn
Sir far below. Then were the Gondothlim glad, and they

made in after days the Eagle a sign of their kindred in token of their joy, and Idril bore it, but Eärendel loved rather the Swan-wing of his father. Now unhampered Galdor's men bore back those that opposed them, for they were not very many and the onset of the Thornhoth affrighted them much; and the company fared forward again, though Glorfindel had fighting enough in the rear. Already the half had passed the perilous way and the falls of Thorn Sir, when that Balrog that was with the rearward foe leapt with great might on certain lofty rocks that stood into the path on the left side upon the lip of the chasm, and thence with a leap of fury he was past Glorfindel's men and among the women and the sick in front, lashing with his whip of flame. Then Glorfindel leapt forward upon him and his golden armour gleamed strangely in the moon, and he hewed at that demon that it leapt again upon a great boulder and Glorfindel after. Now there was a deadly combat upon that high rock above the folk; and these, pressed behind and hindered ahead, were grown so close that well nigh all could see, yet was it over ere Glorfindel's men could leap to his side. The ardour of Glorfindel drove that Balrog from point to point, and his mail fended him from its whip and claw. Now had he beaten a heavy swinge upon its iron helm, now hewn off the creature's whip-arm at the elbow. Then sprang the Balrog in the torment of his pain and fear full at Glorfindel, who stabbed like a dart of a snake; but he found only a shoulder, and was grappled, and they swayed to a fall upon the crag-top. Then Glorfindel's left hand sought a dirk, and this he thrust up that it pierced the Balrog's belly nigh his own face (for that demon was double his stature); and it shrieked, and fell backward from the rock, and falling clutched Glorfindel's yellow locks beneath his cap, and those twain fell into the abyss.

Now this was a very grievous thing, for Glorfindel was most dearly beloved – and lo! the dint of their fall echoed about the hills, and the abyss of Thorn Sir rang. Then at the death-cry of the Balrog the Orcs before and behind wavered and were slain or fled far away, and Thorondor himself, a mighty bird, descended to the abyss and brought up the body of Glorfindel; but the Balrog lay, and the water of Thorn Sir ran black for many a day far below in Tumladen.

Still do the Eldar say when they see good fighting at great odds of power against a fury of evil: 'Alas! It is Glorfindel and the Balrog', and their hearts are still sore for that fair one of the Noldoli. Because of their love, despite the haste and their fear of the advent of new foes, Tuor let raise a great stone-cairn over Glorfindel just there beyond the perilous way by the precipice of Eagle-stream, and Thorondor has let not yet any harm come thereto, but yellow flowers have fared thither and blow ever now about that mound in those unkindly places; but the folk of the Golden Flower wept at its building and might not dry their tears.

Now who shall tell of the wanderings of Tuor and the exiles of Gondolin in the wastes that lie beyond the mountains to the south of the vale of Tumladen? Miseries were theirs and death, colds and hungers, and ceaseless watches. That they won ever through those regions infested by

Melko's evil came from the great slaughter and damage done
to his power in that assault, and from the speed and wariness
with which Tuor led them; for of a certain Melko knew of
that escape and was furious thereat. Ulmo had heard tidings
in the far oceans of the deeds that were done, but he could
not yet aid them for they were far from waters and rivers –
and indeed they thirsted sorely, and they knew not the way.

But after a year and more of wandering, in which many
a time they journeyed long tangled in the magic of those
wastes only to come again upon their own tracks, once more
the summer came, and nigh to its height they came at
last upon a stream, and following this came to better lands
and were a little comforted. Here did Voronwë guide them,
for he had caught a whisper of Ulmo's in that stream one late
summer's night – and he got ever much wisdom from the
sound of waters. Now he led them even till they came down
to Sirion which that stream fed, and then both Tuor and
Voronwë saw that they were not far from the outer issue of
old of the Way of Escape, and were once more in that deep
dale of alders. Here were all the bushes trampled and the
trees burnt, and the dale-wall scarred with flame, and they
wept, for they thought they knew the fate of those who
sundered aforetime from them at the tunnel-mouth.

Now they journeyed down that river but were again in
fear from Melko, and fought affrays with his Orc-bands and
were in peril from the wolfriders, but his firedrakes sought
not at them, both for the great exhaustion of their fires in
the taking of Gondolin, and the increasing power of Ulmo
as the river grew. So came they after many days – for they

went slowly and got their sustenance very hardly – to those great heaths and morasses above the Land of Willows, and Voronwë knew not those regions. Now here goes Sirion a very great way under earth, diving at the great cavern of the Tumultuous Winds, but running clear again above the Pools of Twilight, even where Tulkas after fought with Melko's self. Tuor had fared over these regions by night and dusk after Ulmo came to him amid the reeds, and he remembered not the ways. In places that land is full of deceits and very marshy; and here the host had long delay and was vexed by sore flies, for it was autumn still, and agues and fevers fared amongst them, and they cursed Melko.

Yet came they at last to the great pools and the edges of that most tender Land of Willows; and the very breath of the winds thereof brought rest and peace to them, and for the comfort of that place the grief was assuaged of those who mourned the dead in that great fall. There women and maids grew fair again and their sick were healed, and old wounds ceased to pain; yet they alone who of reason feared their folk living still in bitter thraldom in the Hells of Iron sang not, nor did they smile.

Here they abode very long indeed, and Eärendel was a grown boy ere the voice of Ulmo's conches drew the heart of Tuor, that his sea-longing returned with a thirst the deeper for years of stifling; and all that host arose at his bidding, and got them down Sirion to the Sea.

Now the folk that had passed into the Eagles' Cleft and who saw the fall of Glorfindel had been nigh eight hundreds – a large wayfaring, yet was it a sad remnant of so fair and numerous a city. But they who arose from the grasses of the Land of Willows in years after and fared away to sea, when spring set celandine in the meads and they had held sad festival in memorial of Glorfindel, these numbered but three hundreds and a score of men and man-children, and two hundreds and three score of women and maid-children. Now the number of women was few because of their hiding or being stowed by their kinsfolk in secret places in the city. There were they burned or slain or taken and enthralled, and the rescue-parties found them too seldom; and it is the greatest ruth to think of this, for the maids and women of the Gondothlim were as fair as the sun and as lovely as the moon and brighter than the stars. Glory dwelt in that city of Gondolin of the Seven Names, and its ruin was the most dread of all the sacks of cities upon the face of Earth. Nor Bablon, nor Ninwi, nor the towers of Trui, nor all the many takings of Rûm that is greatest among Men, saw such terror as fell that day upon Amon Gwareth in the kindred of the Gnomes; and this is esteemed the worst work that Melko has yet thought of in the world.

Yet now those exiles of Gondolin dwelt at the mouth of Sirion by the waves of the Great Sea. There they take the name of Lothlim, the people of the flower, for Gondothlim is a name too sore to their hearts; and fair among the Lothlim Eärendel grows in the house of his father, and the great tale of Tuor is come to its waning.'

Then said Littleheart son of Bronweg: 'Alas for Gondolin.'

*

III

THE EARLIEST TEXT

Important elements in the early evolution of the history of the Elder Days are my father's hurried notes. As I have described them elsewhere, these notes were for the most part pencilled at furious speed, the writing now rubbed and faint and in places after long study scarcely decipherable, on slips of paper, disordered and dateless, or in a little notebook; in these, during the years in which he was composing the *Lost Tales*, he jotted down thoughts and suggestions – many of them being no more than simple sentences, or mere isolated names, serving as reminders of work to be done, stories to be told, or changes to be made.

Among these notes is found what must be the earliest trace of the story of the fall of Gondolin:

Isfin daughter of Fingolma loved from afar by Eöl (Arval) of the Mole-kin of the Gnomes. He is strong and in favour with Fingolma and with the Sons of Fëanor (to whom he is akin) because he is a leader of the Miners and searches after hidden jewels, but he is illfavoured and Isfin loathes him.

For an explanation of the choice of the word 'Gnomes' see p.21 (footnote). *Fingolma* was an early name of the later *Finwë* (the leader of the second host of the Elves, the Noldor, on the Great Journey from Palisor, the land of their awakening). Isfin appears in the *Tale of the Fall of Gondolin* as the sister of Turgon King of Gondolin and the mother of Meglin, son of Eöl.

It is obvious that this note is a form of the story told in the Lost Tales, despite the major difference. In the note it is Eöl the miner of the 'Mole-kin' who is the suitor for the daughter of Fingolma, Isfin, who rejects him on account of his ugliness. In the 'Lost Tale', on the other hand, the rejected – and ugly – suitor is Meglin the *son* of Eöl and his mother is Isfin – the sister of Turgon King of Gondolin; and it is said expressly (p.61) that the tale of Isfin and Eöl 'may not here be told' – presumably because my father thought that it would go too far afield.

I think it most probable that the brief note given above was written before the *Tale of the Fall of Gondolin* and before the advent of Maeglin, and that the story in its origin had no association with Gondolin.

(Henceforward I shall usually refer to the 'Lost Tale' of *The Fall of Gondolin* (pp. 37–111) simply as 'the *Tale*'.)

*

TURLIN AND THE EXILES OF GONDOLIN

There is a loose page carrying a short prose piece, unquestionably preserved in its entirety, that bears the title *Turlin and the Exiles of Gondolin*. It can be placed chronologically *after* the *Tale of the Fall of Gondolin*, and was clearly the abandoned start of a new version of the *Tale*.

My father hesitated much over the name of the hero of Gondolin, and in this text he gave him the name *Turlin*, but altered it throughout to *Turgon*. Since this (not rare) interchange of names between characters can be needlessly confusing, I will name him *Tuor* in my text of the piece that follows.

The anger of the Gods (the Valar) against the Gnomes and the sealing of Valinor against all comers, with which this piece begins, arose from their rebellion and their evil deeds at the Haven of the Swans. This is known as the

Kinslaying, and is of importance in the story of the Fall of Gondolin, and indeed of the later history of the Elder Days.

Turlin [Tuor] and the Exiles of Gondolin

'Then' said Ilfiniol son of Bronweg 'know that Ulmo Lord of Waters forgot never the sorrows of the Elven kindreds beneath the power of Melko, but he might do little because of the anger of the other Gods who shut their hearts against the race of the Gnomes, and dwelt behind the veiled hills of Valinor heedless of the Outer World, so deep was their ruth and regret for the death of the Two Trees. Nor did any save Ulmo only dread the power of Melko that wrought ruin and sorrow over all the Earth; but Ulmo desired that Valinor should gather all its might to quench his evil ere it be too late, and it seemed to him that both purposes might perchance be achieved if messengers from the Gnomes should win to Valinor and plead for pardon and for pity upon the Earth; for the love of Palúrien and Oromë her son for those wide realms did but slumber still. Yet hard and evil was the road from the Outer Earth to Valinor, and the Gods themselves had meshed the ways with magic and veiled the encircling hills. Thus did Ulmo seek unceasingly to stir the Gnomes to send messengers unto Valinor, but Melko was cunning and very deep in wisdom, and unsleeping was his wariness in all things that touched the Elven kindreds, and their messengers overcame not the perils and temptations of that longest and most evil of all roads, and many that dared to set forth were lost for ever.

Now tells the tale how Ulmo despaired that any of the Elven race should surpass the dangers of the way, and of the deepest and the latest design that he then fashioned, and of those things which came of it.

In those days the greater part of the kindreds of Men dwelt after the Battle of Unnumbered Tears in that land of the North that has many names, but which the Elves of Kôr have named Hisilómë which is the Twilit Mist, and the Gnomes, who of the Elf-kin know it best, Dor-lómin the Land of Shadows. A people mighty in numbers were there, dwelling about the wide pale waters of Mithrim the great lake that lies in those regions, and other folk named them Tunglin or folk of the Harp, for their joy was in the wild music and minstrelsy of the fells and woodlands, but they knew not and sang not of the sea. Now this folk came into those places after the dread battle, being too late summoned thither from afar, and they bore no stain of treachery against the Elven kin; but indeed many among them clung to such friendship with the hidden Gnomes of the mountains and Dark Elves as might be still for the sorrow and mistrust born of those ruinous deeds in the Vale of Ninniach [the site of the Battle of Unnumbered Tears].

Tuor was a man of that folk, son of Peleg, son of Indor, son of Fengel who was their chief and hearing the summons had marched out of the deeps of the East with all his folk. But Tuor dwelt not much with his kindred, and loved rather solitude and the friendship of the Elves whose tongues he knew, and he wandered alone about the long shores of Mithrim, now hunting in its woods, now making sudden music in the rocks upon his rugged harp of wood strung with the sinews of bears. But he sang not for the ears of Men, and many hearing the power of his rough songs came from afar to hearken to his harping; but Tuor left his singing and departed to lonely places in the mountains.

Many strange things he learned there, broken tidings of far off things, and longing came upon him for deeper lore, but as yet his heart turned not from the long shores and the pale waters of Mithrim in the mists. Yet was he not fated to dwell for ever in those places, for it is said that magic and destiny led him on a day to a cavernous opening in the rocks, down which a hidden river flowed from Mithrim. And Tuor entered that cavern seeking to learn its secret, but having entered the waters of Mithrim drove him forward into the heart of the rock and he might not win back into the light. This men have said was not without the will of Ulmo, at whose prompting maybe the Gnomes had fashioned that deep and hidden way. Then came the Gnomes to Tuor and guided him along the dark passages amid the mountains until he came out once more into the light.

It will be seen that my father had the text of the *Tale* in front of him when he wrote this text (which I will call 'the *Turlin* version'), for phrases of the one reappear in the other (such as 'magic and destiny led him on a day to a cavernous opening', p.37); but in several features there are advances on the earlier text. The original genealogy of Tuor remains (son of Peleg, son of Indor), but more is told of his people: they were Men from the East who came to the aid of the Elves in the vast and ruinous battle against the forces of Melko that came to be known as *The Battle of Unnumbered Tears*. But they came too late; and they settled in great numbers in Hisilómë 'Twilit Mist' (Hithlum), called also Dor-lómin 'Land of Shadows'. An important and decisive element in the early conception of the history of the Elder Days was the overwhelming nature of the victory of Melko in that battle, so sweeping that a great part of the people named Noldoli became his imprisoned slaves; it is said in the *Tale* (p.49): 'Know then that the Gondothlim [the people of Gondolin] were that kin of the Noldoli who alone escaped Melko's power when at the Battle of Unnumbered Tears he slew and enslaved their folk and wove spells about them and caused them to dwell in the Hells of Iron, faring thence at his will and bidding only.'

Notable also is the account in this text of Ulmo's 'design and desire', as his purpose is described in the *Tale* (p.47): but in the *Tale* it is said that 'thereof Tuor understood little' – and we are told no more. In this further brief text, the *Turlin* version, on the other hand, Ulmo spoke of his inability to prevail against the other Valar, isolated in his fear of the power of Melko, and of his wish that Valinor should rise against that power; his attempts also to per- suade the Noldoli to send messengers to Valinor to plead for compassion and help, while the Valar 'dwelt behind the veiled hills of Valinor heedless of the Outer World.' This was the time known as 'The Hiding of Valinor', when, as is said in the *Turlin* version (p.115), 'the Gods themselves had meshed the ways [to Valinor] with magic and veiled the encircling hills' (on this crucial element in the history see *The Evolution of the Story*, pp.223 ff.).

Most significant is this passage (p.116): 'Now tells the tale how Ulmo despaired that any of the Elven race should surpass the dangers of the way, and of the deepest and the latest design that he then fashioned, and of those things which came of it.'

THE STORY TOLD IN THE
SKETCH OF THE MYTHOLOGY

I give now the form of the story of the Fall of Gondolin that
my father wrote in 1926 in a work called *Sketch of the
Mythology*, identifying it later as *The Original Silmarillion*.
A portion of the work was included and its nature explained
in *Beren and Lúthien* (p.89), and I have used a further
portion to serve as a prologue to this book. My father made
later a number of corrections (almost all in the form of
additions), and I include most of these in square brackets.

Ylmir is the Gnomish form for *Ulmo*.

The great river Sirion flowed through the lands south-
west; at its mouth was a great delta, and its lower course ran
through wide green and fertile lands, little peopled save by
birds and beasts because of the Orc-raids; but they were
not inhabited by Orcs, who preferred the northern woods,
and feared the power of Ylmir – for Sirion's mouth was in
the Western Seas.

Turgon Fingolfin's son had a sister Isfin. She was lost in
Taur-na-Fuin after the Battle of Unnumbered Tears. There
she was trapped by the Dark Elf Eöl. Their son was Meglin.
The people of Turgon escaping, aided by the prowess of
Húrin, were lost from the knowledge of Morgoth, and indeed
of all in the world save Ylmir. In a secret place in the hills
their scouts climbing to the tops [had] discovered a broad
valley entirely encircled by the hills in rings ever lower as
they came towards the centre. Amid this ring was a wide land
without hills, except for one rocky hill that stuck up from the
plain, not right at the centre, but nearest to that part of the
outer wall which marched close to the edge of Sirion. [The
hill nearest to Angband was guarded by Fingolfin's cairn.]

Ylmir's messages come up Sirion bidding them take refuge
in this valley, and teaching them spells of enchantment to
place upon all the hills about, to keep off foes and spies.
He foretells that their fortress shall stand longest of all the
refuges of the Elves against Morgoth, and like Doriath never
be overthrown save by treachery from within. The spells
are strongest near to Sirion, although here the encircling
mountains are lowest. Here the Gnomes dig a mighty winding tunnel under the roots of the mountains, that issues at
last in the Guarded Plain. Its outer entrance is guarded by
the spells of Ylmir; its inner is watched unceasingly by the
Gnomes. It is set there in case those within ever need to
escape, and as a way of more rapid exit from the valley for
scouts, wanderers, and messages, and also as an entrance
for fugitives escaping from Morgoth.

Thorondor King of Eagles removes his eyries to the

northern heights of the encircling mountains and guards
them against Orc-spies [sitting upon Fingolfin's cairn]. On
the rocky hill Amon Gwareth, the hill of watching, whose
sides they polish to the smoothness of glass, and whose
top they level, the great city of Gondolin with gates of steel
is built. The plain all about is levelled as flat and smooth
as a lawn of clipped grass to the feet of the hills, so that
nothing can creep over it unawares. The people of Gondolin
grows mighty, and their armouries are filled with weapons.
But Turgon does not march to the aid of Nargothrond,
or Doriath, and after the slaying of Dior he has no more
to do with the sons of Fëanor. Finally he closes the vale to
all fugitives, and forbids the folk of Gondolin to leave the
valley. Gondolin is the only stronghold of the Elves left.
Morgoth has not forgotten Turgon, but his search is in vain.
Nargothrond is destroyed; Doriath desolate; Húrin's children dead; and only scattered and fugitive Elves, Gnomes
and Ilkorins left, except such as work in the smithies and
mines in great numbers. His triumph is nearly complete.

Meglin son of Eöl and Isfin sister of Turgon was sent by
his mother to Gondolin, and there received, although half of
Ilkorin blood, and treated as a prince [last of the fugitives
from without].

Húrin of Hithlum had a brother Huor. The son of Huor
was Tuor, younger than [> cousin of] Túrin son of Húrin.
Rían, Huor's wife, sought her husband's body among the
slain on the field of Unnumbered Tears, and died there. Her
son remaining in Hithlum fell into the hands of the faithless
men whom Morgoth drove into Hithlum after that battle,

and he was made a thrall. Growing wild and rough he fled
into the woods, and became an outlaw, and a solitary, living
alone and communing with none save rarely with wandering
and hidden Elves. On a time Ylmir contrived that he should
be led to a subterranean river-course leading out of Mithrim
into a chasmed river that flowed at last into the Western Sea.
In this way his going was unmarked by Man, Orc, or spy,
and unknown of Morgoth. After long wanderings down the
western shores he came to the mouths of Sirion, and there
fell in with the Gnome Bronweg, who had once been in
Gondolin. They journey secretly up Sirion together. Tuor
lingers long in the sweet land Nan-tathrin 'Valley of
Willows'; but there Ylmir himself comes up the river to visit
him, and tells him of his mission. He is to bid Turgon to
prepare for battle with Morgoth; for Ylmir will turn the
hearts of the Valar to forgive the Gnomes and send them
succour. If Turgon will do this, the battle will be terrible,
but the race of Orcs will perish, and will not in after ages
trouble Elves and Men. If not, the people of Gondolin are to
prepare for flight to Sirion's mouth, where Ylmir will aid
them to build a fleet and guide them back to Valinor. If
Turgon does Ylmir's will Tuor is to abide a while in Gondolin and then go back to Hithlum with a force of Gnomes
and draw Men once more into alliance with the Elves, for
'without Men the Elves shall not prevail against the Orcs
and Balrogs'. This Ylmir does because he knows that ere
seven full years are passed the doom of Gondolin will come
through Meglin [if they sit still in their halls].

Tuor and Bronweg reach the secret way, [which they find

by grace of Ylmir] and come out upon the guarded plain. Taken captive by the watch they are led before Turgon. Turgon is grown old and very mighty and proud, and Gondolin so fair and beautiful, and its people so proud of it and confident in its secret and impregnable strength, that the king and most of the people do not wish to trouble about the Gnomes and Elves without, or care for Men, nor do they long any more for Valinor. Meglin approving, the king rejects Tuor's message in spite of the words of Idril the far-sighted (also called Idril Silverfoot, because she loved to walk barefoot) his daughter, and the wiser of his counsellors. Tuor lives on in Gondolin, and becomes a great chieftain. After three years he weds Idril – Tuor and Beren alone of all mortals ever wedded Elves, and since Elwing daughter of Dior Beren's son wedded Eärendel son of Tuor and Idril of them alone has come the strain of Elfinesse into mortal blood.

Not long after this Meglin going far afield over the mountains is taken by Orcs, and purchases his life when taken to Angband by revealing Gondolin and its secrets. Morgoth promises him the lordship of Gondolin, and possession of Idril. Lust for Idril led him the easier to his treachery, and added to his hatred for Tuor.

Morgoth sends him back to Gondolin. Eärendel is born, having the beauty and light and wisdom of Elfinesse, the hardihood and strength of Men, and the longing for the sea which captured Tuor and held him for ever when Ylmir spoke to him in the Land of Willows.

At last Morgoth is ready, and the attack is made on Gondolin with dragons, Balrogs, and Orcs. After a dreadful fight about the walls the city is stormed, and Turgon perishes with many of the most noble in the last fight in the great square. Tuor rescues Idril and Eärendel from Meglin, and hurls him from the battlements. He then leads the remnant of the people of Gondolin down a secret tunnel previously made by Idril's advice which comes out far in the north of the Plain. Those who would not come with him but fled to the old Way of Escape are caught by the dragon sent by Morgoth to watch that exit.

In the fume of the burning Tuor leads his company into the mountains into the cold pass of Cristhorn (Eagles' Cleft). There they are ambushed, but saved by the valour of Glorfindel (chief of the house of the Golden Flower of Gondolin, who dies in a duel with a Balrog upon a pinnacle) and the intervention of Thorondor. The remnant reaches Sirion and journeys to the land at its mouth – the Waters of Sirion. Morgoth's triumph is now complete.

The story told in this compressed form had not greatly changed from its form in the *Tale of the Fall of Gondolin*, but there are nonetheless significant developments. It is here that Tuor of the *Tale* is placed within the genealogy of the *Edain*, the Elf-friends: he has become the son of Huor the brother of Húrin – who was the father of the tragic hero Túrin Turambar. Thus Tuor was first cousin of Túrin. Here too emerges the story that Huor was slain in the Battle of Unnumbered Tears (see p.122), and that his wife Rían searched for his body on the battlefield, and died there. Tuor their son remained in Hithlum and was enslaved by 'the faithless men whom Morgoth drove into Hithlum after that battle' (p.122), but he escaped from them and took to a solitary life in the wilds.

A major difference in the early versions of the story, in respect of the wider history of the Elder Days, lies in what my father told of the discovery of the vale of Tumladen, hidden in the Encircling Mountains. In the *Sketch of the Mythology* (p.121) it is said that the people of Turgon escaping from the great battle (*Nirnaeth Arnoediad*, Unnumbered Tears) disappeared from the knowledge of Morgoth, because 'in a secret place in the hills their scouts climbing to the tops discovered a broad valley entirely encircled by the hills'. But in the days of the writing of the *Tale of the Fall of Gondolin* the story had been that there was a long age after the terrible battle before the destruction of Gondolin. It was said (p.58) that Tuor heard when he came there 'how unstaying labour through ages of years had not sufficed to its building and adornment whereat folk travailed yet'. The chronological difficulties led my father later to place the discovery of the site of Gondolin – by Turgon – and its building to a time many centuries *before* the Battle of Unnumbered Tears: Turgon led his people fleeing south down Sirion from the battlefield to the hidden city that he had founded a great age before. It was to a very ancient city that Tuor came.

A distinctive change in the story of the attack on Gondolin occurs, as I believe, in the *Sketch of the Mythology*. In *the Tale of The Fall of Gondolin* it was told that Morgoth had discovered Gondolin *before* Meglin was captured by Orcs (pp.63 ff.). He became very suspicious at the strange news that a Man had been seen 'wandering amid the dales of the waters of Sirion'; and to this end he gathered 'a mighty army of spies', of animals and birds and reptiles, who 'through the years untiring' brought back to him a mass of information. From the Encircling Mountains his spies had looked down on the plain of Tumladen; even the 'Way of Escape' had been revealed. When Eärendel was a year old tidings were brought to Gondolin of how the agents of Morgoth had 'encompassed the vale of Tumladen all around'; and Turgon strengthened the defences of the city. In *the Tale of The Fall of Gondolin* the *subsequent* treachery of Meglin lay in his describing in detail the plan of Gondolin and all the preparations for its defence (p.67); with Melko he 'devised a plan for the overthrow of Gondolin'.

But in the condensed account in the *Sketch* (p.124) it is said that when Meglin was captured by Orcs in the mountains 'he purchased his life when taken to Angband *by revealing Gondolin and its secrets*'. The words 'revealing Gondolin' seem to me to show clearly that the change had entered, and the later story was present: Morgoth did not know and could not discover where the Hidden Kingdom lay *until* the capture of Meglin by the Orcs. But there was yet another change to follow: see pp.292–3.

*

THE STORY TOLD IN THE
QUENTA NOLDORINWA

I come now to a major 'Silmarillion' text from which I took passages in *Beren and Lúthien*, and I repeat here a part of the explanatory note from that book.

> After the *Sketch of the Mythology* this text, which I will refer to as 'the *Quenta*', was the only complete and finished version of 'The Silmarillion' that my father achieved: a typescript that he made in (as seems certain) 1930. No preliminary drafts or outlines, if there were any, survive; but it is plain that for a good part of its length he had the *Sketch* before him. It is longer than the *Sketch*, and the 'Silmarillion style' has clearly appeared, but it remains a compression, a compendious account.

In calling this text a compression I do not mean to suggest that it was a hasty piece of work, awaiting a more finished treatment at some later time. Comparison of the two versions Q I and Q II (explained below) shows how attentively he heard and weighed the rhythm of the phrases. But compression there was indeed: witness the twenty or so lines devoted to the battle in the *Quenta* compared with the twelve pages in the *Tale*.

Towards the end of the *Quenta* my father expanded and retyped portions of the text (while preserving the discarded pages); the text as it stood before this rewriting I will call 'Q I'. Near the end of the narrative Q I gives out, and only the rewritten version ('Q II') continues to the end. It seems clear from this that the rewriting (which concerns Gondolin and its destruction) belongs to the same time, and I have given the Q II text throughout, from the point where the tale of Gondolin begins. The name of the King of Eagles, *Thorndor*, was changed throughout the text to *Thorondor*.

It will be seen that in the *Quenta* manuscript as written the story told in the *Sketch* (see p.127) was still present: the vale of Gondolin was discovered by scouts of Turgon's people fleeing from the Battle of Unnumbered Tears. At some later but unidentifiable time, my father rewrote all the relevant passages, and I have shown these revisions in the text that follows here.

Here must be told of Gondolin. The great river Sirion, mightiest in Elvish song, flowed through all the land of Beleriand and its course was south-west; and at its mouth was a great delta and its lower course ran through green and fertile lands, little peopled save by birds and beasts. Yet the

Orcs came seldom there, for it was far from the northern woods and fells, and the power of Ulmo waxed ever in that water, as it drew nigh to the sea; for the mouths of that river were in the western sea, whose uttermost borders are the shores of Valinor.

Turgon, Fingolfin's son, had a sister, Isfin the white-handed. She was lost in Taur-na-Fuin after the Battle of Unnumbered Tears. There she was captured by the Dark-elf Eöl, and it is said that he was of gloomy mood, and had deserted the hosts ere the battle; yet he had not fought on Morgoth's side. But Isfin he took to wife, and their son was Meglin.

Now the people of Turgon escaping from the battle, aided by the prowess of Húrin, as has been told, escaped from the knowledge of Morgoth and vanished from all men's eyes; and Ulmo alone knew whither they had gone. [Their scouts climbing the heights had come upon a secret place in the mountains: a broad valley >] For they returned to the hidden city of Gondolin that Turgon had built. In a secret place in the mountains there was a broad valley entirely circled by the hills, ringed about in a fence unbroken, but falling ever lower as they came towards the middle. In the midmost of this marvellous ring was a wide land and a green plain, wherein was no hill, save for a single rocky height. This stood up dark upon the plain, not right at its centre, but nearest to that part of the outer wall that marched close to the borders of Sirion. Highest were the Encircling Mountains towards the North and the threat of Angband, and on their outer slopes to East and North began the shadow of dread Taur-na-Fuin; but they were crowned with the cairn of Fingolfin, and no evil came that way, as yet.

In this valley [the Gnomes took refuge >] Turgon had taken refuge and spells of hiding and enchantment were set on all the hills about, that foes and spies might never find it. In this Turgon had the aid of the messages of Ulmo, that came now up the river Sirion; for his voice is to be heard in many waters, and some of the Gnomes had yet the lore to harken. In those days Ulmo was filled with pity for the exiled Elves in their need, and in the ruin that had now almost overwhelmed them. He foretold that the fortress of Gondolin should stand longest of all the refuges of the Elves against the might of Morgoth, and like Doriath never be overthrown save by treachery from within. Because of his protecting might the spells of concealment were strongest in those parts nearest to Sirion, though there the Encircling Mountains were at their lowest. In that region the Gnomes dug a great winding tunnel under the roots of the hills, and its issue was in the steep side, tree-clad and dark, of a gorge through which the blissful river ran. There he was still a young stream, but strong, flowing down the narrow vale that lies between the shoulders of the Encircling Mountains and the Mountains of Shadow, Eryd-Lómin [> Eredwethion], the walls of Hithlum [*struck out*: in whose northern heights he took his rise].

That passage they made at first to be a way of return for fugitives and for such as escaped from the bondage of Morgoth; and most as an issue for their scouts and messengers. For Turgon deemed, when first they came into that vale after the dreadful battle,* that Morgoth Bauglir had grown too mighty for Elves and Men, and that it were better to seek the forgiveness and aid of the Valar, if either might be got, ere all was lost. Wherefore some of his folk went down the river Sirion at whiles, ere the shadow of Morgoth yet stretched into the uttermost parts of Beleriand, and a small and secret haven they made at his mouth; thence ever and anon ships would set forth into the West bearing the embassy of the Gnomish king. Some there were that came back driven by contrary winds; but the most never returned again, and none reached Valinor.

The issue of that Way of Escape was guarded and concealed by the mightiest spells they could contrive, and by the power that dwelt in Sirion beloved of Ulmo, and no thing of evil found it; yet its inner gate, which looked upon the vale of Gondolin, was watched unceasingly by the Gnomes.

In those days Thorondor King of Eagles removed his eyries from Thangorodrim, because of the power of Morgoth, and the stench and fumes, and the evil of the dark clouds that lay now ever upon the mountain-towers above his cavernous halls. But Thorondor dwelt upon the northward heights of the Encircling Mountains, and he kept watch and saw many things, sitting upon the cairn of King Fingolfin. And in the vale below dwelt Turgon Fingolfin's son. Upon Amon Gwareth, the Hill of Defence, the rocky height amidst the plain, was built Gondolin the great, whose fame

---

* This sentence marked with an X for rejection, but without replacement.

and glory is mightiest in song of all dwellings of the Elves in these Outer Lands. Of steel were its gates and of marble were its walls. The sides of the hill the Gnomes polished to the smoothness of dark glass, and its top they levelled for the building of their town, save amidmost where stood the tower and palace of the king. Many fountains there were in that city, and white waters fell shimmering down the glistening sides of Amon Gwareth. The plain all about they smoothed till it became as a lawn of shaven grass from the stairways before the gates unto the feet of the mountain wall, and nought might walk or creep across unseen.

In that city the folk waxed mighty, and their armouries were filled with weapons and with shields; for they purposed at first to come forth to war, when the hour was ripe. But as the years drew on, they grew to love that place, the work of their hands, as the Gnomes do, with a great love, and desired no better. Then seldom went any forth from Gondolin on errand of war or peace again. They sent no messengers more into the West, and Sirion's haven was desolate. They shut them behind their impenetrable and enchanted hills, and suffered none to enter, though he fled from Morgoth hate-pursued; tidings of the lands without came to them faint and far, and they heeded them little; and their dwelling became as a rumour, and a secret no man could find. They succoured not Nargothrond nor Doriath, and the wandering Elves sought them in vain; and Ulmo alone knew where the realm of Turgon could be found. Tidings Turgon heard of Thorondor concerning the slaying of Dior, Thingol's heir, and thereafter he shut his ear to word of the woes without;

and he vowed to march never at the side of any son of Fëanor; and his folk he forbade ever to pass the leaguer of the hills.

Gondolin now alone remained of all the strongholds of the Elves. Morgoth forgot not Turgon, and knew that without knowledge of that king his triumph could not be achieved; yet his search unceasing was in vain. Nargothrond was void, Doriath desolate, the sons of Fëanor driven away to a wild woodland life in the South and East, Hithlum was filled with evil men, and Taur-na-Fuin was a place of nameless dread: the race of Hador was at an end, and the house of Finrod; Beren came no more to war, and Huan was slain; and all Elves and Men bowed to his will, or laboured as slaves in the mines and smithies of Angband, save only the wild and wandering, and few there were of these save far in the East of once fair Beleriand. His triumph was near complete, and yet was not quite full.

On a time Eöl was lost in Taur-na-Fuin, and Isfin came through great peril and dread unto Gondolin, and after her coming none entered until the last messenger of Ulmo, of whom the tales speak more ere the end. With her came her son Meglin, and he was there received by Turgon as his sister-son, and though he was half of Dark-elven blood he was treated as a prince of Fingolfin's line. He was swart but comely, wise and eloquent, and cunning to win men's hearts and minds.

Now Húrin of Hithlum had a brother Huor. The son of Huor was Tuor. Rían Huor's wife sought her husband among the slain upon the field of Unnumbered Tears, and there bewailed him, ere she died. Her son was but a child, and remaining in Hithlum fell into the hands of the faithless Men whom Morgoth drove into that land after the battle; and he became a thrall. Growing of age, and he was fair of face and great of stature, and despite his grievous life valiant and wise, he escaped into the woods, and he became an outlaw and a solitary, living alone and communing with none save rarely wandering and hidden Elves.*

On a time Ulmo contrived, as is told in the *Tale of the Fall of Gondolin*, that he should be led to a river-course that flowed underground from Lake Mithrim in the midst of Hithlum into a great chasm, Cris-Ilfing [> Kirith Helvin] the Rainbow-cleft, through which a turbulent water ran at last into the western sea. And the name of this chasm was so devised by reason of the rainbow that shimmered ever in the sun in that place, because of the abundance of the spray of the rapids and the waterfalls.

In this way the flight of Tuor was marked by no Man nor Elf, neither was it known to the Orcs or any spy of Morgoth, with whom the land of Hithlum was filled.

Tuor wandered long by the western shores, journeying ever South; and he came at last to the mouths of Sirion, and

---

* The text here is somewhat confused by hasty changes. In this rewriting it is told that Rían 'went forth into the wild', where Tuor was born; and that 'he was fostered by the Dark-elves; but Rían laid herself down and died upon the Hill of Slain. But Tuor grew up in the woods of Hithlum, and he was fair of face and great of stature ...' There is thus in the rewriting no mention of an enslavement of Tuor.

the sandy deltas peopled by many birds of the sea. There he
fell in with a Gnome, Bronwë, who had escaped from Angband, and being of old of the people of Turgon, sought ever
to find the path to the hidden places of his lord, of which
rumour ran among all captives and fugitives. Now Bronwë
had come thither by far and wandering paths to the East,
and little though any step back nigher to the thraldom from
which he had come was to his liking, he purposed now to
go up Sirion and seek for Turgon in Beleriand. Fearful and
very wary was he, and he aided Tuor in their secret march,
by night and twilight, so that they were not discovered by
the Orcs.

They came first into the fair Land of Willows, Nan-
tathrin which is watered by the Narog and by Sirion; and
there all things were yet green, and the meads were rich
and full of flowers, and there was song of many birds; so that
Tuor lingered there as one enchanted, and it seemed sweet
to him to dwell there after the grim lands of the North and
his weary wandering.

There Ulmo came and appeared before him, as he stood
in the long grass at evening; and the might and majesty of
that vision is told of in the song of Tuor that he made for
his son Eärendel. Thereafter the sound of the sea and the
longing for the sea was ever in Tuor's heart and ear; and an
unquiet was on him at whiles that took him at last into the
depths of the realm of Ulmo. But now Ulmo bade him make
all speed to Gondolin, and gave him guidance for the finding
of the hidden door; and a message he gave him to bear from
Ulmo, friend of Elves, unto Turgon, bidding him to prepare

for war, and battle with Morgoth ere all was lost; and to send again his messengers into the West. Summons too should he send into the East and gather, if he might, Men (who were now multiplying and spreading on the earth) unto his banners; and for that task Tuor was most fit. 'Forget,' counselled Ulmo, 'the treachery of Uldor the accursed, and remember Húrin; for without mortal Men the Elves shall not prevail against the Balrogs and the Orcs.' Nor should the feud with the sons of Fëanor be left unhealed; for this should be the last gathering of the hope of the Gnomes, when every sword should count. A terrible and mortal strife he foretold, but victory if Turgon would dare it, the breaking of Morgoth's power, and the healing of feuds, and friendship between Men and Elves, whereof the greatest good should come into the world, and the servants of Morgoth trouble it no more. But if Turgon would not go forth to this war, then he should abandon Gondolin and lead his people down Sirion, and build there his fleets and seek back to Valinor and the mercy of the Gods. But in this counsel there was danger more dire than in the other, though so it might not seem; and grievous thereafter would be the fate of the Hither Lands.

This errand Ulmo performed out of his love of the Elves, and because he knew that ere many years were passed the doom of Gondolin would come, if its people sat still behind its walls; not thus should anything of joy or beauty in the world be preserved from Morgoth's malice.

Obedient to Ulmo Tuor and Bronwë journeyed North, and came at last to the hidden door; and passing down the tunnel reached the inner gate, and were taken by the guard as prisoners. There they saw the fair vale of Tumladen set like a green jewel amid the hills; and amidst Tumladen Gondolin the great, the city of seven names, white, shining from afar, flushed with the rose of dawn upon the plain. Thither they were led and passed the gates of steel, and were brought before the steps of the palace of the king. There Tuor spoke the embassy of Ulmo, and something of the power and majesty of the Lord of Waters his voice had caught, so that all folk looked in wonder on him, and doubted that this were a Man of mortal race as he declared. But proud was Turgon become, and Gondolin as beautiful as a memory of Tûn, and he trusted in its secret and impregnable strength; so that he and the most part of his folk wished not to imperil it nor leave it, and they desired not to mingle in the woes of Elves and Men without; nor did they any longer desire to return through dread and danger to the West.

Meglin spoke ever against Tuor in the councils of the king, and his words seemed the more weighty in that they went with Turgon's heart. Wherefore Turgon rejected the bidding of Ulmo; though some there were of his wisest counsellors who were filled with disquiet. Wise-hearted even beyond the measure of the daughters of Elfinesse was the daughter of the king, and she spoke ever for Tuor, though it did not avail, and her heart was heavy. Very fair and tall was she, well nigh of warrior's stature, and her hair was a fountain of gold. Idril was she named, and called Celebrindal, Silver-foot, for the whiteness of her foot; and she walked and danced ever unshod in the white ways and green lawns of Gondolin.

Thereafter Tuor sojourned in Gondolin, and went not to summon the Men of the East, for the blissfulness of Gondolin, the beauty and wisdom of its folk, held him enthralled. And he grew high in the favour of Turgon; for he became a mighty man in stature and in mind, learning deeply of the lore of the Gnomes. The heart of Idril was turned to him, and his to her; at which Meglin ground his teeth, for he desired Idril, and despite his close kinship purposed to possess her; and she was the only heir of the king of Gondolin. Indeed in his heart he was already planning how he might oust Turgon and seize his throne; but Turgon loved and trusted him. Nonetheless Tuor took Idril to wife; and the folk of Gondolin made merry feast, for Tuor had won their hearts, all save Meglin and his secret following. Tuor and Beren alone of mortal Men had Elves to wife, and since Elwing daughter of Dior son of Beren after wedded Eärendel son of Tuor and Idril of Gondolin, of them alone has come the elven blood into mortal race. But as yet Eärendel was a little child: surpassing fair was he, a light was in his face as the light of heaven, and he had the beauty and the wisdom of Elfinesse and the strength and hardihood of the Men of old; and the sea spoke ever in his ear and heart, even as with Tuor his father.

On a time when Eärendel was yet young, and the days of Gondolin were full of joy and peace (and yet Idril's heart misgave her, and foreboding crept upon her spirit like a cloud), Meglin was lost. Now Meglin loved mining and quarrying after metals above other craft; and he was master and leader of the Gnomes who worked in the mountains distant from the city, seeking for metals for their smithying of things both of peace and war. But often Meglin went with few of his folk beyond the leaguer of the hills, though the king knew not that his bidding was defied; and so it came to pass, as fate willed, that Meglin was taken prisoner by the Orcs and taken before Morgoth. Meglin was no weakling or craven, but the torment wherewith he was threatened cowed his soul, and he purchased his life and freedom by revealing unto Morgoth the place of Gondolin and the ways whereby it might be found and assailed. Great indeed was the joy of Morgoth; and to Meglin he promised the lordship of Gondolin, as his vassal, and the possession of Idril, when that city should be taken. Lust for Idril and hatred of Tuor led Meglin the easier to his foul treachery. But Morgoth sent him back to Gondolin, lest men should suspect the betrayal, and so that Meglin should aid the assault from within when the hour came; and Meglin abode in the halls of the king with a smile on his face and evil in his heart, while the gloom gathered ever deeper upon Idril.

At last, and Eärendel was then seven years of age, Morgoth was ready, and he loosed upon Gondolin his Orcs and his Balrogs and his serpents; and of these, dragons of many and dire shapes were new devised for the taking of the city. The host of Morgoth came over the Northern hills where the height was greatest and the watch less vigilant, and it came at night at a time of festival, when all the folk of Gondolin were upon the walls to wait upon the rising sun and sing their songs at its uplifting, for the morrow was the feast which they named the Gates of Summer. But the red light mounted the hills in the North and not in the East; and there was no stay in the advance of the foe until they were beneath the very walls of Gondolin, and Gondolin was beleaguered without hope.

Of the deeds of desperate valour there done, by the chieftains of the noble houses and their warriors, and not least by Tuor, is much told in *The Fall of Gondolin*; of the death of Rog without the walls; and of the battle of Ecthelion of the Fountain with Gothmog lord of Balrogs in the very square of the king, where each slew the other; and of the defence of the tower of Turgon by the men of his household, until the tower was overthrown; and mighty was its fall and the fall of Turgon in its ruin.

Tuor sought to rescue Idril from the sack of the city, but Meglin had laid hands upon her and Eärendel; and Tuor fought on the walls with him, and cast him down to death. Then Tuor and Idril led such remnants of the folk of Gondolin as they could gather in the confusion of the burning, down a secret way that Idril had let prepare in the days of her foreboding. This was not yet complete, but its issue was already far beyond the walls and in the North of the plain where the mountains were long distant from Amon Gwareth. Those who would not come with them, but fled to the old Way of Escape that led into the gorge of Sirion, were caught and destroyed by a dragon that Morgoth had sent to watch that gate, being apprised of it by Meglin. But of the new passage Meglin had not heard, and it was not thought that fugitives would take a path towards the North and the highest parts of the mountains and the nighest to Angband.

The fume of the burning, and the steam of the fair

fountains of Gondolin withering in the flame of the dragons of the North, fell upon the vale in mournful mists, and thus was the escape of Tuor and his company aided, for there was still a long and open road to follow from the tunnel's mouth to the foothills of the mountains. They came nonetheless into the mountains, in woe and misery, for the high places were cold and terrible, and they had among them many women and children and many wounded men.

There is a dreadful pass, Cristhorn [> Kirith-thoronath] was it named, the Eagle's Cleft, where beneath the shadow of the highest peaks a narrow path winds its way, walled by a precipice to the right and on the left a dreadful fall leaps into emptiness. Along that narrow way their march was strung when it was ambushed by an outpost of Morgoth's power; and a Balrog was their leader. Then dreadful was their plight, and hardly would it have been saved by the deathless valour of yellow-haired Glorfindel, chief of the House of the Golden Flower of Gondolin, had not Thorondor come timely to their aid.

Songs have been sung of the duel of Glorfindel with the Balrog upon a pinnacle of rock in that high place; and both fell to ruin in the abyss. But Thorondor bore up Glorfindel's body and he was buried in a mound of stones beside the pass, and there came after a turf of green and small flowers like yellow stars bloomed there amid the barrenness of stone. And the birds of Thorondor stooped upon the Orcs and drove them shrieking back; and all were slain or cast into the deeps, and rumour of the escape from Gondolin came not until long after to Morgoth's ears.

Thus by weary and dangerous marches the remnant of Gondolin came unto Nan-tathrin and there rested a while, and were healed of their hurts and weariness, but their sorrow could not be cured. There they made feast in memory of Gondolin and those that had perished, fair maidens, wives, and warriors and their king; but for Glorfindel the well-beloved many and sweet were the songs they sang. And there Tuor spoke in song to Eärendel his son of the coming of Ulmo aforetime, the sea-vision in the midst of the land, and the sea-longing awoke in his heart and in his son's. Wherefore they removed with the most part of the people to the mouths of Sirion by the sea, and there they dwelt, and joined their folk to the slender company of Elwing daughter of Dior, that had fled thither little while before.

Then Morgoth thought in his heart that his triumph was fulfilled, recking little of the sons of Fëanor, and of their oath, which had harmed him never and turned always to his mightiest aid. And in his black thought he laughed, regretting not the one Silmaril he had lost, for by it he deemed the last shreds of the Elvish race should vanish yet from the earth and trouble it no more. If he knew of the dwelling by the waters of Sirion he made no sign, biding his time, and waiting upon the working of oath and lie.

Yet by Sirion and the sea there grew up an elven folk, the gleanings of Gondolin and Doriath, and they took to the waves and to the making of fair ships, dwelling ever nigh unto the shores and under the shadow of Ulmo's hand.

We are now at the same place in the story of Gondolin in the *Quenta Noldorinwa* as that reached in the *Sketch of the Mythology* on p.125. Here I will leave the *Quenta* and turn to the last major text of the story of Gondolin, which is also the last account of the foundation of Gondolin and of how Tuor came to enter the city.

THE LAST VERSION

Many years passed between the story of Gondolin as told in the *Quenta Noldorinwa* and this text, entitled *Of Tuor and the Fall of Gondolin*. It is certain that it was written in 1951 (see *The Evolution of the Story* p.207).

Rían, wife of Huor, dwelt with the people of the house of Hador; but when rumour came to Dor-lómin of the Nirnaeth Arnoediad [the Battle of Unnumbered Tears], and yet she could hear no news of her lord, she became distraught and wandered forth into the wild alone. There she would have perished, but the Grey-elves came to her aid. For there was a dwelling of this people in the mountains westward of Lake Mithrim; and thither they led her, and she was there delivered of a son before the end of the Year of Lamentation.

And Rían said to the Elves: 'Let him be called *Tuor*, for that name his father chose, ere war came between us. And I beg of you to foster him, and to keep him hidden in your care; for I forebode that great good, for Elves and Men, shall come from him. But I must go in search of Huor, my lord.'

Then the Elves pitied her; but one Annael, who alone of all that went to war from that people had returned from the Nirnaeth, said to her: 'Alas, lady, it is known now that Huor fell at the side of Húrin his brother; and he lies, I deem, in the great hill of slain that the Orcs have raised upon the field of battle.'

Therefore Rían arose and left the dwelling of the Elves, and she passed through the land of Mithrim and came at last to the Haudh-en-Ndengin in the waste of Anfauglith, and there she laid her down and died. But the Elves cared for the infant son of Huor, and Tuor grew up among them; and he was fair of face, and golden-haired after the manner of his father's kin, and he became strong and tall and valiant, and being fostered by the Elves he had lore and skill no less than the princes of the Edain, ere ruin came upon the North.

But with the passing of the years the life of the former folk of Hithlum, such as still remained, Elves or Men, became ever harder and more perilous. For as is elsewhere told, Morgoth broke his pledges to the Easterlings that had served him, and he denied to them the rich lands of Beleriand which they had coveted, and he drove away these evil folk into Hithlum, and there commanded them to dwell. And though they loved Morgoth no longer, they served him still in fear, and hated all the Elven-folk; and they despised the remnant of the House of Hador (the aged and women and children, for the most part), and they oppressed them, and wedded their women by force, and took their lands and goods, and enslaved their children. Orcs came and went about the land as they would, pursuing the lingering Elves into the fastnesses of the mountains, and taking many captive to the mines of Angband to labour as the thralls of Morgoth.

Therefore Annael led his small people to the caves of Androth, and there they lived a hard and wary life, until Tuor was sixteen years of age and was become strong and able to wield arms, the axe and bow of the Grey-elves; and his heart grew hot within him at the tale of the griefs of his people, and he wished to go forth and avenge them on the Orcs and Easterlings. But Annael forbade this.

'Far hence, I deem, your doom lies, Tuor son of Huor,' he said. 'And this land shall not be freed from the shadow of Morgoth until Thangorodrim itself be overthrown. There-fore we are resolved at last to forsake it, and to depart into the South; and with us you shall go.'

'But how shall we escape the net of our enemies?' said Tuor. 'For the marching of so many together will surely be marked.'

'We shall not march through the land openly,' said Annael; 'and if our fortune is good we shall come to the secret way which we call Annon-in-Gelydh, the Gate of the Noldor; for it was made by the skill of that people, long ago in the days of Turgon.'

At that name Tuor was stirred, though he knew not why; and he questioned Annael concerning Turgon. 'He is a son of Fingolfin,' said Annael, 'and is now accounted High King of the Noldor, since the fall of Fingon. For he lives yet, most feared of the foes of Morgoth, and he escaped from the ruin of the Nirnaeth, when Húrin of Dor-lómin and Huor your father held the passes of Sirion behind him.'

'Then I will go and seek Turgon,' said Tuor; 'for surely he will lend me aid for my father's sake?'

'That you cannot,' said Annael. 'For his stronghold is hidden from the eyes of Elves and Men, and we know not where it stands. Of the Noldor some, maybe, know the way thither, but they will speak of it to none. Yet if you would have speech with them, then come with me, as I bid you; for in the far havens of the South you may meet with wanderers from the Hidden Kingdom.'

Thus it came to pass that the Elves forsook the caves of Androth, and Tuor went with them. But their enemies kept watch upon their dwellings, and were soon aware of their march; and they had not gone far from the hills into the plain before they were assailed by a great force of Orcs and Easterlings, and they were scattered far and wide, fleeing into the gathering night. But Tuor's heart was kindled with the fire of battle, and he would not flee, but boy as he was he wielded the axe as his father before him, and for long he stood his ground and slew many that assailed him; but at the last he was overwhelmed and taken captive and led before Lorgan the Easterling. Now this Lorgan was held the chief of the Easterlings and claimed to rule all Dor-lómin as a fief under Morgoth; and he took Tuor to be his slave. Hard and bitter then was his life; for it pleased Lorgan to treat Tuor the more evilly as he was of the kin of the former lords, and he sought to break, if he could, the pride of the house of Hador. But Tuor saw wisdom, and endured all pains and taunts with watchful patience; so that in time his lot was somewhat lightened, and at the least he was not starved, as were many of Lorgan's unhappy thralls. For he was strong and skilful, and Lorgan fed his beasts of burden well, while they were young and could work.

But after three years of thraldom Tuor saw at last a chance of escape. He was come now almost to his full stature, taller and swifter than any of the Easterlings; and being sent with other thralls on an errand of labour into the woods he turned suddenly on the guards and slew them with an axe, and fled into the hills. The Easterlings hunted him with dogs, but without avail; for wellnigh all the hounds of Lorgan were his friends, and if they came up with him they would fawn upon him, and then run homeward at his command. Thus he came back at last to the caves of Androth and dwelt there alone. And for four years he was an outlaw in the land of his fathers, grim and solitary; and his name was feared, for he went often abroad, and slew many of the Easterlings that he came upon. Then they set a great price upon his head; but they did not dare to come to his hiding-place, even with strength of men, for they feared the Elven-folk, and shunned the caves where they had dwelt. Yet it is said that Tuor's journeys were not made for the purpose of vengeance; rather he sought ever for the Gate of the Noldor, of which Annael had spoken. But he found it not, for he knew not where to look, and such few of the Elves as lingered in the mountains had not heard of it.

Now Tuor knew that, though fortune still favoured him, yet in the end the days of an outlaw are numbered, and are ever few and without hope. Nor was he willing to live thus for ever a wild man in the houseless hills, and his heart urged him ever to great deeds. Herein, it is said, the power of Ulmo was shown. For he gathered tidings of all that passed in Beleriand, and every stream that flowed from Middle-earth to the Great Sea was to him a messenger, both to and fro; and he remained also in friendship, as of old, with Círdan and the Shipwrights at the Mouths of Sirion. And at this time most of all Ulmo gave heed to the fates of the House of Hador, for in his deep counsels he purposed that they should play great part in his designs for the succour of the Exiles; and he knew well of the plight of Tuor, for Annael and many of his folk had indeed escaped from Dor-lómin and come at last to Círdan in the far South.*

Thus it came to pass that on a day in the beginning of the year (twenty and three since the Nirnaeth) Tuor sat by a spring that trickled forth near to the door of the cave where he dwelt; and he looked out westward towards the cloudy sunset. Then suddenly it came into his heart that he would wait no longer, but would arise and go. 'I will leave now the grey land of my kin that are no more,' he cried, 'and I will go in search of my doom! But whither shall I turn? Long have I sought the Gate and found it not.'

---

* This is Círdan the Shipwright who appears in *The Lord of the Rings* as the lord of the Grey Havens at the end of the Third Age.

Then he took up the harp which he bore ever with him, being skilled in playing upon its strings, and heedless of the peril of his clear voice alone in the waste he sang an elven song of the North for the uplifting of hearts. And even as he sang the well at his feet began to boil with great increase of water, and it overflowed, and a rill ran noisily down the rocky hillside before him. And Tuor took this as a sign, and he arose at once and followed after it. Thus he came down from the tall hills of Mithrim and passed out into the northward plain of Dor-lómin; and ever the stream grew as he followed it westward, until after three days he could descry in the west the long grey ridges of Ered Lómin that in those regions marched north and south, fencing off the far coastlands of the Western Shores. To those hills in all his journeys Tuor had never come.

Now the land became more broken and stony again, as it approached the hills, and soon it began to rise before Tuor's feet, and the stream went down into a cloven bed. But even as dim dusk came on the third day of his journey, Tuor found before him a wall of rock, and there was an opening therein like a great arch; and the stream passed in and was lost. Then Tuor was dismayed, and he said: 'So my hope has cheated me! The sign in the hills has led me only to a dark end in the midst of the land of my enemies.' And grey at heart he sat among the rocks on the high bank of the stream, keeping watch through a bitter fireless night; for it was yet but the month of Súlimë, and no stir of spring had come to that far northern land, and a shrill wind blew from the East.

But even as the light of the coming sun shone pale in the far mists of Mithrim, Tuor heard voices, and looking down he saw in amazement two Elves that waded in the shallow water; and as they climbed up steps hewn in the bank, Tuor stood up and called to them. At once they drew their bright swords and sprang towards him. Then he saw that they were grey-cloaked but mail-clad under; and he marvelled, for they were fairer and more fell to look upon, because of the light of their eyes, than any of the Elven-folk that he yet had known. He stood to his full height and awaited them; but when they saw that he drew no weapon, but stood alone and greeted them in the Elven-tongue, they sheathed their swords and spoke courteously to him. And one said: 'Gelmir and Arminas we are, of Finarfin's people. Are you not one of the Edain of old that dwelt in these lands ere the Nirnaeth? And indeed of the kindred of Hador and Húrin I deem you; for so the gold of your head declares you.'

And Tuor answered: 'Yea, I am Tuor, son of Huor, son of Galdor, son of Hador; but now at last I desire to leave this land where I am outlawed and kinless.'

'Then,' said Gelmir, 'if you would escape and find the havens in the South, already your feet have been guided on the right road.'

'So I thought,' said Tuor. 'For I followed a sudden spring of water in the hills, until it joined this treacherous stream. But now I know not whither to turn, for it has gone into darkness.'

'Through darkness one may come to the light,' said Gelmir.

'Yet one will walk under the Sun while one may,' said Tuor. 'But since you are of that people, tell me if you can where lies the Gate of the Noldor. For I have sought it long, ever since Annael my foster-father of the Grey-elves spoke of it to me.'

Then the Elves laughed, and said: 'Your search is ended; for we have ourselves just passed that Gate. There it stands before you!' And they pointed to the arch into which the water flowed. 'Come now! Through darkness you shall come to the light. We will set your feet on the road, but we cannot guide you far; for we are sent back to the lands whence we fled upon an urgent errand.' 'But fear not,' said Gelmir: 'a great doom is written upon your brow, and it shall lead you far from these lands, far indeed from Middle-earth, as I guess.'

Then Tuor followed the Noldor down the steps and waded in the cold water, until they passed into the shadow beyond the arch of stone. And then Gelmir brought forth one of those lamps for which the Noldor were renowned; for they were made of old in Valinor, and neither wind nor water could quench them, and when they were unhooded they sent forth a clear blue light from a flame imprisoned in white crystal. Now by the light that Gelmir held above his head Tuor saw that the river began to go suddenly down a smooth slope into a great tunnel, but beside its rock-hewn course there ran long flights of steps leading on and downward into a deep gloom beyond the beam of the lamp.

When they had come to the foot of the rapids they stood under a great dome of rock, and there the river rushed over a steep fall with a great noise that echoed in the vault, and it passed then on again under another arch into a further tunnel. Beside the falls the Noldor halted, and bade Tuor farewell.

'Now we must return and go our ways with all speed,' said Gelmir; 'for matters of great peril are moving in Beleriand.'

'Is then the hour come when Turgon shall come forth?' said Tuor.

Then the Elves looked at him in amazement. 'That is a matter which concerns the Noldor rather than the sons of Men,' said Arminas. 'What know you of Turgon?'

'Little,' said Tuor; 'save that my father aided his escape from the Nirnaeth, and that in his stronghold dwells the hope of the Noldor. Yet, though I know not why, ever his name stirs in my heart, and comes to my lips. And had I my will, I would go in search of him, rather than tread this dark way of dread. Unless, perhaps, this secret road is the way to his dwelling?'

'Who shall say?' answered the Elf. 'For since the dwelling of Turgon is hidden, so also are the ways thither. I know them not, though I have sought them long. Yet if I knew them, I would not reveal them to you, nor to any among Men.'

But Gelmir said: 'I have heard that your House has the favour of the Lord of Waters. And if his counsels lead you to Turgon, then surely shall you come to him, whithersoever you turn. Follow now the road to which the water has brought you from the hills, and fear not! You shall not walk long in darkness. Farewell! And think not that our meeting was by chance; for the Dweller in the Deep moves many things in this land still. *Anar kaluva tielyanna!* [The sun will shine upon your path!]'

With that the Noldor turned and went back up the long stairs; but Tuor stood still, until the light of their lamp was lost, and he was alone in a darkness deeper than night amid the roaring of the falls. Then summoning his courage he set his left hand to the rock-wall, and felt his way forward, slowly at first, and then more quickly, as he became more used to the darkness and found nothing to hinder him. And after a great while, as it seemed to him, when he was weary and yet unwilling to rest in the black tunnel, he saw far before him a light; and hastening on he came to a tall and narrow cleft, and followed the noisy stream between its leaning walls out into a golden evening. For he was come into a deep ravine with tall sheer sides, and it ran straight towards the West; and before him the setting sun, going down through a clear sky, shone into the ravine and kindled its walls with yellow fire, and the waters of the river glittered like gold as they broke and foamed upon many gleaming stones.

In that deep place Tuor went on now in great hope and delight, finding a path beneath the southern wall, where there lay a long and narrow strand. And when night came, and the river rushed on unseen, save for a glint of high stars mirrored in dark pools, then he rested, and slept; for he felt no fear beside that water, in which the power of Ulmo ran.

With the coming of day he went on again without haste. The sun rose behind his back and set before his face, and where the water foamed among the boulders or rushed over sudden falls, at morning and evening rainbows were woven across the stream. Wherefore he named that stream Cirith Ninniach [Rainbow Cleft].

Thus Tuor journeyed slowly for three days, drinking the cold water but desiring no food, though there were many fish that shone as gold or silver, or gleamed with colours like to the rainbows in the spray above. And on the fourth day the channel grew wider, and its walls lower and less sheer; but the river ran deeper and more strongly, for high hills now marched on either side, and fresh waters spilled from them into Cirith Ninniach over shimmering falls. There long while Tuor sat, watching the swirling of the stream and listening to its endless voice, until night came again and stars shone cold and white in the dark lane of sky above him. Then he lifted up his voice, and plucked the strings of his harp, and above the noise of the water the sound of his song and the sweet thrilling of the harp were echoed in the stone and multiplied, and went forth and rang in the night-clad hills, until all the empty land was filled with music beneath the stars. For though he knew it not, Tuor was now come to the Echoing Mountains of Lammoth about the Firth of Drengist. There once long ago Fëanor had landed from the sea, and the voices of his host were swelled to a mighty clamour upon the coasts of the North ere the rising of the Moon.

Then Tuor was filled with wonder and stayed his song, and slowly the music died in the hills, and there was silence. And then amid the silence he heard in the air above him a strange cry; and he knew not of what creature that cry came. Now he said: 'It is a fay-voice', now: 'Nay, it is a small beast that is wailing in the waste'; and then, hearing it again, he said: 'Surely, it is the cry of some nightfaring bird that I know not.' And it seemed to him a mournful sound, and yet he desired nonetheless to hear it and follow it, for it called him, he knew not whither.

The next morning he heard the same voice above his head, and looking up he saw three great white birds beating down the ravine against the westerly wind, and their strong wings shone in the new-risen sun, and as they passed over him they wailed aloud. Thus for the first time he beheld the great gulls, beloved of the Teleri. Then Tuor arose to follow them, and so that he might better mark whither they flew he climbed the cliff upon his left hand, and stood upon the top, and felt a great wind out of the West rush against his face; and his hair streamed from his head. And he drank deep of that new air, and said: 'This uplifts the heart like the drinking of cool wine!' But he knew not that the wind came fresh from the Great Sea.

Now Tuor went on once more, seeking the gulls, high above the river; and as he went the sides of the ravine drew together again, and he came to a narrow channel, and it was filled with a great noise of water. And looking down Tuor saw a great marvel, as it seemed to him; for a wild flood came up the narrows and strove with the river that would still press on, and a wave like a wall rose up almost to the cliff-top, crowned with foam-crests flying in the wind. Then the river was thrust back, and the incoming flood swept roaring up the channel, drowning it in deep water, and the rolling of the boulders was like thunder as it passed. Thus Tuor was saved by the call of the sea-birds from death in the rising tide; and that was very great because of the season of the year and of the high wind from the sea.

But now Tuor was dismayed by the fury of the strange waters, and he turned aside and went away southward, and so came not to the long shores of the Firth of Drengist, but wandered still for some days in a rugged country bare of trees; and it was swept by a wind from the sea, and all that grew there, herb or bush, leaned ever to the dawn because of the prevalence of that wind from the West. In this way Tuor passed into the borders of Nevrast, where once Turgon had dwelt; and at last at unawares (for the cliff-tops at the margin of the land were higher than the slopes behind) he came suddenly to the black brink of Middle-earth, and saw the Great Sea, Belegaer the Shoreless. And at that hour the sun went down beyond the rim of the world, as a mighty fire; and Tuor stood alone upon the cliff with outspread arms, and a great yearning filled his heart. It is said that he was the first of Men to reach the Great Sea, and that none, save the Eldar, have ever felt more deeply the longing that it brings.

Tuor tarried many days in Nevrast, and it seemed good to him, for that land, being fenced by mountains from the North and East and nigh to the sea, was milder and more kindly than the plains of Hithlum. He was long used to dwell alone as a hunter in the wild, and he found no lack of food; for spring was busy in Nevrast, and the air was filled with the noise of birds, both those that dwelt in multitudes upon the shores, and those that teemed in the marshes of Linaewen in the midst of the hollow land, but in those days no voice of Elves or Men was heard in all the solitude.

To the borders of the great mere Tuor came, but its waters were beyond his reach, because of the wide mires and the pathless forests of reeds that lay all about; and soon he turned away, and went back to the coast, for the Sea drew him, and he was not willing to dwell long where he could not hear the sound of its waves. And in the shorelands Tuor first found traces of the Noldor of old. For among the tall and sea-hewn cliffs south of Drengist there were many coves and sheltered inlets, with beaches of white sand among the black gleaming rocks, and leading down to such places Tuor found often winding stairs cut in the living stone; and by the water-edge were ruined quays, built of great blocks hewn from the cliffs, where elven ships had once been moored. In those regions Tuor long remained, watching the ever-changing sea, while through spring and summer the slow year wore on, and darkness deepened in Beleriand, and the autumn of the doom of Nargothrond drew near.

And, maybe, birds saw from afar the fell winter that was to come; for those that were wont to go south gathered early to depart, and others that used to dwell in the North came from their homes to Nevrast. And one day, as Tuor sat upon the shore, he heard the rush and whine of great wings, and he looked up and saw seven white swans flying in a swift wedge southward. But as they came above him they wheeled and flew suddenly down, and alighted with a great plash and churning of water.

Now Tuor loved swans, which he knew on the grey pools of Mithrim; and the swan moreover had been the token of Annael and his foster-folk. He rose therefore to greet the birds, and called to them, marvelling to behold that they were greater and prouder than any of their kind that he had seen before; but they beat their wings and uttered harsh cries, as if they were wroth with him and would drive him from the shore. Then with a great noise they rose again from the water and flew above his head, so that the rush of their wings blew upon him as a whistling wind; and wheeling in a wide circle they ascended into the high air and went away south.

Then Tuor cried aloud: 'Here now comes another sign that I have tarried too long!' And straightway he climbed to the cliff-top, and there he beheld the swans still wheeling on high, but when he turned southward and set out to follow them, they flew swiftly away.

Now Tuor journeyed south along the coast for full seven days, and each morning he was aroused by the rush of wings above him in the dawn and each day the swans flew on as he followed after. And as he went the great cliffs became lower, and their tops were clothed deep with flowering turf; and away eastward there were woods turning yellow in the waning of the year. But before him, drawing ever nearer, he saw a line of great hills that barred his way, marching westward until they ended in a tall mountain: a dark and

cloud-helmed tower reared upon mighty shoulders above a great green cape thrust out into the sea.

Those grey hills were indeed the western outliers of Ered Wethrin, the north fence of Beleriand, and the mountain was Mount Taras, westernmost of all the towers of that land, whose head a mariner would first descry across the miles of the sea, as he drew near to the mortal shores. Beneath its long slopes in bygone days Turgon had dwelt in the halls of Vinyamar, eldest of all the works of stone that the Noldor built in the lands of their exile. There it still stood, desolate but enduring, high upon great terraces that looked towards the sea. The years had not shaken it, and the servants of Morgoth had passed it by; but wind and rain and frost had graven it, and upon the coping of its walls and the great shingles of its roof there was a deep growth of grey-green plants that, living upon the salt air, throve even in the cracks of barren stone.

Now Tuor came to the ruins of a lost road, and he passed amid green mounds and leaning stones, and so came as the day was waning to the old hall and its high and windy courts. No shadow of fear or evil lurked there, but an awe fell upon him, thinking of those that had dwelt there and had gone, none knew whither: the proud people, deathless but doomed, from far beyond the Sea. And he turned and looked, as often their eyes had looked, out across the glitter of the unquiet waters to the end of sight. Then he turned back again, and saw that the swans had alighted on the highest terrace, and stood before the west-door of the hall; and they beat their wings, and it seemed to him that they beckoned him to enter. Then Tuor went up the wide stairs, now half-hidden in thrift and campion, and he passed under the mighty lintel and entered the shadows of the house of Turgon; and he came at last to a high-pillared hall. If great it had appeared from without, now vast and wonderful it seemed to Tuor from within, and for awe he wished not to awake the echoes in its emptiness. Nothing could he see there, save at the eastern end a high seat upon a dais, and softly as he might he paced towards it; but the sound of his feet rang upon the paved floor as the steps of doom, and echoes ran before him along the pillared aisles.

As he stood before the great chair in the gloom, and saw that it was hewn of a single stone and written with strange signs, the sinking sun drew level with a high window under the westward gable, and a shaft of light smote the wall before him, and glittered as it were upon burnished metal. Then Tuor marvelling saw that on the wall behind the throne there hung a shield and a great hauberk, and a helm and a long sword in a sheath. The hauberk shone as it were wrought of silver untarnished, and the sunbeam gilded it with sparks of gold. But the shield was of a shape strange to Tuor's eyes, for it was long and tapering; and its field was blue, in the midst of which was wrought an emblem of a white swan's wing. Then Tuor spoke, and his voice rang as a challenge in the roof: 'By this token I will take these arms unto myself, and upon myself whatsoever doom they bear.' And he lifted down the shield and found it light and wieldy beyond his guess; for it was wrought, it seemed, of wood, but overlaid

by the craft of elven-smiths with plates of metal, strong
yet thin as foil, whereby it had been preserved from worm
and weather.

Then Tuor arrayed himself in the hauberk, and set the
helm upon his head, and he girt himself with the sword;
black were sheath and belt with clasps of silver. Thus armed
he went forth from Turgon's hall, and stood upon the high
terraces of Taras in the red light of the sun. None were there
to see him, as he gazed westward, gleaming in silver and
gold, and he knew not that in that hour he appeared as one
of the Mighty of the West, and fit to be the father of the
kings of the Kings of Men beyond the Sea, as it was indeed
his doom to be; but in the taking of those arms a change
came upon Tuor son of Huor, and his heart grew great
within him. And, as he stepped down from the doors the
swans did him reverence, and plucking each a great feather
from their wings they proffered them to him, laying their
long necks upon the stone before his feet; and he took the
seven feathers and set them in the crest of his helm, and
straightway the swans arose and flew north in the sunset,
and Tuor saw them no more.

Now Tuor felt his feet drawn to the sea-strand, and he
went down by long stairs to a wide shore upon the north
side of Taras-ness; and as he went he saw that the sun was
sinking low into a great black cloud that came up over the
rim of the darkening sea; and it grew cold, and there was a
stirring and murmur as of a storm to come. And Tuor stood
upon the shore, and the sun was like a smoky fire behind the

menace of the sky; and it seemed to him that a great wave rose far off and rolled towards the land, but wonder held him, and he remained there unmoved. And the wave came towards him, and upon it lay a mist of shadow. Then suddenly as it drew near it curled, and broke, and rushed forward in long arms of foam; but where it had broken there stood dark against the rising storm a living shape of great height and majesty.

Then Tuor bowed in reverence, for it seemed to him that he beheld a mighty king. A tall crown he wore like silver, from which his long hair fell down as foam glimmering in the dusk; and as he cast back the grey mantle that hung about him like a mist, behold! he was clad in a gleaming coat, close-fitted as the mail of a mighty fish, and in a kirtle of deep green that flashed and flickered with sea-fire as he strode slowly towards the land. In this manner the Dweller of the Deep, whom the Noldor name Ulmo, Lord of Waters, showed himself to Tuor son of Huor of the House of Hador beneath Vinyamar.

He set no foot upon the shore, but standing knee-deep in the shadowy sea he spoke to Tuor, and then for the light of his eyes and for the sound of his deep voice that came as it seemed from the foundations of the world, fear fell upon Tuor and he cast himself down upon the sand.

'Arise, Tuor son of Huor!' said Ulmo. 'Fear not my wrath, though long have I called to thee unheard; and setting out at last thou hast tarried on thy journey hither. In the Spring thou shouldst have stood here; but now a fell winter cometh soon from the land of the Enemy. Haste thou must learn, and the pleasant road that I designed for thee must be changed. For my counsels have been scorned, and a great evil creeps upon the Valley of Sirion, and already a host of foes is come between thee and thy goal.'

'What then is my goal, Lord?' said Tuor.

'That which thy heart hath ever sought,' answered Ulmo: 'to find Turgon, and look upon the hidden city. For thou art arrayed thus to be my messenger, even in the arms which long ago I decreed for thee. Yet now thou must under shadow pass through peril. Wrap thyself therefore in this cloak, and cast it never aside, until thou come to thy journey's end.'

Then it seemed to Tuor that Ulmo parted his grey mantle, and cast to him a lappet, and as it fell about him it was for him a great cloak wherein he might wrap himself over all, from head to foot.

'Thus thou shalt walk under my shadow,' said Ulmo. 'But tarry no more; for in the lands of Anar and in the fires of Melkor it will not endure. Wilt thou take up my errand?'

'I will, Lord,' said Tuor.

'Then I will set words in thy mouth to say unto Turgon,' said Ulmo. 'But first I will teach thee, and some things thou shalt hear which no man else hath heard, nay, not even the mighty among the Eldar.' And Ulmo spoke to Tuor of Valinor and its darkening, and the Exile of the Noldor, and the Doom of Mandos, and the hiding of the Blessed Realm. 'But behold!' said he, 'in the armour of Fate (as the Children of Earth name it) there is ever a rift, and in the walls of Doom a breach, until the full-making, which ye call the End. So it shall be while I endure, a secret voice that gainsayeth, and a light where darkness was decreed. Therefore, though in the days of this darkness I seem to oppose the will of my brethren, the Lords of the West, that is my part among them, to which I was appointed ere the making of the World. Yet Doom is strong, and the shadow of the Enemy lengthens; and I am diminished, until in Middle-earth I am become now no more than a secret whisper. The waters that run westward wither, and their springs are poisoned, and my power withdraws from the land; for Elves and Men grow blind and deaf to me because of the might of Melkor. And now the Curse of Mandos hastens to its fulfilment, and all the works of the Noldor shall perish, and every hope which they build shall crumble. The last hope alone is left, the hope that they have not looked for and have not prepared. And that hope lieth in thee; for so I have chosen.'

'Then shall Turgon not stand against Morgoth, as all the Eldar yet hope?' said Tuor. 'And what wouldst thou of me, Lord, if I come now to Turgon? For though I am indeed willing to do as my father and stand by that king in his need, yet of little avail shall I be, a mortal man alone, among so many and so valiant of the High Folk of the West.'

'If I choose to send thee, Tuor son of Huor, then believe not that thy one sword is not worth the sending. For the valour of the Edain the Elves shall ever remember as the ages lengthen, marvelling that they gave life so freely of which on earth they had so little. But it is not for thy valour only that I send thee, but to bring into the world a hope beyond thy sight, and a light that shall pierce the darkness.'

And as Ulmo said these things the mutter of the storm

rose to a great cry, and the wind mounted, and the sky grew black; and the mantle of the Lord of Waters streamed out like a flying cloud. 'Go now,' said Ulmo, 'lest the Sea devour thee! For Ossë obeys the will of Mandos, and he is wroth, being a servant of the Doom.'

'As thou commandest,' said Tuor. 'But if I escape the Doom, what words shall I say unto Turgon?'

'If thou come to him,' answered Ulmo, 'then the words shall arise in thy mind, and thy mouth shall speak as I would. Speak and fear not! And thereafter do as thy heart and valour lead thee. Hold fast to my mantle, for thus shalt thou be guarded. And I will send one to thee out of the wrath of Ossë, and thus shalt thou be guided: yea, the last mariner of the last ship that shall seek into the West until the rising of the Star. Go now back to the land!'

Then there was a noise of thunder, and lightning flared over the sea; and Tuor beheld Ulmo standing among the waves as a tower of silver flickering with darting flames; and he cried against the wind: 'I go, Lord! Yet now my heart yearneth rather to the Sea.'

And thereupon Ulmo lifted up a mighty horn, and blew upon it a single great note, to which the roaring of the storm was but a wind-flaw upon a lake. And as he heard that note, and was encompassed by it, and filled with it, it seemed to Tuor that the coasts of Middle-earth vanished, and he surveyed all the waters of the world in a great vision: from the veins of the lands to the mouths of the rivers, and from the strands and estuaries out into the deep. The Great Sea he saw through its unquiet regions teeming with strange forms, even to its lightless depths, in which amid the everlasting darkness there echoed voices terrible to mortal ears. Its measureless plains he surveyed with the swift sight of the Valar, lying windless under the eye of Anar, or glittering under the horned Moon, or lifted in hills of wrath that broke upon the Shadowy Isles, until remote upon the edge of sight, and beyond the count of leagues, he glimpsed a mountain, rising beyond his mind's reach into a shining cloud, and at its feet a long surf glimmering. And even as he strained to hear the sound of those far waves, and to see clearer that distant light, the note ended, and he stood beneath the thunder of the storm, and lightning many-branched rent asunder the heavens above him. And Ulmo was gone, and the sea was in tumult, as the wild waves of Ossë rode against the walls of Nevrast.

Then Tuor fled from the fury of the sea, and with labour he won his way back to the high terraces; for the wind drove him against the cliff, and when he came out upon the top it bent him to his knees. Therefore he entered again the dark and empty hall for shelter, and he sat nightlong in the stone seat of Turgon. The very pillars trembled for the violence of the storm, and it seemed to Tuor that the wind was full of wailing and wild cries. Yet being weary he slept at times, and his sleep was troubled with many dreams, of which naught remained in waking memory save one: a vision of an isle, and in the midst of it was a steep mountain, and behind it the sun went down, and shadows sprang into the sky; but above it there shone a single dazzling star.

After this dream Tuor fell into a deep sleep, for before the

night was over the tempest passed, driving the black clouds into the East of the world. He awoke at length in the grey light, and arose, and left the high seat, and as he went down the dim hall he saw that it was filled with sea-birds driven in by the storm; and he went out as the last stars were fading in the West before the coming day. Then he saw that the great waves in the night had ridden high upon the land, and had cast their crests above the cliff-tops, and weed and shingle-drift were flung even upon the terraces before the doors. And Tuor looked down from the lowest terrace and saw, leaning against its wall among the stones and the sea-wrack, an Elf, clad in a grey cloak sodden with the sea. Silent he sat, gazing beyond the ruin of the beaches out over the long ridges of the waves. All was still, and there was no sound save the roaring of the surf below.

As Tuor stood and looked at the silent grey figure he remembered the words of Ulmo, and a name untaught came to his lips, and he called aloud: 'Welcome, Voronwë! I await you.'

Then the Elf turned and looked up, and Tuor met the piercing glance of his sea-grey eyes, and knew that he was of the high folk of the Noldor. But fear and wonder grew in his gaze as he saw Tuor standing high upon the wall above him, clad in his great cloak like a shadow out of which the elven-mail gleamed upon his breast.

A moment thus they stayed, each searching the face of the other, and then the Elf stood up and bowed low before Tuor's feet. 'Who are you, lord?' he said. 'Long have I laboured in the unrelenting sea. Tell me: have great tidings befallen since

I walked the land? Is the Shadow overthrown? Have the Hidden People come forth?'

'Nay,' Tuor answered. 'The Shadow lengthens, and the Hidden remain hid.'

Then Voronwë looked at him long in silence. 'But who are you?' he asked again. 'For many years ago my people left this land, and none have dwelt here since. And now I perceive that despite your raiment you are not of them, as I thought, but are of the kindred of Men.'

'I am,' said Tuor. 'And are you not the last mariner of the last ship that sought the West from the Havens of Círdan?'

'I am,' said the Elf. 'Voronwë son of Aranwë am I. But how you know my name and fate I understand not.'

'I know, for the Lord of Waters spoke to me yestereve,' answered Tuor, 'and he said that he would save you from the wrath of Ossë, and send you hither to be my guide.'

Then in fear and wonder Voronwë cried: 'You have spoken with Ulmo the Mighty? Then great indeed must be your worth and doom! But whither should I guide you, lord? For surely a king of Men you must be, and many must wait upon your word.'

'Nay, I am an escaped thrall,' said Tuor, 'and I am an outlaw alone in an empty land. But I have an errand to Turgon the Hidden King. Know you by what road I should find him?'

'Many are outlaw and thrall in these days who were not born so,' answered Voronwë. 'A lord of Men by right you are, I deem. But were you the highest of all your folk, no right would you have to seek Turgon, and vain would be your quest. For even were I to lead you to his gates, you could not enter in.'

'I do not bid you to lead me further than the gate,' said Tuor. 'There Doom shall strive with the Counsel of Ulmo. And if Turgon will not receive me, then my errand will be ended, and Doom shall prevail. But as for my right to seek Turgon: I am Tuor son of Huor and kin to Húrin, whose names Turgon will not forget. And I seek also by the command of Ulmo. Will Turgon forget that which he spoke to him of old: *Remember that the last hope of the Noldor cometh from the Sea?* Or again: *When peril is nigh one shall come from Nevrast to warn thee?* I am he that should come, and I am arrayed thus in the gear that was prepared for me.'

Tuor marvelled to hear himself speak so, for the words of Ulmo to Turgon at his going from Nevrast were not known to him before, nor to any save the Hidden People. Therefore the more amazed was Voronwë; but he turned away, and looked toward the Sea, and he sighed.

'Alas!' he said. 'I wish never again to return. And often have I vowed in the deeps of the sea that, if ever I set foot on land again, I would dwell at rest far from the Shadow in the North, or by the Havens of Círdan, or maybe in the fair fields of Nan-tathrin, where the spring is sweeter than the heart's desire. But if evil has grown while I have wandered, and the last peril approaches them, then I must go to my people.' He turned back to Tuor. 'I will lead you to the hidden gates,' he said; 'for the wise will not gainsay the counsels of Ulmo.'

'Then we will go together, as we are counselled,' said

Tuor. 'But mourn not, Voronwë! For my heart says to you that far from the Shadow your long road shall lead you, and your hope shall return to the Sea.'

'And yours also,' said Voronwë. 'But now we must leave it, and go in haste.'

'Yea,' said Tuor. 'But whither will you lead me, and how far? Shall we not first take thought how we may fare in the wild, or if the way be long, how pass the harbourless winter?'

But Voronwë would answer nothing clearly concerning the road. 'You know the strength of Men,' he said. 'As for me, I am of the Noldor, and long must be the hunger and cold the winter that shall slay the kin of those who passed the Grinding Ice. Yet how think you that we could labour countless days in the salt wastes of the sea? Or have you not heard of the waybread of the Elves? And I keep still that which all mariners hold until the last.' Then he showed beneath his cloak a sealed wallet clasped upon his belt. 'No water nor weather will harm it while it is sealed. But we must husband it until great need; and doubtless an outlaw and hunter may find other food ere the year worsens.'

'Maybe,' said Tuor. 'But not in all lands is it safe to hunt, be the game never so plentiful. And hunters tarry on the road.'

Now Tuor and Voronwë made ready to depart. Tuor took with him the small bow and arrows that he had brought, beside the gear that he had taken from the hall; but his spear, upon which his name was written in the elven-runes of the

North, he set upon the wall in token that he had passed. No arms had Voronwë save a short sword only.

Before the day was broad they left the ancient dwelling of Turgon, and Voronwë led Tuor about, westward of the steep slopes of Taras, and across the great cape. There once the road from Nevrast to Brithombar had passed, that now was but a green track between old turf-clad dikes. So they came into Beleriand, and the north region of the Falas; and turning eastward they sought the dark eaves of Ered Wethrin, and there they lay hid and rested until day had waned to dusk. For though the ancient dwellings of the Falathrim, Brithombar and Eglarest, were still far distant, Orcs now dwelt there and all the land was infested by the spies of Morgoth: he feared the ships of Círdan that would come at times raiding to the shores, and join with the forays sent forth from Nargothrond.

Now as they sat shrouded in their cloaks as shadows under the hills, Tuor and Voronwë spoke much together. And Tuor questioned Voronwë concerning Turgon, but Voronwë would tell little of such matters, and spoke rather of the dwellings upon the Isle of Balar, and of the Lisgardh, the land of reeds at the Mouths of Sirion.

'There now the numbers of the Eldar increase,' he said, 'for ever more flee thither of either kin from the fear of Morgoth, weary of war. But I forsook not my people of my own choice. For after the Bragollach and the breaking of the Siege of Angband doubt first came into Turgon's heart that Morgoth might prove too strong. In that year he sent out the first of his folk that passed his gates from within: a few only,

upon a secret errand. They went down Sirion to the shores
about the Mouths, and there built ships. But it availed them
nothing, save to come to the great Isle of Balar and there
establish lonely dwellings, far from the reach of Morgoth.
For the Noldor have not the art of building ships that will
long endure the waves of Belegaer the Great.

'But when later Turgon heard of the ravaging of the Falas
and the sack of the ancient Havens of the Shipwrights that
lie away there before us, and it was told that Círdan had
saved a remnant of his people and sailed away south to the
Bay of Balar, then he sent out messengers anew. That was
but a little while ago, yet it seems in memory the longest
portion of my life. For I was one of those that he sent,
being young in years among the Eldar. I was born here in
Middle-earth in the land of Nevrast. My mother was of the
Grey-elves of the Falas, and akin to Círdan himself – there
was much mingling of the peoples in Nevrast in the first
days of Turgon's kingship – and I have the sea-heart of my
mother's people. Therefore I was among the chosen, since
our errand was to Círdan, to seek his aid in our shipbuild-
ing, that some message and prayer for aid might come to the
Lords of the West ere all was lost. But I tarried on the way.
For I had seen little of the lands of Middle-earth, and we
came to Nan-tathrin in the spring of the year. Lovely to
heart's enchantment is that land, Tuor, as you shall find, if
ever your feet go upon the southward roads down Sirion.
There is the cure of all sea-longing, save for those whom
Doom will not release. There Ulmo is but the servant of
Yavanna, and the earth has brought to life a wealth of fair

things that is beyond the thought of hearts in the hard hills of the North. In that land Narog joins Sirion, and they haste no more, but flow broad and quiet through living meads; and all about the shining river are flaglilies like a blossoming forest, and the grass is filled with flowers, like gems, like bells, like flames of red and gold, like a waste of many-coloured stars in a firmament of green. Yet fairest of all are the willows of Nan-tathrin, pale green, or silver in the wind, and the rustle of their innumerable leaves is a spell of music: day and night would flicker by uncounted, while still I stood knee-deep in grass and listened. There I was enchanted, and forgot the Sea in my heart. There I wandered, naming new flowers, or lay adream amid the singing of the birds, and the humming of bees and flies; and there I might still dwell in delight, forsaking all my kin, whether the ships of the Teleri or the swords of the Noldor, but my doom would not so. Or the Lord of Waters himself, maybe; for he was strong in that land.

'Thus it came into my heart to make a raft of willow-boughs and move upon the bright bosom of Sirion; and so I did, and so I was taken. For on a day, as I was in the midst of the river, a sudden wind came and caught me, and bore me away out of the Land of Willows down to the Sea. Thus I came last of the messengers to Círdan; and of the seven ships that he built at Turgon's asking all but one were then full-wrought. And one by one they set sail into the West, and none yet has ever returned, nor has any news of them been heard.

'But the salt air of the sea now stirred anew the heart of

my mother's kin within me, and I rejoiced in the waves, learning all ship-lore, as were it already stored in the mind. So when the last ship, and the greatest, was made ready, I was eager to be gone, saying within my thought: "If the words of the Noldor be true, then in the West there are meads with which the Land of Willows cannot compare. There is no withering nor any end of Spring. And perhaps even I, Voronwë, may come thither. And at the worst to wander on the waters is better far than the Shadow in the North." And I feared not, for the ships of the Teleri no water may drown.

'But the Great Sea is terrible, Tuor son of Huor; and it hates the Noldor, for it works the Doom of the Valar. Worse things it holds than to sink into the abyss and so perish: loathing, and loneliness, and madness; terror of wind and tumult, and silence, and shadows where all hope is lost and all living shapes pass away. And many shores evil and strange it washes, and many islands of danger and fear infest it. I will not darken your heart, son of Middle-earth, with the tale of my labour seven years in the Great Sea from the North even into the South, but never to the West. For that is shut against us.

'At the last, in black despair, weary of all the world, we turned and fled from the doom that so long had spared us, only to strike us more cruelly. For even as we descried a mountain from afar, and I cried: "Lo! There is Taras, the land of my birth," the wind awoke, and great clouds thunder-laden came up from the West. Then the waves hunted us like living things filled with malice, and the lightnings smote us; and when we were broken down to a helpless hull the seas leaped upon us in fury. But as you see, I was spared; for it seemed to me that there came a wave, greater and yet calmer than all the others, and it took me and lifted me from the ship, and bore me high upon its shoulders, and rolling to the land it cast me upon the turf, and then drained away, pouring back over the cliff in a great waterfall. There but one hour had I sat when you came upon me, still dazed by the sea. And still I feel the fear of it, and the bitter loss of all my friends that went with me so long and so far, beyond the sight of mortal lands.'

Voronwë sighed, and spoke then softly as if to himself. 'But very bright were the stars upon the margin of the world, when at times the clouds about the West were drawn aside. Yet whether we saw only clouds still more remote, or glimpsed indeed, as some held, the Mountains of the Pelóri about the lost strands of our long home, I know not. Far, far away they stand, and none from mortal lands shall come there ever again, I deem.' Then Voronwë fell silent; for night had come, and the stars shone white and cold.

Soon after Tuor and Voronwë arose and turned their backs toward the sea, and set out upon their long journey in the dark; of which there is little to tell, for the shadow of Ulmo was on Tuor, and none saw them pass, by wood or stone, by field or fen, between the setting and the rising of the sun. But ever warily they went, shunning the night-eyed hunters of Morgoth, and forsaking the trodden ways of Elves and Men. Voronwë chose their path and Tuor followed. He asked no vain questions, but noted well that they went ever eastward along the march of the rising mountains, and turned never southward: at which he wondered, for he believed, as did well nigh all Elves and Men, that Turgon dwelt far from the battles of the North.

Slow was their going by twilight or by night in the pathless wilds, and the fell winter came down swiftly from the realm of Morgoth. Despite the shelter of the hills the winds were strong and bitter, and soon the snow lay deep upon the heights, or whirled through the passes, and fell upon the woods of Núath ere the full-shedding of their withered leaves. Thus though they set out before the middle of Narquelië, the Hísimë came in with biting frost even as they drew nigh to the Sources of Narog.

There at the end of a weary night in the grey of dawn they halted, and Voronwë was dismayed, looking about him in grief and fear. Where once the fair pool of Ivrin had lain in its great stone basin carved by falling waters, and all about it had been a tree-clad hollow under the hills, now he saw a land defiled and desolate. The trees were burned or uprooted; and the stone-marges of the pool were broken, so that the waters of Ivrin strayed and wrought a great barren marsh amid the ruin. All now was but a welter of frozen mire, and a reek of decay lay like a foul mist upon the ground.

'Alas! Has the evil come even here?' Voronwë cried. 'Once far from the threat of Angband was this place; but ever the fingers of Morgoth grope further.'

'It is even as Ulmo spoke to me,' said Tuor: '*The springs are poisoned, and my power withdraws from the waters of the land.*'

'Yet,' said Voronwë, 'a malice has been here with strength greater than that of Orcs. Fear lingers in this place.' And he searched about the edges of the mire, until suddenly he stood still and cried again: 'Yea, a great evil!' And he beckoned to Tuor, and Tuor coming saw a slot like a huge furrow that passed away southward, and at either side, now blurred, now sealed hard and clear by frost, the marks of great clawed feet. 'See!' said Voronwë, and his face was pale with dread and loathing, 'Here not long since was the Great Worm of Angband, most fell of all the creatures of the Enemy! Late already is our errand to Turgon. There is need of haste.'

Even as he spoke thus, they heard a cry in the woods, and they stood still as grey stones, listening. But the voice was a fair voice, though filled with grief, and it seemed that it called ever upon a name, as one that searches for another who is lost. And as they waited one came through the trees, and they saw that he was a tall Man, armed, clad in black, with a long sword drawn; and they wondered, for the blade of the sword also was black, but the edges shone bright and cold. Woe was graven in his face, and when he beheld the ruin of Ivrin he cried aloud in grief, saying: 'Ivrin, Faelivrin! Gwindor and Beleg! Here once I was healed. But now never shall I drink the draught of peace again.'

Then he went swiftly away towards the North, as one in pursuit, or on an errand of great haste, and they heard him cry *Faelivrin, Finduilas!* until his voice died away in the woods. But they knew not that Nargothrond had fallen, and this was Túrin son of Húrin, the Blacksword. Thus only for a moment, and never again, did the paths of those kinsmen, Túrin and Tuor, draw together.

When the Blacksword had passed, Tuor and Voronwë held on their way for a while, though day had come; for the memory of his grief was heavy upon them, and they could not endure to remain beside the defilement of Ivrin. But before long they sought a hiding-place, for all the land was filled now with a foreboding of evil. They slept little and uneasily, and as the day wore it grew dark and a great snow fell, and with the night came a grinding frost. Thereafter the snow and ice relented not at all, and for five months the Fell Winter, long remembered, held the North in bonds. Now Tuor and Voronwë were tormented by the cold, and feared to be revealed by the snow to hunting enemies, or to fall into hidden dangers treacherously cloaked. Nine days they held on, ever slower and more painfully, and Voronwë turned somewhat north, until they crossed the three well-streams of Teiglin; and then he bore eastward again, leaving the mountains, and went warily, until they passed Glithui and came to the stream of Malduin, and it was frozen black.

Then Tuor said to Voronwë: 'Fell is this frost, and death draws near to me, if not to you.' For they were now in evil case: it was long since they had found any food in the wild, and the waybread was dwindling; and they were cold and weary. 'Ill is it to be trapped between the Doom of the Valar and the Malice of the Enemy,' said Voronwë. 'Have I escaped the mouths of the sea but to lie under the snow?'

But Tuor said: 'How far is now to go? For at last, Voronwë, you must forgo your secrecy with me. Do you lead me straight, and whither? For if I must spend my last strength, I would know to what that may avail.'

'I have led you as straight as I safely might,' answered Voronwë. 'Know then now that Turgon dwells still in the north of the land of the Eldar, though that is believed by few. Already we draw nigh to him. Yet there are many leagues still to go, even as a bird might fly; and for us Sirion is yet to cross, and great evil, maybe, lies between. For we must come soon to the Highway that ran of old down from the Minas of King Finrod to Nargothrond. There the servants of the Enemy will walk and watch.'

'I counted myself the hardiest of Men,' said Tuor, 'and I have endured many winters' woe in the mountains; but I had a cave at my back and fire then, and I doubt now my strength to go much further thus hungry through the fell weather. But let us go on as far as we may before hope fails.'

'No other choice have we,' said Voronwë, 'unless it be to lay us down here and seek the snow-sleep.'

Therefore all through that bitter day they toiled on, deeming the peril of foes less than the winter; but ever as they went they found less snow, for they were now going southward again down into the Vale of Sirion, and the Mountains of Dor-lómin were left far behind. In the deepening dusk they came to the Highway at the bottom of a tall wooded bank. Suddenly they were aware of voices, and looking out warily from the trees they saw a red light below. A company of Orcs was encamped in the midst of the road, huddled about a large wood-fire.

'*Gurth an Glamhoth!* [Death to the Orcs!]' Tuor

muttered. 'Now the sword shall come from under the cloak. I will risk death for mastery of that fire, and even the meat of Orcs would be a prize.'

'Nay!' said Voronwë. 'On this quest only the cloak will serve. You must forgo the fire, or else forgo Turgon. This band is not alone in the wild: cannot your mortal sight see the far flame of other posts to the north and to the south? A tumult will bring a host upon us. Hearken to me, Tuor! It is against the law of the Hidden Kingdom that any should approach the gates with foes at their heels; and that law I will not break, neither for Ulmo's bidding, nor for death. Rouse the Orcs, and I leave you.'

'Then let them be,' said Tuor. 'But may I live yet to see the day when I need not sneak aside from a handful of Orcs like a cowed dog.'

'Come then!' said Voronwë. 'Debate no more, or they will scent us. Follow me!'

He crept then away through the trees, southward down the wind, until they were midway between that Orc-fire and the next upon the road. There he stood a long while listening.

'I hear none moving on the road,' he said, 'but we know not what may be lurking in the shadows.' He peered forward into the gloom and shuddered. 'The air is evil,' he muttered. 'Alas! Yonder lies the land of our quest and hope of life, but death walks between.'

'Death is all about us,' said Tuor. 'But I have strength left only for the shortest road. Here I must cross, or perish. I will trust to the mantle of Ulmo, and you also it shall cover. Now I will lead!'

So saying he stole to the border of the road. Then clasping Voronwë close he cast about them both the folds of the grey cloak of the Lord of Waters, and stepped forth.

All was still. The cold wind sighed as it swept down the ancient road. Then suddenly it too fell silent. In the pause Tuor felt a change in the air as if the breath from the land of Morgoth had failed a while, and faint as a memory of the Sea came a breeze from the West. As a grey mist on the wind they passed over the stony street and entered a thicket on its eastern brink.

All at once from near at hand there came a wild cry, and many others along the borders of the road answered it. A harsh horn blared, and there was the sound of running feet. But Tuor held on. He had learned enough of the tongue of the Orcs in his captivity to know the meaning of those cries: the watchers had scented them and heard them, but they were not seen. The hunt was out. Desperately he stumbled and crept forward with Voronwë at his side, up a long slope deep in whin and whortleberry among knots of rowan and low birch. At the top of the ridge they halted, listening to the shouts behind and the crashing of the Orcs in the undergrowth below.

Beside them was a boulder that reared its head out of a tangle of heath and brambles, and beneath it was such a lair as a hunted beast might seek and hope there to escape pursuit, or at the least with its back to stone to sell its life dearly. Down into the dark shadow Tuor drew Voronwë, and side by side under the grey cloak they lay and panted like tired foxes. No word they spoke; all their heed was in their ears.

The cries of the hunters grew fainter; for the Orcs thrust never deep into the wild lands at either hand, but swept rather down and up the road. They recked little of stray fugitives, but spies they feared and the scouts of armed foes; for Morgoth had set a guard on the highway, not to ensnare Tuor and Voronwë (of whom as yet he knew nothing) nor any coming from the West, but to watch for the Blacksword, lest he should escape and pursue the captives of Nargothrond, bringing help, it might be, out of Doriath.

The night passed, and the brooding silence lay again upon the empty lands. Weary and spent Tuor slept beneath Ulmo's cloak; but Voronwë crept forth and stood like a stone silent, unmoving, piercing the shadows with his Elvish eyes. At the break of day he woke Tuor, and he creeping out saw that the weather had indeed for a time relented, and the black clouds were rolled aside. There was a red dawn, and he could see far before him the tops of strange mountains glinting against the eastern fire.

Then Voronwë said in a low voice: '*Alae! Ered en Echoriath, ered e·mbar nín!* [the Encircling Mountains, the mountains of my home]'. For he knew that he looked on the Encircling Mountains and the walls of the realm of Turgon. Below them, eastward, in a deep and shadowy vale lay Sirion the fair, renowned in song; and beyond, wrapped in mist, a grey land climbed from the river to the broken hills at the mountains' feet. 'Yonder lies Dimbar,' said Voronwë. 'Would we were there! For there our foes seldom dare to walk. Or so it was, while the power of Ulmo was strong in

Sirion. But all may now be changed – save the peril of the river: it is already deep and swift, and even for the Eldar dangerous to cross. But I have led you well; for there gleams the Ford of Brithiach, yet a little southward, where the East Road that of old ran all the way from Taras in the West made the passage of the river. None now dare to use it save in desperate need, neither Elf nor Man nor Orc, since that road leads to Dungortheb and the land of dread between the Gorgoroth and the Girdle of Melian; and long since has it faded into the wild, or dwindled to a track among weeds and trailing thorns.'

Then Tuor looked as Voronwë pointed, and far away he caught the glimmer as of open waters under the brief light of dawn; but beyond loomed a darkness, where the great forest of Brethil climbed away southward into a distant highland. Now warily they made their way down the valley-side, until at last they came to the ancient road descending from the waymeet on the borders of Brethil, where it crossed the highway from Nargothrond. Then Tuor saw that they were come close to Sirion. The banks of its deep channel fell away in that place, and its waters, choked by a great waste of stones, were spread out into broad shallows, full of the murmur of fretting streams. Then after a little the river gathered together again, and delving a new bed flowed away toward the forest, and far off vanished into a deep mist that his eye could not pierce; for there lay, though he knew it not, the north march of Doriath within the shadow of the Girdle of Melian.

At once Tuor would hasten to the ford, but Voronwë

restrained him, saying: 'Over the Brithiach we may not go in open day, nor while any doubt of pursuit remains.'

'Then shall we sit here and rot?' said Tuor. 'For such doubt will remain while the realm of Morgoth endures. Come! Under the shadow of the cloak of Ulmo we must go forward.'

Still Voronwë hesitated, and looked back westward; but the track behind was deserted, and all about was quiet save for the rush of the waters. He looked up, and the sky was grey and empty, for not even a bird was moving. Then suddenly his face brightened with joy, and he cried aloud: 'It is well! The Brithiach is guarded still by the enemies of the Enemy. The Orcs will not follow us here; and under the cloak we may pass now without more doubt.'

'What new thing have you seen?' said Tuor.

'Short is the sight of Mortal Men!' said Voronwë. 'I see the Eagles of the Crissaegrim; and they are coming hither. Watch a while!'

Then Tuor stood at gaze; and soon high in the air he saw three shapes beating on strong wings down from the distant mountain-peaks now wreathed again in cloud. Slowly they descended in great circles, and then stooped suddenly upon the wayfarers; but before Voronwë could call to them they turned with a wide sweep and rush, and flew northward along the line of the river.

'Now let us go,' said Voronwë. 'If there be any Orc nearby, he will lie cowering nose to ground, until the eagles have gone far away.'

Swiftly down a long slope they hastened, and passed over

the Brithiach, walking often dryfoot upon shelves of shingle, or wading in the shoals no more than knee-deep. The water was clear and very cold, and there was ice upon the shallow pools, where the wandering streams had lost their way among the stones; but never, not even in the Fell Winter of the Fall of Nargothrond, could the deadly breath of the North freeze the main flood of Sirion.

On the far side of the ford they came to a gully, as it were the bed of an old stream, in which no water now flowed; yet once, it seemed, a torrent had cloven its deep channel, coming down from the north out of the mountains of the Echoriath, and bearing thence all the stones of the Brithiach down into Sirion.

'At last beyond hope we find it!' cried Voronwë. 'See! Here is the mouth of the Dry River, and that is the road we must take.' Then they passed into the gully, and as it turned north and the slopes of the land went steeply up, so its sides rose on either hand, and Tuor stumbled in the dim light among the stones with which its rough bed was strewn. 'If this is a road,' he said, 'it is an evil one for the weary.'

'Yet it is the road to Turgon,' said Voronwë.

'Then the more do I marvel,' said Tuor, 'that its entrance lies open and unguarded. I had looked to find a great gate, and strength of guard.'

'That you shall yet see,' said Voronwë. 'This is but the approach. A road I named it; yet upon it none have passed for more than three hundred years, save messengers few and secret, and all the craft of the Noldor has been expended to conceal it, since the Hidden People entered in. Does it lie open? Would you have known it, if you had not had one of the Hidden Kingdom for a guide? Or would you have guessed it to be but the work of the weathers and the waters of the wilderness? And are there not the Eagles, as you have seen? They are the folk of Thorondor, who dwelt once even on Thangorodrim ere Morgoth grew so mighty, and dwell now in the Mountains of Turgon since the fall of Fingolfin. They alone save the Noldor know the Hidden Kingdom and guard the skies above it, though as yet no servant of the Enemy has dared to fly into the high airs; and they bring much news to the King of all that moves in the lands without. Had we been Orcs, doubt not that we should have been seized, and cast from a great height upon the pitiless rocks.'

'I doubt it not,' said Tuor. 'But it comes into my mind to wonder also whether news will not now come to Turgon of our approach swifter than we. And if that be good or ill, you alone can say.'

'Neither good nor ill,' said Voronwë. 'For we cannot pass the Guarded Gate unmarked, be we looked for or no; and if we come there the Guards will need no report that we are not Orcs. But to pass we shall need a greater plea than that. For you do not guess, Tuor, the peril that we then shall face. Blame me not, as one unwarned, for what may then betide; may the power of the Lord of Waters be shown indeed! For in that hope alone have I been willing to guide you, and if it fails then more surely shall we die than by all the perils of wild and winter.'

But Tuor said: 'Forebode no more. Death in the wild is

certain; and death at the Gate is yet in doubt to me, for all your words. Lead me still on!'

Many miles they toiled on in the stones of the Dry River, until they could go no further, and the evening brought darkness into the deep cleft; they climbed out then onto the east bank, and they had now come into the tumbled hills that lay at the feet of the mountains. And looking up Tuor saw that they towered up in a fashion other than that of any mountains that he had seen; for their sides were like sheer walls, piled each one above and behind the lower, as were they great towers of many-storeyed precipices. But the day had waned, and all the lands were grey and misty, and the Vale of Sirion was shrouded in shadow. Then Voronwë led him to a shallow cave in a hillside that looked out over the lonely slopes of Dimbar, and they crept within, and there they lay hid; and they ate their last crumbs of food, and were cold, and weary, but slept not. Thus did Tuor and Voronwë come in the dusk of the eighteenth day of Hísimë, the thirty-seventh of their journey, to the towers of the Echoriath and the threshold of Turgon, and by the power of Ulmo escaped both the Doom and the Malice.

When the first glimmer of day filtered grey amid the mists of Dimbar they crept back into the Dry River, and soon after its course turned eastward, winding up to the very walls of the mountains; and straight before them there loomed a great precipice, rising sheer and sudden from a steep slope upon which grew a tangled thicket of thorn-trees. Into this thicket the stony channel entered, and there it was still dark as night; and they halted, for the thorns grew far down the sides of the gully, and their lacing branches were a dense roof above it, so low that often Tuor and Voronwë must crawl under like beasts stealing back to their lair.

But at last, as with great labour they came to the very foot of the cliff, they found an opening, as it were the mouth of a tunnel worn in the hard rock by waters flowing from the heart of the mountains. They entered, and within there was no light, but Voronwë went steadily forward, while Tuor followed with his hand upon his shoulder, bending a little, for the roof was low. Thus for a time they went on blindly, step by step, until presently they felt the ground beneath their feet had become level and free from loose stones. Then they halted and breathed deeply, as they stood listening. The air seemed fresh and wholesome, and they were aware of a great space around and above them; but all was silent, and not even the drip of water could be heard. It seemed to Tuor that Voronwë was troubled and in doubt, and he whispered: 'Where then is the Guarded Gate? Or have we indeed now passed it?'

'Nay,' said Voronwë. 'Yet I wonder, for it is strange that any incomer should creep thus far unchallenged. I fear some stroke in the dark.'

But their whispers aroused the sleeping echoes, and they were enlarged and multiplied, and ran in the roof and the unseen walls, hissing and murmuring as the sound of many stealthy voices. And even as the echoes died in the stone, Tuor heard out of the darkness a voice speak in the

Elven-tongues: first in the High Speech of the Noldor, which he knew not; and then in the tongue of Beleriand, though in a manner somewhat strange to his ears, as of a people long sundered from their kin.

'Stand!' it said. 'Stir not! Or you will die, be you foes or friends.'

'We are friends,' said Voronwë.

'Then do as we bid,' said the voice.

The echo of their voices rolled into silence. Voronwë and Tuor stood still, and it seemed to Tuor that many slow minutes passed, and a fear was in his heart such as no other peril of his road had brought. Then there came the beat of feet, growing to a tramping loud as the march of trolls in that hollow place. Suddenly an elven lantern was unhooded, and its bright ray was turned upon Voronwë before him, but nothing else could Tuor see save a dazzling star in the darkness; and he knew that while that beam was upon him he could not move, neither to flee nor to run forward.

For a moment they were held thus in the eye of the light, and then the voice spoke again, saying: 'Show your faces!' And Voronwë cast back his hood, and his face shone in the ray, hard and clear, as if graven in stone; and Tuor marvelled to see its beauty. Then he spoke proudly, saying: 'Know you not whom you see? I am Voronwë son of Aranwë of the House of Fingolfin. Or am I forgotten in my own land after a few years? Far beyond the thought of Middle-earth I have wandered, yet I remember your voice, Elemmakil.'

'Then Voronwë will remember also the laws of his land,' said the voice. 'Since by command he went forth, he has the right to return. But not to lead hither any stranger. By that deed his right is void, and he must be led as a prisoner to the king's judgement. As for the stranger, he shall be slain or held captive at the judgement of the Guard. Lead him hither that I may judge.'

Then Voronwë led Tuor towards the light, and as they drew near many Noldor, mail-clad and armed, stepped forward out of the darkness and surrounded them with drawn swords. And Elemmakil, captain of the Guard, who bore the bright lamp, looked long and closely at them.

'This is strange in you, Voronwë,' he said. 'We were long friends. Why then would you set me thus cruelly between the law and my friendship? If you had led hither unbidden one of the other houses of the Noldor, that were enough. But you have brought to knowledge of the Way a mortal Man – for by his eyes I perceive his kin. Yet free can he never again go, knowing the secret; and as one of alien kin that has dared to enter, I should slay him – even though he be your friend and dear to you.'

'In the wide lands without, Elemmakil, many strange things may befall one, and tasks unlooked for be laid on one,' Voronwë answered. 'Other shall the wanderer return than as he set forth. What I have done, I have done under command greater than the law of the Guard. The King alone should judge me, and him that comes with me.'

Then Tuor spoke, and feared no longer. 'I come with Voronwë son of Aranwë, because he was appointed to be my guide by the Lord of Waters. To this end was he delivered from the wrath of the Sea and the Doom of the Valar. For

I bear from Ulmo an errand to the son of Fingolfin, and to him will I speak it.'

Thereat Elemmakil looked in wonder upon Tuor. 'Who then are you?' he said. 'And whence come you?'

'I am Tuor son of Huor of the House of Hador and the kindred of Húrin, and these names, I am told, are not unknown in the Hidden Kingdom. From Nevrast I have come through many perils to seek it.'

'From Nevrast?' said Elemmakil. 'It is said that none dwell there, since our people departed.'

'It is said truly,' answered Tuor. 'Empty and cold stand the courts of Vinyamar. Yet thence I come. Bring me now to him that built those halls of old.'

'In matters so great judgement is not mine,' said Elemmakil. 'Therefore I will lead you to the light where more may be revealed, and I will deliver you to the Warden of the Great Gate.'

Then he spoke in command, and Tuor and Voronwë were set between tall guards, two before and three behind them; and their captain led them from the cavern of the Outer Guard, and they passed, as it seemed, into a straight passage, and there walked long upon a level floor until a pale light gleamed ahead. Thus they came at length to a wide arch with tall pillars upon either hand, hewn in the rock, and between hung a great portcullis of crossed wooden bars, marvellously carved and studded with nails of iron.

Elemmakil touched it, and it rose silently, and they passed through; and Tuor saw that they stood at the end of a ravine, the like of which he had never before beheld or imagined in his thought, long though he had walked in the wild mountains of the North; for beside the Orfalch Echor Cirith Ninniach was but a groove in the rock. Here the hands of the Valar themselves, in ancient wars of the world's beginning, had wrested the great mountains asunder, and the sides of the rift were sheer as if axe-cloven, and they towered up to heights unguessable. There far aloft ran a ribbon of sky, and against its deep blue stood black peaks and jagged pinnacles, remote but hard, cruel as spears. Too high were those mighty walls for the winter sun to overlook, and though it was now full morning faint stars glimmered above the mountain-tops, and down below all was dim, but for the pale light of lamps set beside the climbing road. For the floor of the ravine sloped steeply up, eastward, and upon the left hand Tuor saw beside the stream-bed a wide way, laid and paved with stone, winding upward till it vanished into shadow.

'You have passed the First Gate, the Gate of Wood,' said Elemmakil. 'There lies the way. We must hasten.'

How far that deep road ran Tuor could not guess, and as he stared onward a great weariness came upon him like a cloud. A chill wind hissed over the faces of the stones, and he drew his cloak about him. 'Cold blows the wind from the Hidden Kingdom!' he said.

'Yea, indeed,' said Voronwë; 'to a stranger it might seem that pride has made the servants of Turgon pitiless. Long and hard seem the leagues of the Seven Gates to the hungry and wayworn.'

'If our law were less stern, long ago guile and hatred

would have entered and destroyed us. That you know well,' said Elemmakil. 'But we are not pitiless. Here there is no food, and the stranger may not go back through a gate that he has passed. Endure then a little, and at the Second Gate you shall be eased.'

'It is well,' said Tuor, and he went forward as he was bidden. After a little he turned, and saw that Elemmakil alone followed with Voronwë. 'There is no need more of guards,' said Elemmakil, reading his thought. 'From the Orfalch there is no escape for Elf or Man, and no returning.'

Thus they went on up the steep way, sometimes by long stairs, sometimes by winding slopes, under the daunting shadow of the cliff, until some half-league from the Wooden Gate Tuor saw that the way was barred by a great wall built across the ravine from side to side, with stout towers of stone at either hand. In the wall was a great archway above the road, but it seemed that masons had blocked it with a single mighty stone. As they drew near its dark and polished face gleamed in the light of a white lamp that hung above the midst of the arch.

'Here stands the Second Gate, the Gate of Stone,' said Elemmakil; and going up to it he thrust lightly upon it. It turned upon an unseen pivot, until its edge was towards them, and the way was open upon either side; and they passed through, into a court where stood many armed guards clad in grey. No word was spoken, but Elemmakil led his charges to a chamber beneath the northern tower; and there food and wine was brought to them, and they were permitted to rest a while.

'Scant may the fare seem,' said Elemmakil to Tuor. 'But if your claim be proved, hereafter it shall richly be amended.'

'It is enough,' said Tuor. 'Faint were the heart that needed better healing.' And indeed such refreshment did he find in the drink and food of the Noldor that soon he was eager to go on.

After a little space they came to a wall yet higher and stronger than before, and in it was set the Third Gate, the Gate of Bronze: a great twofold door hung with shields and plates of bronze, wherein were wrought many figures and strange signs. Upon the wall above its lintel were three square towers, roofed and clad with copper that by some device of smith-craft were ever bright and gleamed as fire in the rays of the red lamps ranged like torches along the wall. Again silently they passed the gate, and saw in the court beyond a yet greater company of guards in mail that glowed like dull fire; and the blades of their axes were red. Of the kindred of the Sindar of Nevrast for the most part were those that held this gate.

Now they came to the most toilsome road, for in the midst of the Orfalch the slope was at the steepest, and as they climbed Tuor saw the mightiest of the walls looming dark above him. Thus at last they drew near the fourth Gate, the Gate of Writhen Iron. High and black was the wall, and lit with no lamps. Four towers of iron stood upon it, and between the two inner towers was set an image of a great eagle wrought in iron, even the likeness of King Thorondor himself, as he would alight upon a mountain from the high airs. But as Tuor stood before the gate it seemed to his wonder that he was looking through boughs and stems of imperishable trees into a pale glade of the Moon. For a light came through the traceries of the gate, which were wrought and hammered into the shapes of trees with writhing roots and woven branches laden with leaves and flowers. And as he passed through he saw how this could be; for the wall was of great thickness, and there was not one grill, but three in line, so set that to one who approached in the middle of the way each formed part of the device; but the light beyond was the light of day.

For they had climbed now to a great height above the lowlands where they began, and beyond the Iron Gate the road ran almost level. Moreover, they had passed the crown and heart of the Echoriath, and the mountain-towers now fell swiftly down towards the inner hills, and the ravine opened wider, and its sides became less sheer. Its long shoulders were mantled with white snow, and the light of the sky snow-mirrored came white as moonlight through a glimmering mist that filled the air.

Now they passed through the lines of the Iron Guards that stood behind the Gate; black were their mantles and their mail and long shields, and their faces were masked with vizors bearing each an eagle's beak. Then Elemmakil went before them and they followed him into the pale light; and Tuor saw beside the way a sward of grass, where like stars bloomed the white flowers of *uilos*, the Evermind that knows no season and withers not; and thus in wonder and lightening of heart he was brought to the Gate of Silver.

The wall of the Fifth Gate was built of white marble, and

was low and broad, and its parapet was a trellis of silver between five great globes of marble; and there stood many archers robed in white. The gate was in shape as three parts of a circle, and wrought of silver and pearl of Nevrast in likenesses of the Moon; but above the Gate upon the midmost globe stood an image of the White Tree Telperion, wrought of silver and malachite, with flowers made of great pearls of Balar. And beyond the Gate in a wide court paved with marble, green and white, stood archers in silver mail and white-crested helms, a hundred upon either hand. Then Elemmakil led Tuor and Voronwë through their silent ranks, and they entered upon a long white road, that ran straight towards the Sixth Gate; and as they went the grass-sward became wider, and among the white stars of *uilos* there opened many small flowers like eyes of gold.

So they came to the Golden Gate, the last of the ancient gates of Turgon that were wrought before the Nirnaeth; and it was much like the Gate of Silver, save that the wall was built of yellow marble, and the globes and parapet were of red gold; and there were six globes, and in the midst upon a golden pyramid was set an image of Laurelin, the Tree of the Sun, with flowers wrought of topaz in long clusters upon chains of gold. And the Gate itself was adorned with discs of gold, many-rayed, in likenesses of the Sun, set amid devices of garnet and topaz and yellow diamonds. In the court beyond were arrayed three hundred archers with long bows, and their mail was gilded, and tall golden plumes rose from their helmets; and their great round shields were red as flame.

Now sunlight fell upon the further road, for the walls of the hills were low on either side, and green, but for the snows upon their tops; and Elemmakil hastened forward, for the way was short to the Seventh Gate, named the Great, the Gate of Steel that Maeglin wrought after the return from the Nirnaeth, across the wide entrance to the Orfalch Echor.

No wall stood there, but on either hand were two round towers of great height, many-windowed, tapering in seven storeys to a turret of bright steel, and between the towers there stood a mighty fence of steel that rusted not, but glittered cold and white. Seven great pillars of steel there were, tall with the height and girth of strong young trees, but ending in a bitter spike that rose to the sharpness of a needle; and between the pillars were seven cross-bars of steel, and in each space seven times seven rods of steel upright with heads like the broad blades of spears. But in the centre, above the midmost pillar and the greatest, was raised a mighty image of the king-helm of Turgon, the Crown of the Hidden Kingdom, set about with diamonds.

No gate or door could Tuor see in this mighty hedge of steel, but as he drew near through the spaces between the bars there came, as it seemed to him, a dazzling light, and he shaded his eyes, and stood still in dread and wonder. But Elemmakil went forward, and no gate opened to his touch; but he struck upon a bar, and the fence rang like a harp of many strings, giving forth clear notes in harmony that ran from tower to tower.

Straightway there issued riders from the towers, but before those of the north tower came one upon a white horse; and he dismounted and strode towards them. And high and noble as was Elemmakil, greater and more lordly was Ecthelion, Lord of the Fountains, at that time Warden of the Great Gate. All in silver was he clad, and upon his shining helm was set a spike of steel pointed with a diamond; and as his esquire took his shield it shimmered as if it were bedewed with drops of rain, that were indeed a thousand studs of crystal.

Elemmakil saluted him and said: 'Here have I brought Voronwë Aranwion, returning from Balar; and here is the stranger that he has led hither, who demands to see the King.'

Then Ecthelion turned to Tuor, but he drew his cloak about him and stood silent, facing him; and it seemed to Voronwë that a mist mantled Tuor and his stature was increased, so that the peak of his high hood over-topped the helm of the Elf-lord, as it were the crest of a grey sea-wave riding to the land. But Ecthelion bent his bright glance upon Tuor, and after a silence he spoke gravely, saying:* 'You have come to the Last Gate. Know then that no stranger who passes it shall ever go out again, save by the door of death.'

'Speak not ill-boding! If the messenger of the Lord of Waters go by that door, then all those who dwell here will follow him. Lord of the Fountains, hinder not the messenger of the Lord of Waters!'

Then Voronwë and all those who stood near looked again

---

* At this point the carefully written manuscript ends, and there follows only a rough text scribbled on a scrap of paper.

in wonder at Tuor, marvelling at his words and voice. And to Voronwë it seemed as if he heard a great voice, but as of one who called from afar off. But to Tuor it seemed that he listened to himself speaking, as if another spoke with his mouth.

For a while Ecthelion stood silent, looking at Tuor, and slowly awe filled his face, as if in the grey shadow of Tuor's cloak he saw visions from far away. Then he bowed, and went to the fence and laid hands upon it, and gates opened inward on either side of the pillar of the Crown. Then Tuor passed through, and coming to a high sward that looked out over the valley beyond, he beheld a vision of Gondolin amid the white snow. And so entranced was he that for long he could look at nothing else; for he saw before him at last the vision of his desire out of dreams of longing.

Thus he stood and spoke no word. Silent upon either hand stood a host of the army of Gondolin; all of the seven kinds of the Seven Gates were there represented; but their captains and chieftains were upon horses, white and grey. Then even as they gazed on Tuor in wonder, his cloak fell, and he stood there before them in the mighty livery of Nevrast. And many were there who had seen Turgon himself set these things upon the wall behind the High Seat of Vinyamar.

Then Ecthelion said at last: 'Now no further proof is needed; and even the name he claims as son of Huor matters less than this clear proof, that he comes from Ulmo himself.'

*

Here this text comes to an end, but there follow some rapidly written notes sketching out elements of the narrative as my father at that time foresaw it. Tuor asked the name of the city, and was told its seven names (see *The Tale of The Fall of Gondolin* p.51). Ecthelion gave orders for the sounding of the signal, and trumpets were blown on the towers of the Great Gate; then answering trumpets were heard blown far off on the city walls.

On horseback they rode to the city, of which a description was to follow: of the Great Gate, the trees, the Place of the Fountain, and of the King's house; and then would be described the welcome of Tuor by Turgon. Beside the throne would be seen Maeglin on the right and Idril on the left; and Tuor would declare the message of Ulmo. There is also a note saying that there was to be a description of the city as Tuor saw it from afar; and that it was to be recounted why there was no queen of Gondolin.

THE EVOLUTION OF THE STORY

These notes (i.e. at the end of the 'latest Tuor' manuscript) are of slight significance in the history of the legend of *The Fall of Gondolin*, but they show at least that my father did not abandon this work in some sudden unlooked for haste never to take it up again. But any idea that a further fully evolved continuation of the story, after Ecthelion's words to Tuor at the Seventh Gate of Gondolin, has been lost is out of the question.

So there we have it. My father did indeed abandon this essential, and (one may say) definitive, form and treatment of the legend, at the very moment when he had brought Tuor at long last to 'behold a vision of Gondolin amid the white snow.' For me it is perhaps the most grievous of his many abandonments. Why did he stop there? An answer, of a kind, can be found.

This was a deeply distressing time for him, a time of intense frustration. It can be said with certainty that when

The Lord of the Rings was at last completed, he returned to the legends of the Elder days with a strong new energy. I will cite here parts of a remarkable letter that he wrote to Sir Stanley Unwin, the Chairman of Allen and Unwin, on 24 February 1950, for it clearly presents the prospect of publishing as he saw it at that time.

In one of your more recent letters you expressed a desire still to see the MS of my proposed work, *The Lord of the Rings*, originally expected to be a sequel to *The Hobbit*? For eighteen months now I have been hoping for the day when I could call it finished. But it was not until after Christmas [1949] that this goal was reached at last. It is finished, if still partly unrevised, and is, I suppose, in a condition which a reader could read, if he did not wilt at the sight of it.

As the estimate for typing a fair copy was in the neighbourhood of £100 (which I have not to spare), I was obliged to do nearly all myself. And now I look at it, the magnitude of the disaster is apparent to me. My work has escaped from my control, and I have produced a monster: an immensely long, complex, rather bitter, and very terrifying romance, quite unfit for children (if fit for anybody); and it is not really a sequel to *The Hobbit*, but to *The Silmarillion*. My estimate is that it contains, even without certain necessary adjuncts, about 600,000 words. One typist put it even higher. I can see only too clearly how impracticable this is. But I am tired. It is off my chest, and I do not feel that I can do anything more about it, beyond a little revision of inaccuracies. Worse still: I feel that it is tied to the *Silmarillion*.

You may, perhaps, remember about that work, a long legendary of imaginary times in a 'high style', and full of Elves (of a sort). It was rejected on the advice of your reader many years ago. As far as my memory goes he allowed it a kind of Celtic beauty intolerable to Anglo-Saxons in large doses.* He was probably perfectly right and just. And you commented that it was a work to be drawn upon rather than published.

Unfortunately I am not an Anglo-Saxon, and though shelved (until a year ago) the *Silmarillion* and all that has refused to be suppressed. It has bubbled up, infiltrated, and probably spoiled everything (that even remotely approached 'Faery') which I have tried to write since. It was kept out of *Farmer Giles* with an effort, but stopped the continuation. Its shadow was deep on the later parts of *The Hobbit*. It has captured *The Lord of the Rings* so that that has become simply its continuation and completion, requiring *The Silmarillion* to be fully intelligible – without a lot of references and explanations that clutter it in one or two places.

---

* The reader had in fact only seen a few pages of *The Silmarillion*, although he did not know this. As I have mentioned in *Beren and Lúthien* (p.220), he contrasted those pages greatly to the detriment of *The Lay of Leithian*, having no understanding of their relationship; and in his enthusiasm for the *Silmarillion* pages he said absurdly that the tale is 'told with a picturesque brevity and dignity that holds the reader's interest in spite of its eye-splitting Celtic names. It has something of that mad, bright-eyed beauty that perplexes all Anglo-Saxons in the face of Celtic art.'

Ridiculous and tiresome as you may think me, I want to publish them both – *The Silmarillion* and *The Lord of the Rings* – in conjunction or in connexion. 'I want to' – it would be wiser to say 'I should like to', since a little packet of, say, a million words, of matter set out in extenso, that Anglo-Saxons (or the English-speaking public) can only endure in moderation, is not very likely to see the light, even if paper were available at will.

All the same that is what I should like. Or I will let it all be. I cannot contemplate any drastic re-writing or compression. Of course being a writer I should like to see my words printed; but there they are. For me the chief thing is that I feel that the whole matter is now 'exorcized', and rides me no more. I can turn now to other things ...

I will not follow the intricate and painful history through the next two years. My father never relinquished his opinion, in his words in another letter, that '*The Silmarillion* etc. and *The Lord of the Rings* went together, as one long Saga of the Jewels and the Rings': 'I was resolved to treat them as one thing, however they might formally be issued'.

But the costs of production of such a huge work in the years after the War were hopelessly against him. On 22 June 1952 he wrote to Rayner Unwin:

As for *The Lord of the Rings* and *The Silmarillion*, they are where they were. The one finished (and the end revised), and the other still unfinished (or unrevised), and both gathering dust. I have been off and on too unwell, and too burdened to do much about them, and too downhearted. Watching paper-shortages and costs mounting against me. But I have rather modified my views. Better something than nothing! Although to me all are one, and *The Lord of the Rings* would be better far (and eased) as part of the whole, I would gladly consider the publication of any part of this stuff. Years are becoming precious. And retirement (not far off) will, as far as I can see, bring not leisure but a poverty that will necessitate scraping a living by 'examining' and suchlike tasks.

As I said in *Morgoth's Ring* (1993): 'Thus he bowed to necessity, but it was a grief to him'.

I believe that the explanation of his abandonment of 'the Last Version' is to be found in the extracts of correspondence given above. In the first place, there are his words in his letter to Stanley Unwin of 24 February 1950. He announced firmly that *The Lord of the Rings* was finished: 'after Christmas this goal was reached at last.' And he said: 'For me the chief thing is that I feel that the whole matter is now "exorcized", and rides me no more. I can turn now to other things . . .'

In the second place, there is an essential date. The page of the manuscript of the Last Version of *Of Tuor and the Fall of Gondolin*, carrying notes of elements in the story that were never reached in that text (p.202), was a page of an engagement calendar for September 1951; and other pages from this calendar were used for rewriting passages.

In the Foreword to *Morgoth's Ring* I wrote:

But little of all the work begun at that time was completed. The new *Lay of Leithian*, the new tale of Tuor and the Fall of Gondolin, the *Grey Annals* (of Beleriand), the revision of the *Quenta Silmarillion*, were all abandoned. I have little doubt that despair of publication, at least in the form that he regarded as essential, was the prime cause.

As he said in the letter to Rayner Unwin of 22 June 1952 cited above: 'As for *The Lord of the Rings* and *The Silmarillion*, they are where they were. I have been off and on been too unwell, and too burdened to do much about them, and too downhearted.'

It remains therefore to look back at what we do possess of this last story, which never became 'the Fall of Gondolin', but is nevertheless unique among the evocations of Middle-earth in the Elder Days, most especially perhaps in my father's intense awareness of the detail, of the atmosphere, of successive scenes. Reading his account of the coming to Tuor of the God Ulmo, Lord of Waters, of his appearance and of his 'standing knee-deep in the shadowy sea', one may wonder what descriptions there might have been of the colossal encounters in the battle for Gondolin.

As it stands – and stops – it is the story of a journey – a journey on an extraordinary mission, conceived and ordained by one of the greatest of the Valar, and expressly imposed upon Tuor, of a great house of Men, to whom the God ultimately appears at the ocean's edge in the midst of a vast storm. That extraordinary mission is to have a yet more extraordinary outcome, that would change the history of the imagined world.

The profound importance of the journey presses down upon Tuor and Voronwë, the Noldorin Elf who becomes his companion, at every step, and my father felt their growing deadly weariness, in the Fell Winter of that year, as if he himself had in dreams trudged from Vinyamar to Gondolin in hunger and exhaustion, and the fear of Orcs, in the last years of the Elder Days in Middle-earth.

The story of Gondolin has now been repeated from its origin in 1916 to this final but strangely abandoned version of some thirty-five years later. In what follows I will usually refer to the original story as 'the Lost Tale', or for brevity simply as 'the Tale', and the abandoned text as 'the Last Version', or abbreviated 'LV'. Of these two widely separated texts this may be said at once. It seems unquestionable either that my father had the manuscript of the Lost Tale in front of him, or at any rate that he had been reading it not long before, when he wrote the Last Version. This conclusion derives from the very close similarity or even near identity of passages here and there in either text. To cite a single example:

(*The Lost Tale* p.40)
Then Tuor found himself in a rugged country bare of trees, and swept by a wind coming from the set of the sun, and all the shrubs and bushes leaned to the dawn because of the prevalence of that wind.

(*The Last Version* p.158)

[Tuor] wandered still for some days in a rugged country bare of trees; and it was swept by a wind from the sea, and all that grew there, herb or bush, leaned ever to the dawn because of the prevalence of that wind from the West.

All the more interesting is it to compare the two texts, in so far as they are comparable, and observe how essential features of the old story are retained but transformed in their significance, while wholly new elements and dimensions have entered.

In the *Tale* Tuor announces his name and lineage thus (p.54):

I am Tuor son of Peleg son of Indor of the house of the Swan of the sons of the Men of the North who live far hence.

It was also said of him in the *Tale* (p.41) that when he made a dwelling for himself in the cove of Falasquil on the coast of the ocean he adorned it with many carvings, 'and ever among them was the Swan the chief, for Tuor loved this emblem and it became the sign of himself, his kindred and folk thereafter.' Moreover, again in the *Tale*, it was said of him (p.60) that when in Gondolin a suit of armour was made for Tuor 'his helm was adorned with a device of metals and jewels like to two swan-wings, one on either side, and a swan's wing was wrought on his shield.'

And again, at the time of the attack on Gondolin, all the

warriors of Tuor who stood around him 'wore wings as it were of swans or gulls upon their helms, and the emblem of the White Wing was upon their shields' (p.73); they were 'the folk of the Wing'.

Already in the *Sketch of the Mythology*, however, Tuor had been drawn into the evolving *Silmarillion*. The house of the Swan of the Men of the North had disappeared. He had become a member of the House of Hador, the son of Huor who was killed in the Battle of Unnumbered Tears and the cousin of Túrin Turambar. Yet the association of Tuor with the Swan and the Swan's wing was by no means lost in this transformation. It was said in the *Last Version* (p.160):

> Now Tuor loved swans, which he knew on the grey pools of Mithrim; and the swan moreover had been the token of Annael and his foster-folk [for Annael see the *Last Version* p.146].

Then in Vinyamar, the ancient house of Turgon before the discovery of Gondolin, the shield that Tuor found bore upon it the emblem of a white swan's wing, and he said: '*By this token* I will take these arms unto myself, and upon myself whatsoever doom they bear' (LV p.162).

The original *Tale* opened (p.37) with no more than a very slight introduction concerning Tuor, 'who dwelt in very ancient days in that land of the North called Dor-lómin or the Land of Shadows.' He lived alone, a hunter in the lands about Lake Mithrim, singing the songs that he made and playing on his harp; and he became acquainted with 'the wandering Noldoli', from whom he learned greatly and not least much of their language.

But 'it is said that magic and destiny led him on a day to a cavernous opening down which a hidden river flowed from Mithrim', and Tuor entered in. This, it is said, 'was the will of Ulmo Lord of Waters at whose prompting the Noldoli had made that hidden way.'

When Tuor was unable against the strength of the river to retreat from the cavern the Noldoli came and guided him along dark passages amid the mountains until he came out in the light once more.

In the *Sketch* of 1926, where as noted above Tuor's lineage as a descendant of the house of Hador emerged, it is told (pp.122–3) that after the death of Rían his mother he became a slave of the faithless men whom Morgoth drove into Hithlum after the Battle of Unnumbered Tears; but he escaped from them, and Ulmo contrived that he should be led to a subterranean river-course leading out of Mithrim into a chasmed river that flowed at last into the Western Sea. In the *Quenta* of 1930 (pp.134–5) this account was closely followed, and in both texts the only significance in the story that is ascribed to it is the secrecy that it afforded to Tuor's escape, totally unknown to any spy of Morgoth. But both these texts were of their nature largely condensed.

Returning to the *Tale*, Tuor's passage of the river-chasm was told at length, to the point where the incoming tide met the river flowing down swiftly from Lake Mithrim in frightening tumult to one standing in the path: 'but the Ainur [Valar] put it into his heart to climb from the gully when he did, or had he been whelmed in the incoming tide' (p.40). It seems that the guiding Noldoli left Tuor when he came out of the dark cavern: '[The Noldoli] guided him along dark passages amid the mountains until he came out in the light once more' (p.38).

Leaving the river and standing above its ravine Tuor for the first time set his eyes upon the sea. Finding in the coast a sheltered cove (which came to be called *Falasquil*) he built there a dwelling of timber floated down the river to him by the Noldoli (on the Swan amid the carvings of his dwelling see p.210 above). In Falasquil he 'passed a very great while' (*Tale* p.41) until he wearied of his loneliness, and here again the Ainur are said to bear a part ('for Ulmo loved Tuor', *Tale* p.41); he left Falasquil and followed a flight of three swans passing southward down the coast and plainly leading him. His great journey through winter to spring is described, until he reached the Sirion. Thence he went further until he reached the Land of Willows (*Nan-tathrin*, *Tasarinan*), where the butterflies and the bees, the flowers and the singing birds enthralled him, and he gave names to them, and lingered there through spring and summer (*Tale* pp.44–5).

The accounts in the *Sketch* and the *Quenta* are extremely brief, as is to be expected. In the *Sketch* (p.123) it is said of Tuor only that 'after long wanderings down the western shores he came to the mouths of Sirion, and there fell in with the Gnome Bronweg [Voronwë] who had once been in Gondolin. They journey secretly up Sirion together. Tuor lingers long in the sweet land Nan-tathrin "Valley of Willows".' The passage in the *Quenta* (p.135–6) is in content essentially the same. The Gnome, spelled Bronwë, is now said to have escaped from Angband, and 'being of old of the people of Turgon sought ever to find the path to the hidden places of his lord', and so he and Tuor went up Sirion and came to the Land of Willows.

It is curious that in these texts the entry of Voronwë into the narrative takes place before the coming of Tuor to the Land of Willows: for in the primary source, the *Tale*, Voronwë had appeared much later, under wholly different circumstances, *after* the appearance of Ulmo. In the *Tale* (p.45) Tuor's long rapture in Nan-tathrin led Ulmo to fear that he would never leave it; and in his instruction to Tuor he said that the Noldoli would escort him secretly to the city of the people named *Gondothlim* or 'dwellers in stone' (this being the first reference to Gondolin in the *Tale*: in both the *Sketch* and the *Quenta* some account of the hidden city is given before there is any mention of Tuor). In the event, according to the *Tale* (p.48), the Noldoli guiding Tuor on his eastbound journey deserted him out of fear of Melko, and he became lost. But one of the Elves came back to him, and offered to accompany him in his search for Gondolin, of which this Noldo had heard rumour, but nothing else. He was Voronwë.

Advancing now through many years we come to the Last Version (LV), and what is told of Tuor's youth. Neither in the *Sketch* nor the *Quenta* is there any reference to Tuor's fostering by the Grey-elves of Hithlum, but in this final version there enters an extensive account (pp.145–9). This tells of his upbringing among the Elves under Annael, of their oppressed lives and southward flight by the secret way known as Annon-in-Gelydh 'the Gate of the Noldor, for it was made by the skill of that people long ago in the days of Turgon'. There is here also an account of Tuor's slavery and his escape, with the years following as a much feared outlaw.

The most significant development in all this arises from Tuor's determination to flee the land. Following what he had learned from Annael he sought far and wide for the Gate of the Noldor, and the mysterious hidden kingdom of Turgon (LV p.149). This was Tuor's express aim; but he did not know what that 'Gate' might be. He came to the spring of a stream that rose in the hills of Mithrim, and it was here that he made his final decision to depart from Hithlum 'the grey land of my kin', though his search for the Gate of the Noldor had failed. He followed the stream down until he came to a rock wall where it disappeared in 'an opening like a great arch'. There he sat in despair through the night, until at sunrise he saw two Elves climbing up from the arch.

They were Noldorin Elves named Gelmir and Arminas, engaged on an urgent errand which they did not define. From them he learned that the great arch was indeed the Gate of the Noldor, and all unknowing he had found it. Taking the place of the Noldoli who guided him in the old *Tale* (p.38), Gelmir and Arminas guided him through the tunnel to a place where they halted, and he questioned them about Turgon, saying that that name strangely moved him whenever he heard it. To this they gave him no reply, but bade him farewell and went back up the long stairs in the darkness (p.155).

The Last Version introduced little alteration to the narrative of the *Tale* in the account of Tuor's journey, after he had emerged from the tunnel, down the steep-sided ravine. It is notable, however, that whereas in the *Tale* (p.40) 'the Ainur put it into his heart to climb from the gully when he did, or had he been whelmed in the incoming tide', in LV (pp.157–8) he climbed up because he wished to follow the three great gulls, and he 'was saved by the call of the sea-birds from death in the rising tide'. The sea-cove named Falasquil (*Tale* p.41) where Tuor built himself a dwelling and 'passed a very great while', 'by slow labour' adorning it with carvings, had disappeared in the Last Version.

In that text Tuor, dismayed by the fury of the strange waters (LV p.158), set off southwards from the ravine of the river, and passed into the borders of the region of Nevrast in the far west 'where once Turgon had dwelt'; and at last he came at sunset to the shores of Middle-earth and saw the Great Sea. Here the Last Version departs radically from the history of Tuor as told hitherto.

Returning to the *Tale*, and the coming of Ulmo to meet Tuor in the Land of Willows (p.45), there enters my father's original description of the appearance of the great Vala

(*Tale* p.45). The Lord of all seas and rivers, he came to urge Tuor to tarry no longer in that place. This description is an elaborate and sharply defined picture of the god himself, come on a vast voyage across the ocean. He dwells in a 'palace' below the waters of the Outer Sea, he rides in his 'car', made in the fashion of a whale, at a stupendous speed. His hair and his great beard are observed, his mail 'like the scales of blue and silver fishes', his kirtle (coat) of 'shimmering greens', his girdle of great pearls, his shoes of stone. Leaving his 'car' at the mouth of the Sirion he strode up beside the great river, and 'he sat among the reeds at twilight' near the place where Tuor 'stood knee-deep in the grass'; he played upon his strange instrument of music, which was 'made of many long twisted shells pierced with holes' (*Tale* pp.45–6).

Perhaps most notable of all the characters of Ulmo was the fathomless depth of his eyes and his voice when he spoke to Tuor, filling him with fear. Leaving the Land of Willows Tuor, escorted secretly by Noldoli, must seek out the city of the Gondothlim (see p.46 above). In the *Tale* (p.46) Ulmo said 'Words I will set to your mouth there, and there you shall abide awhile.' Of what his words to Turgon would be there is in this version no indication – but it is said that Ulmo spoke to Tuor 'some of his design and desire', which he scarcely understood. Ulmo uttered also an extraordinary prophecy concerning Tuor's child to be, 'than whom no man shall know more of the uttermost deeps, be it of the sea or of the firmament of heaven.' That child was Eärendel.

*

In the *Sketch* of 1926, on the other hand, there is a clear statement (p.123) of Ulmo's purpose that Tuor is to assert in Gondolin: in brief, Turgon must prepare for a terrible battle with Morgoth, in which 'the race of Orcs will perish'; but if Turgon will not accept this, then the people of Gondolin must flee their city and go to the mouth of Sirion, where Ulmo 'will aid them to build a fleet and guide them back to Valinor'. In the *Quenta Noldorinwa* of 1930 (p.137) the prospects held out by Ulmo are essentially the same, though the outcome of such a battle, 'a terrible and mortal strife', is presented as the breaking of Morgoth's power and much else, 'whereof the greatest good should come into the world, and the servants of Morgoth trouble it no more'.

It is convenient at this point to turn to the important manuscript of the later 1930s entitled *Quenta Silmarillion*. This was to be a new prose version of the history of the Elder Days following the *Quenta Noldorinwa* of 1930; but it came to an abrupt end in 1937 with the advent of the 'new story about hobbits' (I have given an account of this strange history in *Beren and Lúthien*, pp.219–21).

From this work I append here passages that bear on the early history of Turgon, his discovery of Tumladen and the building of Gondolin, but which do not appear in the texts of *The Fall of Gondolin*.

It is told in the *Quenta Silmarillion* that Turgon, a leader of the Noldor who dared the terror of the *Helkaraksë* (the Grinding Ice) in the crossing to Middle-earth, dwelt in Nevrast. In this text occurs this passage:

On a time Turgon left Nevrast where he dwelt and went to visit Inglor his friend, and they journeyed southward along Sirion, being weary for a while of the northern mountains, and as they journeyed night came upon them beyond the Meres of Twilight beside the waters of Sirion, and they slept upon his banks beneath the summer stars. But Ulmo coming up the river laid a profound sleep upon them and heavy dreams; and the trouble of the dreams remained after they awoke, but neither said aught to the other, for their memory was not clear, and each deemed that Ulmo had sent a message to him alone. But unquiet was upon them ever after and doubt of what should befall, and they wandered often alone in unexplored country, seeking far and wide for places of hidden strength; for it seemed to each that he was bidden to prepare for a day of evil, and to establish a retreat, lest Morgoth should burst from Angband and overthrow the armies of the North.

Thus it came to pass that Inglor found the deep gorge of Narog and the caves in its western side; and he built there a stronghold and armouries after the fashion of the deep mansions of Menegroth. And he called this place Nargothrond, and made there his home with many of his folk; and the Gnomes of the North, at first in merriment, called him on this account Felagund, or Lord of Caves, and that name he bore thereafter until his end. But Turgon went alone into hidden places, and by the guidance of Ulmo found the secret vale of Gondolin; and of this he said nought as yet, but returned to Nevrast and his folk.

In a further passage of the *Quenta Silmarillion* it is told of Turgon, the second son of Fingolfin, that he ruled over a numerous people, but 'the unquiet of Ulmo increased upon him;'

> he arose, and took with him a great host of Gnomes, even to a third of the people of Fingolfin, and their goods and wives and children, and departed eastward. His going was by night and his march swift and silent, and he vanished out of knowledge of his kindred. But he came to Gondolin, and built there a city like unto Tûn of Valinor, and fortified the surrounding hills; and Gondolin lay hidden for many years.

A third, and essential, citation comes from a different source. There are two texts, bearing the titles *The Annals of Beleriand* and *The Annals of Valinor.* These were begun about 1930, and are extant in subsequent versions. I have said of them: 'The Annals began, perhaps, in parallel with the *Quenta* as a convenient way of driving abreast, and keeping track of, the different elements in the ever more complex narrative web.' The final text of *The Annals of Beleriand,* also named the *Grey Annals,* derive from the time in the early 1950s when my father turned again to the matter of the Elder Days after the completion of *The Lord of the Rings.* It was a major source for the published *Silmarillion.*

There follows here a passage from the *Grey Annals*; it refers to the year 'in which Gondolin was full-wrought, after fifty and two years of secret toil'.

Now therefore Turgon prepared to depart from Nevrast, and leave his fair halls in Vinyamar beneath Mount Taras; and then Ulmo came to him a second time and said: 'Now thou shalt go at last to Gondolin, Turgon; and I will set my power in the Vale of Sirion, so that none shall mark thy going, nor shall any find there the hidden entrance to thy land against thy will. Longest of all the realms of the Eldalië shall Gondolin stand against Melkor. But love it not too well, and remember that the true hope of the Noldor lieth in the West and cometh from the Sea.'*

And Ulmo warned Turgon that he also lay under the Doom of Mandos, which Ulmo had no power to remove. 'Thus it may come to pass,' he said, 'that the curse of the Noldor shall find thee too ere the end, and treason shall awake within thy walls. Then shall they be in peril of fire. But if this peril draweth nigh, then even from Nevrast one shall come to warn thee, and from him beyond ruin and fire hope shall be born for Elves and Men. Leave, therefore, in this house arms and a sword, that in years to come he may find them, and thus shalt thou know him and be not deceived.' And Ulmo showed to Turgon of what kind and stature should be the mail and helm and sword that he left behind.

Then Ulmo returned to the Sea; and Turgon sent forth all his folk ... and they passed away, company by company, secretly, under the shadows of Eryd Wethion, and came unseen with their wives and goods to Gondolin, and none

---

* These words, slightly changed, were spoken by Tuor to Voronwë at Vinyamar, LV p.171.

knew whither they were gone. And last of all Turgon arose and went with his lords and household silently through the hills and passed the gates in the mountains, and they were shut. But Nevrast was empty of folk and so remained until the ruin of Beleriand.

In this last passage is seen the explanation of the shield and sword, the hauberk and helm, that Tuor found when he entered the great hall of Vinyamar (LV p.162).

After the conclusion of the meeting of Ulmo with Tuor in the Land of Willows all the early texts (the *Tale*, the *Sketch*, the *Quenta Noldorinwa*) move on to the journey of Tuor and Voronwë in search of Gondolin. Of the eastward journey itself there is indeed scarcely any mention, the mystery of the hidden city residing in the secret of entry to Tumladen (to which in the *Sketch* and *Quenta Noldorinwa* Ulmo gives them aid).

But here we will return to the Last Version, which I left in this discussion at the coming of Tuor to the coast of the Sea in the region of Nevrast (LV p.158). Here we see the great abandoned house of Vinyamar beneath Mount Taras ('eldest of all the works of stone that the Noldor built in the lands of their exile') where Turgon first dwelt, and which Tuor now entered. Of all that follows ('Tuor in Vinyamar', LV pp.161 ff.) there is no hint or preceding trace in the early texts – save of course the advent of Ulmo, told again after a lapse of thirty-five years.

*

I pause here to observe what is told elsewhere concerning the guidance, indeed the urging, of Tuor in the furtherance of Ulmo's designs.

The origin of his 'designs' that came to be centred on Tuor arose from the massive and far-reaching event that came to be called *The Hiding of Valinor*. There exists an early story, one of the *Lost Tales*, that bears that title, and describes the origin and nature of this alteration of the world in the Elder Days. It arose from the rebellion of the Noldoli (Noldor) under the leadership of Fëanor, maker of the Silmarils, against the Valar, and their intent to leave Valinor. I have described very briefly the consequence of that decision in *Beren and Lúthien*, p.23, and I repeat that here.

Before their departure from Valinor there took place the dreadful event that marred the history of the Noldor in Middle-earth. Fëanor demanded of those Teleri, the third host of the Eldar on the Great Journey [from the place of their Awakening], who dwelt now on the coast of Aman, that they give up to the Noldor their fleet of ships, their great pride, for without ships the crossing to Middle-earth by such a host would not be possible. This the Teleri refused utterly. Then Fëanor and his people attacked the Teleri in their city of Alqualondë, the Haven of the Swans, and took the fleet by force. In that battle, which was known as the Kinslaying, many of the Teleri were slain.

In *The Hiding of Valinor* there is a remarkable description of a very heated and indeed extraordinary meeting of the Valar that bears on the present subject. On this occasion there was present an Elf of Alqualondë named Ainairos whose kin had perished in the battle of the Haven, 'and he sought unceasingly with his words to persuade the [Teleri] to greater bitterness of heart.' This Ainairos spoke at the debate, and his words are recorded in *The Hiding of Valinor*.

He laid before the Gods the mind of the Elves [i.e. the Teleri] concerning the Noldoli and of the nakedness of the land of Valinor toward the world beyond. Thereat arose much tumult and many of the Valar and their folk supported him loudly, and some others of the Eldar cried out that Manwë and Varda had caused their kindred to dwell in Valinor promising them unfailing joy therein – now let the Gods see to it that their gladness was not minished to a little thing, seeing that Melko held the world and they dared not fare forth to the places of their awakening even if they would.

The most of the Valar moreover were fain of their ancient ease and desired only peace, wishing neither rumour of Melko and his violence nor murmur of the restless Gnomes to come ever again among them to disturb their happiness; and for such reasons they also clamoured for the conceal-ment of the land. Not the least among these were Vána and Nessa, albeit most even of the great Gods were of one mind. In vain did Ulmo of his foreknowing plead before them for pity and pardon on the Noldoli, or Manwë unfold the secrets of the Music of the Ainur and the purpose of the world; and long and very full of that noise was that council, and more filled with bitterness and burning words than any that had been; wherefore did Manwë Súlimo depart at length from among them, saying that no walls or bulwarks might now fend Melko's evil from them which lived already among them and clouded all their minds.

So came it that the enemies of the Gnomes carried the council of the Gods and the blood of [the Haven of the Swans] began already its fell work; for now began that which is named the Hiding of Valinor, and Manwë and Varda and Ulmo of the Seas had no part therein, but none others of the Valar or the Elves held aloof therefrom ...

Now Lórien and Vána led the Gods and Aulë lent his skill and Tulkas his strength, and the Valar went not at that time forth to conquer Melko, and the greatest ruth was that to them thereafter, and yet is; for the great glory of the Valar by reason of that error came not to its fullness in many ages of the Earth, and still doth the world await it.

Very striking is this last passage, with its clear representation of the Gods as indolently regarding only their own security and well-being, and expression of the view that they had committed a colossal 'error', for in failing to make war on Melko they left Middle-earth open to the destructive ambitions and hatreds of the arch-enemy. But such condemnation of the Valar is not found in later writing. The Hiding of Valinor is present only as a great fact of legendary antiquity.

There follows in *The Hiding of Valinor* a passage in which the gigantic and manifold works of defence are described –

'new and mighty labours such as had not been seen among them since the days of the first building of Valinor', such as the making of the encircling mountains more utterly impassable on their eastern sides.

> From North to South marched the enchantments and inaccessible magic of the Gods, yet were they not content; and they said: 'Behold, we will cause all the paths that fare to Valinor, both known and secret, to fade utterly from the world, or wander treacherously into blind confusion.'
>
> This then they did, and no channel in the seas was left that was not beset with perilous eddies or with streams of overmastering strength for the confusion of all ships. And spirits of sudden storms and winds unlooked for brooded there by Ossë's will, and others of inextricable mist.

To read of the effects of the Hiding of Valinor on Gondolin one may look ahead to Turgon's words to Tuor in the *Tale*, speaking of the fate of the many messengers that had been sent from Gondolin to build ships for the voyage to Valinor (p.57):

> '... but the paths thereto are forgotten and the highways faded from the world, and the seas and mountains are about it, and they that sit within in mirth reck little of the dread of Melko or the sorrow of the world, but hide their land and weave about it inaccessible magic, that no tidings of evil come ever to their ears. Nay, enough of my people have

for years untold gone out to the wide waters never to
return, but have perished in the deep places or wander now
lost in the shadows that have no paths; and at the coming of
next year no more shall fare to the sea ...'

(It is a very curious fact that Turgon's words here were
uttered in ironic repetition of Tuor's, spoken as Ulmo bade
him, immediately preceding (*Tale* p.56):

'... lo! the paths thereto are forgotten and the highways
faded from the world, and the seas and mountains are
about it, yet still dwell there the Elves on the hill of Kôr
and the Gods sit in Valinor, though their mirth is minished
for sorrow and fear of Melko, and they hide their land and
weave about it inaccessible magic that no evil come to its
shores.')

On pp.115–17 (*Turlin and the Exiles of Gondolin*) I have
given a brief text that was soon abandoned, but was clearly
intended as the beginning of a new version of the *Tale* (but
still with the old version of the genealogy of Tuor, which
was replaced by that of the house of Hador in the *Sketch* of
1926). It is a remarkable feature of this piece that Ulmo is
explicitly represented as altogether alone among the Valar
in his concern for the Elves who lived under the power
of Melko, 'nor did any save Ulmo only dread the power of
Melko that wrought ruin and sorrow over all the Earth; but
Ulmo desired that Valinor should gather all its might to
quench his evil ere it be too late, and it seemed to him that

both his purposes might perchance be achieved if messengers from the Gnomes should win to Valinor and plead for pardon and for pity upon the Earth.'

It was here that the 'isolation' of Ulmo among the Valar first appears, for there is no suggestion of it in the *Tale*. I will conclude this account with a repetition of how Ulmo saw it in his words to Tuor as he stood at the water's edge in the rising storm at Vinyamar (LV pp.165–6).

And Ulmo spoke to Tuor of Valinor and its darkening, and the Exile of the Noldor, and the Doom of Mandos, and the hiding of the Blessed Realm. 'But behold!' said he, 'in the armour of Fate (as the Children of Earth name it) there is ever a rift, and in the walls of Doom a breach, until the full-making, which ye call the End. So it shall be while I endure, a secret voice that gainsayeth, and a light where darkness was decreed. Therefore, though in the days of this darkness I seem to oppose the will of my brethren, the Lords of the West, that is my part among them, to which I was appointed ere the making of the World. Yet Doom is strong, and the shadow of the Enemy lengthens; and I am diminished, until in Middle-earth I am become now no more than a secret whisper. The waters that run westward wither, and their springs are poisoned, and my power withdraws from the land; for Elves and Men grow blind and deaf to me because of the might of Melkor. And now the Curse of Mandos hastens to its fulfilment, and all the works of the Noldor shall perish, and every hope that they build will crumble. The last hope alone is left, the hope that they have not looked for and have not prepared. And that hope lieth in thee; for so I have chosen.'

This leads to a further question: why did he choose Tuor? Or even, why did he choose a Man? To this latter question an answer is given in the *Tale*, p.62:

Behold now many years have gone since Tuor was lost amid the foothills and deserted by those Noldoli; yet many years too have gone since to Melko's ears came first those strange tidings – faint were they and various in form – of a man wandering amid the dales of the waters of Sirion. Now Melko was not much afraid of the race of Men in those days of his great power, and for this reason did Ulmo work through one of this kindred for the better deceiving of Melko, seeing that no Valar and scarce any of the Eldar or Noldoli might stir unmarked of his vigilance.

But to the far more significant question I think that the answer lies in the words of Ulmo to Tuor at Vinyamar (LV p.166), when Tuor said to him: 'Of little avail shall I be, a mortal man alone, among so many and so valiant of the High Folk of West.' To this Ulmo replied:

'If I choose to send thee, *Tuor son of Huor*, then believe not that thy one sword is not worth the sending. For the valour of the Edain the Elves shall ever remember as the ages lengthen, marvelling that they gave life so freely of which on earth they had so little. But it is not for thy valour only that I send thee, but to bring into the world a hope beyond thy sight, and a light that shall pierce the darkness.'

What was that hope? I believe that it was the event that Ulmo declared with such miraculous foresight to Tuor in the *Tale* (p.47):

'... of a surety a child shall come of thee than whom no man shall know more of the uttermost deeps, be it of the sea or of the firmament of heaven.'

As I have observed (p.217 above), the child was Eärendel.

It cannot be doubted that Ulmo's prophetic words 'a light that shall pierce the darkness', sent by Ulmo himself, and brought into the world by Tuor, is Eärendel. But strange indeed as it appears, there is a passage elsewhere showing that Ulmo's 'miraculous foresight', as I have called it, had emerged many years before, independently of Ulmo.

This passage occurs in the version of the text *The Annals of Beleriand* known as the *Grey Annals*, from the period following the completion of *The Lord of the Rings*, on which see *The Evolution of the Story* p.220. The scene is the Battle of Unnumbered Tears, towards its end with the death of Fingon the Elvenking.

The day was lost, but still Húrin and Huor with the men of Hador stood firm, and the Orcs could not yet win the passes of Sirion ... The last stand of Húrin and Huor is the deed of war most renowned among the Eldar that the

Fathers of Men wrought in their behalf. For Húrin spoke to Turgon saying: 'Go now, lord, while time is! For last art thou of the House of Fingolfin, and in thee lives the last hope of the Noldor. While Gondolin stands, strong and guarded, Morgoth shall still know fear in his heart.'

'Yet not long now can Gondolin be hidden, and being discovered it must fall,' said Turgon.

'Yet if it stands but a little while,' said Huor, 'then out of thy house shall come the hope of Elves and Men. This I say to thee, lord, with the eyes of death; though here we part for ever, and I shall never look on thy white walls, <u>from thee and me shall a new star arise</u>.'

Turgon accepted the counsel of Húrin and Huor. He withdrew with all such warriors as he could gather from the host of Fingon and from Gondolin and vanished into the mountains, while Húrin and Huor held the pass behind them against the swarming host of Morgoth. Huor fell with a poisoned arrow in the eye.

We cannot overestimate the divine powers of Ulmo – mightiest of the Gods after Manwë alone: in his vast knowledge and foreknowledge, and in his inconceivable ability to enter the minds of other beings and influence their thoughts and even their understanding from far away. Most notable of course is his speaking through Tuor when he came to Gondolin. This goes back to the *Tale*: 'Words I will set to your mouth there' (p.46); and in the Last Version (p.167), when Tuor asks 'What words shall I say unto

Turgon?', Ulmo replies: 'If thou come to him, then the words shall arise in thy mind, then thy mouth shall speak as I would.' In the *Tale* (p.55) this capacity of Ulmo goes even further: 'Then spoke Tuor, and Ulmo set power in his heart and majesty in his voice.'

In this discursive discussion of Ulmo's designs for Tuor we have come to Vinyamar, and to the second appearance of the God in this narrative that differs profoundly from that in the *Tale* (p.45 and p.216 above). No longer does he come up the great river Sirion and make music sitting in the reeds, but as a great storm of the sea draws near he strides out of a wave, 'a living shape of great height and majesty', seeming to Tuor a mighty king wearing a tall crown; and the God speaks to the Man 'standing knee-deep in the shadowy sea'. But the entire episode of Tuor's coming to Vinyamar was absent from the story as it previously existed; and thus likewise the essential element, in the Last Version, of the arms left for him in the house of Turgon (see LV p.162 and p.221 above).

It is conceivable, however, that the germ of this story was present as far back as the *Tale*, p.55, when Turgon greets Tuor before the doors of his palace: 'Welcome, O Man of the Land of Shadows. Lo! thy coming was set in our books of wisdom, and it has been written that there would come to pass many great things in the homes of the Gondothlim whenso thou faredst hither.'

In the Last Version there appears (p.169) the Noldorin Elf Voronwë in a role that binds him from his first appearance in the narrative to the tale of Tuor and Ulmo, wholly distinct from his entry in earlier texts (see p.48). After the departure of Ulmo

> Tuor looked down from the lowest terrace [of Vinyamar] and saw, leaning against its wall among the stones and the sea-wrack, an Elf, clad in a grey cloak sodden with the sea ... As Tuor stood and looked at the silent grey figure he remembered the words of Ulmo, and a name untaught came to his lips, and he called aloud: 'Welcome, Voronwë! I await you.'

These words of Ulmo were his last to Tuor before his departure (LV p. 167):

> 'I will send one to thee out of the wrath of Ossë, and thus shalt thou be guided: yea, the last mariner of the last ship that shall seek into the West until the rising of the Star.'

And this mariner was Voronwë, who told his story to Tuor beside the sea at Vinyamar (LV pp.173–7). His account of his voyaging over seven years in the Great Sea was a grim one to give to Tuor, so greatly enamoured of the ocean. But before setting forth on his mission, he said (LV p.174 ff.):

> I tarried on the way. For I had seen little of the lands of Middle-earth, and we came to Nan-tathrin in the spring of the year. Lovely to heart's enchantment is that land, Tuor,

as you shall find, if ever your feet go upon the southward roads down Sirion. There is the cure of all sea-longing ...

The story in the *Tale* of Tuor's overlong stay in Nan-tathrin, the Land of Willows, the cause of Ulmo's visitation as originally told, bewitched by its beauty, had now of course disappeared from the narrative; but it was not lost. In the last version it was Voronwë, speaking to Tuor at Vinyamar, who had passed a while in Nan-tathrin, and become enthralled as he 'stood knee-deep in grass' (LV p.175); in the old story it had been Tuor who 'stood knee-deep in the grass' in the Land of Willows (*Tale* p.46). Both Tuor and Voronwë gave names of their own to the flowers and birds and butterflies unknown to them.

Since we shall not in this 'Evolution of the Story' meet again Ulmo in person I attach here a portrait of the great Vala that my father wrote in his work *The Music of the Ainur* (late 1930s):

Ulmo has dwelt ever in the Outer Ocean, and governed the flowing of all waters, and the courses of all rivers, the replenishment of springs and the distilling of rain and dew throughout the world. In the deep places he gives thought to music great and terrible; and the echo thereof runs through all the veins of the world, and its joy is as the joy of a fountain in the sun whose wells are the wells of unfathomed sorrow at the foundations of the world. The Teleri learned much of him, and for this reason their music has both sadness and enchantment.

We come now to the journey of Tuor and Voronwë from Vinyamar in Nevrast, beside the sea in the far West, to find Gondolin. This would take them eastward along the southern side of the great mountain range Ered Wethrin, the Mountains of Shadow, that formed a vast barrier between Hithlum and West Beleriand, and bring them at last to the great river Sirion running from north to south.

The earliest reference, in the *Tale* (p.49), says no more than that 'Long time did Tuor and Voronwë [who in the old story had never been there] seek for the city of that folk [the Gondothlim], until after many days they came upon a deep dale amid the hills'. Likewise the *Sketch*, not surprisingly, says very simply (pp.123–4) that 'Tuor and Bronweg reach the secret way ... and come out upon the guarded plain.' And the *Quenta Noldorinwa* (p.137) is equally brief: 'Obedient to Ulmo Tuor and Bronwë journeyed North, and came at last to the hidden door.'

Beside these terse glances the account in the Last Version of the fearful days passed by Tuor and Voronwë in the bitter winds and biting frosts of the houseless country, their escape from the bands of Orcs and their encampments, the coming of the eagles, may be seen as a significant element in the history of Gondolin. (On the presence of the eagles in that region see *Quenta Noldorinwa* p.132 and LV p.188.) Most notable is their coming to the Pool of Ivrin (p.178), the lake where the river Narog rose, now defiled and made desolate by the passage of the dragon Glaurung (called by Voronwë 'the Great Worm of Angband'). Here the seekers of Gondolin touched the greatest story of the Elder Days: for they saw a tall man passing, bearing a long sword drawn, and the blade was long and black. They did not speak to this man clad in black; and they did not know that he was Túrin Turambar, the Blacksword, fleeing north from the sack of Nargothrond, of which they had not heard. 'Thus only for a moment, and never again, did the paths of those kinsmen, Túrin and Tuor, draw together.' (Húrin the father of Túrin was the brother of Huor the father of Tuor.)

We come now to the last step in the 'Evolution of the Story' (because the Last Version extends no further): the first sight of Gondolin, by way of the hidden and guarded entry into the plain of Tumladen – a 'door' or 'gate' of renown in the history of Middle-earth. In the *Tale* (p.49) Tuor and Voronwë came to a place where the river (Sirion) 'went over a very stony bed'. This was the Ford of Brithiach, not yet so named; 'it was curtained with a heavy growth of alders', but the banks were sheer-sided. There in the 'green wall' Voronwë found 'an opening like a great door with sloping sides, and this was cloaked with thick bushes and long-tangled undergrowth'.

Passing through this opening (p.49) they found themselves in a dark and wandering tunnel. In this they groped their way until they saw a distant light, 'and making for this gleam they came to a gate like that by which they had entered'. Here they were surrounded by armed guards, and found themselves in the sunlight at the feet of steep hills bordering in a circle a wide plain, and in this there stood a city, at the summit of a great hill standing alone.

In the *Sketch* there is of course no description of the entry; but in the *Quenta Noldorinwa* (p.131) this is said of the Way of Escape: in the region where the Encircling Mountains were at their lowest the Elves of Gondolin 'dug a great winding tunnel under the roots of the hills, and its issue was in the steep side, tree-clad and dark, of a gorge through which the blissful river [Sirion] ran.' It is said in the *Quenta* (p.137) that when Tuor and Bronwë (Voronwë) came to the hidden door they passed down the tunnel and 'reached the inner gate', where they were taken prisoner.

The two 'gates' and the tunnel between them were thus present when my father wrote the *Quenta Noldorinwa* in 1930, and on this conception he based the final version of 1951. This is where the resemblance ends.

But it will be seen that in the final version (LV pp.187 ff.) my father introduced a sharp difference into the topography. The entrance was no longer in the eastern bank of the Sirion; it was from a tributary stream. But the dangerous crossing of the Brithiach they made, being fortified by the appearance of the eagles.

On the far side of the ford they came to a gully, as it were the bed of an old stream, in which no water now flowed; yet once, it seemed, a torrent had cloven its deep channel, coming down from the north out of the mountains of the Echoriath, and bearing thence all the stones of the Brithiach down into Sirion.

'At last beyond hope we find it!' cried Voronwë. 'See!

Here is the mouth of the Dry River, and that is the road we must take.'

But the 'road' was full of stones and went sharply up, and Tuor expressed to Voronwë his disgust, and his amazement that this wretched track should be the way of entry to the city of Gondolin.

After many miles, and a night spent, in the Dry River it led them to the walls of the Encircling Mountains, and entering by an opening they were brought at length to what they felt to be a great silent space, in which they could see nothing. The sinister reception of Tuor and Voronwë can scarcely be equalled in the writings of Middle-earth: the dazzling light turned on Voronwë in the huge darkness, the cold menacing, questioning voice. That dreadful interview over, they were led to another entry, or exit.

In the *Quenta Noldorinwa* (p.138) Tuor and Voronwë stepped out from the long twisting black tunnel, where they were taken prisoner by the guard, and saw Gondolin 'shining from afar, flushed with the rose of dawn upon the plain'. Thus the conception at that time was readily described: the wide plain Tumladen wholly encircled by the mountains, the Echoriath, and a tunnel from the outer world running through them. But in the Last Version, when they left the place of their inquisition, Tuor found that they were standing 'at the end of a ravine, the like of which he had never before beheld or imagined in his thought'. Up this ravine, named the Orfalch Echor, a long road climbed through a succession of huge gates magnificently adorned until the top of the rift was reached at the seventh, the Great Gate. It was only then that Tuor 'beheld a vision of Gondolin amid the white snow'; and it was there that Ecthelion said of Tuor that it was certain that 'he comes from Ulmo himself' – the words with which the last text of *The Fall of Gondolin* ends.

CONCLUSION

I mentioned (p.23) that the original title of the *Tale, Tuor and the Exiles of Gondolin*, was followed by the words 'which bringeth in the Great Tale of Eärendel.' Further, the 'Last Tale' that followed *The Fall of Gondolin*, was the *Tale of the Nauglafring* (The Necklace of the Dwarves, on which was set the Silmaril) of which I cited the concluding words in *Beren and Lúthien*, p.246:

> And thus did all the fates of the fairies weave then to one strand, and that strand is the great tale of Eärendel; and to that tale's true beginning are we now come.

We may suppose that the 'true beginning' of the *Tale of Eärendel* was to follow the words with which the *Tale of The Fall of Gondolin* ended (p.111):

Yet now those exiles of Gondolin dwelt at the mouth of
Sirion by the waves of the Great Sea ... and fair among the
Lothlim Eärendel grows in the house of his father, and the
great tale of Tuor is come to its waning.

But the Lost Tale of Eärendel was never written. There
are many notes and outlines from the early period, and
several very early poems: but there is nothing remotely
corresponding to the Tale of *The Fall of Gondolin*. To set
out and discuss these often contradictory outlines in their
clipped phrases would be contrary to the purpose of these
two books: the comparative histories of *narratives* as they
evolved. On the other hand, the story of the destruction of
Gondolin is very fully told in the original *Tale*; the history
of the survivors is an essential continuation of the history
of the Elder Days. I have decided therefore to return to the
two early narratives in which the tale of the end of the Elder
Days is told: the *Sketch of the Mythology* and the *Quenta
Noldorinwa*. (As I have remarked elsewhere, 'It will seem
strange indeed that the *Quenta Noldorinwa* was the only
completed text (after the *Sketch*) that he ever made.')

For this reason there follows here the conclusion of the
Sketch of 1926, following on the words (p.125): 'The remnant
[of the people of Gondolin] reaches Sirion and journeys
to the land at its mouth – the Waters of Sirion. Morgoth's
triumph is now complete.'

THE CONCLUSION OF THE
SKETCH OF THE MYTHOLOGY

At Sirion's mouth Elwing daughter of Dior dwelt, and received the survivors of Gondolin. These become a seafaring folk, building many boats and living far out on the delta, whither the Orcs dare not come.

Ylmir [Ulmo] reproaches the Valar, and bids them rescue the remnants of the Noldoli and the Silmarils in which alone now lives the light of the old days of bliss when the Trees were shining.

The sons of the Valar led by Fionwë Tulkas' son lead forth a host, in which all the Quendi march, but remembering Swanhaven few of the Teleri go with them. Côr is deserted.

Tuor growing old cannot forbear the call of the sea, and builds Eärámë and sails West with Idril and is heard of no more. Eärendel weds Elwing. The call of the sea is born also in him. He builds Wingelot and wishes to sail in search of his father. Here follow the marvellous adventures of

Wingelot in the seas and isles, and of how Eärendel slew Ungoliant in the South. He returned home and found the Waters of Sirion desolate. The sons of Fëanor learning of the dwelling of Elwing and the Nauglafring [on which was set the Silmaril of Beren] had come down on the people of Gondolin. In a battle all the sons of Fëanor save Maidros and Maglor were slain, but the last folk of Gondolin were destroyed or forced to go away and join the people of Maidros. Maglor sat and sang by the sea in repentance. Elwing cast the Nauglafring into the sea and leapt after it, but was changed into a white sea-bird by Ylmir, and flew to seek Eärendel, seeking about all the shores of the world.

Their son Elrond who is part mortal and part elven, a child, was saved however by Maidros. When later the Elves return to the West, bound by his mortal half he elects to stay on earth . . .

Eärendel learning of these things from Bronweg, who dwelt in a hut, a solitary, at the mouth of Sirion, is overcome with sorrow. With Bronweg he sets sail in Wingelot once more in search of Elwing and of Valinor.

He comes to the magic isles, and to the Lonely Isle, and at last to the Bay of Faërie. He climbs the hill of Kôr, and walks in the deserted ways of Tûn, and his raiment becomes encrusted with the dust of diamonds and of jewels. He dares not go further into Valinor. He builds a tower on an isle in the northern seas, to which all the seabirds of the world repair. He sails by the aid of their wings even over the airs in search of Elwing, but is scorched by the Sun and hunted from the sky by the Moon, and for a long while he wanders the sky as a fugitive star.

The march of Fionwë into the North is then told, and of the Terrible or Last Battle. The Balrogs are all destroyed, and the Orcs destroyed or scattered. Morgoth himself makes a last sally with all his dragons; but they are destroyed, all save two which escape, by the sons of the Valar, and Morgoth is overthrown and bound by the chain Angainor, and his iron crown is made into a collar for his neck. The two Silmarils are rescued. The Northern and Western parts of the world are rent and broken in the struggle, and the fashion of their lands altered.

The Gods and Elves release Men from Hithlum, and march through the lands summoning the remnants of the Gnomes and Ilkorins to join them. All do so except the people of Maidros. Maidros prepares to perform his oath, though now at last weighed down by sorrow because of it. He sends to Fionwë reminding him of the oath and begging for the Silmarils. Fionwë replies that he has lost his right to them because of the evil deeds of Fëanor, and of the slaying of Dior, and of the plundering of Sirion. He must submit, and come back to Valinor; in Valinor only and at the judgement of the Gods shall they be handed over ...

On the last march Maglor says to Maidros that there are two sons of Fëanor left, and two Silmarils; one is his. He steals it, and flies, but it burns him so that he knows he no longer has a right to it. He wanders in pain over the earth and casts it into a fiery pit. One Silmaril is now in the sea, and one in the earth. Maglor sings now ever in sorrow by the sea.

The judgement of the Gods takes place. The earth is to be for Men, and the Elves who do not set sail for the Lonely Isle or Valinor shall slowly fade and fail. For a while the last dragons and Orcs shall grieve the earth, but in the end all shall perish by the valour of Men.

Morgoth is thrust through the Door of Night into the outer dark beyond the Walls of the World, and a guard set for ever on that Door. The lies that he sowed in the hearts of Men and Elves do not die and cannot all be slain by the Gods, but live on and bring much evil even to this day. Some say also that secretly Morgoth or his black shadow and spirit in spite of the Valar creeps back over the Walls of the World in the North and East and visits the world, others that this is Thû his great chief who escaped the Last Battle and dwells still in dark places, and perverts Men to his dreadful worship. When the world is much older, and the Gods weary, Morgoth will come back through the Door, and the last battle of all will be fought. Fionwë will fight Morgoth on the plain of Valinor, and the spirit of Túrin shall be beside him; it shall be Túrin who with his black sword will slay Morgoth, and thus the children of Húrin shall be avenged.

In those days the Silmarils shall be recovered from sea and earth and air, and Maidros shall break them and Palúrien with their fire rekindle the Two Trees, and the great light shall come forth again, and the Mountains of Valinor shall be levelled so that it goes out over the world, and Gods and

Elves shall grow young again, and all their dead awake. But of Men in that Day the prophecy speaks not.

And thus it was that the last Silmaril came into the air. The Gods adjudged the last Silmaril to Eärendel – 'until many things shall come to pass' – because of the deeds of the sons of Fëanor. Maidros is sent to Eärendel and with the aid of the Silmaril Elwing is found and restored. Eärendel's boat is drawn over Valinor to the Outer Seas, and Eärendel launches it into the outer darkness high above Sun and Moon. There he sails with the Silmaril upon his brow and Elwing at his side, the brightest of all stars, keeping watch upon Morgoth and the Door of Night. So he shall sail until he sees the last battle gathering upon the plains of Valinor. Then he will descend.

And this is the last end of the tales of the days before the days, in the Northern regions of the Western world.

It would take this story very much too far afield to enter into any general discussion of this most complex and obscure part of the history of the 'First Age': its end. I will only mention a few aspects of the narrative in the *Sketch of the Mythology* given here. What little writing on the subject that survives from the earliest period of my father's work had very largely been abandoned, and the account in the *Sketch* is effectively the first witness to wholly new features, among which is the emergence of the fate of the Silmarils as a central element in the story of the final war. This is borne out by a question that my father asked himself in a very early, isolated note: 'What became of the

Silmarils after the capture of Melko?' (Indeed, it may well be said that the very existence of the Silmarils was of far less radical significance in the original conception of the mythology than it was to become.)

In the account in the *Sketch* Maglor says to Maidros (p.244) that 'there are two sons of Fëanor left, and two Silmarils; one is his'. The third is lost, because it has been told in the *Sketch* (p.243) that 'Elwing cast the Nauglafring into the sea and leapt after it'. That was the Silmaril of Beren and Lúthien. When Maglor cast into a fiery pit the Silmaril from the Iron Crown that he had stolen from the keeping of Fionwë 'one Silmaril was now in the sea and one in the earth' (pp.244–5). The third was the other from the Iron Crown; and it was this that the Gods adjudged to Eärendel, who wearing it upon his brow 'launched it into the outer darkness high above Sun and Moon'.

That it was the Silmaril wrested by Beren and Lúthien from Morgoth in Angband that Eärendel wore and became the Morning and Evening Star had not been achieved at this stage, though when achieved it seems a necessity of the myth.

It is also very striking that Eärendel Half-elven is not as yet the voice that interceded before the Valar on behalf of Men and Elves.

THE CONCLUSION OF THE
QUENTA NOLDORINWA

I take up this second citation of the *Quenta* from the point at which the first citation ended (p.143), where it was told that the Elves who survived the destruction of Doriath and of Gondolin became a small people of shipbuilders at the mouths of Sirion, where they dwelt 'ever nigh unto the shores and under the shadow of Ulmo's hand.' I give now the *Quenta* to its end, following as before (see p.129) the rewritten text 'Q II'.

In Valinor Ulmo spoke unto the Valar of the need of the Elves, and he called on them to forgive and send succour unto them and rescue them from the overmastering might of Morgoth, and win back the Silmarils wherein alone now bloomed the light of the days of bliss when the Two Trees still were shining. Or so it is said, among the Gnomes, who after had tidings of many things from their kinsfolk the Quendi, the Light-elves beloved of Manwë, who ever knew something of the mind of the Lord of the Gods. But as yet Manwë moved not, and the counsels of his heart what tale shall tell? The Quendi have said that the hour was not yet come, and that only one speaking in person for the cause of both Elves and Men, pleading for pardon upon their misdeeds and pity on their woes, might move the counsels of the Powers; and the oath of Fëanor perchance even Manwë could not loose, until it found its end, and the sons of Fëanor relinquished the Silmarils, upon which they had laid their ruthless claim. For the light which lit the Silmarils the Gods had made.

In those days Tuor felt old age creep upon him, and ever a longing for the deeps of the sea grew stronger in his heart. Wherefore he built a great ship, Eärámë, Eagle's Pinion, and with Idril he set sail into the sunset and the West, and came no more into any tale or song. [*Later addition*: But Tuor alone of mortal Men was numbered among the elder race, and joined with the Noldoli whom he loved, and in aftertime dwelt still, or so it hath been said, ever upon his ship voyaging the seas of the Elven-lands, or resting a while in the harbours of the Gnomes of Tol Eressëa, and his fate is sundered from the fate of Men.] Bright Eärendel was then lord of the folk of Sirion and their many ships; and he took to wife Elwing the fair, and she bore him Elrond Half-elven [> Elrond and Elros who are called the Half-elven]. Yet Eärendel could not rest, and his voyages about the shores of the Hither Lands [Middle-earth] eased not his unquiet. Two purposes grew in his heart, blended as one in longing for the wide sea: he sought to sail thereon, seeking after Tuor and

Idril Celebrindal who returned not; and he thought to find perhaps the last shore and bring ere he died the message of Elves and Men unto the Valar of the West, that should move the hearts of Valinor and of the Elves of Tûn to pity on the world and the sorrows of Mankind.

Wingelot he built, fairest of the ships of song, the Foamflower; white were its timbers as the argent moon, golden were its oars, silver were its shrouds, its masts were crowned with jewels like stars. In the Lay of Eärendel is many a thing sung of his adventures in the deep and in lands untrodden, and in many seas and many isles. Ungoliant in the South he slew, and her darkness was destroyed, and light came to many regions which had yet long been hid. But Elwing sat sorrowing at home.

Eärendel found not Tuor nor Idril, nor came he ever on that journey to the shores of Valinor, defeated by shadows and enchantment, driven by repelling winds, until in longing for Elwing he turned him homeward toward the East. And his heart bade him haste, for a sudden fear was fallen on him out of dreams, and the winds that before he had striven with might not now bear him back as swift as his desire.

Upon the havens of Sirion new woe had fallen. The dwelling of Elwing there, where she still possessed the Nauglamír and the glorious Silmaril, became known unto the remaining sons of Fëanor, Maidros and Maglor and Damrod and Díriel; and they gathered together from their wandering hunting-paths, and messages of friendship and yet stern demand they sent unto Sirion. But Elwing and the folk of

Sirion would not yield that jewel which Beren had won and Lúthien had worn, and for which Dior the Fair was slain; and least of all while Eärendel their lord was in the sea, for it seemed to them that in that jewel lay the gift of bliss and healing that had come upon their houses and their ships.

And so came in the end to pass the last and cruellest of the slayings of Elf by Elf; and that was the third of the great wrongs achieved by the accursed oath. For the sons of Fëanor came down upon the exiles of Gondolin and the remnant of Doriath and destroyed them. Though some of their folk stood aside, and some few rebelled and were slain upon the other part aiding Elwing against their own lords (for such was the sorrow and confusion of the hearts of Elfinesse in those days), yet Maidros and Maglor won the day. Alone they now remained of the sons of Fëanor, for in that battle Damrod and Díriel were slain; but the folk of Sirion perished or fled away, or departed of need to join the people of Maidros, who claimed now the lordship of all the Elves of the Hither Lands. And yet Maidros gained not the Silmaril, for Elwing seeing that all was lost and her child Elrond taken captive, eluded the host of Maidros, and with the Nauglamír upon her breast she cast herself into the sea and perished, as folk thought.

But Ulmo bore her up and he gave unto her the likeness of a great white bird, and upon her breast there shone as a star the shining Silmaril, as she flew over the water to seek Eärendel her beloved. And on a time of night Eärendel at the helm saw her come towards him, as a white cloud under moon exceeding swift, as a star over the sea moving in strange course, a pale flame on wings of storm. And it is sung that she fell from the air upon the timbers of Wingelot, in a swoon, nigh unto death for the urgency of her speed, and Eärendel took her unto his bosom. And in the morn with marvelling eyes he beheld his wife in her own form beside him with her hair upon his face; and she slept.

But great was the sorrow of Eärendel and Elwing for the ruin of the havens of Sirion, and the captivity of their son, for whom they feared death, and yet it was not so. For Maidros took pity on Elrond, and he cherished him, and love grew after between them, as little might be thought; but Maidros' heart was sick and weary with the burden of the dreadful oath.

[*This passage was rewritten thus*:
But great was the sorrow of Eärendel and Elwing for the ruin of the havens of Sirion, and the captivity of their sons; and they feared that they would be slain. But it was not so. For Maglor took pity on Elros and Elrond, and he cherished them, and love grew after between them, as little might be thought; but Maglor's heart was sick and weary, &c.]

Yet Eärendel saw now no help left in the lands of Sirion, and he turned again in despair and came not home, but sought back once more to Valinor with Elwing at his side. He stood now most often at the prow, and the Silmaril he bound upon his forehead; and ever its light grew greater as they drew unto the West. Maybe it was due in part to the puissance of that holy jewel that they came in time to the waters that as yet no vessels save those of the Teleri had known; and they came unto the Magic Isles and escaped their magic, and they came into the Shadowy Seas and passed their shadows; and they looked upon the Lonely Isle and they tarried not there, and they cast anchor in the Bay of Faërie [> Bay of Elvenhome] upon the borders of the world. And the Teleri saw the coming of that ship and were amazed, gazing from afar upon the light of the Silmaril, and it was very great.

But Eärendel landed on the immortal shores alone of living Men; and neither Elwing nor any of his small company would he suffer to go with him, lest they fell beneath the wrath of the Gods, and he came at a time of festival even as Morgoth and Ungoliant had in ages past, and the watchers upon the hill of Tûn were few, for the Quendi were most in the halls of Manwë on Tindbrenting's height.

The watchers rode therefore in haste to Valmar, or hid them in the passes of the hills; and all the bells of Valmar pealed; but Eärendel climbed the marvellous hill of Kôr and found it bare, and he entered into the streets of Tûn and they were empty; and his heart sank. He walked now in the deserted ways of Tûn and the dust upon his raiment and his shoes was a dust of diamonds, yet no one heard his call. Wherefore he went back unto the shores and would climb once more upon Wingelot his ship; but one came unto the strand and cried unto him: 'Hail Eärendel, star most radiant, messenger most fair! Hail thou bearer of light before the Sun and Moon, the looked-for that comest unawares, the

longed-for that comest beyond hope! Hail thou splendour of
the children of the world, thou slayer of the dark! Star of the
sunset, hail! Hail herald of the morn!'

And that was Fionwë the son of Manwë, and he summoned Eärendel before the Gods; and Eärendel went unto
Valinor and to the halls of Valmar, and came never again
back into the lands of Men. But Eärendel spoke the embassy
of the two kindreds before the faces of the Gods, and asked
for pardon upon the Gnomes and pity for the exiled Elves
and for unhappy Men, and succour in their need.

Then the sons of the Valar prepared for battle, and the
captain of their host was Fionwë son of Manwë. Beneath
his white banner marched also the host of the Quendi, the
Light-elves, the folk of Ingwë, and among them such of
the Gnomes of old as had never departed from Valinor; but
remembering Swan Haven the Teleri went not forth save
very few, and these manned the ships wherewith the most of
that army came into the Northern lands; but they themselves
would set foot never on those shores.

*Eärendel was their guide; but the Gods would not suffer
him to return again, and he built him a white tower upon the
confines of the outer world in the Northern regions of the
Sundering Seas; and there all the sea-birds of the earth at
times repaired. And often was Elwing in the form and likeness of a bird; and she devised wings for the ship of Eärendel,
and it was lifted even into the oceans of the air. Marvellous
and magical was that ship, a starlit flower in the sky, bearing
a wavering and holy flame; and the folk of Earth beheld it
from afar and wondered, and looked up from despair, saying

surely a Silmaril is in the sky, a new star is risen in the West. Maidros said unto Maglor:

[*This passage, from the asterisk, was rewritten thus*:
In those days the ship of Eärendel was drawn by the Gods beyond the edge of the world, and it was lifted even into the oceans of the air. Marvellous and magical was that ship ... [*&c. as first written*] ... a new star is risen in the West. But Elwing mourned for Eärendel yet found him never again, and they are sundered till the world endeth. Therefore she built a white tower upon the confines of the outer world in the Northern regions of the Sundering Seas; and there all the sea-birds of the earth at times repaired. And Elwing devised wings for herself, and desired to fly to Eärendel's ship. But [*illegible: ?she fell back ....*] But when the flame of it appeared on high Maglor said unto Maidros:]

'If that be the Silmaril that riseth by some power divine out of the sea into which we saw it fall, then let us be glad, that its glory is seen now by many.' Thus hope arose and a promise of betterment; but Morgoth was filled with doubt.

Yet it is said that he looked not for the assault that came upon him from the West. So great was his pride become that he deemed none would ever again come against him in open war; moreover he thought that he had estranged for ever the Gnomes from the Gods and from their kin, and that content in their Blissful Realm the Valar would heed no more his kingdom in the world without. For heart that is pitiless counteth not the power that pity hath, of which stern anger may be forged and a lightning kindled before which mountains fall.

Of the march of the host of Fionwë to the North little is said, for in his armies came none of those Elves who had dwelt and suffered in the Hither Lands, and who made these tales; and tidings only long after did they learn of these things from their kinsfolk the Light-elves of Valinor. But Fionwë came, and the challenge of his trumpets filled the sky, and he summoned unto him all Men and Elves from Hithlum unto the East; and Beleriand was ablaze with the glory of his arms, and the mountains rang.

The meeting of the hosts of the West and of the North is named the Great Battle, the Battle Terrible, the Battle of Wrath and Thunder. There was marshalled the whole power of the Throne of Hate, and well nigh measureless had it become, so that Dor-na-Fauglith could not contain it, and all the North was aflame with war. But it availed not. All the Balrogs were destroyed, and the uncounted hosts of the Orcs perished like straw in fire, or were swept like shrivelled leaves before a burning wind. Few remained to trouble the world thereafter. And it is said that there many Men of Hithlum repentant of their evil servitude did deeds of valour, and many beside of Men new come out of the East; and so were fulfilled in part the words of Ulmo; for by Eärendel son of Tuor was help brought unto the Elves, and by the swords of Men were they strengthened on the fields of war.

[*Later addition*: But most Men, and especially those new come out of the East, were on the side of the Enemy.] But Morgoth quailed and he came not forth; and he loosed his last assault, and that was the winged dragons [*Later addition*: for as yet had none of these creatures of his cruel thought assailed the air]. So sudden and so swift and ruinous was the onset of that fleet, as a tempest of a hundred thunders winged with steel, that Fionwë was driven back; but Eärendel came and a myriad of birds were about him, and the battle lasted all through the night of doubt. And Eärendel slew Ancalagon the black and the mightiest of all the dragon-horde, and cast him from the sky, and in his fall the towers of Thangorodrim were thrown down. Then the sun rose of the second day and the sons of the Valar prevailed, and all the dragons were destroyed save two alone; and they fled into the East. Then were all the pits of Morgoth broken and unroofed, and the might of Fionwë descended into the deeps of the Earth, and there Morgoth was thrown down.

[*The words* and there Morgoth was thrown down were *rejected and replaced by this passage*:
and there Morgoth stood at last at bay; and yet not valiant. He fled unto the deepest of his mines and sued for peace and pardon. But his feet were hewn from under him, and he was hurled upon his face.]

He was bound with the chain Angainor, which long had been prepared, and his iron crown they beat into a collar for his neck, and his head was bowed unto his knees. But Fionwë took the two Silmarils that remained and guarded them.

Thus perished the power and woe of Angband in the North, and its multitude of thralls came forth beyond all hope into the light of day, and they looked upon a world all changed; for so great was the fury of those adversaries that the Northern regions of the Western world were rent and riven, and the sea roared in through many chasms, and there was confusion and great noise; and the rivers perished or found new paths, and the valleys were upheaved and the hills trod down; and Sirion was no more. Then Men fled away, such as perished not in the ruin of those days, and long was it ere they came back over the mountains to where Beleriand once had been, and not until the tale of those wars had faded to an echo seldom heard.

But Fionwë marched through the Western lands summoning the remnants of the Gnomes, and the Dark-elves that had yet not looked on Valinor, to join with the thralls released and to depart. But Maidros would not harken, and he prepared, though with weary loathing and despair, to perform even yet the obligation of his oath. For Maidros and Maglor would have given battle for the Silmarils, were they withheld, even against the victorious host of Valinor, and though they stood alone in all the world. And they sent unto Fionwë and bade him yield now up those jewels which of old Morgoth stole from Fëanor. But Fionwë said that the right to the work of their hands which Fëanor and his sons had formerly possessed now had perished, because of their many and evil deeds blinded by their oath, and most of all the slaying of Dior and the assault upon Elwing; the light of the Silmarils should go now to the Gods whence it came, and to Valinor must Maidros and Maglor return and there abide the judgement of the Gods, by whose decree alone would Fionwë yield the jewels from his charge.

Maglor was minded to submit, for he was sad at heart, and he said: 'The oath says not that we may not bide our time, and maybe in Valinor all shall be forgiven and forgot, and we shall come into our own.' But Maidros said that if once they returned and the favour of the Gods were withheld from them, then would their oath still remain, to be fulfilled in despair yet greater; 'and who can tell to what dreadful doom we shall come, if we disobey the Powers in their own land, or purpose ever to bring war again into their Guarded Realm?' And so it came that Maidros and Maglor crept into the camps of Fionwë, and laid hands on the Silmarils, and slew the guards; and there they prepared to defend themselves to the death. But Fionwë stayed his folk; and the brethren departed and fled far away.

Each took a single Silmaril, saying that one was lost unto them and two remained, and but two brethren. But the jewel burned the hand of Maidros in pain unbearable (and he had but one hand as has before been told); and he perceived that it was as Fionwë had said, and that his right thereto had become void, and that the oath was vain. And being in anguish and despair he cast himself into a gaping chasm filled with fire, and so ended; and his Silmaril was taken into the bosom of the Earth.

And it is told also of Maglor that he could not bear the pain with which the Silmaril tormented him; and he cast it at last into the sea, and thereafter wandered ever upon the shore singing in pain and regret beside the waves; for Maglor was the mightiest of the singers of old, but he came never back among the folk of Elfinesse.

In those days there was a mighty building of ships on the shores of the Western Sea, and especially upon the great isles, which in the disruption of the Northern world were fashioned of ancient Beleriand. Thence in many a fleet the survivors of the Gnomes and of the Western companies of the Dark-elves set sail into the West and came not again into the lands of weeping and of war; but the Light-elves marched back beneath the banners of their king following in the train of Fionwë's victory, and they were borne back in triumph unto Valinor. [*Later addition*: Yet little joy had they in their return, for they came without the Silmarils, and these could not be again found, unless the world was broken and remade anew.] But in the West the Gnomes and Dark-elves rehabited for the most part the Lonely Isle, that looks both East and West; and very fair did that land become, and so remains. But some returned even unto Valinor, as all were free to do who willed; and the Gnomes were admitted again to the love of Manwë and the pardon of the Valar, and the Teleri forgave their ancient grief, and the curse was laid to rest.

Yet not all would forsake the Outer Lands where they had long suffered and long dwelt; and some lingered many an age in the West and North, and especially in the western isles. And among these were Maglor as has been told; and with him Elrond the Half-elven, who after went among mortal Men again, and from whom alone the blood of the Firstborn and the seed divine of Valinor have come among Mankind (for he was son of Elwing, daughter of Dior, son of Lúthien, child of Thingol and Melian; and Eärendel his sire was son of Idril Celebrindal, the fair maid of Gondolin). But ever as the ages drew on and the Elf-folk faded on the Earth, they would still set sail at eve from our Western shores; as still they do, when now there linger few anywhere of their lonely companies.

This was the judgement of the Gods, when Fionwë and the sons of the Valar had returned unto Valmar: thereafter the Outer Lands should be for Mankind, the younger children of the world; but to the Elves alone should the gateways of the West stand ever open; and if they would not come thither and tarried in the world of Men, then they should slowly fade and fail. This is the most grievous of the fruits of the lies and works that Morgoth wrought, that the Eldalië should be sundered and estranged from Men. For a while his Orcs and his Dragons breeding again in dark places affrighted the world, and in sundry regions do so yet; but ere the End all shall perish by the valour of mortal Men.

But Morgoth the Gods thrust through the Door of Timeless Night into the Void, beyond the Walls of the World, and a guard is set for ever on that door, and Eärendel keeps watch upon the ramparts of the sky. Yet the lies that Melko, Moeleg the mighty and accursed, Morgoth Bauglir the Dark Power Terrible, sowed in the hearts of Elves and Men have not all died and cannot by the Gods be slain, and they live to work much evil even to this later day. Some say also that Morgoth at whiles secretly as a cloud that cannot be seen or felt, and yet is venomous, creeps back surmounting the Walls and visiteth the world; *but others say that this is the black shadow of Thû, whom Morgoth made, and who escaped from the Battle Terrible, and dwells in dark places and perverts Men to his dreadful allegiance and his foul worship.

[*This passage, from the asterisk, was rewritten thus*:
but others say that this is the black shadow of Sauron, who served Morgoth and became the greatest and most evil of his underlings; and Sauron escaped from the Great Battle, and dwelt in dark places and perverted Men to his dreadful allegiance and his foul worship.]

After the triumph of the Gods Eärendel sailed still in the seas of heaven, but the Sun scorched him and the Moon hunted him in the sky. Then the Valar drew his white ship Wingelot over the land of Valinor, and they filled it with radiance and hallowed it, and launched it through the Door of Night. And long Eärendel set sail into the starless vast, [*struck out*: Elwing at his side, *see the rewritten passage on p.255*] the Silmaril upon his brow voyaging the Dark behind the world, a glimmering and fugitive star. And ever and anon he returns and shines behind the courses of the Sun and Moon above the ramparts of the Gods, brighter than all other stars, the mariner of the sky, keeping watch against Morgoth upon the confines of the world. Thus shall he sail until he sees the Last Battle fought upon the plains of Valinor.

Thus spoke the prophecy of Mandos, which he declared in Valmar at the judgement of the Gods, and the rumour of it was whispered among all the Elves of the West: when the world is old and the Powers grow weary, then Morgoth shall come back through the Door out of the Timeless Night; and he shall destroy the Sun and the Moon, but Eärendel shall come upon him as a white flame and drive him from the airs. Then shall the last battle be gathered on the fields of Valinor. In that day Tulkas shall strive with Melko, and on his right shall stand Fionwë and on his left Túrin Turambar, son of Húrin, Conqueror of Fate; and it shall be the black sword of Túrin that deals unto Melko his death and final end; and so shall the children of Húrin and all Men be avenged.

Thereafter shall the Silmarils be recovered out of sea and earth and air; for Eärendel shall descend and yield up that flame that he hath had in keeping. Then Fëanor shall bear the Three and yield them unto Yavanna Palúrien; and she will break them and with their fire rekindle the Two Trees, and a great light shall come forth; and the Mountains of Valinor shall be levelled, so that the light goes out over all the world. In that light the Gods will again grow young, and

the Elves awake and all their dead arise, and the purpose of
Ilúvatar be fulfilled concerning them.

Such is the end of the tales of the days before the days
in the Northern regions of the Western world.

*

My history of a history thus ends with a prophecy, the
prophecy of Mandos. I will end the book with a repetition
of what I wrote in my edition of the Great Tale of *The
Children of Húrin*. 'It is to be borne in mind that at that
time the *Quenta Noldorinwa* represented (if only in a
somewhat bare structure) the full extent of my father's
"imagined world". It was not the history of the First Age,
as it afterwards became, for there was as yet no Second
Age, nor Third Age; there was no Númenor, no hobbits,
and of course no Ring.'

LIST OF NAMES

At the end of the main list that follows here are listed the seven longer additional notes to which a few of the names in the main list are extended. Names that appear in the map of Beleriand are followed by an asterisk.

Ainairos An Elf of Alqualondë.
Ainur See the additional note on p.287.
Almaren The isle of Almaren was the first dwelling of the Valar in Arda.
Alqualondë See *Swanhaven*.
Aman The land in the West beyond the Great Sea in which was Valinor.
Amnon The words of the Prophecy of Amnon, 'Great is the fall of Gondolin', uttered by Turgon in the midst of the battle for the city, are cited in two closely similar forms in isolated jottings under this title. Both begin with the words under the title 'Great is the fall of Gondolin', and then follow in the one case 'Turgon shall not fade till the lily of the valley fadeth' and in the other 'When the lily of the valley withers then shall Turgon fade'.

The lily of the valley is Gondolin, one of the seven names of the city, the Flower of the Plain. There are references also in notes to the prophecies of Amnon, and to the places of the prophecies; but nowhere, it seems, is there any explanation of who Amnon was or when he uttered these words.

Amon Gwareth   'The Hill of Watch', or 'The Hill of Defence', a tall and isolated rocky height in the Guarded Plain of Gondolin, on which the city was built.

Anar   The Sun.

Ancalagon the black   The greatest of Morgoth's winged dragons, destroyed by Eärendel in the Great Battle.

Androth   Caves in the hills of Mithrim where Tuor dwelt with Annael and the Grey-elves, and afterwards as a solitary outlaw.

*Anfauglith**   Once the great grassy plain of Ard-galen north of Taur-na-Fuin before its desolation by Morgoth.

Angainor   The name of the chain, wrought by Aulë, with which Morgoth was twice bound: for he had been forced to wear it when imprisoned by the Valar in a very remote age, and again in his final defeat.

Angband   The great dungeon-fortress of Morgoth in the North-west of Middle-earth.

Annael   Grey-elf of Mithrim, fosterfather of Tuor.

Annon-in-Gelydh   'Gate of the Noldor': the entrance to the subterranean river rising in the lake of Mithrim and leading to the Rainbow Cleft.

Aranwë   Elf of Gondolin, father of Voronwë.

Aranwion   'Son of Aranwë'. See *Voronwë*.

Arlisgion   A region, translated 'the place of reeds', through which Tuor passed on his great southward journey; but the name is not found on any map. It seems impossible to trace the way that Tuor took until he reached the Land of Willows after many days; but it is clear that in this account Arlisgion was somewhere to the north of that land. The only other reference to this place seems to be in the Last Version (p.173), where Voronwë spoke to Tuor of the Lisgardh, 'the land of reeds at the Mouths of Sirion'. Arlisgion 'place of reeds' is clearly the same as Lisgardh 'land of reeds'; but the geography of this region at this time is very unclear.

Arvalin   A desolate region of wide and misty plains between the Pelóri (the Mountains of Valinor) and the sea. Its name, meaning 'near Valinor', was later replaced by *Avathar*, 'the shadows'. It was here that Morgoth met with Ungoliant, and it was said that the Doom of Mandos was spoken in Arvalin. See *Ungoliant*.

Aulë   He is one of the great Valar, called 'the Smith', of might little less than Ulmo. The following is taken from the portrait of him, in the text named *Valaquenta*:

> His lordship is over all the substances of which Arda is made. In the beginning he wrought much in fellowship with Manwë and Ulmo; and the fashioning of all lands was his labour. He is a smith and a master of all crafts, and he delights in works of skill, however small, as much as in the mighty building of old. His are the gems that lie deep in the Earth and the gold that is fair in the hand, no less than the walls of the mountains and the basins of the sea.

Bablon, Ninwi, Trui, Rûm   Babylon, Nineveh, Troy, Rome. A note on *Bablon* reads: '*Bablon* was a city of Men, and more rightly *Babylon*, but such is the Gnomes' name as they now shape it, and they got it from aforetime.'

Bad Uthwen   See *The Way of Escape*.

Balar, Isle of   An island far out in the Bay of Balar. See *Círdan the Shipwright*.

Balcmeg   An Orc slain by Tuor.

Balrogs   'Demons with whips of flame and claws of steel'.

Battle of Unnumbered Tears   See the note on p.295.

Bauglir   A name frequently added to *Morgoth*; translated 'The Constrainer'.

Bay of Faërie   A great bay in the eastern face of Aman.

Beleg   A great archer of Doriath and close friend of Túrin, whom he slew in darkness thinking him a foe.

Belegaer   See *Great Sea*.

*Beleriand**   The great north-western region of Middle-earth, extending from the Blue Mountains in the East to include all the inner lands south of Hithlum and the coasts south of Drengist.

Beren   Man of the House of Bëor, lover of Lúthien, who cut the Silmaril from Morgoth's crown. Slain by Carcharoth the wolf of Angband; he alone of mortal Men returned from the dead.

The Blacksword (Mormegil)   A name given to Túrin on account of his sword Gurthang ('Iron of Death').

The Blessed Realm   See *Aman*.

Bragollach   Short form of *Dagor Bragollach*, 'The Battle of Sudden Flame', in which the Siege of Angband was ended.

Bredhil   Gnomish name of Varda (also Bridhil).

*Brethil**   The forest between the rivers Teiglin and Sirion.

*Brithiach**   The ford over Sirion leading into Dimbar.

*Brithombar**   The northernmost of the Havens of the Falas.

Bronweg   The Gnomish name of *Voronwë*.

Celegorm   Son of Fëanor; called the Fair.

Círdan the Shipwright   Lord of the Falas (the western coasts of Beleriand); at the destruction of the Havens in that region by Morgoth after the Battle of Unnumbered Tears Círdan escaped to the Isle of Balar and the region of the Mouths of Sirion, and continued the building of ships. This is the Círdan the Shipwright who appears in *The Lord of the Rings* as the lord of the Grey Havens at the end of the Third Age.

Cirith Ninniach   The 'Rainbow Cleft'; see *Cris-Ilfing*.

City of Stone   Gondolin; see *Gondothlim*.

Cleft of Eagles   In the southernmost of the Encircling Mountains about Gondolin. Elvish name *Cristhorn*.

Cranthir   Son of Fëanor, called the Dark; changed to Caranthir.

Cris-Ilfing   'Rainbow Cleft': the ravine in which flowed the river from Lake Mithrim. Replaced by the name *Kirith Helvin*, and finally *Cirith Ninniach*.

*Crissaegrim** The mountain-peaks south of Gondolin, where were the eyries of Thorondor, the Lord of the Eagles.

Cristhorn Elvish name of the *Cleft of Eagles*. Replaced by the name *Kirith-thoronath*.

Cuiviénen The 'waters of awakening' of the Elves in the far distant East of Middle-earth: 'a dark lake amid mighty rocks, and the stream that feeds that water falls therein down a deep cleft, a pale and slender thread'.

Curufin Son of Fëanor; called the Crafty.

Damrod and Díriel Twin brothers, youngest of the sons of Fëanor; later changed to Amrod and Amras.

Deep-elves A name of the second host of the Elves on the great journey. See *Noldoli*, *Noldor*, and the note on p.300.

*Dimbar** The land between the rivers Sirion and Mindeb.

Dior The son of Beren and Lúthien and possessor of their Silmaril; known as 'Thingol's Heir'. He was the father of Elwing; and was slain by the sons of Fëanor.

Doom of Mandos See note on p.299.

The Door of Night See the entry *Outer Seas*. In the text named *Ambarkanta* that I have cited there, concerning *Ilurambar*, the Walls of the World, and *Vaiya*, the Enfolding Ocean or Outer Sea, it is further said:

> In the midst of Valinor is Ando Lómen, the Door of Timeless Night that pierces the Walls and opens upon the Void. For the World is set amid Kúma, the Void, the Night without form or time. But none can pass the chasm and the belt of Vaiya and come to that Door, save the great Valar only. And they made that Door when Melko was overcome and put forth into the Outer Dark, and it is guarded by Eärendel.

*Doriath** The great forested region of Beleriand, ruled by Thingol and Melian. The Girdle of Melian gave rise to the later name *Doriath* (*Dor-iâth* 'Land of the Fence').

*Dor-lómin** 'The Land of Shadows': region in the south of Hithlum.

Dor-na-Fauglith   The great northern grassy plain named Ard-galen; utterly destroyed by Morgoth it was named Dor-na-Fauglith, translated as 'the land under choking ash'.

Dramborleg   Tuor's axe. A note on this name says: '*Dramborleg* means "Thudder-sharp", and was the axe of Tuor that smote both a heavy dint as of a club and cleft as a sword'.

Drengist   A long firth of the sea penetrating the Echoing Mountains. The river from Mithrim that Tuor followed through the Rainbow Cleft would have brought him to the sea by that route, 'but he was dismayed by the fury of the strange waters, and he turned aside and went away southward, and so came not to the long shores of the Firth of Drengist' (p. 158).

The Dry River   The bed of the river that once flowed out from the Encircling Mountains to join Sirion; forming the entrance to Gondolin.

Duilin   Lord of the people of the Swallow in Gondolin.

Dungortheb   Shortened form of *Nan Dungortheb*, 'the valley of dreadful death', between Ered Gorgoroth, the Mountains of Terror, and the Girdle of Melian protecting Doriath from the north.

The Dweller in the Deep   Ulmo.

Eagle-stream   See *Thorn Sir*.

Eärámë   'Eagle's Pinion', Tuor's ship.

Eärendel   (later form *Eärendil*) 'Halfelven': the son of Tuor and Idril Turgon's daughter; the father of Elrond and Elros. See the note on p.296.

Easterlings   Name given to Men who followed the Edain into Beleriand; they fought on both sides in the Battle of Unnumbered Tears, and were given Hithlum by Morgoth, where they oppressed the remnant of the People of Hador.

*Echoing Mountains of Lammoth**   The Echoing Mountains (Ered Lómin) formed the 'west wall' of Hithlum; Lammoth was the region between those mountains and the sea.

Echoriath   See *Encircling Mountains*.

Ecthelion   Lord of the people of the Fountain in Gondolin.

Edain   The Men of the Three Houses of the Elf-friends.

Egalmoth   Lord of the people of the Heavenly Arch in Gondolin.

*Eglarest**   The southern Haven of the Falas.

Eldalië   'Elven folk', a name used interchangeably with *Eldar*.

Eldar   In early writings the name *Eldar* meant the Elves of the great journey from Cuiviénen, which was divided into three hosts: see *Light-elves, Deep-elves, and Sea-elves*: on these names see the remarkable passage in *The Hobbit* given in the note on p.300. Subsequently it could be used as distinct from *Noldoli*, and of the language of the Eldar as opposed to Gnomish (the language of the Noldoli).

Elemmakil   Elf of Gondolin, captain of the guard of the outer gate.

Elfinesse   An inclusive name for all the lands of the Elves.

Elrond and Elros   The sons of Eärendel and Elwing. Elrond elected to belong to the Firstborn; he was the master of Rivendell and keeper of the ring Vilya. Elros was numbered among Men and became the first King of Númenor.

Elwing   Daughter of Dior, wedded Eärendel; mother of Elrond and Elros.

Encircling Mountains, ~Hills   The mountains encircling the plain of Gondolin. Elvish name *Echoriath*.

Eöl   The 'dark Elf' of the forest who ensnared Isfin; father of Maeglin.

Ered Wethrin   (earlier form *Eredwethion*) Mountains of Shadow ('The walls of Hithlum'). See the note on *Iron Mountains*, p.293.

Evermind   White flower that was continuously in bloom.

The Exiles   The rebellious Noldor who returned to Middle-earth from Aman.

*Falas**   The western coastlands of Beleriand, south of Nevrast.

Falasquil   A cove of the sea-coast where Tuor dwelt for a time. This was clearly a small bay, marked without a name on a map made by my father, on the long firth (named Drengist) running

east to Hithlum and Dor-lómin. The wood for Eärendel's ship
Wingilot ('Foam-flower') was said to have come from Falasquil.

Falathrim   The Telerin Elves of the Falas.

Fëanor   The eldest son of Finwë; maker of the Silmarils.

Finarfin   The third son of Finwë; father of Finrod Felagund and
Galadriel. He remained in Aman after the flight of the Noldor.

Finduilas   Daughter of Orodreth, King of Nargothrond after
Finrod Felagund. *Faelivrin* was a name given to her; the meaning is 'the gleam of the sun on the pools of Ivrin'.

Fingolfin   The second son of Finwë; father of Fingon and Turgon;
High King of the Noldor in Beleriand; slain by Morgoth in
single combat at the gates of Angband (described in *The Lay of
Leithian, Beren and Lúthien* pp.190 ff.).

Fingolma   Early name of Finwë.

Fingon   The elder son of Fingolfin; brother of Turgon; High King
of the Noldor after the death of Fingolfin; slain in the Battle of
Unnumbered Tears.

Finn   Gnomish form of Finwë.

Finrod Felagund   Eldest son of Finarfin; founder and King of
Nargothrond, whence his name *Felagund* 'cave-hewer'. See
Inglor.

Finwë   Leader of the second host (Noldoli) on the great journey
from Cuiviénen; father of Fëanor, Fingolfin and Finarfin.

Fionwë   Son of Manwë; captain of the host of the Valar in the
Great Battle.

The Fountain   Name of one of the kindreds of the Gondothlim.
See *Ecthelion*.

Galdor   The father of Húrin and Huor; see *Tuor*.

Galdor   Lord of the people of the Tree in Gondolin.

Gar Ainion   'The Place of the Gods' (*Ainur*) in Gondolin.

Gate of the Noldor   See *Annon-in-Gelydh*.

Gates of Summer   See *Tarnin Austa*.

Gelmir and Arminas   Noldorin Elves who came upon Tuor at the
Gate of the Noldor when on their way to Nargothrond to warn

Orodreth (the second king, following Felagund) of its peril, of which they did not speak to Tuor.

Girdle of Melian   See *Melian*.

Glamhoth   Orcs; translated 'the barbaric host', 'hosts of hate'.

Glaurung   The most celebrated of all the dragons of Morgoth.

Glingol and Bansil   The gold and silver trees at the doors of the King's palace in Gondolin. Originally these were shoots of old from the Two Trees of Valinor before Melko and Gloomweaver withered them, but later the story was that they were images made by Turgon in Gondolin.

Glithui*   A river flowing down from Ered Wethrin, a tributary of Teiglin.

Gloomweaver   See *Ungoliant*.

Glorfalc   'Golden Cleft': Tuor's name for the ravine through which flowed the river that rose in Lake Mithrim.

Glorfindel   Lord of the people of the Golden Flower in Gondolin.

Gnomes   This was the early translation of the name of the Elves called *Noldoli* (later *Noldor*). For explanation of this use of 'Gnomes' see *Beren and Lúthien* pp.32–3. Their language was Gnomish.

The Golden Flower   Name of one of the kindreds of the Gondothlim.

Gondolin*   For the name see *Gondothlim*. For the other names see p.51.

Gondothlim   The people of Gondolin; translated 'the dwellers in stone'. Other names of related form are *Gondobar* meaning 'City of Stone' and *Gondothlimbar* ' City of the Dwellers in Stone'. Both these names are included in the Seven Names of the city cited to Tuor by the guard at the gate of Gondolin (p.51). The element *gond* meant 'stone', as in *Gondor*. *Gondolin* was interpreted at the time of writing the *Lost Tales* as 'Stone of Song', which was said to mean 'stone carved and wrought to great beauty.' A later interpretation was 'the Hidden Rock'.

Gondothlimbar   See *Gondothlim*.

Gorgoroth   Shortened form of *Ered Gorgoroth*, the Mountains of Terror; see *Dungortheb*.

Gothmog   Lord of Balrogs, captain of the hosts of Melkor; son of Melkor, slain by Ecthelion.

The Great Battle   The world-changing battle that finally overthrew Morgoth and brought the First Age of the World to its end. It may also be said to have ended the Elder Days, for 'in the Fourth Age the earlier Ages were often called the *Elder Days*; but that name was properly given only to the days before the casting out of Morgoth' (*The Tale of Years*, appendix to *The Lord of the Rings*). That is why Elrond said at the great council in Rivendell: 'My memory reaches back *even to the Elder Days*. Eärendil was my sire, who was born in Gondolin before its fall.'

*Great Sea**   The Great Sea of the West, whose name was *Belegaer*, extended from the western coasts of Middle-earth to the coasts of Aman.

Great Worm of Angband   See *Glaurung*.

Grey Annals   See p.220.

Grey-elves   The Sindar. This name was given to the Eldar who remained in Beleriand and did not go further into the West.

The Grinding Ice   In the far north of Arda there was a strait between the 'western world' and the coast of Middle-earth, and in one of the accounts of the 'Grinding Ice' it is described thus:

> Through these narrows the chill waters of the Encircling Sea [see *Outer Seas*] and the waves of the Great Sea of the West flow together, and there are vast mists of deathly cold, and the sea-streams are filled with clashing hills of ice and the grinding of ice submerged. This strait was named *Helkaraksë*.

Guarded Plain   Tumladen, the plain of Gondolin.

Gwindor   Elf of Nargothrond, lover of Finduilas.

Hador   See *Tuor*. The House of Hador was called The Third House of the Edain. His son Galdor was the father of Húrin and Huor.

The Hammer of Wrath   Name of one of the kindreds of the Gondothlim.

The Harp   Name of one of the kindreds of the Gondothlim.

Haudh-en-Ndengin   'The Hill of Slain': a great mound in which were laid all the Elves and Men who died in the Battle of Unnumbered Tears. This was in the desert of Anfauglith.

Heavenly Arch   Name of one of the kindreds of the Gondothlim.

Hells of Iron   Angband. See the note on *Iron Mountains,* p.293.

Hendor   A servant of Idril who carried Eärendel in the flight from Gondolin.

The Hidden King   Turgon.

The Hidden Kingdom   Gondolin.

The Hidden People   See *Gondothlim.*

Hill of Watch   See *Amon Gwareth.*

Hisilómë   The Gnomish form of the name *Hithlum.*

Hísimë   The eleventh month, corresponding to November.

Hither Lands   Middle-earth.

*Hithlum**   The great region, translated 'Land of Mist', 'Twilit Mist', extending northward from the great wall of Ered Wethrin, the Mountains of Shadow; in the south of the region lay Dor-lómin and Mithrim. See *Hisilómë.*

Huor   The brother of Húrin, husband of Rían, and father of Tuor; slain in the Battle of Unnumbered Tears. See the note on *Húrin and Gondolin,* p.290.

Húrin   The father of Túrin Turambar and brother of Huor father of Tuor; see the note *Húrin and Gondolin,* p.290.

Idril   Called *Celebrindal* 'Silverfoot', the daughter of Turgon. Her mother was Elenwë, who perished in the crossing of the Helcaraxë, the Grinding Ice. It is told in a very late note that 'Turgon had himself come near to death in the bitter waters when he attempted to save her and his daughter Idril, whom the breaking of treacherous ice had cast into the cruel sea. Idril he saved; but the body of Elenwë was covered in fallen ice.' She was the wife of Tuor and the mother of Eärendel.

Ilfiniol   Elvish name of *Littleheart*.

Ilkorindi, Ilkorins   Elves who never dwelt in Kôr in Valinor.

Ilúvatar   The Creator. The elements are *Ilu* 'the Whole, the Universe'; and *atar* 'father'.

Inglor   Earlier name for Finrod Felagund.

Ingwë   Leader of the Light-elves on the great journey from Cuiviénen. It is told in the *Quenta Noldorinwa* that 'he entered into Valinor and sits at the feet of the Powers, and all Elves revere his name, but he has come never back to the Outer Lands.'

Iron Mountains   'Morgoth's mountains' in the far North. But the occurrence of the name in the text of the original *Tale* on p.43 derives from an earlier time when *Iron Mountains* was applied to the range later named *Shadowy Mountains* (*Ered Wethrin*): see the note on *Iron Mountains* on p.293. I have emended the text on p.43 at this point.

Isfin   Sister of King Turgon; mother of Maeglin, wife of Eöl.

Ivrin   The lake and falls beneath Ered Wethrin where the river Narog rose.

Kôr   The hill in Valinor overlooking the Bay of Faërie on which was built the Elvish city of Tûn, later Tirion; also as the name of the city itself. See *Ilkorindi*.

Land of Shadows   See *Dor-lómin*.

*Land of Willows**   The beautiful land where the river Narog flowed into the Sirion, south of Nargothrond. Its Elvish names were *Nan-tathrin* 'Willow-vale' and *Tasarinan*. In *The Two Towers* (Book 3, chapter 4), when Treebeard was carrying Merry and Pippin in the forest of Fangorn he chanted to them, and the first words were

> In the willow-meads of Tasarinan I walked in the Spring.

> Ah! the sight and the smell of the Spring in Nan-tasarion!

Laurelin   Name of the Golden Tree of Valinor.

Legolas Greenleaf   An Elf of the House of the Tree in Gondolin, gifted with extraordinary night-sight.

Light-elves A name of the first host of the Elves on the great journey from Cuiviénen. See *Quendi*, and the note on p.300.

Linaewen The great mere in Nevrast 'in the midst of the hollow land'.

Lisgardh 'The land of reeds at the Mouths of Sirion'. See *Arlisgion*.

Littleheart Elf of Tol Eressëa who told the original tale of *The Fall of Gondolin*. He is described thus in the *Lost Tales*: 'He had a weatherworn face and blue eyes of great merriment, and was very slender and small, nor might one say if he were fifty or ten thousand'; and it is also said that he owed his name to 'the youth and wonder of his heart'. In the *Lost Tales* he has many Elvish names, but *Ilfiniol* is the only one that appears in this book.

Lonely Isle *Tol Eressëa*: a large island in the Western Ocean, within remote sight of the coasts of Aman. For its early history see p.26.

Lord of Waters See *Ulmo*.

Lords of the West The Valar.

Lorgan Easterling chief in Hithlum who enslaved Tuor.

Lórien The Valar Mandos and Lórien were called brothers, and bore the name *Fanturi*. Mandos was *Nefantur* and Lórien was *Olofantur*. Like Mandos, Lórien was the name of his dwelling but was also used as his own name. He was 'the master of visions and dreams'.

Lothlim 'People of the Flower': the name taken by the survivors of Gondolin in their dwellings at the Mouths of Sirion.

Lug An Orc slain by Tuor.

Maglor Son of Fëanor, called the Mighty; a great singer and minstrel.

Maidros Eldest son of Fëanor, called the Tall.

*Malduin** A tributary of the Teiglin.

Malkarauki Elvish name for *Balrogs*.

Mandos The dwelling, by which he himself is always named, of the great Vala Namo. I give here the portrait of Mandos in the brief text *Valaquenta*:

[Mandos] is the keeper of the Houses of the Dead, and the summoner of the spirits of the slain. He forgets nothing; and he knows all things that shall be, save only those that lie still in the freedom of Ilúvatar. He is the Doomsman of the Valar; but he pronounces his dooms and his judgements only at the bidding of Manwë. Vairë the Weaver is his spouse, who weaves all things that have ever been in Time into her storied webs, and the halls of Mandos that ever widen as the ages pass are clothed with them.

See *Lórien*.

Manwë   The chief of the Valar and the spouse of Varda; Lord of the realm of Arda. See *Súlimo*.

Meglin (and later *Maeglin*)   Son of Eöl and Isfin sister of King Turgon; he betrayed Gondolin to Morgoth, the most infamous treachery in the history of Middle-earth; slain by Tuor.

Meleth   The nurse of Eärendel.

Melian   A Maia from the company of the Vala Lórien in Valinor, who came to Middle-earth and became the Queen of Doriath. 'She put forth her power' [as told in the *Grey Annals*, see p.220] 'and fenced all that region about with an unseen wall of shadow and bewilderment: the Girdle of Melian, that none thereafter could pass against her will or the will of King Thingol'. See *Thingol* and *Doriath*.

Melko (later form *Melkor*)   'He who arises in might'; the name of the great evil Ainu before he became 'Morgoth'. 'The mightiest of those Ainur who came into the World was in his beginning Melkor. [He] is counted no longer among the Valar, and his name is not spoken upon Earth.' (From the text named *Valaquenta*.)

*Menegroth**   See *Thousand Caves*.

Meres of Twilight   Aelin-uial, a region of great pools and marshes, wrapped in mists, where Aros, flowing out of Doriath, met Sirion.

Mighty of the West   The Valar.

Minas of King Finrod   The tower (Minas Tirith) built by Finrod Felagund. This was a great watch-tower that he built on Tol Sirion, the isle in the Pass of Sirion that became after its capture by Sauron *Tol-in-Gaurhoth*, the Isle of Werewolves.

Mithrim*   The great lake in the south of Hithlum, and also the region in which it lay and the mountains to the west.

Moeleg   The Gnomish form of Melko, which the Gnomes would not speak, calling him Morgoth Bauglir, the Dark Power Terrible.

The Mole   A sable Mole was the sign of Meglin and his house.

Morgoth   This name ('the Black Foe' and other translations) only occurs once in the *Lost Tales*. It was first given by Fëanor after the rape of the Silmarils. See *Melko* and *Bauglir*.

Mountains of Darkness   The Iron Mountains.

Mountains of Shadow*   See *Ered Wethrin*.

Mountains of Turgon   See *Echoriath*.

Mountains of Valinor   The great range of mountains that were raised by the Valar when they came to Aman. Called also the *Pelóri*, they extended in a vast crescent from north to south not far from the eastern shores of Aman.

Nan-tathrin*   Elvish name of the *Land of Willows*.

Nargothrond*   The great underground fortress city on the river Narog in West Beleriand, founded by Finrod Felagund and destroyed by the dragon Glaurung.

Narog*   The river that rose in the lake of Ivrin under Ered Wethrin and flowed into Sirion in the Land of Willows.

Narquelië   The tenth month, corresponding to October.

Nessa   A 'Queen of the Valar', the sister of Vána and spouse of Tulkas.

Nevrast*   The region south-west of Dor-lómin where Turgon dwelt before his departure to Gondolin.

Ninniach, Vale of   The site of the Battle of Unnumbered Tears, but found only here under this name.

Nirnaeth Arnoediad The Battle of Unnumbered Tears. Often referred to as 'the Nirnaeth'. See the note on p.295.

Noldoli, Noldor The earlier and later forms of the name of the second host of the Elves on the great journey from Cuiviénen. See *Gnomes, Deep-elves*.

Nost-na-Lothion 'The Birth of Flowers', a festival of spring in Gondolin.

Orcobal A great champion of Orcs, slain by Ecthelion.

Orcs In a note on the word my father wrote: 'A folk devised and brought into being by Morgoth to make war on Elves and Men; sometimes translated "Goblins", but they were of nearly human stature.' See *Glamhoth*.

Orfalch Echor The great ravine in the Encircling Mountains by which Gondolin was approached.

Oromë Vala, the son of Yavanna, renowned as the greatest of all hunters; he and Yavanna alone of the Valar came at times to Middle-earth in the Elder Days. On Nahar his white horse he led the Elves on the great journey from Cuiviénen.

Ossë He is a Maia, a vassal of Ulmo, and is thus described in the *Valaquenta*:

> He is master of the seas that wash the shores of Middle-earth.
> He does not go in the deeps, but loves the coasts and the isles,
> and rejoices in the winds of Manwë; for in storm he delights,
> and laughs amid the roaring of the waves.

Othrod A lord of Orcs, slain by Tuor.

Outer Lands The lands east of the Great Sea (Middle-earth).

Outer Seas I quote from a passage in a text named *Ambarkanta* ('Shape of the World') of the 1930s, probably later than the *Quenta Noldorinwa*: 'About all the world are the Ilurambar, or Walls of the World ['the final Wall' in the *Prologue*, p.24] ... They cannot be seen, nor can they be passed, save by the Door of Night. Within these Walls the Earth is globed: above, below, and upon all sides is *Vaiya*, the Enfolding Ocean [which is the *Outer Sea*]. But this is more like to sea below the Earth and more like to air above the Earth. In *Vaiya* below the Earth dwells Ulmo.'

In the *Lost Tale* of *The Coming of the Valar* Rúmil, who tells the tale, says: 'Beyond Valinor I have never seen or heard, save that of a surety there are the dark waters of the Outer Seas, that have no tides, and they are very cool and thin, that no boat can sail upon their bosom or fish swim within their depths, save the enchanted fish of Ulmo and his magic car.'

Outer World, Outer Earth   The lands east of the Great Sea (Middle-earth).

Palisor   The distant land in the East of Middle-earth where the Elves awoke.

Palúrien   A name of Yavanna; both names are often conjoined. *Palúrien* was replaced later by *Kementári*; both names bear such meanings as 'Queen of the Earth', 'Lady of the Wide Earth'.

Peleg son of Indor son of Fengel   Peleg was the father of Tuor in the first genealogy. (See *Tunglin*)

Pelóri   See *Mountains of Valinor*.

Penlod   Lord of the peoples of the Pillar and the Tower of Snow in Gondolin.

The Pillar   Name of one of the kindreds of the Gondothlim. See *Penlod*.

Prophecy of Mandos   See note on p.299.

Quendi   An early name for all Elves, meaning 'Those who have voices'; later, the name of the first of the three hosts on the great journey from Cuiviénen. See *Light-elves*.

Rían   Wife of Huor, mother of Tuor; died in Anfauglith after the death of Huor.

Rog   Lord of the people of the Hammer of Wrath in Gondolin.

Salgant   Lord of the people of the Harp in Gondolin. Described as 'a craven'.

Sea-elves   A name of the third host of the Elves on the great journey from Cuiviénen. See *Teleri*, and the note on p.300.

Silpion   The White Tree; see *Trees of Valinor* and *Telperion*.

Sindar   See *Grey-elves*.

*Sirion**   The Great River that rose at Eithel Sirion ('Sirion's Well') and dividing West from East Beleriand flowed into the Great Sea in the Bay of Balar.

Sorontur   'King of Eagles'. See *Thorondor*.

The Stricken Anvil   Emblem of the people of the Hammer of Wrath in Gondolin.

Súlimë   The third month, corresponding to March.

Súlimo   This name, referring to Manwë as a wind-god, is very frequently attached to his name. He is called 'Lord of the Airs'; but only once does there seem to be a translation specifically of *Súlimo*: 'Lord of the Breath of Arda'. Related words are *súya* 'breath' and *súle* 'breathe'.

The Swallow   Name of one of the kindreds of the Gondothlim.

Swanhaven   The chief city of the Teleri (Sea-elves), on the coast north of Kôr. Elvish *Alqualondë*.

Taniquetil   The highest of the Pelóri (the Mountains of Valinor) and the highest mountain of Arda, on which Manwë and Varda had their dwelling (Ilmarin).

Taras   A great mountain on the western headland of Nevrast, beyond which was Vinyamar.

Tarnin Austa   'The Gates of Summer', a festival in Gondolin.

*Taur-na-Fuin**   'Forest of Night', previously called *Dorthonion* 'Land of Pines', the great forested highlands to the north of Beleriand.

*Teiglin**   A tributary of Sirion, rising in Ered Wethrin.

Teleri   The third host of the Elves on the great journey from Cuiviénen.

Telperion   Name of the White Tree of Valinor.

Thingol A leader of the third host (Teleri) on the great journey from Cuiviénen; his earlier name *Tinwelint*. He never came to Kôr, but became the King of Doriath in Beleriand.

Thorn Sir Falling stream below Cristhorn.

Thornhoth 'The people of the Eagles'.

Thorondor 'King of Eagles', Gnomish name of Eldarin *Sorontur*; earlier form *Thorndor*.

Thousand Caves *Menegroth*, the hidden halls of Thingol and Melian.

Timbrenting The Old English name of Taniquetil.

The Tower of Snow Name of one of the kindreds of the Gondothlim. See *Penlod*.

The Tree Name of one of the kindreds of the Gondothlim. See *Galdor*.

Trees of Valinor *Silpion* the White Tree and *Laurelin* the Golden Tree; see p.24, where they are described, and *Glingol and Bansil*.

Tulkas Of this Vala, 'the greatest in strength and deeds of prowess', it is said in the *Valaquenta*:

> He came last to Arda, to aid the Valar in the first battles with Melkor. He delights in wrestling and in contests of strength; and he rides no steed, for he can outrun all things that go on feet, and he is tireless. He has little heed for either the past or the future, and is of no avail as a counsellor, but is a hardy friend.

Tumladen 'Valley of smoothness', the 'Guarded Plain' of Gondolin.

Tûn The Elvish city in Valinor; see *Kôr*.

Tunglin 'The folk of the Harp': in an early and soon abandoned text of *The Fall of Gondolin* a name given to the people living in Hithlum after the Battle of Unnumbered Tears. Tuor was of that people (see *Peleg*).

Tuor Tuor was a descendant (great-grandson) of the renowned Hador Lórindol ('Hador Goldenhead'). In *The Lay of Leithian* it is said of Beren:

As fearless Beren was renowned:
when men most hardy upon ground
were reckoned folk would speak his name,
foretelling that his after-fame
would even golden Hador pass ...

To Hador was given the lordship of Dor-lómin by Fingolfin, and his successors were the House of Hador. Tuor's father Huor was slain in the Battle of Unnumbered Tears, and his mother, Rían, died of grief. Huor and Húrin were brothers, the sons of Galdor of Dor-lómin, son of Hador; and Húrin was the father of Túrin Turambar; thus Tuor and Túrin were first cousins. But only once did they meet, and they did not know each other as they passed: this is told in *The Fall of Gondolin*.

Turgon The second son of Fingolfin, founder and king of Gondolin, father of Idril.

Turlin A name briefly preceding *Tuor*.

Uinen 'Lady of the Seas'; a Maia, the spouse of Ossë. This is said of her in the text named *Valaquenta*:

> [Her] hair lies spread through all waters under sky. All creatures she loves that live in the salt streams, and all weeds that grow there; to her mariners cry, for she can lay calm upon the waves, restraining the wildness of Ossë.

Uldor the accursed He was a leader among certain Men moving into the West of Middle-earth who treacherously allied themselves with Morgoth in the Battle of Unnumbered Tears.

Ulmo The following text is taken from the portrait of the great Vala, who was 'next in might to Manwë', from the text named *Valaquenta*, an account of each individual Vala.

> [Ulmo] kept all Arda in thought, and he has no need of any resting-place. Moreover he does not love to walk upon land, and will seldom clothe himself in a body after the manner of his peers. If [Men or Elves] beheld him they were filled with a great dread; for the arising of the King of the Sea was terrible, as a mounting wave that strides to the land, with dark helm

foam-crested and raiment of mail shimmering from silver down into shadows of green. The trumpets of Manwë are loud, but Ulmo's voice is deep as the deeps of the ocean which he only has seen.

Nonetheless Ulmo loves both Elves and Men, and never abandoned them, not even when they lay under the wrath of the Valar. At times he will come unseen to the shores of Middle-earth, or pass far inland up firths of the sea, and there make music upon his great horns, the Ulumúri, that are wrought of white shell; and those to whom that music comes hear it ever after in their hearts, and longing for the sea never leaves them again. But mostly Ulmo speaks to those who dwell in Middle-earth with voices that are heard only as the music of water. For all seas, lakes, rivers, fountains and springs are in his government; so that the Elves say that the spirit of Ulmo runs in all the veins of the world. Thus news comes to Ulmo, even in the deeps, of all the needs and griefs of Arda.

Ulmonan   Ulmo's halls in the Outer Sea.

Ungoliant   The great spider, called Gloomweaver, who dwelt in Arvalin. This is said of Ungoliant in the *Quenta Noldorinwa*: There [in Arvalin] secret and unknown dwelt Ungoliant, Gloomweaver, in spider's form. It is not told whence she is, from the outer darkness, maybe, that lies beyond the Walls of the World [see *Outer Seas*].

Valar   The ruling powers of Arda; sometimes referred to as 'the Powers'. In the beginning there were nine Valar, as stated in the *Sketch*, but Melkor (Morgoth) ceased to be numbered among them.

Valinor   The land of the Valar in Aman. See *Mountains of Valinor.*

Valmar   The city of the Valar in Valinor.

Vána   A 'Queen of the Valar', spouse of Oromë; called 'the Ever-Young'.

Varda   Spouse of Manwë, with whom she dwelt on Taniquetil;

greatest of the Queens of the Valar; maker of the stars. In Gnomish her name was *Bredhil* or *Bridhil*.

*Vinyamar** The house of Turgon in Nevrast under Mount Taras before his departure to Gondolin.

Voronwë Elf of Gondolin, the only mariner to survive from the seven ships sent into the West by Turgon after the Nirnaeth Arnoediad, who guided Tuor to the hidden city. The name means 'steadfast'.

The Way of Escape The tunnel under the Encircling Mountains leading into the plain of Gondolin. Elvish name *Bad Uthwen*.

The Western Sea(s) See *Great Sea*.

The Wing Emblem of Tuor and his followers.

Wingelot 'Foam-flower', the ship of Eärendel.

Yavanna After Varda, Yavanna was the greatest of the Queens of the Valar. She was 'the Giver of Fruits' (the meaning of her name) and 'the lover of all things that grow in the earth'. Yavanna brought into being the Trees that gave light to Valinor, growing near the gates of Valmar. See *Palúrien*.

Ylmir Gnomish form for *Ulmo*.

ADDITIONAL NOTES

Ainur

The name *Ainur*, translated 'the Holy Ones', derives from my father's myth of the Creation of the World. He set down the original conception, according to a letter of 1964 (from which I have cited a passage on p.21), when at Oxford he was 'employed on the staff of the then still incomplete great Dictionary' from 1918–20. 'In Oxford', the letter continues, 'I wrote a cosmogonical myth, "The Music of the Ainur", defining the relation of The One, the transcendental Creator, to the Valar, the "Powers", the angelical First-created, and their part in ordering and carrying out the Primeval Design.'

It may seem an excessive departure from the tale of the Fall of Gondolin to his myth of the Creation of the World, but I hope it will soon be apparent why I have made it.

The central conception of the 'cosmogonical myth' is

declared in the title: *The Music of the Ainur*. It was not until the 1930s that my father composed a further version, the *Ainulindalë* (The Music of the Ainur), in substance closely following the original text. It is from this version that I have taken the quotations in the very brief account that follows.

The Creator is Eru, the One, also and more frequently named Ilúvatar, meaning 'the Father of All', of the Universe. It is told in this work that before all else Eru made the Ainur 'that were the offspring of his thought, and they were with him before Time. And he spoke to them, propounding to them themes of music. And they sang before him, each one alone, while the rest hearkened.' This was the beginning of the Music of the Ainur: for Ilúvatar summoned them all, and he declared to them a mighty theme, of which they must make in harmony together 'a Great Music'.

When Ilúvatar brought this great music to an end he made it known to the Ainur that he being the Lord of All had transformed all that they had sung and played: he had caused them to be: to have shape and reality, as had the Ainur themselves. He led them then out into the darkness.

But when they came into the midmost Void they beheld a sight of surpassing beauty, where before had been emptiness. And Ilúvatar said: 'Behold your music! For of my will it has taken shape, and even now the history of the world is beginning.'

I conclude this account with a passage of great significance in this book. There is speech between Ilúvatar and Ulmo concerning the realm of the Lord of Waters. Then follows:

And even as Ilúvatar spoke to Ulmo, the Ainur beheld the unfolding of the world, and the beginning of that history which Ilúvatar had propounded to them as a theme of song. Because of their memory of the speech of Ilúvatar, and the knowledge that each has of the music which he played, the Ainur know much of what is to come, and few things are unforeseen by them.

If we set this passage beside the foresight of Ulmo concerning Eärendel, which I have characterised (p.230) as 'miraculous', it seems that Ulmo was looking very far back in time to know for a certainty what the near future was portending.

There remains a further aspect of the Ainur to notice. To quote the *Ainulindalë* once more, it is told that

Even as they gazed, many became enamoured of the beauty of the world and engrossed in the history which came there to being, and there was unrest among them. Thus it came to pass that some abode still with Ilúvatar beyond the world ... But others, and among them were many of the wisest and fairest of the Ainur, craved leave of Ilúvatar to enter into the world and dwell there, and put on the form and raiment of Time ...

Then those that wished descended, and entered into the world. But this condition Ilúvatar made, that their power should thenceforth be contained and bounded by the world, and fail with it; and his purpose with them afterward Ilúvatar has not revealed.

Thus the Ainur came into the world, whom we call the Valar, or the Powers, and they dwelt in many places: in the firmament, or in the deeps of the sea, or upon Earth, or in Valinor upon the borders of Earth. And the four greatest were Melko and Manwë and Ulmo and Aulë.

This is followed by the portrait of Ulmo that is given in *The Music of the Ainur* (p.234).

It follows from the foregoing that the term *Ainur*, singular *Ainu*, may be used in the place of *Valar*, *Vala* now and again: so for example 'but the Ainur put it into his heart', p.40.

I must add finally that in this sketch of the Music of the Ainur I have deliberately omitted a major strand in the story of the Creation: the huge and destructive part played by Melko/Morgoth.

Húrin and Gondolin

This story is found in the relatively late text which my father called the *Grey Annals* (see p.220). It tells that Húrin and his brother Huor (the father of Tuor) 'went both to battle with the Orcs, even Huor, for he would not be restrained, though he was but thirteen years of age. And being with a company that was cut off from the rest, they were pursued to the ford of Brithiach; and there they would have been taken or slain, but for the power of Ulmo, which was still strong in Sirion. Therefore a mist arose from the river and hid them from their enemies, and they escaped into Dimbar, and wandered in the hills beneath the sheer walls of the Crissaegrim. There Thorondor espied them, and sent two Eagles that took them and bore them up and brought them beyond the mountains to the secret vale of Tumladen and the hidden city of Gondolin, which no man else yet had seen.'

King Turgon welcomed them, for Ulmo had counselled him to deal kindly with the house of Hador whence help should come at need. They dwelt in Gondor a year, and it is said that at this time Húrin learned something of the counsels and purposes of Turgon; for he had great liking for them, and wished to keep them in Gondolin. But they desired to return to their own kin, and share in the wars and griefs that now beset them. Turgon yielded to their wish and he said: 'By the way that you came you have leave to depart, if Thorondor is willing. I grieve at this parting, yet in a little while, as the Eldar account it, we may meet again.'

The story ends with the hostile words of Maeglin, who greatly opposed the king's generosity towards them. 'The law is become less stern than aforetime,' he said, 'or else no choice would be given you but to abide here to your life's end.' To this Húrin replied that if Maeglin did not trust them, they would take oaths; and they swore never to reveal the counsels of Turgon and to keep secret all that they had seen in his realm.

Years later Tuor would say to Voronwë, as they stood beside the sea at Vinyamar (p.171): 'But as for my right to seek Turgon: I am Tuor son of Huor and kin to Húrin, whose names Turgon will not forget.'

*

Húrin was taken alive in the Battle of Unnumbered Tears. Morgoth offered him his freedom, or else power as the greatest of Morgoth's captains, 'if he would but reveal where Turgon had his stronghold'. This proposal Húrin refused to Morgoth's face with the utmost boldness and scorn. Then Morgoth set him in a high place of Thangorodrim, to sit there upon a chair of stone; and he said to Húrin that seeing with the eyes of Morgoth he should look out upon the evil fates of those he loved and nothing would escape him. Húrin endured this for twenty-eight years. At the end of that time Morgoth released him. He feigned that he was moved by pity for an enemy utterly defeated, but he lied. He had further evil purpose; and Húrin knew that Morgoth was without pity. But he took his freedom. In the extension of the *Grey Annals* in which this story is told, 'The Wanderings of Húrin', he came at length to the Echoriath, the Encircling Mountains of Gondolin. But he could find no way further, and he stood at last in despair 'before the stern silence of the mountains ... He stood at last upon a great stone, and spreading wide his arms, looking towards Gondolin, he called in a great voice: "Turgon! Húrin calls you. O Turgon, will you not hear in your hidden halls?" But there was no answer, and all that he heard was wind in the dry grasses ... Yet there were ears that had heard the words that Húrin spoke, and eyes that marked well his gestures; and report of all came soon to the Dark Throne in the North. Then Morgoth smiled, and knew now clearly in what region Turgon dwelt, though because of the Eagles no spy of his could yet come within sight of the land behind the encircling mountains.'

So here again we meet my father's shifting perception of how Morgoth discovered where the Hidden Kingdom lay (see pp.126–7). The story in the present text is clearly at odds with the passage in the *Quenta Noldorinwa* (p.140), where the treachery of Maeglin, taken prisoner by the Orcs, is told in this clear form: 'he purchased his life and freedom by revealing unto Morgoth the place of Gondolin and the ways whereby it might be found and assailed. Great indeed was the joy of Morgoth . . .'

The story was in fact, I think, now taking a further step in the light of the end of the passage given above, where Húrin's cries revealed the place of Gondolin 'to the joy of Morgoth'. This is seen from what my father added at this point in the manuscript:

> Later when captured and Maeglin wished to buy his release with treachery, Morgoth must answer laughing, saying: 'Stale news will buy nothing. I know this already, I am not easily blinded!' So Maeglin was obliged to offer more - to undermine resistance in Gondolin.

Iron Mountains

At first sight it appeared from early texts that *Hisilómë* (*Hithlum*) was a region distinct from the later Hithlum, since it was placed *beyond* the Iron Mountains. I concluded however that what was involved was simply a change of names, and this is certainly the truth of the matter. It is told elsewhere in the *Lost Tales* that after the escape of Melko from his imprisonment in Valinor he made for himself 'new dwellings in that region of the North where stand the Iron Mountains very high and terrible to see'; and also that Angband lay beneath the roots of the northernmost fortresses of the Iron Mountains: those mountains were so named from 'the Hells of Iron' beneath them.

The explanation is that the name 'Mountains of Iron' was originally applied to the range later called 'Shadowy Mountains' or 'Mountains of Shadow', *Ered Wethrin*. (It might be that while these mountains were regarded as a continuous range, the southern extension, the southern and eastern walls of Hithlum, came to be distinguished in name from the terrible northern peaks above Angband, the mightiest of them being Thangorodrim.)

Unhappily I failed to alter the List of Names in the entry *Hisilómë* in *Beren and Lúthien*, which states that that region owes its name to 'the scanty sun which peeps over the Iron Mountains to the east and south of it.' At p.43 in the present text I have replaced 'Iron' by 'Shadowy'.

Nirnaeth Arnoediad: The Battle of
Unnumbered Tears

It is said in the *Quenta Noldorinwa*:

> Now it must be told that Maidros, son of Fëanor, perceived
> that Morgoth was not unassailable after the deeds of Huan
> and Lúthien and the breaking of the towers of Thû [Tol
> Sirion, Isle of Werewolves; later > Sauron's tower], but that
> he would destroy them all, one by one, if they did not form
> again a league and council. This was the Union of Maidros
> and wisely planned.

The gigantic battle that ensued was the most disastrous
in the history of the wars of Beleriand. References to the
Nirnaeth Arnoediad abound in the texts, for Elves and
Men were utterly defeated and the ruin of the Noldor was
achieved. Fingon, king of the Noldor, a son of Fingolfin and
brother of Turgon was slain, and his realm was no more. But
a very notable event, early in the battle, was the intervention
of Turgon, breaking the leaguer of Gondolin: this event is
told thus in the *Grey Annals* (on which see *The Evolution of
the Story* p.220):

> To the joy and wonder of all there was a sounding of great
> trumpets, and there marched up to war a host unlooked
> for. This was the army of Turgon that issued from Gondo-
> lin, ten thousand strong, with bright mail and long swords,

and they were stationed southwards guarding the passes of Sirion.

There is also in the *Grey Annals* a very noteworthy passage on the subject of Turgon and Morgoth.

> But one thought troubled Morgoth deeply, and marred his triumph; Turgon had escaped the net, whom he most desired to take. For Turgon came of the great house of Fingolfin, and was now by right King of all the Noldor, and Morgoth feared and hated most the house of Fingolfin, because they had scorned him in Valinor, and had the friendship of Ulmo, and because of the wounds that Fingolfin gave him in battle. Moreover of old his eye had lighted on Turgon, and a dark shadow fell on his heart, foreboding that, in some time that lay yet hidden in doom, from Turgon ruin should come to him.

The Origins of Eärendel

The text that follows here is derived from a lengthy letter written by my father in 1967 on the subject of his construction of names within his history and his adoption of names exterior to his history.

He remarked at the outset that the name *Eärendil* (the later form) was very plainly derived from the Old English word *Éarendel* – a word that he felt to be of peculiar beauty in that language. 'Also' (he continued) 'its form strongly suggests that it is in origin a proper name and not a common noun.' From related forms in other languages he thought it certain that it belonged to astronomical myth, and was the name of a star or star-group.

'To my mind', he wrote, 'the Old English uses seem plainly to indicate that it was a star presaging the dawn (at any rate in English tradition): that is what we call *Venus*: the morning star as it may be seen shining brilliantly in the dawn, before the actual rising of the Sun. That is at any rate how I took it. Before 1914 I wrote a "poem" upon Eärendel who launched his ship like a bright spark from the havens of the Sun. I adopted him into my mythology – in which he became a prime figure as a mariner, eventually as a herald star, and a sign of hope to men. *Aiya Eärendil Elenion Ancalima* "hail Eärendel brightest of Stars" is derived at long remove from *Éala Éarendel engla beorhtast*.'

It was indeed a long remove. These Old English words are taken from the poem *Crist*, which reads at this point *Éala! Éarendel engla beorhtast ofer middangeard monnum sended*. But, extraordinary as it seems at first sight, in the Elvish words *Aiya Eärendil Elenion Ancalima* cited by my father in this letter he was referring to a passage in the chapter *Shelob's Lair* in *The Lord of the Rings*. As Shelob approached Sam and Frodo in the darkness Sam cried out 'The Lady's gift! The star-glass! A light to you in dark places, she said it was to be. The star-glass!' In amazement at his forgetfulness 'slowly Frodo's hand went to his bosom, and slowly he held aloft the Phial of Galadriel' ... 'The darkness receded from it, until it seemed to shine in the centre of a globe of airy crystal, and the hand that held it sparkled with white fire.

'Frodo gazed in wonder at this marvellous gift that he had so long carried, not guessing its full worth and potency. Seldom had he remembered it on the road, until they came to Morgul Vale, and never had he used it for fear of its revealing light. *Aiya Eärendil Elenion Ancalima!* he cried, and knew not what he had spoken; for it seemed that another voice spoke through his, clear, untroubled by the foul air of the pit.'

In the letter of 1967 my father went on to say that 'the name could not be adopted just like that: it had to be accommodated to the Elvish linguistic situation, at the same time as a place for this person was made in legend. From this, far back in the history of "Elvish", which was beginning, after many tentative starts in boyhood, to take definite shape at the time of the name's adoption, arose eventually the Common Elvish stem AYAR "sea", primarily applied to the Great Sea of the West and the verbal element (N)DIL, meaning "to love, be devoted to". Eärendil became a character in the earliest written (1916–17) of the major legends ... Tuor had been visited by Ulmo one of the greatest Valar, the lord of seas and waters, and sent by him to Gondolin. The visitation had set in Tuor's heart an insatiable sea-longing, hence the choice of name for his son, to whom this longing was transmitted.'

The Prophecy of Mandos

In the extract from the *Sketch of the Mythology* given in the Prologue it is told (p.32) that as the Noldoli sailed from Valinor in their rebellion against the Valar Mandos sent an emissary, who speaking from a high cliff as they sailed by warned them to return, and when they refused he spoke the Prophecy of Mandos concerning their fate in afterdays. I give here a passage that gives an account of it. The text is the first version of *The Annals of Valinor* – the last version being the *Grey Annals* (see *The Evolution of the Story* p.220. This earliest version belongs to the same period as the *Quenta Noldorinwa*.

They [the departing Noldoli] came to a place where a high rock stands above the shores, and there stood either Mandos or his messenger and spoke the Doom of Mandos. For the kin-slaying he cursed the house of Fëanor, and to a less degree all who followed them, or shared in their emprise, unless they would return to abide the doom and pardon of the Valar. But if they would not, then should evil fortune and disaster befall them, and ever from treachery of kin towards kin; and their oath should turn against them; and a measure of mortality should visit them, that they should be lightly slain with weapons, or torments, or sorrow, and in the end fade and wane before the younger race. And much else he foretold darkly that after befell, warning them that the Valar would fence Valinor against their return.

But Fëanor hardened his heart and held on, and so also but reluctantly did Fingolfin's folk, feeling the constraint of their kindred and fearing for the doom of the Gods (for not all of Fingolfin's house had been guiltless of the kin-slaying).

See also the words of Ulmo to Tuor at Vinyamar, LV p.166.

The Three Kindreds of the Elves in The Hobbit

In *The Hobbit*, not far from the end of Chapter 8, *Flies and Spiders*, occurs this passage.

The feasting people were Wood-elves, of course ... They differed from the High Elves of the West, and were more dangerous and less wise. For most of them (together with their scattered relations in the hills and mountains) were descended from the ancient tribes that never went to Faerie in the West. There the Light-elves and the Deep-elves and the Sea-elves went and lived for ages, and grew fairer and wiser and more learned, and invented their magic and their cunning craft in the making of beautiful and marvellous things, before some came back into the Wide World.

These last words refer to the rebellious Noldor who left Valinor and in Middle-earth became known as the Exiles.

SHORT GLOSSARY OF OBSOLETE, ARCHAIC AND RARE WORDS

affray   attack, assault
ambuscaded   placed in *ambuscade,* ambushed
ardour   burning heat (of breath)
argent   silver or silvery-white
astonied   earlier form of *astonished*
bested   beset [also spelt *bestead*]
blow   bloom
boss   raised centre of a shield
broidure   embroidery
burg   a walled town
byrnie   coat of mail
car   chariot
carle   peasant or servant
chrysoprase   a golden-green precious stone
conch   shellfish used as a musical instrument or instrument
   of call
cravenhood   cowardice [apparently unique here]
damascened   etched or inlaid with gold or silver
descry   catch sight of
diapered   diamond-patterned
dight   arrayed
drake   dragon. Old English *draca.*
drolleries   something amusing or funny
emprise   enterprise
fain   gladly, willingly
fell   (1) cruel, terrible   (2) mountain
glistering   sparkling
greave   armour for the shin
hauberk   defensive armour, long tunic of chain-mail
illfavoured   having an unpleasant appearance; ugly

kirtle   garment reaching to the knees or lower
lappet   small fold of a garment
leaguer/-ed [lands] besiege/-d
lealty   faithfulness, loyalty
let   allowed (if occasion let, let fashion)
malachite   a green mineral
marges   margins or edges
mattock   two-headed agricultural tool
mead   meadow
meshed   entangled inextricably
plash   splash
plenished   filled up
puissance   power, strength, force
reck   take thought of
rede   counsel
repair   go frequently to
repast   food; meal, feast
rowan   mountain ash
ruth   sorrow, distress
sable   black
scathe   harm
sojourned   stayed
sward   expanse of short grass
swart   dark-hued
tarry/-ied   linger/-ed
thrall/thralldom   slave/slavery
twain   two
vambrace   armour for the fore-arm
weird   fate
whin   gorse
whortleberry   bilberry
writhen   twisted, arranged in coils

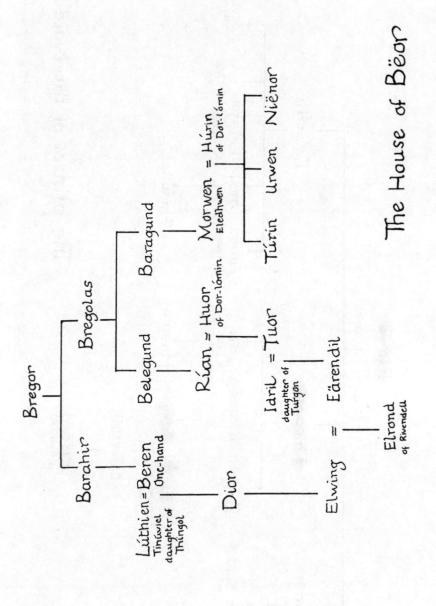

The House of Bëor

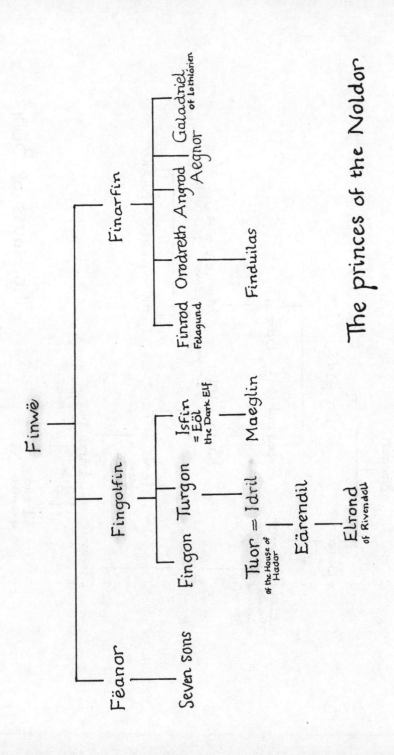

The princes of the Noldor

THE CHILDREN OF HÚRIN

WORKS BY J.R.R. TOLKIEN

THE HOBBIT
LEAF BY NIGGLE
ON FAIRY-STORIES
FARMER GILES OF HAM
THE HOMECOMING OF BEORHTNOTH
THE LORD OF THE RINGS
THE ADVENTURES OF TOM BOMBADIL
THE ROAD GOES EVER ON (WITH DONALD SWANN)
SMITH OF WOOTON MAJOR

WORKS PUBLISHED POSTHUMOUSLY

SIR GAWAIN AND THE GREEN KNIGHT, PEARL,
   AND SIR ORFEO
THE FATHER CHRISTMAS LETTERS
THE SILMARILLION
PICTURES BY J.R.R. TOLKIEN
UNFINISHED TALES
THE LETTERS OF J.R.R. TOLKIEN
FINN AND HENGEST
MR BLISS
THE MONSTERS AND THE CRITICS & OTHER ESSAYS
ROVERANDOM
THE CHILDREN OF HÚRIN
THE LEGEND OF SIGURD AND GUDRÚN
THE FALL OF ARTHUR
BEOWULF: A TRANSLATION AND COMMENTARY

THE HISTORY OF MIDDLE-EARTH
BY CHRISTOPHER TOLKIEN

I · THE BOOK OF LOST TALES, PART ONE
II · THE BOOK OF LOST TALES, PART TWO
III · THE LAYS OF BELERIAND
IV · THE SHAPING OF MIDDLE-EARTH
V · THE LOST ROAD AND OTHER WRITINGS
VI · THE RETURN OF THE SHADOW
VII · THE TREASON OF ISENGARD
VIII · THE WAR OF THE RING
IX · SAURON DEFEATED
X · MORGOTH'S RING
XI · THE WAR OF THE JEWELS
XII · THE PEOPLES OF MIDDLE-EARTH

NARN I CHÎN HÚRIN

The Tale of the Children of Húrin

J.R.R. TOLKIEN

Edited by Christopher Tolkien

Illustrated by Alan Lee

HOUGHTON MIFFLIN HARCOURT

BOSTON • NEW YORK

To
BAILLIE TOLKIEN

First published in Great Britain by HarperCollins Publishers, 2007

For information about permission to reproduce selections from this book, write to
trade.permissions@hmhco.com or to Permissions, Houghton Mifflin Harcourt
Publishing Company,3 Park Avenue, 19th Floor, New York, New York 10016.

www.hmhco.com

Library of Congress Cataloging-in-Publication Data
Tolkien, J. R. R. (John Ronald Reuel), date.
Narn i chîn Húrin : the tale of the children of Húrin / by J.R.R.
Tolkien ; edited by Christopher Tolkien ; illustrated by Alan Lee.
p. cm.
Includes index.
ISBN 978-0-618-89464-2
ISBN 978-0-618-90441-9 (deluxe edition)
1. Middle Earth (Imaginary place) — Fiction. I. Tolkien, Christopher.
II. Title.
PR6039.032N37 2007
823'.912 — dc22   2007001420

Printed in the United States of America
22 23 24 25 26 LSB 23 22 21 20 19

CONTENTS

PREFACE

It is undeniable that there are a very great many readers of *The Lord of the Rings* for whom the legends of the Elder Days (as previously published in varying forms in *The Silmarillion, Unfinished Tales,* and *The History of Middle-earth*) are altogether unknown, unless by their repute as strange and inaccessible in mode and manner. For this reason it has seemed to me for a long time that there was a good case for presenting my father's long version of the legend of the Children of Húrin as an independent work, between its own covers, with a minimum of editorial presence, and above all in continuous narrative without gaps or interruptions, if this could be done without distortion or invention, despite the unfinished state in which he left some parts of it.

I have thought that if the story of the fate of Túrin and Niënor, the children of Húrin and Morwen, could be presented in this way, a window might be opened onto a scene and a story set in an unknown Middle-earth that are vivid and immediate, yet conceived as handed down from remote ages: the drowned lands in the west beyond the Blue Mountains where Treebeard walked in his youth, and the life of Túrin Turambar, in Dor-lómin, Doriath, Nargothrond, and the Forest of Brethil.

This book is thus primarily addressed to such readers as may perhaps recall that the hide of Shelob was so horrendously hard that it 'could not be pierced by any strength of men, not though Elf or Dwarf should forge the steel or the hand of Beren or of Túrin wield it', or that Elrond named Túrin to Frodo at Rivendell as one of 'the mighty Elf-friends of old'; but know no more of him.

When my father was a young man, during the years of the First World War and long before there was any inkling of the tales that were to form the narrative of *The Hobbit* or *The Lord of the Rings*, he began the writing of a collection of stories that he called *The Book of Lost Tales*. That was his first work of imaginative literature, and a substantial one, for though it was left unfinished there are fourteen completed tales. It was in *The Book of Lost Tales* that there first appeared in narrative the Gods, or Valar; Elves and Men as the Children of Ilúvatar (the Creator); Melkor-Morgoth the great Enemy; Balrogs and Orcs; and the lands in which the Tales are set, Valinor 'land of the Gods' beyond the western ocean, and the 'Great Lands' (afterwards called 'Middle-earth', between the seas of east and west).

Among the *Lost Tales* three were of much greater length and fullness, and all three are concerned with Men as well as Elves: they are *The Tale of Tinúviel* (which appears in brief form in *The Lord of the Rings* as the story of Beren and Lúthien that Aragorn told to the hobbits on Weathertop; this my father wrote in 1917), *Turambar and the Foalókë* (Túrin Turambar and the Dragon, certainly in existence by 1919, if not before), and *The Fall of Gondolin* (1916–17). In an often-quoted passage of a long letter describing his work that my father wrote in 1951, three years before the publication of *The Fellowship of the Ring*, he told of his early ambition: 'once upon a time (my crest has long since fallen) I had a mind to make a body of more or less connected legend, ranging from the large and cosmogonic, to the level of romantic fairy-story – the larger founded on the lesser in contact with the earth, the lesser drawing splendour from the vast backcloths . . . I would draw some of the great tales in fullness, and leave many only placed in the scheme, and sketched.'

It is seen from this reminiscence that from far back it was a part of his conception of what came to be called *The Silmarillion* that some of the 'Tales' should be told in much fuller form; and indeed in that same letter of 1951 he referred expressly to the three stories which I have mentioned above as being much the longest in *The Book of Lost Tales.* Here he called the tale of Beren and Lúthien 'the chief of the stories of *The Silmarillion*', and of it he said: 'the story is (I think a beautiful and powerful) heroic-fairy-romance, receivable in itself with only a very general vague knowledge of the background. But it is also a fundamental link in the cycle, deprived of its full significance out of its place therein.' 'There are other stories almost equally full in treatment,' he went on, 'and equally independent, and yet linked to the general history': these are *The Children of Húrin* and *The Fall of Gondolin.*

It thus seems unquestionable, from my father's own words, that if he could achieve final and finished narratives on the scale he desired, he saw the three 'Great Tales' of the Elder Days (Beren and Lúthien, the Children of Húrin, and the Fall of Gondolin) as works sufficiently complete in themselves as not to demand knowledge of the great body of legend known as *The Silmarillion.* On the other hand, as my father observed in the same place, the tale of the Children of Húrin is integral to the history of Elves and Men in the Elder Days, and there are necessarily a good many references to events and circumstances in that larger story.

It would be altogether contrary to the conception of this book to burden its reading with an abundance of notes giving information about persons and events that are in any case seldom of real importance to the immediate narrative. However, it may be found helpful here and there if some such assistance is provided, and I have accordingly given in the Introduction a very brief sketch of Beleriand and its peoples near the end of the Elder Days, when Túrin and Niënor were born; and, as well as a map of Beleriand and the lands to the North, I have included a list of all names occurring in the text with very concise indications concerning each, and simplified genealogies.

At the end of the book is an Appendix in two parts: the first concerned with my father's attempts to achieve a final form for the three tales, and the second with the composition of the text in this book, which differs in many respects from that in *Unfinished Tales*.

I am very grateful to my son Adam Tolkien for his indispensable help in the arrangement and presentation of the material in the Introduction and Appendix, and for easing the book into the (to me) daunting world of electronic transmission.

INTRODUCTION

Middle-earth in the Elder Days

The character of Túrin was of deep significance to my father, and in dialogue of directness and immediacy he achieved a poignant portrait of his boyhood, essential to the whole: his severity and lack of gaiety, his sense of justice and his compassion; of Húrin also, quick, gay, and sanguine, and of Morwen his mother, reserved, courageous, and proud; and of the life of the household in the cold country of Dorlómin during the years, already full of fear, after Morgoth broke the Siege of Angband, before Túrin was born.

But all this was in the Elder Days, the First Age of the world, in a time unimaginably remote. The depth in time to which this story reaches back was memorably conveyed in a passage in *The Lord of the Rings*. At the great council in Rivendell Elrond spoke of the Last Alliance of

Elves and Men and the defeat of Sauron at the end of the
Second Age, more than three thousand years before:

> Thereupon Elrond paused a while and sighed. 'I
> remember well the splendour of their banners,' he said.
> 'It recalled to me the glory of the Elder Days and the hosts
> of Beleriand, so many great princes and captains were
> assembled. And yet not so many, nor so fair, as when
> Thangorodrim was broken, and the Elves deemed that evil
> was ended for ever, and it was not so.'
>
> 'You remember?' said Frodo, speaking his thought
> aloud in his astonishment. 'But I thought,' he stammered
> as Elrond turned towards him, 'I thought that the fall of
> Gil-galad was a long age ago.'
>
> 'So it was indeed,' answered Elrond gravely. 'But my
> memory reaches back even to the Elder Days. Eärendil was
> my sire, who was born in Gondolin before its fall; and my
> mother was Elwing, daughter of Dior, son of Lúthien of
> Doriath. I have seen three ages in the West of the world, and
> many defeats, and many fruitless victories.'

Some six and a half thousand years before the Council
of Elrond was held in Rivendell, Túrin was born in Dor-
lómin, 'in the winter of the year,' as is recorded in the
Annals of Beleriand, 'with omens of sorrow'.
But the tragedy of his life is by no means comprehended solely in the portrayal of character, for he was
condemned to live trapped in a malediction of huge and
mysterious power, the curse of hatred set by Morgoth

upon Húrin and Morwen and their children, because
Húrin defied him, and refused his will. And Morgoth, the
Black Enemy, as he came to be called, was in his origin, as
he declared to Húrin brought captive before him, 'Melkor,
first and mightiest of the Valar, who was before the
world.' Now become permanently incarnate, in form a
gigantic and majestic, but terrible, King in the north-west
of Middle-earth, he was physically present in his huge
fortress of Angband, the Hells of Iron: the black reek that
issued from the summits of Thangorodrim, the mountains
that he piled above Angband, could be seen far off staining the northern sky. It is said in the *Annals of Beleriand*
that 'the gates of Morgoth were but one hundred and fifty
leagues distant from the bridge of Menegroth; far and yet
all too near.' These words refer to the bridge leading to the
dwellings of the Elvish king Thingol, who took Túrin to
be his fosterson: they were called Menegroth, the Thousand Caves, far south and east of Dor-lómin.

But being incarnate Morgoth was afraid. My father
wrote of him: 'As he grew in malice, and sent forth from
himself the evil that he conceived in lies and creatures of
wickedness, his power passed into them and was dispersed, and he himself became ever more earth-bound,
unwilling to issue from his dark strongholds.' Thus when
Fingolfin, High King of the Noldorin Elves, rode alone to
Angband to challenge Morgoth to combat, he cried at the
gate: 'Come forth, thou coward king, to fight with thine

own hand! Den-dweller, wielder of thralls, liar and lurker, foe of Gods and Elves, come! For I would see thy craven face.' Then (it is told) 'Morgoth came. For he could not refuse such a challenge before the face of his captains.' He fought with the great hammer <u>Grond</u>, which at each blow made a great pit, and he beat Fingolfin to the ground; but as he died he pinned the great foot of Morgoth to the earth, 'and the black blood gushed forth and filled the pits of Grond. Morgoth went ever halt thereafter.' So also, <u>when Beren and Lúthien, in the shapes of a wolf and a bat, made their way into the deepest hall in Angband</u>, where Morgoth sat, <u>Lúthien cast a spell on him</u>: and 'suddenly he <u>fell, as a hill sliding in avalanche, and hurled like thunder from his throne</u> lay prone upon the floors of hell. The iron crown rolled echoing from his head.'

The curse of such a being, who can claim that 'the shadow of my purpose lies upon Arda [the Earth], and all that is in it bends slowly and surely to my will', is unlike the curses or imprecations of beings of far less power. Morgoth is not 'invoking' evil or calamity on Húrin and his children, he is not 'calling on' a higher power to be the agent: for he, 'Master of the fates of Arda' as he named himself to Húrin, intends to bring about the ruin of his enemy by the force of his own gigantic will. Thus he <u>'designs' the future of those whom he hates</u>, and so he says to Húrin: 'Upon all whom you love *my thought* shall weigh as *a cloud of Doom*, and it shall bring them down into darkness and despair.'

The torment that he devised for Húrin was 'to see with Morgoth's eyes'. My father gave a definition of what this meant: if one were forced to look into Morgoth's eye he would 'see' (or receive in his mind from Morgoth's mind) a compellingly credible picture of events, distorted by Morgoth's bottomless malice; and if indeed any could refuse Morgoth's command, Húrin did not. This was in part, my father said, because his love of his kin and his anguished anxiety for them made him desire to learn all that he could of them, no matter what the source; and in part from pride, believing that he had defeated Morgoth in debate, and that he could 'outstare' Morgoth, or at least retain his critical reason and distinguish between fact and malice.

Throughout Túrin's life from the time of his departure from Dor-lómin, and the life of his sister Niënor who never saw her father, this was the fate of Húrin, seated immovably in a high place of Thangorodrim in increasing bitterness inspired by his tormentor.

In the tale of Túrin, who named himself Turambar 'Master of Fate', the curse of Morgoth seems to be seen as power unleashed to work evil, seeking out its victims; so the fallen Vala himself is said to fear that Túrin 'would grow to such a power that the curse that he had laid upon him would become void, and he would escape the doom that had been designed for him' (p. 147). And afterwards in Nargothrond Túrin concealed his true name, so that when Gwindor revealed it he was angered: 'You have done ill to me, friend, to betray my right name, and call down my doom upon me, from which I would lie hid.' It was Gwindor who had told Túrin of the rumour that ran through Angband, where Gwindor had been held prisoner, that Morgoth had laid a curse on Húrin and all his kin. But now he replied to Túrin's wrath: 'the doom lies in yourself, not in your name.'

So essential is this complex conception in the story that my father even proposed an alternative title to it: *Narn e·'Rach Morgoth*, The Tale of the Curse of Morgoth. And his view of it is seen in these words: 'So ended the tale of Túrin the hapless; the worst of the works of Morgoth among Men in the ancient world.'

When Treebeard strode through the forest of Fangorn carrying Merry and Pippin each in the crook of his arm he sang to them of places that he had known in remote times, and of the trees that grew there:

> *In the willow-meads of Tasarinan I walked in the Spring.*
> *Ah! the sight and the smell of the Spring in Nan-tasarion!*
> *And I said that was good.*
> *I wandered in Summer in the elm-woods of Ossiriand.*
> *Ah! the light and the music in the Summer by the Seven*
> *   Rivers of Ossir!*
> *And I thought that was best.*
> *To the beeches of Neldoreth I came in the Autumn.*
> *Ah! the gold and the red and the sighing of leaves in the*
> *   Autumn in Taur-na-Neldor!*
> *It was more than my desire.*

To the pine-trees upon the highland of Dorthonion I
* climbed in the Winter.*
Ah! the wind and the whiteness and the black branches
* of Winter upon Orod-na-Thôn!*
My voice went up and sang in the sky.
And now all those lands lie under the wave,
And I walk in Ambarona, in Tauremorna, in Aldalómë,
In my own land, in the country of Fangorn,
Where the roots are long,
And the years lie thicker than the leaves
In Tauremornalómë.

The memory of Treebeard, 'Ent the earthborn, old as
mountains', was indeed long. He was remembering
ancient forests in the great country of Beleriand, which
was destroyed in the tumults of the Great Battle at the end
of the Elder Days. The Great Sea poured in and drowned
all the lands west of the Blue Mountains, called Ered Luin
and Ered Lindon: so that the map accompanying *The
Silmarillion* ends in the east with that mountain-chain,
whereas the map accompanying *The Lord of the Rings*
ends in the west with the same range; and the coastal lands
beyond the mountains named on that map Forlindon and
Harlindon (North Lindon and South Lindon) were all
that remained in the Third Age of the country called both
Ossiriand, Land of Seven Rivers, and also Lindon, in
whose elm-woods Treebeard once walked.

He walked also among the great pine-trees on the highland of Dorthonion ('Land of Pines'), which afterwards

came to be called Taur-nu-Fuin, 'the Forest under Night', when Morgoth turned it into 'a region of dread and dark enchantment, of wandering and despair' (p. 152); and he came to Neldoreth, the northern forest of Doriath, realm of Thingol.

It was in Beleriand and the lands to the north that Túrin's terrible destiny was played out; and indeed both Dorthonion and Doriath where Treebeard walked were crucial in his life. He was born into a world of warfare, though he was still a child when the last and greatest battle in the wars of Beleriand was fought. A very brief sketch of how this came about will answer questions that arise and references that are made in the course of the narrative.

In the north the boundaries of Beleriand seem to have been formed by the Ered Wethrin, the Mountains of Shadow, beyond which lay Húrin's country, Dor-lómin, a part of Hithlum; while in the east Beleriand extended to the feet of the Blue Mountains. Further east lay lands that scarcely appear in the history of the Elder Days; but the peoples that shaped that history came out of the east by the passes of the Blue Mountains.

The Elves appeared on earth far off in the distant east, beside a lake that was named Cuiviénen, Water of Awakening; and thence they were summoned by the Valar to leave Middle-earth, and passing over the Great Sea to come to the 'Blessed Realm' of Aman in the west of the world, the land of the Gods. Those who accepted the summons

were led on a great march across Middle-earth from Cuiviénen by the Vala Oromë, the Hunter, and they are called
the Eldar, the Elves of the Great Journey, the High Elves:
distinct from those who, refusing the summons, chose
Middle-earth for their land and their destiny. They are the
'lesser Elves', called Avari, the Unwilling.

But not all the Eldar, though they had crossed the Blue
Mountains, departed over the Sea; and those who
remained in Beleriand are named the Sindar, the Grey
Elves. Their high king was Thingol (which means 'Grey-
cloak'), who ruled from Menegroth, the Thousand Caves
in Doriath. And not all the Eldar who crossed the Great
Sea remained in the land of the Valar; for one of their great
kindreds, the Noldor (the 'Loremasters'), returned to
Middle-earth, and they are called the Exiles. The prime
mover in their rebellion against the Valar was Fëanor,
'Spirit of Fire': he was the eldest son of Finwë, who had
led the host of the Noldor from Cuiviénen, but was now
dead. This cardinal event in the history of the Elves was
thus briefly conveyed by my father in Appendix A to *The
Lord of the Rings*:

> Fëanor was the greatest of the Eldar in arts and lore,
> but also the proudest and most selfwilled. He wrought
> the Three Jewels, the *Silmarilli*, and filled them with
> the radiance of the Two Trees, Telperion and Laurelin,
> that gave light to the land of the Valar. The Jewels were
> coveted by Morgoth the Enemy, who stole them and, after

destroying the Trees, took them to Middle-earth, and guarded them in his great fortress of Thangorodrim [the mountains above Angband]. Against the will of the Valar Fëanor forsook the Blessed Realm and went in exile to Middle-earth, leading with him a great part of his people; for in his pride he purposed to recover the Jewels from Morgoth by force. Thereafter followed the hopeless war of the Eldar and the Edain against Thangorodrim, in which they were at last utterly defeated.

Fëanor was slain in battle soon after the return of the Noldor to Middle-earth, and his seven sons held wide lands in the east of Beleriand, between Dorthonion (Taur-nu-Fuin) and the Blue Mountains; but their power was destroyed in the terrible Battle of Unnumbered Tears which is described in *The Children of Húrin*, and thereafter 'the Sons of Fëanor wandered as leaves before the wind' (p. 61).

The second son of Finwë was Fingolfin (the half-brother of Fëanor), who was held the overlord of all the Noldor; and he with his son Fingon ruled Hithlum, which lay to the north and west of the great chain of Ered Wethrin, the Mountains of Shadow. Fingolfin dwelt in Mithrim, by the great lake of that name, while Fingon held Dor-lómin in the south of Hithlum. Their chief fortress was Barad Eithel (the Tower of the Well) at Eithel Sirion (Sirion's Well), where the river Sirion rose in the east face of the Mountains of Shadow: Sador, the old crippled servant of Húrin and Morwen, served as a soldier

there for many years, as he told Túrin (pp. 41–42). After
Fingolfin's death in single combat with Morgoth Fingon
became the High King of the Noldor in his stead. Túrin
saw him once, when he 'and many of his lords had ridden
through Dor-lómin and passed over the bridge of Nen
Lalaith, glittering in silver and white' (p. 40).

The second son of Fingolfin was Turgon. He dwelt at
first, after the return of the Noldor, in the house named
Vinyamar, beside the sea in the region of Nevrast, west of
Dor-lómin; but he built in secret the hidden city of Gondolin, which stood on a hill in the midst of the plain called
Tumladen, wholly surrounded by the Encircling Mountains, east of the river Sirion. When Gondolin was built,
after many years of labour, Turgon removed from Vinyamar and dwelt with his people, both Noldor and Sindar,
in Gondolin; and for centuries this Elvish redoubt of great
beauty was preserved in the most profound secrecy, its
only entry undiscoverable and heavily guarded, so that no
stranger could ever pass in; and Morgoth was unable to
learn where it lay. Not until the Battle of Unnumbered
Tears, when more than three hundred and fifty years had
passed since he left Vinyamar, did Turgon emerge with his
great army from Gondolin.

The third son of Finwë, the brother of Fingolfin and
half-brother of Fëanor, was Finarfin. He did not return to
Middle-earth, but his sons and daughter came with the host
of Fingolfin and his sons. The eldest son of Finarfin was
Finrod, who, inspired by the magnificence and beauty of

Menegroth in Doriath, founded the underground fortress-city of Nargothrond, for which he was named Felagund, interpreted to mean 'Lord of Caves' or 'Cave-hewer' in the tongue of the Dwarves. The doors of Nargothrond opened onto the gorge of the river Narog in West Beleriand, where that river passed through the high hills called Taur-en-Faroth, or the High Faroth; but Finrod's realm extended far and wide, east to the river Sirion, and west to the river Nenning that reached the sea at the haven of Eglarest. But Finrod was slain in the dungeons of Sauron, chief servant of Morgoth, and Orodreth, the second son of Finarfin, took the crown of Nargothrond: this took place in the year following the birth of Túrin in Dor-lómin.

The other sons of Finarfin, Angrod and Aegnor, vassals of their brother Finrod, dwelt on Dorthonion, looking northwards over the vast plain of Ard-galen. Galadriel, Finrod's sister, dwelt long in Doriath with Melian the Queen. Melian was a Maia, a spirit of great power who took human form and dwelt in the forests of Beleriand with King Thingol: she was the mother of Lúthien, and the fore-mother of Elrond. Not long before the return of the Noldor from Aman, when great armies out of Angband came south into Beleriand, Melian (in the words of *The Silmarillion*) 'put forth her power and fenced all that dominion [the forests of Neldoreth and Region] round about with an unseen wall of shadow and bewilderment: the Girdle of Melian, that none thereafter could pass against her will or the will of King Thingol, unless one should come with a

24

power greater than that of Melian the Maia.' Thereafter the land was named Doriath, 'the Land of the Fence'.

In the sixtieth year after the return of the Noldor, ending many years of peace, a great host of Orcs came down from Angband, but was utterly defeated and destroyed by the Noldor. This was called *Dagor Aglareb*, the Glorious Battle; but the Elvish lords took warning from it, and set the Siege of Angband, which lasted for almost four hundred years.

It was said that Men (whom the Elves called *Atani* 'the Second', and *Hildor* 'the Followers') arose far off in the east of Middle-earth towards the end of the Elder Days; but of their earliest history the Men who entered Beleriand in the days of the Long Peace, when Angband was besieged and its gates shut, would never speak. The leader of these first Men to cross the Blue Mountains was named Bëor the Old; and to Finrod Felagund, King of Nargothrond, who first encountered them Bëor declared: 'A darkness lies behind us; and we have turned our backs on it, and we do not desire to return thither even in thought. Westwards our hearts have been turned, and we believe that there we shall find Light.' Sador, the old servant of Húrin, spoke in the same way to Túrin in his boyhood (p. 43). But it was said afterwards that when Morgoth learned of the arising of Men he left Angband for the last time and went into the East; and that the first Men to enter Beleriand 'had repented and rebelled against the Dark

Power, and were cruelly hunted and oppressed by those that worshipped it, and its servants'.

These Men belonged to three Houses, known as the House of Bëor, the House of Hador, and the House of Haleth. Húrin's father Galdor the Tall was of the House of Hador, being indeed his son; but his mother was of the House of Haleth, while Morwen his wife was of the House of Bëor, and related to Beren.

The people of the Three Houses were the *Edain* (the Sindarin form of *Atani*), and they were called Elf-friends. Hador dwelt in Hithlum and was given the lordship of Dor-lómin by King Fingolfin; the people of Bëor settled in Dorthonion; and the people of Haleth at this time dwelt in the Forest of Brethil. After the ending of the Siege of Angband Men of a very different sort came over the mountains; they were commonly referred to as Easterlings, and some of them played an important part in the story of Túrin.

The Siege of Angband ended with a terrible suddenness (though long prepared) on a night of midwinter, 395 years after it had begun. Morgoth released rivers of fire that ran down from Thangorodrim, and the great grassy plain of Ard-galen that lay to the north of the highland of Dorthonion was transformed into a parched and arid waste, known thereafter by a changed name, *Anfauglith*, the Gasping Dust.

This catastrophic assault was called *Dagor Bragollach*, the Battle of Sudden Flame. Glaurung Father of Dragons emerged from Angband now for the first time in his full might; vast armies of Orcs poured southwards; the Elvish lords of Dorthonion were slain, and a great part of the warriors of Bëor's people. King Fingolfin and his son Fingon were driven back with the warriors of Hithlum to the fortress of Eithel Sirion in the east face of the Mountains of Shadow, and in its defence Hador Goldenhead was killed. Then Galdor, Húrin's father, became the lord of Dor-lómin; for the torrents of fire were stopped by the barrier of the Mountains of Shadow, and Hithlum and Dor-lómin remained unconquered.

It was in the year after the Bragollach that Fingolfin, in a fury of despair, rode to Angband and challenged Morgoth. Two years later Húrin and Huor went to Gondolin. After four more years, in a renewed assault on Hithlum, Húrin's father Galdor was slain in the fortress of Eithel Sirion: Sador was there, as he told Túrin (p. 42), and saw Húrin (then a young man of twenty-one) 'take up his lordship and his command'.

All these things were fresh in memory in Dor-lómin when Túrin was born, nine years after the Battle of Sudden Flame.

NOTE ON PRONUNCIATION

The following note is intended to clarify a few main features in the pronunciation of names.

Consonants

C   always has the value of *k*, never of *s*; thus *Celebros* is '*Kelebros*', not '*Selebros*'.

CH   always has the value of *ch* in Scots *loch* or German *buch*, never that of *ch* in English *church*; examples are *Anach, Narn i Chîn Húrin*.

DH   is always used to represent the sound of a voiced ('soft') *th* in English, that is the *th* in *then*, not the *th* in *thin*. Examples are *Glóredhel, Eledhwen, Maedhros*.

G   always has the sound of English *g* in *get*; thus *Region* is not pronounced like English *region*, and the first syllable of *Ginglith* is as in English *begin*, not as in *gin*.

Vowels

AI   has the sound of English *eye*; thus the second syllable of *Edain* is like English *dine*, not *Dane*.

AU   has the value of English *ow* in *town*; thus the first vowel of *Sauron* is like English *sour*, not *sore*.

EI   as in *Teiglin* has the sound of English *grey*.

IE   should not be pronounced as in English *piece*, but with both the vowels *i* and *e* sounded, and run together; thus *Ni-enor*, not '*Neenor*'.

AE   as in *Aegnor*, *Nirnaeth*, is a combination of the individual vowels, *a-e*, but may be pronounced in the same way as AI.

EA and EO   are not run together, but constitute two syllables; these combinations are written *ëa* and *ëo*, as in *Bëor*, or at the beginning of names *Eä*, *Eö*, as in *Eärendil*.

Ú   in names like *Húrin*, *Túrin*, should be pronounced *oo*; thus '*Toorin*', not '*Tyoorin*'.

IR, UR   before a consonant (as in *Círdan*, *Gurthang*) should not be pronounced as in English *fir*, *fur*, but as in English, *eer*, *oor*.

E   at the end of words is always pronounced as a distinct vowel, and in this position is written *ë*. It is always pronounced in the middle of words like *Celebros*, *Menegroth*.

NARN I CHÎN HÚRIN

The Tale of the Children of Húrin

CHAPTER I

THE CHILDHOOD OF TÚRIN

Hador Goldenhead was a lord of the Edain and well-beloved by the Eldar. He dwelt while his days lasted under the lordship of Fingolfin, who gave to him wide lands in that region of Hithlum which was called Dor-lómin. His daughter Glóredhel wedded Haldir son of Halmir, lord of the Men of Brethil; and at the same feast his son Galdor the Tall wedded Hareth, the daughter of Halmir.

Galdor and Hareth had two sons, Húrin and Huor. Húrin was by three years the elder, but he was shorter in stature than other men of his kin; in this he took after his mother's people, but in all else he was like Hador, his grandfather, strong in body and fiery of mood. But the fire in him burned steadily, and he had great endurance of will. Of all Men of the North he knew most of the counsels of the Noldor. Huor his brother was tall, the tallest of all the Edain save his own son Tuor only, and a swift runner; but if the race were long and hard Húrin would be the first home, for he ran as strongly at the end of the course as at the beginning. There was great love between the brothers, and they were seldom apart in their youth.

Húrin wedded Morwen, the daughter of Baragund son of Bregolas of the House of Bëor; and she was thus of close kin to Beren One-hand. Morwen was dark-haired and tall, and for the light of her glance and the beauty of her face men called her Eledhwen, the elven-fair; but she was somewhat stern of mood and proud. The sorrows of the House of Bëor saddened her heart; for she came as an exile to Dorlómin from Dorthonion after the ruin of the Bragollach.

Túrin was the name of the eldest child of Húrin and Morwen, and he was born in that year in which Beren came to Doriath and found Lúthien Tinúviel, Thingol's daughter. Morwen bore a daughter also to Húrin, and she was named Urwen; but she was called Lalaith, which is Laughter, by all that knew her in her short life.

Huor wedded Rían, the cousin of Morwen; she was the daughter of Belegund son of Bregolas. By hard fate was she born into such days, for she was gentle of heart and loved neither hunting nor war. Her love was given to trees and to the flowers of the wild, and she was a singer and a maker of songs. Two months only had she been wedded to Huor when he went with his brother to the Nirnaeth Arnoediad, and she never saw him again.

But now the tale returns to Húrin and Huor in the days of their youth. It is said that for a while the sons of Galdor dwelt in Brethil as foster-sons of Haldir their uncle, after the custom of Northern men in those days. They often went to battle with the Men of Brethil against the Orcs, who now harried the northern borders of their land; for Húrin, though only seventeen years of age, was strong, and Huor the younger was already as tall as most full-grown men of that people.

On a time Húrin and Huor went with a company of scouts, but they were ambushed by the Orcs and scattered, and the brothers were pursued to the ford of Brithiach. There they would have been taken or slain but for the power of Ulmo that was still strong in the waters of Sirion; and it is said that a mist arose from the river and hid them from their enemies, and they escaped over the Brithiach into Dimbar. There they wandered in great hardship among the hills beneath the sheer walls of the Crissaegrim, until they were bewildered in the deceits of that land and knew not the way to go on or to return. There Thorondor espied them, and he sent two of his Eagles to their aid; and the Eagles bore them up and brought them beyond the Encircling Mountains to the secret vale of Tumladen and the hidden city of Gondolin, which no Man had yet seen.

There Turgon the King received them well, when he learned of their kin; for Hador was an Elf-friend, and Ulmo, moreover, had counselled Turgon to deal kindly with the sons of that House, from whom help should come to him at need. Húrin and Huor dwelt as guests in the King's house for well nigh a year; and it is said that in this time Húrin, whose mind was swift and eager, gained much lore of the Elves, and learned also something of the counsels and purposes of the King. For Turgon took great liking for the sons of Galdor, and spoke much with them; and he wished indeed to keep them in Gondolin out of love, and not only for his law that no stranger, be he Elf or Man, who found the way to the secret kingdom or looked upon the city should ever depart again, until the King should open the leaguer, and the hidden people should come forth.

But Húrin and Huor desired to return to their own people and share in the wars and griefs that now beset them. And Húrin said to Turgon: 'Lord, we are but mortal Men, and unlike the Eldar. They may endure for long years awaiting battle with their enemies in some far distant day; but for us the time is short, and our hope and strength soon wither. Moreover we did not find the road to Gondolin, and indeed we do not know surely where this city stands; for we were brought in fear and wonder by the high ways of the air, and in mercy our eyes were veiled.' Then Turgon granted his prayer, and he said: 'By the way that you came you have leave to return, if Thorondor is willing. I grieve at this parting; yet in a little while, as the Eldar account it, we may meet again.'

But Maeglin, the King's sister-son, who was mighty in Gondolin, grieved not at all at their going, though he begrudged them the favour of the King, for he had no love for any of the kindred of Men; and he said to Húrin: 'The King's grace is greater than you know, and some might wonder wherefore the strict law is abated for two knave-children of Men. It would be safer if they had no choice but to abide here as our servants to their life's end.'

'The King's grace is great indeed,' answered Húrin, 'but if our word is not enough, then we will swear oaths to you.' And the brothers swore never to reveal the counsels of Turgon, and to keep secret all that they had seen in his realm. Then they took their leave, and the Eagles coming bore them away by night, and set them down in Dor-lómin before the dawn. Their kinsfolk rejoiced to see them, for messengers from Brethil had reported that they were lost; but they would not tell even to their father where they had been, save that they were rescued in the wilderness by the Eagles that brought them home. But Galdor said: 'Did you then dwell a year in the wild? Or did the Eagles house you in their eyries? But you found food and fine raiment, and return as young princes, not as waifs of the wood.' 'Be content, father,' said Húrin, 'that we have returned; for only under an oath of silence was this permitted. That oath is still on us.' Then Galdor questioned them no more, but he and many others guessed at the truth. For both the oath of silence and the Eagles pointed to Turgon, men thought.

So the days passed, and the shadow of the fear of Morgoth lengthened. But in the four hundred and sixty-ninth year after the return of the Noldor to Middle-earth there was a stirring of hope among Elves and Men; for the rumour ran among them of the deeds of Beren and Lúthien, and the putting to shame of Morgoth even upon his throne in Angband, and some said that Beren and Lúthien yet lived, or had returned from the Dead. In that year also the great counsels of Maedhros were almost complete, and with the reviving strength of the Eldar and the Edain the advance of Morgoth was stayed, and the Orcs were driven back from Beleriand. Then some began to speak of victories to come, and of redressing the Battle of the Bragollach, when Maedhros should lead forth the united hosts, and drive Morgoth underground, and seal the Doors of Angband.

But the wiser were uneasy still, fearing that Maedhros revealed his growing strength too soon, and that Morgoth would be given time enough to take counsel against him. 'Ever will some new evil be hatched in Angband beyond the guess of Elves and Men,' they said. And in the autumn of that year, to point their words, there came an ill wind from the North under leaden skies. The Evil Breath it was called, for it was pestilent; and many sickened and died in the fall of the year in the northern lands that bordered on the Anfauglith, and they were for the most part the children or the rising youth in the houses of Men.

In that year Túrin son of Húrin was yet only five years old, and Urwen his sister was three in the beginning of spring. Her hair was like the yellow lilies in the grass as she ran in the fields, and her laughter was like the sound of the merry stream that came singing out of the hills past the walls of her father's house. Nen Lalaith it was named, and after it all the people of the household called the child Lalaith, and their hearts were glad while she was among them.

But Túrin was loved less than she. He was dark-haired as his mother, and promised to be like her in mood also; for he was not merry, and spoke little, though he learned to speak early and ever seemed older than his years. Túrin was slow to forget injustice or mockery; but the fire of his father was also in him, and he could be sudden and fierce. Yet he was quick to pity, and the hurts or sadness of living things might move him to tears; and he was like his father in this also, for Morwen was stern with others as with herself. He loved his mother, for her speech to him was forthright and plain; but his father he saw little, for Húrin was often long away from home with the host of Fingon that guarded Hithlum's eastern borders, and when he returned his quick speech, full of strange words and jests and half-meanings, bewildered Túrin and made him uneasy. At that time all the warmth of his heart was for Lalaith his sister; but he played with her seldom, and liked better to guard her unseen and to watch her going upon grass or under tree, as she sang such songs as the children of the Edain made long ago when the tongue of the Elves was still fresh upon their lips.

'Fair as an Elf-child is Lalaith,' said Húrin to Morwen; 'but briefer, alas! And so fairer, maybe, or dearer.' And Túrin hearing these words pondered them, but could not understand them. For he had seen no Elf-children. None of the Eldar at that time dwelt in his father's lands, and once only had he seen them, when King Fingon and many of his lords had ridden through Dor-lómin and passed over the bridge of Nen Lalaith, glittering in silver and white.

But before the year was out the truth of his father's words was shown; for the Evil Breath came to Dor-lómin, and Túrin took sick, and lay long in a fever and dark dream. And when he was healed, for such was his fate and the strength of life that was in him, he asked for Lalaith. But his nurse answered: 'Speak no more of Lalaith, son of Húrin; but of your sister Urwen you must ask tidings of your mother.'

And when Morwen came to him, Túrin said to her: 'I am no longer sick, and I wish to see Urwen; but why must I not say Lalaith any more?'

'Because Urwen is dead, and laughter is stilled in this house,' she answered. 'But you live, son of Morwen; and so does the Enemy who has done this to us.'

She did not seek to comfort him any more than herself; for she met her grief in silence and coldness of heart. But Húrin mourned openly, and he took up his harp and would make a song of lamentation; but he could not, and he broke his harp, and going out he lifted up his hand towards the North, crying: 'Marrer of Middle-earth, would that I might see you face to face, and mar you as my lord Fingolfin did!'

But Túrin wept bitterly at night alone, though to Morwen he never again spoke the name of his sister. To

one friend only he turned at that time, and to him he
spoke of his sorrow and the emptiness of the house. This
friend was named Sador, a house-man in the service of
Húrin; he was lame, and of small account. He had been a
woodman, and by ill-luck or the mishandling of his axe he
had hewn his right foot, and the footless leg had shrunken;
and Túrin called him Labadal, which is 'Hopafoot',
though the name did not displease Sador, for it was given
in pity and not in scorn. Sador worked in the outbuild-
ings, to make or mend things of little worth that were
needed in the house, for he had some skill in the working
of wood; and Túrin would fetch him what he lacked, to
spare his leg, and sometimes he would carry off secretly
some tool or piece of timber that he found unwatched, if
he thought his friend might use it. Then Sador smiled, but
bade him return the gifts to their places; 'Give with a free
hand, but give only your own,' he said. He rewarded as he
could the kindness of the child, and carved for him the
figures of men and beasts; but Túrin delighted most in
Sador's tales, for he had been a young man in the days of
the Bragollach, and loved now to dwell upon the short
days of his full manhood before his maiming.

'That was a great battle, they say, son of Húrin. I was
called from my tasks in the wood in the need of that year;
but I was not in the Bragollach, or I might have got my
hurt with more honour. For we came too late, save to bear
back the bier of the old lord, Hador, who fell in the guard
of King Fingolfin. I went for a soldier after that, and I was

41

in Eithel Sirion, the great fort of the Elf-kings, for many years; or so it seems now, and the dull years since have little to mark them. In Eithel Sirion I was when the Black King assailed it, and Galdor your father's father was the captain there in the King's stead. He was slain in that assault; and I saw your father take up his lordship and his command, though but new come to manhood. There was a fire in him that made the sword hot in his hand, they said. Behind him we drove the Orcs into the sand; and they have not dared to come within sight of the walls since that day. But alas! my love of battle was sated, for I had seen spilled blood and wounds enough; and I got leave to come back to the woods that I yearned for. And there I got my hurt; for a man that flies from his fear may find that he has only taken a short cut to meet it.'

In this way Sador would speak to Túrin as he grew older; and Túrin began to ask many questions that Sador found hard to answer, thinking that others nearer akin should have had the teaching. And one day Túrin said to him: 'Was Lalaith indeed like an Elf-child, as my father said? And what did he mean, when he said that she was briefer?'

'Very like,' said Sador; 'for in their first youth the children of Men and Elves seem close akin. But the children of Men grow more swiftly, and their youth passes soon; such is our fate.'

Then Túrin asked him: 'What is fate?'

'As to the fate of Men,' said Sador, 'you must ask those that are wiser than Labadal. But as all can see, we weary soon

Turin's name for Sador

and die; and by mischance many meet death even sooner. But the Elves do not weary, and they do not die save by great hurt. From wounds and griefs that would slay Men they may be healed; and even when their bodies are marred they return again, some say. It is not so with us.'

'Then Lalaith will not come back?' said Túrin. 'Where has she gone?'

'She will not come back,' said Sador. 'But where she has gone no man knows; or I do not.'

'Has it always been so? Or do we suffer some curse of the wicked King, perhaps, like the Evil Breath?'

'I do not know. A darkness lies behind us, and out of it few tales have come. The fathers of our fathers may have had things to tell, but they did not tell them. Even their names are forgotten. The Mountains stand between us and the life that they came from, flying from no man now knows what.'

'Were they afraid?' said Túrin.

'It may be,' said Sador. 'It may be that we fled from the fear of the Dark, only to find it here before us, and nowhere else to fly to but the Sea.'

'We are not afraid any longer,' said Túrin, 'not all of us. My father is not afraid, and I will not be; or at least, as my mother, I will be afraid and not show it.'

It seemed then to Sador that Túrin's eyes were not the eyes of a child, and he thought: 'Grief is a hone to a hard mind.' But aloud he said: 'Son of Húrin and Morwen, how it will be with your heart Labadal cannot guess; but seldom and to few will you show what is in it.'

43

Then Túrin said: 'Perhaps it is better not to tell what you wish, if you cannot have it. But I wish, Labadal, that I were one of the Eldar. Then Lalaith might come back, and I should still be here, even if she were long away. I shall go as a soldier with an Elf-king as soon as I am able, as you did, Labadal.'

'You may learn much of them,' said Sador, and he sighed. 'They are a fair folk and wonderful, and they have a power over the hearts of Men. And yet I think sometimes that it might have been better if we had never met them, but had walked in lowlier ways. For already they are ancient in knowledge; and they are proud and enduring. In their light we are dimmed, or we burn with too quick a flame, and the weight of our doom lies the heavier on us.'

'But my father loves them,' said Túrin, 'and he is not happy without them. He says that we have learned nearly all that we know from them, and have been made a nobler people; and he says that the Men that have lately come over the Mountains are hardly better than Orcs.'

'That is true,' answered Sador; 'true at least of some of us. But the up-climbing is painful, and from high places it is easy to fall low.'

At this time Túrin was almost eight years old, in the month of Gwaeron in the reckoning of the Edain, in the year that cannot be forgotten. Already there were rumours among his elders of a great mustering and gathering of arms, of which Túrin heard nothing; though he marked

44

that his father often looked steadfastly at him, as a man might look at something dear that he must part from.

Now Húrin, knowing her courage and her guarded tongue, often spoke with Morwen of the designs of the Elven-kings, and of what might befall, if they went well or ill. His heart was high with hope, and he had little fear for the outcome of the battle; for it did not seem to him that any strength in Middle-earth could overthrow the might and splendour of the Eldar. 'They have seen the Light in the West,' he said, 'and in the end Darkness must flee from their faces.' Morwen did not gainsay him; for in Húrin's company the hopeful ever seemed the more likely. But there was knowledge of Elven-lore in her kindred also, and to herself she said: 'And yet did they not leave the Light, and are they not now shut out from it? It may be that the Lords of the West have put them out of their thought; and how then can even the Elder Children over-come one of the Powers?'

No shadow of such doubt seemed to lie on Húrin Thalion; yet one morning in the spring of that year he awoke heavy as after unquiet sleep, and a cloud lay on his brightness that day; and in the evening he said suddenly: 'When I am summoned, Morwen Eledhwen, I shall leave in your keeping the heir of the House of Hador. The lives of Men are short, and in them there are many ill chances, even in time of peace.'

'That has ever been so,' she answered. 'But what lies under your words?'

'Prudence, not doubt,' said Húrin; yet he looked troubled. 'But one who looks forward must see this: that things will not remain as they were. This will be a great throw, and one side must fall lower than it now stands. If it be the Elven-kings that fall, then it must go evilly with the Edain; and we dwell nearest to the Enemy. This land might pass into his dominion. But if things do go ill, I will not say to you: *Do not be afraid!* For you fear what should be feared, and that only; and fear does not dismay you. But I say: *Do not wait!* I shall return to you as I may, but do not wait! Go south as swiftly as you can – if I live I shall follow, and I shall find you, though I have to search through all Beleriand.'

'Beleriand is wide, and houseless for exiles,' said Morwen. 'Whither should I flee, with few or with many?'

Then Húrin thought for a while in silence. 'There is my mother's kin in Brethil,' he said. 'That is some thirty leagues, as the eagle flies.'

'If such an evil time should indeed come, what help would there be in Men?' said Morwen. 'The House of Bëor has fallen. If the great House of Hador falls, in what holes shall the little Folk of Haleth creep?'

'In such as they can find,' said Húrin. 'But do not doubt their valour, though they are few and unlearned. Where else is hope?'

'You do not speak of Gondolin,' said Morwen.

'No, for that name has never passed my lips,' said Húrin. 'Yet the word is true that you have heard: I have been there. But I tell you now truly, as I have told no other, and will not: I do not know where it stands.'

'But you guess, and guess near, I think,' said Morwen.

'It may be so,' said Húrin. 'But unless Turgon himself released me from my oath, I could not tell that guess, even to you; and therefore your search would be vain. But were I to speak, to my shame, you would at best but come at a shut gate; for unless Turgon comes out to war (and of that no word has been heard, and it is not hoped) no one will come in.'

'Then if your kin are not hopeful, and your friends deny you,' said Morwen, 'I must take counsel for myself; and to me now comes the thought of Doriath.'

'Ever your aim is high,' said Húrin.

'Over-high, you would say?' said Morwen. 'But last of all defences will the Girdle of Melian be broken, I think; and the House of Bëor will not be despised in Doriath. Am I not now kin of the king? For Beren son of Barahir was grandson of Bregor, as was my father also.'

'My heart does not lean to Thingol,' said Húrin. 'No help will come from him to King Fingon; and I know not what shadow falls on my spirit when Doriath is named.'

'At the name of Brethil my heart also is darkened,' said Morwen.

Then suddenly Húrin laughed, and he said: 'Here we sit debating things beyond our reach, and shadows that come out of dream. Things will not go so ill; but if they do, then to your courage and counsel all is committed. Do then what your heart bids you; but do it swiftly. And if we gain our ends, then the Elven-kings are resolved to restore all the fiefs of Bëor's house to his heir; and that is you, Morwen daughter of Baragund. Wide lordships we should then wield, and a high inheritance come to our son. Without the malice in the North he should come to great wealth, and be a king among Men.'

'Húrin Thalion,' said Morwen, 'this I judge truer to say: that you look high, but I fear to fall low.'

'That at the worst you need not fear,' said Húrin.

That night Túrin half-woke, and it seemed to him that his father and mother stood beside his bed, and looked down on him in the light of the candles that they held; but he could not see their faces.

On the morning of Túrin's birthday Húrin gave his son a gift, an Elf-wrought knife, and the hilt and the sheath were silver and black; and he said: 'Heir of the House of Hador, here is a gift for the day. But have a care! It is a bitter blade, and steel serves only those that can wield it. It will cut your hand as willingly as aught else.' And setting Túrin on a table he kissed his son, and said: 'You overtop me already, son of Morwen; soon you will be as high on your own feet. In that day many may fear your blade.'

Then Túrin ran from the room and went away alone, and in his heart was a warmth like the warmth of the sun upon the cold earth that sets growth astir. He repeated to himself his father's words, Heir of the House of Hador; but other words came also to his mind: Give with a free hand, but give of your own. And he went to Sador and cried: 'Labadal, it is my birthday, the birthday of the heir of the House of Hador! And I have brought you a gift to mark the day. Here is a knife, just such as you need; it will cut anything that you wish, as fine as a hair.'

Then Sador was troubled, for he knew well that Túrin had himself received the knife that day; but men held it a grievous thing to refuse a free-given gift from any hand. He spoke then to him gravely: 'You come of a generous kin, Túrin son of Húrin. I have done nothing to equal your gift, and I cannot hope to do better in the days that are left to me; but what I can do, I will.' And when Sador drew the knife from the sheath he said: 'This is a gift indeed: a blade of elven steel. Long have I missed the feel of it.'

Húrin soon marked that Túrin did not wear the knife, and he asked him whether his warning had made him fear it. Then Túrin answered: 'No; but I gave the knife to Sador the woodwright.'

'Do you then scorn your father's gift?' said Morwen; and again Túrin answered: 'No; but I love Sador, and I am sorry for him.'

Then Húrin said: 'All three gifts were your own to give, Túrin: love, pity, and the knife the least.'

'Yet I doubt if Sador deserves them,' said Morwen. 'He is self-maimed by his own want of skill, and he is slow with his tasks, for he spends much time on trifles unbidden.'

'Give him pity nonetheless,' said Húrin. 'An honest hand and a true heart may hew amiss; and the harm may be harder to bear than the work of a foe.'

'But you must wait now for another blade,' said Morwen. 'Thus the gift shall be a true gift and at your own cost.'

Nonetheless Túrin marked that Sador was treated more kindly thereafter, and was set now to the making of a great chair for the lord to sit on in his hall.

There came a bright morning in the month of Lothron when Túrin was roused by sudden trumpets; and running to the doors he saw in the court a great press of men on foot and on horse, and all fully armed as for war. There also stood Húrin, and he spoke to the men and gave commands; and Túrin learned that they were setting out that day for Barad Eithel. These were Húrin's guards and household men; but all the men of his land that could be spared were summoned. Some had gone already with Huor his father's brother; and many others would join the Lord of Dor-lómin on the road, and go behind his banner to the great muster of the King.

Then Morwen bade farewell to Húrin without tears; and she said: 'I will guard what you leave in my keeping, both what is and what shall be.'

And Húrin answered her: 'Farewell, Lady of Dor-lómin; we ride now with greater hope than ever we have known before. Let us think that at this midwinter the feast shall be merrier than in all our years yet, with a fearless spring to follow after!' Then he lifted Túrin to his shoulder, and cried to his men: 'Let the heir of the House of Hador see the light of your swords!' And the sun glittered on fifty blades as they leaped forth, and the court rang with the battle-cry of the Edain of the North: *Lacho calad! Drego morn!* Flame Light! Flee Night!

Then at last Húrin sprang into his saddle, and his golden banner was unfurled, and the trumpets sang again in the morning; and thus Húrin Thalion rode away to the Nirnaeth Arnoediad. — *The Battle of Unumbered tears.*

But Morwen and Túrin stood still by the doors, until far away they heard the faint call of a single horn on the wind: Húrin had passed over the shoulder of the hill, beyond which he could see his house no more.

CHAPTER II

THE BATTLE OF UNNUMBERED TEARS

Many songs are yet sung and many tales are yet told by the Elves of the Nirnaeth Arnoediad, the Battle of Unnumbered Tears, in which Fingon fell and the flower of the Eldar withered. If all were now retold a man's life would not suffice for the hearing. Here then shall be recounted only those deeds which bear upon the fate of the House of Hador and the children of Húrin the Steadfast.

Having gathered at length all the strength that he could Maedhros appointed a day, the morning of Midsummer. On that day the trumpets of the Eldar greeted the rising of the Sun, and in the east was raised the standard of the sons of Fëanor; and in the west the standard of Fingon, King of the Noldor.

Then Fingon looked out from the walls of Eithel Sirion, and his host was arrayed in the valleys and woods upon the east of Ered Wethrin, well hid from the eyes of the Enemy; but he knew that it was very great. For there all the Noldor of Hithlum were assembled, and to them were gathered many Elves of the Falas and of Nargothrond; and he had great strength of Men. Upon the right were stationed the host of Dor-lómin and all the valour of Húrin and Huor his brother, and to them had come Haldir of Brethil, their kinsman, with many men of the woods.

Then Fingon looked east and his elven-sight saw far off a dust and the glint of steel like stars in a mist, and he knew that Maedhros had set forth; and he rejoiced. Then he looked towards Thangorodrim, and there was a dark cloud about it and a black smoke went up; and he knew that the wrath of Morgoth was kindled and that their challenge would be accepted, and a shadow of doubt fell upon his heart. But at that moment a cry went up, passing on the wind from the south from vale to vale, and Elves and Men lifted up their voices in wonder and joy. For unsummoned and unlooked-for Turgon had opened the leaguer of Gondolin, and was come with an army, ten thousand strong, with bright mail and long swords and spears like a forest. Then when Fingon heard afar the great trumpet of Turgon, the shadow passed and his heart was uplifted, and he shouted aloud: '*Utúlie'n aurë! Aiya Eldalië ar Atanatarni, utúlie'n aurë!* The day has come! Behold, people of the Eldar and Fathers of Men, the day has come!' And all those who heard his great voice echo in the hills answered crying: '*Auta i lómë!* The night is passing!'

It was not long before the great battle was joined. For Morgoth knew much of what was done and designed by his foes and had laid his plans against the hour of their assault. Already a great force out of Angband was drawing near to Hithlum, while another and greater went to meet Maedhros to prevent the union of the powers of the kings. And those that came against Fingon were clad all in dun raiment and showed no naked steel, and thus were already far over the sands of Anfauglith before their approach became known.

Then the hearts of the Noldor grew hot, and their captains wished to assail their foes on the plain; but Fingon spoke against this.

'Beware of the guile of Morgoth, lords!' he said. 'Ever his strength is more than it seems, and his purpose other than he reveals. Do not reveal your own strength, but let the enemy spend his first in assault on the hills.' For it was the design of the kings that Maedhros should march openly over the Anfauglith with all his strength, of Elves and of Men and of Dwarves; and when he had drawn forth, as he hoped, the main armies of Morgoth in answer, then Fingon should come on from the West, and so the might of Morgoth should be taken as between hammer and anvil and be broken to pieces; and the signal for this was to be the firing of a great beacon in Dorthonion.

But the Captain of Morgoth in the west had been commanded to draw out Fingon from his hills by whatever means he could. He marched on, therefore, until the front of his battle was drawn up before the stream of Sirion, from the walls of the Barad Eithel to the Fen of Serech; and the outposts of Fingon could see the eyes of their enemies. But there was no answer to his challenge, and the taunts of his Orcs faltered as they looked upon the silent walls and the hidden threat of the hills.

Then the Captain of Morgoth sent out riders with tokens of parley, and they rode up before the very walls of the outworks of the Barad Eithel. With them they brought Gelmir son of Guilin, a lord of Nargothrond, whom they had captured in the Bragollach, and had blinded; and their heralds showed him forth crying: 'We have many more such at home, but you must make haste if you would find them. For we shall deal with them all when we return, even so.' And they hewed off Gelmir's arms and legs, and left him.

By ill chance at that point in the outposts stood Gwindor son of Guilin with many folk of Nargothrond; and indeed he had marched to war with such strength as he could gather because of his grief for the taking of his brother. Now his wrath was like a flame, and he leapt forth upon horse-back, and many riders with him, and they pursued the heralds of Angband and slew them; and all the folk of Nargothrond followed after, and they drove on deep into the ranks of Angband. And seeing this the host of the Noldor was set on fire, and Fingon put on his white helm, and sounded his trumpets, and all his host leapt forth from the hills in sudden onslaught.

The light of the drawing of the swords of the Noldor was like a fire in a field of reeds; and so fell and swift was their onset that almost the designs of Morgoth went astray. Before the decoying army that he had sent west could be strengthened it was swept away and destroyed, and the banners of Fingon passed over the Anfauglith and were raised before the walls of Angband.

Ever in the forefront of that battle went Gwindor and the folk of Nargothrond, and even now they could not be restrained; and they burst through the outer gates and slew the guards within the very courts of Angband; and Morgoth trembled upon his deep throne, hearing them beat upon his doors. But Gwindor was trapped there and taken alive and his folk slain; for Fingon could not come to his aid. By many secret doors in Thangorodrim Morgoth let forth his main strength that he had held in waiting, and Fingon was beaten back with great loss from the walls of Angband.

Then in the plain of the Anfauglith, on the fourth day of the war, there began the Nirnaeth Arnoediad, all the sorrow of which no tale can contain. Of all that befell in the eastward battle: of the routing of Glaurung the Dragon by the Dwarves of Belegost; of the treachery of the Easterlings and the overthrow of the host of Maedhros and the flight of the sons of Fëanor, no more is here said. In the west the host of Fingon retreated over the sands, and there fell Haldir son of Halmir and most of the Men of Brethil. But on the fifth day as night fell, and they were

still far from Ered Wethrin, the armies of Angband surrounded the army of Fingon, and they fought until day,
pressed ever closer. In the morning came hope, for the
horns of Turgon were heard, as he marched up with the
main host of Gondolin; for Turgon had been stationed
southward guarding the passes of Sirion, and he had
restrained most of his folk from the rash onslaught. Now
he hastened to the aid of his brother; and the Noldor of
Gondolin were strong and their ranks shone like a river
of steel in the sun, for the sword and harness of the least
of the warriors of Turgon was worth more than the
ransom of any king among Men.

Now the phalanx of the guard of the King broke
through the ranks of the Orcs, and Turgon hewed his way
to the side of his brother. And it is said that the meeting of
Turgon with Húrin who stood beside Fingon was glad in
the midst of the battle. For a while then the hosts of
Angband were driven back, and Fingon again began his
retreat. But having routed Maedhros in the east Morgoth
had now great forces to spare, and before Fingon and
Turgon could come to the shelter of the hills they were
assailed by a tide of foes thrice greater than all the force
that was left to them. Gothmog, high-captain of Angband,
was come; and he drove a dark wedge between the Elven-
hosts, surrounding King Fingon, and thrusting Turgon
and Húrin aside towards the Fen of Serech. Then he
turned upon Fingon. That was a grim meeting. At last
Fingon stood alone with his guard dead about him, and he

fought with Gothmog, until a Balrog came behind him and cast a thong of steel round him. Then Gothmog hewed him with his black axe, and a white flame sprang up from the helm of Fingon as it was cloven. Thus fell the King of the Noldor; and they beat him into the dust with their maces, and his banner, blue and silver, they trod into the mire of his blood.

The field was lost; but still Húrin and Huor and the remnant of the House of Hador stood firm with Turgon of Gondolin; and the hosts of Morgoth could not yet win the passes of Sirion. Then Húrin spoke to Turgon, saying: 'Go now, lord, while time is! For you are the last of the House of Fingolfin, and in you lives the last hope of the Eldar. While Gondolin stands Morgoth shall still know fear in his heart.'

'Not long now can Gondolin remain hidden, and being discovered it must fall,' said Turgon.

'Yet if it stands only a little while,' said Huor, 'then out of your house shall come the hope of Elves and Men. This I say to you, lord, with the eyes of death: though we part here for ever, and I shall not look on your white walls again, from you and from me a new star shall arise. Farewell!'

Maeglin, Turgon's sister-son, who stood by, heard these words and did not forget them.

Then Turgon took the counsel of Húrin and Huor, and he gave orders that his host should begin a retreat into the passes of Sirion; and his captains Ecthelion and Glorfindel guarded the flanks to right and left so that none of the enemy should pass them by, for the only road in that region was narrow and ran near the west bank of the growing stream of Sirion. But the Men of Dor-lómin held the rearguard, as Húrin and Huor desired; for they did not wish in their hearts to escape from the Northlands; and if they could not win back to their homes, there they would stand to the end. So it was that Turgon fought his way southward, until coming behind the guard of Húrin and Huor, he passed down Sirion and escaped; and he vanished into the mountains and was hidden from the eyes of Morgoth. But the brothers drew the remnant of the mighty men of the House of Hador about them, and foot by foot they withdrew, until they came behind the Fen of Serech, and had the stream of Rivil before them. There they stood and gave way no more.

Then all the hosts of Angband swarmed against them, and they bridged the stream with their dead, and encircled the remnant of Hithlum as a gathering tide about a rock. There, as the Sun westered and the shadows of the Ered Wethrin grew dark, Huor fell pierced with a venomed arrow in the eye, and all the valiant men of Hador were slain about him in a heap; and the Orcs hewed their heads and piled them as a mound of gold in the sunset.

Last of all Húrin stood alone. Then he cast aside his shield, and seized the axe of an orc-captain and wielded it two-handed; and it is sung that the axe smoked in the black blood of the troll-guard of Gothmog until it withered, and each time that he slew Húrin cried aloud: '*Aure entuluva!*

Day shall come again!' Seventy times he uttered that cry; but they took him at last alive, by the command of Morgoth, who thought thus to do him more evil than by death. Therefore the Orcs grappled Húrin with their hands, which clung to him still, though he hewed off their arms; and ever their numbers were renewed, till he fell buried beneath them. Then Gothmog bound him and dragged him to Angband with mockery.

Thus ended the Nirnaeth Arnoediad, as the Sun went down beyond the Sea. Night fell in Hithlum, and there came a great storm of wind out of the West.

Great was the triumph of Morgoth, though all the purposes of his malice were not yet accomplished. One thought troubled him deeply and marred his victory with unquiet: Turgon had escaped his net, of all his foes the one whom he had most desired to take or destroy. For Turgon of the great House of Fingolfin was now by right King of all the Noldor; and Morgoth feared and hated the House of Fingolfin, because they had scorned him in Valinor and had the friendship of Ulmo his foe; and because of the wounds that Fingolfin gave him in battle. And most of all Morgoth feared Turgon, for of old in Valinor his eye had lighted on him, and whenever he drew near a dark shadow had fallen on his spirit, foreboding that in some time that yet lay hidden in doom, from Turgon ruin should come to him.

CHAPTER III

THE WORDS OF HÚRIN AND MORGOTH

Now by the command of Morgoth the Orcs with great labour gathered all the bodies of their enemies, and all their harness and weapons, and piled them in a mound in the midst of the plain of Anfauglith, and it was like a great hill that could be seen from afar, and the Eldar named it Haudh-en-Nirnaeth. But grass came there and grew again long and green upon that hill alone in all the desert; and no servant of Morgoth thereafter trod upon the earth beneath which the swords of the Eldar and the Edain crumbled into rust. The realm of Fingon was no more, and the Sons of Fëanor wandered as leaves before the wind. To Hithlum none of the Men of Hador's House returned, nor any tidings of the battle and the fate of their lords. But Morgoth sent thither Men who were under his dominion, swarthy Easterlings; and he shut them in that land and forbade them to leave it. This was all that he gave them of the rich rewards that he had promised them for their treachery to Maedhros: to plunder and harass the old and the children and womenfolk of Hador's people. The remnant of the Eldar of Hithlum, all those who did not escape into the wilds and the mountains, he took to the mines of Angband and they became his thralls. But the Orcs went freely through all the North and pressed ever southward into Beleriand. There Doriath yet remained, and Nargothrond; but Morgoth gave little heed to them, either because he knew little of them, or because their hour was not yet come in the designs of his malice. But his thought ever returned to Turgon.

Therefore Húrin was brought before Morgoth, for Morgoth knew by his arts and his spies that Húrin had the friendship of the King; and he sought to daunt him with his eyes. But Húrin could not yet be daunted, and he defied Morgoth. Therefore Morgoth had him chained and set in slow torment; but after a while he came to him, and offered him his choice to go free whither he would, or to receive power and rank as the greatest of Morgoth's captains, if he would but reveal where Turgon had his stronghold, and aught else that he knew of the King's counsels. But Húrin the Steadfast mocked him, saying: 'Blind you are, Morgoth Bauglir, and blind shall ever be, seeing only the dark. You know not what rules the hearts of Men, and if you knew you could not give it. But a fool is he who accepts what Morgoth offers. You will take first the price and then withhold the promise; and I should get only death, if I told you what you ask.'

Then Morgoth laughed, and he said: 'Death you may yet crave of me as a boon.' Then he took Húrin to the Haudh-en-Nirnaeth, and it was then new-built and the reek of death was upon it; and Morgoth set Húrin upon its top and bade him look west towards Hithlum, and think of his wife and his son and other kin. 'For they dwell now in my realm,' said Morgoth, 'and they are at my mercy.'

'You have none,' answered Húrin. 'But you will not come at Turgon through them; for they do not know his secrets.'

Then wrath mastered Morgoth, and he said: 'Yet I may come at you, and all your accursed house; and you shall be broken on my will, though you all were made of steel.' And he took up a long sword that lay there and broke it before the eyes of Húrin, and a splinter wounded his face; but Húrin did not blench. Then Morgoth stretching out his long arm towards Dor-lómin cursed Húrin and Morwen and their offspring, saying: 'Behold! The shadow of my thought shall lie upon them wherever they go, and my hate shall pursue them to the ends of the world.'

But Húrin said: 'You speak in vain. For you cannot see them, nor govern them from afar: not while you keep this shape, and desire still to be a King visible on earth.'

Then Morgoth turned upon Húrin, and he said: 'Fool, little among Men, and they are the least of all that speak! Have you seen the Valar, or measured the power of Manwë and Varda? Do you know the reach of their thought? Or do you think, perhaps, that their thought is upon you, and that they may shield you from afar?'

'I know not,' said Húrin. 'Yet so it might be, if they willed. For the Elder King shall not be dethroned while Arda endures.'

'You say it,' said Morgoth. 'I am the Elder King: Melkor, first and mightiest of all the Valar, who was before the world, and made it. The shadow of my purpose lies upon Arda, and all that is in it bends slowly and surely to my will. But upon all whom you love my thought shall weigh as a cloud of Doom, and it shall bring them down into darkness and despair. Wherever they go, evil shall arise. Whenever they speak, their words shall bring ill counsel. Whatsoever they do shall turn against them. They shall die without hope, cursing both life and death.'

But Húrin answered: 'Do you forget to whom you speak? Such things you spoke long ago to our fathers; but we escaped from your shadow. And now we have knowledge of you, for we have looked on the faces that have seen the Light, and heard the voices that have spoken with Manwë. Before Arda you were, but others also; and you did not make it. Neither are you the most mighty; for you have spent your strength upon yourself and wasted it in your own emptiness. No more are you now than an escaped thrall of the Valar, and their chain still awaits you.'

'You have learned the lessons of your masters by rote,' said Morgoth. 'But such childish lore will not help you, now they are all fled away.'

THE Torment of Húrin

'This last then I will say to you, thrall Morgoth,' said
Húrin, 'and it comes not from the lore of the Eldar, but is
put into my heart in this hour. You are not the Lord of
Men, and shall not be, though all Arda and Menel fall in
your dominion. Beyond the Circles of the World you
shall not pursue those who refuse you.'

'Beyond the Circles of the World I will not pursue
them,' said Morgoth. 'For beyond the Circles of the
World there is Nothing. But within them they shall not
escape me, until they enter into Nothing.'

'You lie,' said Húrin.

'You shall see and you shall confess that I do not lie,'
said Morgoth. And taking Húrin back to Angband he set
him in a chair of stone upon a high place of Thangorodrim, from which he could see afar the land of Hithlum in
the west and the lands of Beleriand in the south. There he
was bound by the power of Morgoth; and Morgoth standing beside him cursed him again and set his power upon
him, so that he could not move from that place, nor die,
until Morgoth should release him.

'Sit now there,' said Morgoth, 'and look out upon the
lands where evil and despair shall come upon those whom
you have delivered to me. For you have dared to mock
me, and have questioned the power of Melkor, Master of
the fates of Arda. Therefore with my eyes you shall see,
and with my ears you shall hear, and nothing shall be
hidden from you.'

CHAPTER IV

THE DEPARTURE OF TÚRIN

To Brethil three men only found their way back at last
through Taur-nu-Fuin, an evil road; and when Glóredhel
Hador's daughter learned of the fall of Haldir she grieved
and died.

To Dor-lómin no tidings came. Rían wife of Huor fled
into the wild distraught; but she was aided by the Grey-
elves of Mithrim, and when her child, Tuor, was born they
fostered him. But Rían went to the Haudh-en-Nirnaeth,
and laid herself down there, and died.

Morwen Eledhwen remained in Hithlum, silent in grief.
Her son Túrin was only in his ninth year, and she was again
with child. Her days were evil. The Easterlings came into
the land in great numbers and they dealt cruelly with the
people of Hador, and robbed them of all that they possessed
and enslaved them. All the people of Húrin's homelands

that could work or serve any purpose they took away, even young girls and boys, and the old they killed or drove out to starve. But they dared not yet lay hands on the Lady of Dor-lómin, or thrust her from her house; for the word ran among them that she was perilous, and a witch who had dealings with the white-fiends: for so they named the Elves, hating them, but fearing them more. For this reason they also feared and avoided the mountains, in which many of the Eldar had taken refuge, especially in the south of the land; and after plundering and harrying the Easterlings drew back northwards. For Húrin's house stood in the south-east of Dor-lómin, and the mountains were near; Nen Lalaith indeed came down from a spring under the shadow of Amon Darthir, over whose shoulder there was a steep pass. By this the hardy could cross Ered Wethrin and come down by the wells of Glithui into Beleriand. But this was not known to the Easterlings, nor to Morgoth yet; for all that country, while the House of Fingolfin stood, was secure from him, and none of his servants had ever come there. He trusted that Ered Wethrin was a wall insurmountable, both against escape from the north and against assault from the south; and there was indeed no other pass, for the unwinged, between Serech and far westward where Dor-lómin marched with Nevrast.

Thus it came to pass that after the first inroads Morwen was let be, though there were men that lurked in the woods about and it was perilous to stir far abroad. There still remained under Morwen's shelter Sador the woodwright and a few old men and women, and Túrin, whom she kept close within the garth. But the homestead of Húrin soon fell into decay, and though Morwen laboured hard she was poor, and would have gone hungry but for the help that was sent to her secretly by Aerin, Húrin's kinswoman; for a certain Brodda, one of the Easterlings, had taken her by force to be his wife. Alms were bitter to Morwen; but she took this aid for the sake of Túrin and her unborn child, and because, as she said, it came of her own. For it was this Brodda who had seized the people, the goods, and the cattle of Húrin's homelands, and carried them off to his own dwellings. He was a bold man, but of small account among his own people before they came to Hithlum; and so, seeking wealth, he was ready to hold lands that others of his sort did not covet. Morwen he had seen once, when he rode to her house on a foray; but a great dread of her had seized him. He thought that he had looked in the fell eyes of a white-fiend, and he was filled with a mortal fear lest some evil should overtake him; and he did not ransack her house, nor discover Túrin, else the life of the heir of the true lord would have been short.

Brodda made thralls of the Strawheads, as he named the people of Hador, and set them to build him a wooden hall in the land to the northward of Húrin's house; and within a stockade his slaves were herded like cattle in a byre, but ill guarded. Among them some could still be found uncowed and ready to help the Lady of Dor-lómin, even at their peril; and from them came secretly tidings of

68

the land to Morwen, though there was little hope in the news they brought. But Brodda took Aerin as a wife and not a slave, for there were few women amongst his own following, and none to compare with the daughters of the Edain; and he hoped to make himself a lordship in that country, and have an heir to hold it after him.

Of what had happened and of what might happen in the days to come Morwen said little to Túrin; and he feared to break her silence with questions. When the Easterlings first came into Dor-lómin he said to his mother: 'When will my father come back, to cast out these ugly thieves? Why does he not come?'

Morwen answered: 'I do not know. It may be that he was slain, or that he is held captive; or again it may be that he was driven far away, and cannot yet return through the foes that surround us.'

'Then I think that he is dead,' said Túrin, and before his mother he restrained his tears; 'for no one could keep him from coming back to help us, if he were alive.'

'I do not think that either of those things are true, my son,' said Morwen.

As the time lengthened the heart of Morwen grew darker for her son Túrin, heir of Dor-lómin and Ladros; for she could see no hope for him better than to become a slave of the Easterling men, before he was much older. Therefore she remembered her words with Húrin, and her thought turned again to Doriath; and she resolved at last to send Túrin away in secret, if she could, and to beg King Thingol to harbour him. And as she sat and pondered how this might be done, she heard clearly in her thought the voice of Húrin saying to her: *Go swiftly! Do not wait for me!* But the birth of her child was drawing near, and the road would be hard and perilous; the more that went the less hope of escape. And her heart still cheated her with hope unadmitted; her inmost thought foreboded that Húrin was not dead, and she listened for his footfall in the sleepless watches of the night, or would wake thinking that she had heard in the courtyard the neigh of Arroch his horse. Moreover, though she was willing that her son should be fostered in the halls of another, after the manner of that time, she would not yet humble her pride to be an alms-guest, not even of a king. Therefore the voice of Húrin, or the memory of his voice, was denied, and the first strand of the fate of Túrin was woven.

Autumn of the Year of Lamentation was drawing on before Morwen came to this resolve, and then she was in haste; for the time for journeying was short, but she dreaded that Túrin would be taken, if she waited over winter. Easterlings were prowling round the garth and spying on the house. Therefore she said suddenly to Túrin: 'Your father does not come. So you must go, and soon. It is as he would wish.'

'Go?' cried Túrin. 'Whither shall we go? Over the Mountains?'

'Yes,' said Morwen, 'over the Mountains, away south.
South – that way some hope may lie. But I did not say *we*,
my son. You must go, but I must stay.'

'I cannot go alone!' said Túrin. 'I will not leave you.
Why should we not go together?'

'I cannot go,' said Morwen. 'But you will not go alone.
I shall send Gethron with you, and Grithnir too, perhaps.'

'Will you not send Labadal?' said Túrin.

'No, for Sador is lame,' said Morwen, 'and it will be
a hard road. And since you are my son and the days are
grim, I will not speak softly: you may die on that road.
The year is getting late. But if you stay, you will come
to a worse end: to be a thrall. If you wish to be a man,
when you come to a man's age, you will do as I bid,
bravely.'

'But I shall leave you only with Sador, and blind
Ragnir, and the old women,' said Túrin. 'Did not my
father say that I am the heir of Hador? The heir should
stay in Hador's house to defend it. Now I wish that I still
had my knife!'

'The heir should stay, but he cannot,' said Morwen.
'But he may return one day. Now take heart! I will follow
you, if things grow worse; if I can.'

'But how will you find me, lost in the wild? said Túrin;
and suddenly his heart failed him, and he wept openly.

'If you wail, other things will find you first,' said
Morwen. 'But I know whither you are going, and if you
come there, and if you remain there, there I will find you,

if I can. For I am sending you to King Thingol in Doriath. Would you not rather be a king's guest than a thrall?'

'I do not know,' said Túrin. 'I do not know what a thrall is.'

'I am sending you away so that you need not learn it,' Morwen answered. Then she set Túrin before her and looked into his eyes, as if she were trying to read some riddle there. 'It is hard, Túrin, my son,' she said at length. 'Not hard for you only. It is heavy on me in evil days to judge what is best to do. But I do as I think right; for why else should I part with the thing most dear that is left to me?'

They spoke no more of this together, and Túrin was grieved and bewildered. In the morning he went to find Sador, who had been hewing sticks for firing, of which they had little, for they dared not stray out in the woods; and now he leant on his crutch and looked at the great chair of Húrin, which had been thrust unfinished in a corner. 'It must go,' he said, 'for only bare needs can be served in these days.'

'Do not break it yet,' said Túrin. 'Maybe he will come home, and then it will please him to see what you have done for him while he was away.'

'False hopes are more dangerous than fears,' said Sador, 'and they will not keep us warm this winter.' He fingered the carving on the chair, and sighed. 'I wasted my time,' he said, 'though the hours seemed pleasant. But all such things are short-lived; and the joy in the making is their only true end, I guess. And now I might as well give you back your gift.'

Túrin put out his hand, and quickly withdrew it. 'A man does not take back his gifts,' he said.

'But if it is my own, may I not give it as I will?' said Sador.

'Yes,' said Túrin, 'to any man but me. But why should you wish to give it?'

'I have no hope of using it for worthy tasks,' Sador said. 'There will be no work for Labadal in days to come but thrall-work.'

'What is a thrall?' said Túrin.

'A man who was a man but is treated as a beast,' Sador answered. 'Fed only to keep alive, kept alive only to toil, toiling only for fear of pain or death. And from these robbers he may get pain or death just for their sport. I hear that they pick some of the fleet-footed and hunt them with hounds. They have learned quicker from the Orcs than we learnt from the Fair Folk.'

'Now I understand things better,' said Túrin.

'It is a shame that you should have to understand such things so soon,' said Sador; then seeing the strange look on Túrin's face: 'What do you understand now?'

'Why my mother is sending me away,' said Túrin, and tears filled his eyes.

'Ah!' said Sador, and he muttered to himself: 'But why so long delayed?' Then turning to Túrin he said: 'That does not seem news for tears to me. But you should not speak your mother's counsels aloud to Labadal, or to anyone. All walls and fences have ears these days, ears that do not grow on fair heads.'

'But I must speak with someone!' said Túrin. 'I have always told things to you. I do not want to leave you, Labadal. I do not want to leave this house or my mother.'

'But if you do not,' said Sador, 'soon there will be an end of the House of Hador for ever, as you must understand now. Labadal does not want you to go; but Sador servant of Húrin will be happier when Húrin's son is out of the reach of the Easterlings. Well, well, it cannot be helped: we must say farewell. Now will you not take my knife as a parting gift?'

'No!' said Túrin. 'I am going to the Elves, to the King of Doriath, my mother says. There I may get other things like it. But I shall not be able to send you any gifts, Labadal. I shall be far away and all alone.' Then Túrin wept; but Sador said to him: 'Hey now! Where is Húrin's son? For I heard him say, not long ago: *I shall go as a soldier with an Elf-king, as soon as I am able.*'

Then Túrin stayed his tears, and he said: 'Very well: if those were the words of the son of Húrin, he must keep them, and go. But whenever I say that I will do this or that, it looks very different when the time comes. Now I am unwilling. I must take care not to say such things again.'

'It would be best indeed,' said Sador. 'So most men teach, and few men learn. Let the unseen days be. Today is more than enough.'

Now Túrin was made ready for the journey, and he bade
farewell to his mother, and departed in secret with his two
companions. But when they bade Túrin turn and look back
upon the house of his father, then the anguish of parting
smote him like a sword, and he cried: 'Morwen, Morwen,
when shall I see you again?' But Morwen standing on her
threshold heard the echo of that cry in the wooded hills,
and she clutched the post of the door so that her fingers
were torn. This was the first of the sorrows of Túrin.

Early in the year after Túrin was gone Morwen gave
birth to her child, and she named her Niënor, which is
Mourning; but Túrin was already far away when she was
born. Long and evil was his road, for the power of Morgoth
was ranging far abroad; but he had as guides Gethron and
Grithnir, who had been young in the days of Hador, and
though they were now aged they were valiant, and they
knew well the lands, for they had journeyed often through
Beleriand in former times. Thus by fate and courage they
passed over the Shadowy Mountains, and coming down
into the Vale of Sirion they passed into the Forest of
Brethil; and at last, weary and haggard, they reached the
confines of Doriath. But there they became bewildered, and
were enmeshed in the mazes of the Queen, and wandered
lost amid the pathless trees, until all their food was spent.
There they came near to death, for winter came cold from
the North; but not so light was Túrin's doom. Even as they
lay in despair they heard a horn sounded. Beleg the Strongbow was hunting in that region, for he dwelt ever on the

THE CHILDREN OF HÚRIN

marches of Doriath, and he was the greatest woodsman of those days. He heard their cries and came to them, and when he had given them food and drink he learned their names and whence they came, and he was filled with wonder and pity. And he looked with liking upon Túrin, for he had the beauty of his mother and the eyes of his father, and he was sturdy and strong.

'What boon would you have of King Thingol?' said Beleg to the boy.

'I would be one of his knights, to ride against Morgoth, and avenge my father,' said Túrin.

'That may well be, when the years have increased you,' said Beleg. 'For though you are yet small you have the makings of a valiant man, worthy to be a son of Húrin the Steadfast, if that were possible.' For the name of Húrin was held in honour in all the lands of the Elves. Therefore Beleg gladly became the guide of the wanderers, and he led them to a lodge where he dwelt at that time with other hunters, and there they were housed while a messenger went to Menegroth. And when word came back that Thingol and Melian would receive the son of Húrin and his guardians, Beleg led them by secret ways into the Hidden Kingdom.

Thus Túrin came to the great bridge over the Esgalduin, and passed the gates of Thingol's halls; and as a child he gazed upon the marvels of Menegroth, which no mortal Man before had seen, save Beren only. Then Gethron spoke the message of Morwen before Thingol and Melian;

and Thingol received them kindly, and set Túrin upon his knee in honour of Húrin, mightiest of Men, and of Beren his kinsman. And those that saw this marvelled, for it was a sign that Thingol took Túrin as his foster-son; and that was not at that time done by kings, nor ever again by Elf-lord to a Man. Then Thingol said to him: 'Here, son of Húrin, shall your home be; and in all your life you shall be held as my son, Man though you be. Wisdom shall be given you beyond the measure of mortal Men, and the weapons of the Elves shall be set in your hands. Perhaps the time may come when you shall regain the lands of your father in Hithlum; but dwell now here in love.'

Thus began the sojourn of Túrin in Doriath. With him remained for a while Gethron and Grithnir his guardians, though they yearned to return again to their lady in Dor-lómin. Then age and sickness came upon Grithnir, and he stayed beside Túrin until he died; but Gethron departed, and Thingol sent with him an escort to guide him and guard him, and they brought words from Thingol to Morwen. They came at last to Húrin's house, and when Morwen learned that Túrin was received with honour in the halls of Thingol her grief was lightened; and the Elves brought also rich gifts from Melian, and a message bidding her return with Thingol's folk to Doriath. For Melian was wise and foresighted, and she hoped thus to avert the evil that was prepared in the thought of Morgoth. But Morwen would not depart from her house, for her heart was yet

unchanged and her pride still high; moreover Niënor was
a babe in arms. Therefore she dismissed the Elves of
Doriath with her thanks, and gave them in gift the last
small things of gold that remained to her, concealing her
poverty; and she bade them take back to Thingol the Helm
of Hador. But Túrin watched ever for the return of
Thingol's messengers; and when they came back alone he
fled into the woods and wept, for he knew of Melian's
bidding and he had hoped that Morwen would come. This
was the second sorrow of Túrin. When the messengers
spoke Morwen's answer, Melian was moved with pity, perceiving her mind; and she saw that the fate which she foreboded could not lightly be set aside.

The Helm of Hador was given into Thingol's hands.
That helm was made of grey steel adorned with gold, and
on it were graven runes of victory. A power was in it that
guarded any who wore it from wound or death, for the
sword that hewed it was broken, and the dart that smote
it sprang aside. It was wrought by Telchar, the smith of
Nogrod, whose works were renowned. It had a visor
(after the manner of those that the Dwarves used in their
forges for the shielding of their eyes), and the face of one
that wore it struck fear into the hearts of all beholders, but
was itself guarded from dart and fire. Upon its crest was
set in defiance a gilded image of Glaurung the dragon; for
it had been made soon after he first issued from the gates
of Morgoth. Often Hador, and Galdor after him, had
borne it in war; and the hearts of the host of Hithlum were

uplifted when they saw it towering high amid the battle, and they cried: 'Of more worth is the Dragon of Dorlómin than the gold-worm of Angband!' But Húrin did not wear the Dragon-helm with ease, and in any case he would not use it, for he said: 'I would rather look on my foes with my true face.' Nonetheless he accounted the helm among the greatest heirlooms of his house.

Now Thingol had in Menegroth deep armouries filled with great wealth of weapons: metal wrought like fishes' mail and shining like water in the moon; swords and axes, shields and helms, wrought by Telchar himself or by his master Gamil Zirak the old, or by elven-wrights more skilful still. For some things he had received in gift that came out of Valinor and were wrought by Fëanor in his mastery, than whom no craftsman was greater in all the days of the world. Yet Thingol handled the Helm of Hador as though his hoard were scanty, and he spoke courteous words, saying: 'Proud were the head that bore this helm, which the sires of Húrin bore.'

Then a thought came to him, and he summoned Túrin, and told him that Morwen had sent to her son a mighty thing, the heirloom of his fathers. 'Take now the Dragon-head of the North,' he said, 'and when the time comes wear it well.' But Túrin was yet too young to lift the helm, and he heeded it not because of the sorrow of his heart.

CHAPTER V

TÚRIN IN DORIATH

In the years of his childhood in the kingdom of Doriath
Túrin was watched over by Melian, though he saw her
seldom. But there was a maiden named Nellas, who lived
in the woods; and at Melian's bidding she would follow
Túrin if he strayed in the forest, and often she met him
there, as it were by chance. Then they played together, or
walked hand in hand; for he grew swiftly, whereas she
seemed no more than a maiden of his own age, and was so
in heart for all her elven-years. From Nellas Túrin learned
much concerning the ways and the wild things of Doriath,
and she taught him to speak the Sindarin tongue after the
manner of the ancient realm, older, and more courteous,
and richer in beautiful words. Thus for a little while his
mood was lightened, until he fell again under shadow, and
that friendship passed like a morning of spring. For Nellas

80

did not go to Menegroth, and was unwilling ever to walk under roofs of stone; so that as Túrin's boyhood passed and he turned his thoughts to deeds of men, he saw her less and less often, and at last called for her no more. But she watched over him still, though now she remained hidden.

Nine years Túrin dwelt in the halls of Menegroth. His heart and thought turned ever to his own kin, and at times he had tidings of them for his own comfort. For Thingol sent messengers to Morwen as often as he might, and she sent back words for her son; thus Túrin heard that Morwen's plight was eased, and that his sister Niënor grew in beauty, a flower in the grey North. And Túrin grew in stature until he became tall among Men and surpassed that of the Elves of Doriath, and his strength and hardihood were renowned in the realm of Thingol. In those years he learned much lore, hearing eagerly the histories of ancient days and great deeds of old, and he became thoughtful, and sparing in speech. Often Beleg Strongbow came to Menegroth to seek him, and led him far afield, teaching him woodcraft and archery and (which he liked more) the handling of swords; but in crafts of making he had less skill, for he was slow to learn his own strength, and often marred what he made with some sudden stroke. In other matters also it seemed that fortune was unfriendly to him, so that often what he designed went awry, and what he desired he did not gain; neither did he win friendship easily, for he was not merry, and laughed seldom, and a shadow lay on his youth. Nonetheless he was held in love and esteem by those who knew him well, and he had honour as the fosterling of the King.

Yet there was one in Doriath that begrudged him this, and ever the more as Túrin drew nearer to manhood; Saeros was his name. He was proud, dealing haughtily with those whom he deemed of lesser state and worth than himself. He became a friend of Daeron the minstrel, for he also was skilled in song; and he had no love for Men, and least of all for any kinsman of Beren One-hand. 'Is it not strange,' said he, 'that this land should be opened to yet another of this unhappy race? Did not the other do harm enough in Doriath?' Therefore he looked askance at Túrin and on all that he did, saying what ill he could of it; but his words were cunning and his malice veiled. If he met with Túrin alone, he spoke haughtily to him and showed plain his contempt; and Túrin grew weary of him, though for long he returned ill words with silence, for Saeros was great among the people of Doriath and a counsellor of the King. But the silence of Túrin displeased Saeros as much as his words.

In the year that Túrin was seventeen years old, his grief was renewed; for all tidings from his home ceased at that time. The power of Morgoth had grown yearly, and all Hithlum was now under his shadow. Doubtless he knew much of the doings of Húrin's people and kin, and had not molested them for a while, so that his design might be fulfilled; but now in pursuit of this purpose he set a close watch on all the passes of the Shadowy Mountains, so that none might come out of Hithlum nor enter it, save at great peril, and the Orcs swarmed about the sources of Narog and Teiglin and the upper waters of Sirion. Thus there came a time when the messengers of Thingol did not return, and he would send no more. He was ever loath to let any stray beyond the guarded borders, and in nothing had he shown greater good will to Húrin and his kin than in sending his people on the dangerous roads to Morwen in Dor-lómin.

Now Túrin grew heavy-hearted, not knowing what new evil was afoot, and fearing that an ill fate had befallen Morwen and Niënor; and for many days he sat silent, brooding on the downfall of the House of Hador and the Men of the North. Then he rose up and went to seek Thingol; and he found him sitting with Melian under Hirilorn, the great beech of Menegroth.

Thingol looked on Túrin in wonder, seeing suddenly before him in the place of his fosterling a Man and a stranger, tall, dark-haired, looking at him with deep eyes in a white face, stern and proud; but he did not speak.

'What do you desire, foster-son?' said Thingol, and guessed that he would ask for nothing small.

'Mail, sword, and shield of my stature, lord,' answered Túrin. 'Also by your leave I will now reclaim the Dragon-helm of my sires.'

'These you shall have,' said Thingol. 'But what need have you yet of such arms?'

'The need of a man,' said Túrin; 'and of a son who has kin to remember. And I need also companions valiant in arms.'

'I will appoint you a place among my knights of the sword, for the sword will ever be your weapon,' said Thingol. 'With them you may make trial of war upon the marches, if that is your desire.'

'Beyond the marches of Doriath my heart urges me,' said Túrin. 'For onset against our foe I long, rather than defence.'

'Then you must go alone,' said Thingol. 'The part of my people in the war with Angband I rule according to my wisdom, Túrin son of Húrin. No force of the arms of Doriath will I send out at this time; nor at any time that I can yet foresee.'

'Yet you are free to go as you will, son of Morwen,' said Melian. 'The Girdle of Melian does not hinder the going of those that passed in with our leave.'

'Unless wise counsel will restrain you,' said Thingol.

'What is your counsel, lord?' said Túrin.

'A Man you seem in stature, and indeed more than many already,' Thingol answered; 'but nonetheless you have not come to the fullness of your manhood that shall be. Until that is achieved, you should be patient, testing and training your strength. Then, maybe, you can remember your kin; but there is little hope that one Man alone can do more against the Dark Lord than to aid the Elf-lords in their defence, as long as that may last.'

Then Túrin said: 'Beren my kinsman did more.'

'Beren, and Lúthien,' said Melian. 'But you are over-bold to speak so to the father of Lúthien. Not so high is your destiny, I think, Túrin son of Morwen, though greatness is in you, and your fate is twined with that of the Elven-folk, for good or for ill. Beware of yourself, lest it be ill.' Then after a silence she spoke to him again, saying: 'Go now, fosterson; and take the advice of the King. That will ever be wiser than your own counsel. Yet I do not think that you will long abide with us in Doriath beyond the coming of manhood. If in days to come you remember the words of Melian, it will be for your good: fear both the heat and the cold of your heart, and strive for patience, if you can.'

Then Túrin bowed before them, and took his leave. And soon after he put on the Dragon-helm, and took arms, and went away to the north-marches, and was joined to the elven-warriors who there waged unceasing war upon the Orcs and all servants and creatures of Morgoth. Thus while yet scarcely out of his boyhood his strength and courage were proved; and remembering the wrongs of his kin he was ever forward in deeds of daring, and he received many wounds by spear or arrow or the crooked blades of the Orcs.

But his doom delivered him from death; and word ran through the woods, and was heard far beyond Doriath, that the Dragon-helm of Dor-lómin was seen again. Then many wondered, saying: 'Can the spirit of any man return from death; or has Húrin of Hithlum escaped indeed from the pits of Hell?'

One only was mightier in arms among the march-wardens of Thingol at that time than Túrin, and that was Beleg Strongbow; and Beleg and Túrin were companions in every peril, and walked far and wide in the wild woods together.

Thus three years passed, and in that time Túrin came seldom to Thingol's halls; and he cared no longer for his looks or his attire, but his hair was unkempt, and his mail covered with a grey cloak stained with the weather. But it chanced in the third summer after Túrin's departure, when he was twenty years old, that desiring rest and needing smithwork for the repair of his arms he came unlooked for to Menegroth, and went one evening into the hall. Thingol was not there, for he was abroad in the greenwood with Melian, as was his delight at times in the high summer. Túrin took a seat without heed, for he was wayworn, and filled with thought; and by ill-luck he set himself at a board among the elders of the realm, and in that place where Saeros was accustomed to sit. Saeros, entering late, was angered, believing that Túrin had done this in pride, and with intent to affront him; and his anger was not lessened to find that Túrin was not rebuked by those that sat there, but was welcomed as one worthy to sit among them.

For a while therefore Saeros feigned to be of like mind, and took another seat, facing Túrin across the board.

'Seldom does the march-warden favour us with his company,' he said; 'and I gladly yield my accustomed seat for the chance of speech with him.' But Túrin, who was in converse with Mablung the Hunter, did not rise, and said only a curt 'I thank you'.

Saeros then plied him with questions, concerning the news from the borders, and his deeds in the wild; but though his words seemed fair, the mockery in his voice could not be mistaken. Then Túrin became weary, and he looked about him, and knew the bitterness of exile; and for all the light and laughter of the Elven-halls his thought turned to Beleg and their life in the woods, and thence far away, to Morwen in Dor-lómin in the house of his father; and he frowned, because of the darkness of his thoughts, and made no answer to Saeros. At this, believing the frown aimed at himself, Saeros restrained his anger no longer; and he took out a golden comb, and cast it on the board before Túrin, crying: 'Doubtless, Man of Hithlum, you came in haste to this table, and may be excused your ragged cloak; but there is no need to leave your head untended as a thicket of brambles. And maybe if your ears were uncovered you would heed better what is said to you.'

Túrin said nothing, but turned his eyes upon Saeros, and there was a glint in their darkness. But Saeros did not heed the warning, and returned the gaze with scorn, saying for all to hear: 'If the Men of Hithlum are so wild and fell, of what sort are the women of that land? Do they run like the deer clad only in their hair?'

Then Túrin took up a drinking-vessel and cast it in Saeros' face, and he fell backward with great hurt; and Túrin drew his sword and would have run at him, but Mablung restrained him. Then Saeros rising spat blood upon the board, and spoke as best he could with a broken mouth: 'How long shall we harbour this woodwose? Who rules here tonight? The King's law is heavy upon those who hurt his lieges in the hall; and for those who draw blades there outlawry is the least doom. Outside the hall I could answer you, Woodwose!'

But when Túrin saw the blood upon the table his mood became cold; and with a shrug he released himself from Mablung and left the hall without a word.

Then Mablung said to Saeros: 'What ails you tonight? For this evil I hold you to blame; and maybe the King's law will judge a broken mouth a just return for your taunting.'

'If the cub has a grievance, let him bring it to the King's judgement,' answered Saeros. 'But the drawing of swords here is not to be excused for any such cause. Outside the hall, if the woodwose draws on me, I shall kill him.'

'It might well go otherwise,' said Mablung. 'But if either be slain it will be an evil deed, more fit for Angband than Doriath, and more evil will come of it. Indeed I feel that some shadow of the North has reached out to touch us tonight. Take heed, Saeros, lest you do the will of Morgoth in your pride, and remember that you are of the Eldar.'

Túrin causes Saeros' death

'I do not forget it,' said Saeros; but he did not abate his wrath, and through the night his malice grew, nursing his injury.

In the morning he waylaid Túrin, as he set off early from Menegroth, intending to go back to the marches. Túrin had gone only a little way when Saeros ran out upon him from behind with drawn sword and shield on arm. But Túrin, trained in the wild to wariness, saw him from the corner of his eye, and leaping aside he drew swiftly and turned upon his foe. 'Morwen!' he cried, 'now your mocker shall pay for his scorn!' And he clove Saeros' shield, and then they fought together with swift blades. But Túrin had been long in a hard school, and had grown as agile as any Elf, but stronger. He soon had the mastery, and wounding Saeros' sword-arm he had him at his mercy. Then he set his foot on the sword that Saeros had let fall. 'Saeros,' he said, 'there is a long race before you, and clothes will be a hindrance; hair must suffice.' And suddenly throwing him to the ground he stripped him, and Saeros felt Túrin's great strength, and was afraid. But Túrin let him up, and then 'Run, run, mocker of women!' he cried. 'Run! And unless you go swift as the deer I shall prick you on from behind.' Then he set the point of the sword in Saeros' buttock; and he fled into the wood, crying wildly for help in his terror; but Túrin came after him like a hound, and however he ran, or swerved, still the sword was behind him to egg him on.

The cries of Saeros brought many others to the chase, and they followed after, but only the swiftest could keep

89

up with the runners. Mablung was in the forefront of these, and he was troubled in mind, for though the taunting had seemed evil to him, 'malice that wakes in the morning is the mirth of Morgoth ere night'; and it was held moreover a grievous thing to put any of the Elven-folk to shame, self-willed, without the matter being brought to judgement. None knew at that time that Túrin had been assailed first by Saeros, who would have slain him.

'Hold, hold, Túrin!' he cried. 'This is Orc-work in the woods!' 'Orc-work there was; this is only Orc-play,' Túrin called back. Before Mablung spoke he had been on the point of releasing Saeros, but now with a shout he sprang after him again; and Saeros, despairing at last of aid and thinking his death close behind, ran wildly on, until he came suddenly to a brink where a stream that fed Esgalduin flowed in a deep cleft through high rocks, and it was wide for a deer-leap. In his terror Saeros attempted the leap; but he failed of his footing on the far side and fell back with a cry, and was broken on a great stone in the water. So he ended his life in Doriath; and long would Mandos hold him.

Túrin looked down on his body lying in the stream, and he thought: 'Unhappy fool! From here I would have let him walk back to Menegroth. Now he has laid a guilt upon me undeserved.' And he turned and looked darkly on Mablung and his companions, who now came up and stood near him on the brink. Then after a silence Mablung said gravely: 'Alas! But come back now with us, Túrin, for the King must judge these deeds.'

Túrin Leaves Doriath

But Túrin said: 'If the King were just, he would judge me guiltless. But was not this one of his counsellors? Why should a just king choose a heart of malice for his friend? I abjure his law and his judgement.'

'Your words are too proud,' said Mablung, though he pitied the young man. 'Learn wisdom! You shall not turn runagate. I bid you return with me, as a friend. And there are other witnesses. When the King learns the truth you may hope for his pardon.'

But Túrin was weary of the Elven-halls, and he feared lest he be held captive; and he said to Mablung: 'I refuse your bidding. I will not seek King Thingol's pardon for nothing; and I will go now where his doom cannot find me. You have but two choices: to let me go free, or to slay me, if that would fit your law. For you are too few to take me alive.'

They saw by the fire in his eyes that this was true, and they let him pass. 'One death is enough,' said Mablung.

'I did not will it, but I do not mourn it,' said Túrin. 'May Mandos judge him justly; and if ever he return to the lands of the living, may he prove wiser. Farewell!'

'Fare free!' said Mablung; 'for that is your wish. To say *well* would be vain, if you go in this way. A shadow is over you. When we meet again, may it be no darker.'

To that Túrin made no answer, but left them, and went swiftly away, alone, none knew whither.

It is told that when Túrin did not return to the north-marches of Doriath and no tidings could be heard of him,

Beleg Strongbow came himself to Menegroth to seek him; and with heavy heart he gathered news of Túrin's deeds and flight. Soon afterwards Thingol and Melian came back to their halls, for the summer was waning; and when the King heard report of what had passed he said: 'This is a grievous matter, which I must hear in full. Though Saeros, my counsellor, is slain, and Túrin my foster-son has fled, tomorrow I will sit in the seat of judgement, and hear again all in due order, before I speak my doom.'

Next day the King sat upon his throne in his court, and about him were all the chiefs and elders of Doriath. Then many witnesses were heard, and of these Mablung spoke most and clearest. And as he told of the quarrel at table, it seemed to the King that Mablung's heart leaned to Túrin.

'You speak as a friend of Túrin son of Húrin?' said Thingol. 'I was, but I have loved truth more and longer,' Mablung answered. 'Hear me to the end, lord!'

When all was told, even to the parting words of Túrin, Thingol sighed; and he looked on those that sat before him, and he said: 'Alas! I see a shadow on your faces. How has it stolen into my realm? Malice is at work here. Saeros I accounted faithful and wise; but if he lived he would feel my anger, for his taunting was evil, and I hold him to blame for all that chanced in the hall. So far Túrin has my pardon. But I cannot pass over his later deeds, when wrath should have cooled. The shaming of Saeros and the hounding of him to his death were wrongs greater than the offence. They show a heart hard and proud.'

Then Thingol sat for a while in thought, and spoke sadly at last. 'This is an ungrateful foster-son, and in truth a man too proud for his state. How can I still harbour one who scorns me and my law, or pardon one who will not repent? This must be my doom. I will banish Túrin from Doriath. If he seeks entry he shall be brought to judgement before me; and until he sues for pardon at my feet he is my son no longer. If any here accounts this unjust, let him speak now!'

Then there was silence in the hall, and Thingol lifted up his hand to pronounce his doom. But at that moment Beleg entered in haste, and cried: 'Lord, may I yet speak?'

'You come late,' said Thingol. 'Were you not bidden with the others?'

'Truly, lord,' answered Beleg, 'but I was delayed; I sought for one whom I knew. Now I bring at last a witness who should be heard, ere your doom falls.'

'All were summoned who had aught to tell,' said the King. 'What can he tell now of more weight than those to whom I have listened?'

'You shall judge when you have heard,' said Beleg. 'Grant this to me, if I have ever deserved your grace.'

'To you I grant it,' said Thingol. Then Beleg went out, and led in by the hand the maiden Nellas, who dwelt in the woods, and came never into Menegroth; and she was afraid, as much of the great pillared hall and the roof of stone as of the company of many eyes that watched her. And when Thingol bade her speak, she said: 'Lord, I was sitting in a tree'; but then she faltered in awe of the King, and could say no more.

At that the King smiled, and said: 'Others have done this also, but have felt no need to tell me of it.'

'Others indeed,' said she, taking courage from his smile. 'Even Lúthien! And of her I was thinking that morning, and of Beren the Man.'

To that Thingol said nothing, and he smiled no longer, but waited until Nellas should speak again.

'For Túrin reminded me of Beren,' she said at last. 'They are akin, I am told, and their kinship can be seen by some: by some that look close.'

Then Thingol grew impatient. 'That may be,' he said. 'But Túrin son of Húrin is gone in scorn of me, and you will see him no more to read his kindred. For now I will speak my judgement.'

'Lord King!' she cried then. 'Bear with me, and let me speak first. I sat in a tree to look on Túrin as he went away; and I saw Saeros come out from the wood with sword and shield, and spring on Túrin at unawares.'

At that there was a murmur in the hall; and the King lifted his hand, saying: 'You bring graver news to my ear than seemed likely. Take heed now to all that you say; for this is a court of doom.'

'So Beleg has told me,' she answered, 'and only for that have I dared to come here, so that Túrin shall not be ill judged. He is valiant, but he is merciful. They fought, lord, these two, until Túrin had bereft Saeros of both shield and sword; but he did not slay him. Therefore I do not believe that he willed his death in the end. If Saeros were put to shame, it was shame that he had earned.'

'Judgement is mine,' said Thingol. 'But what you have told shall govern it.' Then he questioned Nellas closely; and at last he turned to Mablung, saying: 'It is strange to me that Túrin said nothing of this to you.'

'Yet he did not,' said Mablung, 'or I should have recounted it. And otherwise should I have spoken to him at our parting.'

'And otherwise shall my doom now be,' said Thingol. 'Hear me! Such fault as can be found in Túrin I now pardon, holding him wronged and provoked. And since it was indeed, as he said, one of my council who so misused him, he shall not seek for this pardon, but I will send it to him, wherever he may be found; and I will recall him in honour to my halls.'

But when the doom was pronounced, suddenly Nellas wept. 'Where can he be found?' she said. 'He has left our land, and the world is wide.'

'He shall be sought,' said Thingol. Then he rose, and Beleg led Nellas forth from Menegroth; and he said to her: 'Do not weep; for if Túrin lives or walks still abroad, I shall find him, though all others fail.'

On the next day Beleg came before Thingol and Melian, and the King said to him: 'Counsel me, Beleg; for

I am grieved. I took Húrin's son as my son, and so he shall remain, unless Húrin himself should return out of the shadows to claim his own. I would not have any say that Túrin was driven forth unjustly into the wild, and gladly would I welcome him back; for I loved him well.'

'Give me leave, lord,' said Beleg, 'and on your behalf I will redress this evil, if I can. For such manhood as he promised should not run to nothing in the wild. Doriath has need of him, and the need will grow more. And I love him also.'

Then Thingol said to Beleg: 'Now I have hope in the quest! Go with my good will, and if you find him, guard him and guide him as you may. Beleg Cúthalion, long have you been foremost in the defence of Doriath, and for many deeds of valour and wisdom have earned my thanks. Greatest of all I shall hold the finding of Túrin. At this parting ask for any gift, and I will not deny it to you.'

'I ask then for a sword of worth,' said Beleg; 'for the Orcs come now too thick and close for a bow only, and such blade as I have is no match for their armour.'

'Choose from all that I have,' said Thingol, 'save only Aranrúth, my own.'

Then Beleg chose Anglachel; and that was a sword of great fame, and it was so named because it was made of iron that fell from heaven as a blazing star; it would cleave all earth-dolven iron. One other sword only in Middle-earth was like to it. That sword does not enter into this tale, though it was made of the same ore by the same

96

smith; and that smith was Eöl the Dark Elf, who took Aredhel Turgon's sister to wife. He gave Anglachel to Thingol as fee, which he begrudged, for leave to dwell in Nan Elmoth; but the other sword, Anguirel, its mate, he kept, until it was stolen from him by Maeglin, his son.

But as Thingol turned the hilt of Anglachel towards Beleg, Melian looked at the blade; and she said: 'There is malice in this sword. The heart of the smith still dwells in it, and that heart was dark. It will not love the hand that it serves; neither will it abide with you long.'

'Nonetheless I will wield it while I may,' said Beleg; and thanking the king he took the sword and departed. Far across Beleriand he sought in vain for tidings of Túrin, through many perils; and that winter passed away, and the spring after.

CHAPTER VI

TÚRIN AMONG THE OUTLAWS

Now the tale turns again to Túrin. He, believing himself an outlaw whom the King would pursue, did not return to Beleg on the north-marches of Doriath, but went away westward, and passing secretly out of the Guarded Realm came into the woodlands south of Teiglin. There before the Nirnaeth many men had dwelt in scattered homesteads; they were of Haleth's folk for the most part, but owned no lord, and they lived both by hunting and husbandry, keeping swine in the mast-lands, and tilling clearings in the forest which were fenced from the wild. But most were now destroyed, or had fled into Brethil, and all that region lay under the fear of Orcs, and of outlaws. For in that time of ruin houseless and desperate men went astray: remnants of battle and defeat, and lands laid waste; and some were men driven into the wild for evil deeds. They hunted and gathered such food as they could; but many took to robbery and became cruel, when hunger or other need drove them. In winter they were most to be feared, like wolves; and Gaurwaith, wolf-men, they were called by those who still defended their homes. Some sixty of these men had joined in one band, wandering in the woods beyond the western marches of Doriath; and they were hated scarcely less than Orcs, for there were among them outcasts hard of heart, bearing a grudge against their own kind.

The hardest of heart was one named Andróg, who had been hunted from Dor-lómin for the slaying of a woman; and others also came from that land: old Algund, the oldest of the fellowship, who had fled from the Nirnaeth, and Forweg, as he named himself, a man with fair hair and unsteady glittering eyes, big and bold, but far fallen from the ways of the Edain of the people of Hador. Yet he could still be wise and generous at times; and he was the captain of the fellowship. They had dwindled now to some fifty men, by deaths in hardship or affrays; and they were become wary, and set scouts or a watch about them, whether moving or at rest. Thus they were soon aware of Túrin when he strayed into their haunts. They trailed him, and they drew a ring about him, so that suddenly, as he came out into a glade beside a stream, he found himself within a circle of men with bent bows and drawn swords.

Then Túrin halted, but he showed no fear. 'Who are you?' he said. 'I thought that only Orcs waylaid men; but I see that I am mistaken.'

'You may rue the mistake,' said Forweg, 'for these are our haunts, and my men do not allow other men to walk in them. We take their lives as forfeit, unless they can ransom them.'

Then Túrin laughed grimly: 'You will get no ransom from me, an outcast and an outlaw. You may search me when I am dead, but it may cost you dearly to prove my words true. Many of you are likely to die first.'

Nonetheless his death seemed near, for many arrows were notched to the string, waiting for the word of the captain, and though Túrin wore elven-mail under his grey tunic and cloak, some would find a deadly mark. None of his enemies stood within reach of a leap with drawn sword. But suddenly Túrin stooped, for he had espied some stones at the stream's edge before his feet. At that moment an outlaw, angered by his proud words, let fly a shaft aimed at his face; but it passed over him, and he sprang up again like a bowstring released and cast a stone at the bowman with great force and true aim; and he fell to the ground with broken skull.

'I might be of more service to you alive, in the place of that luckless man,' said Túrin; and turning to Forweg he said: 'If you are the captain here, you should not allow your men to shoot without command.'

'I do not,' said Forweg; 'but he has been rebuked swiftly enough. I will take you in his stead, if you will heed my words better.'

'I will,' said Túrin, 'as long as you are captain, and in

all that belongs to a captain. But the choice of a new man to a fellowship is not his alone, I judge. All voices should be heard. Are there any here who do not welcome me?'

Then two of the outlaws cried out against him; and one was a friend of the fallen man. Ulrad was his name. 'A strange way to gain entry to a fellowship,' he said, 'the slaying of one of our best men!'

'Not unchallenged,' said Túrin. 'But come then! I will endure you both together, with weapons or with strength alone. Then you shall see if I am fit to replace one of your best men. But if there are bows in this test, I must have one too.' Then he strode towards them; but Ulrad gave back and would not fight. The other threw down his bow and walked up to meet Túrin. This man was Andróg of Dor-lómin. He stood before Túrin and looked him up and down.

'Nay,' he said at length, shaking his head. 'I am not a chicken-heart, as men know; but I am not your match. There is none here, I think. You may join us, for my part. But there is a strange light in your eyes; you are a danger-ous man. What is your name?'

'Neithan, the Wronged, I call myself,' said Túrin, and Neithan he was afterwards called by the outlaws; but though he claimed to have suffered injustice (and to any who claimed the like he ever lent too ready an ear), no more would he reveal concerning his life or his home. Yet they saw that he had fallen from high state, and that though he had nothing but his arms, those were made by elven-smiths. He soon won their praise, for he was strong and valiant, and had more skill in the woods than they, and they trusted him, for he was not greedy, and took little thought for himself; but they feared him, because of his sudden angers, which they seldom understood.

To Doriath Túrin could not, or in pride would not, return; to Nargothrond since the fall of Felagund none were admitted. To the lesser folk of Haleth in Brethil he did not deign to go; and to Dor-lómin he did not dare, for it was closely beset, and one man alone could not hope at that time, as he thought, to come through the passes of the Mountains of Shadow. Therefore Túrin abode with the outlaws, since the company of any men made the hardship of the wild more easy to endure; and because he wished to live and could not be ever at strife with them, he did little to restrain their evil deeds. Thus he soon became hardened to a mean and often cruel life, and yet at times pity and disgust would wake in him, and then he was perilous in his anger. In this evil and dangerous way Túrin lived to that year's end and through the need and hunger of winter, until stirring came and then a fair spring.

Now in the woods of Teiglin, as has been told, there were still some homesteads of Men, hardy and wary, though now few in number. Though they loved them not at all and pitied them little, they would in bitter winter put out such food as they could well spare where the Gaur-waith might find it; and so they hoped to avoid the banded attack of the famished. But they earned less gratitude so from the outlaws than from beasts and birds, and they were saved rather by their dogs and their fences. For each homestead had great hedges about its cleared land, and about the houses was a ditch and a stockade; and there were paths from stead to stead, and men could summon help at need by horn-calls.

But when spring was come it was perilous for the Gaurwaith to linger so near to the houses of the woodmen, who might gather and hunt them down; and Túrin wondered therefore that Forweg did not lead them away. There was more food and game, and less peril, away south where no Men remained. Then one day Túrin missed Forweg, and also Andróg his friend; and he asked where they were, but his companions laughed.

'Away on business of their own, I guess,' said Ulrad. 'They will be back before long, and then we shall move. In haste, maybe; for we shall be lucky if they do not bring the hive-bees after them.'

The sun shone and the young leaves were green, and Túrin was irked by the squalid camp of the outlaws, and he wandered away alone far into the forest. Against his will he remembered the Hidden Kingdom, and he seemed to hear the names of the flowers of Doriath as echoes of an old tongue almost forgotten. But on a sudden he heard cries, and from a hazel-thicket a young woman ran out; her clothes were rent by thorns, and she was in great fear, and stumbling she fell gasping to the ground. Then Túrin springing towards the thicket with drawn sword hewed down a man that burst from the hazels in pursuit; and he saw only in the very stroke that it was Forweg.

But as he stood looking down in amaze at the blood upon the grass, Andróg came out, and halted also astounded. 'Evil work, Neithan!' he cried, and drew his sword; but Túrin's mood ran cold, and he said to Andróg: 'Where are the Orcs, then? Have you outrun them to help her?'

'Orcs?' said Andróg. 'Fool! You call yourself an outlaw. Outlaws know no law but their needs. Look to your own, Neithan, and leave us to mind ours.'

'I will do so,' said Túrin. 'But today our paths have crossed. You will leave the woman to me, or you will join Forweg.'

Andróg laughed. 'If that is the way of it, have your will,' he said. 'I make no claim to match you, alone; but our fellows may take this slaying ill.'

Then the woman rose to her feet and laid her hand on Túrin's arm. She looked at the blood and she looked at Túrin, and there was delight in her eyes. 'Kill him, lord!' she said. 'Kill him too! And then come with me. If you bring their heads, Larnach my father will not be displeased. For two "wolf-heads" he has rewarded men well.'

But Túrin said to Andróg: 'Is it far to her home?'

'A mile or so,' he answered, 'in a fenced homestead yonder. She was straying outside.' 'Go then quickly,' said Túrin, turning back to the woman. 'Tell your father to keep you better. But I will not cut off the heads of my fellows to buy his favour, or aught else.'

Then he put up his sword. 'Come!' he said to Andróg. 'We will return. But if you wish to bury your captain, you must do so yourself. Make haste, for a hue and cry may be raised. Bring his weapons!'

The woman went off through the woods, and she looked back many times before the trees hid her. Then Túrin went on his way without more words, and Andróg watched him go, and he frowned as one pondering a riddle.

When Túrin came back to the camp of the outlaws he found them restless and ill at ease; for they had stayed too long already in one place, near to homesteads well-guarded, and they murmured against Forweg. 'He runs hazards to our cost', they said; 'and others may have to pay for his pleasures.'

'Then choose a new captain!' said Túrin, standing before them. 'Forweg can lead you no longer; for he is dead.'

'How do you know that?' said Ulrad. 'Did you seek honey from the same hive? Did the bees sting him?'

'No,' said Túrin. 'One sting was enough. I slew him. But I spared Andróg, and he will soon return.' Then he told all that was done, rebuking those that did such deeds; and while he yet spoke Andróg returned bearing Forweg's weapons. 'See, Neithan!' he cried. 'No alarm has been raised. Maybe she hopes to meet with you again.'

'If you jest with me,' said Túrin, 'I shall regret that I grudged her your head. Now tell your tale, and be brief.'

Then Andróg told truly enough all that had befallen. 'What business Neithan had there I now wonder,' he said. 'Not ours, it seems. For when I came up, he had already slain Forweg. The woman liked that well, and offered to go with him, begging our heads as a bride-price. But he did not want her, and sped her off; so what grudge he had against the captain I cannot guess. He left my head on my shoulders, for which I am grateful, though much puzzled.'

'Then I deny your claim to come of the People of Hador,' said Túrin. 'To Uldor the Accursed you belong rather, and should seek service with Angband. But hear me now!' he cried to them all. 'These choices I give you. You must take me as your captain in Forweg's place, or else let me go. I will govern this fellowship now, or leave it. But if you wish to kill me, set to! I will fight you all until I am dead – or you.'

Then many men seized their weapons, but Andróg cried out: 'Nay! The head that he spared is not witless. If we fight, more than one will die needlessly, before we kill the best man among us.' Then he laughed. 'As it was when he joined us, so it is again. He kills to make room. If it proved well before, so may it again; and he may lead us to better fortune than prowling about other men's middens.'

And old Algund said: 'The best man among us. Time was when we would have done the same, if we dared; but we have forgotten much. He may bring us home in the end.'

At that the thought came to Túrin that from this small band he might rise to build himself a free lordship of his own. But he looked at Algund and Andróg, and he said: 'Home, do you say? Tall and cold stand the Mountains of Shadow between. Behind them are the people of Uldor, and about them the legions of Angband. If such things do not daunt you, seven times seven men, then I may lead you homewards. But how far, before we die?'

All were silent. Then Túrin spoke again. 'Do you take me to be your captain? Then I will lead you first away into the wild, far from the homes of Men. There we may find better fortune, or not; but at the least we shall earn less hatred of our own kind.'

Then all those that were of the People of Hador gathered to him, and took him as their captain; and the others with less good will agreed. And at once he led them away out of that country.

Many messengers had been sent out by Thingol to seek Túrin within Doriath and in the lands near its borders; but in the year of his flight they searched for him in vain, for none knew or could guess that he was with the outlaws and enemies of Men. When winter came on they returned to the King, save Beleg only. After all others had departed still he went on alone.

But in Dimbar and along the north-marches of Doriath things had gone ill. The Dragon-helm was seen there in battle no longer, and the Strongbow also was missed; and the servants of Morgoth were heartened and increased ever in numbers and in daring. Winter came and passed, and with Spring their assault was renewed: Dimbar was overrun, and the Men of Brethil were afraid, for evil roamed now upon all their borders, save in the south.

It was now almost a year since Túrin had fled, and still Beleg sought for him, with ever lessening hope. He passed northwards in his wanderings to the Crossings of Teiglin, and there, hearing ill news of a new inroad of Orcs out of Taur-nu-Fuin, he turned back, and came as it chanced to the homes of the Woodmen soon after Túrin had left that region. There he heard a strange tale that went among them. A tall and lordly Man, or an Elf-warrior, some said, had appeared in the woods, and had slain one of the Gaurwaith, and rescued the daughter of Larnach whom they were pursuing. 'Very proud he was,' said Larnach's daughter to Beleg, 'with bright eyes that scarcely deigned to look at me. Yet he called the Wolf-men his fellows, and would not slay another that stood by, and knew his name. Neithan, he called him.'

'Can you read this riddle?' asked Larnach of the Elf.

'I can, alas,' said Beleg. 'The Man that you tell of is one whom I seek.' No more of Túrin did he tell the Woodmen; but he warned them of evil gathering northward. 'Soon the Orcs will come ravening in this country in strength too great for you to withstand,' he said. 'This year at last you must give up your freedom or your lives. Go to Brethil while there is time!'

Then Beleg went on his way in haste, and sought for the lairs of the outlaws, and such signs as might show him whither they had gone. These he soon found; but Túrin was now several days ahead, and moved swiftly, fearing the pursuit of the Woodmen, and he had used all the arts that he knew to defeat or mislead any that tried to follow him. He led his men westward, away from the Woodmen and from the borders of Doriath, until they came to the northern end of the great highlands that rose between the Vales of Sirion and Narog. There the land was drier, and the forest ceased suddenly on the brink of a ridge. Below it could be seen the ancient South Road, climbing up from the Crossings of Teiglin to pass along the western feet of the moorlands on its way to Nargothrond. There for a time the outlaws lived warily, remaining seldom two nights in one camp, and leaving little trace of their going or staying. So it was that even Beleg hunted them in vain. Led by signs that he could read, or by the rumour of the passing of Men among the wild things with whom he could speak, he came often near, but always their lair was deserted when he came to it; for they kept a watch about them by day and night, and at any rumour of approach they were swiftly up and away. 'Alas!' he cried. 'Too well did I teach this child of Men craft in wood and field! An Elvish band almost one might think this to be.' But they for their part became aware that they were trailed by some tireless pursuer, whom they could not see, and yet could not shake off; and they grew uneasy.

Not long afterwards, as Beleg had feared, the Orcs came across the Brithiach, and being resisted with all the force that he could muster by Handir of Brethil, they passed south over the Crossings of Teiglin in search of plunder. Many of the Woodmen had taken Beleg's counsel and sent their woman and children to ask for refuge in Brethil. These and their escort escaped, passing over the Crossings in time; but the armed men that came behind were met by the Orcs, and the men were worsted. A few fought their way through and came to Brethil, but many were slain or captured; and the Orcs passed on to the homesteads, and sacked them and burned them. Then at once they turned back westwards, seeking the Road, for they wished now to return back north as swiftly as they could with their booty and their captives.

But the scouts of the outlaws were soon aware of them; and though they cared little enough for the captives, the plunder of the Woodmen aroused their greed. To Túrin it seemed perilous to reveal themselves to the Orcs, until their numbers were known; but the outlaws would not heed him, for they had need of many things in the wild, and already some began to regret his leading. Therefore taking one Orleg as his only companion Túrin went forth to spy upon the Orcs; and giving command of the band to Andróg he charged him to lie close and well hid while they were gone.

Now the Orc-host was far greater than the band of outlaws, but they were in lands to which Orcs had seldom dared to come, and they knew also that beyond the Road lay the Talath Dirnen, the Guarded Plain, upon which the scouts and spies of Nargothrond kept watch; and fearing danger they were wary, and their scouts went creeping through the trees on either side of the marching lines. Thus it was that Túrin and Orleg were discovered, for three scouts stumbled upon them as they lay hid; and though they slew two the third escaped, crying as he ran *Golug! Golug!* Now that was a name which they had for the Noldor. At once the forest was filled with Orcs, scattering silently and hunting far and wide. Then Túrin, seeing that there was small hope of escape, thought at least to deceive them and to lead them away from the hiding-place of his men; and perceiving from the cry of *Golug!* that they feared the spies of Nargothrond, he fled with Orleg westward. The pursuit came swiftly after them, until turn and dodge as they would they were driven at last out of the forest; and then they were espied, and as they sought to cross the Road Orleg was shot down by many arrows. But Túrin was saved by his elven-mail, and escaped alone into the wilds beyond; and by speed and craft he eluded his enemies, fleeing far into lands that were strange to him. Then the Orcs, fearing that the Elves of Nargothrond might be aroused, slew their captives and made haste away into the North.

Now when three days had passed, and yet Túrin and Orleg did not return, some of the outlaws wished to depart from the cave where they lay hid; but Andróg spoke against it. And while they were in the midst of this debate, suddenly a grey figure stood before them. Beleg had found them at last. He came forward with no weapon in his hands, and held the palms turned towards them; but they leapt up in fear and Andróg coming behind cast a noose over him, and drew it so that it pinioned his arms.

'If you do not wish for guests, you should keep better watch,' said Beleg. 'Why do you welcome me thus? I come as a friend, and seek only a friend. Neithan, I hear that you call him.'

'He is not here,' said Ulrad. 'But unless you have long spied on us, how know you that name?'

'He has long spied on us,' said Andróg. 'This is the shadow that has dogged us. Now perhaps we shall learn his true purpose.' Then he bade them tie Beleg to a tree beside the cave; and when he was hard bound hand and foot they questioned him. But to all their questions Beleg would give one answer only: 'A friend I have been to this Neithan since I first met him in the woods, and he was then but a child. I seek him only in love, and to bring him good tidings.'

'Let us slay him, and be rid of his spying,' said Andróg in wrath; and he looked on the great bow of Beleg and coveted it, for he was an archer. But some of better heart spoke against him, and Algund said to him: 'The captain may return yet; and then you will rue it, if he learns that he has been robbed at once of a friend and of good tidings.'

'I do not believe the tale of this Elf,' said Andróg. 'He is a spy of the King of Doriath. But if he has indeed any tidings, he shall tell them to us; and we shall judge if they give us reason to let him live.'

'I shall wait for your captain,' said Beleg.

'You shall stand there until you speak,' said Andróg.

Then at the egging of Andróg they left Beleg tied to the tree without food or water, and they sat near eating and drinking; but he said no more to them. When two days and nights had passed in this way they became angry and fearful, and were eager to be gone; and most were now ready to slay the Elf. As night drew down they were all gathered about him, and Ulrad brought a brand from the little fire that was lit in the cave-mouth. But at that moment Túrin returned. Coming silently, as was his custom, he stood in the shadows beyond the ring of men, and he saw the haggard face of Beleg in the light of the brand.

Then he was stricken as with a shaft, and as if at the sudden melting of a frost tears long unshed filled his eyes. He sprang out and ran to the tree. 'Beleg! Beleg!' he cried. 'How have you come hither? And why do you stand so?' At once he cut the bonds from his friend, and Beleg fell forward into his arms.

When Túrin heard all that the men would tell, he was angry and grieved; but at first he gave heed only to Beleg. While he tended him with what skill he had, he thought of his life in the woods, and his anger turned upon himself. For often strangers had been slain, when caught near the lairs of the outlaws, or waylaid by them, and he had not hindered it; and often he himself had spoken ill of King Thingol and of the Grey-elves, so that he must share the blame, if they were treated as foes. Then with bitterness he turned to the men. 'You were cruel,' he said, 'and cruel without need. Never until now have we tormented a prisoner; but to this Orc-work such a life as we lead has brought us. Lawless and fruitless all our deeds have been, serving only ourselves, and feeding hate in our hearts.'

But Andróg said: 'But whom shall we serve, if not ourselves? Whom shall we love, when all hate us?'

'At least my hands shall not again be raised against Elves or Men,' said Túrin. 'Angband has servants enough. If others will not take this vow with me, I will walk alone.'

Then Beleg opened his eyes and raised his head. 'Not alone!' he said. 'Now at last I can tell my tidings. You are no outlaw, and Neithan is a name unfit. Such fault as was found in you is pardoned. For a year you have been sought, to recall you to honour and to the service of the King. The Dragon-helm has been missed too long.'

But Túrin showed no joy in this news, and sat long in silence; for at Beleg's words a shadow fell upon him again. 'Let this night pass,' he said at length. 'Then I will choose. However it goes, we must leave this lair tomorrow; for not all who seek us wish us well.'

'Nay, none,' said Andróg, and he cast an evil look at Beleg.

In the morning Beleg, being swiftly healed of his pains, after the manner of the Elven-folk of old, spoke to Túrin apart.

'I looked for more joy at my tidings,' he said. 'Surely you will return now to Doriath?' And he begged Túrin to do this in all ways that he could; but the more he urged it, the more Túrin hung back. Nonetheless he questioned Beleg closely concerning the judgement of Thingol. Then Beleg told him all that he knew, and at the last Túrin said: 'Then Mablung proved my friend, as he once seemed?'

'The friend of truth, rather,' said Beleg, 'and that was best, in the end; though the doom would have been less just, were it not for the witness of Nellas. Why, why, Túrin, did you not speak of Saeros' assault to Mablung? All otherwise might things have gone. And,' he said, looking at the men sprawled near the mouth of the cave, 'you might have held your helm still high, and not fallen to this.'

'That may be, if fall you call it,' said Túrin. 'That may be. But so it went; and words stuck in my throat. There was reproof in his eyes, without question asked of me, for a deed I had not done. My Man's heart was proud, as the Elf-king said. And so it still is, Beleg Cúthalion. Not yet will it suffer me to go back to Menegroth and bear looks of pity and pardon, as for a wayward boy amended. I should give pardon, not receive it. And I am a boy no longer, but a man, according to my kind; and a hard man by my fate.'

Then Beleg was troubled. 'What will you do, then?' he asked.

'Fare free,' said Túrin. 'That wish Mablung gave me at our parting. The grace of Thingol will not stretch to receive these companions of my fall, I think; but I will not part with them now, if they do not wish to part with me. I love them in my way, even the worst a little. They are of my own kind, and there is some good in each that might grow. I think that they will stand by me.'

'You see with other eyes than mine,' said Beleg. 'If you try to wean them from evil, they will fail you. I doubt them, and one most of all.'

'How shall an Elf judge of Men?' said Túrin.

'As he judges of all deeds, by whomsoever done,' answered Beleg, but he said no more, and did not speak of Andróg's malice, to which his evil handling had been chiefly due; for perceiving Túrin's mood he feared to be disbelieved and to hurt their old friendship, driving Túrin back to his evil ways.

'Fare free, you say, Túrin, my friend,' he said. 'What is your meaning?'

'I would lead my own men, and make war in my own way,' Túrin answered. 'But in this at least my heart is changed: I repent every stroke save those dealt against the Enemy of Men and Elves. And above all else I would have you beside me. Stay with me!'

'If I stayed beside you, love would lead me, not wisdom,' said Beleg. 'My heart warns me that we should return to Doriath. Elsewhere a shadow lies before us.'

'Nonetheless, I will not go there,' said Túrin.

'Alas!' said Beleg. 'But as a fond father who grants his son's desire against his own foresight, I yield to your will. At your asking, I will stay.'

'That is well indeed!' said Túrin. Then all at once he fell silent, as if he himself were aware of the shadow, and strove with his pride, which would not let him turn back. For a long while he sat, brooding on the years that lay behind.

Coming suddenly out of thought he looked at Beleg, and said: 'The elf-maiden that you named, though I forget how: I owe her well for her timely witness; yet I cannot recall her. Why did she watch my ways?' Then Beleg looked strangely at him. 'Why indeed?' he said. 'Túrin, have you lived always with your heart and half your mind far away? As a boy you used to walk with Nellas in the woods.'

'That must have been long ago,' said Túrin. 'Or so my childhood now seems, and a mist is over it – save only the memory of my father's house in Dor-lómin. Why would I walk with an elf-maiden?'

'To learn what she could teach, maybe,' said Beleg, 'if no more than a few elven-words of the names of woodland flowers. Their names at least you have not forgotten. Alas! child of Men, there are other griefs in Middle-earth than yours, and wounds made by no weapon. Indeed I begin to think that Elves and Men should not meet or meddle.'

Túrin said nothing, but looked long in Beleg's face, as if he would read in it the riddle of his words. Nellas of

Doriath never saw him again, and his shadow passed from her. Now Beleg and Túrin turned to other matters, debating where they should dwell. 'Let us return to Dimbar, on the north-marches, where once we walked together!' said Beleg eagerly. 'We are needed there. For of late the Orcs have found a way down out of Taur-nu-Fuin, making a road through the Pass of Anach.'

'I do not remember it,' said Túrin.

'No, we never went so far from the borders,' said Beleg. 'But you have seen the peaks of the Crissaegrim far off, and to their east the dark walls of the Gorgoroth. Anach lies between them, above the high springs of Mindeb. A hard and dangerous way; and yet many come by it now, and Dimbar which used to lie in peace is falling under the Dark Hand, and the Men of Brethil are troubled. To Dimbar I call you!'

'Nay, I will not walk backward in life,' said Túrin. 'Nor can I come easily to Dimbar now. Sirion lies between, unbridged and unforded below the Brithiach far northward; it is perilous to cross. Save in Doriath. But I will not pass into Doriath, and make use of Thingol's leave and pardon.'

'A hard man you have called yourself, Túrin. Truly, if by that you meant stubborn. Now the turn is mine. I will go, by your leave, as soon as I may, and bid you farewell. If you wish indeed to have the Strongbow beside you, look for me in Dimbar.' At that time Túrin said no more.

The next day Beleg set out, and Túrin went with him a bowshot from the camp, but said nothing. 'Is it farewell, then, son of Húrin?' said Beleg.

'If you wish indeed to keep your word and stay beside me,' answered Túrin, 'then look for me on Amon Rûdh!' Thus he spoke, being fey and unwitting of what lay before him. 'Else, this is our last farewell.'

'Maybe that is best,' said Beleg, and went his way.

It is said that Beleg went back to Menegroth, and came before Thingol and Melian and told them of all that had happened, save only his evil handling by Túrin's companions. Then Thingol sighed, and he said: 'I took up the fathering of the son of Húrin, and that cannot be laid down for love or hate, unless Húrin the Valiant himself should return. What more would he have me do?'

But Melian said: 'A gift you shall now have of me, Cúthalion, for your help, and your honour, for I have none worthier to give.' And she gave him a store of *lembas*, the waybread of the Elves, wrapped in leaves of silver; and the threads that bound it were sealed at the knots with the seal of the Queen, a wafer of white wax shaped as a single flower of Telperion. For according to the customs of the Eldalië the keeping and the giving of this food belonged to the Queen alone. 'This waybread, Beleg,' she said, 'shall be your help in the wild and the winter, and the help also of those whom you choose. For I commit this now to you, to apportion as you will in my stead.' In nothing did Melian show greater favour to Túrin than in this gift; for the Eldar had never before allowed Men to use this waybread, and seldom did so again.

Then Beleg departed from Menegroth and went back to the north-marches, where he had his lodges, and many friends; but when winter came, and war was stilled, suddenly his companions missed Beleg, and he returned to them no more.

CHAPTER VII

OF MÎM THE DWARF

Now the tale turns to Mîm the Petty-dwarf. The Petty-dwarves are long out of mind, for Mîm was the last. Little was known of them even in days of old. The Nibin-nogrim the Elves of Beleriand called them long ago, but they did not love them; and the Petty-dwarves loved none but themselves. If they hated and feared the Orcs, they hated also the Eldar, and the Exiles most of all; for the Noldor, they said, had stolen their lands and their homes. Nargothrond was first found and its delving begun by the Petty-dwarves, long before Finrod Felagund came over the Sea.

They came, some said, of Dwarves that had been banished from the Dwarf-cities of the east in ancient days. Long before the return of Morgoth they had wandered westward. Being masterless and few in number, they found it hard to come by the ore of metals, and their smith-craft and store of weapons dwindled; and they took to lives of stealth, and became somewhat smaller in stature than their eastern kin, walking with bent shoulders and quick, furtive steps. Nonetheless, as all the Dwarf-kind, they were far stronger than their stature promised, and they could cling to life in great hardship. But now at last they had dwindled and died out of Middle-earth, all save Mîm and his two sons; and Mîm was old even in the reckoning of Dwarves, old and forgotten.

After the departure of Beleg (and that was in the second summer after the flight of Túrin from Doriath) things went ill for the outlaws. There were rains out of season, and Orcs in greater numbers than before came down from the North and along the old South Road over Teiglin, troubling all the woods on the west borders of Doriath. There was little safety or rest, and the company were more often hunted than hunters.

One night as they lay lurking in the fireless dark, Túrin looked on his life, and it seemed to him that it might well be bettered. 'I must find some secure refuge,' he thought, 'and make provision against winter and hunger.' But he did not know whither to turn.

Next day he led his men away southward, further than they had yet come from the Teiglin and the marches of Doriath; and after three days' journeying they halted at the western edge of the woods of Sirion's Vale. There the land was drier and barer, as it began to climb up into the moorlands.

Soon after, it chanced that as the grey light of a day of rain was failing Túrin and his men were sheltering in a holly-thicket; and beyond it was a treeless space, in which there were many great stones, leaning or tumbled together. All was still, save for the drip of rain from the leaves.

Suddenly a watchman gave a call, and leaping up they saw three hooded shapes, grey-clad, going stealthily among the stones. They were burdened each with a great sack, but they went swiftly for all that. Túrin cried to them to halt, and the men ran out on them like hounds; but they held on their way, and though Andróg shot at them two vanished in the dusk. One lagged behind, being slower or more heavily burdened; and he was soon seized and thrown down, and held by many hard hands, though he struggled and bit like a beast. But Túrin came up, and rebuked his men. 'What have you there?' he said. 'What need to be so fierce? It is old and small. What harm is in it?'

'It bites,' said Andróg, nursing a bleeding hand. 'It is an Orc, or of Orc-kin. Kill it!'

'It deserves no less, for cheating our hope,' said another, who had taken the sack. 'There is nothing here but roots and small stones.'

'Nay,' said Túrin, 'it is bearded. It is only a Dwarf, I guess. Let him up, and speak.'

So it was that Mîm came into the Tale of the Children of Húrin. For he stumbled up on his knees before Túrin's feet

and begged for his life. 'I am old,' he said, 'and poor. Only
a Dwarf, as you say, not an Orc. Mîm is my name. Do not
let them slay me, master, for no cause, as Orcs would.'

Then Túrin pitied him in his heart, but he said: 'Poor
you seem, Mîm, though that would be strange in a Dwarf;
but we are poorer, I think: houseless and friendless Men.
If I said that we do not spare for pity's sake only, being in
great need, what would you offer for ransom?'

'I do not know what you desire, lord,' said Mîm warily.

'At this time, little enough!' said Túrin, looking about
him bitterly with rain in his eyes. 'A safe place to sleep in
out of the damp woods. Doubtless you have such for
yourself.'

'I have,' said Mîm; 'but I cannot give it in ransom. I am
too old to live under the sky.'

'You need grow no older,' said Andróg, stepping up
with a knife in his unharmed hand. 'I can spare you that.'

'Lord!' cried Mîm in great fear, clinging to Túrin's
knees. 'If I lose my life, you lose the dwelling; for you will
not find it without Mîm. I cannot give it, but I will share
it. There is more room in it than once there was, so many
have gone for ever,' and he began to weep.

'Your life is spared, Mîm,' said Túrin.

'Till we come to his lair, at least,' said Andróg.

But Túrin turned upon him, and said: 'If Mîm brings
us to his home without trickery, and it is good, then his
life is ransomed; and he shall not be slain by any man who
follows me. So I swear.'

Then Mîm kissed Túrin's knees and said: 'Mîm will be your friend, lord. At first he thought you were an Elf, by your speech and your voice. But if you are a Man, that is better. Mîm does not love Elves.'

'Where is this house of yours?' said Andróg. 'It must be good indeed to share it with a Dwarf. For Andróg does not like Dwarves. His people brought few good tales of that race out of the East.'

'They left worse tales of themselves behind them,' said Mîm. 'Judge my home when you see it. But you will need light on your way, you stumbling Men. I will return in good time and lead you.' Then he rose and picked up his sack.

'No, no!' said Andróg. 'You will not allow this, surely, captain? You would never see the old rascal again.'

'It is growing dark,' said Túrin. 'Let him leave us some pledge. Shall we keep your sack and its load, Mîm?'

But at this the Dwarf fell on his knees again in great trouble. 'If Mîm did not mean to return, he would not return for an old sack of roots,' he said. 'I will come back. Let me go!'

'I will not,' said Túrin. 'If you will not part with your sack, you must stay with it. A night under the leaves will make you pity us in your turn, maybe.' But he marked, and others also, that Mîm set more store by the sack and his load than it seemed worth to the eye.

They led the old Dwarf away to their dismal camp, and as he went he muttered in a strange tongue that seemed harsh with ancient hatred; but when they put bonds on his legs he went suddenly quiet. And those who were on the watch saw him sitting on through the night silent and still as a stone, save for his sleepless eyes that glinted as they roved in the dark.

Before morning the rain ceased, and a wind stirred in the trees. Dawn came more brightly than for many days, and light airs from the South opened the sky, pale and clear about the rising of the sun. Mîm sat on without moving, and he seemed as if dead; for now the heavy lids of his eyes were closed, and the morning-light showed him withered and shrunken with age. Túrin stood and looked down on him. 'There is light enough now,' he said.

Then Mîm opened his eyes and pointed to his bonds; and when he was released he spoke fiercely. 'Learn this, fools!' he said. 'Do not put bonds on a Dwarf! He will not forgive it. I do not wish to die, but for what you have done my heart is hot. I repent my promise.'

'But I do not,' said Túrin. 'You will lead me to your home. Till then we will not speak of death. That is *my* will.' He looked steadfastly in the eyes of the Dwarf, and Mîm could not endure it; few indeed could challenge the eyes of Túrin in set will or in wrath. Soon he turned away his head, and rose. 'Follow me, lord!' he said.

'Good!' said Túrin. 'But now I will add this: I understand your pride. You may die, but you shall not be set in bonds again.'

'I will not,' said Mîm. 'But come now!' And with that he led them back to the place where he had been captured, and he pointed westward. 'There is my home!' he said. 'You have often seen it, I guess, for it is tall. Sharbhund we called it, before the Elves changed all the names.' Then they saw that he was pointing to Amon Rûdh, the Bald Hill, whose bare head watched over many leagues of the wild.

'We have seen it, but never nearer,' said Andróg. 'For what safe lair can be there, or water, or any other thing that we need? I guessed that there was some trick. Do men hide on a hill-top?'

'Long sight may be safer than lurking,' said Túrin. 'Amon Rûdh gazes far and wide. Well, Mîm, I will come and see what you have to show. How long will it take us, stumbling Men, to come thither?'

'All this day until dusk, if we start now,' answered Mîm.

Soon the company set out westward, and Túrin went at the head with Mîm at his side. They walked warily when they left the woods, but all the land seemed empty and quiet. They passed over the tumbled stones, and began to climb; for Amon Rûdh stood upon the eastern edge of the high moorlands that rose between the vales of Sirion and Narog, and even above the stony heath at its base its crown was reared up a thousand feet and more. Upon the eastern side a broken land climbed slowly up to the high ridges among knots of birch and rowan, and ancient thorn-trees rooted in rock. Beyond, upon the moors and about the lower slopes of Amon Rûdh, there grew thickets of *aeglos*; but its steep grey head was bare, save for the red *seregon* that mantled the stone.

As the afternoon was waning the outlaws drew near to the roots of the hill. They came now from the north, for so Mîm had led them, and the light of the westering sun fell upon the crown of Amon Rûdh, and the *seregon* was all in flower.

'See! There is blood on the hill-top,' said Andróg.

'Not yet,' said Túrin.

The sun was sinking and light was failing in the hollows. The hill now loomed up before them and above them, and they wondered what need there could be of a guide to so plain a mark. But as Mîm led them on, and they began to climb the last steep slopes, they perceived that he was following some path by secret signs or old custom. Now his course wound to and fro, and if they looked aside they saw that at either hand dark dells and chines opened, or the land ran down into wastes of great stones with falls and holes masked by bramble and thorn. There without a guide they might have laboured and clambered for days to find a way.

At length they came to steeper but smoother ground. They passed under the shadows of ancient rowan-trees, into aisles of long-legged *aeglos*: a gloom filled with a sweet scent. Then suddenly there was a rock-wall before

them, flat-faced and sheer, forty feet high, maybe, but dusk
dimmed the sky above them and guess was uncertain.

'Is this the door of your house?' said Túrin. 'Dwarves
love stone, it is said.' He drew close to Mîm, lest he should
play them some trick at the last.

'Not the door of the house, but the gate of the garth,'
said Mîm. Then he turned to the right along the cliff-foot,
and after twenty paces he halted suddenly; and Túrin saw
that by the work of hands or of weather there was a cleft so
shaped that two faces of the wall overlapped, and an
opening ran back to the left between them. Its entrance was
shrouded by long trailing plants rooted in crevices above,
but within there was a steep stony path going upward in the
dark. Water trickled down it, and it was dank.

One by one they filed up. At the top the path turned
right and south again, and brought them through a thicket
of thorns out upon a green flat, through which it ran on
into the shadows. They had come to Mîm's house, Bar-en-
Nibin-noeg, which only ancient tales in Doriath and Nargothrond remembered, and no Men had seen. But night
was falling, and the east was starlit, and they could not yet
see how this strange place was shaped.

Amon Rûdh had a crown: a great mass like a steep cap
of stone with a bare flattened top. Upon its north side
there stood out from it a shelf, level and almost square,
which could not be seen from below; for behind it stood
the hill-crown like a wall, and west and east from its brink
sheer cliffs fell. Only from the north, as they had come,

could it be reached with ease by those who knew the way. From the 'gate' a path led, and passed soon into a little grove of dwarfed birches growing about a clear pool in a rock-hewn basin. This was fed by a spring at the foot of the wall behind, and through a runnel it spilled like a white thread over the western brink of the shelf. Behind the screen of the trees, near the spring between two tall buttresses of rock, there was a cave. No more than a shallow grot it looked, with a low broken arch; but further in it had been deepened and bored far under the hill by the slow hands of the Petty-dwarves, in the long years that they had dwelt there, untroubled by the Grey-elves of the woods.

Through the deep dusk Mîm led them past the pool, where now the faint stars were mirrored among the shadows of the birch-boughs. At the mouth of the cave he turned and bowed to Túrin. 'Enter, lord!' he said: 'Bar-en-Danwedh, the House of Ransom. For so it shall be called.'

'That may be,' said Túrin. 'I will look at it first.' Then he went in with Mîm, and the others, seeing him unafraid, followed behind, even Andróg, who most misdoubted the Dwarf. They were soon in a black dark; but Mîm clapped his hands, and a little light appeared, coming round a corner: from a passage at the back of the outer grot there stepped another Dwarf bearing a small torch.

'Ha! I missed him, as I feared!' said Andróg. But Mîm spoke quickly with the other in their own harsh tongue, and seeming troubled or angered by what he heard, he darted into the passage and disappeared. Now Andróg was all for going forward. 'Attack first!' he cried. 'There may be a hive of them; but they are small.'

'Three only, I guess,' said Túrin; and he led the way, while behind him the outlaws groped along the passage by the feel of the rough walls. Many times it bent this way and that at sharp angles; but at last a faint light gleamed ahead, and they came into a small but lofty hall, dim-lit by lamps hanging down out of the roof-shadow upon fine chains. Mîm was not there, but his voice could be heard, and led by it Túrin came to the door of a chamber opening at the back of the hall. Looking in, he saw Mîm kneeling on the floor. Beside him stood silent the Dwarf with the torch; but on a stone couch by the far wall lay another. 'Khîm, Khîm, Khîm!' the old Dwarf wailed, tearing at his beard.

'Not all your shots went wild,' said Túrin to Andróg. 'But this may prove an ill hit. You loose shaft too lightly; but you may not live long enough to learn wisdom.'

Leaving the others, Túrin entered softly and stood behind Mîm, and spoke to him. 'What is the trouble, master?' he said. 'I have some healing arts. May I help you?'

Mîm turned his head, and his eyes had a red light. 'Not unless you can turn back time and cut off the cruel hands of your men,' he answered. 'This is my son. An arrow was in his breast. Now he is beyond speech. He died at sunset. Your bonds held me from healing him.'

Again pity long hardened welled in Túrin's heart as water from rock. 'Alas!' he said. 'I would recall that shaft, if I could. Now Bar-en-Danwedh, House of Ransom, shall this be called in truth. For whether we dwell here or no, I will hold myself in your debt; and if ever I come to any wealth, I will pay you a *danwedh* of heavy gold for your son, in token of sorrow, even if it gladdens your heart no more.'

Then Mîm rose and looked long at Túrin. 'I hear you,' he said. 'You speak like a dwarf-lord of old; and at that I marvel. Now my heart is cooled, though it is not glad. My own ransom I will pay, therefore: you may dwell here, if you will. But this I will add: he that loosed the shaft shall break his bow and his arrows and lay them at my son's feet; and he shall never take an arrow nor bear bow again. If he does, he shall die by it. That curse I lay on him.'

Andróg was afraid when he heard of this curse; and though he did so with great grudge, he broke his bow and his arrows and laid them at the dead Dwarf's feet. But as he came out from the chamber, he glanced evilly at Mîm, and muttered: 'The curse of a dwarf never dies, they say; but a Man's too may come home. May he die with a dart in his throat!'

That night they lay in the hall and slept uneasily for the wailing of Mîm and of Ibun, his other son. When that ceased they could not tell; but when they woke at last the Dwarves were gone and the chamber was closed by a stone. The day was fair again, and in the morning sunshine the outlaws washed in the pool and prepared such food as they had; and as they ate Mîm stood before them.

He bowed to Túrin. 'He is gone and all is done,' he said. 'He lies with his fathers. Now we turn to such life as is left, though the days before us may be short. Does Mîm's home please you? Is the ransom paid and accepted?'

'It is,' said Túrin.

'Then all is yours, to order your dwelling here as you will, save this: the chamber that is closed, none shall open it but me.'

'We hear you,' said Túrin. 'But as for our life here, we are secure, or so it seems; but still we must have food, and other things. How shall we go out; or still more, how shall we return?'

To their disquiet Mîm laughed in his throat. 'Do you fear that you have followed a spider to the heart of his web?' he said. 'Nay, Mîm does not eat Men. And a spider could ill deal with thirty wasps at a time. See, you are armed, and I stand here bare. No, we must share, you and I: house, food, and fire, and maybe other winnings. The house, I guess, you will guard and keep secret for your own good, even when you know the ways in and out. You will learn them in time. But in the meantime Mîm must guide you, or Ibun his son, when you go out; and one will go where you go and return when you return – or await you at some point that you know and can find unguided. Ever nearer and nearer home will that be, I guess.'

To this Túrin agreed, and he thanked Mîm, and most of his men were glad; for under the sun of morning, while summer was yet high, it seemed a fair place to dwell in. Andróg alone was ill-content. 'The sooner we are masters of our own goings and comings the better,' he said. 'Never before have we taken a prisoner with a grievance to and fro on our ventures.'

That day they rested, and cleaned their arms and mended their gear; for they had food to last a day or two yet, and Mîm added to what they had. Three great cooking-pots he lent to them, and firing; and he brought out a sack. 'Rubbish,' he said. 'Not worth the stealing. Only wild roots.'

But when they were washed the roots proved white and fleshy with their skins, and when boiled they were good to eat, somewhat like bread; and the outlaws were glad of them, for they had long lacked bread save when they could steal it. 'Wild Elves know them not; Grey-elves have not found them; the proud ones from over the Sea are too proud to delve,' said Mîm.

'What is their name?' said Túrin.

Mîm looked at him sidelong. 'They have no name, save in the dwarf-tongue, which we do not teach,' he said. 'And we do not teach Men to find them, for Men are greedy and thriftless, and would not spare till all the plants had perished; whereas now they pass them by as they go blundering in the wild. No more will you learn of me; but you may have enough of my bounty, as long as you speak fair and do not spy or steal.' Then again he laughed in his throat. 'They are of great worth,' he said. 'More than gold in the hungry winter, for they may be hoarded like the nuts of a squirrel, and already we were building our store from the first that are ripe. But you are fools, if you think that I would not be parted from one small load even for the saving of my life.'

'I hear you,' said Ulrad, who had looked in the sack when Mîm was taken. 'Yet you would not be parted, and your words only make me wonder the more.'

Mîm turned and looked at him darkly. 'You are one of the fools that spring would not mourn if you perished in winter,' he said to him. 'I had spoken my word, and so must have returned, willing or not, with sack or without, let a lawless and faithless man think what he will! But I love not to be parted from my own by force of the wicked, be it no more than a shoe-thong. Do I not remember that your hands were among those that put bonds upon me, and so held me that I did not speak again with my son? Ever when I deal out the earth-bread from my store you will be counted out, and if you eat it, you shall eat by the bounty of your fellows, not of me.'

Then Mîm went away; but Ulrad, who had quailed under his anger, spoke to his back: 'High words! Nonetheless the old rogue had other things in his sack, of like shape but harder and heavier. Maybe there are other things beside earth-bread in the wild which Elves have not found and Men must not know!'

'That may be,' said Túrin. 'Nonetheless the Dwarf spoke the truth in one point at least, calling you a fool. Why must you speak your thoughts? Silence, if fair words stick in your throat, would serve all our ends better.'

The day passed in peace, and none of the outlaws desired to go abroad. Túrin paced much upon the green sward of the shelf, from brink to brink; and he looked out east, and west, and north, and wondered to find how far were the views in the clear air. Northward, and seeming strangely near, he could descry the forest of Brethil climbing green about the Amon Obel. Thither he found that his eyes would stray more often than he wished, though he knew not why; for his heart was set rather to the north-west, where league upon league away on the skirts of the sky it seemed to him that he could glimpse the Mountains of Shadow and the borders of his home. But at evening Túrin looked west into the sunset, as the sun rode down red into the hazes above the far distant coasts, and the Vale of Narog lay deep in the shadows between.

So began the abiding of Túrin son of Húrin in the halls of Mîm, in Bar-en-Danwedh, the House of Ransom.

For a long while the life of the outlaws went well to their liking. Food was not scarce, and they had good shelter, warm and dry, with room enough and to spare; for they found that the caves could have housed a hundred or more at need. There was another smaller hall further in. It had a hearth at one side, above which a smoke-shaft ran up through the rock to a vent cunningly hidden in a crevice on the hillside. There were also many other chambers, opening out of the halls or the passage between them, some for dwelling, some for works or for stores. In storage Mîm had more arts than they, and he had many vessels and chests of stone and wood that looked to be of great age. But most of the chambers were now empty: in the armouries hung axes and other gear rusted and dusty, shelves and aumbries were bare; and the smithies were idle. Save one: a small room that led out of the inner hall and had a hearth which shared the smoke-vent of the hearth in the hall. There Mîm would work at times, but would not allow others to be with him; and he did not tell of a secret hidden stair that led from his house to the flat summit of Amon Rûdh. This Andróg came upon when seeking in hunger to find Mîm's stores of food he became lost in the caves; but he kept this discovery to himself.

During the rest of that year they went on no more raids, and if they stirred abroad for hunting or gathering of food they went for the most part in small parties. But for a long while they found it hard to retrace their road, and beside Túrin not more than six of his men became ever sure of the way. Nonetheless, seeing that those skilled in such things could come to their lair without Mîm's help, they set a watch by day and night near to the cleft in the north-wall. From the south they expected no enemies, nor was there fear of any climbing Amon Rûdh from that quarter; but by day there was at most times a watchman set on the top of the crown, who could look far all about. Steep as were the sides of the crown, the summit could be reached, for to the east of the cave-mouth rough steps had been hewn leading up to slopes where men could clamber unaided.

So the year wore on without hurt or alarm. But as the days drew in, and the pool became grey and cold and the birches bare, and great rains returned, they had to pass more time in shelter. Then they soon grew weary of the dark under hill, or the dim half-light of the halls; and to most it seemed that life would be better if it were not shared with Mîm. Too often he would appear out of some shadowy corner or doorway when they thought him else-where; and when Mîm was near unease fell on their talk. They took to speaking ever to one another in whispers.

Yet, and strange it seemed to them, with Túrin it went otherwise; and he became ever more friendly with the old Dwarf, and listened more and more to his counsels. In the winter that followed he would sit for long hours with Mîm, listening to his lore and the tales of his life; nor did Túrin rebuke him if he spoke ill of the Eldar. Mîm seemed well pleased, and showed much favour to Túrin in return; him only would he admit to his smithy at times, and there they would talk softly together.

But when autumn was passed the winter pressed them hard. Before Yule snow came down from the North heavier than they had known it in the river-vales; at that time, and ever the more as the power of Angband grew, the winters worsened in Beleriand. Amon Rûdh was covered deep, and only the hardiest dared stir abroad. Some fell sick, and all were pinched with hunger.

In the dim dusk of a day in midwinter there appeared suddenly among them a Man, as it seemed, of great bulk and girth, cloaked and hooded in white. He had eluded their watchmen, and he walked up to their fire without a word. When men sprang up he laughed and threw back his hood, and they saw that it was Beleg Strongbow. Under his wide cloak he bore a great pack in which he had brought many things for the help of men.

In this way Beleg came back to Túrin, yielding to his love against his wisdom. Túrin was glad indeed, for he had often regretted his stubbornness; and now the desire of his heart was granted without the need to humble himself or to yield his own will. But if Túrin was glad, not so was Andróg, nor some others of his company. It seemed to them that there had been a tryst between Beleg and their captain, which he had kept secret from them; and Andróg watched them jealously as the two sat apart in speech together.

Beleg had brought with him the Helm of Hador; for he hoped that it might lift Túrin's thought again above his life in the wild as the leader of a petty company. 'This is your own which I bring back to you,' he said to Túrin as he took out the helm. 'It was left in my keeping on the north-marches; but was not forgotten, I think.'

'Almost,' said Túrin; 'but it shall not be so again'; and he fell silent, looking far away with the eyes of his thought, until suddenly he caught the gleam of another thing that Beleg held in his hand. It was the gift of Melian; but the silver leaves were red in the firelight, and when Túrin saw the seal his eyes darkened. 'What have you there?' he said.

'The greatest gift that one who loves you still has to give,' answered Beleg. 'Here is *lembas in·Elidh*, the waybread of the Eldar that no man has yet tasted.'

'The helm of my fathers I take, with good will for your keeping,' said Túrin. 'But I will not receive gifts out of Doriath.'

'Then send back your sword and your arms,' said Beleg. 'Send back also the teaching and fostering of your youth. And let your men, who (you say) have been faithful, die in the desert to please your mood! Nonetheless this waybread was a gift not to you but to me, and I may do with it as I will. Eat it not, if it sticks in your throat; but others may be more hungry and less proud.'

Túrin's eyes glinted, but as he looked in Beleg's face the fire in them died, and they went grey, and he said in a voice hardly to be heard: 'I wonder, friend, that you deign to come back to such a churl. From you I will take whatever you give, even rebuke. Henceforward you shall counsel me in all ways, save the road to Doriath only.'

CHAPTER VIII

THE LAND OF BOW AND HELM

In the days that followed Beleg laboured much for the good of the Company. Those that were hurt or sick he tended, and they were quickly healed. For in those days the Grey-elves were still a high people, possessing great power, and they were wise in the ways of life and of all living things; and though they were less in crafts and lore than the Exiles from Valinor they had many arts beyond the reach of Men. Moreover Beleg the Archer was great among the people of Doriath; he was strong, and enduring, and far-sighted in mind as well as eye, and at need he was valiant in battle, relying not only upon the swift arrows of his long bow, but also upon his great sword Anglachel. And ever the more did hatred grow in the heart of Mîm, who hated all Elves, as has been told, and who looked with a jealous eye on the love that Túrin bore to Beleg.

When winter passed, and the stirring came, and the spring, the outlaws soon had sterner work to do. Morgoth's might was moved; and as the long fingers of a groping hand the forerunners of his armies probed the ways into Beleriand.

Who knows now the counsels of Morgoth? Who can measure the reach of his thought, who had been Melkor, mighty among the Ainur of the Great Song, and sat now, the dark lord upon a dark throne in the North, weighing in his malice all the tidings that came to him, whether by spy or by traitor, seeing in the eyes of his mind and understanding far more of the deeds and purposes of his enemies than even the wisest of them feared, save Melian the Queen. To her often his thought reached out, and there was foiled.

In this year, therefore, he turned his malice towards the lands west of Sirion, where there was still power to oppose him. Gondolin still stood, but it was hidden. Doriath he knew, but could not enter yet. Further still lay Nargothrond, to which none of his servants had yet found the way, a name of fear to them; there the people of Finrod dwelt in hidden strength. And far away from the South, beyond the white woods of the birches of Nimbrethil, from the coast of Arvernien and the mouths of Sirion, came rumour of the Havens of the Ships. Thither he could not reach until all else had fallen.

So now the Orcs came down out of the North in ever greater numbers. Through Anach they came, and Dimbar was taken, and all the north-marches of Doriath were infested. Down the ancient road they came that led through the long defile of Sirion, past the isle where Minas Tirith of Finrod had stood, and so through the land between Malduin and Sirion and then on through the eaves of Brethil to the Crossings of Teiglin. Thence of old the road passed on into the Guarded Plain, and then, along the feet of the highlands watched over by Amon Rûdh, it ran down into the vale of Narog and came at last to Nargothrond. But the Orcs did not go far upon that road as yet; for there dwelt now in the wild a terror that was hidden, and upon the red hill were watchful eyes of which they had not been warned.

In that spring Túrin put on again the Helm of Hador, and Beleg was glad. At first their company had less than fifty men, but the woodcraft of Beleg and the valour of Túrin made them seem to their enemies as a host. The scouts of the Orcs were hunted, their camps were espied, and if they gathered to march in force in some narrow place, out of the rocks or from the shadow of the trees there leaped the Dragon-helm and his men, tall and fierce. Soon at the very sound of his horn in the hills their captains would quail and the Orcs would turn to flight before any arrow whined or sword was drawn.

It has been told that when Mîm surrendered his hidden dwelling on Amon Rûdh to Túrin and his company, he demanded that he who had loosed the arrow that slew his son should break his bow and his arrows and lay them at the feet of Khîm; and that man was Andróg. Then with great ill-will Andróg did as Mîm bade. Moreover Mîm declared that Andróg must never again bear bow and arrow, and he laid a curse on him, that if nevertheless he should do so, then would he meet his own death by that means.

Now in the spring of that year Andróg defied the curse of Mîm and took up a bow again in a foray from Bar-en-Danwedh; and in that foray he was struck by a poisoned orc-arrow, and was brought back dying in pain. But Beleg healed him of his wound. And now the hatred that Mîm bore to Beleg was increased still more, for he had thus undone his curse; but 'it will bite again,' he said.

In that year far and wide in Beleriand the whisper went, under wood and over stream and through the passes of the hills, saying that the Bow and Helm that had fallen in Dimbar (as was thought) had arisen again beyond hope. Then many, both Elves and Men, who went leaderless, dispossessed but undaunted, remnants of battle and defeat and lands laid waste, took heart again, and came to seek the Two Captains, though where they had their stronghold none yet knew. Túrin received gladly all who came to him, but by the counsel of Beleg he admitted no newcomer to his refuge upon Amon Rûdh (and that was now named Echad i Sedryn, Camp of the Faithful); the way thither only those of the Old Company knew and no others were admitted. But other guarded camps and forts were established round about: in the forest eastward, or in the highlands, or in the southward fens, from Methed-en-glad ('the End of the Wood') south of the Crossings of Teiglin to Bar-erib some leagues south of Amon Rûdh in the once fertile land between Narog and the Meres of Sirion. From all these places men could see the summit of Amon Rûdh, and by signals receive tidings and commands.

In this way, before the summer had passed, the following of Túrin had swelled to a great force, and the power of Angband was thrown back. Word of this came even to Nargothrond, and many there grew restless, saying that if an outlaw could do such hurt to the Enemy, what might not the Lord of Narog do. But Orodreth King of Nargothrond would not change his counsels. In all things he followed Thingol, with whom he exchanged messengers by secret ways; and he was a wise lord, according to the wisdom of those who considered first their own people, and how long they might preserve their life and wealth against the lust of the North. Therefore he allowed none of his people to go to Túrin, and he sent messengers to say to him that in all that he might do or devise in his war he should not set foot in the land of Nargothrond, nor drive Orcs thither. But help other than in arms he offered to the Two Captains, should they have need (and in this, it is thought, he was moved by Thingol and Melian).

Then Morgoth withheld his hand; though he made frequent feint of attack, so that by easy victory the confidence of these rebels might become overweening. As it proved indeed. For Túrin now gave the name of Dor-Cúarthol to all the land between Teiglin and the west march of Doriath; and claiming the lordship of it he named himself anew, Gorthol, the Dread Helm; and his heart was high. But to Beleg it seemed now that the Helm had wrought otherwise with Túrin than he had hoped; and looking into the days to come he was troubled in mind.

One day as summer was wearing on he and Túrin were sitting in the Echad resting after a long affray and march. Túrin said then to Beleg: 'Why are you sad, and thoughtful? Does not all go well, since you returned to me? Has not my purpose proved good?'

'All is well now,' said Beleg. 'Our enemies are still surprised and afraid. And still good days lie before us – for a while.'

'And what then?' said Túrin.

'Winter,' said Beleg. 'And after that another year, for those who live to see it.'

'And what then?'

'The wrath of Angband. We have burned the fingertips of the Black Hand – no more. It will not withdraw.'

'But is not the wrath of Angband our purpose and delight?' said Túrin. 'What else would you have me do?'

'You know full well,' said Beleg. 'But of that road you have forbidden me to speak. But hear me now. A king or the lord of a great host has many needs. He must have a secure refuge; and he must have wealth, and many whose work is

not in war. With numbers comes the need of food, more than
the wild will furnish to hunters. And there comes the passing
of secrecy. Amon Rûdh is a good place for a few – it has eyes
and ears. But it stands alone, and is seen far off; and no great
force is needed to surround it – unless a host defends it,
greater far than ours is yet or than it is likely ever to be.'

'Nonetheless, I will be the captain of my own host,'
said Túrin; 'and if I fall, then I fall. Here I stand in the path
of Morgoth, and while I so stand he cannot use the southward road.'

Report of the Dragon-helm in the land west of Sirion
came swiftly to the ear of Morgoth, and he laughed, for
now Túrin was revealed to him again, who had long been
lost in the shadows and under the veils of Melian. Yet he
began to fear that Túrin would grow to such a power that
the curse that he had laid upon him would become void,
and he would escape the doom that had been designed for
him, or else that he might retreat to Doriath and be lost to
his sight again. Now therefore he had a mind to seize
Túrin and afflict him even as his father, to torment him
and enslave him.

Beleg had spoken truly when he said to Túrin that they
had but scorched the fingers of the Black Hand, and that
it would not withdraw. But Morgoth concealed his
designs, and for that time contented himself with the
sending out of his most skilled scouts; and ere long Amon
Rûdh was surrounded by spies, lurking unobserved in the

wilderness and making no move against the parties of men that went in and out.

But Mîm was aware of the presence of Orcs in the lands about Amon Rûdh, and the hatred that he bore to Beleg led him now in his darkened heart to an evil resolve. One day in the waning of the year he told the men in Bar-en-Danwedh that he was going with his son Ibun to search for roots for their winter store; but his true purpose was to seek out the servants of Morgoth, and to lead them to Túrin's hiding-place.(*)

Nevertheless he attempted to impose certain conditions on the Orcs, who laughed at him, but Mîm said that they knew little if they believed that they could gain anything from a Petty-dwarf by torture. Then they asked him what these conditions might be, and Mîm declared his demands: that they pay him the weight in iron of each man whom they caught or slew, but of Túrin and Beleg in gold; that Mîm's house, when rid of Túrin and his company, be left to him, and himself unmolested; that Beleg be left behind, bound, for Mîm to deal with; and that Túrin be let go free.

To these conditions the emissaries of Morgoth readily agreed, with no intention of fulfilling either the first or the second. The Orc-captain thought that the fate of Beleg

---

(*) But another tale is told, which has it that Mîm did not encounter the Orcs with deliberate intent. It was the capture of his son and their threat to torture him that led Mîm to his treachery.

might well be left to Mîm; but as to letting Túrin go free, 'alive to Angband' were his orders. While agreeing to the conditions he insisted that they keep Ibun as hostage; and then Mîm became afraid, and tried to back out of his undertaking, or else to escape. But the Orcs had his son, and so Mîm was obliged to guide them to Bar-en-Danwedh. Thus was the House of Ransom betrayed.

It has been told that the stony mass that was the crown or cap of Amon Rûdh had a bare or flattened top, but that steep as were its sides men could reach the summit by climbing a stair cut into the rock, leading up from the shelf or terrace before the entrance to Mîm's house. On the summit watchmen were set, and they gave warning of the approach of the enemies. But these, guided by Mîm, came onto the level shelf before the doors, and Túrin and Beleg were driven back to the entrance of Bar-en-Danwedh. Some of the men who tried to climb up the steps cut in the rock were shot down by the arrows of the Orcs.

Túrin and Beleg retreated into the cave, and rolled a great stone across the passage. In these straits Andróg revealed to them the hidden stair leading to the flat summit of Amon Rûdh which he had found when lost in the caves, as has been told. Then Túrin and Beleg with many of their men went up by this stair and came out on the summit, surprising those few of the Orcs who had already come there by the outer path, and driving them over the edge. For a little while they held off the Orcs climbing up the rock, but they had no shelter on the bare summit, and many were shot from below. Most valiant of these was Andróg, who fell mortally wounded by an arrow at the head of the outside stair.

Then Túrin and Beleg with the ten men left to them drew back to the centre of the summit, where there was a standing stone, and making a ring about it they defended themselves until all were slain save Beleg and Túrin, for over them the Orcs cast nets. Túrin was bound and carried off; Beleg who was wounded was bound likewise, but he was laid on the ground with wrists and ankles tied to iron pins driven in to the rock.

Now the Orcs, finding the issue of the secret stair, left the summit and entered Bar-en-Danwedh, which they defiled and ravaged. They did not find Mîm, lurking in his caves, and when they had departed from Amon Rûdh Mîm appeared on the summit, and going to where Beleg lay prostrate and unmoving he gloated over him while he sharpened a knife.

But Mîm and Beleg were not the only living beings on that stony height. Andróg, though himself wounded to the death, crawled among the dead bodies towards them, and seizing a sword he thrust it at the Dwarf. Shrieking in fear Mîm ran to the brink of the cliff and disappeared: he fled down a steep and difficult goat's path that was known to him. But Andróg putting forth his last strength cut through the wristbands and fetters that bound Beleg, and so released him; but dying he said: 'My hurts are too deep even for your healing.'

CHAPTER IX

THE DEATH OF BELEG

Beleg sought among the dead for Túrin, to bury him;
but he could not discover his body. He knew then that
Húrin's son was still alive, and taken to Angband; but
he remained perforce in Bar-en-Danwedh until his
wounds were healed. He set out then with little hope to
try to find the trail of the Orcs, and he came upon their
tracks near the Crossings of Teiglin. There they divided,
some passing along the eaves of the Forest of Brethil
towards the Ford of Brithiach, while others turned
away westwards; and it seemed plain to Beleg that he
must follow those that went direct with greatest speed
to Angband, making for the Pass of Anach. Therefore
he journeyed on through Dimbar, and up to the Pass of
Anach in Ered Gorgoroth, the Mountains of Terror, and
so to the highlands of Taur-nu-Fuin, the Forest under

Night, a region of dread and dark enchantment, of wandering and despair.

Benighted in that evil land, it chanced that Beleg saw a small light among the trees, and going towards it he found an Elf, lying asleep beneath a great dead tree: beside his head was a lamp, from which the covering had slipped off. Then Beleg woke the sleeper, and gave him *lembas*, and asked him what fate had brought him to this terrible place; and he named himself Gwindor, son of Guilin.

Grieving Beleg looked at him, for Gwindor was but a bent and timid shadow of his former shape and mood, when in the Battle of Unnumbered Tears that lord of Nargothrond rode to the very doors of Angband, and there was taken. For few of the Noldor whom Morgoth took captive were put to death, because of their skill in mining for metals and gems; and Gwindor was not slain, but put to labour in the mines of the North. These Noldor possessed many of the Fëanorian lamps, which were crystals hung in a fine chain net, the crystals being ever-shining with an inner blue radiance marvellous for finding the way in the darkness of night or in tunnels; of these lamps they themselves did not know the secret. Many of the mining Elves thus escaped from the darkness of the mines, for they were able to bore their way out; but Gwindor received a small sword from one who worked in the forges, and when working in a stone-gang turned suddenly on the guards. He escaped, but with one hand cut off; and now he lay exhausted under the great pines of Taur-nu-Fuin.

From Gwindor Beleg learned that the small company of Orcs ahead of them, from whom he had hidden, had no captives, and were going with speed: an advance guard, perhaps, bearing report to Angband. At this news Beleg despaired: for he guessed that the tracks that he had seen turning away westwards after the Crossings of Teiglin were those of a greater host, who had in orc-fashion gone marauding in the lands seeking food and plunder, and might now be returning to Angband by way of 'the Narrow Land', the long defile of Sirion, much further to the west. If this were so, his sole hope lay in returning to the Ford of Brithiach, and then going north to Tol Sirion. But scarcely had he determined on this than they heard the noise of a great host approaching through the forest from the south; and hiding in the boughs of a tree they watched the servants of Morgoth pass, moving slowly, laden with booty and captives, surrounded by wolves. And they saw Túrin with chained hands being driven on with whips.

Then Beleg told him of his own errand in Taur-nu-Fuin; and Gwindor sought to dissuade him from his quest, saying that he would but join Túrin in the anguish that awaited him. But Beleg would not abandon Túrin, and despairing himself he aroused hope again in Gwindor's heart; and together they went on, following the Orcs until they came out of the forest on the high slopes that ran down to the barren dunes of the Anfauglith. There within sight of the peaks of Thangorodrim the Orcs made their encampment in a bare dale, and set wolf-sentinels all about its rim. There they fell to carousing and feasting on their booty; and after tormenting their prisoners most fell drunkenly asleep. By that time day was failing and it became very dark. A great storm rode up out of the West, and thunder rumbled far off as Beleg and Gwindor crept towards the camp.

When all in the camp were sleeping Beleg took up his bow and in the darkness shot four of the wolf-sentinels on the south side, one by one and silently. Then in great peril they entered in, and they found Túrin fettered hand and foot and tied to a tree. All about knives that had been cast at him by his tormentors were embedded in the trunk, but he was not hurt; and he was senseless in a drugged stupor or swooned in a sleep of utter weariness. Then Beleg and Gwindor cut the bonds from the tree, and bore Túrin out of the camp. But he was too heavy to carry far, and they could go no further than to a thicket of thorn trees high on the slopes above the camp. There they laid him down; and now the storm drew nearer, and lightning flashed on Thangorodrim. Beleg drew his sword Anglachel, and with it he cut the fetters that bound Túrin; but fate was that day more strong, for the blade of Eöl the Dark Elf slipped in his hand, and pricked Túrin's foot.

Then Túrin was roused into a sudden wakefulness of rage and fear, and seeing a form bending over him in the gloom with a naked blade in hand he leapt up with a great cry, believing that Orcs were come again to torment him; and grappling with him in the darkness he seized Anglachel, and slew Beleg Cúthalion thinking him a foe.

But as he stood, finding himself free, and ready to sell his life dearly against imagined foes, there came a great flash of lightning above them, and in its light he looked down on Beleg's face. Then Túrin stood stonestill and silent, staring on that dreadful death, knowing what he had done; and so terrible was his face, lit by the lightning that flickered all about them, that Gwindor cowered down upon the ground and dared not raise his eyes.

But now in the camp beneath the Orcs were roused, both by the storm and by Túrin's cry, and discovered that Túrin was gone; but no search was made for him, for they were filled with terror by the thunder that came out of the West, believing that it was sent against them by the great Enemies beyond the Sea. Then a wind arose, and great rains fell, and torrents swept down from the heights of Taur-nu-Fuin; and though Gwindor cried out to Túrin, warning him of their utmost peril, he made no answer, but sat unmoving and unweeping beside the body of Beleg Cúthalion, lying in the dark forest slain by his hand even as he cut the bonds of thraldom from him.

When morning came the storm was passed away eastward over Lothlann, and the sun of autumn rose hot and bright; but the Orcs hating this almost as much as the thunder, and believing that Túrin would have fled far from that place and all trace of his flight be washed away, they departed in haste, eager to return to Angband. Far off Gwindor saw them marching northward over the steaming sands of Anfauglith. Thus it came to pass that they returned to Morgoth empty-handed, and left behind them the son of Húrin, who sat crazed and unwitting on the slopes of Taur-nu-Fuin, bearing a burden heavier than their bonds.

Then Gwindor roused Túrin to aid him in the burial of Beleg, and he rose as one that walked in sleep; and together they laid Beleg in a shallow grave, and placed beside him Belthronding his great bow, that was made of black yew-wood. But the dread sword Anglachel Gwindor took, saying that it were better that it should take vengeance on the servants of Morgoth than lie useless in the earth; and he took also the *lembas* of Melian to strengthen them in the wild.

Thus ended Beleg Strongbow, truest of friends, greatest in skill of all that harboured in the woods of Beleriand in the Elder Days, at the hand of him whom he most loved; and that grief was graven on the face of Túrin and never faded.

But courage and strength were renewed in the Elf of Nargothrond, and departing from Taur-nu-Fuin he led Túrin far away. Never once as they wandered together on long and grievous paths did Túrin speak, and he walked as one without wish or purpose, while the year waned and winter drew on over the northern lands. But Gwindor was ever beside him to guard him and guide him; and thus they passed westward over Sirion and came at length to

the Beautiful Mere and Eithel Ivrin, the springs whence
Narog rose beneath the Mountains of Shadow. There
Gwindor spoke to Túrin, saying: 'Awake, Túrin son of
Húrin! On Ivrin's lake is endless laughter. She is fed from
crystal fountains unfailing, and guarded from defilement
by Ulmo, Lord of Waters, who wrought her beauty in
ancient days.' Then Túrin knelt and drank from that
water; and suddenly he cast himself down, and his tears
were unloosed at last, and he was healed of his madness.

There he made a song for Beleg, and he named it *Laer
Cú Beleg*, the Song of the Great Bow, singing it aloud
heedless of peril. And Gwindor gave the sword Anglachel
into his hands, and Túrin knew that it was heavy and
strong and had great power; but its blade was black and
dull and its edges blunt. Then Gwindor said: 'This is a
strange blade, and unlike any that I have seen in Middle-
earth. It mourns for Beleg even as you do. But be comforted; for I return to Nargothrond of the House of
Finarfin, where I was born and dwelt before my grief. You
shall come with me, and be healed and renewed.'

'Who are you?' said Túrin.

'A wandering Elf, a thrall escaped, whom Beleg met
and comforted,' said Gwindor. 'Yet once I was Gwindor
son of Guilin, a lord of Nargothrond, until I went to the
Nirnaeth Arnoediad, and was enslaved in Angband.'

'Then have you seen Húrin son of Galdor, the warrior
of Dor-lómin?' said Túrin.

'I have not seen him,' said Gwindor. 'But the rumour

runs through Angband that he still defies Morgoth; and Morgoth has laid a curse upon him and all his kin.'

'That I do believe,' said Túrin.

And now they arose, and departing from Eithel Ivrin they journeyed southward along the banks of Narog, until they were taken by scouts of the Elves and brought as prisoners to the hidden stronghold.

Thus did Túrin come to Nargothrond.

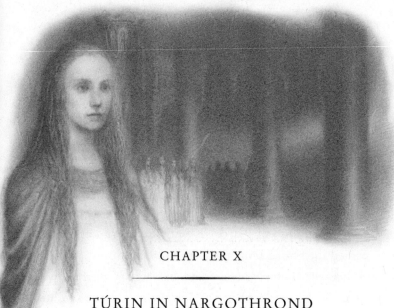

CHAPTER X

TÚRIN IN NARGOTHROND

At first his own people did not know Gwindor, who went out young and strong, and returned now seeming as one of the aged among mortal Men, because of his torments and his labours; and now also he was maimed. But Finduilas daughter of Orodreth the King knew him and welcomed him, for she had loved him, and indeed they were betrothed, before the Nirnaeth, and so greatly did Gwindor love her beauty that he named her Faelivrin, which is the sheen of the sun upon the pools of Ivrin.

Thus Gwindor came home, and for his sake Túrin was admitted with him; for Gwindor said that he was a valiant man, dear friend of Beleg Cúthalion of Doriath. But when Gwindor would tell his name Túrin checked him, saying: 'I am Agarwaen, the son of Úmarth (which is the Bloodstained, son of Ill-fate), a hunter in the woods.' But though the Elves guessed that he took these names because of the slaying of his friend (not knowing other reasons), they questioned him no more.

The sword Anglachel was forged anew for him by the cunning smiths of Nargothrond, and though ever black its edges shone with pale fire. Then Túrin himself became known in Nargothrond as Mormegil, the Black Sword, for the rumour of his deeds with that weapon; but he named the sword Gurthang, Iron of Death.

Because of his prowess and his skill in warfare with Orcs Túrin found favour with Orodreth, and was admitted to his council. Now Túrin had no liking for the manner of fighting of the Elves of Nargothrond, of ambush and stealth and secret arrow, and he urged that it be abandoned, and that they should use their strength to attack the servants of the Enemy, to open battle and pursuit. But Gwindor spoke ever against Túrin in this matter in the council of the King, saying that he had been in Angband and had had a glimpse of the power of Morgoth, and had some inkling of his designs. 'Petty victories will prove profitless at the last,' he said; 'for thus Morgoth learns where the boldest of his enemies are to be found, and gathers strength great enough to destroy them. All the might of the Elves and Edain united sufficed only to contain him, and to gain the peace of a siege; long indeed, but only so long as Morgoth bided his time before he broke the leaguer; and never again can such a union be made. Only in secrecy lies hope of survival. Until the Valar come.'

'The Valar!' said Túrin. 'They have forsaken you, and they hold Men in scorn. What use to look westward across the endless Sea to a dying sunset in the West? There is but one Vala with whom we have to do, and that is Morgoth; and if in the end we cannot overcome him, at least we can hurt him and hinder him. For victory is victory, however small, nor is its worth only from what follows from it. But it is expedient also. Secrecy is not finally possible: arms are the only wall against Morgoth. If you do nothing to halt him, all Beleriand will fall under his shadow before many years are passed, and then one by one he will smoke you out of your earths. And what then? A pitiable remnant will fly south and west, to cower on the shores of the Sea, caught between Morgoth and Ossë. Better then to win a time of glory, though it be shortlived; for the end will be no worse. You speak of secrecy, and say that therein lies the only hope; but could you ambush and waylay every scout and spy of Morgoth to the last and least, so that none came ever back with tidings to Angband, yet from that he would learn that you lived and guess where. And this also I say: though mortal Men have little life beside the span of the Elves, they would rather spend it in battle than fly or submit. The defiance of Húrin Thalion is a great deed; and though Morgoth slay the doer he cannot make the deed not to have been. Even the Lords of the West will honour it; and is it not written into the history of Arda, which neither Morgoth nor Manwë can unwrite?'

'You speak of high things,' Gwindor answered, 'and plain it is that you have lived among the Eldar. But a darkness is on you if you set Morgoth and Manwë together, or speak of the Valar as the foes of Elves and Men; for the Valar scorn nothing, and least of all the Children of Ilúvatar. Nor do you know all the hopes of the Eldar. It is a prophecy among us that one day a messenger from Middle-earth will come through the shadows to Valinor, and Manwë will hear, and Mandos relent. For that time shall we not attempt to preserve the seed of the Noldor, and of the Edain also? And Círdan dwells now in the South, and there is building of ships; but what know you of ships, or of the Sea? You think of yourself and of your own glory, and bid us each do likewise; but we must think of others beside ourselves, for not all can fight and fall, and those we must keep from war and ruin, while we can.'

'Then send them to your ships, while there is yet time,' said Túrin.

'They will not be parted from us,' said Gwindor, 'even could Círdan sustain them. We must abide together as long as we may, and not court death.'

'All this I have answered,' said Túrin. 'Valiant defence of the borders and hard blows ere the enemy gathers; in that course lies the best hope of your long abiding together. And do those that you speak of love such skulkers in the woods, hunting strays like a wolf, better than one who puts on his helm and figured shield, and drives away the foe, be they far greater than all his host? At least the women of the Edain do not. They did not hold back the men from the Nirnaeth Arnoediad.'

'But they suffered greater woe than if that field had not been fought,' said Gwindor.

But Túrin advanced greatly in the favour of Orodreth, and he became the chief counsellor of the King, who submitted all things to his advice. In that time the Elves of Nargothrond forsook their secrecy, and great store of weapons were made; and by the counsel of Túrin the Noldor built a mighty bridge over the Narog from the Doors of Felagund for the swifter passage of their arms, since war was now chiefly east of Narog in the Guarded Plain. As its northmarch Nargothrond now held the 'Debatable Land' about the sources of Ginglith, Narog, and the fringes of the Woods of Núath. Between Nenning and Narog no Orc came; and east of Narog their realm went to the Teiglin and the borders of the Moors of the Nibin-noeg.

Gwindor fell into dishonour, for he was no longer forward in arms, and his strength was small; and the pain of his maimed left arm was often upon him. But Túrin was young, and only now reached his full manhood; and he was in truth the son of Morwen Eledhwen to look upon: tall, dark-haired and pale-skinned, with grey eyes, and his face more beautiful than any other among mortal men, in the Elder Days. His speech and bearing were those of the ancient kingdom of Doriath, and even among the Elves he might be taken at first meeting for one from the great houses of the Noldor. So valiant was Túrin, and so exceedingly skilled in arms, especially with sword and shield, that the Elves said that he could not be slain, save by mischance, or an evil arrow from afar. Therefore they gave him dwarf-mail, to guard him; and in a grim mood he found in the armouries a dwarf-mask all gilded, and he put it on before battle, and his enemies fled before his face.

Now that he had his way, and all went well, and he had work to do after his heart, and had honour in it, he was courteous to all, and less grim than of old, so that well nigh all hearts were turned to him; and many called him Adanedhel, the Elf-man. But most of all Finduilas the daughter of Orodreth found her heart moved whenever he came near, or was in hall. She was golden-haired after the manner of the house of Finarfin, and Túrin began to take pleasure in the sight of her and in her company; for she reminded him of his kindred and the women of Dor-lómin in his father's house.

At first he met her only when Gwindor was by; but after a while she sought him out, so that they met at times alone, though it seemed to be by chance. Then she would question him about the Edain, of whom she had seen few and seldom, and about his country and his kin.

Then Túrin spoke freely to her concerning these things, though he did not name the land of his birth, nor any of his kindred; and on a time he said to her: 'I had a sister, Lalaith, or so I named her; and of her you put me in mind. But Lalaith was a child, a yellow flower in the green grass of spring; and had she lived she would now, maybe, have become dimmed with grief. But you are queenly, and as a golden tree; I would I had a sister so fair.'

'But you are kingly,' said she, 'even as the lords of the people of Fingolfin; I would I had a brother so valiant. And I do not think that Agarwaen is your name, nor is it fit for you, Adanedhel. I call you Thurin, the Secret.'

At this Túrin started, but he said: 'That is not my name; and I am not a king, for our kings are of the Eldar, as I am not.'

Now Túrin marked that Gwindor's friendship grew cooler towards him; and he wondered also that whereas at first the woe and horror of Angband had begun to be lifted from him, now he seemed to slip back into care and sorrow. And he thought, it may be that he is grieved that I oppose his counsels, and have overcome him; I would it were not so. For he loved Gwindor as his guide and healer, and was filled with pity for him. But in those days the radiance of Finduilas also became dimmed, her footsteps slow and her face grave, and she grew wan and thin; and Túrin perceiving this surmised that the words of Gwindor had set fear in her heart of what might come to pass.

In truth Finduilas was torn in mind. For she honoured Gwindor and pitied him, and wished not to add one tear to his suffering; but against her will her love for Túrin grew day by day, and she thought of Beren and Lúthien. But Túrin was not like Beren! He did not scorn her, and was glad in her company; yet she knew that he had no love of the kind she wished. His mind and heart were elsewhere, by rivers in springs long past.

Then Túrin spoke to Finduilas, and said: 'Do not let the words of Gwindor affright you. He has suffered in the darkness of Angband; and it is hard for one so valiant to be thus crippled and backward perforce. He needs all solace, and a longer time for healing.'

'I know it well,' she said.

'But we will win that time for him!' said Túrin. 'Nargothrond shall stand! Never again will Morgoth the Craven come forth from Angband, and all his reliance must be on his servants; thus says Melian of Doriath. They are the fingers of his hands; and we will smite them, and cut them off, till he draws back his claws. Nargothrond shall stand!'

'Perhaps,' said she. 'It shall stand, if you can achieve it. But have a care, Thurin; my heart is heavy when you go out to battle, lest Nargothrond be bereaved.'

Afterwards Túrin sought out Gwindor, and said to him: 'Gwindor, dear friend, you are falling back into sadness; do not so! For your healing will come in the houses of your kin, and in the light of Finduilas.'

Then Gwindor stared at Túrin, but he said nothing, and his face was clouded.

'Why do you look upon me so?' said Túrin. 'Often your eyes have gazed at me strangely of late. How have I grieved you? I have opposed your counsels; but a man must speak as he sees, nor hide the truth that he believes, for any private cause. I would that we were one in mind; for to you I owe a great debt, and I shall not forget it.'

'Will you not?' said Gwindor. 'Nonetheless your deeds and your counsels have changed my home and my kin. Your shadow lies upon them. Why should I be glad, who have lost all to you?'

Túrin did not understand these words, and did but guess that Gwindor begrudged him his place in the heart and counsels of the King.

But Gwindor, when Túrin had gone, sat alone in dark thought, and he cursed Morgoth who could thus pursue his enemies with woe, whithersoever they might run. 'And now at last,' he said, 'I believe the rumour of Angband that Morgoth has cursed Húrin and all his kin.' And going to find Finduilas he said to her: 'A sadness and doubt is upon you; and too often now I miss you, and begin to guess that you are avoiding me. Since you tell me not the cause, I must guess. Daughter of the house of Finarfin, let no grief lie between us; for though Morgoth has laid my life in ruin, you still I love. But go whither love leads you; for I am become unfit to wed you; and neither my prowess nor my counsel have any honour more.'

Then Finduilas wept. 'Weep not yet!' said Gwindor. 'But beware lest you have cause. Not fitting is it that the Elder Children of Ilúvatar should wed the Younger; nor is it wise, for they are brief, and soon pass, to leave us in widowhood while the world lasts. Neither will fate suffer it, unless it be once or twice only, for some high cause of doom that we do not perceive.

'But this man is not Beren, even if he be both as fair and as brave. A doom lies on him; a dark doom. Enter not into it! And if you will, your love shall betray you to bitterness and death. For hearken to me! Though he be indeed *agarwaen* son of *úmarth*, his right name is Túrin son of Húrin, whom Morgoth holds in Angband, and has cursed all his kin. Doubt not the power of Morgoth Bauglir! Is it not written in me?'

Then Finduilas rose, and queenly indeed she looked. 'Your eyes are dimmed, Gwindor,' she said. 'You do not see or understand what has here come to pass. Must I now be put to double shame to reveal the truth to you? For I love you, Gwindor, and I am ashamed that I love you not more, but have taken a love even greater, from which I cannot escape. I did not seek it, and long I put it aside. But if I have pity for your hurts, have pity on mine. Túrin loves me not, nor will.'

'You say this,' said Gwindor, 'to take the blame from him whom you love. Why does he seek you out, and sit long with you, and come ever more glad away?'

'Because he also needs solace,' said Finduilas, 'and is bereaved of his kin. You both have your needs. But what of Finduilas? Now is it not enough that I must confess myself to you unloved, but that you should say that I speak so to deceive?'

'Nay, a woman is not easily deceived in such a case,' said Gwindor. 'Nor will you find many who will deny that they are loved, if that is true.'

'If any of us three be faithless, it is I: but not in will. But what of your doom and rumours of Angband? What of death and destruction? The Adanedhel is mighty in the tale of the World, and his stature shall reach yet to Morgoth in some far day to come.'

'He is proud,' said Gwindor.

'But also he is merciful,' said Finduilas. 'He is not yet awake, but still pity can ever pierce his heart, and he will never deny it. Pity maybe shall be ever the only entry. But he does not pity me. He holds me in awe, as were I both his mother and a queen.'

Maybe Finduilas spoke truly, seeing with the keen eyes of the Eldar. And now Túrin, not knowing what had passed between Gwindor and Finduilas, was ever gentler towards her as she seemed more sad. But on a time Finduilas said to him: 'Thurin Adanedhel, why did you hide your name from me? Had I known who you were I should not have honoured you less, but I should better have understood your grief.'

'What do you mean?' he said. 'Whom do you make me?'

'Túrin son of Húrin Thalion, captain of the North.'

Now when Túrin learned from Finduilas of what had passed, he was wrathful, and he said to Gwindor: 'In love I hold you for rescue and safe-keeping. But now you have done ill to me, friend, to betray my right name, and call down my doom upon me, from which I would lie hid.'

But Gwindor answered: 'The doom lies in yourself, not in your name.'

In that time of respite and hope, when because of the deeds of the Mormegil the power of Morgoth was stemmed west of Sirion, and all the woods had peace, Morwen fled at last from Dor-lómin with Niënor her daughter, and adventured the long journey to Thingol's halls. There new grief awaited her, for she found Túrin gone, and to Doriath there had come no tidings since the Dragon-helm had vanished from the lands west of Sirion; but Morwen remained in Doriath with Niënor as guests of Thingol and Melian, and were treated with honour.

CHAPTER XI

THE FALL OF NARGOTHROND

When five years had passed since Túrin came to Nargothrond, in the spring of the year, there came two Elves,
and they named themselves Gelmir and Arminas, of the
people of Finarfin; and they said that they had an errand
to the Lord of Nargothrond. Túrin now commanded all
the forces of Nargothrond, and ruled all matters of war;
indeed he was become stern and proud, and would order
all things as he wished or thought good. They were
brought therefore before Túrin; but Gelmir said: 'It is to
Orodreth, Finarfin's son, that we would speak.'

And when Orodreth came, Gelmir said to him: 'Lord,
we were of Angrod's people, and we have wandered far
since the Nirnaeth; but of late we have dwelt among
Círdan's following by the Mouths of Sirion. And on a day
he called us, and bade us go to you; for Ulmo himself, the

Lord of Waters, had appeared to him and warned him of great peril that draws near to Nargothrond.'

But Orodreth was wary, and he answered: 'Why then do you come hither out of the North? Or perhaps you had other errands also?'

Then Arminas said: 'Yes, lord. Ever since the Nirnaeth I have sought for the hidden kingdom of Turgon, and I have found it not; and in this search I fear now that I have delayed our errand hither over long. For Círdan sent us along the coast by ship, for secrecy and speed, and we were put ashore in Drengist. But among the sea-folk were some that came south in past years as messengers from Turgon, and it seemed to me from their guarded speech that maybe Turgon dwells still in the North, and not in the South as most believe. But we have found neither sign nor rumour of what we sought.'

'Why do you seek Turgon?' said Orodreth.

'Because it is said that his kingdom shall stand longest against Morgoth,' answered Arminas. And these words seemed to Orodreth ill-omened, and he was displeased.

'Then tarry not in Nargothrond,' said he; 'for here you will hear no news of Turgon. And I need none to teach me that Nargothrond stands in peril.'

'Be not angered, lord,' said Gelmir, 'if we answer your questions with truth. And our wandering from the straight path hither has not been fruitless, for we have passed beyond the reach of your furthest scouts; we have traversed Dor-lómin and all the lands under the eaves of

Ered Wethrin, and we have explored the Pass of Sirion spying out the ways of the Enemy. There is a great gathering of Orcs and evil creatures in those regions, and a host is mustering about Sauron's Isle.'

'I know it,' said Túrin. 'Your news is stale. If the message of Círdan was to any purpose, it should have come sooner.'

'At least, lord, you shall hear the message now,' said Gelmir to Orodreth. 'Hear then the words of the Lord of Waters! Thus he spoke to Círdan: "The Evil of the North has defiled the springs of Sirion, and my power withdraws from the fingers of the flowing waters. But a worse thing is yet to come forth. Say therefore to the Lord of Nargothrond: Shut the doors of the fortress, and go not abroad. Cast the stones of your pride into the loud river, that the creeping evil may not find the gate."'

These words seemed dark to Orodreth, and he turned as ever to Túrin for counsel. But Túrin mistrusted the messengers, and he said in scorn: 'What does Círdan know of our wars, who dwell nigh to the Enemy? Let the mariner look to his ships! But if in truth the Lord of Waters would send us counsel, let him speak more plainly. Otherwise to one trained in war it will still seem better in our case to muster our strength, and go boldly to meet our foes, ere they come too nigh.'

Then Gelmir bowed before Orodreth, and said: 'I have spoken as I was bidden, lord'; and he turned away. But Arminas said to Túrin: 'Are you indeed of the House of Hador, as I have heard said?'

'Here I am named Agarwaen, the Black Sword of Nargothrond,' answered Túrin. 'You deal much, it seems, in
guarded speech, friend Arminas. It is well that Turgon's
secret is hid from you, or soon it would be heard in
Angband. A man's name is his own, and should the son of
Húrin learn that you have betrayed him when he would be
hid, then may Morgoth take you and burn out your tongue!'

Arminas was dismayed by the black wrath of Túrin; but
Gelmir said: 'He shall not be betrayed by us, Agarwaen.
Are we not in council behind closed doors, where speech
may be plainer? And Arminas, I deem, questioned you,
since it is known to all that dwell by the Sea that Ulmo has
great love for the House of Hador, and some say that Húrin
and Huor his brother came once into the Hidden Realm.'

'If that were so, then he would speak of it to none,
neither the great nor the less, and least of all to his son in
childhood,' answered Túrin. 'Therefore I do not believe
that Arminas asked this of me in order to learn aught of
Turgon. I mistrust such messengers of mischief.'

'Save your mistrust!' said Arminas in anger. 'Gelmir
mistakes me. I asked because I doubted what here seems
believed; for little indeed do you resemble the kin of
Hador, whatever your name.'

'And what do you know of them?' said Túrin.

'Húrin I have seen,' answered Arminas, 'and his fathers
before him. And in the wastes of Dor-lómin I met with
Tuor, son of Huor, Húrin's brother; and he is like his
fathers, as you are not.'

'That may be,' said Túrin, 'though of Tuor I have heard no word ere now. But if my head be dark and not golden, of that I am not ashamed. For I am not the first of sons in the likeness of his mother; and I come through Morwen Eledhwen of the House of Bëor and the kindred of Beren Camlost.'

'I spoke not of the difference between the black and the gold,' said Arminas. 'But others of the House of Hador bear themselves otherwise, and Tuor among them. For they use courtesy, and they listen to good counsel, holding the Lords of the West in awe. But you, it seems, will take counsel with your own wisdom, or with your sword only; and you speak haughtily. And I say to you, Agarwaen Mormegil, that if you do so, other shall be your doom than one of the Houses of Hador and Bëor might look for.'

'Other it has ever been,' answered Túrin. 'And if, as it seems, I must bear the hate of Morgoth because of the valour of my father, shall I also endure the taunts and ill-boding of a runagate from war, though he claim the kinship of kings? Get you back to the safe shores of the Sea!'

Then Gelmir and Arminas departed, and went back to the South; but despite Túrin's taunts they would gladly have awaited battle beside their kin, and they went only because Círdan had bidden them under the command of Ulmo to bring back word to him of Nargothrond and of the speeding of their errand there. And Orodreth was much troubled by the words of the messengers; but all the more fell became the mood of Túrin, and he would by no means listen to their counsels, and least of all would he suffer the great bridge to be cast down. For so much at least of the words of Ulmo were read aright.

Soon after the departure of the messengers Handir Lord of Brethil was slain; for the Orcs invaded his land, seeking to secure the Crossings of Teiglin for their further advance. Handir gave them battle, but the Men of Brethil were worsted and driven back into their woods. The Orcs did not pursue them, for they had achieved their purpose for that time; and they continued to muster their strength in the Pass of Sirion.

In the autumn of the year, biding his hour, Morgoth loosed upon the people of Narog the great host that he had long prepared; and Glaurung the Father of Dragons passed over Anfauglith, and came thence into the north vales of Sirion and there did great evil. Under the shadows of Ered Wethrin, leading a great army of Orcs in his train, he defiled the Eithel Ivrin, and thence he passed into the realm of Nargothrond, burning the Talath Dirnen, the Guarded Plain, between Narog and Teiglin.

Then the warriors of Nargothrond went forth, and tall and terrible on that day looked Túrin, and the heart of the host was uplifted as he rode on the right hand of Orodreth. But greater far was the host of Morgoth than any scouts had told, and none but Túrin defended by his dwarf-mask could withstand the approach of Glaurung.

The Elves were driven back and defeated on the field of Tumhalad; and there all the pride and host of Nargothrond withered away. Orodreth the King was slain in the forefront of the battle, and Gwindor son of Guilin was wounded to the death. But Túrin came to his aid, and all fled before him; and he bore Gwindor out of the rout, and escaping to a wood there laid him on the grass.

Then Gwindor said to Túrin: 'Let bearing pay for bearing! But ill-fated was mine, and vain is yours; for my body is marred beyond healing, and I must leave Middle-earth. And though I love you, son of Húrin, yet I rue the day that I took you from the Orcs. But for your prowess and your pride, still I should have love and life, and Nargothrond should yet stand a while. Now if you love me, leave me! Haste you to Nargothrond, and save Finduilas. And this last I say to you: she alone stands between you and your doom. If you fail her, it shall not fail to find you. Farewell!'

Then Túrin sped back to Nargothrond, mustering such of the rout as he met with on the way; and the leaves fell from the trees in a great wind as they went, for the autumn was passing to a dire winter. But Glaurung and his host of Orcs were there before him, because of his rescue of Gwindor, and they came suddenly, ere those that were left on guard were aware of what had befallen on the field of Tumhalad. In that day the bridge that Túrin had caused to be built over Narog proved an evil; for it was great and mightily made and could not swiftly be destroyed, and thus the enemy came readily over the deep river, and Glaurung came in full fire against the Doors of Felagund, and overthrew them, and passed within.

And even as Túrin came up the ghastly sack of Nargothrond was well-nigh achieved. The Orcs had slain or driven off all that remained in arms, and they were even then ransacking the great halls and chambers, plundering and destroying; but those of the women and maidens that were not burned or slain they had herded on the terrace before the doors, as slaves to be taken to Angband. Upon this ruin and woe Túrin came, and none could withstand him; or would not, though he struck down all before him, and passed over the bridge, and hewed his way towards the captives.

And now he stood alone, for the few that had followed him had fled into hiding. But in that moment Glaurung the fell issued from the gaping Doors of Felagund, and lay behind, between Túrin and the bridge. Then suddenly he spoke by the evil spirit that was in him, saying: 'Hail, son of Húrin. Well met!'

Then Túrin sprang about, and strode against him, and fire was in his eyes, and the edges of Gurthang shone as with flame. But Glaurung withheld his blast, and opened wide his serpent-eyes and gazed upon Túrin. Without fear Túrin looked in those eyes as he raised up his sword; and straightway he fell under the dreadful spell of the dragon, and was as one turned to stone. Thus long they stood unmoving, silent before the great Doors of Felagund. Then

Glaurung spoke again, taunting Túrin. 'Evil have been all your ways, son of Húrin,' said he. 'Thankless fosterling, outlaw, slayer of your friend, thief of love, usurper of Nargothrond, captain foolhardy, and deserter of your kin. As thralls your mother and your sister live in Dor-lómin, in misery and want. You are arrayed as a prince, but they go in rags. For you they yearn, but you care not for that. Glad may your father be to learn that he has such a son: as learn he shall.' And Túrin being under the spell of Glaurung hearkened to his words, and he saw himself as in a mirror misshapen by malice, and he loathed what he saw.

And while he was yet held by the eyes of Glaurung in torment of mind, and could not stir, at a sign from the Dragon the Orcs drove away the herded captives, and they passed nigh to Túrin and went over the bridge. And among them was Finduilas, and she held out her arms to Túrin, and called him by name. But not until her cries and the wailing of the captives was lost upon the northward road did Glaurung release Túrin, and he might not stop his ears against that voice that haunted him after.

Then suddenly Glaurung withdrew his glance, and waited; and Túrin stirred slowly as one waking from a hideous dream. Then coming to himself with a loud cry he sprang upon the Dragon. But Glaurung laughed, saying: 'If you wish to be slain, I will slay you gladly. But small help will that be to Morwen and Niënor. No heed did you give to the cries of the Elf-woman. Will you deny also the bond of your blood?'

But Túrin drawing back his sword stabbed at his eyes; and Glaurung coiling back swiftly towered above him, and said: 'Nay! At least you are valiant. Beyond all whom I have met. And they lie who say that we of our part do not honour the valour of foes. See now! I offer you freedom. Go to your kin, if you can. Get you gone! And if Elf or Man be left to make tale of these days, then surely in scorn they will name you, if you spurn this gift.'

Then Túrin, being yet bemused by the eyes of the dragon, as if he were treating with a foe that could know pity, believed the words of Glaurung, and turning away he sped over the bridge. But as he went, Glaurung spoke behind him, saying in a fell voice: 'Haste you now, son of Húrin, to Dor-lómin! Or perhaps the Orcs shall come before you, once again. And if you tarry for Finduilas, then never shall you see Morwen or Niënor again; and they will curse you.'

But Túrin passed away on the northward road, and Glaurung laughed once more, for he had accomplished the errand of his Master. Then he turned to his own pleasure, and sent forth his blast, and burned all about him. But all the Orcs that were busy in the sack he routed forth, and drove them away, and denied them their plunder even to the last thing of worth. The bridge then he broke down and cast into the foam of Narog; and being thus secure he gathered all the hoard and riches of Felagund and heaped them, and lay upon them in the innermost hall, and rested a while.

And Túrin hastened along the ways to the North, through the lands now desolate between Narog and Teiglin,

and the Fell Winter came down to meet him; for that year
snow fell ere autumn was passed, and spring came late and
cold. Ever it seemed to him as he went that he heard the
cries of Finduilas, calling his name by wood and hill, and
great was his anguish; but his heart being hot with the lies
of Glaurung, and seeing ever in his mind the Orcs burning
the house of Húrin or putting Morwen and Niënor to
torment, he held on his way, turning never aside.

CHAPTER XII

THE RETURN OF TÚRIN TO DOR-LÓMIN

At last worn by haste and the long road (for forty leagues and more had he journeyed without rest) he came with the first ice of winter to the pools of Ivrin, where before he had been healed. But they were now only a frozen mire, and he could drink there no more.

Thence he came to the passes into Dor-lómin, and snow came bitterly from the North, and the ways were perilous and cold. Though three and twenty years were gone since he had trodden that path, it was graven in his heart, so great was the sorrow of each step at the parting from Morwen. Thus at last he came back to the land of his childhood. It was bleak and bare; and the people there were few and churlish, and they spoke the harsh tongue of the Easterlings, and the old tongue was become the language of serfs, or of foes. Therefore Túrin walked warily, hooded and silent, and he came at last to the house that he sought. It stood empty and dark, and no living thing dwelt near it; for Morwen was gone, and Brodda the Incomer (he that took by force Aerin, Húrin's kinswoman, to wife) had plundered her house, and taken all that was left to her of goods or of servants. Brodda's house stood nearest to the old house of Húrin, and thither Túrin came, spent with wandering and grief, begging for shelter; and it was granted to him, for some of the kindlier manners of old were still kept there by Aerin. He was given a seat by the fire by the servants, and a few vagabonds as grim and wayworn as he; and he asked news of the land.

At that the company fell silent, and some drew away, looking askance at the stranger. But one old vagabond man, with a crutch, said: 'If you must speak the old tongue, master, speak it softer, and ask for no tidings. Would you be beaten for a rogue, or hung for a spy? For both you may well be by the looks of you. Which is but to say,' he said, coming near and speaking low in Túrin's ear, 'one of the kindly folk of old that came with Hador in the days of gold, before heads wore wolf-hair. Some here are of like sort, though now made beggars and slaves, and but for the Lady Aerin would get neither this fire nor this broth. Whence are you, and what news would you have?'

'There was a lady called Morwen,' answered Túrin, 'and long ago I lived in her house. Thither after far wandering I came to seek welcome, but neither fire nor folk are there now.'

'Nor have been this long year and more,' answered the old man. 'But scant were both fire and folk in that house since the deadly war; for she was of the old people — as doubtless you know, the widow of our lord, Húrin Galdor's son. They dared not touch her, though, for they feared her; proud and fair as a queen, before sorrow marred her. Witchwife they called her, and shunned her. Witchwife: it is but "elf-friend" in the new language. Yet they robbed her. Often would she and her daughter have gone hungry, but for the Lady Aerin. She aided them in secret, it is said, and was often beaten for it by the churl Brodda, her husband by need.'

'And this long year and more?' said Túrin. 'Are they dead, or made thralls? Or have the Orcs assailed her?'

'It is not known for sure,' said the old man. 'But she is gone with her daughter; and this Brodda has plundered her and stripped what remained. Not a dog is left, and her few folk made his slaves; save some that have gone begging, as have I. I served her many a year, and the great master before, Sador Onefoot: a cursed axe in the woods long ago, or I would be lying in the Great Mound now. Well I remember the day when Húrin's boy was sent away, and how he wept; and she, when he was gone. To the Hidden Kingdom he went, it was said.'

With that the old man stayed his tongue, and eyed Túrin doubtfully. 'I am old and I babble, master,' he said. 'Mind me not! But though it be pleasant to speak the old tongue with one that speaks it fair as in time past, the days are ill, and one must be wary. Not all that speak the fair tongue are fair at heart.'

'Truly,' said Túrin. 'My heart is grim. But if you fear that I am a spy of the North or the East, then you have learned little more wisdom than you had long ago, Sador Labadal.'

The old man eyed him agape; then trembling he spoke. 'Come outside! It is colder, but safer. You speak too loud, and I too much, for an Easterling's hall.'

When they were come into the court he clutched at Túrin's cloak. 'Long ago you dwelt in that house, you say. Lord Túrin, why have you come back? My eyes are opened, and my ears at last: you have the voice of your father. But young Túrin alone ever gave me that name, Labadal. He meant no ill: we were merry friends in those days. What does he seek here now? Few are we left; and we are old and weaponless. Happier are those in the Great Mound.'

'I did not come with thought of battle,' said Túrin, 'though your words have waked the thought in me now, Labadal. But it must wait. I came seeking the Lady Morwen and Niënor. What can you tell me, and swiftly?'

'Little, lord,' said Sador. 'They went away secretly. It was whispered among us that they were summoned by the Lord Túrin; for we did not doubt that he had grown great in the years, a king or a lord in some south country. But it seems this is not so.'

'It is not,' answered Túrin. 'A lord I was in a south country, though now I am a vagabond. But I did not summon them.'

'Then I know not what to tell you,' said Sador. 'But the Lady Aerin will know, I doubt not. She knew all the counsel of your mother.'

'How can I come to her?'

'That I know not. It would cost her much pain were she caught whispering at a door with a wandering wretch of the downtrod people, even could any message call her forth. And such a beggarman as you are will not walk far up the hall towards the high board before the Easterlings seize him and beat him, or worse.'

Then in anger Túrin cried: 'May I not walk up Brodda's hall, and will they beat me? Come, and see!'

Thereupon he went into the hall, and cast back his hood, and thrusting aside all in his path he strode towards the board where sat the master of the house and his wife, and other Easterling lords. Then some rose to seize him, but he flung them to the ground, and cried: 'Does no one rule this house, or is it an Orc-hold rather? Where is the master?'

Then Brodda rose in wrath. 'I rule this house,' said he. But before he could say more, Túrin said: 'Then you have not yet learned the courtesy that was in this land before you. Is it now the manner of men to let lackeys mishandle the kinsmen of their wives? Such am I, and I have an errand to the Lady Aerin. Shall I come freely, or shall I come as I will?'

'Come,' said Brodda, scowling; but Aerin turned pale.

Then Túrin strode to the high board and stood before it, and bowed. 'Your pardon, Lady Aerin,' he said, 'that I

break in upon you thus; but my errand is urgent and has
brought me far. I seek Morwen, Lady of Dor-lómin, and
Niënor her daughter. But her house is empty and plundered. What can you tell me?'

'Nothing,' said Aerin in great fear, for Brodda watched
her narrowly.

'That I do not believe,' said Túrin.

Then Brodda sprang forth, and he was red with
drunken rage. 'No more!' he cried. 'Shall my wife be
gainsaid before me, by a beggar that speaks the serf-
tongue? There is no Lady of Dor-lómin. But as for
Morwen, she was of the thrall-folk, and has fled as thralls
will. Do you likewise, and swiftly, or I will have you
hung on a tree!'

Then Túrin leapt at him, and drew his black sword,
and seized Brodda by the hair and laid back his head. 'Let
no one stir,' said he, 'or this head will leave its shoulders!
Lady Aerin, I would beg your pardon once more, if I
thought that this churl had ever done you anything but
wrong. But speak now, and do not deny me! Am I not
Túrin, Lord of Dor-lómin? Shall I command you?'

'Command me,' she said.

'Who plundered the house of Morwen?'

'Brodda,' she answered.

'When did she flee, and whither?'

'A year and three months gone,' said Aerin. 'Master
Brodda and others of the Incomers of the East hereabout
oppressed her sorely. Long ago she was bidden to the

Hidden Kingdom; and she went forth at last. For the lands between were then free of evil for a while, because of the prowess of the Blacksword of the south country, it is said; but that is now ended. She looked to find her son there awaiting her. But if you are he, then I fear that all has gone awry.'

Then Túrin laughed bitterly. 'Awry, awry?' he cried. 'Yes, ever awry: as crooked as Morgoth!' And suddenly a black wrath shook him; for his eyes were opened, and the spell of Glaurung loosed its last threads, and he knew the lies with which he had been cheated. 'Have I been cozened, that I might come and die here dishonoured, who might at least have ended valiantly before the Doors of Nargothrond?' And out of the night about the hall it seemed to him that he heard the cries of Finduilas.

'Not first will I die here!' he cried. And he seized Brodda, and with the strength of his great anguish and wrath he lifted him on high and shook him, as if he were a dog. 'Morwen of the thrall-folk, did you say? You son of dastards, thief, slave of slaves!' Thereupon he flung Brodda head foremost across his own table, full in the face of an Easterling that rose to assail Túrin. In that fall Brodda's neck was broken; and Túrin leapt after his cast and slew three more that cowered there, for they were caught weaponless. There was tumult in the hall. The Easterlings that sat there would have come against Túrin, but many others were gathered there who were of the elder people of Dor-lómin: long had they been tame servants, but now they rose with shouts of rebellion. Soon there was great fighting in the hall, and though the thralls had but meat-knives and such things as they could snatch up against daggers and swords, many were quickly slain on either hand, before Túrin leapt down among them and slew the last of the Easterlings that remained in the hall.

Then he rested, leaning against a pillar, and the fire of his rage was as ashes. But old Sador crept up to him and clutched him about the knees, for he was wounded to the death. 'Thrice seven years and more, it was long to wait for this hour,' he said. 'But now go, go, lord! Go, and do not come back, unless with greater strength. They will raise the land against you. Many have run from the hall. Go, or you will end here. Farewell!' Then he slipped down and died.

'He speaks with the truth of death,' said Aerin. 'You have learned what you would. Now go swiftly! But go first to Morwen and comfort her, or I will hold all the wrack you have wrought here hard to forgive. For ill though my life was, you have brought death to me with your violence. The Incomers will avenge this night on all that were here. Rash are your deeds, son of Húrin, as if you were still but the child that I knew.'

'And faint heart is yours, Aerin Indor's daughter, as it was when I called you aunt, and a rough dog frightened you,' said Túrin. 'You were made for a kinder world. But come away! I will bring you to Morwen.'

'The snow lies on the land, but deeper upon my head,' she answered. 'I should die as soon in the wild with you, as with the brute Easterlings. You cannot mend what you have done. Go! To stay will make all the worse, and rob Morwen to no purpose. Go, I beg you!'

Then Túrin bowed low to her, and turned, and left the hall of Brodda; but all the rebels that had the strength followed him. They fled towards the mountains, for some among them knew well the ways of the wild, and they blessed the snow that fell behind them and covered their trail. Thus though soon the hunt was up, with many men and dogs and braying of horses, they escaped south into the hills. Then looking back they saw a red light far off in the land they had left.

'They have fired the hall,' said Túrin. 'To what purpose is that?'

'They? No, lord: she, I guess,' said one, Asgon by name. 'Many a man of arms misreads patience and quiet. She did much good among us at much cost. Her heart was not faint, and patience will break at the last.'

Now some of the hardiest that could endure the winter stayed with Túrin and led him by strange paths to a refuge in the mountains, a cave known to outlaws and runagates; and some store of food was hidden there. There they waited until the snow ceased, and they gave him food and took him to a pass little used that led south to Sirion's Vale, where the snow had not come. On the downward path they parted.

'Farewell now, Lord of Dor-lómin,' said Asgon. 'But do not forget us. We shall be hunted men now; and the Wolf-folk will be crueller because of your coming. Therefore go, and do not return, unless you come with strength to deliver us. Farewell!'

CHAPTER XIII

THE COMING OF TÚRIN INTO BRETHIL

Now Túrin went down towards Sirion, and he was torn in mind. For it seemed to him that whereas before he had two bitter choices, now there were three, and his oppressed people called him, upon whom he had brought only increase of woe. This comfort only he had: that beyond doubt Morwen and Niënor had come long since to Doriath, and only by the prowess of the Blacksword of Nargothrond had their road been made safe. And he said in his thought: 'Where else better might I have bestowed them, had I come indeed sooner? If the Girdle of Melian be broken, then all is ended. Nay, it is better as things be; for by my wrath and rash deeds I cast a shadow wherever I dwell. Let Melian keep them! And I will leave them in peace unshadowed for a while.'

But too late now Túrin sought for Finduilas, roaming the

woods under the eaves of Ered Wethrin, wild and wary as a beast; and he waylaid all the roads that went north to the Pass of Sirion. Too late. For all trails had been washed away by the rains and the snows. But thus it was that Túrin passing down Teiglin came upon some of the People of Haleth from the Forest of Brethil. They were dwindled now by war to a small people, and dwelt for the most part secretly within a stockade upon Amon Obel deep in the forest. Ephel Brandir that place was named; for Brandir son of Handir was now their lord, since his father was slain. And Brandir was no man of war, being lamed by a leg broken in a misadventure in childhood; and he was moreover gentle in mood, loving wood rather than metal, and the knowledge of things that grow in the earth rather than other lore.

But some of the woodmen still hunted the Orcs on their borders; and thus it was that as Túrin came thither he heard the sound of an affray. He hastened towards it, and coming warily through the trees he saw a small band of men surrounded by Orcs. They defended themselves desperately, with their backs to a knot of trees that grew apart in a glade; but the Orcs were in great number, and they had little hope of escape, unless help came. Therefore, out of sight in the underwood, Túrin made a great noise of stamping and crashing, and then he cried in a loud voice, as if leading many men: 'Ha! Here we find them! Follow me all! Out now, and slay!'

At that many of the Orcs looked back in dismay, and then out came Túrin leaping, waving as if to men behind, and the edges of Gurthang flickered like flame in his hand. Too well was that blade known to the Orcs, and even before he sprang among them many scattered and fled. Then the woodmen ran to join him, and together they hunted their foes into the river: few came across. At last they halted on the bank, and Dorlas, leader of the woodmen, said: 'You are swift in the hunt, lord; but your men are slow to follow.'

'Nay,' said Túrin, 'we all run together as one man, and will not be parted.'

Then the Men of Brethil laughed, and said: 'Well, one such is worth many. And we owe you great thanks. But who are you, and what do you here?'

'I do but follow my trade, which is Orc-slaying,' said Túrin. 'And I dwell where my trade is. I am Wildman of the Woods.'

'Then come and dwell with us,' said they. 'For we dwell in the woods, and we have need of such craftsmen. You would be welcome!'

Then Túrin looked at them strangely, and said: 'Are there then any left who will suffer me to darken their doors? But, friends, I have still a grievous errand: to find Finduilas, daughter of Orodreth of Nargothrond, or at least to learn news of her. Alas! Many weeks is it since she was taken from Nargothrond, but still I must go seeking.'

Then they looked on him with pity, and Dorlas said: 'Seek no more. For an Orc-host came up from Nargothrond towards the Crossings of Teiglin, and we had long warning of it: it marched very slow, because of the number of captives that were led. Then we thought to deal our small stroke in the war, and we ambushed the Orcs with all the bowmen we could muster, and hoped to save some of the prisoners. But alas! as soon as they were assailed the foul Orcs slew first the women among their captives; and the daughter of Orodreth they fastened to a tree with a spear.'

Túrin stood as one mortally stricken. 'How do you know this?' he said.

'Because she spoke to me, before she died,' said Dorlas. 'She looked upon us as though seeking one whom she had expected, and she said: "Mormegil. Tell the Mormegil that Finduilas is here." She said no more. But because of her latest words we laid her where she died. She lies in a mound beside Teiglin. Yes, it is a month now ago.'

'Bring me there,' said Túrin; and they led him to a hillock by the Crossings of Teiglin. There he laid himself down, and a darkness fell on him, so that they thought he was dead. But Dorlas looked down at him as he lay, and then he turned to his men and said: 'Too late! This is a piteous chance. But see: here lies the Mormegil himself, the great captain of Nargothrond. By his sword we should have known him, as did the Orcs.' For the fame of the Black Sword of the South had gone far and wide, even into the deeps of the wood.

Now therefore they lifted him with reverence and bore him to Ephel Brandir; and Brandir coming to meet them

wondered at the bier that they bore. Then drawing back
the coverlet he looked on the face of Túrin son of Húrin;
and a dark shadow fell on his heart. 'O cruel Men of
Haleth!' he cried. 'Why did you hold back death from this
man? With great labour you have brought hither the last
bane of our people.'

But the woodmen said: 'Nay, it is the Mormegil of
Nargothrond, a mighty Orc-slayer, and he shall be a great
help to us, if he lives. And were it not so, should we leave
a man woe-stricken to lie as carrion by the way?'

'You should not indeed,' said Brandir. 'Doom willed it
not so.' And he took Túrin into his house and tended him
with care.

But when at last Túrin shook off the darkness, spring
was returning; and he awoke and saw sun on the green
buds. Then the courage of the House of Hador awoke in
him also, and he arose and said in his heart: 'All my deeds
and past days were dark and full of evil. But a new day is
come. Here I will stay at peace, and renounce name and
kin; and so I will put my shadow behind me, or at the least
not lay it upon those that I love.'

Therefore he took a new name, calling himself Turambar, which in the High-elven speech signified Master of
Doom; and he dwelt among the woodmen, and was loved
by them, and he charged them to forget his name of old,
and to count him as one born in Brethil. Yet with the
change of a name he could not change wholly his temper,
nor forget his old griefs against the servants of Morgoth;

and he would go hunting the Orcs with a few of the same mind, though this was displeasing to Brandir. For he hoped rather to preserve his people by silence and secrecy.

'The Mormegil is no more,' said he, 'yet have a care lest the valour of Turambar bring a like vengeance on Brethil!'

Therefore Turambar laid his black sword by, and took it no more to battle, and wielded rather the bow and the spear. But he would not suffer the Orcs to use the Crossings of Teiglin or draw near the mound where Finduilas was laid. Haudh-en-Elleth it was named, the Mound of the Elf-maid, and soon the Orcs learned to dread that place, and shunned it. And Dorlas said to Turambar: 'You have renounced the name, but the Blacksword you are still; and does not rumour say truly that he was the son of Húrin of Dor-lómin, lord of the House of Hador?'

And Turambar answered: 'So I have heard. But publish it not, I beg you, as you are my friend.'

CHAPTER XIV

Mother of Turin β Nienor

THE JOURNEY OF MORWEN AND NIËNOR TO NARGOTHROND

When the Fell Winter withdrew new tidings of Nargothrond came to Doriath. For some that escaped from the sack, and had survived the winter in the wild, came at last seeking refuge with Thingol, and the march-wards brought them to the King. And some said that all the enemy had withdrawn northwards, and others that Glaurung abode still in the halls of Felagund; and some said that the Mormegil was slain, and others that he was cast under a spell by the Dragon and dwelt there yet, as one changed to stone. But all declared that it was known in Nargothrond ere the end that the Blacksword was none other than Túrin son of Húrin of Dor-lómin.

Then great was the fear and sorrow of Morwen and of Niënor; and Morwen said: 'Such doubt is the very work of Morgoth! May we not learn the truth, and know surely the worst that we must endure?'

Now Thingol himself desired greatly to know more of the fate of Nargothrond, and had in mind already the sending out of some that might go warily thither, but he believed that Túrin was indeed slain or beyond rescue, and he was loath to see the hour when Morwen should know this clearly. Therefore he said to her: 'This is a perilous matter, Lady of Dor-lómin, and must be pondered. Such doubt may in truth be the work of Morgoth, to draw us on to some rashness.'

But Morwen being distraught cried: 'Rashness, lord! If my son lurks in the woods hungry, if he lingers in bonds, if his body lies unburied, then I would be rash. I would lose no hour to go to seek him.'

'Lady of Dor-lómin,' said Thingol, 'that surely the son of Húrin would not desire. Here would he think you better bestowed than in any other land that remains: in the keeping of Melian. For Húrin's sake and Túrin's I would not have you wander abroad in the black peril of these days.'

'You did not hold Túrin from peril, but me you will hold from him,' cried Morwen. 'In the keeping of Melian! Yes, a prisoner of the Girdle! Long did I hold back before I entered it, and now I rue it.'

'Nay, if you speak so, Lady of Dor-lómin,' said Thingol, 'know this: the Girdle is open. Free you came hither: free you shall stay – or go.'

Then Melian, who had remained silent, spoke: 'Go not hence, Morwen. A true word you said: this doubt is of Morgoth. If you go, you go at his will.'

'Fear of Morgoth will not withhold me from the call of my kin,' Morwen answered. 'But if you fear for me, lord, then lend me some of your people.'

'I command you not,' said Thingol. 'But my people are my own to command. I will send them at my own advice.'

Then Morwen said no more, but wept; and she left the presence of the King. Thingol was heavy-hearted, for it seemed to him that the mood of Morwen was fey; and he asked Melian whether she would not restrain her by her power. 'Against the coming in of evil I may do much,' she answered. 'But against the going out of those who will go, nothing. That is your part. If she is to be held here, you must hold her with strength. Yet maybe thus you will overthrow her mind.'

Now Morwen went to Niënor, and said: 'Farewell, daughter of Húrin. I go to seek my son, or true tidings of him, since none here will do aught, but tarry till too late. Await me here until haply I return.' Then Niënor in dread and distress would restrain her, but Morwen answered nothing, and went to her chamber; and when morning came she had taken horse and gone.

Now Thingol had commanded that none should stay her, or seem to waylay her. But as soon as she went forth, he gathered a company of the hardiest and most skilled of his march-wards, and he set Mablung in charge.

'Follow now speedily,' he said, 'yet let her not be aware of you. But when she is come into the wild, if danger

threatens, then show yourselves; and if she will not return,
then guard her as you may. But some of you I would have
go forward as far as you can, and learn all that you may.'

Thus it was that Thingol sent out a larger company
than he had at first intended, and there were ten riders
among them with spare horses. They followed after
Morwen; and she went south through Region, and so
came to the shores of Sirion above the Twilit Meres; and
there she halted, for Sirion was wide and swift, and she did
not know the way. Therefore now the guards must needs
reveal themselves; and Morwen said: 'Will Thingol stay
me? Or late does he send me the help he denied?'

'Both,' answered Mablung. 'Will you not return?'

'No,' she said.

'Then I must help you,' said Mablung, 'though it is
against my own will. Wide and deep here is Sirion, and
perilous to swim for beast or man.'

'Then bring me over by whatever way the Elven-folk
are used to cross,' said Morwen; 'or else I will try the
swimming.'

Therefore Mablung led her to the Twilit Meres. There
amid creeks and reeds ferries were kept hidden and
guarded on the east shore; for by that way messengers
would pass to and fro between Thingol and his kin in Nargothrond. Now they waited until the starlit night was late,
and they passed over in the white mists before the dawn.
And even as the sun rose red beyond the Blue Mountains,
and a strong morning-wind blew and scattered the mists,

the guards went up onto the west shore, and left the Girdle of Melian. Tall Elves of Doriath they were, grey-clad, and cloaked over their mail. Morwen from the ferry watched them as they passed silently, and then suddenly she gave a cry, and pointed to the last of the company that went by.

'Whence came he?' she said. 'Thrice ten you came to me. Thrice ten and one you go ashore!'

Then the others turned, and saw that the sun shone upon a head of gold: for it was Niënor, and her hood was blown back by the wind. Thus it was revealed that she had followed the company, and joined them in the dark before they crossed the river. They were dismayed, and none more than Morwen. 'Go back! Go back! I command you!' she cried.

'If the wife of Húrin can go forth against all counsel at the call of kindred,' said Niënor, 'then so also can Húrin's daughter. Mourning you named me, but I will not mourn alone, for father, brother, and mother. But of these you only have I known, and above all do I love. And nothing that you fear not do I fear.'

In truth little fear was seen in her face or her bearing. Tall and strong she seemed; for of great stature were those of Hador's house, and thus clad in Elvish raiment she matched well with the guards, being smaller only than the greatest among them.

'What would you do?' said Morwen.

'Go where you go,' said Niënor. 'This choice indeed I bring. To lead me back and bestow me safely in the keeping of Melian; for it is not wise to refuse her counsel.

Or to know that I shall go into peril, if you go.' For in truth Niënor had come most in hope that for fear and love of her her mother would turn back; and Morwen was indeed torn in mind.

'It is one thing to refuse counsel,' said she. 'It is another to refuse the command of your mother. Go now back!'

'No,' said Niënor. 'It is long since I was a child. I have a will and wisdom of my own, though until now it has not crossed yours. I go with you. Rather to Doriath, for reverence of those that rule it; but if not, then westward. Indeed, if either of us should go on, it is I rather, in the fullness of strength.'

Then Morwen saw in the grey eyes of Niënor the steadfastness of Húrin; and she wavered, but she could not overcome her pride, and would not (save the fair words) seem thus to be led back by her daughter, as one old and doting. 'I go on, as I have purposed,' she said. 'Come you also, but against my will.'

'Let it be so,' said Niënor.

Then Mablung said to his company: 'Truly, it is by lack of counsel not of courage that Húrin's kin bring woe to others! Even so with Túrin; yet not so with his fathers. But now they are all fey, and I like it not. More do I dread this errand of the King than the hunting of the Wolf. What is to be done?'

But Morwen, who had come ashore and now drew near, heard the last of his words. 'Do as you are bidden by the King,' said she. 'Seek for tidings of Nargothrond, and of Túrin. For this end are we all come together.'

'It is yet a long way and dangerous,' said Mablung. 'If you go further, you shall both be horsed and go among the riders, and stray no foot from them.'

Thus it was that with the full day they set forth, and passed slowly and warily out of the country of reeds and low willows, and came to the grey woods that covered much of the southern plain before Nargothrond. All day they went due west, and saw nothing but desolation, and heard nothing; for the lands were silent, and it seemed to Mablung that a present fear lay upon them. That same way had Beren trodden years before, and then the woods were filled with the hidden eyes of the hunters; but now all the people of Narog were gone, and the Orcs, it seemed, were not yet roaming so far southward. That night they encamped in the grey wood without fire or light.

The next two days they went on, and by evening of the third day from Sirion they were come across the plain and were drawing near to the east shores of Narog. Then so great an unease came upon Mablung that he begged Morwen to go no further. But she laughed, and said: 'You will be glad soon to be rid of us, as is likely enough. But you must endure us a little longer. We are come too near now to turn back in fear.'

Then Mablung cried: 'Fey are you both, and foolhardy. You help not but hinder any gathering of news. Now hear me! I was bidden not to stay you with strength; but I was bidden also to guard you, as I might. In this pass, one only can I do. And I will guard you. Tomorrow I will lead you to Amon Ethir, the Spyhill, which is near; and there you shall sit under guard, and go no further while I command here.' Now Amon Ethir was a mound as great as a hill that long ago Felagund had caused to be raised with great labour in the plain before his Doors, a league east of Narog. It was tree-grown, save on the summit, whence a wide view might be had all ways of the roads that led to the great bridge of Nargothrond and of the lands round about. To this hill they came late in the morning and climbed up from the east. Then looking out towards the High Faroth, brown and bare beyond the river, Mablung saw with elven-sight the terraces of Nargothrond on the steep west bank, and as a small black hole in the hill-wall the gaping Doors of Felagund. But he could hear no sound, and he could see no sign of any foe, nor any token of the Dragon, save the burning about the Doors that he had wrought in the day of the sack. All lay quiet under a pale sun.

Now therefore Mablung, as he had said, commanded his ten riders to keep Morwen and Niënor on the hill-top, and not to stir thence until he returned, unless some great peril arose: and if that befell, the riders should set Morwen and Niënor in their midst and flee as swiftly as they might, east-away towards Doriath, sending one ahead to bring news and seek aid.

Then Mablung took the other score of his company, and they crept down from the hill; and then passing into the fields westward, where trees were few, they scattered and made each his way, daring but stealthy, to the banks of Narog. Mablung himself took the middle way, going towards the bridge, and so came to its hither end and found it all broken down; and the deep-cloven river, running wild after rains far away northward, was foaming and roaring among the fallen stones.

But Glaurung lay there, just within the shadow of the great passage that led inward from the ruined Doors, and he had long been aware of the spies, though few other eyes in Middle-earth would have discerned them. But the glance of his fell eyes was keener than that of the eagles, and outreached the far sight of the Elves; and indeed he knew also that some remained behind and sat upon the bare top of Amon Ethir.

Thus, even as Mablung crept among the rocks, seeking whether he could ford the wild river upon the fallen stones of the bridge, suddenly Glaurung came forth with a great blast of fire, and crawled down into the stream. Then straightway there was a vast hissing and huge vapours arose, and Mablung and his followers that lurked near were engulfed in a blinding steam and foul stench; and the most fled as best they could guess towards the Spyhill. But as Glaurung was passing over Narog, Mablung drew aside and lay under a rock, and remained; for it seemed to him that he had an errand yet to do. He knew now indeed that Glaurung abode in Nargothrond, but he was bidden also to learn the truth concerning Húrin's son, if he might; and in the stoutness of his heart, therefore, he purposed to cross the river, as soon as Glaurung was gone, and search the halls of Felagund. For he thought that all had been done that could be for the keeping of Morwen and Niënor: the coming of Glaurung would be marked, and even now the riders should be speeding towards Doriath.

Glaurung therefore passed Mablung by, a vast shape in the mist; and he went swiftly, for he was a mighty Worm, and yet lithe. Then Mablung behind him forded Narog in great peril; but the watchers upon Amon Ethir beheld the issuing of the Dragon, and were dismayed. At once they bade Morwen and Niënor mount, without debate, and prepared to flee eastward as they were bidden. But even as they came down from the hill into the plain, an ill wind blew the great vapours upon them, bringing a stench that no horses would endure. Then, blinded by the fog and in mad terror of the dragon-reek, the horses soon became ungovernable, and went wildly this way and that; and the guards were dispersed, and were dashed against trees to great hurt, or sought vainly one for another. The neighing of the horses and the cries of the riders came to the ears of Glaurung; and he was well pleased.

One of the Elf-riders, striving with his horse in the fog, saw suddenly the Lady Morwen passing near, a grey wraith upon a mad steed, but she vanished in the mist, crying *Niënor*, and they saw her no more.

But when the blind terror came upon the riders, Niënor's horse, running wild, stumbled, and she was thrown. Falling softly into grass she was unhurt; but when she got to her feet she was alone: lost in the mist without horse or companion.

Her heart did not fail her, and she took thought; and it seemed to her vain to go towards this cry or that, for cries were all about her, but growing ever fainter. Better it seemed to her in such case to seek again for the hill: thither doubtless Mablung would come before he went away, if only to be sure that none of his company had remained there.

Therefore walking at guess she found the hill, which was indeed close at hand, by the rising of the ground before her feet; and slowly she climbed the path that led up from the east. And as she climbed so the fog grew thinner, until she came at last out into the sunlight on the bare summit. Then she stepped forward and looked westward. And there right before her was the great head of Glaurung, who had even then crept up from the other side; and before she was aware her eyes had looked in the fell spirit of his eyes, and they were terrible, being filled with the fell spirit of Morgoth, his master.

Strong was the will and heart of Niënor, and she strove against Glaurung; but he put forth his power against her. 'What seek you here?' he said.

And constrained to answer she said: 'I do but seek one Túrin that dwelt here a while. But he is dead, maybe.'

'I know not,' said Glaurung. 'He was left here to defend the women and weaklings; but when I came he deserted them and fled. A boaster but a craven, it seems. Why seek you such a one?'

'You lie,' said Niënor. 'The children of Húrin at least are not craven. We fear you not.'

Then Glaurung laughed, for so was Húrin's daughter revealed to his malice. 'Then you are fools, both you and your brother,' said he. 'And your boast shall be made vain. For I am Glaurung!'

Then he drew her eyes into his, and her will swooned. And it seemed to her that the sun sickened and all became dim about her; and slowly a great darkness drew down on her and in that darkness there was emptiness; she knew nothing, and heard nothing, and remembered nothing.

Long Mablung explored the halls of Nargothrond, as well he might for the darkness and the stench; but he found no living thing there: nothing stirred among the bones, and none answered his cries. At last, being oppressed by the horror of the place, and fearing the return of Glaurung, he came back to the Doors. The sun was sinking west, and the shadows of the Faroth behind lay dark on the terraces and the wild river below; but away beneath Amon Ethir he descried, as it seemed, the evil shape of the Dragon. Harder and more perilous was the return over Narog in such haste and fear; and scarcely had he reached the east shore and crept aside under the bank when Glaurung drew nigh. But he was slow now and stealthy; for all the fires in him were burned low: great power had gone out of him, and he would rest and sleep in the dark. Thus he writhed through the water and slunk up to the Doors like a huge snake, ashen-grey, sliming the ground with his belly.

But he turned before he went in and looked back eastward, and there came from him the laughter of Morgoth, dim but horrible, as an echo of malice out of the black depths far away. And this voice, cold and low, came after: 'There you lie like a vole under the bank, Mablung the mighty! Ill do you run the errands of Thingol. Haste you now to the hill and see what is become of your charge!'

Then Glaurung passed into his lair, and the sun went down and grey evening came chill over the land. But Mablung hastened back to Amon Ethir, and as he climbed to the top the stars came out in the east. Against them he saw there standing, dark and still, a figure as it were an image of stone. Thus Nienor stood, and heard nothing that he said, and made him no answer. But when at last he took her hand, she stirred, and suffered him to lead her away; and while he held her she followed, but if he loosed her, she stood still.

Then great was Mablung's grief and bewilderment; but no other choice had he but to lead Nienor so upon the long eastward way, without help or company. Thus they passed away, walking like dreamers, out into the night-shadowed plain. And when morning returned Nienor stumbled and fell, and lay still; and Mablung sat beside her in despair.

'Not for nothing did I dread this errand,' he said. 'For it will be my last, it seems. With this unlucky child of Men I shall perish in the wilderness, and my name shall be held in scorn in Doriath: if any tidings indeed are ever heard of our fate. All else doubtless are slain, and she alone spared, but not in mercy.'

Thus they were found by three of the company that had fled from Narog at the coming of Glaurung, and after much wandering, when the mist had passed, went back to the hill; and finding it empty they had begun to seek their way home. Hope then returned to Mablung; and they went on now together steering northward and eastward, for there was no road back into Doriath in the south, and since the fall of Nargothrond the ferry-wards were forbidden to set any across save those that came from within.

Slow was their journey, as for those that lead a weary child. But ever as they passed further from Nargothrond and drew nearer to Doriath, so little by little strength returned to Niënor, and she would walk hour by hour obediently, led by the hand. Yet her wide eyes saw nothing, and her ears heard no words, and her lips spoke no words.

And now at length after many days they came nigh to the west border of Doriath, somewhat south of the Teiglin; for they intended to pass the fences of the little land of Thingol beyond Sirion and so come to the guarded bridge near the inflowing of Esgalduin. There a while they halted; and they laid Niënor on a couch of grass, and she closed her eyes, as she had not yet done, and it seemed that she slept. Then the Elves rested also, and for very weariness were unheedful. Thus they were assailed at unawares by a band of orc-hunters, such as now roamed much in that region, as nigh to the fences of Doriath as they dared to go. In the midst of the affray suddenly Niënor leapt up from her couch, as one waking out of sleep to an alarm by night, and with a cry she sped away into the forest. Then the Orcs turned and gave chase, and the Elves after them. But a strange change had come upon Niënor and now she outran them all, flying like a deer among the trees with her hair streaming in the wind of her speed. The Orcs indeed Mablung and his companions swiftly overtook, and they slew them one and all, and hastened on. But by then Niënor had passed away like a wraith; and neither sight nor slot of her could they find, though they hunted far northward and searched for many days.

Then at last Mablung returned to Doriath bowed with grief and with shame. 'Choose you a new master of your hunters, lord,' he said to the King. 'For I am dishonoured.'

But Melian said: 'It is not so, Mablung. You did all that you could, and none other among the King's servants would have done so much. But by ill chance you were matched against a power too great for you, too great indeed for all that now dwell in Middle-earth.'

'I sent you to win tidings, and that you have done,' said Thingol. 'It is no fault of yours that those whom your tidings touch nearest are now beyond hearing. Grievous indeed is this end of all Húrin's kin, but it lies not at your door.'

For not only was Niënor now run witless into the wild, but Morwen also was lost. Neither then nor after did any certain news of her fate come to Doriath or to Dorlómin. Nonetheless Mablung would not rest, and with a small company he went into the wild and for three years wandered far, from Ered Wethrin even to the Mouths of Sirion, seeking for sign or tidings of the lost.

CHAPTER XV

NIËNOR IN BRETHIL

But as for Niënor, she ran on into the wood, hearing the shouts of pursuit come behind; and her clothing she tore off, casting away her garments one by one as she fled, until she went naked; and all that day still she ran, as a beast that is hunted to heart-bursting, and dare not stay or draw breath. But at evening suddenly her madness passed. She stood still a moment as in wonder, and then, in a swoon of utter weariness, she fell as one stricken down into a deep brake of fern. And there amid the old bracken and the swift fronds of spring she lay and slept, heedless of all.

In the morning she woke, and rejoiced in the light as one first called to life; and all things that she saw seemed to her new and strange, and she had no names for them. For behind her lay only an empty darkness, through which came no memory of anything she had ever known, nor any echo of any word. A shadow of fear only she remembered, and so she was wary, and sought ever for hidings: she would climb into trees or slip into thickets, swift as a squirrel or fox, if any sound or shadow frightened her; and thence she would peer long through the leaves with shy eyes, before she went on again.

Thus going forward in the way she first ran, she came to the river Teiglin, and stayed her thirst; but no food she found, nor knew how to seek it, and she was famished and cold. And since the trees across the water seemed closer and darker (as indeed they were, being the eaves of Brethil forest) she crossed over at last, and came to a green mound and there cast herself down: for she was spent, and it seemed to her that the darkness that lay behind her was overtaking her again, and the sun going dark.

But indeed it was a black storm that came up out of the South, laden with lightning and great rain; and she lay there cowering in terror of the thunder, and the dark rain smote her nakedness, and she watched without words as a wild thing that is trapped.

Now it chanced that some of the woodmen of Brethil came by in that hour from a foray against Orcs, hastening over the Crossings of Teiglin to a shelter that was near; and there came a great flash of lightning, so that the Haudh-en-Elleth was lit as with a white flame. Then Turambar who led the men started back and covered his eyes, and trembled; for it seemed that he saw the wraith of a slain maiden that lay on the grave of Finduilas.

But one of the men ran to the mound, and called to him: 'Hither, lord! Here is a young woman lying, and she lives!' and Turambar coming lifted her, and the water dripped from her drenched hair, but she closed her eyes and quivered and strove no more. Then marvelling that she lay thus naked Turambar cast his cloak about her and bore her away to the hunters' lodge in the woods. There they lit a fire and wrapped coverlets about her, and she opened her eyes and looked upon them; and when her glance fell on Turambar a light came in her face and she put out a hand towards him, for it seemed to her that she had found at last something that she had sought in the darkness, and she was comforted. But Turambar took her hand, and smiled, and said: 'Now, lady, will you not tell us your name and your kin, and what evil has befallen you?'

Then she shook her head, and said nothing, but began to weep; and they troubled her no more, until she had eaten hungrily of what food they could give her. And when she had eaten she sighed, and laid her hand again in Turambar's; and he said: 'With us you are safe. Here you may rest this night, and in the morning we will lead you to our homes up in the high forest. But we would know your name and your kin, so that we may find them, maybe, and bring them news of you. Will you not tell us?' But again she made no answer, and wept.

'Do not be troubled!' said Turambar. 'Maybe the tale is too sad yet to tell. But I will give you a name, and call you

Níniel, Maid of Tears.' And at that name she looked up, and she shook her head, but said: 'Níniel.' And that was the first word that she spoke after her darkness, and it was her name among the woodmen ever after.

In the morning they bore Níniel towards Ephel Brandir, and the road went steeply up until it came to a place where it must cross the tumbling stream of Celebros. There a bridge of wood had been built, and below it the stream went over a lip of worn stone, and fell down by many foaming steps into a rocky bowl far below; and all the air was filled with spray like rain. There was a wide green sward at the head of the falls, and birches grew about it, but over the bridge there was a wide view towards the ravines of Teiglin some two miles to the west. There the air was ever cool, and there wayfarers in summer would rest and drink of the cold water. Dimrost, the Rainy Stair, those falls were called, but after that day Nen Girith, the Shuddering Water; for Turambar and his men halted there, but as soon as Níniel came to that place she grew cold and shivered, and they could not warm her or comfort her. Therefore they hastened on their way; but before they came to Ephel Brandir Níniel was wandering in a fever. Long she lay in her sickness, and Brandir used all his skill in her healing, and the wives of the woodmen watched over her by night and by day. But only when Turambar stayed near her would she lie at peace, or sleep without moaning; and this thing all marked that watched her:

throughout all her fever, though often she was much troubled, she murmured never a word in any tongue of Elves
or of Men. And when health slowly returned to her, and
she waked, and began to eat again, then as with a child the
women of Brethil must teach her to speak, word by word.
But in this learning she was quick and took great delight,
as one that finds again treasures, great and small, that were
mislaid; and when at length she had learned enough to
speak with her friends she would say: 'What is the name of
this thing? For in my darkness I lost it.' And when she was
able to go about again, she would seek the house of
Brandir; for she was most eager to learn the names of all
living things, and he knew much of such matters; and they
would walk together in the gardens and the glades.

Then Brandir grew to love her; and when she grew
strong she would lend him her arm for his lameness, and
she called him her brother. But to Turambar her heart was
given, and only at his coming would she smile, and only
when he spoke gaily would she laugh.

One evening of the golden autumn they sat together,
and the sun set the hillside and the houses of Ephel
Brandir aglow, and there was a deep quiet. Then Níniel
said to him: 'Of all things I have now asked the name, save
you. What are you called?'

'Turambar,' he answered.

Then she paused as if listening for some echo; but she
said: 'And what does that say, or is it just the name for you
alone?'

'It means,' said he, 'Master of the Dark Shadow. For I also, Níniel, had my darkness, in which dear things were lost; but now I have overcome it, I deem.'

'And did you also flee from it, running, until you came to these fair woods?' she said. 'And when did you escape, Turambar?'

'Yes,' he answered. 'I fled for many years. And I escaped when you did so. For it was dark when you came, Níniel, but ever since it has been light. And it seems to me that what I long sought in vain has come to me.' And as he went back to his house in the twilight, he said to himself: 'Haudh-en-Elleth! From the green mound she came. Is that a sign, and how shall I read it?'

Now that golden year waned and passed to a gentle winter, and there came another bright year. There was peace in Brethil, and the woodmen held themselves quiet and went not abroad, and they heard no tidings of the lands that lay about them. For the Orcs that at that time came southward to the dark reign of Glaurung, or were sent to spy on the borders of Doriath, shunned the Crossings of Teiglin, and passed westward far beyond the river.

And now Níniel was fully healed, and was grown fair and strong, and Turambar restrained himself no longer, but asked her in marriage. Then Níniel was glad; but when Brandir heard of it his heart was sick within him, and he said to her: 'Be not in haste! Think me not unkindly, if I counsel you to wait.'

'Nothing that you do is done unkindly,' she said. 'But why then do you give me such counsel, wise brother?'

'Wise brother?' he answered. 'Lame brother, rather, unloved and unlovely. And I scarce know why. Yet there lies a shadow on this man, and I am afraid.'

'There was a shadow,' said Níniel, 'for so he told me. But he has escaped from it, even as I. And is he not worthy of love? Though he now holds himself at peace, was he not once the greatest captain, from whom all our enemies would flee, if they saw him?'

'Who told you this?' said Brandir.

'It was Dorlas,' she said. 'Does he not speak truth?'

'Truth indeed,' said Brandir, but he was ill pleased, for Dorlas was chief of that party that wished for war on the Orcs. And yet he sought still for reasons to delay Níniel; and he said therefore: 'The truth, but not the whole truth; for he was the Captain of Nargothrond, and came before out of the North, and was (it is said) son of Húrin of Dor-lómin of the warlike House of Hador.' And Brandir, seeing the shadow that passed over her face at that name, misread her, and said more: 'Indeed, Níniel, well may you think that such a one is likely ere long to go back to war, far from this land, maybe. And if so, how long will you endure it? Have a care, for I forebode that if Turambar goes again to battle, then not he but the Shadow shall have the mastery.'

'Ill would I endure it,' she answered; 'but unwedded no better than wedded. And a wife, maybe, would better restrain him, and hold off the shadow.' Nonetheless she was troubled by the words of Brandir, and she bade Turambar wait yet a while. And he wondered and was downcast; but when he learned from Níniel that Brandir had counselled her to wait he was ill pleased.

But when the next spring came he said to Níniel: 'Time passes. We have waited, and now I will wait no longer. Do as your heart bids you, Níniel most dear, but see: this is the choice before me. I will go back now to war in the wild; or I will wed you, and go never to war again – save only to defend you, if some evil assails our home.'

Then she was glad indeed, and she plighted her troth, and at the mid-summer they were wedded; and the woodmen made a great feast, and they gave them a fair house which they had built for them upon Amon Obel. There they dwelt in happiness, but Brandir was troubled, and the shadow on his heart grew deeper.

CHAPTER XVI

THE COMING OF GLAURUNG

Now the power and malice of Glaurung grew apace, and
he waxed fat, and he gathered Orcs to him, and ruled as a
dragon-king, and all the realm of Nargothrond that had
been was laid under him. And before this year ended, the
third of Turambar's dwelling among the woodmen, he
began to assail their land, which for a while had had peace;
for indeed it was well known to Glaurung and to his
Master that in Brethil there abode a remnant of free men,
the last of the Three Houses to defy the power of the
North. And this they would not brook; for it was the
purpose of Morgoth to subdue all Beleriand and to search
out its every corner, so that none in any hole or hiding
might live that were not thrall to him. Thus, whether
Glaurung guessed where Túrin was hidden, or whether
(as some hold) he had indeed for that time escaped from

the eye of Evil that pursued him, is of little matter. For in the end the counsels of Brandir must prove vain, and at the last two choices only could there be for Turambar: to sit deedless until he was found, driven forth like a rat; or to go forth soon to battle, and be revealed.

But when tidings of the coming of the Orcs were first brought to Ephel Brandir, he did not go forth and yielded to the prayers of Níniel. For she said: 'Our homes are not yet assailed, as your word was. It is said that the Orcs are not many. And Dorlas told me that before you came such affrays were not seldom, and the woodmen held them off.'

But the woodmen were worsted, for these Orcs were of a fell breed, fierce and cunning; and indeed they came with a purpose to invade the Forest of Brethil, not as before passing through its eaves on other errands, or hunting in small bands. Therefore Dorlas and his men were driven back with loss, and the Orcs came over Teiglin and roamed far into the woods. And Dorlas came to Turambar and showed his wounds, and he said: 'See, lord, now is the time of our need come upon us, after a false peace, even as I foreboded. Did you not ask to be counted one of our people, and no stranger? Is this peril not yours also? For our homes will not remain hidden, if the Orcs come further into our land.'

Therefore Turambar arose, and took up again his sword Gurthang, and he went to battle; and when the woodmen learned this they were greatly heartened, and they gathered to him, till he had a force of many hundreds. Then they hunted through the forest and slew all the Orcs that crept there, and hung them on the trees near the Crossings of Teiglin. And when a new host came against them, they trapped it, and being surprised both by the numbers of the woodmen and by the terror of the Black Sword that had returned, the Orcs were routed and slain in great number. Then the woodmen made great pyres and burned the bodies of the soldiers of Morgoth in heaps, and the smoke of their vengeance rose black into heaven, and the wind bore it away westward. But few living went back to Nargothrond with these tidings.

Then Glaurung was wrathful indeed; but for a while he lay still and pondered what he had heard. Thus the winter passed in peace, and men said: 'Great is the Black Sword of Brethil, for all our enemies are overcome.' And Níniel was comforted, and she rejoiced in the renown of Turambar; but he sat in thought, and he said in his heart: 'The die is cast. Now comes the test, in which my boast shall be made good, or fail utterly. I will flee no more. Turambar indeed I will be, and by my own will and prowess I will surmount my doom – or fall. But falling or riding, Glaurung at least I will slay.'

Nonetheless he was unquiet, and he sent out men of daring as scouts far afield. For indeed, though no word was said, he now ordered things as he would, as if he were lord of Brethil, and no man heeded Brandir.

Spring came hopefully, and men sang at their work. But in that spring Níniel conceived, and she became pale and wan, and all her happiness was dimmed. And soon after there came strange tidings, from the men that had gone abroad beyond Teiglin, that there was a great burning far out in the woods of the plain towards Nargothrond, and men wondered what it might be.

But before long there came more reports: that the fires drew ever northward, and that indeed Glaurung himself made them. For he had left Nargothrond, and was abroad again on some errand. Then the more foolish or more hopeful said: 'His army is destroyed, and now at last he sees wisdom, and is going back whence he came.' And others said: 'Let us hope that he will pass us by.' But Turambar had no such hope, and knew that Glaurung was coming to seek him. Therefore though he masked his mind because of Níniel, he pondered ever by day and by night what counsel he should take; and spring turned towards summer.

A day came when two men returned to Ephel Brandir in terror, for they had seen the Great Worm himself. 'In truth, lord,' they said, 'he draws now near to Teiglin, and turns not aside. He lay in the midst of a great burning, and the trees smoked about him. The stench of him is scarce to be endured. And all the long leagues back to Nargothrond his foul swath lies, we deem, in a line that swerves not, but points straight to us. What is to be done?'

'Little,' said Turambar, 'but to that little I have already given thought. The tidings you bring give me hope rather than dread; for if indeed he goes straight, as you say, and

does not swerve, then I have some counsel for hardy hearts.'

The men wondered, for he said no more at that time; but they took heart from his steadfast bearing.

Now the river Teiglin ran in this manner. It flowed down from Ered Wethrin swift as Narog, but at first between low shores, until after the Crossings, gathering power from other streams, it clove a way through the feet of the highlands upon which stood the Forest of Brethil. Thereafter it ran in deep ravines, whose great sides were like walls of rock, but pent at the bottom the waters flowed with great force and noise. And right in the path of Glaurung there lay now one of these gorges, by no means the deepest, but the narrowest, just north of the inflow of Celebros. Therefore Turambar sent out three hardy men to keep watch from the brink on the movements of the Dragon; but he himself would ride to the high fall of Nen Girith, where news could find him swiftly, and whence he himself could look far across the lands.

But first he gathered the woodmen together in Ephel Brandir and spoke to them, saying: 'Men of Brethil, a deadly peril has come upon us, which only great hardihood shall turn aside. But in this matter numbers will avail little; we must use cunning, and hope for good fortune. If we went up against the Dragon with all our strength, as against an army of Orcs, we should but offer ourselves all to death, and so leave our wives and kin defenceless. Therefore I say that you should stay here, and prepare for flight. For if Glaurung comes, then you must abandon this place, and scatter far and wide; and so may some escape and live. For certainly, if he can, he will destroy it, and all that he espies; but afterwards he will not abide here. In Nargothrond lies all his treasure, and there are the deep halls in which he can lie safe, and grow.'

Then the men were dismayed, and were utterly downcast, for they trusted in Turambar, and had looked for more hopeful words. But he said: 'Nay, that is the worst. And it shall not come to pass, if my counsel and fortune are good. For I do not believe that this Dragon is unconquerable, though he grows greater in strength and malice with the years. I know somewhat of him. His power is rather in the evil spirit that dwells within him than in the might of his body, great though that be. For hear now this tale that I was told by some that fought in the year of the Nirnaeth, when I and most that hear me were children. In that field the Dwarves withstood him and Azaghâl of Belegost pricked him so deep that he fled back to Angband. But here is a thorn sharper and longer than the knife of Azaghâl.'

And Turambar swept Gurthang from its sheath and stabbed with it up above his head, and it seemed to those that looked on that a flame leapt from Turambar's hand many feet into the air. Then they gave a great cry: 'The Black Thorn of Brethil!'

'The Black Thorn of Brethil,' said Turambar: 'well may he fear it. For know this: it is the doom of this Dragon (and all his brood, it is said) that how great so ever be his armour of horn, harder than iron, below he must go with the belly of a snake. Therefore, Men of Brethil, I go now to seek the belly of Glaurung, by what means I may. Who will come with me? I need but a few with strong arms and stronger hearts.'

Then Dorlas stood forth and said: 'I will go with you, lord: for I would ever go forward rather than wait for a foe.'

But no others were so swift to the call, for the dread of Glaurung lay on them, and the tale of the scouts that had seen him had gone about and grown in the telling. Then Dorlas cried out: 'Hearken, Men of Brethil, it is now well seen that for the evil of our times the counsels of Brandir were vain. There is no escape by hiding. Will none of you take the place of the son of Handir, that the house of Haleth be not put to shame?' Thus Brandir, who sat indeed in the high-seat of the lord of the assembly, but unheeded, was scorned, and he was bitter in his heart; for Turambar did not rebuke Dorlas. But one Hunthor, Brandir's kinsman, arose and said: 'You do evilly, Dorlas, to speak thus to the shame of your lord, whose limbs by ill hazard cannot do as his heart would. Beware lest the contrary be seen in you at some turn! And how can it be said that his counsels were vain, when they were never taken? You, his liege, have ever set them at naught. I say to you that Glaurung comes now to us, as to Nargothrond before, because our deeds have betrayed us, as he feared. But since this woe is now come, with your leave, son of Handir, I will go on behalf of Haleth's house.'

Then Turambar said: 'Three is enough! You twain will I take. But, lord, I do not scorn you. See! We must go in great haste, and our task will need strong limbs. I deem that your place is with your people. For you are wise, and are a healer; and it may be that there will be great need of wisdom and healing ere long.' But these words, though fair spoken, did but embitter Brandir the more, and he said to Hunthor: 'Go then, but not with my leave. For a shadow lies on this man, and it will lead you to evil.'

Now Turambar was in haste to go; but when he came to Níniel to bid her farewell, she clung to him, weeping grievously. 'Go not forth, Turambar, I beg!' she said. 'Challenge not the shadow that you have fled from! Nay, nay, flee still, and take me with you, far away!'

'Níniel most dear,' he answered, 'we cannot flee further, you and I. We are hemmed in this land. And even should I go, deserting the people that befriended us, I could but take you forth into the houseless wild, to your death and the death of our child. A hundred leagues lie between us and any land that is yet beyond the reach of the Shadow. But take heart, Níniel. For I say to you: neither you nor I shall be slain by this Dragon, nor by any foes of the North.' Then Níniel ceased to weep and fell silent, but her kiss was cold as they parted.

Then Turambar with Dorlas and Hunthor went away hotfoot to Nen Girith, and when they came there the sun was westering and shadows were long; and the last two of the scouts were there awaiting them.

'You come not too soon, lord,' said they. 'For the Dragon has come on, and already when we left he had reached the brink of the Teiglin, and glared across the water. He moves ever by night, and we may look then for some stroke before tomorrow's dawn.'

Turambar looked out over the falls of Celebros and saw the sun going down to its setting, and black spires of smoke rising by the borders of the river. 'There is no time to lose,' he said; 'yet these tidings are good. For my fear was that he would seek about; and if he passed northward and came to the Crossings and so to the old road in the lowland, then hope would be dead. But now some fury of pride and malice drives him headlong.' But even as he spoke, he wondered, and mused in his mind: 'Or can it be that one so evil and fell shuns the Crossings, even as the Orcs? Haudh-en-Elleth! Does Finduilas lie still between me and my doom?'

Then he turned to his companions and said: 'This task now lies before us. We must wait yet a little, for too soon in this case were as ill as too late. When dusk falls, we must creep down, with all stealth, to Teiglin. But beware! For the ears of Glaurung are as keen as his eyes, and they are deadly. If we reach the river unmarked, we must then climb down into the ravine, and cross the water, and so come in the path that he will take when he stirs.'

'But how can he come forward so?' said Dorlas. 'Lithe he may be, but he is a great Dragon, and how shall he climb down the one cliff and up the other, when part must again be climbing before the hinder part is yet descended? And if he can so, what will it avail us to be in the wild water below?'

'Maybe he can so,' answered Turambar, 'and indeed if he does, it will go ill with us. But it is my hope from what we learn of him, and from the place where he now lies, that his purpose is otherwise. He is come to the brink of Cabed-en-Aras, over which, as you tell, a deer once leaped from the huntsmen of Haleth. So great is he now that I think he will seek to cast himself across there. That is all our hope, and we may trust to it.'

Dorlas' heart sank at these words; for he knew better than any all the land of Brethil, and Cabed-en-Aras was a grim place indeed. On the east side was a sheer cliff of some forty feet, bare but tree-grown at the crown; on the other side was a bank somewhat less sheer and less high, shrouded with hanging trees and bushes, but between them the water ran fiercely between rocks, and though a man bold and sure-footed might ford it by day, it was perilous to dare it at night. But this was the counsel of Turambar, and it was useless to gainsay him.

They set out therefore at dusk, and they did not go straight towards the Dragon, but took first the path towards the Crossings; then, before they came so far, they turned southward by a narrow track and passed into the twilight of the woods above Teiglin. And as they drew near to Cabed-en-Aras, step by step, halting often to listen, the reek of burning came to them, and a stench that sickened them. But all was deadly still, and there was no stir of air. The first stars glimmered in the east before them, and faint spires of smoke rose straight and unwavering against the last light in the west.

Now when Turambar was gone Níniel stood silent as a stone; but Brandir came to her and said: 'Níniel, fear not the worst until you must. But did I not counsel you to wait?'

'You did so,' she answered. 'Yet how would that profit me now? For love may abide and suffer unwedded.'

'That I know,' said Brandir. 'Yet wedding is not for nothing.'

'No,' said Níniel. 'For now I am two months gone with his child. But it does not seem to me that my fear of loss is the more heavy to bear. I understand you not.'

'Nor I myself,' said he. 'And yet I am afraid.'

'What a comforter you are!' she cried. 'But Brandir, friend: wedded or unwedded, mother or maid, my dread is beyond enduring. The Master of Doom is gone to challenge his doom far hence, and how shall I stay here and wait for the slow coming of tidings, good or ill? This night, it may be, he will meet with the Dragon, and how shall I stand or sit, or pass the dreadful hours?'

'I know not,' said he, 'but somehow the hours must pass, for you and for the wives of those that went with him.'

'Let them do as their hearts bid!' she cried. 'But for me, I shall go. The miles shall not lie between me and my lord's peril. I will go to meet the tidings!'

Then Brandir's dread grew black at her words, and he cried: 'That you shall not do, if I may hinder it. For thus will you endanger all counsel. The miles that lie between may give time for escape, if ill befall.'

'If ill befall, I shall not wish to escape,' she said. 'And now your wisdom is vain, and you shall not hinder me.' And she stood forth before the people that were still gathered in the open place of the Ephel, and she cried: 'Men of Brethil! I will not wait here. If my lord fails, then all hope is false. Your land and woods shall be burned utterly, and all your houses laid in ashes, and none, none, shall escape. Therefore why tarry here? Now I go to meet the tidings and whatever doom may send. Let all those of like mind come with me!'

Then many were willing to go with her: the wives of Dorlas and Hunthor because those whom they loved were gone with Turambar; others for pity of Níniel and desire to befriend her; and many more that were lured by the very rumour of the Dragon, in their hardihood or their folly (knowing little of evil) thinking to see strange and glorious deeds. For indeed so great in their minds had the Black Sword become that few could believe that even Glaurung would conquer him. Therefore they set forth soon in haste, a great company, towards a peril that they did not understand; and going with little rest they came wearily at last, just at nightfall, to Nen Girith but a little while after Turambar had departed. But night is a cold counsellor, and many were now amazed at their own rashness; and when they heard from the scouts that remained there how near Glaurung was come, and the desperate purpose of Turambar, their hearts were chilled, and they dared go no further. Some looked out towards Cabed-en-Aras with anxious eyes, but nothing could they see, and nothing hear save the cold voice of the falls. And Níniel sat apart, and a great shuddering seized her.

When Níniel and her company had gone, Brandir said to those that remained: 'Behold how I am scorned, and all my counsel disdained! Choose you another to lead you: for here I renounce both lordship and people. Let Turambar be your lord in name, since already he has taken all my authority. Let none seek of me ever again either counsel or healing!' And he broke his staff. To himself he thought: 'Now nothing is left to me, save only my love of Níniel: therefore where she goes, in wisdom or folly, I must go. In this dark hour nothing can be foreseen; but it may well chance that even I could ward off some evil from her, if I were nigh.'

He girt himself therefore with a short sword, as seldom before, and took his crutch, and went with what speed he might out of the gate of the Ephel, limping after the others down the long path to the west march of Brethil.

CHAPTER XVII

THE DEATH OF GLAURUNG

At last, even as full night closed over the land, Turambar and his companions came to Cabed-en-Aras, and they were glad of the great noise of the water; for though it promised peril below, it covered all other sounds. Then Dorlas led them a little aside, southwards, and they climbed down by a cleft to the cliff-foot; but there his heart quailed, for many rocks and great stones lay in the river, and the water ran wild about them, grinding its teeth. 'This is a sure way to death,' said Dorlas.

'It is the only way, to death or to life,' said Turambar, 'and delay will not make it seem more hopeful. Therefore follow me!' And he went on before them, and by skill and hardihood, or by fate, he came across, and in the deep dark he turned to see who came after. A dark form stood beside him. 'Dorlas?' he said.

'No, it is I,' said Hunthor. 'Dorlas failed at the crossing, I think. For a man may love war, and yet dread many things. He sits shivering on the shore, I guess; and may shame take him for his words to my kinsman.'

Now Turambar and Hunthor rested a little, but soon the night chilled them, for they were both drenched with water, and they began to seek a way along the stream northwards towards the lodgement of Glaurung. There the chasm grew darker and narrower, and as they felt their way forward they could see a flicker above them as of smouldering fire, and they heard the snarling of the Great Worm in his watchful sleep. Then they groped for a way up, to come nigh under the brink; for in that lay all their hope to come at their enemy beneath his guard. But so foul now was the reek that their heads were dizzy, and they slipped as they clambered, and clung to the tree-stems, and retched, forgetting in their misery all fear save the dread of falling into the teeth of Teiglin.

Then Turambar said to Hunthor: 'We spend our waning strength to no avail. For till we be sure where the Dragon will pass, it is vain to climb.'

'But when we know,' said Hunthor, 'then there will be no time to seek a way up out of the chasm.'

'Truly,' said Turambar. 'But where all lies on chance, to chance we must trust.' They halted therefore and waited, and out of the dark ravine they watched a white star far above creep across the faint strip of sky; and then slowly Turambar sank into a dream, in which all his will was given to clinging, though a black tide sucked and gnawed at his limbs.

Suddenly there was a great noise and the walls of the chasm quivered and echoed. Turambar roused himself, and said to Hunthor: 'He stirs. The hour is upon us. Strike deep, for two must strike now for three!'

And with that Glaurung began his assault upon Brethil; and all passed much as Turambar had hoped. For now the Dragon crawled with slow weight to the edge of the cliff, and he did not turn aside, but made ready to spring over the chasm with his great forelegs and then draw his bulk after. Terror came with him; for he did not begin his passage right above, but a little to the northward, and the watchers from beneath could see the huge shadow of his head against the stars; and his jaws gaped, and he had seven tongues of fire. Then he sent forth a blast, so that all the ravine was filled with a red light, and black shadows flying among the rocks; but the trees before him withered and went up in smoke, and stones crashed down into the river. And thereupon he hurled himself forward, and grappled the further cliff with his mighty claws, and began to heave himself across.

Now there was need to be bold and swift, for though Turambar and Hunthor had escaped the blast, since they were not right in Glaurung's path, they yet had to come at him, before he passed over, or all their hope failed. Heedless of peril therefore Turambar clambered along the cliff to come beneath him; but there so deadly was the heat and the stench that he tottered and would have fallen if Hunthor, following stoutly behind, had not seized his arm and steadied him.

'Great heart!' said Turambar. 'Happy was the choice that took you for a helper!' But even as he spoke, a great stone hurtled from above and smote Hunthor on the head, and he fell into the water, and so ended: not the least valiant of the House of Haleth. Then Turambar cried: 'Alas! It is ill to walk in my shadow! Why did I seek aid? For now you are alone, O Master of Doom, as you should have known it must be. Now conquer alone!'

Then he summoned to him all his will, and all his hatred of the Dragon and his Master, and it seemed to him that suddenly he found a strength of heart and of body that he had not known before; and he climbed the cliff, from stone to stone, and root to root, until he seized at last a slender tree that grew a little beneath the lip of the chasm, and though its top was blasted it still held fast by its roots. And even as he steadied himself in a fork of its boughs, the midmost parts of the Dragon came above him, and swayed down with their weight almost upon his head, ere Glaurung could heave them up. Pale and wrinkled was their underside, and all dank with a grey slime, to which clung all manner of dropping filth; and it stank of death. Then Turambar drew the Black Sword of Beleg and stabbed upwards with all the might of his arm, and of his hate, and the deadly blade, long and greedy, went into the belly even to its hilts.

Then Glaurung, feeling his death-pang, gave forth a scream, whereat all the woods were shaken, and the watchers at Nen Girith were aghast. Turambar reeled as from a blow, and slipped down, and his sword was torn from his grasp, and clave to the belly of the Dragon. For Glaurung in a great spasm bent up all his shuddering bulk and hurled it over the ravine, and there upon the further shore he writhed, screaming, lashing and coiling himself in his agony, until he had broken a great space all about him, and lay there at last in a smoke and a ruin, and was still.

Now Turambar clung to the roots of the tree, stunned and well-nigh overcome. But he strove against himself and drove himself on, and half sliding and half climbing he came down to the river, and dared again the perilous crossing, crawling now on hands and feet, clinging, blinded with spray, until he came over at last, and climbed wearily up the cleft by which they had descended. Thus he came at length to the place of the dying Dragon, and he looked on his stricken enemy without pity, and was glad.

There now Glaurung lay, with jaws agape; but all his fires were burned out, and his evil eyes were closed. He was stretched out in his length, and had rolled upon one side, and the hilts of Gurthang stood in his belly. Then the heart of Turambar rose high within him, and though the Dragon still breathed he would recover his sword, which if he prized it before was now worth to him all the treasure of Nargothrond. True proved the words spoken at its forging that nothing, great or small, should live that once it had bitten.

Therefore going up to his foe he set foot upon his belly, and seizing the hilts of Gurthang he put forth his strength to withdraw it. And he cried in mockery of Glaurung's words at Nargothrond: 'Hail, Worm of Morgoth! Well met again! Die now and the darkness have you! Thus is Túrin son of Húrin avenged.' Then he wrenched out the sword, and even as he did so a spout of black blood followed it, and fell upon his hand, and his flesh was burned by the venom, so that he cried aloud at the pain. Thereat Glaurung stirred and opened his baleful eyes and looked upon Turambar with such malice that it seemed to him that he was smitten by an arrow; and for that and for the anguish of his hand he fell in a swoon, and lay as one dead beside the Dragon, and his sword was beneath him.

Now the screams of Glaurung came to the people at Nen Girith, and they were filled with terror; and when the watchers beheld from afar the great breaking and burning that the Dragon made in his throes, they believed that he was trampling and destroying those that had assailed him. Then indeed they wished the miles longer that lay between them; but they dared not leave the high place where they were gathered, for they remembered the words of Turambar that, if Glaurung conquered, he would go first to Ephel Brandir. Therefore they watched in fear for any sign of his movement, but none were so hardy as to go down and seek for tidings in the place of the battle. And Níniel sat, and did not move, save that she shuddered and could not still her limbs; for when she heard the voice of Glaurung her heart died within her, and she felt her darkness creeping upon her again.

Thus Brandir found her. For he came at last to the bridge over Celebros, slow and weary; all the long way alone he had limped on his crutch, and it was five leagues at the least from his home. Fear for Níniel had driven him on, and now the tidings that he learned were no worse than he had dreaded. 'The Dragon has crossed the river,' men told him, 'and the Black Sword is surely dead, and those that went with him.' Then Brandir stood by Níniel, and guessed her misery, and he yearned to her; but he thought nonetheless: 'The Black Sword is dead, and Níniel lives.' And he shuddered, for suddenly it seemed cold by the waters of Nen Girith; and he cast his cloak about Níniel. But he found no words to say; and she did not speak.

Time passed, and still Brandir stood silent beside her, peering into the night and listening; but he could see nothing, and could hear no sound but the falling of the waters of Nen Girith, and he thought: 'Now surely Glaurung has gone and has passed into Brethil.' But he pitied his people no more, fools that had flouted his counsel, and had scorned him. 'Let the Dragon go to Amon Obel, and there will be time then to escape, and to lead Níniel away.' Whither, he scarce knew, for he had never journeyed beyond Brethil.

At last he bent down and touched Níniel on the arm, and said to her: 'Time passes, Níniel! Come! It is time to go. If you will let me, I will lead you.' Then silently she arose, and took his hand, and they passed over the bridge and went down the path to the Crossings of Teiglin. But those that saw them moving as shadows in the dark knew not who they were, and cared not. And when they had gone some little way through the silent trees, the moon rose beyond Amon Obel, and the glades of the forest were filled with a grey light. Then Níniel halted and said to Brandir: 'Is this the way?'

And he answered: 'What is the way? For all our hope in Brethil is ended. We have no way, save to escape the Dragon, and flee far from him while there is yet time.'

Níniel looked at him in wonder and said: 'Did you not offer to lead me to him? Or would you deceive me? The Black Sword was my beloved and my husband, and only to find him do I go. What else could you think? Now do as you will, but I must hasten.'

And even as Brandir stood a moment amazed, she sped from him; and he called after her, crying: 'Wait, Níniel! Go not alone! You know not what you will find. I will come with you!' But she paid no heed to him, and went now as though her blood burned her, which before had been cold; and though he followed as he could she passed soon out of his sight. Then he cursed his fate and his weakness; but he would not turn back.

Now the moon rose white in the sky, and was near the full, and as Níniel came down from the upland towards the land near the river, it seemed to her that she remembered it, and feared it. For she was come to the Crossings of Teiglin, and Haudh-en-Elleth stood there before her, pale in the moonlight, with a black shadow cast athwart it; and out of the mound came a great dread.

Then she turned with a cry and fled south along the river, and cast her cloak as she ran, as though casting off a darkness that clung to her; and beneath she was all clad in white, and she shone in the moon as she flitted among the trees. Thus Brandir above on the hill-side saw her, and turned to cross her course, if he could; and finding by fortune the narrow path that Turambar had used, for it left the more beaten road and went steeply down southward to the river, he came at last close behind her again. But though he called, she did not heed, or did not hear, and soon once more she passed on ahead; and so they drew near to the woods beside Cabed-en-Aras and the place of the agony of Glaurung.

The moon was then riding in the south unclouded, and the light was cold and clear. Coming to the edge of the ruin that Glaurung had wrought, Níniel saw his body lying there, and his belly grey in the moon-sheen; but beside him lay a man. Then forgetting her fear she ran on amid the smouldering wrack and so came to Turambar. He was fallen on his side, and his sword lay beneath him, but his face was wan as death in the white light. Then she threw herself down by him weeping, and kissed him; and it seemed to her that he breathed faintly, but she thought it but a trickery of false hope, for he was cold, and did not move, nor did he answer her. And as she caressed him she found that his hand was blackened as if it had been scorched, and she washed it with her tears, and tearing a strip from her raiment she bound it about. But still he did not move at her touch, and she kissed him again, and cried aloud: 'Turambar, Turambar, come back! Hear me! Awake! For it is Níniel. The Dragon is dead, dead, and I alone am here by you.' But he answered nothing. Her cry Brandir heard, for he had come to the edge of the ruin; but even as he stepped forward towards Níniel he was halted, and stood still. For at the cry of Níniel Glaurung stirred for the last time, and a quiver ran through all his body; and he opened his baleful eyes a slit, and the moon gleamed in them, as gasping he spoke:

'Hail, Niënor, daughter of Húrin. We meet again ere we end. I give you joy that you have found your brother at last. And now you shall know him: a stabber in the dark, treacherous to foes, faithless to friends, and a curse unto his kin, Túrin son of Húrin! But the worst of all his deeds you shall feel in yourself.'

Then Niënor sat as one stunned, but Glaurung died; and with his death the veil of his malice fell from her, and all her memory grew clearer before her, from day unto day, neither did she forget any of those things that had befallen her since she lay on Haudh-en-Elleth. And her whole body shook with horror and anguish. But Brandir, who had heard all, was stricken, and leaned against a tree.

Then suddenly Niënor started to her feet, and stood pale as a wraith in the moon, and looked down on Túrin, and cried: 'Farewell, O twice beloved! *A Túrin Turambar turún*' *ambartanen*: master of doom by doom mastered! O happy to be dead!' Then distraught with woe and the horror that had overtaken her she fled wildly from that place; and Brandir stumbled after her, crying: 'Wait! Wait, Níniel!'

One moment she paused, looking back with staring eyes. 'Wait?' she cried. 'Wait? That was ever your counsel. Would that I had heeded! But now it is too late. And now I will wait no more upon Middle-earth.' And she sped on before him.

Swiftly she came to the brink of Cabed-en-Aras, and there stood and looked on the loud water crying: 'Water, water! Take now Níniel Niënor daughter of Húrin; Mourning, Mourning daughter of Morwen! Take me and bear me down to the Sea!'

With that she cast herself over the brink: a flash of white swallowed in the dark chasm, a cry lost in the roaring of the river.

The waters of Teiglin flowed on, but Cabed-en-Aras was no more: Cabed Naeramarth, the Leap of Dreadful Doom, thereafter it was named by men; for no deer would ever leap there again, and all living things shunned it, and no man would walk upon its shore. Last of men to look down into its darkness was Brandir son of Handir; and he turned away in horror, for his heart quailed, and though he hated now his life, he could not there take the death that he desired. Then his thought turned to Túrin Turambar, and he cried: 'Do I hate you, or do I pity you? But you are dead. I owe you no thanks, taker of all that I had or would have. But my people owe you a debt. It is fitting that from me they should learn it.'

And so he began to limp back to Nen Girith, avoiding the place of the Dragon with a shudder; and as he climbed the steep path again he came on a man that peered through the trees, and seeing him drew back. But he had marked his face in a gleam of the sinking moon.

'Ha, Dorlas!' he cried. 'What news can you tell? How came you off alive? And what of my kinsman?'

'I know not,' answered Dorlas sullenly.

'Then that is strange,' said Brandir.

'If you will know,' said Dorlas, 'the Black Sword would have us ford the races of Teiglin in the dark. Is it strange that I could not? I am a better man with an axe than some, but I am not goat-footed.'

'So they went on without you to come at the Dragon?' said Brandir. 'But how when he passed over? At the least you would stay near, and would see what befell.'

But Dorlas made no answer, and stared only at Brandir with hatred in his eyes. Then Brandir understood, perceiving suddenly that this man had deserted his companions, and unmanned by shame had then hidden in the woods. 'Shame on you, Dorlas!' he said. 'You are the begetter of our woes: egging on the Black Sword, bringing the Dragon upon us, putting me to scorn, drawing Hunthor to his death, and then you flee to skulk in the woods!' And as he spoke another thought entered his mind, and he said in great anger: 'Why did you not bring tidings? It was the least penance that you could do. Had you done so, the Lady Níniel would have had no need to seek them herself. She need never have seen the Dragon. She might have lived. Dorlas, I hate you!'

'Keep your hate!' said Dorlas. 'It is as feeble as all your counsels. But for me the Orcs would have come and hung you as a scarecrow in your garden. Take the name skulker to yourself!' And with that, being for his shame the readier to wrath, he aimed a blow at Brandir with his great fist, and so ended his life, before the look of amazement left his eyes: for Brandir drew his sword and hewed him his death-blow. Then for a moment he stood trembling, sickened by the blood; and casting down his sword he turned, and went on his way, bowed upon his crutch.

As Brandir came to Nen Girith the pallid moon was gone down, and the night was fading; morning was opening in the east. The people that cowered there still by the bridge saw him come like a grey shadow in the dawn, and some called to him in wonder: 'Where have you been? Have you seen her? For the Lady Níniel is gone.'

'Yes,' said Brandir, 'she is gone. Gone, gone, never to return! But I am come to bring you tidings. Hear now, people of Brethil, and say if there was ever such a tale as the tale that I bear! The Dragon is dead, but dead also is Turambar at his side. And those are good tidings: yes, both are good indeed.'

Then the people murmured, wondering at his speech, and some said that he was mad; but Brandir cried: 'Hear me to the end! Níniel too is dead, Níniel the fair whom you loved, whom I loved dearest of all. She leaped from the brink of the Deer's Leap, and the teeth of Teiglin have taken her. She is gone, hating the light of day. For this she learned before she fled: Húrin's children were they both, sister and brother. The Mormegil he was called, Turambar he named himself, hiding his past: Túrin son of Húrin. Níniel we named her, not knowing her past: Niënor she was, daughter of Húrin. To Brethil they brought their dark doom's shadow. Here their doom has fallen, and of grief this land shall never again be free. Call it not Brethil, not the land of the Halethrim, but *Sarch nia Chîn Húrin*, Grave of the Children of Húrin!'

Then though they did not understand yet how this evil had come to pass, the people wept as they stood, and some said: 'A grave there is in Teiglin for Níniel the beloved, a grave shall there be for Turambar, most valiant of men. Our deliverer shall not be left to lie under the sky. Let us go to him.'

CHAPTER XVIII

THE DEATH OF TÚRIN

Now even as Níniel fled away, Túrin stirred, and it seemed to him that out of his deep darkness he heard her call to him far away; but as Glaurung died, the black swoon left him, and he breathed deep again, and sighed, and passed into a slumber of great weariness. But before dawn it grew bitter cold, and he turned in his sleep, and the hilts of Gurthang drove into his side, and suddenly he awoke. Night was going, and there was a breath of morning in the air; and he sprang to his feet, remembering his victory, and the burning venom on his hand. He raised it up, and looked at it, and marvelled. For it was bound about with a strip of white cloth, yet moist, and it was at ease; and he said to himself: 'Why should one tend me so, and yet leave me here to lie cold amid the wrack and the dragon-stench? What strange things have chanced?'

Then he called aloud, but there was no answer. All was black and drear about him, and there was a reek of death. He stooped and lifted his sword, and it was whole, and the light of its edges was undimmed. 'Foul was the venom of Glaurung,' he said, 'but you are stronger than I, Gurthang. All blood will you drink. Yours is the victory. But come! I must go seek for aid. My body is weary, and there is a chill in my bones.'

Then he turned his back upon Glaurung and left him to rot; but as he passed from that place each step seemed more heavy, and he thought: 'At Nen Girith, maybe, I will find one of the scouts awaiting me. But would I were soon in my own house, and might feel the gentle hands of Níniel, and the good skill of Brandir!' And so at last, walking wearily, leaning on Gurthang, through the grey light of early day he came to Nen Girith, and even as men were setting forth to seek his dead body, he stood before the people.

Then they gave back in terror, believing that it was his unquiet spirit, and the women wailed and covered their eyes. But he said: 'Nay, do not weep, but be glad! See! Do I not live? And have I not slain the Dragon that you feared?'

Then they turned upon Brandir, and cried: 'Fool, with your false tales, saying that he lay dead. Did we not say that you were mad?' Then Brandir was aghast, and stared at Túrin with fear in his eyes, and he could say nothing.

But Túrin said to him: 'It was you then that were there, and tended my hand? I thank you. But your skill is failing, if you cannot tell swoon from death.' Then he turned to the people: 'Speak not so to him, fools all of you. Which of you would have done better? At least he had the heart to come down to the place of battle, while you sit wailing!

'But now, son of Handir, come! There is more that I would learn. Why are you here, and all this people, whom I left at the Ephel? If I may go into the peril of death for your sakes, may I not be obeyed when I am gone? And where is Níniel? At the least I may hope that you did not bring her hither, but left her where I bestowed her, in my house, with true men to guard it?'

And when no one answered him, 'Come, say where is Níniel?' he cried. 'For her first I would see; and to her first will I tell the tale of the deeds in the night.'

But they turned their faces from him, and Brandir said at last: 'Níniel is not here.'

'That is well then,' said Túrin. 'Then I will go to my home. Is there a horse to bear me? Or a bier would be better. I faint with my labours.'

'Nay, nay!' said Brandir in anguish of heart. 'Your house is empty. Níniel is not there. She is dead.'

But one of the women – the wife of Dorlas, who loved Brandir little – cried shrilly: 'Pay no heed to him, lord! For he is crazed. He came crying that you were dead, and called it good tidings. But you live. Why then should his tale of Níniel be true: that she is dead, and yet worse?'

Then Túrin strode towards Brandir: 'So my death was good tidings?' he cried. 'Yes, ever you did begrudge her to me, that I knew. Now she is dead, you say. And yet worse? What lie have you begotten in your malice, Clubfoot? Would you slay us then with foul words, since you can wield no other weapon?'

Then anger drove pity from Brandir's heart, and he cried: 'Crazed? Nay, crazed are you, Black Sword of black doom! And all this dotard people. I do not lie! Níniel is dead, dead, dead! Seek her in Teiglin!'

Then Túrin stood still and cold. 'How do you know?' he said softly. 'How did you contrive it?'

'I know because I saw her leap,' answered Brandir. 'But the contriving was yours. She fled from you, Túrin son of Húrin, and in Cabed-en-Aras she cast herself, that she might never see you again. Níniel! Níniel? Nay, Niënor daughter of Húrin.'

Then Túrin seized him and shook him; for in those words he heard the feet of his doom overtaking him, but in horror and fury his heart would not receive them, as a beast hurt to death that will wound ere it dies all that are near it.

'Yes, I am Túrin son of Húrin,' he cried. 'So long ago you guessed. But nothing do you know of Niënor my sister. Nothing! She dwells in the Hidden Kingdom, and is safe. It is a lie of your own vile mind, to drive my wife witless, and now me. You limping evil – would you dog us both to death?'

But Brandir shook him off. 'Touch me not!' he said. 'Stay your raving. She that you name wife came to you and tended you, and you did not answer her call. But one answered for you. Glaurung the Dragon, who I deem bewitched you both to your doom. So he spoke, before he ended: "Niënor daughter of Húrin, here is your brother: treacherous to foes, faithless to friends, a curse unto his kin, Túrin son of Húrin."' Then suddenly a fey laughter seized on Brandir. 'On their deathbed men will speak true, they say,' he cackled. 'And even a Dragon too, it seems. Túrin son of Húrin, a curse unto your kin and unto all that harbour you!'

Then Túrin grasped Gurthang and a fell light was in his eyes. 'And what shall be said of you, Club-foot?' he said slowly. 'Who told her secretly behind my back my right name? Who brought her to the malice of the Dragon? Who stood by and let her die? Who came hither to publish this horror at the swiftest? Who would now gloat upon me? Do men speak true before death? Then speak it now quickly.'

Then Brandir, seeing his death in Túrin's face, stood still and did not quail, though he had no weapon but his crutch; and he said: 'All that has chanced is a long tale to tell, and I am weary of you. But you slander me, son of Húrin. Did Glaurung slander you? If you slay me, then all shall see that he did not. Yet I do not fear to die, for then I will go to seek Níniel whom I loved, and perhaps I may find her again beyond the Sea.'

'Seek Níniel!' cried Túrin. 'Nay, Glaurung you shall find, and breed lies together. You shall sleep with the

Worm, your soul's mate, and rot in one darkness!' Then
he lifted up Gurthang and hewed Brandir, and smote him
to death. But the people hid their eyes from that deed, and
as he turned and went from Nen Girith they fled from
him in terror.

Then Túrin went as one witless through the wild
woods, now cursing Middle-earth and all the life of Men,
now calling upon Níniel. But when at last the madness of
his grief left him he sat awhile and pondered all his deeds,
and he heard himself crying: 'She dwells in the Hidden
Kingdom, and is safe!' And he thought that now, though
all his life was in ruin, he must go thither; for all the lies of
Glaurung had ever led him astray. Therefore he arose and
went to the Crossings of Teiglin, and as he passed by
Haudh-en-Elleth he cried: 'Bitterly have I paid, O Finduilas! that ever I gave heed to the Dragon. Send me now
counsel!'

But even as he cried out he saw twelve huntsmen well-
armed that came over the Crossings, and they were Elves;
and as they drew near he knew one, for it was Mablung,
chief huntsman of Thingol. And Mablung hailed him,
crying: 'Túrin! Well met at last. I seek you, and glad I am to
see you living, though the years have been heavy on you.'

'Heavy!' said Túrin. 'Yes, as the feet of Morgoth. But
if you are glad to see me living, you are the last in Middle-
earth. Why so?'

'Because you were held in honour among us,'
answered Mablung; 'and though you have escaped many

perils, I feared for you at the last. I watched the coming forth of Glaurung, and I thought that he had fulfilled his wicked purpose and was returning to his Master. But he turned towards Brethil, and at the same time I learned from wanderers in the land that the Black Sword of Nargothrond had appeared there again, and the Orcs shunned its borders as death. Then I was filled with dread, and I said: "Alas! Glaurung goes where his Orcs dare not, to seek out Túrin." Therefore I came hither as swift as might be, to warn you and aid you.'

'Swift, but not swift enough,' said Túrin. 'Glaurung is dead.'

Then the Elves looked at him in wonder, and said: 'You have slain the Great Worm! Praised for ever shall your name be among Elves and Men!'

'I care not,' said Túrin. 'For my heart also is slain. But since you come from Doriath, give me news of my kin. For I was told in Dor-lómin that they had fled to the Hidden Kingdom.'

The Elves made no answer, but at length Mablung spoke: 'They did so indeed, in the year before the coming of the Dragon. But they are not there now, alas!' Then Túrin's heart stood still, hearing the feet of doom that would pursue him to the end. 'Say on!' he cried. 'And be swift!'

'They went out into the wild seeking you,' said Mablung. 'It was against all counsel; but they would go to Nargothrond, when it was known that you were the Black Sword; and Glaurung came forth, and all their guard were scattered. Morwen none have seen since that day; but Niënor had a spell of dumbness upon her, and fled north into the woods like a wild deer, and was lost.' Then to the wonder of the Elves Túrin laughed loud and shrill. 'Is not that a jest?' he cried. 'O the fair Niënor! So she ran from Doriath to the Dragon, and from the Dragon to me. What a sweet grace of fortune! Brown as a berry she was, dark was her hair; small and slim as an Elf-child, none could mistake her!'

Then Mablung was amazed, and he said: 'But some mistake is here. Not such was your sister. She was tall, and her eyes were blue, her hair fine gold, the very likeness in woman's form of Húrin her father. You cannot have seen her!'

'Can I not, can I not, Mablung?' cried Túrin. 'But why no! For see, I am blind! Did you not know? Blind, blind, groping since childhood in a dark mist of Morgoth! Therefore leave me! Go, go! Go back to Doriath, and may winter shrivel it! A curse upon Menegroth! And a curse on your errand! This only was wanting. Now comes the night!'

Then he fled from them, like the wind, and they were filled with wonder and fear. But Mablung said: 'Some strange and dreadful thing has chanced that we know not. Let us follow him and aid him if we may: for now he is fey and witless.'

But Túrin sped far before them, and came to Cabed-en-Aras, and stood still; and he heard the roaring of the water, and saw that all the trees near and far were withered, and their sere leaves fell mournfully, as though winter had come in the first days of summer.

'Cabed-en-Aras, Cabed Naeramarth!' he cried. 'I will not defile your waters where Níniel was washed. For all my deeds have been ill, and the latest the worst.'

Then he drew forth his sword, and said: 'Hail Gurthang, iron of death, you alone now remain! But what lord or loyalty do you know, save the hand that wields you? From no blood will you shrink. Will you take Túrin Turambar? Will you slay me swiftly?'

And from the blade rang a cold voice in answer: 'Yes, I will drink your blood, that I may forget the blood of Beleg my master, and the blood of Brandir slain unjustly. I will slay you swiftly.'

Then Túrin set the hilts upon the ground, and cast himself upon the point of Gurthang, and the black blade took his life.

But Mablung came and looked on the hideous shape of Glaurung lying dead, and he looked upon Túrin and was grieved, thinking of Húrin as he had seen him in the Nirnaeth Arnoediad, and the dreadful doom of his kin. As the Elves stood there, men came down from Nen Girith to look upon the Dragon, and when they saw to what end the life of Túrin Turambar had come they wept; and the Elves learning at last the reason of Túrin's words to them were aghast. Then Mablung said bitterly: 'I also have been

meshed in the doom of the Children of Húrin, and thus with words have slain one that I loved.'

Then they lifted up Túrin, and saw that his sword was broken asunder. So passed all that he possessed.

With toil of many hands they gathered wood and piled it high and made a great burning and destroyed the body of the Dragon, until he was but black ash and his bones beaten to dust, and the place of that burning was ever bare and barren thereafter. But Túrin they laid in a high mound where he had fallen, and the shards of Gurthang were set beside him. And when all was done, and the minstrels of Elves and Men had made lament, telling of the valour of Turambar and the beauty of Níniel, a great grey stone was brought and set upon the mound; and thereon the Elves carved in the Runes of Doriath:

TÚRIN TURAMBAR DAGNIR GLAURUNGA

and beneath they wrote also:

NIËNOR NÍNIEL

But she was not there, nor was it ever known whither the cold waters of Teiglin had taken her.

Here ends the Tale of the Children of Húrin, longest of all the lays of Beleriand.

After the deaths of Túrin and Niënor Morgoth released Húrin from bondage in furtherance of his evil purpose. In the course of his wanderings he reached the Forest of Brethil, and came up in the evening from the Crossings of Teiglin to the place of the burning of Glaurung and the great stone standing on the brink of Cabed Naeramarth. Of what befell there this is told.

But Húrin did not look at the stone, for he knew what was written there; and his eyes had seen that he was not alone. Sitting in the shadow of the stone there was a figure bent over its knees. Some homeless wanderer broken with age it seemed, too wayworn to heed his coming; but its rags were the remnants of a woman's garb. At length as Húrin stood there silent she cast back her tattered hood and lifted up her face slowly, haggard and hungry as a long-hunted wolf. Grey she was, sharp-nosed with broken teeth, and with a lean hand she clawed at the cloak upon her breast. But suddenly her eyes looked into his, and then Húrin knew her; for though they were wild now and full of fear, a light still gleamed in them hard to endure: the elven-light that long ago had earned her her name, Eledhwen, proudest of mortal women in the days of old.

'Eledhwen! Eledhwen!' Húrin cried; and she rose and stumbled forward, and he caught her in his arms.

'You come at last,' she said. 'I have waited too long.'

'It was a dark road. I have come as I could,' he answered.

'But you are late,' she said, 'too late. They are lost.'

'I know,' he said. 'But you are not.'

'Almost,' she said. 'I am spent utterly. I shall go with the sun. They are lost.' She clutched at his cloak. 'Little time is left,' she said. 'If you know, tell me! How did she find him?'

But Húrin did not answer, and he sat beside the stone with Morwen in his arms; and they did not speak again. The sun went down, and Morwen sighed and clasped his hand and was still; and Húrin knew that she had died.

GENEALOGIES

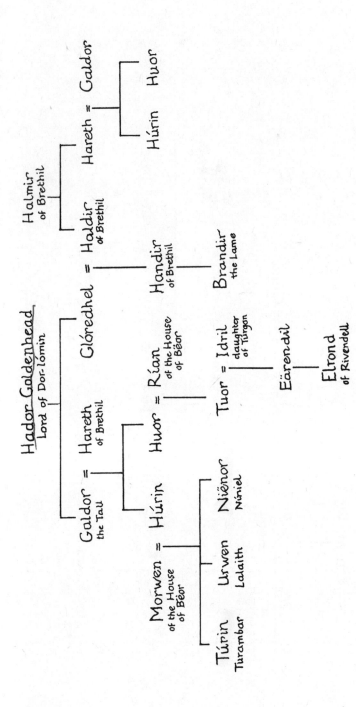

The House of Hador & the People of Haleth

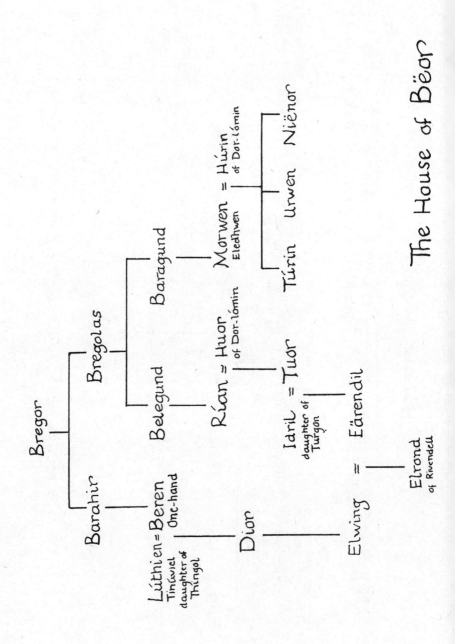

The House of Bëor

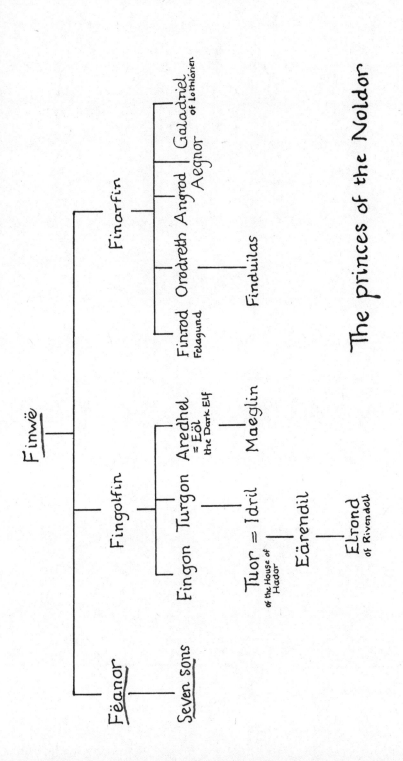

The princes of the Noldor

APPENDIX

THE EVOLUTION OF
THE GREAT TALES

These interrelated but independent stories had from far
back stood out from the long and complex history of Valar,
Elves and Men in Valinor and the Great Lands; and in the
years that followed his abandonment of the *Lost Tales*
before they were completed my father turned away from
prose composition and began work on a long poem with
the title *Túrin son of Húrin and Glórund the Dragon*, later
changed in a revised version to *The Children of Húrin*.
This was in the earlier 1920s, when he held appointments
at the University of Leeds. For this poem he employed the
ancient English alliterative metre (the verse form of
Beowulf and other Anglo-Saxon poetry), imposing on
modern English the demanding patterns of stress and
'initial rhyme' observed by the old poets: a skill in which
he achieved great mastery, in very different modes, from
the dramatic dialogue of *The Homecoming of Beorhtnoth*
to the elegy for the men who died in the battle of the
Pelennor Fields. The alliterative *Children of Húrin* was by
far the longest of his poems in this metre, running to well
over two thousand lines; yet he conceived it on so lavish a
scale that even so he had reached no further in the narrative than the assault of the Dragon on Nargothrond when

he abandoned it. With so much more of the *Lost Tale* still to come it would have needed on this scale many more thousands of lines; while a second version, abandoned at an earlier point in the narrative, is about double the length of the first version to that same point.

In that part of the legend of the Children of Húrin that my father achieved in the alliterative poem the old story in *The Book of Lost Tales* was substantially extended and elaborated. Most notably, it was now that the great underground fortress-city of Nargothrond emerged, and the wide lands of its dominion (a central element not only in the legend of Túrin and Niënor but in the history of the Elder Days of Middle-earth), with a description of the farmlands of the Elves of Nargothrond that gives a rare suggestion of the 'arts of peace' in the ancient world, such glimpses being few and far between. Coming south along the river Narog Túrin and his companion (Gwindor in the text in this book) found the lands near the entrance to Nargothrond to all appearance deserted:

> . . . *they came to a country   kindly tended;*
> *through flowery frith   and fair acres*
> *they fared, and found   of folk empty*
> *the leas and leasows   and the lawns of Narog,*
> *the teeming tilth   by trees enfolded*
> *twixt hills and river.   The hoes unrecked*
> *in the fields were flung,   and fallen ladders*
> *in the long grass lay   of the lush orchards;*

every tree there turned   its tangled head
and eyed them secretly,   and the ears listened
of the nodding grasses;   though noontide glowed
on land and leaf,   their limbs were chilled.

And so the two travellers came to the doors of Nargothrond, in the gorge of the Narog:

there steeply stood   the strong shoulders
of the hills, o'erhanging   the hurrying water;
there shrouded in trees   a sheer terrace,
wide and winding,   worn to smoothness,
was fashioned in the face   of the falling slope.
Doors there darkly   dim gigantic
were hewn in the hillside;   huge their timbers,
and their posts and lintels   of ponderous stone.

Seized by Elves they were haled through the portal, which closed behind them:

Ground and grumbled   on its great hinges
the door gigantic;   with din ponderous
it clanged and closed   like clap of thunder,
and echoes awful   in empty corridors
there ran and rumbled   under roofs unseen;
the light was lost.   Then led them on
down long and winding   lanes of darkness
their guards guiding   their groping feet,

till the faint flicker   of fiery torches
flared before them;   fitful murmur
as of many voices   in meeting thronged
they heard as they hastened.   High sprang the roof.
Round a sudden turning   they swung amazed,
and saw a solemn   silent conclave,
where hundreds hushed   in huge twilight
neath distant domes   darkly vaulted
them wordless waited.

But in the text of *The Children of Húrin* given in this book we are told no more than this (p. 158):

> And now they arose, and departing from Eithel Ivrin they journeyed southward along the banks of Narog, until they were taken by scouts of the Elves and brought as prisoners to the hidden stronghold.
> Thus did Túrin come to Nargothrond.

How did this come about? In what follows I shall try to answer that question.

It seems virtually certain that all that my father wrote of his alliterative poem on Túrin was accomplished at Leeds, and that he abandoned it at the end of 1924 or early in 1925; but why he did so must remain unknown. What he then turned to is however not mysterious: in the summer of 1925 he embarked on a new poem in a wholly different metre, octosyllabic rhyming couplets, entitled *The Lay of Leithian* 'Release from Bondage'. Thus he took up now another of the tales that he described years later, in 1951, as I have already noted, as full in treatment, independent, and yet linked to 'the general history'; for the subject of *The Lay of Leithian* is the legend of Beren and Lúthien. He worked on this second long poem for six years, and in its turn abandoned it, in September 1931, having written more than 4000 lines. As does the alliterative *Children of Húrin* which it succeeded and supplanted, this poem represents a substantial advance in the evolution of the legend from the original *Lost Tale* of Beren and Lúthien.

While *The Lay of Leithian* was in progress, in 1926, he wrote a 'Sketch of the Mythology', expressly intended for R.W. Reynolds, who had been his teacher at King Edward's school in Birmingham, 'to explain the background of the alliterative version of Túrin and the Dragon'. This brief manuscript, which would run to some twenty printed pages, was avowedly written as a synopsis, in the present tense and in a succinct style; and yet it was the starting-point of the subsequent 'Silmarillion' versions (though that name was not yet given). But while the entire mythological conception was set out in this text, the tale of Túrin has very evidently pride of place – and indeed the title in the manuscript is 'Sketch of the mythology with especial reference to the "Children of Húrin"', in keeping with his purpose in writing it.

In 1930 there followed a much more substantial work, the *Quenta Noldorinwa* (the History of the Noldor: for the history of the Noldorin Elves is the central theme of

'The Silmarillion'). This was directly derived from the 'Sketch', and while much enlarging the earlier text and writing in a more finished manner, my father nonetheless still saw the *Quenta* very much as a *summarising* work, an epitome of far richer narrative conceptions: as is in any case clearly shown by the sub-title that he gave to it, in which he declared that it was 'a *brief history* [of the Noldor] drawn from the Book of Lost Tales'.

It is to be borne in mind that at that time the *Quenta* represented (if only in a somewhat bare structure) the full extent of my father's 'imagined world'. It was not the history of the First Age, as it afterwards became, for there was as yet no Second Age, nor Third Age; there was no Númenor, no hobbits, and of course no Ring. The history ended with the Great Battle, in which Morgoth was finally defeated by the other Gods (the Valar), and by them 'thrust through the Door of Timeless Night into the Void, beyond the Walls of the World'; and my father wrote at the end of the *Quenta*: 'Such is *the end of the tales* of the days before the days in the Northern regions of the Western world.'

Thus it will seem strange indeed that the *Quenta* of 1930 was nonetheless the only completed text (after the 'Sketch') of 'The Silmarillion' that he ever made; but as was so often the case, external pressures governed the evolution of his work. The *Quenta* was followed later in the 1930s by a new version in a beautiful manuscript, bearing at last the title *Quenta Silmarillion, History of the Silmarilli*. This was, or was to be, much longer than the preceding *Quenta Noldorinwa*, but the conception of the work as essentially a *summarising* of myths and legends (themselves of an altogether different nature and scope if fully told) was by no means lost, and is again defined in the title: 'The *Quenta Silmarillion* .... This is a *history in brief* drawn from many older tales; for all the matters that it contains were of old, and still are among the Eldar of the West, recounted more fully in other histories and songs.'

It seems at least probable that my father's view of *The Silmarillion* did actually arise from the fact that what may be called the '*Quenta* phase' of the work in the 1930s began in a condensed synopsis serving a particular purpose, but then underwent expansion and refinement in successive stages until it lost the appearance of a synopsis, but nonetheless retaining, from the form of its origin, a characteristic 'evenness' of tone. I have written elsewhere that 'the compendious or epitomising form and manner of *The Silmarillion*, with its suggestion of ages of poetry and "lore" behind it, strongly evokes a sense of "untold tales", even in the telling of them; "distance" is never lost. There is no narrative urgency, the pressure and fear of the immediate and unknown event. We do not actually see the Silmarils as we see the Ring.'

However, the *Quenta Silmarillion* in this form came to an abrupt and, as it turned out, a decisive end in 1937. *The Hobbit* was published by George Allen and Unwin on 21 September of that year, and not long afterwards, at the invitation of the publisher, my father sent in a number of his manuscripts, which were delivered in London on 15 November 1937. Among these was the *Quenta Silmarillion*, so far as it then went, ending in the middle of a sentence at the foot of a page. But while it was gone he continued the narrative in draft form as far as Túrin's flight from Doriath and his taking up the life of an outlaw:

> passing the borders of the realm he gathered to himself a company of such houseless and desperate folk as could be found in those evil days lurking in the wild; and their hands were turned against all who came in their path, Elves, Men, or Orcs.

This is the forerunner of the passage, in the text in this book p. 98, at the beginning of *Túrin among the Outlaws*.

My father had reached these words when the *Quenta Silmarillion* and the other manuscripts were returned to him; and three days later, on 19 December 1937, he wrote to Allen and Unwin saying: 'I have written the first chapter of a new story about Hobbits – "A long expected party".'

It was at this point that the continuous and evolving tradition of *The Silmarillion* in the summarising, *Quenta* mode came to an end, brought down in full flight, at Túrin's departure from Doriath. The further history from that point remained during the years that followed in the simple, compressed, and undeveloped form of the *Quenta* of 1930, frozen, as it were, while the great structures of the Second and Third Ages arose with the writing of *The Lord of the Rings*. But that further history was of cardinal importance in the ancient legends, for the concluding stories (deriving from the original *Book of Lost Tales*) told of the disastrous history of Húrin, father of Túrin, after Morgoth released him, and of the ruin of the Elvish kingdoms of Nargothrond, Doriath, and Gondolin, of which Gimli chanted in the mines of Moria many thousands of years afterwards.

> *The world was fair, the mountains tall,*
> *In Elder Days before the fall*
> *Of mighty kings in Nargothrond*
> *And Gondolin, who now beyond*
> *The Western Seas have passed away. . . .*

And this was to be the crown and completion of the whole: the doom of the Noldorin Elves in their long struggle against the power of Morgoth, and the parts that Húrin and Túrin played in that history; ending with the tale of Eärendil, who escaped from the burning ruin of Gondolin.

When, many years later, early in 1950, *The Lord of the Rings* was finished, my father turned with energy and confidence to 'the Matter of the Elder Days', now become 'the First Age'; and in the years immediately following he took out many old manuscripts from where they had long lain. Turning to *The Silmarillion*, he covered at this time the beautiful manuscript of the *Quenta Silmarillion* with corrections and expansions; but that revision ceased in 1951 before he reached the story of Túrin, where the *Quenta Silmarillion* was abandoned in 1937 with the advent of 'the new story about Hobbits'.

He began a revision of the *Lay of Leithian* (the poem in rhyming verse telling the story of Beren and Lúthien that was abandoned in 1931) that soon became almost a new poem, of much greater accomplishment; but this petered out and was ultimately abandoned. He embarked on what was to be a long saga of Beren and Lúthien in prose, closely based on the rewritten form of the Lay; but that too was abandoned. Thus his desire, shown in successive attempts, to render the first of the 'great tales' on the scale that he sought was never fulfilled.

At that time also he turned again at last to the 'great tale' of the Fall of Gondolin, still extant only in the *Lost Tale* from some thirty-five years before and in the few pages devoted to it in the *Quenta Noldorinwa* of 1930. This was to be the presentation, when he was at the height of his powers, in close narrative and in all its bearings, of the extraordinary tale that he had read to the Essay Society of his college at Oxford in 1920, and which remained throughout his life a vital element in his imagination of the

Elder Days. The special link with the tale of Túrin lies in the brothers Húrin, father of Túrin, and Huor, father of Tuor. Húrin and Huor in their youth entered the Elvish city of Gondolin, hidden within a circle of high mountains, as is told in *The Children of Húrin* (p. 35); and afterwards, in the battle of Unnumbered Tears, they met again with Turgon, King of Gondolin, and he said to them (p. 58): 'Not long now can Gondolin remain hidden, and being discovered it must fall.' And Huor replied: 'Yet if it stands only a little while, then out of your house shall come the hope of Elves and Men. This I say to you, lord, with the eyes of death: though we part here for ever, and I shall not look on your white walls again, from you and from me a new star shall arise.'

This prophecy was fulfilled when Tuor, first cousin to Túrin, came to Gondolin and wedded Idril, daughter of Turgon; for their son was Eärendil: the 'new star', 'hope of Elves and Men', who escaped from Gondolin. In the prose saga of *The Fall of Gondolin* that was to be, begun probably in 1951, my father recounted the journey of Tuor and his Elvish companion, Voronwë, who guided him; and on the way, alone in the wilderness, they heard a cry in the woods:

And as they waited one came through the trees, and they saw that he was a tall Man, armed, clad in black, with a long sword drawn; and they wondered, for the blade of the sword also was black, but the edges shone bright and cold.

That was Túrin, hastening from the sack of Nargothrond (pp. 180–1); but Tuor and Voronwë did not speak to him as he passed, and 'they knew not that Nargothrond had fallen, and this was Túrin son of Húrin, the Blacksword. Thus only for a moment, and never again, did the paths of those kinsmen, Túrin and Tuor, draw together.'

In the new tale of Gondolin my father brought Tuor to the high place in the Encircling Mountains from where the eye could travel across the plain to the Hidden City; and there, grievously, he stopped, and never went further. And so in *The Fall of Gondolin* likewise he failed of his purpose; and we see neither Nargothrond nor Gondolin with his later vision.

I have said elsewhere that 'with the completion of the great "intrusion" and departure of *The Lord of the Rings*, it seems that he returned to the Elder Days with a desire to take up again the far more ample scale with which he had begun long before, in *The Book of Lost Tales*. The completion of the *Quenta Silmarillion* remained an aim; but the "great tales", vastly developed from their original forms, *from which its later chapters should be derived*, were never achieved.' These remarks are true of the 'great tale' of *The Children of Húrin* as well; but in this case my father achieved much more, even though he was never able to bring a substantial part of the later and hugely extended version to final and finished form.

At the same time as he turned again to the *Lay of Leithian* and *The Fall of Gondolin* he began his new work on *The Children of Húrin*, not with Túrin's childhood, but with the latter part of the story, the culmination of his disastrous history after the destruction of Nargothrond. This is the text in this book from *The Return of Túrin to Dor-lómin* (p. 182) to his death. Why my father should have proceeded in this way, so unlike his usual practice of starting again at the beginning, I cannot explain. But in this case he left also among his papers a mass of later but undated writing concerned with the story from Túrin's birth to the sack of Nargothrond, with great elaboration of the old versions and expansion into narrative previously unknown.

By far the greater part of this work, if not all of it, belongs to the time following the actual publication of *The Lord of the Rings*. In those years *The Children of Húrin* became for him the dominant story of the end of the Elder Days, and for a long time he devoted all his thought to it. But he found it hard now to impose a firm narrative structure as the tale grew in complexity of character and event; and indeed in one long passage the story is contained in a patchwork of disconnected drafts and plot-outlines.

Yet *The Children of Húrin* in its latest form is the chief narrative fiction of Middle-earth after the conclusion of *The Lord of the Rings*; and the life and death of Túrin is portrayed with a convincing power and an immediacy scarcely to be found elsewhere among the peoples of Middle-earth. For this reason I have attempted in this book, after long study of the manuscripts, to form a text that provides a continuous narrative from start to finish, without the introduction of any elements that are not authentic in conception.

(2)

THE COMPOSITION OF THE TEXT

In *Unfinished Tales*, published more than a quarter of a century ago, I presented a partial text of the long version of this tale, known as the *Narn*, from the Elvish title *Narn i Chîn Húrin*, the Tale of the Children of Húrin. But that was one element in a large book of various content, and the text was very incomplete, in keeping with the general purpose and nature of the book: for I omitted a number of substantial passages (and one of them very long) where the *Narn* text and that in the much briefer version in *The Silmarillion* are very similar, or where I decided that no distinctive 'long' text could be provided.

The form of the *Narn* in this book therefore differs in a number of ways from that in *Unfinished Tales*, some of them deriving from the far more thorough study of the formidable complex of manuscripts that I made after that book was published. This led me to different conclusions about the relations and sequence of some of the texts, chiefly in the extremely confusing evolution of the legend in the period of 'Túrin among the Outlaws'. A description and explanation of the composition of this new text of *The Children of Húrin* follows here.

An important element in all this is the peculiar status of the published *Silmarillion*; for as I have mentioned in the first part of this Appendix my father abandoned the *Quenta Silmarillion* at the point that he had reached (Túrin's becoming an outlaw after his flight from Doriath) when he began *The Lord of the Rings* in 1937. In the formation of a narrative for the published work I made much use of *The Annals of Beleriand*, originally a 'Tale of Years', but which in successive versions grew and expanded into annalistic narrative in parallel with the successive 'Silmarillion' manuscripts, and which extended to the freeing of Húrin by Morgoth after the deaths of Túrin and Niënor.

Thus the first passage that I omitted from the version of the *Narn i Chîn Húrin* in *Unfinished Tales* (p. 58 and note 1) is the account of the sojourn of Húrin and Huor in Gondolin in their youth; and I did so simply because the tale is told in *The Silmarillion* (pp. 158–9). But my father did in fact write two versions: one of them was expressly intended for the opening of the *Narn*, but was very closely based on a passage in *The Annals of Beleriand*, and indeed for most of its length differs little. In *The Silmarillion* I used both texts, but here I have followed the *Narn* version.

The second passage that I omitted from the *Narn* in *Unfinished Tales* (pp. 65–6 and note 2) is the account of the Battle of Unnumbered Tears, an omission made for the same reason; and here again my father wrote two versions, one in the *Annals*, and a second, much later but with the *Annals* text in front of him, and for the most part closely followed. This second narrative of the great battle was, again, expressly intended as a constituent element in the *Narn* (the text is headed *Narn II*, i.e. the second section of the *Narn*), and states at the outset (p. 52 in the text in this book): 'Here there shall be recounted only those deeds which bear upon the fate of the House of Hador and the children of Húrin the Steadfast.' In pursuit of this my father retained from the *Annals* account only the description of the 'westward battle' and the destruction of the host of Fingon; and by this simplification and reduction of the narrative he altered the course of the battle as told in the *Annals*. In *The Silmarillion* I of course followed the *Annals*, though with some features taken from the *Narn* version; but in this book I have kept to the text that my father thought appropriate to the *Narn* as a whole.

From *Túrin in Doriath* the new text is a good deal changed in relation to that in *Unfinished Tales*. There is here a range of writing, much of it very rough, concerned with the same narrative elements at different stages of development, and in such a case it is obviously possible to take different views on how the original material should be treated. I have come to think that when I composed the text in *Unfinished Tales* I allowed myself more editorial freedom than was necessary. In this book I have reconsidered the original manuscripts and reconstituted the text, in many (usually very minor) places restoring the original words, introducing sentences or brief passages that should not have been omitted, correcting a few errors, and making different choices among the original readings.

As regards the structure of the narrative in this period of Túrin's life, from his flight out of Doriath to the lair of the outlaws on Amon Rûdh, my father had certain narrative 'elements' in mind: the trial of Túrin before Thingol; the gifts of Thingol and Melian to Beleg; the maltreatment of Beleg by the outlaws in Túrin's absence; the meetings of Túrin and Beleg. He moved these 'elements' in relation to each other, and placed passages of dialogue in different contexts; but found it difficult to compose them into a settled 'plot' – 'to find out what really happened'. But it seems now clear to me, after much further study, that my father did achieve a satisfying structure and sequence for this part of the story before he abandoned it; and also that the narrative in much reduced form that I composed for the published *Silmarillion* conforms to this – but with one difference.

In *Unfinished Tales* there is a third gap in the narrative on p. 96: the story breaks off at the point where Beleg, having at last found Túrin among the outlaws, cannot persuade him to return to Doriath (pp. 115–19 in the new text), and does not take up again until the outlaws encounter the Petty-dwarves. Here I referred again to *The Silmarillion* for the filling of the gap, noting that there follows in the story Beleg's farewell to Túrin and his return to Menegroth 'where he received the sword Anglachel from Thingol and *lembas* from Melian'. But it is in fact demonstrable that my father rejected this; for 'what really happened' was that Thingol gave Anglachel to Beleg after the trial of Túrin, when Beleg first set off to find him. In the present text therefore the gift of the sword is placed at that point (p. 96), and there is no mention there of the gift of *lembas*. In the later passage, when Beleg returned to Menegroth after the finding of Túrin, there is of course no reference to Anglachel in the new text, but only to Melian's gift.

This is a convenient point to notice that I have omitted from the text two passages that I included in *Unfinished Tales* but which are parenthetical to the narrative: these are the history of how the Dragon-helm came into the possession of Hador of Dor-lómin (*Unfinished Tales*, p. 75), and the origin of Saeros (*Unfinished Tales*, p. 77). It seems, incidentally, certain from a closer understanding of the relations of the manuscripts that my father rejected the name *Saeros* and replaced it by *Orgol*, which by 'linguistic accident' coincides with Old English *orgol, orgel* 'pride'. But it seems to me too late now to remove *Saeros*.

The major lacuna in the narrative as given in *Unfinished Tales* (p. 104) is filled in the new text on pages 141 to 181, from the end of the section *Of Mîm the Dwarf* and through *The Land of Bow and Helm, The Death of Beleg, Túrin in Nargothrond*, and *The Fall of Nargothrond*.

There is a complex relationship in this part of the 'Túrin saga' between the original manuscripts, the story as it is told in *The Silmarillion*, the disconnected passages collected in the appendix to the *Narn* in *Unfinished Tales*, and the new text in this book. I have always supposed that it was my father's general intention, in the fullness of time, when he had achieved to his satisfaction the 'great tale' of Túrin, to derive from it a much briefer form of the story in what one may call 'the *Silmarillion* mode'. But of course this did not happen; and so I undertook, now more than thirty years ago, the strange task of trying to simulate what he did not do: the writing of a 'Silmarillion' version of the latest form of the story, but deriving this from the heterogeneous materials of the 'long version', the *Narn*. That is Chapter 21 in the published *Silmarillion*.

Thus the text in this book that fills the long gap in the story in *Unfinished Tales* is derived from the same original materials as is the corresponding passage in *The Silmarillion* (pp. 204–15), but they are used for a different purpose in each case, and in the new text with a better understanding of the labyrinth of drafts and notes and their sequence. Much in the original manuscripts that was omitted or compressed in *The Silmarillion* remains available; but where there was nothing to be added to the *Silmarillion* version (as in the tale of the death of Beleg, derived from the *Annals of Beleriand*) that version is simply repeated.

In the result, while I have had to introduce bridging passages here and there in the piecing together of different drafts, there is no element of extraneous 'invention' of any kind, however slight, in the longer text here presented. The text is nonetheless artificial, as it could not be otherwise: the more especially since this great body of manuscript represents a continual evolution in the actual story. Drafts that are essential to the formation of an uninterrupted narrative may in fact belong to an earlier stage. Thus, to give an example from an earlier point, a primary text for the story of the coming of Túrin's band to the hill of Amon Rûdh, the dwelling place that they found upon it and their life there, and the ephemeral success of the land of Dor-Cúarthol, was written before there was any suggestion of the Petty-dwarves; and indeed a fully-developed description of Mîm's house beneath the summit appears before Mîm himself.

In the remainder of the story, from Túrin's return to Dor-lómin, to which my father gave a finished form, there are naturally very few differences from the text in *Unfinished Tales*. But there are two matters of detail in the account of the attack on Glaurung at Cabed-en-Aras where I have emended the original words and which should be explained.

The first concerns the geography. It is said (p. 230) that when Túrin and his companions set out from Nen Girith on the fateful evening they did not go straight towards the Dragon, lying on the further side of the ravine, but took first the path towards the Crossings of Teiglin; and 'then, before they came so far, they turned southward by a narrow track' and went through the woods above the river towards Cabed-en-Aras. As they approached, in the original text of the passage, 'the first stars glimmered in the east behind them'.

When I prepared the text for *Unfinished Tales* I did not observe that this could not be right, since they were certainly not moving in a westerly direction, but east, or south-east, away from the Crossings, and the first stars in the east must have been before them, not behind them. When discussing this in *The War of the Jewels* (1994, p. 157) I accepted the suggestion that the 'narrow track' going southward turned again westward to reach the Teiglin. But this seems to me now to be improbable, as being without point in the narrative, and that a much simpler solution is to emend 'behind them' to 'before them', as I have done in the new text.

The sketch map that I drew in *Unfinished Tales* (p. 149) to illustrate the lie of the land is not in fact well oriented. It is seen from my father's map of Beleriand, and is so reproduced in my map for *The Silmarillion*, that Amon Obel was almost due east from the Crossings of Teiglin ('the moon rose beyond Amon Obel', p. 241), and the Teiglin was flowing south-east or south-south-east in the ravines. I have now redrawn the sketch map,

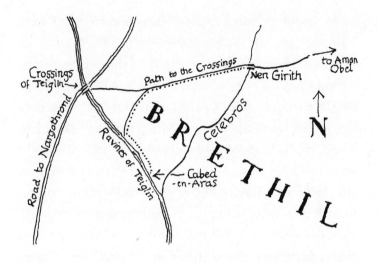

and have entered also the approximate place of Cabed-en-Aras (it is said in the text, p. 225, that 'right in the path of Glaurung there lay now one of these gorges, by no means the deepest, but the narrowest, just north of the inflow of Celebros').

The second matter concerns the story of the slaying of Glaurung at the crossing of the ravine. There are here a draft and a final version. In the draft, Túrin and his companions climbed up the further side of the chasm until they came beneath the brink; they hung there as the night passed, and Túrin 'strove with dark dreams of dread in which all his will was given to clinging and holding'. When day came Glaurung prepared to cross at a point 'many paces to the northward', and so Túrin had to climb down to the river-bed and then up the cliff again to get beneath the Dragon's belly.

In the final version (p. 235) Túrin and Hunthor were only part way up the further side when Túrin said that they were wasting their strength in climbing up now, before they knew where Glaurung would cross; 'they halted therefore and waited'. It is not said that they descended from where they were when they ceased to climb, and the passage concerning Túrin's dream 'in which all his will was given to clinging' reappears from the draft text. But in the revised story there was no need for them to cling: they could and surely would have descended to the bottom and waited there. In fact, this is what they did: it is said in the final text (*Unfinished Tales*, p. 134) that they were not standing in Glaurung's path and that Túrin 'clambered along the water-edge to come beneath him'. It seems then that the final story carries an unneeded trait from the previous draft. To give it coherence I have emended (p. 236) 'since they were not standing right in Glaurung's path' to 'since they were not right in Glaurung's path', and 'clambered along the water-edge' to 'clambered along the cliff'.

These are small matters in themselves, but they clarify what are perhaps the most sharply visualised scenes in the legends of the Elder Days, and one of the greatest events.

LIST OF NAMES IN
THE TALE OF
THE CHILDREN OF HÚRIN

Names that appear in the map of Beleriand are followed by an asterisk.

Adanedhel	'Elf-man', name given to Túrin in Nargothrond.
Aerin	A kinswoman of Húrin in Dor-lómin, taken as wife by Brodda the Easterling.
Agarwaen	'Bloodstained', name taken by Túrin when he came to Nargothrond.
Ainur	'The Holy Ones', the first beings created by Ilúvatar, who were before the World: the Valar and the Maiar ('spirits of the same order as the Valar but of less degree').
Algund	Man of Dor-lómin, member of the outlaw band that Túrin joined.
Amon Darthir *	A peak in the range of Ered Wethrin south of Dor-lómin.
Amon Ethir	'Hill of Spies', a great earthwork raised by Finrod Felagund a league to the east of Nargothrond.
Amon Obel *	A hill in the midst of the Forest of Brethil, on which was built Ephel Brandir.
Amon Rûdh *	'The Bald Hill', a lonely height in the lands south of Brethil, abode of Mîm.
Anach *	Pass leading down from Taur-nu-Fuin at the western end of Ered Gorgoroth.
Andróg	Man of Dor-lómin, a leader of the outlaw band that Túrin joined.

Anfauglith *	'Gasping Dust', the great plain north of Taur-nu-Fuin, once grassy and named *Ard-galen*, but transformed into a desert by Morgoth in the Battle of Sudden Flame.
Angband	The great fortress of Morgoth in the North-west of Middle-earth.
Anglachel	Beleg's sword, the gift of Thingol; after its reforging for Túrin named *Gurthang*.
Angrod	Third son of Finarfin, slain in the Dagor Bragollach.
Anguirel	Eöl's sword.
Aranrúth	'King's Ire', Thingol's sword.
Arda	The Earth.
Aredhel	Sister of Turgon, wife of Eöl.
Arminas	Noldorin Elf who came with Gelmir to Nargothrond to warn Orodreth of its peril.
Arroch	Húrin's horse.
Arvernien *	The coastlands of Beleriand west of Sirion's mouths; named in Bilbo's song in Rivendell.
Asgon	Man of Dor-lómin who aided Túrin's escape after the slaying of Brodda.
Azaghâl	Lord of the Dwarves of Belegost.
Barad Eithel	'Tower of the Well', the fortress of the Noldor at Eithel Sirion.
Baragund	Father of Morwen; cousin of Beren.
Barahir	Father of Beren; brother of Bregolas.

Bar-en-Danwedh   'House of Ransom', name given by Mîm to his house.

Bar-en-Nibin-noeg   'House of the Petty-dwarves' on Amon Rûdh.

Bar Erib   A stronghold of Dor-Cúarthol south of Amon Rûdh.

Battle of Unnumbered Tears   See *Nirnaeth Arnoediad*.

Bauglir   'The Constrainer', name given to Morgoth.

Beleg   Elf of Doriath, a great archer; friend and companion of Túrin. Called *Cúthalion* 'Strongbow'.

Belegost   'Great Fortress', one of the two cities of the Dwarves in the Blue Mountains.

Belegund   Father of Rían; brother of Baragund.

Beleriand *   Lands west of the Blue Mountains in the Elder Days.

Belthronding   Beleg's bow.

Bëor   Leader of the first Men to enter Beleriand; progenitor of the House of Bëor, one of the three Houses of the Edain.

Beren   Man of the House of Bëor, lover of Lúthien, who cut a Silmaril from Morgoth's crown; called 'One-hand' and *Camlost* 'Empty-handed'.

Black King, The   Morgoth.

Black Sword, The   Túrin's name in Nargothrond; also the sword itself. See *Mormegil*.

Blue Mountains   The great mountain chain (called *Ered Luin* and *Ered Lindon*) between Beleriand and Eriador in the Elder Days.

Bragollach   See *Dagor Bragollach.*

Brandir   Ruler of the People of Haleth in Brethil when Túrin came; son of Handir.

Bregolas   Father of Baragund; Morwen's grandfather.

Bregor   Father of Barahir and Bregolas.

Brethil *   Forest between the rivers Teiglin and Sirion; *Men of Brethil*, the People of Haleth.

Brithiach *   Ford over Sirion north of the Forest of Brethil.

Brodda   An Easterling in Hithlum after the Nirnaeth Arnoediad.

Cabed-en-Aras   'The Deer's Leap', a deep gorge of the river Teiglin where Túrin slew Glaurung.

Cabed Naeramarth   'The Leap of Dreadful Doom', name given to Cabed-en-Aras after Niënor leapt from its cliffs.

Celebros   Stream in Brethil falling down to Teiglin near the Crossings.

Children of Ilúvatar   Elves and Men.

Círdan   Called 'the Shipwright'; lord of the Falas; at the destruction of the Havens after the Nirnaeth Arnoediad he escaped to the Isle of Balar in the south.

Crissaegrim *   The mountain peaks south of Gondolin, where were the eyries of Thorondor.

Crossings of Teiglin *   Fords where the old South Road to Nargothrond crossed the Teiglin.

Cúthalion   'Strongbow', name of Beleg.

Daeron   Minstrel of Doriath.

Dagor Bragollach (also *the Bragollach*)   The Battle of Sudden Flame, in which Morgoth ended the Siege of Angband.

Dark Lord, The   Morgoth.

Deer's Leap, The   See *Cabed-en-Aras*.

Dimbar *   The land between the rivers Sirion and Mindeb.

Dimrost   'The Rainy Stair', the falls of Celebros in the Forest of Brethil, afterwards called *Nen Girith*.

Dor Cúarthol   'Land of Bow and Helm', name given to the country defended by Túrin and Beleg from their lair on Amon Rûdh.

Doriath *   The kingdom of Thingol and Melian in the forests of Neldoreth and Region, ruled from Menegroth on the river Esgalduin.

Dorlas   A man of consequence among the People of Haleth in the Forest of Brethil.

Dor-lómin *   Region in the south of Hithlum given by King Fingolfin as a fief to the House of Hador; the home of Húrin and Morwen.

Dorthonion *	'Land of Pines', great forested highlands on the northern borders of Beleriand, afterwards named *Taur-nu-Fuin*.
Drengist *	Long firth of the sea piercing Ered Lómin, the Echoing Mountains.
Easterlings	Tribes of Men who followed the Edain into Beleriand.
Echad i Sedryn	(also *the Echad*) 'Camp of the Faithful', name given to Mîm's house on Amon Rûdh.
Ecthelion	Elf-lord of Gondolin.
Edain	(singular *Adan*) The Men of the Three Houses of the Elf-friends.
Eithel Ivrin *	'Ivrin's Well', the source of the river Narog beneath Ered Wethrin.
Eithel Sirion *	'Sirion's Well', in the eastern face of Ered Wethrin; the fortress of the Noldor in that place, also called *Barad Eithel*.
Eldalië	The Elven-folk, equivalent to *Eldar*.
Eldar	The Elves of the Great Journey out of the East to Beleriand.
Elder Children	The Elves. See *Children of Ilúvatar*.
Eledhwen	Name of Morwen, 'Elfsheen'.
Encircling Mountains	The mountains encircling Tumladen, the plain of Gondolin.
Enemy, The	Morgoth.

Eöl	Called 'the Dark Elf', a great smith who dwelt in Nan Elmoth; maker of the sword Anglachel; father of Maeglin.
Ephel Brandir	'The Fence of Brandir', the enclosed dwellings of the Men of Brethil upon Amon Obel; also *the Ephel.*
Ered Gorgoroth *	'Mountains of Terror', the vast precipices in which Taur-nu-Fuin fell southward; also *the Gorgoroth.*
Ered Wethrin	'Shadowy Mountains', 'Mountains of Shadow', the great range forming the boundary of Hithlum on the east and south.
Esgalduin *	The river of Doriath, dividing the forests of Neldoreth and Region and flowing into Sirion.
Exiles, The	The Noldor who rebelled against the Valar and returned to Middle-earth.
Faelivrin	Name given to Finduilas by Gwindor.
Fair Folk	The Eldar.
Falas *	The coastlands of Beleriand in the West.
Fëanor	Eldest son of Finwë, the first leader of the Noldor; half-brother of Fingolfin; maker of the Silmarils; leader of the Noldor in their rebellion against the Valar, but slain in battle soon after his return to Middle-earth. See *Sons of Fëanor.*

Felagund	'Hewer of caves', name given to King Finrod after the establishment of Nargothrond and often used alone.
Finarfin	Third son of Finwë, brother of Fingolfin and half-brother of Fëanor; father of Finrod Felagund and Galadriel. Finarfin did not return to Middle-earth.
Finduilas	Daughter of Orodreth, second King of Nargothrond.
Fingolfin	Second son of Finwë, the first leader of the Noldor; High King of the Noldor, dwelling in Hithlum; father of Fingon and Turgon.
Fingon	Eldest son of King Fingolfin, and High King of the Noldor after his death.
Finrod	Son of Finarfin; founder and king of Nargothrond, brother of Orodreth and Galadriel; often called *Felagund.*
Forweg	Man of Dor-lómin, captain of the outlaw band that Túrin joined.
Galdor the Tall	Son of Hador Goldenhead; father of Húrin and Huor; slain at Eithel Sirion.
Gamil Zirak	Dwarf smith, teacher of Telchar of Nogrod.
Gaurwaith	'Wolf-men', the outlaw band that Túrin joined in the woodlands beyond the western borders of Doriath.
Gelmir (1)	Elf of Nargothrond, brother of Gwindor.
Gelmir (2)	Noldorin Elf who came with Arminas to Nargothrond to warn Orodreth of its peril.

Gethron	One of Túrin's companions on the journey to Doriath.
*Ginglith**	River flowing into the Narog above Nargothrond.
Girdle of Melian	See *Melian*.
Glaurung	'Father of Dragons', the first of the Dragons of Morgoth.
*Glithui**	River flowing down from Ered Wethrin and joining Teiglin north of the inflow of Malduin.
Glóredhel	Daughter of Hador, sister of Galdor Húrin's father; wife of Haldir of Brethil.
Glorfindel	Elf-lord of Gondolin.
*Gondolin**	The hidden city of King Turgon.
Gorgoroth	See *Ered Gorgoroth*.
Gorthol	'Dread Helm', name taken by Túrin in the land of Dor Cúarthol.
Gothmog	Lord of Balrogs; slayer of King Fingon.
Great Mound, The	See *Haudh-en-Nirnaeth*.
Great Song, The	The Music of the Ainur, in which the World was begun.
Grey-elves	The Sindar, name given to the Eldar who remained in Beleriand and did not cross the Great Sea into the West.
Grithnir	One of Túrin's companions on the journey to Doriath, where he died.
*Guarded Plain, The**	See *Talath Dirnen*.

Guarded Realm, The   Doriath.

Guilin   Elf of Nargothrond, father of Gwindor and Gelmir.

Gurthang   'Iron of Death', Túrin's name for the sword Anglachel after it was reforged in Nargothrond.

Gwaeron   The 'windy month', March.

Gwindor   Elf of Nargothrond, lover of Finduilas, companion of Túrin.

Hador Goldenhead   Elf-friend, lord of Dor-lómin, vassal of King Fingolfin; father of Galdor father of Húrin and Huor; slain at Eithel Sirion in the Dagor Bragollach. *House of Hador*, one of the Houses of the Edain.

Haldir   Son of Halmir of Brethil; wedded Glóredhel daughter of Hador of Dor-lómin.

Haleth   The Lady Haleth, who early became the leader of the Second House of the Edain, the *Halethrim* or *People of Haleth*, who dwelt in the Forest of Brethil.

Halmir   Lord of the Men of Brethil.

Handir of Brethil   Son of Haldir and Glóredhel; father of Brandir.

Hareth   Daughter of Halmir of Brethil, wife of Galdor of Dor-lómin; mother of Húrin.

Haudh-en-Elleth   'The Mound of the Elf-maid' near the Crossings of Teiglin, in which Finduilas was buried.

Haudh-en-Nirnaeth 'The Mound of Tears' in the desert of Anfauglith.

Hidden Kingdom, The Doriath.

Hidden Realm, The Gondolin.

High Faroth, The * Highlands to the west of the river Narog above Nargothrond; also *the Faroth*.

Hirilorn A great beech-tree in the Forest of Neldoreth with three trunks.

Hithlum * 'Land of Mist', northern region bounded by the Mountains of Shadow.

Hunthor Man of Dor-lómin, companion of Túrin in the attack on Glaurung.

Huor Húrin's brother; father of Tuor father of Eärendil; slain in the Battle of Unnumbered Tears.

Húrin Lord of Dor-lómin, husband of Morwen and father of Túrin and Niënor; called *Thalion* 'the Steadfast'.

Ibun One of the sons of Mîm the Petty-dwarf.

Ilúvatar 'The Father of All'.

Indor Man of Dor-lómin, father of Aerin.

Ivrin * Lake and falls beneath Ered Wethrin where the river Narog rose.

Khîm One of the sons of Mîm the Petty-dwarf, slain by Andróg's arrow.

Labadal   Túrin's name for Sador.

Ladros *   Lands to the north-east of Dorthonion
               that were granted by the Noldorin kings
               to the Men of the House of Bëor.

Lady of Dor-lómin   Morwen.

Lalaith   'Laughter', name given to Urwen.

Larnach   One of the Woodmen in the lands south
               of Teiglin.

Lord of Waters   The Vala Ulmo.

Lords of the West   The Valar.

Lothlann   A great plain to the east of Dorthonion
               (*Taur-nu-Fuin*).

Lothron   The fifth month.

Lúthien   Daughter of Thingol and Melian, who
               after the death of Beren chose to become
               mortal and to share his fate. Called
               Tinúviel 'daughter of twilight',
               nightingale.

Mablung   Elf of Doriath, chief captain of Thingol,
               friend of Túrin; called 'the Hunter'.

Maedhros   Eldest son of Fëanor, with lands in the
               east beyond Dorthonion.

Maeglin   Son of Eöl 'the Dark Elf' and Aredhel
               Turgon's sister; betrayer of Gondolin.

Malduin *   A tributary of the Teiglin.

Mandos   A Vala: the Judge, and Keeper of the
               Houses of the Dead in Valinor.

Manwë   The chief of the Valar; called *the Elder
               King*.

Melian	A Maia (see entry *Ainur*); the queen of King Thingol in Doriath, about which she set an invisible barrier of protection, the Girdle of Melian; mother of Lúthien.
Melkor	The Quenya name of Morgoth.
*Menegroth**	'The Thousand Caves', the halls of Thingol and Melian on the river Esgalduin in Doriath.
Menel	The heavens, region of the stars.
Methed-en-glad	'End of the wood', a stronghold of Dor Cúarthol at the edge of the forest south of Teiglin.
Mîm	The Petty-dwarf, dwelling on Amon Rûdh.
Minas Tirith	'Tower of Watch', built by Finrod Felagund on Tol Sirion.
*Mindeb**	A tributary of Sirion, between Dimbar and the Forest of Neldoreth.
*Mithrim**	The south-eastern region of Hithlum, separated from Dor-lómin by the Mountains of Mithrim.
Morgoth	The great rebellious Vala, in his origin the mightiest of the Powers; called *the Enemy*, *the Dark Lord*, *the Black King*, *Bauglir*.
Mormegil	'Black Sword', name given to Túrin in Nargothrond.
Morwen	Daughter of Baragund of the House of Bëor; wife of Húrin and mother of Túrin and Niënor; called *Eledhwen* 'Elfsheen' and *Lady of Dor-lómin*.
*Mountains of Shadow**	See *Ered Wethrin*.

Nan Elmoth *	A forest in East Beleriand; dwelling-place of Eöl.
Nargothrond *	'The great underground fortress on the river Narog', founded by Finrod Felagund, destroyed by Glaurung; also the realm of Nargothrond extending east and west of the river.
Narog *	The chief river of West Beleriand, rising at Ivrin and flowing into Sirion near its mouths. *People of Narog*, the Elves of Nargothrond.
Neithan	'The Wronged', name given to himself by Túrin among the outlaws.
Nellas	Elf of Doriath, friend of Túrin in his boyhood.
Nen Girith	'Shuddering Water', name given to Dimrost, the falls of Celebros in Brethil.
Nen Lalaith	Stream rising under Amon Darthir, a peak in Ered Wethrin, and flowing past Húrin's house in Dor-lómin.
Nenning *	River in West Beleriand, reaching the Sea at the Haven of Eglarest.
Nevrast *	Region west of Dor-lómin, beyond the Echoing Mountains* (*Ered Lómin*).
Nibin-noeg, Nibin-nogrim	Petty-dwarves.
Niënor	'Mourning', daughter of Húrin and Morwen, and sister of Túrin; see *Níniel*.
Nimbrethil *	Birchwoods in Arvernien; named in Bilbo's song in Rivendell.
Níniel	'Maid of Tears', name that Túrin gave to Niënor in Brethil.

Nirnaeth Arnoediad   The Battle of 'Unnumbered Tears', also *the Nirnaeth.*

Nogrod   One of the two cities of the Dwarves in the Blue Mountains.

Noldor   The second host of the Eldar on the Great Journey out of the East to Beleriand; the 'Deep Elves', 'the Loremasters'.

Núath, Woods of *   Woods extending westward from the upper waters of the Narog.

Orleg   A man of Túrin's outlaw band.

Orodreth   King of Nargothrond after the death of his brother Finrod Felagund; father of Finduilas.

Ossë   A Maia (see entry *Ainur*); vassal of Ulmo Lord of Waters.

Petty-dwarves   A race of Dwarves in Middle-earth of whom Mîm and his two sons were the last survivors.

Powers, The   The Valar.

Ragnir   A blind servant in Húrin's house in Dor-lómin.

Region *   The southern forest of Doriath.

Rían   Cousin of Morwen; wife of Huor Húrin's brother; mother of Tuor.

Rivil *   Stream falling from Dorthonion to join Sirion in the Fen of Serech.

Sador	Woodwright, serving-man of Húrin's in Dor-lómin and friend of Túrin in his childhood, by whom he was called *Labadal*.
Saeros	Elf of Doriath, a counsellor of Thingol, hostile to Túrin.
Sauron's Isle	Tol Sirion.
Serech *	The great fen north of the Pass of Sirion, where the river Rivil flowed in from Dorthonion.
Shadowy Mountains	See *Ered Wethrin*.
Sharbhund	Dwarvish name of Amon Rûdh.
Sindarin	Grey-elven, the Elvish tongue of Beleriand. See *Grey-elves*.
Sirion *	The great river of Beleriand, rising at Eithel Sirion.
Sons of Fëanor	See *Fëanor*. The seven sons held lands in East Beleriand.
South Road *	The ancient road from Tol Sirion to Nargothrond by the Crossings of Teiglin.
Spyhill, The	See *Amon Ethir*.
Strawheads	Name given to the People of Hador by the Easterlings in Hithlum.
Strongbow	Name of Beleg; see *Cúthalion*.
Talath Dirnen *	'The Guarded Plain', north of Nargothrond.
Taur-nu-Fuin *	'Forest under Night', later name of Dorthonion.

Teiglin *	A tributary of Sirion rising in the Shadowy Mountains and flowing through the Forest of Brethil. See *Crossings of Teiglin*.
Telchar	Renowned smith of Nogrod.
Telperion	The White Tree, elder of the Two Trees that gave light to Valinor.
Thangorodrim	'Mountains of Tyranny', reared by Morgoth over Angband.
Thingol	'Greycloak', King of Doriath, overlord of the Grey-elves (Sindar); wedded to Melian the Maia; father of Lúthien.
Thorondor	'King of Eagles' (cf. *The Return of the King* VI.4: 'old Thorondor, who built his eyries in the inaccessible peaks of the Encircling Mountains when Middle-earth was young').
Three Houses (of the Edain)	The Houses of Bëor, Haleth, and Hador.
Thurin	'The Secret', name given to Túrin by Finduilas.
Tol Sirion *	Island in the river in the Pass of Sirion on which Finrod built the tower of Minas Tirith; afterwards taken by Sauron.
Tumhalad *	Valley in West Beleriand between the rivers Ginglith and Narog where the host of Nargothrond was defeated.
Tumladen	The hidden vale in the Encircling Mountains where the city of Gondolin stood.
Tuor	Son of Huor and Rían; cousin of Túrin and father of Eärendil.

Turambar	'Master of Doom', name taken by Túrin among the Men of Brethil.
Turgon	Second son of King Fingolfin and brother of Fingon; founder and king of Gondolin.
Túrin	Son of Húrin and Morwen, chief subject of the lay named *Narn i Chîn Húrin*. For his other names see *Neithan, Gorthol, Agarwaen, Thurin, Adanedhel, Mormegil (Black Sword), Wild Man of the Woods, Turambar*.
Twilit Meres *	Region of marshes and pools where the Aros flowed into Sirion.
Uldor the Accursed	A leader of the Easterlings who was slain in the Battle of Unnumbered Tears.
Ulmo	One of the great Valar, 'Lord of Waters'.
Ulrad	A member of the outlaw band that Túrin joined.
Úmarth	'Ill-fate', a fictitious name for his father given out by Túrin in Nargothrond.
Unnumbered Tears	The battle of *Nirnaeth Arnoediad*.
Urwen	Daughter of Húrin and Morwen who died in childhood; called *Lalaith* 'Laughter'.
Valar	'The Powers', those great spirits that entered the World at the beginning of time.
Valinor	The land of the Valar in the West, beyond the Great Sea.

Varda   The greatest of the Queens of the Valar,
                   the spouse of Manwë.

Wildman of the Woods   Name taken by Túrin when he
                   first came among the Men of Brethil.

Wolf-men   See *Gaurwaith*.

Woodmen   Dwellers in the woods south of Teiglin,
                   plundered by the Gaurwaith.

Year of Lamentation   The year of the *Nirnaeth Arnoediad*.

Younger Children   Men. See *Children of Ilúvatar*.

NOTE ON THE MAP

This map is closely based on that in the published *Silmar-illion*, which was itself derived from the map that my father made in the 1930s, and which he never replaced, but used for all his subsequent work. The formalised, and obviously very selective, representations of mountains, hills and forests are imitated from his style.

In this redrawing I have introduced certain differences, intended to simplify it and to make it more expressly applicable to the tale of *The Children of Húrin*. Thus it does not extend eastward to include Ossiriand and the Blue Mountains, and certain geographical features are omitted; while (with a few exceptions) only names that actually occur in the text of the tale are marked.

BEREN AND LÚTHIEN

Works by J.R.R. Tolkien

THE HOBBIT
LEAF BY NIGGLE
ON FAIRY-STORIES
FARMER GILES OF HAM
THE HOMECOMING OF BEORHTNOTH
THE LORD OF THE RINGS
THE ADVENTURES OF TOM BOMBADIL
THE ROAD GOES EVER ON (WITH DONALD SWANN)
SMITH OF WOOTTON MAJOR

Works published posthumously

SIR GAWAIN AND THE GREEN KNIGHT, PEARL AND SIR ORFEO*
THE FATHER CHRISTMAS LETTERS
THE SILMARILLION*
PICTURES BY J.R.R. TOLKIEN*
UNFINISHED TALES*
THE LETTERS OF J.R.R. TOLKIEN*
FINN AND HENGEST
MR BLISS
THE MONSTERS AND THE CRITICS & OTHER ESSAYS*
ROVERANDOM
THE CHILDREN OF HÚRIN*
THE LEGEND OF SIGURD AND GUDRÚN*
THE FALL OF ARTHUR*
BEOWULF: A TRANSLATION AND COMMENTARY*
THE STORY OF KULLERVO

The History of Middle-earth – by Christopher Tolkien

I THE BOOK OF LOST TALES, PART ONE
II THE BOOK OF LOST TALES, PART TWO
III THE LAYS OF BELERIAND
IV THE SHAPING OF MIDDLE-EARTH
V THE LOST ROAD AND OTHER WRITINGS
VI THE RETURN OF THE SHADOW
VII THE TREASON OF ISENGARD
VIII THE WAR OF THE RING
IX SAURON DEFEATED
X MORGOTH'S RING
XI THE WAR OF THE JEWELS
XII THE PEOPLES OF MIDDLE-EARTH

* EDITED BY CHRISTOPHER TOLKIEN

BEREN AND LÚTHIEN

BY

J.R.R. Tolkien

Edited by Christopher Tolkien

With illustrations by Alan Lee

HOUGHTON MIFFLIN HARCOURT
BOSTON   NEW YORK

First U.S. edition

For information about permission to reproduce selections from this book, write
to trade.permissions@hmhco.com or to Permissions, Houghton Mifflin Harcourt
Publishing Company, 3 Park Avenue, 19th Floor, New York, New York 10016.

First published by HarperCollins*Publishers* 2017

Library of Congress Cataloging-in-Publication Data is available.
ISBN 978-1-328-79182-5

Printed in the United States of America
22 23 24 25 26 LSB 15 14 13 12 11

For Baillie

CONTENTS

PLATES

PREFACE

After the publication of *The Silmarillion* in 1977 I spent several years investigating the earlier history of the work, and writing a book which I called *The History of The Silmarillion*. Later this became the (somewhat shortened) basis of the earlier volumes of *The History of Middle-earth*.

In 1981 I wrote at length to Rayner Unwin, the chairman of Allen and Unwin, giving him an account of what I had been, and was still, doing. At that time, as I informed him, the book was 1,968 pages long and sixteen and a half inches across, and obviously not for publication. I said to him: 'If and/or when you see this book, you will perceive immediately why I have said that it is in no conceivable way publishable. The textual and other discussions are far too detailed and minute; the size of it is (and will become progressively more so) prohibitive. It is done partly for my own satisfaction in getting things right, and because I wanted to know how the whole conception did in reality evolve from the earliest origins. . . .

9

'If there is a future for such enquiries, I want to make as sure as I can that any later research into JRRT's "literary history" is not turned into a nonsense by mistaking the actual course of its evolution. The chaos and intrinsic difficulty of many of the papers (the layer upon layer of changes in a single manuscript page, the vital clues on scattered scraps found anywhere in the archive, the texts written on the backs of other works, the disordering and separation of manuscripts, the near or total illegibility in places, is simply inexaggerable. . . .

'In theory, I could produce a lot of books out of the *History*, and there are many possibilities and combinations of possibilities. For example, I could do "Beren", with the original Lost Tale*, *The Lay of Leithian*, and an essay on the development of the legend. My preference, if it came to anything so positive, would probably be for the treating of one legend as a developing entity, rather than to give all the Lost Tales at one go; but the difficulties of exposition in detail would in such a case be great, because one would have to explain so often what was happening elsewhere, in other unpublished writings.'

I said that I would enjoy writing a book called 'Beren' on the lines I suggested: but 'the problem would be its organisation, so that the matter was comprehensible without the editor becoming overpowering.'

When I wrote this I meant what I said about publication: I had no thought of its possibility, other than my idea of

---

* 'The Lost Tales' is the name of the original versions of the legends of *The Silmarillion.*

selecting a single legend 'as a developing entity'. I seem now
to have done precisely that – though with no thought of what
I had said in my letter to Rayner Unwin thirty-five years ago:
I had altogether forgotten it, until I came on it by chance
when this book was all but completed.

There is however a substantial difference between it and
my original idea, which is a difference of context. Since then,
a large part of the immense store of manuscripts pertaining
to the First Age, or Elder Days, has been published, in close
and detailed editions: chiefly in volumes of *The History of
Middle-earth.* The idea of a book devoted to the evolving
story of 'Beren' that I ventured to mention to Rayner Unwin
as a possible publication would have brought to light much
hitherto unknown and unavailable writing. But this book
does not offer a single page of original and unpublished work.
What then is the need, now, for such a book?

I will attempt to provide an (inevitably complex) answer, or
several answers. In the first place, an aspect of those editions
was the presentation of the texts in a way that adequately
displayed my father's apparently eccentric mode of composition (often in fact imposed by external pressures), and so
to discover the sequence of stages in the development of a
narrative, and to justify my interpretation of the evidence.

At the same time, the First Age in *The History of Middle-
earth* was in those books conceived as a *history* in two senses.
It was indeed a history – a chronicle of lives and events in
Middle-earth; but it was also a history of the changing literary conceptions in the passing years; and therefore the story
of Beren and Lúthien is spread over many years and several

books. Moreover, since that story became entangled with the slowly evolving 'Silmarillion', and ultimately an essential part of it, its developments are recorded in successive manuscripts primarily concerned with the whole history of the Elder Days.

To follow the story of Beren and Lúthien, as a single and well-defined narrative, in *The History of Middle-earth* is therefore not easy.

In an often quoted letter of 1951 my father called it 'the chief of the stories of the *Silmarillion*', and he said of Beren that he is 'the outlawed mortal who succeeds (with the help of Lúthien, a mere maiden even if an elf of royalty) where all the armies and warriors have failed: he penetrates the stronghold of the Enemy and wrests one of the Silmarilli from the Iron Crown. Thus he wins the hand of Lúthien and the first marriage of mortal and immortal is achieved.

'As such the story is (I think a beautiful and powerful) heroic-fairy-romance, receivable in itself with only a very general vague knowledge of the background. But it is also a fundamental link in the cycle, deprived of its full significance out of its place therein.'

In the second place, my purpose in this book is twofold. On the one hand I have tried to separate the story of Beren and Tinúviel (Lúthien) so that it stands alone, so far as that can be done (in my opinion) without distortion. On the other hand, I have wished to show how this fundamental story evolved over the years. In my foreword to the first volume of *The Book of Lost Tales* I said of the changes in the stories:

In the history of the history of Middle-earth the development was seldom by outright rejection – far more often it was by subtle transformation in stages, so that the growth of the legends (the process, for instance, by which the Nargothrond story made contact with that of Beren and Lúthien, a contact not even hinted at in the *Lost Tales*, though both elements were present) can seem like the growth of legends among peoples, the product of many minds and generations.

It is an essential feature of this book that these developments in the legend of Beren and Lúthien are shown in my father's own words, for the method that I have employed is the extraction of passages from much longer manuscripts in prose or verse written over many years.

In this way, also, there are brought to light passages of close description or dramatic immediacy that are lost in the summary, condensed manner characteristic of so much *Silmarillion* narrative writing; there are even to be discovered elements in the story that were later altogether lost. Thus, for example, the cross-examination of Beren and Felagund and their companions, disguised as Orcs, by Thû the Necromancer (the first appearance of Sauron), or the entry into the story of the appalling Tevildo, Prince of Cats, who clearly deserves to be remembered, short as was his literary life.

Lastly, I will cite another of my prefaces, that to *The Children of Húrin* (2007):

It is undeniable that there are a great many readers of *The Lord of the Rings* for whom the legends of the Elder Days are altogether unknown, unless by their repute as strange and inaccessible in mode and manner.

It is also undeniable that the volumes of *The History of Middle-earth* in question may well present a deterrent aspect. This is because my father's mode of composition was intrinsically difficult: and a primary purpose of the *History* was to try to disentangle it: thereby (it may seem) exhibiting the tales of the Elder Days as a creation of unceasing fluidity. I believe that he might have said, in explanation of some rejected element in a tale: I came to see that it was not like that; or, I realised that that was not the right name. The fluidity should not be exaggerated: there were nonetheless great, essential, permanences. But it was certainly my hope, in composing this book, that it would show how the creation of an ancient legend of Middle-earth, changing and growing over many years, reflected the search of the author for a presentation of the myth nearer to his desire.

In my letter to Rayner Unwin of 1981 I observed that in the event of my restricting myself to a single legend from among the legends that make up the *Lost Tales* 'the difficulties of exposition in detail would in such a case be great, because one would have to explain so often what was happening elsewhere, in other unpublished writings'. This has proved an accurate prediction in the case of *Beren and Lúthien*. A solution of some sort must be achieved, for Beren and Lúthien

did not live, love, and die, with their friends and foes, on an
empty stage, alone and with no past. I have therefore followed
my own solution in *The Children of Húrin*. In my preface to
that book I wrote:

> It seems unquestionable, from my father's own words, that
> if he could achieve final and finished narratives on the scale
> he desired, he saw three 'Great Tales' of the Elder Days
> (Beren and Lúthien, the Children of Húrin, and the Fall of
> Gondolin) as works sufficiently complete in themselves as
> not to demand knowledge of the great body of legend known
> as *The Silmarillion*. On the other hand . . . the tale of the
> Children of Húrin is integral to the history of Elves and Men
> in the Elder Days, and there are necessarily a good many
> references to events and circumstances in that larger story.

I therefore gave 'a very brief sketch of Beleriand and its
peoples near the end of the Elder Days', and I included 'a list
of all names occurring in the texts with very concise indications concerning each.' In this book I have adopted from *The
Children of Húrin* that brief sketch, adapting and shortening
it, and I have likewise provided a list of all names occurring
in the texts, in this case with explanatory indications of a very
varied nature. None of this ancillary matter is essential, but is
intended merely as an assistance if desired.

A further problem which I should mention arose from the
very frequent changes of names. To follow with exactness
and consistency the succession of names in texts of different dates would not serve the purpose of this book. I have

therefore observed no rule in this respect, but distinguished old and new in some cases but not in others, for various reasons. In a great many cases my father would alter a name in a manuscript at some later, or even much later, time, but not consistently: for example, *Elfin* to *Elven*. In such cases I have made *Elven* the sole form, or *Beleriand* for earlier *Broseliand*; but in others I have retained both, as in *Tinwelint/Thingol, Artanor/Doriath*.

The purpose of this book, then, is altogether different from that of the volumes of *The History of Middle-earth* from which it is derived. It is emphatically not intended as an adjunct to those books. It is an attempt to extract one narrative element from a vast work of extraordinary richness and complexity; but that narrative, the story of Beren and Lúthien, was itself continually evolving, and developing new associations as it became more embedded in the wider history. The decision of what to include and what to exclude of that ancient world 'at large' could only be a matter of personal and often questionable judgement: in such an attempt there can be no attainable 'correct way'. In general, however, I have erred on the side of clarity, and resisted the urge to explain, for fear of undermining the primary purpose and method of the book.

In my ninety-third year this is (presumptively) my last book in the long series of editions of my father's writings, very largely previously unpublished, and is of a somewhat curious nature. This tale is chosen *in memoriam* because of its deeply-rooted presence in his own life, and his intense thought on the union of Lúthien, whom he called 'the greatest of the Eldar', and of Beren the mortal man, of their fates, and of their second lives.

It goes back a long way in my life, for it is my earliest actual recollection of some element in a story that was being told to me – not simply a remembered image of the scene of the storytelling. My father told it to me, or parts of it, speaking it without any writing, in the early 1930s.

The element in the story that I recall, in my mind's eye, is that of the eyes of the wolves as they appeared one by one in the darkness of the dungeon of Thû.

In a letter to me on the subject of my mother, written in the year after her death, which was also the year before his own, he wrote of his overwhelming sense of bereavement, and of his wish to have *Lúthien* inscribed beneath her name on the grave. He returned in that letter, as in that cited on p. 29 of this book, to the origin of the tale of Beren and Lúthien in a small woodland glade filled with hemlock flowers near Roos in Yorkshire, where she danced; and he said: 'But the story has gone crooked, and I am left, and *I* cannot plead before the inexorable Mandos.'

NOTES ON THE ELDER DAYS

The depth in time to which this story reaches back was memorably conveyed in a passage in *The Lord of the Rings*. At the great council in Rivendell Elrond spoke of the Last Alliance of Elves and Men and the defeat of Sauron at the end of the Second Age, more than three thousand years before:

> Thereupon Elrond paused a while and sighed. 'I remember well the splendour of their banners,' he said. 'It recalled to me the glory of the Elder Days and the hosts of Beleriand, so many great princes and captains were assembled. And yet not so many, nor so fair, as when Thangorodrim was broken, and the Elves believed that evil was ended for ever, and it was not so.'
>
> 'You remember?' said Frodo, speaking his thought aloud in his astonishment. 'But I thought,' he stammered as Elrond turned towards him, 'I thought that the fall of Gil-galad was a long age ago.'

'So it was indeed,' answered Elrond gravely. 'But my memory reaches back even to the Elder Days. Eärendil was my sire, who was born in Gondolin before its fall; and my mother was Elwing, daughter of Dior, son of Lúthien of Doriath. I have seen three ages in the West of the world, and many defeats, and many fruitless victories.'

Of Morgoth

Morgoth, the Black Enemy, as he came to be called, was in his origin, as he declared to Húrin brought captive before him, 'Melkor, first and mightiest of the Valar, who was before the world.' Now become permanently incarnate, in form a gigantic and majestic, but terrible, King in the north-west of Middle-earth, he was physically present in his huge fortress of Angband, the Hells of Iron: the black reek that issued from the summits of Thangorodrim, the mountains that he piled above Angband, could be seen far off staining the northern sky. It is said in the *Annals of Beleriand* that 'the gates of Morgoth were but one hundred and fifty leagues from the bridge of Menegroth; far and yet all too near.' These words refer to the bridge leading to the dwellings of the Elvish king Thingol; they were called Menegroth, the Thousand Caves.

But being incarnate Morgoth was afraid. My father wrote of him:

'As he grew in malice, and sent forth from himself the evil that he conceived in lies and creatures of wickedness, his power passed into them and was dispersed, and he himself

19

became ever more earth-bound, unwilling to issue from his dark strongholds.' Thus when Fingolfin, High King of the Noldorin Elves rode alone to Angband to challenge Morgoth to combat, he cried at the gate: Come forth, thou coward king, to fight with thine own hand! Den-dweller, wielder of thralls, liar and lurker, foe of Gods and Elves, come! For I would see thy craven face. Then (it is told) Morgoth came. For he could not refuse such a challenge before the face of his captains. He fought with the great hammer Grond, which at each blow made a great pit, and he beat Fingolfin to the ground; but as he died he pinned the great foot of Morgoth to the earth, and the black blood gushed forth and filled the pits of Grond. Morgoth went ever halt thereafter. So also, when Beren and Lúthien made their way into the deepest hall in Angband where Morgoth sat, Lúthien cast a spell on him; and suddenly he fell, as a hill sliding in avalanche, and hurled like thunder from his throne lay prone upon the floors of hell.

Of Beleriand

When Treebeard strode through the forest of Fangorn carrying Merry and Pippin each in the crook of his arm he sang to them of ancient forests in the great country of Beleriand, which was destroyed in the tumults of the Great Battle at the end of the Elder Days. The Great Sea poured in and drowned all the lands west of the Blue Mountains, called Ered Luin and Ered Lindon; so that the map accompanying *The Silmarillion* ends in the east with that mountain-chain, whereas the map accompanying *The Lord of the Rings* ends in the west, also with the Blue Mountains. The coastal lands beyond them on their western sides were all that remained in the Third Age of that country, called Ossiriand, Land of Seven Rivers, in which Treebeard once walked:

> *I wandered in Summer in the elm-woods of Ossiriand.*
> *Ah! the light and the music in the Summer by the Seven*
> *Rivers of Ossir!*
> *And I thought that was best.*

It was over the passes of the Blue Mountains that Men entered Beleriand; in those mountains were the cities of the Dwarves, Nogrod and Belegost; and it was in Ossiriand that Beren and Lúthien dwelt after they were permitted by Mandos to return to Middle-earth (p. 235).

Treebeard walked also among the pine-trees of Dorthonion ('Land of Pines'):

> *To the pine-trees upon the highland of Dorthonion I climbed*
> *in the Winter.*
> *Ah! the wind and the whiteness and the black branches of*
> *Winter upon Orod-na-Thôn!*
> *My voice went up and sang in the sky.*

That country came afterwards to be called Taur-nu-Fuin, 'the Forest under Night', when Morgoth turned into 'a region of dread and dark enchantment, of wandering and despair' (see p. 107).

Of the Elves

The Elves appeared on earth far off in a distant land (Palisor) beside a lake named Cuiviénen, the Water of Awakening; and thence they were summoned by the Valar to leave Middle-earth, and passing over the Great Sea to come to the 'Blessed Realm' of Aman in the west of the world, the land of the Gods. Those who accepted the summons were led on a great march across Middle-earth by the Vala Oromë, the Hunter, and they are called the Eldar, the Elves of the Great Journey, the High Elves, distinct from those who, refusing the summons, chose Middle-earth for their land and their destiny.

But not all the Eldar, though they had crossed the Blue Mountains, departed over the sea; and those who remained in Beleriand are named the Sindar, the Grey Elves. Their high king was Thingol (which means 'Grey-cloak'), who ruled from Menegroth, the Thousand Caves in Doriath (Artanor). And not all the Eldar who crossed the Great Sea remained in the land of the Valar; for one of their great kindreds, the Noldor (the 'Loremasters'), returned to Middle-earth, and they are called the Exiles.

The prime mover in their rebellion against the Valar was Fëanor, maker of the Silmarils; he was the eldest son of Finwë, who had led the host of the Noldor from Cuiviénen, but was now dead. In my father's words:

> The Jewels were coveted by Morgoth the Enemy, who stole them and, after destroying the Trees, took them to Middle-earth, and guarded them in his great fortress of

Thangorodrim. Against the will of the Valar Fëanor forsook
the Blessed Realm and went in exile to Middle-earth, leading
with him a great part of his people, for in his pride he purposed to recover the Jewels from Morgoth by force.

Thereafter followed the hopeless war of the Eldar and
the Edain [the Men of the Three Houses of the Elf-friends]
against Thangorodrim, in which they were at last utterly
defeated.

[handwritten annotation: 3 mountains of slag built over Angband - destroyed by fall of Ancalagon on it in the Great Battle]

Before their departure from Valinor there took place the
dreadful event that marred the history of the Noldor in
Middle-earth. Fëanor demanded of those Teleri, the third
host of the Eldar on the Great Journey, who dwelt now on
the coast of Aman, that they give up to the Noldor their fleet
of ships, their great pride, for without ships the crossing to
Middle-earth by such a host would not be possible. This the
Teleri refused utterly.

Then Fëanor and his people attacked the Teleri in their city
of Alqualondë, the Haven of the Swans, and took the fleet
by force. In that battle, which was known as The Kinslaying,
many of the Teleri were slain. This is referred to in *The Tale
of Tinúviel* (p. 42): 'the evil deeds of the Gnomes at the Haven
of the Swans', and see p. 130, lines 514–19. *

Fëanor was slain in battle soon after the return of the
Noldor to Middle-earth, and his seven sons held wide lands
in the east of Beleriand, between Dorthonion (Taur-na-fuin)
and the Blue Mountains.

The second son of Finwë was Fingolfin (the half-brother
of Fëanor), who was held the overlord of all the Noldor; and

*[handwritten annotation at bottom: * Only a portion of Fëanor's people could sit in the ships - so they stole them - and on landing in middlearth they burnt 23 - the others were forced to travel along the cold lands of the north]*

he with his son Fingon ruled Hithlum, which lay to the north
and west of the great chain of Ered Wethrin, the Mountains of
Shadow. Fingolfin died in single combat with Morgoth. The
second son of Fingolfin, the brother of Fingon, was Turgon,
the founder and ruler of the hidden city of Gondolin.

The third son of Finwë, the brother of Fingolfin and half-
brother of Fëanor, was in earlier texts Finrod, later Finarfin
(see p. 104). The eldest son of Finrod/Finarfin was in earlier
texts Felagund, but later Finrod; he, inspired by the magnificence and beauty of Menegroth in Doriath, founded the
underground fortress-city of Nargothrond, for which he was
named Felagund, 'Lord of Caves': thus earlier Felagund =
later Finrod Felagund.

The doors of Nargothrond opened onto the gorge of the
river Narog in West Beleriand; but Felagund's realm extended
far and wide, east to the river Sirion and west to the river
Nenning that reached the sea at the haven of Eglarest. But
Felagund was slain in the dungeons of Thû the Necromancer,
later Sauron; and Orodreth, the second son of Finarfin, took
the crown of Nargothrond, as told in this book (pp. 109, 120).

The other sons of Finarfin, Angrod and Egnor, vassals of
their brother Finrod Felagund, dwelt on Dorthonion, looking northwards over the vast plain of Ard-galen. Galadriel,
the sister of Finrod Felagund, dwelt long in Doriath with
Melian the Queen. Melian (in early texts Gwendeling and
other forms) was a Maia, a spirit of great power who took
human form and dwelt in the forests of Beleriand with King
Thingol: she was the mother of Lúthien and the foremother
of Elrond.

In the sixtieth year after the return of the Noldor, ending many years of peace, a great host of Orcs came down from Angband, but was utterly defeated and destroyed by the Noldor. This was called *Dagor Aglareb*, the Glorious Battle; but the Elvish lords took warning from it, and set the Siege of Angband, which lasted for almost four hundred years.

The Siege of Angband ended with a terrible suddenness (though long prepared) on a night of midwinter. Morgoth released rivers of fire that ran down from Thangorodrim, and the great grassy plain of Ard-galen that lay to the north of Dorthonion was transformed into a parched and arid waste, known thereafter by a changed name, *Anfauglith*, the Gasping Dust.

This catastrophic assault was called *Dagor Bragollach*, the Battle of Sudden Flame (p. 106). Glaurung Father of Dragons emerged from Angband now for the first time in his full might; vast armies of Orcs poured southwards; the Elvish lords of Dorthonion were slain, and a great part of the warriors of Bëor's people (pp. 105–6). King Fingolfin and his son Fingon were driven back with the warriors of Hithlum to the fortress of Eithel Sirion (Sirion's Well), where the great river rose in the east face of the Mountains of Shadow. The torrents of fire were stopped by the Mountains of Shadow, and Hithlum and Dor-lómin remained unconquered.

It was in the year after the *Bragollach* that Fingolfin, in a fury of despair, rode to Angband and challenged Morgoth.

*

BEREN AND LÚTHIEN

IN A LETTER of my father's written on the 16th of July 1964 he said:

> The germ of my attempt to write legends of my own to fit my private languages was the tragic tale of the hapless Kullervo in the Finnish *Kalevala*. It remains a major matter in the legends of the First Age (which I hope to publish as *The Silmarillion*), though as 'The Children of Húrin' it is entirely changed except in the tragic ending. The second point was the writing, 'out of my head', of 'The Fall of Gondolin', the story of Idril and Earendel, during sick-leave from the army in 1917; and by the original version of the 'Tale of Lúthien Tinúviel and Beren' later in the same year. That was founded on a small wood with a great undergrowth of 'hemlock' (no doubt many other related plants were also there) near Roos in Holderness, where I was for a while on the Humber Garrison.

My father and mother were married in March 1916, when he was twenty-four and she was twenty-seven. They lived at first in the village of Great Haywood in Staffordshire; but he embarked for France and the battle of the Somme early in June of that year. Taken ill, he was sent back to England at the beginning of November 1916; and in the spring of 1917 he was posted to Yorkshire.

This primary version of *The Tale of Tinúviel*, as he called it, written in 1917, does not exist – or more precisely, exists only in the ghostly form of a manuscript in pencil that he all but entirely erased for most of its length; over this he wrote the text that is for us the earliest version. *The Tale of Tinúviel* was one of the constituent stories of my father's major early work of his 'mythology', *The Book of Lost Tales*, an exceedingly complex work which I edited in the first two volumes of *The History of Middle-earth*, 1983–4. But since the present book is expressly devoted to the evolution of the legend of Beren and Lúthien I will here very largely pass by the strange setting and audience of the *Lost Tales*, for *The Tale of Tinúviel* is in itself almost entirely independent of that setting.

Central to *The Book of Lost Tales* was the story of an English mariner of the 'Anglo-Saxon' period named Eriol or Ælfwine who, sailing far westwards over the ocean, came at last to Tol Eressëa, the Lonely Isle, where dwelt Elves who had departed from 'the Great Lands', afterwards 'Middle-Earth' (a term not used in the *Lost Tales*). During his sojourn in Tol Eressëa he learned from them the true and ancient history of the Creation, of the Gods, of the Elves, and of England. This history is 'The Lost Tales of Elfinesse'.

The work is extant in a number of battered little 'exercise books' in ink and pencil, often formidably difficult to read, though after many hours of peering at the manuscript with a lens I was able, many years ago, to elucidate all the texts with only occasional unsolved words. *The Tale of Tinúviel* is one of the stories that was told to Eriol by the Elves in the Lonely Isle, in this case by a maiden named Vëannë: there were many children present at these story-tellings. Sharply observant of detail (a striking feature), it is told in an extremely individual style, with some archaisms of word and construction, altogether unlike my father's later styles, intense, poetic, at times deeply 'elvish-mysterious'. There is also an undercurrent of sardonic humour in the expression here and there (in the terrible confrontation with the demonic wolf Karkaras as she fled with Beren from Melko's hall Tinúviel enquires 'Wherefore this surliness, Karkaras?').

Rather than awaiting the conclusion of the *Tale* I think it may be helpful to draw attention here to certain aspects of this earliest version of the legend, and to give brief explanations of some names important in the narrative (which are also to be found in the List of Names at the end of the book). *The Tale of Tinúviel* in its rewritten form, which is the earliest form for us, was by no means the earliest of the *Lost Tales*, and light is shed on it by features in other *Tales*. To speak only of narrative structure, some of them, such as the tale of Túrin, are not very far removed from the version in the published *Silmarillion*; some, notably the Fall of Gondolin, the first to be written, is present in the published work only in a severely compressed form; and some, most remarkably the present Tale, are strikingly different in certain aspects.

A fundamental change in the evolution of the legend of Beren and Tinúviel (Lúthien) was the entry into it later of the story of Felagund of Nargothrond and the sons of Fëanor; but equally significant, in a different aspect, was the alteration in the identity of Beren. In the later versions of the legend it was an altogether essential element that Beren was a mortal man, whereas Lúthien was an immortal Elf; but this was not present in the *Lost Tale*: Beren, also, was an Elf. (It is seen, however, from my father's notes to other Tales, that he was originally a Man; and it is clear that this was true also in the erased manuscript of *The Tale of Tinúviel.*) Beren the Elf was of the Elvish people named the Noldoli (later Noldor), which in the *Lost Tales* (and later) is translated 'Gnomes': Beren was a Gnome. This translation later became a problem for my father. He was using another word *Gnome*, wholly distinct in origin and meaning from those Gnomes who nowadays are small figures specially associated with gardens. This other *Gnome* was derived from a Greek word gnōmē 'thought, intelligence'; it barely survives in modern English, with the meaning 'aphorism, maxim', together with the adjective *gnomic.*

In a draft for Appendix F of *The Lord of the Rings* he wrote:

> I have sometimes (not in this book) used 'Gnomes' for *Noldor* and 'Gnomish' for *Noldorin*. This I did, for to some 'Gnome' will still suggest knowledge. Now the High-elven name of this people, Noldor, signifies Those who Know; for of the three kindreds of the Eldar from

their beginning the Noldor were ever distinguished, both by their knowledge of the things that are and were in this world, and by their desire to know more. Yet they in no way resembled the Gnomes either of learned theory or popular fancy; and I have now abandoned this rendering as too misleading.

(In passing, I would mention that he said also [in a letter of 1954] that he greatly regretted having used the word 'Elves', which has become 'overloaded with regrettable tones' that are 'too much to overcome'.)

The hostility shown to Beren, as an Elf, is explained thus in the old Tale (p. 42): 'all the Elves of the woodland thought of the Gnomes of Dor-lómin as treacherous creatures, cruel and faithless'.

It may well seem somewhat puzzling that the word 'fairy, fairies' is frequently used of Elves. Thus, of the white moths that flew in the woods 'Tinúviel being a fairy minded them not' (p. 41); she names herself 'Princess of Fairies' (p. 64); it is said of her (p. 72) that she 'put forth her skill and fairy-magic'. In the first place, the word *fairies* in the *Lost Tales* is synonymous with *Elves*; and in those tales there are several references to the relative physical stature of Men and Elves. In those early days my father's conceptions on such matters were somewhat fluctuating, but it is clear that he conceived a changing relation as the ages passed. Thus he wrote:

33

Men were almost of a stature at first with Elves, the fairies being far greater and Men smaller than now.

But the evolution of Elves was greatly influenced by the coming of Men:

Ever as Men wax more numerous and powerful so the fairies fade and grow small and tenuous, filmy and transparent, but Men larger and more dense and gross. At last Men, or almost Men, can no longer see the fairies.

There is thus no need to suppose, on account of the word, that my father thought of the 'Fairies' of this tale as filmy and transparent; and of course years later, when the Elves of the Third Age had entered the history of Middle-earth, there was nothing 'fairylike', in the modern sense, about them.

The word *fay* is more obscure. In *The Tale of Tinúviel* it is used frequently of Melian (the mother of Lúthien), who came from Valinor (and is called [p. 40] 'a daughter of the Gods'), but also of Tevildo, who was said to be 'an evil fay in beastlike shape' (p. 69). Elsewhere in the *Tales* there are references to 'the wisdom of fays and of Eldar', to 'Orcs and dragons and evil fays', and to 'a fay of the woods and dells'. Most notable perhaps is the following passage from the *Tale of the Coming of the Valar*:

About them fared a great host who are the sprites [spirits] of trees and woods, of dale and forest and mountain-side, or those that sing amid the grass at morning and chant among the standing corn at eve. These are the Nermir and the Tavari, Nandini and Orossi [fays (?) of the meads, of the woods, of the valleys, of the mountains], fays, pixies, leprawns, and what else are they not called, for their number is very great; yet must they not be confused with the Eldar [Elves], for they were born before the world, and are older than its oldest, and are not of it.

Another puzzling feature, appearing not only in *The Tale of Tinúviel*, of which I have found no explanation, nor any more general observation, concerns the power that the Valar possess over the affairs of Men and Elves, and indeed over their minds and hearts, in the far distant Great Lands (Middle-earth). To give examples: on p. 78 'the Valar brought [Huan] to a glade' where Beren and Lúthien were lying on the ground in their flight from Angband; and she said to her father (p. 82): 'The Valar alone saved [Beren] from a bitter death'. Or again, in the account of Lúthien's flight from Doriath (p. 57), 'she entered not that dark region, and regaining heart pressed on' was later changed to 'she entered not that dark region, and the Valar set a new hope in her heart, so that she pressed on once more.'

As regards the names that appear in the Tale, I will note here that *Artanor* corresponds to later *Doriath* and was also called *The Land Beyond*; to the north lay the barrier of the *Iron Mountains*, also called the *Bitter Hills*, over which Beren came: afterwards they became *Ered Wethrin, the Mountains of Shadow*. Beyond the mountains lay *Hisilómë (Hithlum)* the Land of Shadow, also called *Dor-lómin*. *Palisor* (p. 37) is the land where the Elves awoke.

The Valar are often referred to as the Gods, and are called also the *Ainur* (singular *Ainu*). *Melko* (later *Melkor*) is the great evil Vala, called *Morgoth*, the Black Foe, after his theft of the Silmarils. *Mandos* is the name both of the Vala and the place of his abode. He is the keeper of the Houses of the Dead.

Manwë is the lord of the Valar; Varda, maker of the stars, is the spouse of Manwë and dwells with him on the summit of Taniquetil, the highest mountain of Arda. The Two Trees are the great trees whose flowers gave light to Valinor, destroyed by Morgoth and the monstrous spider Ungoliant.

Lastly, this is a convenient place to say something of the Silmarils, fundamental to the legend of Beren and Lúthien: they were the work of Fëanor, greatest of the Noldor: 'the mightiest in skill of word and of hand'; his name means 'Spirit of Fire'. I will quote here a passage from the later (1930) 'Silmarillion' text entitled *Quenta Noldorinwa,* on which see p. 103.

In those far days Fëanor began on a time a long and marvellous labour, and all his power and all his subtle magic he called upon, for he purposed to make a thing more fair than any of the Eldar yet had made, that should last beyond the end of all. Three jewels he made, and named them Silmarils. A living fire burned within them that was blended of the light of the Two Trees; of their own radiance they shone even in the dark; no mortal flesh impure could touch them, but was withered and was scorched. These jewels the Elves prized beyond all the works of their hands, and Manwë hallowed them, and Varda said: 'The fate of the Elves is locked herein, and the fate of many things beside.' The heart of Fëanor was wound about the things he himself had made.

A terrible and deeply destructive oath was sworn by Fëanor and his seven sons in assertion of their sole and inviolable right to the Silmarils, which were stolen by Morgoth.

Vëannë's tale was expressly addressed to Eriol (Ælfwine), who had never heard of Tinúviel, but as she tells it there is no formal opening: she begins with an account of Tinwelint and Gwendeling (afterwards known as Thingol and Melian). I will however turn again to the *Quenta Noldorinwa* for this essential element in the legend. In the *Tale* the formidable Tinwelint (Thingol) is a central figure: the king of the Elves who dwelt in the deep woodlands of Artanor, ruling from his vast cavern in the heart of the forest. But the queen was also a personage of great significance, although seldom seen, and I give here the account of her given in the *Quenta Noldorinwa*.

In this it is told that on the Great Journey of the Elves from far off Palisor, the place of their awakening, with the ultimate goal of reaching Valinor in the far West beyond the great Ocean

[many Elves] were lost upon the long dark roads, and they wandered in the woods and mountains of the world, and never came to Valinor, nor saw the light of the Two Trees.

Therefore they are called Ilkorindi, the Elves that dwelt never in Kôr, the city of the Eldar [Elves] in the land of the Gods. The Dark-elves are they, and many are their scattered tribes, and many are their tongues.

Of the Dark-elves the chief in renown was Thingol. For this reason he came never to Valinor. Melian was a fay. In the gardens of [the Vala] Lórien she dwelt, and among all his fair folk none were there that surpassed her beauty, nor none more wise, nor none more skilled in magical and enchanting song. It is told that the Gods would leave their business and the birds of Valinor their mirth, that Valmar's bells were silent, and the fountains ceased to flow, when at the mingling of the light Melian sang in the gardens of the God of Dreams. Nightingales went always with her, and their song she taught them. But she loved deep shadow, and strayed on long journeys into the Outer Lands [Middle-earth], and there filled the silence of the dawning world with her voice and the voices of her birds.

The nightingales of Melian Thingol heard and was enchanted and left his folk. Melian he found beneath the trees and was cast into a dream and a great slumber, so that his people sought him in vain.

In Vëannë's account, when Tinwelint awoke from his mythically long sleep 'he thought no more of his people (and indeed it had been vain, for long now had those reached Valinor)', but desired only to see the lady of the twilight. She was not far off, for she had watched over him as he slept. 'But more of their story I know not, O Eriol, save that in the end she became his wife, for Tinwelint and Gwendeling very long indeed were king and queen of the Lost Elves of Artanor or the Land Beyond, or so it is said here.'

Vëannë said further that the dwelling of Tinwelint 'was hidden from the vision and knowledge of Melko by the magics of Gwendeling the fay, and she wove spells about the paths thereto that none but the Eldar [Elves] might tread them easily, and so was the king secured from all dangers save it be treachery alone. Now his halls were builded in a deep cavern of great size, and they were nonetheless a kingly and a fair abode. This cavern was in the heart of the mighty forest of Artanor that is the mightiest of forests, and a stream ran before its doors, but none could enter that portal save across the stream, and a bridge spanned it narrow and well guarded.' Then Vëannë exclaimed: 'Lo, now I will tell you of things that happened in the halls of Tinwelint'; and this seems to be the point at which the tale proper can be said to begin.

THE TALE OF TINÚVIEL

Two children had Tinwelint then, Dairon and Tinúviel, and Tinúviel was a maiden, and the most beautiful of all the maidens of the hidden Elves, and indeed few have been so fair, for her mother was a fay, a daughter of the Gods; but Dairon was then a boy strong and merry, and above all things he delighted to play upon a pipe of reeds or other woodland instruments, and he is named now among the three most magic players of the Elves, and the others are Tinfang Warble and Ivárë who plays beside the sea. But Tinúviel's joy was rather in the dance, and no names are set with hers for the beauty and subtlety of her twinkling feet.

Now it was the delight of Dairon and Tinúviel to fare away from the cavernous palace of Tinwelint their father and together spend long time amid the trees. There often would Dairon sit upon a tussock or a tree-root and make music while Tinúviel danced thereto, and when she danced to the play-ing of Dairon more lissom was she than Gwendeling, more magical than Tinfang Warble neath the moon, nor may any see such lilting save be it only in the rose gardens of Valinor where Nessa dances on the lawns of never-fading green.

Even at night when the moon shone pale still would they play and dance, and they were not afraid as I should be, for the rule of Tinwelint and of Gwendeling held evil from the woods and Melko troubled them not as yet, and Men were hemmed beyond the hills.

Now the place that they loved the most was a shady spot, and elms grew there, and beech too, but these were not very tall, and some chestnut trees there were with white flowers, but the ground was moist and a great misty growth of hemlocks rose beneath the trees. On a time of June they were playing there, and the white umbels of the hemlocks were like a cloud about the boles of the trees, and there Tinúviel danced until the evening faded late, and there were many white moths abroad. Tinúviel being a fairy minded them not as many of the children of Men do, although she loved not beetles, and spiders will none of the Eldar touch because of Ungweliantë – but now the white moths flittered about her head and Dairon trilled an eerie tune, when suddenly that strange thing befell.

Never have I heard how Beren came thither over the hills; yet was he braver than most, as thou shalt hear, and 'twas the love of wandering maybe alone that had sped him through the terrors of the Iron Mountains until he reached the Lands Beyond.

Now Beren was a Gnome, son of Egnor the forester who hunted in the darker places in the north of Hisilómë. Dread and suspicion was between the Eldar and those of their kindred that had tasted the slavery of Melko, and in this did the evil deeds of the Gnomes at the Haven of the Swans revenge itself. Now the lies of Melko ran among Beren's folk so that they believed evil things of the secret Elves, yet now did he see Tinúviel dancing in the twilight, and Tinúviel was in a silver-pearly dress, and her bare white feet were twinkling among the hemlock-stems. Then Beren cared not whether she were Vala or Elf or child of Men and crept near to see; and he leant against a young elm that grew upon a mound so that he might look down into the little glade where she was dancing, for the enchantment made him faint. So slender was she and so fair that at length he stood heedlessly in the open the better to gaze upon her, and at that moment the full moon came brightly through the boughs and Dairon caught sight of Beren's face. Straightway did he perceive that he was none of their folk, and all the Elves of the woodland thought of the Gnomes of Dor-lómin as treacherous creatures, cruel and faithless, wherefore Dairon dropped his instrument and crying 'Flee, flee, O Tinúviel, an enemy walks this wood' he was gone swiftly through the trees. Then Tinúviel in her amaze followed not straightway, for she understood not his words at once, and knowing she could not run or leap so hardily as her brother she slipped suddenly down among the white hemlocks and hid herself beneath a very tall flower with many spreading leaves; and here she looked in her white raiment like a spatter of moonlight shimmering through the leaves upon the floor.

Then Beren was sad, for he was lonely and was grieved at their fright, and he looked for Tinúviel everywhere about, thinking her not fled. Thus suddenly did he lay his hand upon her slender arm beneath the leaves, and with a cry she started away from him and flitted as fast as she could in the wan light, darting and wavering in the moonbeams as only the Eldar can, in and about the tree-trunks and the hemlock-stalks. The tender touch of her arm made Beren yet more eager than before to find her, and he followed swiftly and yet not swiftly enough, for in the end she escaped him, and reached the dwellings of her father in fear; nor did she dance alone in the woods for many a day after.

This was a great sorrow to Beren, who would not leave those places, hoping to see that fair elven maiden dance yet again, and he wandered in the wood growing wild and lonely for many a day and searching for Tinúviel. By dawn and dusk he sought her, but ever more hopefully when the moon shone bright. At last one night he caught a sparkle afar off, and lo, there she was dancing alone on a little treeless knoll and Dairon was not there. Often and often she came there after and danced and sang to herself, and sometimes Dairon would be nigh, and then Beren watched from the wood's edge afar, and sometimes he was away and Beren crept then closer. Indeed for long Tinúviel knew of his coming and feigned otherwise, and for long her fear had departed by reason of the wistful hunger of his face lit by the moonlight; and she saw that he was kind and in love with her beautiful dancing.

Then Beren took to following Tinúviel secretly through the woods even to the entrance of the cave and the bridge's head, and when she was gone in he would cry across the stream, softly saying 'Tinúviel', for he had caught the name from Dairon's lips; and although he knew it not Tinúviel often hearkened from within the shadows of the cavernous doors and laughed softly or smiled. At length one day as she danced alone he stepped out more boldly and said to her: 'Tinúviel, teach me to dance.' 'Who art thou?' said she. 'Beren. I am from across the Bitter Hills.' 'Then if thou wouldst dance, follow me,' said the maiden, and she danced before Beren away, and away into the woods, nimbly and yet not so fast that he could not follow, and ever and anon she would look back and laugh at him stumbling after, saying 'Dance, Beren, dance! as they dance beyond the Bitter Hills!' In this way they came by winding paths to the abode of Tinwelint, and Tinúviel beckoned Beren beyond the stream, and he followed her wondering down into the cave and the deep halls of her home.

When however Beren found himself before the king he was abashed, and of the stateliness of Queen Gwendeling he was in great awe, and behold when the king said: 'Who art thou that stumbleth into my halls unbidden?' he had nought to say. Tinúviel answered therefore for him, saying: 'This, my father, is Beren, a wanderer from beyond the hills, and he would learn to dance as the elves of Artanor can dance,' and she laughed, but the king frowned when he heard whence Beren came, and he said: 'Put away thy light words, my child, and say has this wild Elf of the shadows sought to do thee any harm?'

'Nay, father,' said she, 'and I think there is not evil in his heart at all, and be thou not harsh with him, unless thou desirest to see thy daughter Tinúviel weep, for more wonder has he at my dancing than any that I have known.' Therefore said Tinwelint now: 'O Beren son of the Noldoli, what does thou desire of the Elves of the wood ere thou returnest whence thou camest?'

So great was the amazed joy of Beren's heart when Tinúviel spake thus for him to her father that his courage rose within him, and his adventurous spirit that had brought him out of Hisilómë and over the Mountains of Iron awoke again, and looking boldly upon Tinwelint he said: 'Why, O king, I desire thy daughter Tinúviel, for she is the fairest and most sweet of all maidens I have seen or dreamed of.'

Then was there a silence in the hall, save that Dairon laughed, and all who heard were astounded, but Tinúviel cast down her eyes, and the king glancing at the wild and rugged aspect of Beren burst also into laughter, whereat Beren flushed for shame, and Tinúviel's heart was sore for him. 'Why! wed my Tinúviel fairest of the maidens of the world, and become a prince of the woodland Elves – 'tis but a little boon for a stranger to ask,' quoth Tinwelint. 'Haply I may with right ask somewhat in return. Nothing great shall it be, a token only of thy esteem. Bring me a Silmaril from the Crown of Melko, and that day Tinúviel weds thee, an she will.'

Then all in that place knew that the king treated the matter as an uncouth jest, having pity on the Gnome, and they smiled, for the fame of the Silmarils of Fëanor was now great throughout the world, and the Noldoli had told tales of them, and many that had escaped from Angamandi had seen them now blazing lustrous in the iron crown of Melko.

Never did this crown leave his head, and he treasured those jewels as his eyes, and no one in the world, or fay or elf or man, could hope ever to set finger even on them and live. This indeed did Beren know, and he guessed the meaning of their mocking smiles, and aflame with anger he cried; 'Nay, but 'tis too small a gift to the father of so sweet a bride. Strange nonetheless seem to me the customs of the woodland Elves, like to the rude laws of the folk of Men, that thou shouldst name the gift unoffered, yet lo! I Beren, a huntsman of the Noldoli, will fulfil thy small desire,' and with that he burst from the hall while all stood astonished; but Tinúviel wept suddenly. ''Twas ill done, O my father,' she cried, 'to send one to his death with thy sorry jesting – for now methinks he will attempt the deed, being maddened by thy scorn, and Melko will slay him, and none will look ever again with such love upon my dancing.'

Then said the king: ''Twill not be the first of Gnomes that Melko has slain and for less reason. It is well for him that he lies not bound here in grievous spells for his trespass in my halls and for his insolent speech'; yet Gwendeling said nought, neither did she chide Tinúviel or question her sudden weeping for this unknown wanderer.

Beren however going from before the face of Tinwelint was carried by his wrath far through the woods, until he drew nigh to the lower hills and treeless lands that warned of the approach of the bleak Iron Mountains. Only then did he feel his weariness and stay his march, and thereafter did his greater travails begin. Nights of deep despondency were his and he saw no hope whatever in his quest, and indeed there

46

was little, and soon, as he followed the Iron Mountains till he drew nigh to the terrible regions of Melko's abode, the greatest fears assailed him. Many poisonous snakes were in those places and wolves roamed about, and more fearsome still were the wandering bands of the goblins and the Orcs – foul broodlings of Melko who fared abroad doing his evil work, snaring and capturing beasts, and Men, and Elves, and dragging them to their lord.

Many times was Beren near to capture by the Orcs, and once he escaped the jaws of a great wolf only after a combat wherein he was armed but with an ashen club, and other perils and adventures did he know each day of his wandering to Angamandi. Hunger and thirst too tortured him often, and often he would have turned back had not that been well nigh as perilous as going on; but the voice of Tinúviel pleading with Tinwelint echoed in his heart, and at night time it seemed to him that his heart heard her sometimes weeping softly for him far away in the woodlands of her home: and this was indeed true.

One day he was driven by great hunger to search amid a deserted camping of some Orcs for scraps of food, but some of these returned unawares and took him prisoner, and they tormented him but did not slay him, for their captain seeing his strength, worn though he was with hardships, thought that Melko might perchance be pleasured if he was brought before him and might set him to some heavy thrall-work in his mines or in his smithies. So came it that Beren was dragged before Melko, and he bore a stout heart within him nonetheless, for it was a belief among his father's kindred that the power of

Melko would not abide for ever, but the Valar would hearken at last to the tears of the Noldoli, and would arise and bind Melko and open Valinor once more to the weary Elves, and great joy should come back upon Earth.

Melko however looking upon him was wroth, asking how a Gnome, a thrall by birth of his, had dared to fare away into the woods unbidden, but Beren answered that he was no runagate but came of a kindred of Gnomes that dwelt in Aryador and mingled much there among the folk of Men. Then was Melko yet more angry, for he sought ever to destroy the friendship and intercourse of Elves and Men, and said that evidently here was a plotter of deep treacheries against Melko's lordship, and one worthy of the tortures of the Balrogs; but Beren seeing his peril answered: 'Think not, O most mighty Ainu Melko, Lord of the World, that this can be true, for if it were then should I not be here unaided and alone. No friendship has Beren son of Egnor for the kindred of Men; nay indeed, wearying utterly of the lands infested by that folk he has wandered out of Aryador. Many a great tale has my father made to me aforetime of thy splendour and glory, wherefore, albeit I am no renegade thrall, I do desire nothing so much as to serve thee in what small manner I may,' and Beren said therewith that he was a great trapper of small animals and a snarer of birds, and had become lost in the hills in these pursuits until after much wandering he had come into strange lands, and even had not the Orcs seized him he would indeed have had no other rede of safety but to approach the majesty of Ainu Melko and beg him to grant him some humble office – as a winner of meats for his table perchance.

Now the Valar must have inspired that speech, or perchance it was a spell of cunning words cast on him in compassion by Gwendeling, for indeed it saved his life, and Melko marking his hardy frame believed him, and was willing to accept him as a thrall of his kitchens. Flattery savoured ever sweet in the nostrils of that Ainu, and for all his unfathomed wisdom many a lie of those whom he despised deceived him, were they clothed sweetly in words of praise; therefore now he gave orders for Beren to be made a thrall of Tevildo Prince of Cats. Now Tevildo was a mighty cat – the mightiest of all – and possessed of an evil sprite, as some say, and he was in Melko's constant following; and that cat had all cats subject to him, and he and his subjects were the chasers and getters of meat for Melko's table and for his frequent feasts. Wherefore is it that there is hatred still between the Elves and all cats even now when Melko rules no more, and his beasts are become of little account.

When therefore Beren was led away to the halls of Tevildo, and these were not utterly distant from the place of Melko's throne, he was much afraid, for he had not looked for such a turn in things, and those halls were ill-lighted and were full of growling and of monstrous purrings in the dark.

All about shone cats' eyes glowing like green lamps or red or yellow where Tevildo's thanes sat waving and lashing their beautiful tails, but Tevildo himself sat at their head and he was a mighty cat and coal-black and evil to look upon. His eyes were long and very narrow and slanted, and gleamed both red and green, but his great grey whiskers were as stout and as sharp as needles. His purr was like the roll of drums and his growl like thunder, but when he yelled in wrath it turned the blood cold, and indeed small beasts and birds were frozen as to stone, or dropped lifeless often at the very sound. Now Tevildo seeing Beren narrowed his eyes until they seemed to shut, and said: 'I smell dog', and he took dislike to Beren from that moment. Now Beren had been a lover of hounds in his own wild home.

'Why,' said Tevildo, 'do ye dare to bring such a creature before me, unless perchance it is to make meat of him?' But those who led Beren said: 'Nay, 'twas the word of Melko that this unhappy Elf wear out his life as a catcher of beasts and birds in Tevildo's employ.' Then indeed did Tevildo screech in scorn and said: 'Then in sooth was my lord asleep or his thoughts were settled elsewhere, for what use think ye is a child of the Eldar to aid the Prince of Cats and his thanes in the catching of birds or of beasts – as well had ye brought some clumsy-footed Man, for none are there either of Elves or Men that can vie with us in our pursuit.' Nonetheless he set Beren to a test, and he bade him go catch three mice, 'for my hall is infested with them,' said he. This indeed was not true, as might be imagined, yet a certain few there were – a very wild, evil, and magic kind that dared to dwell there in dark holes, but they were larger than rats and very fierce, and Tevildo harboured them for his own private sport and suffered not their numbers to dwindle.

Three days did Beren hunt them, but having nothing wherewith to devise a trap (and indeed he did not lie to Melko saying that he had cunning in such contrivances) he hunted in vain getting nothing better than a bitten finger for all his labour. Then was Tevildo scornful and in great anger, but Beren got no harm of him or his thanes at that time because of Melko's bidding other than a few scratches. Evil however were his days thereafter in the dwellings of Tevildo. They made him a scullion, and his days passed miserably in the washing of floors and vessels, in the scrubbing of tables and the hewing of wood and the drawing of water. Often too he would be set to the turning of spits whereon birds and fat mice were daintily roasted for the cats, yet seldom did he get food or sleep himself, and he became haggard and unkempt, and wished often that never straying out of Hisilómë he had not even caught sight of the vision of Tinúviel.

Now that fair maiden wept for a very great while after Beren's departure and danced no more about the woods, and Dairon grew angry and could not understand her, but she had grown to love the face of Beren peeping through the branches and the crackle of his feet as they followed her through the wood; and his voice that called wistfully 'Tinúviel, Tinúviel' across the stream before her father's doors she longed to hear again, and she would not now dance when Beren was fled to the evil halls of Melko and maybe had already perished. So bitter did this thought become at last that that most tender maiden went to her mother, for to her father she dared not go nor even suffer him to see her weep.

'O Gwendeling, my mother,' said she, 'tell me of thy magic, if thou canst, how doth Beren fare. Is all yet well with him?' 'Nay,' said Gwendeling. 'He lives indeed, but in an evil captivity, and hope is dead in his heart, for behold, he is a slave in the power of Tevildo Prince of Cats.'

'Then,' said Tinúviel, 'I must go and succour him, for none else do I know that will.'

Now Gwendeling laughed not, for in many matters she was wise, and forewise, yet it was a thing unthought in a mad dream that any Elf, still less a maiden, the daughter of the king, should fare untended to the halls of Melko, even in those earlier days before the Battle of Tears when Melko's power had not grown great and he veiled his designs and spread his net of lies. Wherefore did Gwendeling softly bid her not to speak such folly; but Tinúviel said: 'Then must thou plead with my father for aid, that he send warriors to Angamandi and demand the freedom of Beren from Ainu Melko.'

This indeed did Gwendeling do, of love for her daughter, and so wroth was Tinwelint that Tinúviel wished that never had her desire been made known; and Tinwelint bade her nor speak nor think of Beren more, and swore he would slay him an he trod those halls again. Now then Tinúviel pondered much what she might do, and going to Dairon she begged him to aid her, or indeed to fare away with her to Angamandi an he would; but Dairon thought with little love of Beren, and he said: 'Wherefore should I go into the direst peril that there is in the world for the sake of a wandering Gnome of the woods? Indeed I have no love for him, for he has destroyed our play together, our music and our dancing.' But Dairon moreover told the king of what Tinúviel had desired of him – and this he did not of ill intent but fearing lest Tinúviel fare away to her death in the madness of her heart.

Now when Tinwelint heard this he called Tinúviel and said: 'Wherefore, O maiden of mine, does thou not put this folly away from thee, and seek to do my bidding?' But Tinúviel would not answer, and the king bade her promise him that neither would she think more on Beren, nor would she seek in her folly to follow after him to the evil lands whether alone or tempting any of his folk with her. But Tinúviel said that the first she would not promise and the second only in part, for she would not tempt any of the folk of the woodlands to go with her.

Then was her father mightily angry, and beneath his anger not a little amazed and afraid, for he loved Tinúviel; but this was the plan he devised, for he might not shut his daughter for ever in the caverns where only a dim and flickering light ever came. Now above the portals of his cavernous hall was a steep slope falling to the river, and there grew mighty beeches; and one there was that was named Hirilorn, the Queen of Trees, for she was very mighty, and so deeply cloven was her bole that it seemed as if three shafts sprang from the ground together and they were of like size, round and straight, and their grey rind was smooth as silk, unbroken by branch or twig for a very great height above men's heads.

Now Tinwelint let build high up in that strange tree, as high as men could fashion their longest ladders to reach, a little house of wood, and it was above the first branches and was sweetly veiled in leaves. Now that house had three corners and three windows in each wall, and at each corner was one of the shafts of Hirilorn. There then did Tinwelint bid Tinúviel dwell until she would consent to be wise, and when she fared up the ladders of tall pine these were taken from beneath and no way had she to get down again. All that she required was brought to her, and folk would scale the ladders and give her food or whatever else she wished for, and then descending again take away the ladders, and the king promised death to any who left one leaning against the tree or who should try by stealth to place one there at night. A guard therefore was set nigh the tree's foot, and yet came Dairon often thither in sorrow at what he had brought to pass, for he was lonely without Tinúviel; but Tinúviel had at first much pleasure in her house among the leaves, and would gaze out of her little window while Dairon made his sweetest melodies beneath.

But one night a dream of the Valar came to Tinúviel and she dreamt of Beren, and her heart said: 'Let me be gone to seek him whom all others have forgot'; and waking, the moon was shining through the trees, and she pondered very deeply how she might escape. Now Tinúviel daughter of Gwendeling was not ignorant of magics or of spells, as may well be believed, and after much thought she devised a plan. The next day she asked those who came to her to bring, if they would, some of the clearest water of the stream below, 'but this,' she said, 'must be drawn at midnight in a silver bowl, and brought to my hand with no word spoken,' and after that she desired wine to be brought, 'but this,' she said, 'must be borne hither in a flagon of gold at noon, and he who brings it must sing as he comes,' and they did as they were bid, but Tinwelint was not told.

Then said Tinúviel, 'Go now to my mother and say to her that her daughter desires a spinning wheel to pass her weary hours,' but Dairon secretly she begged fashion her a tiny loom, and he did this even in the little house of Tinúviel in the tree. 'But wherewith will you spin and wherewith weave?' said he; and Tinúviel answered: 'With spells and magics,' but Dairon knew not her design, nor said more to the king or to Gwendeling.

Now Tinúviel took the wine and water when she was alone, and singing a very magic song the while, she mingled them together, and as they lay in the bowl of gold she sang a song of growth, and as they lay in the bowl of silver she sang another song, and the names of all the tallest and longest things upon Earth were set in that song; the beards of the Indravangs, the tail of Karkaras, the body of Glorund, the bole of Hirilorn, and the sword of Nan she named, nor did she forget the chain Angainu that Aulë and Tulkas made or the neck of Gilim the giant, and last and longest of all she spake of the hair of Uinen the lady of the sea that is spread through all the waters. Then did she lave her head with the mingled water and wine, and as she did so she sang a third song, a song of uttermost sleep, and the hair of Tinúviel which was dark and finer than the most delicate threads of twilight began suddenly to grow very fast indeed, and after twelve hours had passed it nigh filled the little room, and then Tinúviel was very pleased and she lay down to rest; and when she awoke the room was full as with a black mist and she was deep hidden under it, and lo! her hair was trailing out of the windows and blowing about the tree boles in the morning. Then with difficulty she found her little shears and cut the threads of that growth nigh to her head, and after that her hair grew only as it was wont before.

Then was the labour of Tinúviel begun, and though she

laboured with the deftness of an Elf long was the spinning and longer weaving still, and did any come and hail her from below she bid them be gone, saying: 'I am abed, and desire only to sleep,' and Dairon was much amazed, and called often up to her, but she did not answer.

Now of that cloudy hair Tinúviel wove a robe of misty black soaked with drowsiness more magical far than even that one that her mother had worn and danced in long ago, and therewith she covered her garments of shimmering white, and magic slumbers filled the air about her; but of what remained she twisted a mighty strand, and this she fastened to the bole of the tree within her house, and then was her labour ended, and she looked out of her window westward to the river. Already the sunlight was fading in the trees, and as dusk filled the woods she began a song very soft and low, and as she sang she cast out her long hair from the window so that its slumbrous mist touched the heads and faces of the guards below, and they listening to her voice fell suddenly into a fathomless sleep. Then did Tinúviel clad in her garments of darkness slip down that rope of hair light as a squirrel, and away she danced to the bridge, and before the bridgewards could cry out she was among them dancing; and as the hem of her black robe touched them they fell asleep, and Tinúviel fled very far away as fast as her dancing feet would flit.

Now when the escape of Tinúviel reached the ears of Tinwelint great was his mingled grief and wrath, and all his court was in uproar, and all the woods ringing with the search, but Tinúviel was already far away drawing nigh to the gloomy foothills where the Mountains of Night begin; and 'tis said that Dairon following after her became utterly lost, and came never back to Elfinesse, but turned towards Palisor, and there plays subtle magic musics still, wistful and lonely in the woods and forests of the south.

Yet ere long as Tinúviel went forward a sudden dread overtook her at the thought of what she had dared to do and what lay before; then did she turn back for a while, and she wept, wishing Dairon were with her, and it is said that he indeed was not far off, but was wandering lost in the great pines, the Forest of Night, where afterward Túrin slew Beleg by mishap.

Nigh was Tinúviel now to those places, but she entered not that dark region, and regaining heart pressed on, and by reason of the greater magic of her being and because of the spell of wonder and of sleep that fared about her no such dangers assailed her as did Beren before; yet was it a long and evil and weary journey for a maiden to tread.

Now is it to be told that in those days Tevildo had but one trouble in the world, and that was the kindred of the Dogs. Many indeed of these were neither friends nor foes of the Cats, for they had become subject to Melko and were as savage and cruel as any of his animals; indeed from the most cruel and most savage he bred the race of wolves, and they were very dear indeed to him. Was it not the great grey wolf Karkaras Knife-fang, father of wolves, who guarded the gates of Angamandi in those days and long had done so? Many were there however who would neither bow to Melko nor live wholly in fear of him, but dwelt either in the dwellings of Men and guarded them from much evil that had otherwise befallen them, or roamed the woods of Hisilómë or passing the mountainous places fared even at times into the region of Artanor and the lands beyond and to the south.

Did ever any of these view Tevildo or any of his thanes or subjects, then there was a great baying and a mighty chase, and albeit seldom was any cat slain by reason of their skill in climbing and in hiding and because of the protecting might of Melko, yet was great enmity between them, and some of those hounds were held in dread among the cats. None however did Tevildo fear, for he was as strong as any among them, and more agile and more swift save only than Huan Captain of Dogs. So swift was Huan that on a time he had tasted the fur of Tevildo, and though Tevildo had paid him for that with a gash from his great claws, yet was the pride of the Prince of Cats unappeased and he lusted to do a great harm to Huan of the Dogs.

Great therefore was the good fortune that befell Tinúviel in meeting with Huan in the woods, although at first she was mortally afraid and fled. But Huan overtook her in two leaps, and speaking soft and deep the tongue of the Lost Elves he bid her be not afraid, and 'Wherefore,' said he, 'do I see an Elven maiden, and one most fair, wandering alone so nigh to the abodes of the Ainu of Evil? Knowest thou not that these are very evil places to be in, little one, even with a companion, and they are death to the lonely?'

'That know I,' said she, 'and I am not here for the love of wayfaring, but I seek only Beren.'

'What knowest thou then,' said Huan, 'of Beren – or indeed meanest thou Beren son of the huntsman of the Elves, Egnor bo-Rimion, a friend of mine since very ancient days?'

'Nay, I know not even whether my Beren be thy friend, for I seek only Beren from beyond the Bitter Hills, whom I knew in the woods near to my father's home. Now is he gone, and my mother Gwendeling says of her wisdom that he is a thrall in the cruel house of Tevildo Prince of Cats; and whether this be true or yet worse be now befallen him I do not know, and I go to discover him – though plan I have none.'

'Then will I make thee one,' said Huan, 'but do thou trust in me, for I am Huan of the Dogs, chief foe of Tevildo. Rest thee now with me a while within the shadows of the wood, and I will think deeply.'

Then Tinúviel did as he said, and indeed she slept long while Huan watched, for she was very weary. But after a while awakening she said: 'Lo, I have tarried over long. Come, what is thy thought, O Huan?'

And Huan said: 'A dark and difficult matter is this, and no other rede can I devise but this. Creep now if thou hast the heart to the abiding place of that Prince while the sun is high, and Tevildo and the most of his household drowze upon the terraces before his gates. There discover in what manner thou mayst whether Beren be indeed within, as thy mother said to thee. Now I will lie not far hence in the woods, and thou wilt do me a pleasure and aid thy own desires if going before Tevildo, be Beren there or be he not, thou tellest him how thou hast stumbled upon Huan of the Dogs lying sick in the woods at this place. Do not indeed direct him hither, for thou must guide him, if it may be, thyself. Then wilt thou see what I contrive for thee and for Tevildo. Methinks that bearing such tidings Tevildo will not entreat thee ill within his halls nor seek to hold thee there.'

In this way did Huan design both to do Tevildo a hurt, or perchance if it might so be to slay him, and to aid Beren whom he guessed in truth to be that Beren son of Egnor whom the hounds of Hisilómë loved. Indeed hearing the name of Gwendeling and knowing thereby that this maiden was a princess of the woodland fairies he was eager to aid her, and his heart warmed to her sweetness.

Now Tinúviel taking heart stole near to the halls of Tevildo, and Huan wondered much at her courage, following unknown to her, as far as he might for the success of his design. At length however she passed beyond his sight, and leaving the shelter of the trees came to a region of long grass dotted with bushes that sloped ever upward toward a shoulder of the hills. Now upon that rocky spur the sun shone, but over all the hills and mountains at its back a black cloud brooded, for there was Angamandi; and Tinúviel fared on not daring to look up at that gloom, for fear oppressed her, and as she went the ground rose and the grass grew more scant and rock-strewn until it came even to a cliff, sheer of one side, and there upon a stony shelf was the castle of Tevildo. No pathway led thereto, and the place where it stood fell towards the woods in terrace after terrace so that none might reach its gates save by many great leaps, and those became ever steeper as the castle drew more nigh. Few were the windows of that house and upon the ground there were none – indeed the very gate was in the air where in the dwellings of Men are wont to be the windows of the upper floor; but the roof had many wide and flat spaces open to the sun.

Now does Tinúviel wander disconsolate upon the lowest terrace and look in dread at the dark house upon the hill, when behold, she came at a bend in the rock upon a lone cat lying in the sun and seemingly asleep. As she approached he opened a yellow eye and blinked at her, and thereupon rising and stretching he stepped up to her and said: 'Whither away, little maid – dost not know that you trespass on the sunning ground of his highness Tevildo and his thanes?'

Now Tinúviel was very much afraid, but she made as bold an answer as she was able, saying: 'That know I not, my lord' – and this pleased the old cat greatly, for he was in truth only Tevildo's doorkeeper – 'but I would indeed of your goodness be brought to Tevildo's presence now – nay, even if he sleeps,' said she, for the doorkeeper lashed his tail in astonished refusal.

'I have words of immediate import for his private ear. Lead me to him, my lord,' she pleaded, and thereat the cat purred so loudly that she dared to stroke his ugly head, and this was much larger than her own, being greater than that of any dog that is now on Earth. Thus entreated, Umuiyan, for such was his name, said: 'Come then with me,' and seizing Tinúviel suddenly by her garments at the shoulder to her great terror he tossed her upon his back and leaped upon the second terrace. There he stopped, and as Tinúviel scrambled from his back he said: 'Well is it for thee that this afternoon my lord Tevildo lieth upon this lowly terrace far from his house, for a great weariness and a desire for sleep has come upon me, so that I fear me I should not be willing to carry thee much farther'; now Tinúviel was robed in her robe of <u>sable mist</u>.

So saying Umuiyan yawned mightily and stretched himself before he led her along that terrace to an open space, where upon a wide couch of baking stones lay the horrible form of Tevildo himself, and both his evil eyes were shut. Going up to him the door-cat Umuiyan spoke in his ear softly, saying: 'A maiden awaits thy pleasure, my lord, who hath news of importance to deliver to thee, nor would she take my refusal.' Then did Tevildo angrily lash his tail, half opening an eye – 'What is it – be swift,' said he, 'for this is no hour to come desiring audience of Tevildo Prince of Cats.'

'Nay, lord,' said Tinúviel trembling, 'be not angry; nor do I think that thou wilt when thou hearest, yet is the matter such that it were better not even whispered here where the breezes blow,' and Tinúviel cast a glance as it were of apprehension toward the woods.

'Nay, get thee gone,' said Tevildo, 'thou smellest of dog, and what news of good came ever to a cat from a fairy that had had dealings with the dogs?'

'Why, sir, that I smell of dogs is no matter of wonder, for I have just escaped from one – and it is indeed of a certain very mighty dog whose name thou knowest that I would speak.' Then up sat Tevildo and opened his eyes, and he looked all about him, and stretched three times, and at last bade the door-cat lead Tinúviel within; and Umuiyan caught her upon his back as before. Now was Tinúviel in the sorest dread, for having gained what she desired, a chance of entering Tevildo's stronghold and maybe of discovering whether Beren were there, she had no plan more, and knew not what would become of her – indeed had she been able she would have fled; yet now do those cats begin to ascend the terraces towards the castle, and one leap does Umuiyan make bearing Tinúviel upwards and then another, and at the third he stumbled so that Tinúviel cried out in fear, and Tevildo said: 'What ails thee, Umuiyan, thou clumsy-foot? It is time that thou left my employ if age creeps on thee so swiftly.' But Umuiyan said: 'Nay, lord, I know not what it is, but a mist is before my eyes and my head is heavy,' and he staggered as one drunk, so that Tinúviel slid from his back, and thereupon he laid him down as if in a dead sleep; but Tevildo was wroth and seized Tinúviel and none too gently, and himself bore her to the gates. Then with a mighty leap he sprang within, and bidding that maiden alight he set up a yell that echoed fearsomely in the dark ways and passages. Forthwith they hastened to him from within, and some he bid descend to Umuiyan and bind him and cast him from the rocks 'on the northern side where they fall most sheer, for he is of no use more to me,' he said, 'for his age has robbed him of his sureness of foot'; and Tinúviel quaked to hear the ruthlessness of this beast. But even as he spoke he himself yawned and stumbled as with a sudden drowziness, and he bid others to lead Tinúviel away to a certain chamber within, and that was the one where Tevildo was accustomed to sit at meat with his greatest thanes. It was full of bones and smelt evilly; no windows were there and but one door; but a hatchway gave from it upon the great kitchens, and a red light crept thence and dimly lit the place.

Now so adread was Tinúviel when those catfolk left her

there that she stood a moment unable to stir, but soon becoming used to the darkness she looked about and espying the hatchway that had a wide sill she sprang thereto, for it was not over high and she was a nimble Elf. Now gazing therethrough, for it was ajar, she saw the wide vaulted kitchens and the great fires that burnt there, and those that toiled always within, and the most were cats – but behold, there by a great fire stooped Beren, and he was grimed with labour, and Tinúviel sat and wept, but as yet dared nothing. Indeed even as she sat the harsh voice of Tevildo sounded suddenly within that chamber: 'Nay, where then in Melko's name has that mad Elf fled,' and Tinúviel hearing shrank against the wall, but Tevildo caught sight of her where she was perched and cried: 'Then the little bird sings not any more; come down or I must fetch thee, for behold, I will not encourage the Elves to seek audience of me in mockery.'

Then partly in fear, and part in hope that her clear voice might carry even to Beren, Tinúviel began suddenly to speak very loud and to tell her tale so that the chambers rang; but 'Hush, dear maiden,' said Tevildo, 'if the matter were secret without it is not one for bawling within.' Then said Tinúviel: 'Speak not thus to me, O cat, mighty Lord of Cats though thou be, for am I not Tinúviel Princess of Fairies that have stepped out of my way to do thee a pleasure?' Now at those words, and she had shouted them even louder than before, a great crash was heard in the kitchens as of a number of vessels of metal and earthenware let suddenly fall, but Tevildo snarled: 'There trippeth that fool Beren the Elf. Melko rid me of such folk' – yet Tinúviel, guessing that Beren had heard

and been smitten with astonishment, put aside her fears and repented her daring no longer. Tevildo nonetheless was very wroth at her haughty words, and had he not been minded first to discover what good he might get from her tale, it had fared ill with Tinúviel straightway. Indeed from that moment she was in great peril, for Melko and all his vassals held Tinwelint and his folk as outlaws, and great was their joy to ensnare them and cruelly entreat them, so that much favour would Tevildo have gained had he taken Tinúviel before his lord. Indeed, so soon as she named herself, this did he purpose to do when his own business had been done, but of a truth his wits were drowzed that day, and he forgot to marvel more why Tinúviel sat perched upon the sill of the hatchway; nor did he think more of Beren, for his mind was bent only to the tale Tinúviel bore to him. Wherefore said he, dissembling his evil mood, 'Nay, Lady, be not angry, but come, delay whetteth my desire – what is it that thou hast for my ears, for they twitch already.'

But Tinúviel said: 'There is a great beast, rude and violent, and his name is Huan' – and at that name, Tevildo's back curved, and his hair bristled and crackled, and the light of his eyes was red – 'and', she went on, 'it seems to me a shame that such a brute be suffered to infect the woods so nigh even to the abode of the powerful Prince of Cats, my lord Tevildo'; but Tevildo said: 'Nor is he suffered, and cometh never there save it be by stealth.'

'Howso that may be,' said Tinúviel, 'there he is now, yet methinks that at last may his life be brought utterly to an end; for lo, as I was going through the woods I saw where

a great animal lay upon the ground moaning as in sickness –
and behold, it was Huan, and some evil spell or malady has
him in its grip, and still he lies helpless in a dale not a mile
westward in the woods from this hall. Now with this perhaps
I would not have troubled your ears, had not the brute when
I approached to succour him snarled upon me and essayed to
bite me, and meseems that such a creature deserves whatever
come to him.'

Now all this that Tinúviel spake was a great lie in whose
devising Huan had guided her, and maidens of the Eldar are
not wont to fashion lies; yet have I never heard that any of the
Eldar blamed her therein nor Beren afterward, and neither do
I, for Tevildo was an evil cat and Melko the wickedest of all
beings, and Tinúviel was in dire peril at their hands. Tevildo
however, himself a great and skilled liar, was so deeply versed
in the lies and subtleties of all the beasts and creatures that he
seldom knew whether to believe what was said to him or not,
and was wont to disbelieve all things save those he wished to
believe true, and so was he often deceived by the more honest.
Now the story of Huan and his helplessness so pleased him
that he was fain to believe it true, and determined at least to
test it; yet at first he feigned indifference, saying this was a
small matter for such secrecy and might have been spoken
outside without further ado. But Tinúviel said she had not
thought that Tevildo Prince of Cats needed to learn that the
ears of Huan heard the slightest sounds a league away, and the
voice of a cat further than any sound else.

Now therefore Tevildo sought to discover from Tinúviel
under pretence of mistrusting her tale where exactly Huan

might be found, but she made only vague answers, seeing in this her only hope of escaping from the castle, and at length Tevildo, overcome by curiosity and threatening evil things if she should prove false, summoned two of his thanes to him, and one was Oikeroi, a fierce and warlike cat. Then did the three set out with Tinúviel from that place, but Tinúviel took off her magical garment of black and folded it, so that for all its size and density it appeared no more than the smallest kerchief (for so was she able), and thus was she borne down the terraces upon the back of Oikeroi without mishap, and no drowziness assailed her bearer. Now crept they through the woods in the direction she had named, and soon does Tevildo smell dog and bristles and lashes his great tail, but after he climbs a lofty tree and looks down from thence into that dale that Tinúviel had shown to them. There he does indeed see the great form of Huan lying prostrate groaning and moaning, and he comes down in much glee and haste, and indeed in his eagerness he forgets Tinúviel, who now in great fear for Huan lies hidden in a bank of fern. The design of Tevildo and his two companions was to enter that dale silently from different quarters and so come all suddenly upon Huan unawares and slay him, or if he were too stricken to make fight to make sport of him and torment him. This did they now, but even as they leapt out upon him Huan sprang up into the air with a mighty baying, and his jaws closed in the back close to the neck of that cat Oikeroi, and Oikeroi died; but the other thane fled howling up a great tree, and so was Tevildo left alone face to face with Huan, and such an encounter was not much to his mind, yet was Huan upon him too swiftly for flight, and they fought fiercely in that glade, and the noise that Tevildo made was very hideous; but at length Huan had him by the throat, and that cat might well have perished had not his claws as he struck out blindly pierced Huan's eye. Then did Huan give tongue, and Tevildo screeching fearsomely got himself loose with a great wrench and leapt up a tall and smooth tree that stood by, even as his companion had done. Despite his grievous hurt Huan now leaps beneath that tree baying mightily, and Tevildo curses him and casts evil words upon him from above.

Then said Huan: 'Lo, Tevildo, these are the words of Huan whom thou thoughtest to catch and slay helpless as the miserable mice it is thy wont to hunt – stay for ever up thy lonely tree and bleed to death of thy wounds, or come down and feel again my teeth. But if neither are to thy liking, then tell me where is Tinúviel Princess of Fairies and Beren son of Egnor, for these are my friends. Now these shall be set as ransom against thee – though it be valuing thee far over thy worth.'

'As for that cursed Elf, she lies whimpering in the ferns yonder, an my ears mistake not,' said Tevildo, 'and Beren methinks is being soundly scratched by Miaulë my cook in the kitchens of my castle for his clumsiness there an hour ago.'

'Then let them be given to me in safety,' said Huan, 'and thou mayest return thyself to thy halls and lick thyself unharmed.'

'Of a surety my thane who is here with me shall fetch them for thee,' said Tevildo, but growled Huan: 'Ay, and fetch also all thy tribe and hosts of the Orcs and the plagues of Melko.

Nay, I am no fool; rather shalt thou give Tinúviel a token and she shall fetch Beren, or thou shalt stay here if thou likest not the other way.' Then was Tevildo forced to cast down his golden collar – a token no cat dare dishonour, but Huan said: 'Nay, more yet is needed, for this will arouse all thy folk to seek thee,' and this Tevildo knew and had hoped. So was it that in the end weariness and hunger and fear prevailed upon that proud cat, a prince of the service of Melko, to reveal the secret of the cats and the spell that Melko had entrusted to him; and those were words of magic whereby the stones of his evil house were held together, and whereby he held all beasts of the catfolk under his sway, filling them with an evil power beyond their nature; for long has it been said that Tevildo was an evil fay in beastlike shape. When therefore he had told it Huan laughed till the woods rang, for he knew that the days of the power of the cats were over.

Now sped Tinúviel with the golden collar of Tevildo back to the lowest terrace before the gates, and standing she spake the spell in her clear voice. Then behold, the air was filled with the voices of cats and the house of Tevildo shook; and there came therefrom a host of indwellers and they were shrunk to puny size and were afeared of Tinúviel, who waving the collar of Tevildo spake before them certain of the words that Tevildo had said in her hearing to Huan, and they cowered before her. But she said: 'Lo, let all those of the folk of the Elves or of the children of Men that are bound within these halls be brought forth,' and behold, Beren was brought forth, but of other thralls there were none, save only Gimli, an aged Gnome, bent in thraldom and grown blind, but whose hearing was the keenest that has been in the world, as all songs say. Gimli came leaning upon a stick and Beren aided him, but Beren was clad in rags and haggard, and he had in his hand a great knife he had caught up in the kitchen, fearing some new ill when the house shook and all the voices of the cats were heard; but when he beheld Tinúviel standing amid the host of cats that shrank from her and saw the great collar of Tevildo, then was he amazed utterly, and knew not what to think. But Tinúviel was very glad, and spoke saying: 'O Beren from beyond the Bitter Hills, wilt thou now dance with me – but let it not be here.' And she led Beren far away, and all those cats set up a howling and wailing, so that Huan and Tevildo heard it in the woods, but none followed or molested them, for they were afraid, and the magic of Melko was fallen from them.

This indeed they rued afterward when Tevildo returned home followed by his trembling comrade, for Tevildo's wrath was terrible, and he lashed his tail and dealt blows at all who stood nigh. Now Huan of the dogs, though it might seem a folly, when Beren and Tinúviel came to that glade had suffered that evil Prince to return without further war, but the great collar of gold he had set about his own neck, and at this was Tevildo more angry than all else, for a great magic of strength and power lay therein. Little to Huan's liking was it that Tevildo lived still, but now no longer did he fear the cats, and that tribe has fled before the dogs ever since, and the dogs hold them still in scorn since the humbling of Tevildo in the woods nigh Angamandi; and Huan has not done any greater deed. Indeed afterward Melko heard all and he cursed Tevildo and his folk and banished them, nor have they since that day had lord or master or any friend, and their voices wail and screech for their hearts are very lonely and bitter and full of loss, yet there is only darkness therein and no kindliness.

At the time however whereof the tale tells it was Tevildo's chief desire to recapture Beren and Tinúviel and to slay Huan, that he might regain the spell and magic he had lost, for he was in great fear of Melko, and he dared not seek his master's aid and reveal his defeat and the betrayal of his spell. Unwitting of this Huan feared those places, and was in great dread lest those doings come swiftly to Melko's ear, as did most things that came to pass in the world; wherefore now Tinúviel and Beren wandered far away with Huan, and they became great in friendship with him, and in that life Beren grew strong again and his thraldom fell from him, and Tinúviel loved him.

Yet wild and rugged and very lonely were those days, for never a face of Elf or of Man did they see, and Tinúviel grew at last to long sorely for Gwendeling her mother and the songs of sweet magic she was used to sing to her children as twilight fell in the woodlands by their ancient halls. Often she half fancied she heard the flute of Dairon her brother, in pleasant glades wherein they sojourned, and her heart grew heavy. At length she said to Beren and to Huan: 'I must return home,' and now is it Beren's heart that is overcast with sorrow, for he loved that life in the woods with the dogs (for by now many others had become joined to Huan), yet not if Tinúviel were not there.

Nonetheless said he: 'Never may I go back with thee to the land of Artanor – nor come there ever after to seek thee,

71

sweet Tinúviel, save only bearing a Silmaril; nor may that ever now be achieved, for am I not a fugitive from the very halls of Melko, and in danger of the most evil pains do any of his servants spy me.' Now this he said in the grief of his heart at parting with Tinúviel, and she was torn in mind, abiding not the thought of leaving Beren nor yet of living ever thus in exile. So sat she a great while in sad thought and she spoke not, but Beren sat nigh and at length said: 'Tinúviel, one thing only can we do – go get a Silmaril'; and she sought thereupon Huan, asking his aid and advice, but he was very grave and saw nothing but folly in the matter. Yet in the end Tinúviel begged of him the fell of Oikeroi that he slew in the affray of the glade; now Oikeroi was a very mighty cat and Huan carried that fell with him as a trophy.

Now doth Tinúviel put forth her skill and fairy-magic, and she sews Beren into this fell and makes him to the likeness of a great cat, and she teaches him how to sit and sprawl, to step and bound and trot in the semblance of a cat, till Huan's very whiskers bristled at the sight, and thereat Beren and Tinúviel laughed. Never however could Beren learn to screech or wail or to purr like any cat that ever walked, nor could Tinúviel awaken a glow in the dead eyes of the catskin – 'but we must put up with that,' said she, 'and thou hast the air of a very noble cat if thou but hold thy tongue.'

Then did they bid farewell to Huan and set out for the halls of Melko by easy journeys, for Beren was in great dis-comfort and heat within the fur of Oikeroi, and Tinúviel's heart became lighter awhile than it had been for long, and she stroked Beren or pulled his tail, and Beren was angry because

72

he could not lash it in answer as fiercely as he wished. At length however they drew near to Angamandi, as indeed the rumblings and deep noises, and the sound of mighty hammerings of ten thousand smiths labouring unceasingly, declared to them. Nigh were the sad chambers where the thrall-Noldoli laboured bitterly under the Orcs and goblins of the hills, and here the gloom and darkness was great so that their hearts fell, but Tinúviel arrayed her once more in her dark garment of deep sleep. Now the gates of Angamandi were of iron wrought hideously and set with knives and spikes, and before them lay the greatest wolf the world has ever seen, even Karkaras Knife-fang who had never slept; and Karkaras growled when he saw Tinúviel approach, but of the cat he took not much heed, for he thought little of cats and they were ever passing in and out.

'Growl not, O Karkaras,' said she, 'for I go to seek my lord Melko, and this thane of Tevildo goeth with me as escort.' Now the dark robe veiled all her shimmering beauty, and Karkaras was not much troubled in mind, yet nonetheless he approached as was his wont to snuff the air of her, and the sweet fragrance of the Eldar that garment might not hide. Therefore straightway did Tinúviel begin a magic dance, and the black strands of her dark veil she cast in his eyes so that his legs shook with a drowziness and he rolled over and was asleep. But not until he was fast in dreams of great chases in the woods of Hisilómë when he was yet a whelp did Tinúviel cease, and then did those twain enter that black portal, and winding down many shadowy ways they stumbled at length into the very presence of Melko.

In that gloom Beren passed well enough as a very thane of Tevildo, and indeed Oikeroi had aforetime been much about the halls of Melko, so that none heeded him and he slunk under the very chair of the Ainu unseen, but the adders and evil things there lying set him in great fear so that he durst not move.

Now all this fell out most fortunately, for had Tevildo been with Melko their deceit would have been discovered – and indeed of that danger they had thought, not knowing that Tevildo sat now in his halls and knew not what to do should his discomfiture become noised in Angamandi; but behold, Melko espieth Tinúviel and saith: 'Who art thou that flittest about my halls like a bat? How camest thou in, for of a surety thou dost not belong here?'

'Nay, that I do not yet,' saith Tinúviel, 'though I may perchance hereafter, of thy goodness, my lord Melko. Knowest thou not that I am Tinúviel daughter of Tinwelint the outlaw, and he hath driven me from his halls, for he is an overbearing Elf and I give not my love at his command.'

Now in truth was Melko amazed that the daughter of Tinwelint came thus of her free will to his dwelling, Angamandi the terrible, and suspecting something untoward he asked what was her desire: 'for knowest thou not,' saith he, 'that there is no love here for thy father or his folk, nor needest thou hope for soft words and good cheer from me.'

'So hath my father said,' saith she, 'but wherefore need I believe him? Behold, I have a skill of subtle dances, and I would dance now before you, my lord, for then methinks I might readily be granted some humble corner of your halls wherein to dwell until such times as you should call for the little dancer Tinúviel to lighten your cares.'

'Nay,' saith Melko, 'such things are little to my mind; but as thou hast come thus far to dance, dance, and after we will see,' and with that he leered horribly, for his dark mind pondered some evil.

Then did Tinúviel begin such a dance as neither she nor any other sprite or fay or elf danced ever before or has done since, and after a while even Melko's gaze was held in wonder. Round the hall she fared, swift as a swallow, noiseless as a bat, magically beautiful as only Tinúviel ever was, and now she was at Melko's side, now before him, now behind, and her misty draperies touched his face and waved before his eyes, and the folk that sat about the walls or stood in that place were whelmed one by one in sleep, falling down into deep dreams of all that their ill hearts desired.

Beneath his chair the adders lay like stones, and the wolves before his feet yawned and slumbered, and Melko gazed on enchanted, but he did not sleep. Then began Tinúviel to dance a yet swifter dance before his eyes, and even as she danced she sang in a voice very low and wonderful a song which Gwendeling had taught her long ago, a song that the youths and maidens sang beneath the cypresses of the gardens of Lórien when the Tree of Gold had waned and Silpion was gleaming. The voices of nightingales were in it, and many subtle odours seemed to fill the air of that noisome place as she trod the floor lightly as a feather in the wind; nor has any voice or sight of such beauty ever again been seen there, and Ainu Melko for all his power and majesty succumbed to the magic of that Elf-maid, and indeed even the eyelids of Lórien had grown heavy had he been there to see. Then did Melko fall forward drowzed, and sank at last in utter sleep down from his chair upon the floor, and his iron crown rolled away.

Suddenly Tinúviel ceased. In the hall no sound was heard save of slumbrous breath; even Beren slept beneath the very seat of Melko, but Tinúviel shook him so that he awoke at last. Then in fear and trembling he tore asunder his disguise and freeing himself from it leapt to his feet. Now does he draw that knife that he had from Tevildo's kitchens and he seizes the mighty iron crown, but Tinúviel could not move it and scarcely might the thews of Beren avail to turn it. Great is the frenzy of their fear as in that dark hall of sleeping evil Beren labours as noiselessly as may be to prise out a Silmaril with his knife. Now does he loosen the great central jewel and the sweat pours from his brow, but even as he forces it from the crown lo! his knife snaps with a loud crack.

Tinúviel smothers a cry thereat and Beren springs away with the one Silmaril in his hand, and the sleepers stir and Melko groans as though ill thoughts disturbed his dreams, and a black look comes upon his sleeping face. Content now with that one flashing gem those twain fled desperately from the hall, stumbling wildly down many dark passages till from the glimmering of grey light they knew they neared the gates – and behold! Karkaras lies across the threshold, awake once more and watchful.

Straightway Beren thrust himself before Tinúviel although she said him nay, and this proved in the end ill, for Tinúviel had not time to cast her spell of slumber over the beast again, ere seeing Beren he bared his teeth and growled angrily. 'Wherefore this surliness, Karkaras?' said Tinúviel. 'Wherefore this Gnome who entered not and yet now issueth in haste?' quoth Knife-fang, and with that he leapt upon Beren, who struck straight between the wolf's eyes with his fist, catching for his throat with the other hand.

Then Karkaras seized that hand in his dreadful jaws, and it was the hand wherein Beren clasped the blazing Silmaril, and both hand and jewel Karkaras bit off and took into his red maw. Great was the agony of Beren and the fear and anguish of Tinúviel, yet even as they expect to feel the teeth of the wolf a new thing strange and terrible comes to pass. Behold now that Silmaril blazeth with a white and hidden fire of its own nature and is possessed of a fierce and holy magic – for did it not come from Valinor and the blessed realms, being fashioned with spells of the Gods and Gnomes before evil came there; and it doth not tolerate the touch of evil flesh or of unholy hand. Now cometh it into the foul body of Karkaras, and suddenly that beast is burnt with a terrible anguish and the howling of his pain is ghastly to hear as it echoeth in those rocky ways, so that all the sleeping court within awakes. Then did Tinúviel and Beren flee like the wind from the gates, yet was Karkaras far before them raging and in madness as a beast pursued by Balrogs; and after when they might draw breath Tinúviel wept over the maimed arm of Beren kissing it often, so that behold it bled not, and pain left it, and was healed by the tender healing of her love; yet was Beren ever after surnamed among all folk Ermabwed the One-handed, which in the language of the Lonely Isle is Elmavoitë.

Now however must they bethink them of escape – if such may be their fortune, and Tinúviel wrapped part of her dark mantle about Beren, and so for a while flitting by dusk and dark amid the hills they were seen by none, albeit Melko had raised all his Orcs of terror against them; and his fury at the rape of that jewel was greater than the Elves had ever seen it yet.

Even so it seems soon to them that the net of hunters drew ever more tightly upon them, and though they had reached the edge of the more familiar woods and passed the glooms of the forest of Taurfuin, still were there many leagues of peril yet to pass between them and the caverns of the king, and even did they reach ever there it seemed like they would but draw the chase behind them thither and Melko's hate upon all that woodland folk. So great indeed was the hue and cry that Huan learnt of it far away, and he marvelled much at the daring of those twain, and still more that ever they had escaped from Angamandi.

Now goes he with many dogs through the woods hunting Orcs and thanes of Tevildo, and many hurts he got thus, and many of them he slew or put to fear and flight, until one even at dusk the Valar brought him to a glade in that northward region of Artanor that was called afterward Nan Dumgorthin, the land of the dark idols, but that is a matter that concerns not this tale. Howbeit it was even then a dark land and gloomy and foreboding, and dread wandered beneath its lowering trees no less even than in Taurfuin; and those two Elves Tinúviel and Beren were lying therein weary and without hope, and Tinúviel wept but Beren was fingering his knife.

78

Now when Huan saw them he would not suffer them to speak or to tell any of their tale, but straightway took Tinúviel upon his mighty back and bade Beren run as best he could beside him, 'for,' said he, 'a great company of the Orcs are drawing swiftly hither, and wolves are their trackers and their scouts.' Now doth Huan's pack run about them, and they go very swiftly along quick and secret paths towards the homes of the folk of Tinwelint far away. Thus was it that they eluded the host of their enemies, but had nonetheless many an encounter afterward with wandering things of evil, and Beren slew an Orc that came nigh to dragging off Tinúviel, and that was a good deed. Seeing then that the hunt still pressed them close, once more did Huan lead them by winding ways, and dared not yet straightly to bring them to the land of the woodland fairies. So cunning however was his leading that at last after many days the chase fell far away, and no longer did they see or hear anything of the bands of Orcs; no goblins waylaid them nor did the howling of any evil wolves come upon the airs at night, and belike that was because already they had stepped within the circle of Gwendeling's magic that hid the paths from evil and kept harm from the regions of the woodelves.

Then did Tinúviel breathe freely once more as she had not done since she fled from her father's halls, and Beren rested in the sun far from the glooms of Angband until the last bitterness of thraldom left him. Because of the light falling through green leaves and the whisper of clean winds and the song of birds once more are they wholly unafraid.

At last came there nevertheless a day whereon waking out of a deep slumber Beren started up as one who leaves a dream of happy things coming suddenly to his mind, and he said: 'Farewell, O Huan, most trusty comrade, and thou, little Tinúviel, whom I love, fare thee well. This only I beg of thee, get thee now straight to the safety of thy home, and may good Huan lead thee. But I – lo, I must away into the solitude of the woods, for I have lost that Silmaril which I had, and never dare I draw near to Angamandi more, wherefore neither will I enter the halls of Tinwelint.' Then he wept to himself, but Tinúviel who was nigh and had hearkened to his musing came beside him and said; 'Nay, now is my heart changed, and if thou dwellest in the woods, O Beren Ermabwed, then so will I, and if thou wilt wander in the wild places there will I wander also, or with thee or after thee: – yet never shall my father see me again save only if thou takest me to him.' Then indeed was Beren glad of her sweet words, and fain would he have dwelt with her as a huntsman of the wild, but his heart smote him for all that she had suffered for him, and for her he put away his pride. Indeed she reasoned with him, saying it would be folly to be stubborn, and that her father would greet them with nought but joy, being glad to see his daughter yet alive – 'and maybe,' said she, 'he will have shame that his jesting has given thy fair hand to the jaws of Karkaras.' But Huan also she implored to return with them a space, for 'my father owes thee a very great reward, O Huan,' saith she, 'an he loves his daughter at all.'

So came it that those three set forward once again together, and came at last back to the woodlands that Tinúviel knew and loved nigh to the dwellings of her folk and to the deep halls of her home. Yet even as they approach they find fear and tumult among that people such as had not been for a long age, and asking some that wept before their doors they learned that ever since the day of Tinúviel's secret flight ill-fortune had befallen them. Lo, the king had been distraught with grief and had relaxed his ancient wariness and cunning; indeed his warriors had been sent hither and thither deep into the unwholesome woods searching for that maiden, and many had been slain or lost for ever, and war there was with Melko's servants about all their northern and eastern borders, so that the folk feared mightily lest that Ainu upraise his strength and come utterly to crush them and Gwendeling's magic have not the strength to withhold the numbers of the Orcs. 'Behold,' said they, 'now is the worst of all befallen, for long has Queen Gwendeling sat aloof and smiled not nor spoken, looking as it were to a great distance with haggard eyes, and the web of her magic has blown thin about the woods, and the woods are dreary, for Dairon comes not back, neither is his music heard ever in the glades. Behold now the crown of all our evil tidings, for know that there has broken upon us raging from the halls of Evil a great grey wolf filled with an evil spirit, and he fares as though lashed by some hidden madness, and none are safe. Already has he slain many as he runs wildly snapping and yelling through the woods, so that the very banks of the stream that flows before the king's halls has become a lurking-place of danger. There comes the awful wolf oftentimes to drink, looking as the evil Prince himself with bloodshot eyes and tongue lolling out, and never can he slake his desire for water as though some inward fire devours him.'

Then was Tinúviel sad at the thought of the unhappiness that had come upon her folk, and most of all was her heart bitter at the story of Dairon, for of this she had not heard any murmur before. Yet could she not wish Beren had come never to the lands of Artanor, and together they made haste to Tinwelint; and already to the Elves of the wood it seemed that the evil was at an end now that Tinúviel was come back among them unharmed. Indeed they scarce had hoped for that.

In great gloom do they find King Tinwelint, yet suddenly is his sorrow melted to tears of gladness, and Gwendeling sings again for joy when Tinúviel enters there and casting away her raiment of dark mist she stands before them in her pearly radiance of old. For a while all is mirth and wonder in that hall, and yet at length the king turns his eyes to Beren and says: 'So thou hast returned too – bringing a Silmaril, beyond doubt, in recompense for all the ill thou hast wrought my land; or an thou hast not, I know not wherefore thou art here.'

Then Tinúviel stamped her foot and cried so that the king and all about him wondered at her new and fearless mood: 'For shame, my father – behold, here is Beren the brave whom thy jesting drove into dark places and foul captivity and the Valar alone saved from a bitter death. Methinks 'twould rather befit a king of the Eldar to reward him than revile him.'

'Nay,' said Beren, 'the king thy father hath the right. Lord,' said he, 'I have a Silmaril in my hand even now.'

'Show me then,' said the king in amaze.

'That I cannot,' said Beren, 'for my hand is not here', and he held forth his maimed arm.

Then was the king's heart turned to him by reason of his stout and courteous demeanour, and he bade Beren and Tinúviel relate to him all that had befallen either of them, and he was eager to hearken, for he did not fully comprehend the meaning of Beren's words. When however he had heard all yet more was his heart turned to Beren, and he marvelled at the love that had awakened in the heart of Tinúviel so that she had done greater deeds and more daring than any of the warriors of his folk.

'Never again,' said he, 'O Beren I beg of thee, leave this court nor the side of Tinúviel, for thou art a great Elf and thy name will ever be great among the kindreds.' Yet Beren answered him proudly, and said: 'Nay, O King, I hold to my word and thine, and I will get thee that Silmaril or ever I dwell in peace in thy halls.' And the king entreated him to journey no more into the dark and unknown realms, but Beren said: 'No need is there thereof, for behold that jewel is even now nigh to thy caverns,' and he made clear to Tinwelint that that beast that ravaged his land was none other than Karkaras, the wolfward of Melko's gates – and this was not known to all, but Beren knew it taught by Huan, whose cunning in the reading of track and slot was greatest among all the hounds, and therein are none of them unskilled. Huan indeed was with Beren now in the halls, and when those twain spoke of a chase and a great hunt he begged to be in that deed; and it was granted gladly. Now do those three prepare themselves to harry that beast, that all the folk be rid of the terror of the wolf, and Beren keep his word, bringing a Silmaril to shine once more in Elfinesse. King Tinwelint himself led that chase, and Beren was beside him, and Mablung the heavy-handed, chief of the king's thanes, leaped up and grasped a spear – a mighty weapon captured in battle with the distant Orcs – and with those three stalked Huan mightiest of dogs, but others they would not take according to the desire of the king, who said: 'Four is enough for the slaying even of the Hell-wolf' – but only those who had seen knew how fear-some was that beast, nigh as large as a horse among Men, and so great was the ardour of his breath that it scorched what-soever it touched. About the hour of sunrise they set forth, and soon after Huan espied a new slot beside the stream, not far from the king's doors, 'and,' quoth he, 'this is the print of Karkaras.' Thereafter they followed that stream all day, and at many places its banks were new-trampled and torn and the water of the pools that lay about it was fouled as though some beasts possessed of madness had rolled and fought there not long before.

Now sinks the sun and fades beyond the western trees and darkness is creeping down from Hisilómë so that the light of the forest dies. Even so they come to a place where the spoor swerves from the stream or perchance is lost in its waters and Huan may no longer follow it; and here therefore they encamp, sleeping in turns beside the stream, and the early night wears away.

Suddenly in Beren's watch a sound of great terror leaped up from far away – a howling as of seventy maddened wolves – then lo! the brushwood cracks and saplings snap as the terror

draweth near, and Beren knows that Karkaras is upon them.
Scarce had he time to rouse the others, and they were but
just sprung up and half-awake, when a great form loomed in
the wavering moonlight filtering there, and it was fleeing like
one mad, and its course was bent towards the water. Thereat
Huan gave tongue, and straightway the beast swerved aside
towards them, and foam was dripping from his jaws and a red
light shining from his eyes, and his face was marred with mingled terror and with wrath. No sooner did he leave the trees
than Huan rushed upon him fearless of heart, but he with a
mighty leap sprang right over that great dog, for all his fury
was kindled suddenly against Beren whom he recognized as
he stood behind, and to his dark mind it seemed that there was
the cause of all his agony. Then Beren thrust swiftly upward
with a spear into his throat, and Huan leapt again and had
him by a hind leg, and Karkaras fell like a stone, for at that
same moment the king's spear found his heart, and his evil
spirit gushed forth and sped howling faintly as it fared over
the dark hills to Mandos; but Beren lay under him crushed
beneath his weight. Now they roll back that carcase and fall
to cutting it open, but Huan licks Beren's face whence blood
is flowing. Soon is the truth of Beren's words made clear, for
the vitals of the wolf are half-consumed as though an inner
fire had long been smouldering there, and suddenly the night
is filled with a wondrous lustre, shot with pale and secret colours, as Mablung draws forth the Silmaril. Then holding it
out he said: 'Behold, O King', but Tinwelint said: 'Nay, never
will I handle it save only if Beren give it to me.' But Huan
said: 'and that seems likely never to be, unless ye tend him

swiftly, for methinks he is hurt sorely'; and Mablung and the king were ashamed.

Therefore now they raised Beren gently up and tended him and washed him, and he breathed, but he spoke not nor opened his eyes, and when the sun arose and they had rested a little they bore him as softly as might be upon a bier of boughs back through the woodlands; and nigh midday they drew near the homes of the folk again, and then were they deadly weary, and Beren had not moved nor spoken, but groaned thrice.

There did all the people flock to meet them when their approach was noised among them, and some bore them meat and cool drinks and salves and healing things for their hurts, and but for the harm that Beren had met great indeed had been their joy. Now then they covered the leafy boughs whereon he lay with soft raiment, and they bore him away to the halls of the king, and there was Tinúviel awaiting them in great distress; and she fell upon Beren's breast and wept and kissed him, and he awoke and knew her, and after Mablung gave him that Silmaril, and he lifted it above him gazing at its beauty, ere he said slowly and with pain: 'Behold, O King, I give thee the wondrous jewel thou didst desire, and it is but a little thing found by the wayside, for once methinks thou hadst one beyond thought more beautiful, and she is now mine.' Yet even as he spake the shadows of Mandos lay upon his face, and his spirit fled in that hour to the margin of the world, and Tinúviel's tender kisses called him not back.

*

86

[Here Vëannë suddenly ceased speaking, but she wept, and after a while she said 'Nay, that is not all the tale; but here endeth all that I rightly know'. In the conversation that followed one Ausir said: 'I have heard that the magic of Tinúviel's tender kisses healed Beren, and recalled his spirit from the gates of Mandos, and long time he dwelt among the Lost Elves . . .']

But another said: 'Nay, that was not so, O Ausir, and if thou wilt listen I will tell the true and wondrous tale; for Beren died there in Tinúviel's arms even as Vëannë has said, and Tinúviel crushed with sorrow and finding no comfort or light in all the world followed him swiftly down those dark ways that all must tread alone. Now her beauty and tender loveliness touched even the cold heart of Mandos, so that he suffered her to lead Beren forth once more into the world, nor has this ever been done since to Man or Elf, and many songs and stories are there of the prayer of Tinúviel before the throne of Mandos that I remember not right well. Yet said Mandos to those twain: "Lo, O Elves, it is not to any life of perfect joy that I dismiss you, for such may no longer be found in all the world where sits Melko of the evil heart – and know that ye will become mortal even as Men, and when ye fare hither again it will be for ever, unless the Gods summon you indeed to Valinor." Nonetheless those twain departed hand in hand, and they fared together through the northern woods, and oftentimes were they seen dancing magic dances down the hills, and their name became heard far and wide.'

[Then Vëannë said:] 'Aye, and they did more than dance, for their deeds afterward were very great, and many tales are

there thereof that thou must hear, O Eriol Melinon, upon
another time of tale-telling. For these twain it is that stories
name i-Cuilwarthon, which is to say the dead that live again,
and they became mighty fairies in the lands about the north
of Sirion. Behold now all is ended – and doth it like thee?'

[Then Eriol said that he had not expected to hear such
an astonishing story from one such as Vëannë, to which she
answered:]

'Nay, but I fashioned it not with words of myself; but it
is dear to me – and indeed all the children know of the deeds
that it relates – and I have learned it by heart, reading it in the
great books, and I do not comprehend all that is set therein.'

*

DURING THE 1920s my father was engaged in the casting
of the Lost Tales of Turambar and Tinúviel into verse. The
first of these poems, *The Lay of the Children of Húrin*, in
the Old English alliterative metre, was begun in 1918, but
when far from completion he abandoned it, very probably
when he left the University of Leeds. In the summer of 1925,
the year in which he took up his appointment to the professorship of Anglo-Saxon at Oxford, he began 'the poem
of Tinúviel', called *The Lay of Leithian*. This he translated
'Release from Bondage', but he never explained the title.

Remarkably and uncharacteristically he inserted dates at
many points. The first of these, at line 557 (in the numbering
of the poem as a whole) is 23 August 1925; and the last, 17
September 1931, is written against line 4085. Not far beyond

this, at line 4223, the poem was abandoned, at the point in the narrative where 'the fangs of Carcharoth crashed together like a trap' on Beren's hand bearing the Silmaril, as he fled from Angband. For the remainder of the poem that was never written there are prose synopses.

In 1926 he sent many of his poems to R.W. Reynolds, who had been his teacher at King Edward's School in Birmingham. In that year he composed a substantial text with the title *Sketch of the mythology with especial reference to The Children of Húrin*, and on the envelope containing this manuscript he wrote later that this text was 'the original Silmarillion', and that he had written it for Mr Reynolds in order to 'explain the background of the "alliterative version" of Túrin and the Dragon.'

This *Sketch of the Mythology* was 'the original Silmarillion' because from it there was a direct line of evolution; whereas there is no stylistic continuity with the Lost Tales. The *Sketch* is what its name implies: it is a synopsis, composed in a terse, present-tense manner. I give here the passage in the text that tells in briefest form the tale of Beren and Lúthien.

A PASSAGE FROM THE
'SKETCH OF THE MYTHOLOGY'

The power of Morgoth begins to spread once more. One by one he overthrows Men and Elves in the North. Of these a famous chieftain of Men was Barahir, who had been a friend of Celegorm of Nargothrond.

Barahir is driven into hiding, his hiding betrayed, and Barahir slain; his son Beren after a life outlawed flees south, crosses the Shadowy Mountains, and after grievous hardships comes to Doriath. Of this and his other adventures is told in *The Lay of Leithian*. He gains the love of Tinúviel 'the nightingale' – his own name for Lúthien – the daughter of Thingol. To win her Thingol, in mockery, requires a Silmaril from the crown of Morgoth. Beren sets out to achieve this, is captured, and set in dungeon in Angband, but conceals his real identity and is given as a slave to Thû the hunter. Lúthien is imprisoned by Thingol, but escapes and goes in search of Beren. With the aid of Huan lord of dogs she rescues Beren, and gains entrance to Angband where Morgoth is enchanted and finally wrapped in slumber by her dancing. They get a Silmaril and escape, but are barred at gates of Angband by Carcaras the Wolf-ward. He bites off Beren's hand which holds the Silmaril, and goes mad with the anguish of its burning within him.

They escape and after many wanderings get back to Doriath. Carcaras ravening through the woods bursts into Doriath. There follows the Wolf-hunt of Doriath, in which Carcaras is slain, and Huan is killed in defence of Beren. Beren is however mortally wounded and dies in Lúthien's arms. Some songs say that Lúthien went even over the Grinding Ice, aided by the power of her divine mother, Melian, to Mandos' halls and won him back; others that Mandos hearing his tale released him. Certain it is that he alone of mortals came back from Mandos and dwelt with Lúthien and never spoke to Men again, living in the woods of Doriath and in the Hunters' Wold, west of Nargothrond.

It will be seen that there have been great changes in the legend, the most immediately evident being that of Beren's captor: here we meet Thû 'the hunter'. At the end of the *Sketch* it is said of Thû that he was the 'great chief' of Morgoth, and that he 'escaped the Last Battle and dwells still in dark places, and perverts Men to his dreadful worship'. In *The Lay of Leithian* Thû emerges as the fearful Necromancer, Lord of Wolves, who dwelt in Tol Sirion, the island in the river Sirion with an Elvish watchtower, which came to be Tol-in-Gaurhoth, the Isle of Werewolves. He is, or will be, Sauron. Tevildo and his realm of cats have disappeared.

But in the background another significant element in the legend had emerged after *The Tale of Tinúviel* was written: this concerns the father of Beren. Egnor the forester, the Gnome 'who hunted in the darker places of Hisilómë' (p.41) has gone. Now, in the passage from the *Sketch* just given, his father is Barahir, 'a famous chieftain of *Men*': driven into hiding by the growing hostile power of Morgoth, his hiding was betrayed, and he was slain. 'His son Beren after a life outlawed flees south, crosses the Shadowy Mountains, and after grievous hardships comes to Doriath. Of this and his other adventures is told in *The Lay of Leithian*.'

A PASSAGE EXTRACTED FROM
THE LAY OF LEITHIAN

I give here the passage in the *Lay* (written in 1925; see p. 88)
that describes the treachery of Gorlim, known as Gorlim
the Unhappy, who betrayed to Morgoth the hiding place of
Barahir and his companions, and the aftermath. I should mention here that the textual detail of the poem is very complex,
but since my (ambitious) purpose in this book is to make a
readily readable text that shows the narrative evolution of the
legend at different stages, I have neglected virtually all detail
of this nature, which could only confuse that purpose. An
account of the textual history of the poem will be found in
my book *The Lays of Beleriand* (*The History of Middle-earth*,
Vol. III, 1985). I have taken the extracts from the *Lay* in the
present book word for word from the text that I prepared for
The Lays of Beleriand. The line-numbers are simply those of
the extracts, and have no relation to those of the whole poem.

The extract that follows is taken from Canto II of the *Lay*.
It is preceded by a description of the ferocious tyranny of

93

Morgoth over the northern lands at the time of Beren's coming
into Artanor (Doriath), and of the survival in hiding of Barahir
and Beren and ten others, hunted in vain by Morgoth for many
years, until at last 'their feet were caught in Morgoth's snare'.

>   Gorlim it was, who wearying
> of toil and flight and harrying
> one night by chance did turn his feet
> o'er the dark fields by stealth to meet
> with hidden friends within a dale,   5
> and found a homestead looming pale
> against the misty stars, all dark
> save one small window, whence a spark
> of fitful candle strayed without.
> Therein he peeped, and filled with doubt   10
> he saw, as in a dreaming deep
> when longing cheats the heart in sleep,
> his wife beside a dying fire
> lament him lost; her thin attire
> and greying hair and paling cheek   15
> of tears and loneliness did speak.
> 'A! fair and gentle Eilinel,
> whom I had thought in darkling hell
> long since emprisoned! Ere I fled
> I deemed I saw thee slain and dead   20
> upon that night of sudden fear
> when all I lost that I held dear':
> thus thought his heavy heart amazed
> outside in darkness as he gazed.

But ere he dared to call her name,   25
or ask how she escaped and came
to this far vale beneath the hills,
he heard a cry beneath the hills!
There hooted near a hunting owl
with boding voice. He heard the howl   30
of the wild wolves that followed him
and dogged his feet through shadows dim.
Him unrelenting, well he knew,
the hunt of Morgoth did pursue.
Lest Eilinel with him they slay   35
without a word he turned away,
and like a wild thing winding led
his devious ways o'er stony bed
of stream, and over quaking fen,
until far from the homes of men   40
he lay beside his fellows few
in a secret place; and darkness grew,
and waned, and still he watched unsleeping,
and saw the dismal dawn come creeping
in dank heavens above gloomy trees.   45
A sickness held his soul for ease,
and hope, and even thraldom's chain
if he might find his wife again.
But all he thought twixt love of lord
and hatred of the king abhorred   50
and anguish for fair Eilinel
who drooped alone, what tale shall tell?

Yet at the last, when many days
of brooding did his mind amaze,
he found the servants of the king   55
and bade them to their master bring
a rebel who forgiveness sought,
if haply forgiveness might be bought
with tidings of Barahir the bold,
and where his hidings and his hold   60
might best be found by night or day.
And thus sad Gorlim, led away
unto those dark deep-dolven halls,
before the knees of Morgoth falls,
and puts his trust in that cruel heart   65
wherein no truth had ever part.
Quoth Morgoth: 'Eilinel the fair
thou shalt most surely find, and there
where she doth dwell and wait for thee
together shall ye ever be,   70
and sundered shall ye sigh no more.
Thus guerdon shall he have that bore
these tidings sweet, O traitor dear!
For Eilinel she dwells not here,
but in the shades of death doth roam   75
widowed of husband and of home –
a wraith of that which might have been,
methinks, it is that thou hast seen!
Now shalt thou through the gates of pain
the land thou askest grimly gain;   80

thou shalt to the moonless mists of hell
descend and seek thy Eilinel.'

    Thus Gorlim died a bitter death
and cursed himself with dying breath,
and Barahir was caught and slain,   85
and all good deeds were made in vain.
But Morgoth's guile for ever failed,
nor wholly o'er his foes prevailed;
and some were ever that still fought
unmaking that which malice wrought.   90
Thus Men believed that Morgoth made
the fiendish phantom that betrayed
the soul of Gorlim, and so brought
the lingering hope forlorn to nought
that lived amid the lonely wood;   95
yet Beren had by fortune good
long hunted far afield that day,
and benighted in strange places lay
far from his fellows. In his sleep
he felt a dreadful darkness creep   100
upon his heart, and thought the trees
were bare and bent in mournful breeze;
no leaves they had, but ravens dark
sat thick as leaves on bough and bark,
and croaked, and as they croaked each neb   105
let fall a gout of blood; a web
unseen entwined him hand and limb,
until worn out, upon the rim

of stagnant pool he lay and shivered.
There saw he that a shadow quivered   110
far out upon the water wan,
and grew to a faint form thereon
that glided o'er the silent lake
and coming slowly, softly spake
and sadly said; 'Lo! Gorlim here,   115
traitor betrayed, now stands! Nor fear,
but haste! For Morgoth's fingers close
upon thy father's throat. He knows
your secret tryst, your hidden lair',
and all the evil he laid bare   120
that he had done and Morgoth wrought.
Then Beren waking swiftly sought
his sword and bow, and sped like wind
that cuts with knives the branches thinned
of autumn trees. At last he came,   125
his heart afire with burning flame,
where Barahir his father lay;
he came too late. At dawn of day
he found the homes of hunted men,
a wooded island in the fen   130
and birds rose up in sudden cloud –
no fen-fowl were they crying loud.
The raven and the carrion-crow
sat in the alders all a-row;
one croaked: 'Ha! Beren comes too late',   135
and answered all: 'Too late! Too late!'
There Beren buried his father's bones,

and piled a heap of boulder-stones,
and cursed the name of Morgoth thrice,
but wept not, for his heart was ice.   140

    Then over fen and field and mountain
he followed, till beside a fountain
upgushing hot from fires below
he found the slayers and his foe,
the murderous soldiers of the king.   145
And one there laughed, and showed a ring
he took from Barahir's dead hand.
'This ring in far Beleriand,
now mark ye, mates,' he said, 'was wrought.
Its like with gold could not be bought,   150
for this same Barahir I slew,
this robber fool, they say, did do
a deed of service long ago
for Felagund. It may be so;
for Morgoth bade me bring it back,   155
and yet, methinks, he has no lack
of weightier treasure in his hoard.
Such greed befits not such a lord,
and I am minded to declare
the hand of Barahir was bare!'   160
Yet as he spake an arrow sped;
with riven heart he crumpled dead.
Thus Morgoth loved that his own foe
should in his service deal the blow
that punished the breaking of his word.   165

But Morgoth laughed not when he heard
that Beren like a wolf alone
sprang madly from behind a stone
amid that camp beside the well,
and seized the ring, and ere the yell   170
of wrath and rage had left their throat
had fled his foes. His gleaming coat
was made of rings of steel no shaft
could pierce, a web of dwarvish craft;
and he was lost in rock and thorn,   175
for in charméd hour was Beren born;
their hungry hunting never learned
the way his fearless feet had turned.

As fearless Beren was renowned,
as man most hardy upon ground,   180
while Barahir yet lived and fought;
but sorrow now his soul had wrought
to dark despair, and robbed his life
of sweetness, that he longed for knife,
or shaft, or sword, to end his pain,   185
and dreaded only thraldom's chain.
Danger he sought and death pursued,
and thus escaped the fate he wooed,
and deeds of breathless wonder dared
whose whispered glory widely fared,   190
and softly songs were sung at eve
of marvels he did once achieve
alone, beleaguered, lost at night

by mist or moon, or neath the light
of the broad eye of day. The woods   195
that northward looked with bitter feuds
he filled and death for Morgoth's folk;
his comrades were the beech and oak,
who failed him not, and many things
with fur and fell and feathered wings;   200
and many spirits, that in stone
in mountains old and wastes alone,
do dwell and wander, were his friends.
Yet seldom well an outlaw ends,
and Morgoth was a king more strong   205
than all the world has since in song
recorded, and his wisdom wide
slow and surely who him defied
did hem and hedge. Thus at the last
must Beren flee the forest fast   210
and lands he loved where lay his sire
by reeds bewailed beneath the mire.
Beneath a heap of mossy stones
now crumble those once most mighty bones.
but Beren flees the friendless North   215
one autumn night, and creeps him forth;
the leaguer of his watchful foes
he passes – silently he goes.
No more his hidden bowstring sings,
no more his shaven arrow wings,   220
no more his hunted head doth lie
upon the heath beneath the sky.

The moon that looked amid the mist
upon the pines, the wind that hissed
among the heather and the fern   225
found him no more. The stars that burn
about the North with silver fire
in frosty airs, the Burning Briar
that men did name in days long gone,
were set behind his back, and shone   230
o'er land and lake and darkened hill,
forsaken fen and mountain rill.

    His face was South from the Land of Dread
whence only evil pathways led,
and only the feet of men most bold   235
might cross the Shadowy Mountains cold.
Their northern slopes were filled with woe,
with evil and with mortal foe;
their southern faces mounted sheer
in rocky pinnacle and pier,   240
whose roots were woven with deceit
and washed with waters bitter-sweet.
There magic lurked in gulf and glen,
for far away beyond the ken
of searching eyes, unless it were   245
from dizzy tower that pricked the air
where only eagles lived and cried,
might grey and gleaming be descried
Beleriand, Beleriand,
the borders of the faëry land.   250

THE QUENTA NOLDORINWA

After the *Sketch of the Mythology* this text, which I will refer to as 'the *Quenta*', was the only complete and finished version of 'The Silmarillion' that my father achieved: a typescript that he made in (as seems certain) 1930. No preliminary drafts or outlines, if there were any, survive; but it is plain that for a good part of its length he had the *Sketch* before him. It is longer than the *Sketch*, and the 'Silmarillion style' has clearly appeared, but it remains a compression, a compendious account. In the sub-title it is said that it is 'the brief history of the Noldoli or Gnomes', drawn from the *Book of Lost Tales* which Eriol [Ælfwine] wrote. The long poems were of course now in being, substantial but massively unfinished, and my father was still working on *The Lay of Leithian*.

In the *Quenta* there emerges the major transformation of the legend of Beren and Lúthien by the entry of the Noldorin prince, Felagund, son of Finrod. To explain how this could come about I will give here a passage from this text, but a note on names is needed. The leader of the Noldor in the great journey of the Elves from Cuiviénen, the Water of Awakening in the furthest East, was Finwë; his three sons were Fëanor, Fingolfin, and Finrod, who was the father of Felagund. (Later the names were changed: The third son of Finwë became *Finarfin*, and *Finrod* the name of his son; but Finrod was also *Felagund*. This name meant 'Lord of Caves' or 'Cave-hewer' in the language of the Dwarves, for he was the founder of Nargothrond. The sister of Finrod Felagund was Galadriel.)

A PASSAGE EXTRACTED
FROM THE *QUENTA*

This was the time that songs call the Siege of Angband. The swords of the Gnomes then fenced the earth from the ruin of Morgoth, and his power was shut behind the walls of Angband. The Gnomes boasted that never could he break their leaguer, and that none of his folk could ever pass to work evil in the ways of the world. . . .

In those days Men came over the Blue Mountains into Beleriand, bravest and fairest of their race. Felagund it was that found them, and he was ever their friend. On a time he was the guest of Celegorm in the East, and rode a-hunting with him. But he became separated from the others, and at a time of night he came upon a dale in the western foothills of the Blue Mountains. There were lights in the dale and the sound of rugged song. Then Felagund marvelled, for the tongue of those songs was not the tongue of Eldar or of Dwarves. Nor was it the tongue of Orcs, though this at first he feared. There were camped the people of Bëor, a mighty warrior of Men, whose son was Barahir the bold. They were the first of Men to come into Beleriand. . . .

That night Felagund went among the sleeping men of Bëor's host and sat by their dying fires where none kept watch, and he took a harp which Bëor had laid aside, and he played music on it such as mortal ear had never heard, having learned the strains of music from the Dark-elves alone. Then men woke and listened and marvelled, for great wisdom was in that song, as well as beauty, and the heart grew wiser that listened to it. Thus came it that Men called Felagund, whom they met first of the Noldoli, Wisdom, and after him they called his race the Wise, whom we call the Gnomes.

Bëor lived till death with Felagund, and Barahir his son was the greatest friend of the sons of Finrod.

Now began the time of the ruin of the Gnomes. It was long before this was achieved, for great was their power grown, and they were very valiant, and their allies were many and bold, Dark-elves and Men.

But the tide of their fortune took a sudden turn. Long had Morgoth prepared his forces in secret. On a time of night at winter he let forth great rivers of flame that poured over all the plain before the Mountains of Iron and burned it to a desolate waste. Many of the Gnomes of Finrod's sons perished in that burning, and the fumes of it wrought darkness and confusion among the foes of Morgoth. In the train of the fire came the black armies of the Orcs in numbers such as the Gnomes had never before seen or imagined. In this way Morgoth broke the leaguer of Angband and slew by the hands of the Orcs a great slaughter of the bravest of the besieging hosts. His enemies were scattered far and wide, Gnomes, Ilkorins and Men. Men he drove for the most part over the Blue Mountains, save the children of Bëor and of Hador who took refuge in Hithlum beyond the Shadowy Mountains, where as yet the Orcs came not in force. The Dark-elves fled south to Beleriand and beyond, but many went to Doriath, and the kingdom and power of Thingol grew great in that time, till he became a bulwark and a refuge of the Elves. The magics of Melian that were woven about the borders of Doriath fenced evil from his halls and realm.

The pine-forest Morgoth took and turned it into a place of dread, and the watchtower of Sirion he took and made it into a stronghold of evil and of menace. There dwelt Thû the chief servant of Morgoth, sorcerer of dreadful power, the lord of wolves. Heaviest had the burden of that dreadful battle, the second battle and the first defeat of the Gnomes, fallen upon the sons of Finrod. There were Angrod and Egnor slain. There too would Felagund have been taken or slain, but Barahir came up with all his men and saved the Gnomish king and made a wall of spears about him; and though grievous was their loss they fought their way from the Orcs and fled to the fens of Sirion to the South. There Felagund swore an oath of undying friendship and aid in time of need to Barahir and all his kin and seed, and in token of his vow he gave to Barahir his ring.

Then Felagund went South, and on the banks of Narog established after the manner of Thingol a hidden and cavernous city and a realm. Those deep places were called Nargothrond. There came Orodreth [son of Finrod, brother of Felagund] after a time of breathless flight and perilous wanderings, and with him Celegorm and Curufin, the sons of Fëanor, his friends. The people of Celegorm swelled the strength of Felagund, but it would have been better if they had gone rather to their own kin, who fortified the hill of Himling east of Doriath and filled the Gorge of Aglon with hidden arms. . . .

In these days of doubt and fear, after the [Battle of Sudden Flame], many dreadful things befell of which but few are here told. It is told that Bëor was slain and Barahir yielded not to Morgoth, but all his land was won from him and his people scattered, enslaved or slain, and he himself went in outlawry with his son Beren and ten faithful men. Long they hid and did secret and valiant deeds of war against the Orcs. But in the end, as is told in the beginning of the lay of Lúthien and Beren, the hiding place of Barahir was betrayed, and he was slain and his comrades, all save Beren who by fortune was that day hunting afar. Thereafter Beren lived an outlaw alone, save for the help he had from birds and beasts which he loved; and seeking for death in desperate deeds found it not, but glory and renown in the secret songs of fugitives and hidden enemies of Morgoth, so that the tale of his deeds came even to Beleriand, and was rumoured in Doriath. At length Beren fled south from the ever-closing circle of those that hunted him, and crossed the dreadful Mountains of Shadow, and came at last worn and haggard into Doriath. There in secret he won the love of Lúthien daughter of Thingol, and he named her Tinúviel, the nightingale, because of the beauty of her singing in the twilight beneath the trees; for she was the daughter of Melian.

But Thingol was wroth and he dismissed him in scorn, but did not slay him because he had sworn an oath to his daughter. But he desired nonetheless to send him to his death. And he thought in his heart of a quest that could not be achieved, and he said: If thou bring me a Silmaril from the crown of Morgoth, I will let Lúthien wed thee, if she will. And Beren vowed to achieve this, and went from Doriath to Nargothrond bearing the ring of Barahir. The quest of the Silmaril there aroused the oath from sleep that the sons of Fëanor had sworn, and evil began to grow from it. Felagund, though he knew the quest to be beyond his power, was willing to lend all his aid to Beren, because of his own oath to Barahir. But Celegorm and Curufin dissuaded his people and roused up rebellion against him. And evil thoughts awoke in their hearts, and they thought to usurp the throne of Nargothrond, because they were sons of the eldest line. Rather than a Silmaril should be won and given to Thingol, they would ruin the power of Doriath and Nargothrond.

So Felagund gave his crown to Orodreth and departed from his people with Beren and ten faithful men of his own board. They waylaid an Orc-band and slew them, and disguised themselves by the aid of Felagund's magic as Orcs. But they were seen by Thû from his watchtower, which once had been Felagund's own, and were questioned by him, and their magic was overthrown in a contest between Thû and Felagund. Thus they were revealed as Elves, but the spells of Felagund concealed their names and quest. Long were they tortured in the dungeons of Thû, but none betrayed the other.

The oath referred to at the end of this passage was sworn by Fëanor and his seven sons, in the words of the *Quenta*, 'to pursue with hate and vengeance to the ends of the world Vala, Demon, Elf, or Man, or Orc who hold or take or keep a Silmaril against their will.' See pp. 117–18, lines 171–80.

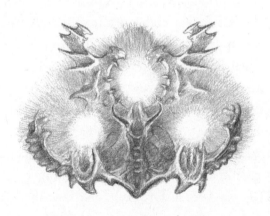

A SECOND EXTRACT FROM
THE LAY OF LEITHIAN

I give now a further passage of *The Lay of Leithian* (see
pp. 91, 93) telling the story that has just been given in its
very compressed form in the *Quenta*. I take up the poem
where the Siege of Angband was ended in what was later
called the Battle of Sudden Flame. According to the dates
that my father wrote on the manuscript the whole passage
was composed in March–April 1928. At line 246 Canto VI
of the *Lay* ends and Canto VII begins.

> An end there came, when fortune turned
> and flames of Morgoth's vengeance burned,
> and all the might which he prepared
> in secret in his fastness flared
> and poured across the Thirsty Plain;   5
> and armies black were in his train.
>   The leaguer of Angband Morgoth broke;
> his enemies in fire and smoke

were scattered, and the Orcs there slew,
and slew, until the blood like dew   10
dripped from each cruel and crooked blade.
Then Barahir the bold did aid
with mighty spear, with shield and men,
Felagund wounded. To the fen
escaping, there they bound their troth,   15
and Felagund deeply swore an oath
of friendship to his kin and seed
of love and succour in time of need.
But there of Finrod's children four
were Angrod slain and proud Egnor.   20
Felagund and Orodreth then
gathered the remnant of their men,
their maidens and their children fair;
forsaking war they made their lair
and cavernous hold far in the south.   25
On Narog's towering bank its mouth
was opened; which they hid and veiled,
and mighty doors, that unassailed
till Túrin's day stood vast and grim,
they built by trees o'ershadowed dim.   30
And with them dwelt a long time there
Curufin, and Celegorm the fair;
and a mighty folk grew neath their hands
in Narog's secret halls and lands.

  Thus Felagund in Nargothrond   35
still reigned, a hidden king whose bond

was sworn to Barahir the bold.
And now his son through forests cold
wandered alone as in a dream.
Esgalduin's dark and shrouded stream   40
he followed, till its waters frore
were joined to Sirion, Sirion hoar,
pale silver water wide and free
rolling in splendour to the sea.

    Now Beren came unto the pools,   45
wide shallow meres where Sirion cools
his gathered tide beneath the stars,
ere chafed and sundered by the bars
of reedy banks a mighty fen
he feeds and drenches, plunging then   50
into vast chasms underground,
where many miles his way is wound.
Umboth-Muilin, Twilight Meres,
those great wide waters grey as tears
the Elves then named. Through driving rain   55
from thence across the Guarded Plain
the Hills of the Hunters Beren saw
with bare tops bitten bleak and raw
by western winds, but in the mist
of streaming rains that flashed and hissed   60
into the meres he knew there lay
beneath those hills the cloven way
of Narog, and the watchful halls
of Felagund beside the falls
of Ingwil tumbling from the wold.   65

An everlasting watch they hold,
the Gnomes of Nargothrond renowned,
and every hill is tower-crowned,
where wardens sleepless peer and gaze
guarding the plain and all the ways   70
between Narog swift and Sirion pale;
and archers whose arrows never fail
there range the woods, and secret kill
all who creep thither against their will.

 Yet now he thrusts into that land   75
bearing the gleaming ring on hand
of Felagund, and oft doth cry:
'Here comes no wandering Orc or spy,
but Beren son of Barahir
who once to Felagund was dear.'   80
 So ere he reached the eastward shore
of Narog, that doth foam and roar
o'er boulders black, those archers green
came round him. When the ring was seen
they bowed before him, though his plight   85
was poor and beggarly. Then by night
they led him northward, for no ford
nor bridge was built where Narog poured
before the gates of Nargothrond,
and friend nor foe might pass beyond.   90
 To northward, where that stream yet young
more slender flowed, below the tongue
of foam-splashed land that Ginglith pens
when her brief golden torrent ends

and joins the Narog, there they wade.   95
Now swiftest journey thence they made
to Nargothrond's sheer terraces
and dim gigantic palaces.
    They came beneath a sickle moon
to doors there darkly hung and hewn   100
with posts and lintels of ponderous stone
and timbers huge. Now open thrown
were gaping gates, and in they strode
where Felagund on throne abode.

    Fair were the words of Narog's king   105
to Beren, and his wandering
and all his feuds and bitter wars
recounted soon. Behind closed doors
they sat, while Beren told his tale
of Doriath; and words him fail   110
recalling Lúthien dancing fair
with wild white roses in her hair,
remembering her elven voice that rung
while stars in twilight round her hung.
He spake of Thingol's marvellous halls   115
by enchantment lit, where fountain falls
and ever the nightingale doth sing
to Melian and to her king.
The quest he told that Thingol laid
in scorn on him; how for love of maid   120
more fair than ever was born to Men,
of Tinúviel, of Lúthien,

he must essay the burning waste,
and doubtless death and torment taste.

This Felagund in wonder heard,   125
and heavily spoke at last this word:
'It seems that Thingol doth desire
thy death. The everlasting fire
of those enchanted jewels all know
is cursed with an oath of endless woe,   130
and Fëanor's sons alone by right
are lords and masters of their light.
He cannot hope within his hoard
to keep this gem, nor is he lord
of all the folk of Elfinesse.   135
And yet thou saist for nothing less
can thy return to Doriath
be purchased? Many a dreadful path
in sooth there lies before thy feet –
and after Morgoth, still a fleet   140
untiring hate, as I know well,
would hunt thee from heaven unto hell.
Fëanor's sons would, if they could,
slay thee or ever thou reached his wood
or laid in Thingol's lap that fire,   145
or gained at least thy sweet desire.
Lo! Celegorm and Curufin
here dwell this very realm within,
and even though I, Finrod's son,
am king, a mighty power have won   150

and many of their own folk lead.
Friendship to me in every need
they yet have shown, but much I fear
that to Beren son of Barahir
mercy or love they will not show   155
if once thy dreadful quest they know.'

   True words he spoke. For when the king
to all his people told this thing,
and spake of the oath to Barahir,
and how that mortal shield and spear   160
had saved them from Morgoth and from woe
on Northern battlefields long ago,
then many were kindled in their hearts
once more to battle. But up there starts
amid the throng, and loudly cries   165
for hearing, one with flaming eyes,
proud Celegorm with gleaming hair
and shining sword. Then all men stare
upon his stern unyielding face,
and a great hush falls upon that place.   170

   'Be he friend or foe, or demon wild
of Morgoth, Elf, or mortal child,
or any that here on earth may dwell,
no law, nor love, nor league of hell,
no might of Gods, no binding spell,   175
shall him defend from hatred fell
of Fëanor's sons, whoso take or steal

or finding keep a Silmaril.
These we alone do claim by right,
our thrice enchanted jewels bright.'   180

    Many wild and potent words he spoke,
and as before in Tûn awoke
his father's voice their hearts to fire,
so now dark fear and brooding ire
he cast on them, foreboding war   185
of friend with friend; and pools of gore
their minds imagined lying red
in Nargothrond about the dead,
did Narog's host with Beren go;
or haply battle, ruin, and woe   190
in Doriath where great Thingol reigned,
if Fëanor's fatal jewel he gained.
And even such as were most true
to Felagund his oath did rue,
and thought with terror and despair   195
of seeking Morgoth in his lair
with force or guile. This Curufin
when his brother ceased did then begin
more to impress upon their minds;
and such a spell he on them binds   200
that never again till Túrin's day
would Gnome of Narog in array
of open battle go to war.
With secrecy, ambush, spies and lore
of wizardry, with silent leaguer   205

of wild things wary, watchful, eager,
of phantom hunters, venomed darts,
and unseen stealthy creeping arts,
with padding hatred that its prey
with feet of velvet all the day   210
followed remorseless out of sight
and slew it unawares at night –
thus they defended Nargothrond,
and forgot their kin and solemn bond
for dread of Morgoth that the art   215
of Curufin set within their heart.

   So would they not that angry day
King Felagund their lord obey,
but sullen murmured that Finrod
nor yet his son were as a god.   220
Then Felagund took off his crown
and at his feet he cast it down,
the silver helm of Nargothrond:
'Yours ye may break, but I my bond
must keep, and kingdom here forsake.   225
If hearts here were that did not quake,
or that to Finrod's son were true,
then I at least should find a few
to go with me, not like a poor
rejected beggar scorn endure,   230
turned from my gates to leave my town,
my people, and my realm and crown!'

Hearing these words there swiftly stood
beside him ten tried warriors good,
men of his house who had ever fought 235
wherever his banners had been brought.
One stooped and lifted up his crown,
and said: 'O king, to leave this town
is now our fate, but not to lose
thy rightful lordship. Thou shalt choose 240
one to be steward in thy stead.'
Then Felagund upon the head
of Orodreth set it: 'Brother mine,
till I return this crown is thine.'
Then Celegorm no more would stay, 245
and Curufin smiled and turned away.

* * * * *

Thus twelve alone there ventured forth
from Nargothrond, and to the North
they turned their silent secret way,
and vanished in the fading day. 250
No trumpet sounds, no voice there sings,
as robed in mail of cunning rings
now blackened dark with helmets grey
and sombre cloaks they steal away.
    Far-journeying Narog's leaping course 255
they followed till they found his source,
the flickering falls, whose freshets sheer
a glimmering goblet glassy-clear

with crystal waters fill that shake
and quiver down from Ivrin's lake,   260
from Ivrin's mere that mirrors dim
the pallid faces bare and grim
of Shadowy Mountains neath the moon.

   Now far beyond the realm immune
from Orc and demon and the dread   265
of Morgoth's might their ways had led.
In woods o'er shadowed by the heights
they watched and waited many nights,
till on a time when hurrying cloud
did moon and constellation shroud,   270
and winds of autumn's wild beginning
soughed in the boughs, and leaves went spinning
down the dark eddies rustling soft,
they heard a murmur hoarsely waft
from far, a croaking laughter coming;   275
now louder; now they heard the drumming
of hideous stamping feet that tramp
the weary earth. Then many a lamp
of sullen red they saw draw near,
swinging, and glistening on spear   280
and scimitar. There hidden nigh
they saw a band of Orcs go by
with goblin faces swart and foul.
Bats were about them, and the owl,
the ghostly forsaken night-bird cried   285
from trees above. The voices died,

the laughter like clash of stone and steel
passed and faded. At their heel
the Elves and Beren crept more soft
than foes stealing through a croft   290
in search of prey. Thus to the camp
lit by flickering fire and lamp
they stole, and counted sitting there
full thirty Orcs in the red flare
of burning wood. Without a sound   295
they one by one stood silent round,
each in the shadow of a tree;
each slowly, grimly, secretly
bent then his bow and drew the string.

    Hark! how they sudden twang and sing,   300
when Felagund lets forth a cry;
and twelve Orcs sudden fall and die.
Then forth they leap casting their bows.
Out their bright swords, and swift their blows!
The stricken Orcs now shriek and yell   305
as lost things deep in lightless hell.
Battle there is beneath the trees
bitter and swift, but no Orc flees;
there left their lives that wandering band
and stained no more the sorrowing land   310
with rape and murder. Yet no song
of joy, or triumph over wrong,
the Elves there sang. In peril sore
they were, for never alone to war

so small an Orc-band went, they knew.   315
Swiftly the raiment off they drew
and cast the corpses in a pit.
This desperate counsel had the wit
of Felagund for them devised:
as Orcs his comrades he disguised.   320

    The poisoned spears, the bows of horn,
the crooked swords their foes had borne
they took; and loathing each him clad
in Angband's raiment foul and sad.
They smeared their hands and faces fair   325
with pigment dark; the matted hair
all lank and black from goblin head
they shore, and joined it thread by thread
with Gnomish skill. As each one leers
at each dismayed, about his ears   330
he hangs it noisome, shuddering.
    Then Felagund a spell did sing
of changing and of shifting shape;
their ears grew hideous, and agape
their mouths did start, and like a fang   335
each tooth became, as slow he sang.
Their Gnomish raiment then they hid
and one by one behind him slid,
behind a foul and goblin thing
that once was elven-fair and king.   340

Northward they went; and Orcs they met
who passed, nor did their going let,
but hailed them in greeting; and more bold
they grew as past the long miles rolled.
  At length they came with weary feet   345
beyond Beleriand. They found the fleet
young waters, rippling, silver-pale
of Sirion hurrying through that vale
where Taur-na-Fuin, Deadly Night,
the trackless forest's pine-clad height,   350
falls dark forbidding slowly down
upon the east, while westward frown
the northward-bending Mountains grey
and bar the westering light of day.

  An isléd hill there stood alone   355
amid the valley, like a stone
rolled from the mountains vast
when giants in tumult hurtled past.
Around its feet the river looped
a stream divided, that had scooped   360
the hanging edges into caves.
There briefly shuddered Sirion's waves
and ran to other shores more clean.
  An elven watchtower had it been,
and strong it was, and still was fair;   365
but now did grim with menace stare
one way to pale Beleriand,
the other to that mournful land

beyond the valley's northern mouth.
Thence could be glimpsed the fields of drouth,   370
the dusty dunes, the desert wide;
and further far could be descried
the brooding cloud that hangs and lowers
on Thangorodrim's thunderous towers.

    Now in that hill was the abode   375
of one most evil; and the road
that from Beleriand thither came
he watched with sleepless eyes of flame.
    Men called him Thû, and as a god
in after days beneath his rod   380
bewildered bowed to him, and made
his ghastly temples in the shade.
Not yet by Men enthralled adored,
now was he Morgoth's mightiest lord,
Master of Wolves, whose shivering howl   385
for ever echoed in the hills, and foul
enchantments and dark sigaldry
did weave and wield. In glamoury
that necromancer held his hosts
of phantoms and of wandering ghosts,   390
of misbegotten or spell-wronged
monsters that about him thronged,
working his bidding dark and vile:
the werewolves of the Wizard's Isle.

From Thû their coming was not hid   395
and though beneath the eaves they slid
of the forest's gloomy-hanging boughs,
he saw them afar, and wolves did rouse:
'Go! fetch me those sneaking Orcs,' he said,
'that fare thus strangely, as if in dread,   400
and do not come, as all Orcs use
and are commanded, to bring me news
of all their deeds, to me, to Thû.'

From his tower he gazed, and in him grew
suspicion and a brooding thought,   405
waiting, leering, till they were brought.
Now ringed about with wolves they stand,
and fear their doom. Alas! the land,
the land of Narog left behind!
Foreboding evil weights their mind,   410
as downcast, halting, they must go
and cross the stony bridge of woe
to Wizard's Isle, and to the throne
there fashioned of blood-darkened stone.

'Where have ye been? What have ye seen?'   415

'In Elfinesse; and tears and distress,
the fire blowing and the blood flowing,
these have we seen, there have we been.
Thirty we slew and their bodies threw

in a dark pit. The ravens sit   420
and the owl cries where our swath lies.'

　　'Come, tell me true, O Morgoth's thralls,
what then in Elfinesse befalls?
What of Nargothrond? Who reigneth there?
Into that realm did your feet dare?'   425

　　'Only its borders did we dare.
There reigns King Felagund the fair.'

　　'Then heard ye not that he is gone,
that Celegorm sits his throne upon?'

　　'That is not true! If he is gone,   430
then Orodreth sits his throne upon.'

　　'Sharp are your ears, swift have they got
tidings of realms ye entered not!
What are your names, O spearmen bold?
Who your captain, ye have not told.'   435

　　'Nereb and Dungalef and warriors ten,
so we are called, and dark our den
under the mountains. Over the waste
we march on an errand of need and haste.
Boldog the captain awaits us there   440
where fires from under smoke and flare.'

'Boldog, I heard, was lately slain
warring on the borders of that domain
where Robber Thingol and outlaw folk
cringe and crawl beneath elm and oak   445
in drear Doriath. Heard ye not then
of that pretty fay, of Lúthien?
Her body is fair, very white and fair.
Morgoth would possess her in his lair.
Boldog he sent, but Boldog was slain: 450
strange ye were not in Boldog's train.

    Nereb looks fierce, his frown is grim.
Little Lúthien! What troubles him?
Why laughs he not to think of his lord
crushing a maiden in his hoard,   455
that foul should be what once was clean,
that dark should be where light has been?

    Whom do ye serve, Light or Mirk?
Who is the maker of mightiest work?
Who is the king of earthly kings,   460
the greatest giver of gold and rings?
Who is the master of the wide earth?
Who despoiled them of their mirth,
the greedy Gods! Repeat your vows,
Orcs of Bauglir! Do not bend your brows!   465
Death to light, to law, to love!
Cursed be moon and stars above!
May darkness everlasting old
that waits outside in surges cold

drown Manwë, Varda, and the sun!   470
May all in hatred be begun
and all in evil ended be,
in the moaning of the endless Sea!'

But no true Man nor Elf yet free
would ever speak that blasphemy,   475
and Beren muttered: 'Who is Thû
to hinder work that is to do?
Him we serve not, nor to him owe
obeisance, and we now would go.'

Thû laughed: 'Patience! Not very long   480
shall ye abide. But first a song
I will sing to you, to ears intent.'
Then his flaming eyes he on them bent
and darkness black fell round them all.
Only they saw as through a pall   485
of eddying smoke those eyes profound
in which their senses choked and drowned.
   He chanted a song of wizardry,
of piercing, opening, of treachery,
revealing, uncovering, betraying.   490
Then sudden Felagund there swaying
sang in answer a song of staying,
resisting, battling against power,
of secrets kept, strength like a tower,
and trust unbroken, freedom, escape;   500

of changing and of shifting shape,
of snares eluded, broken traps,
the prison opening, the chain that snaps.
    Backwards and forwards swayed their song.
Reeling and foundering, as ever more strong   505
Thû's chanting swelled, Felagund fought,
and all the magic and might he brought
of Elfinesse into his words.
Softly in the gloom they heard the birds
singing afar in Nargothrond,   510
the sighing of the sea beyond,
beyond the western world, on sand,
on sand of pearls in Elvenland.

    Then the gloom gathered: darkness growing
in Valinor, the red blood flowing   515
beside the sea, where the Gnomes slew
the Foamriders, and stealing drew
their white ships with their white sails
from lamplit havens. The wind wails.
The wolf howls. The ravens flee.   520
The ice mutters in the mouths of the sea.
The captives sad in Angband mourn.
Thunder rumbles, the fires burn,
a vast smoke gushes out, a roar –
and Felagund swoons upon the floor.   525

    Behold! they are in their own fair shape,
fairskinned, brighteyed. No longer gape

Orclike their mouths; and now they stand
betrayed into the wizard's hand.
Thus came they unhappy into woe,   530
to dungeons no hope nor glimmer know,
where chained in chains that eat the flesh
and woven in webs of strangling mesh
they lay forgotten, in despair.

    Yet not all unavailing were   535
the spells of Felagund; for Thû
neither their names nor purpose knew.
These much he pondered and bethought,
and in their woeful chains them sought,
and threatened all with dreadful death,   540
if one would not with traitor's breath
reveal this knowledge. Wolves should come
and slow devour them one by one
before the others' eyes, and last
should one alone be left aghast,   545
then in a place of horror hung
with anguish should his limbs be wrung,
in the bowels of the earth be slow
endlessly, cruelly, put to woe
and torment, till he all declared.   550

    Even as he threatened, so it fared.
From time to time in the eyeless dark
two eyes would grow, and they would hark
to frightful cries, and then a sound

of rending, a slavering on the ground,   555
and blood flowing they would smell.
But none would yield, and none would tell.

Here Canto VII ends. I return now to the *Quenta*, and
take it up from the words 'Long were they tortured in the
dungeons of Thû, but none betrayed the other' with which
the previous extract ends (p. 110); and as previously I follow
the *Quenta* account with the vastly different passage in
the *Lay*.

A FURTHER EXTRACT FROM
THE *QUENTA*

In the meanwhile Lúthien, learning by the far sight of Melian that Beren had fallen into the power of Thû, sought in her despair to fly from Doriath. This became known to Thingol, who imprisoned her in a house in the tallest of his mighty beeches far above the ground. How she escaped and came into the woods, and was found there by Celegorm as they hunted on the borders of Doriath, is told in *The Lay of Leithian*. They took her treacherously to Nargothrond, and Curufin the crafty became enamoured of her beauty. From her tale they learned that Felagund was in the hands of Thû; and they purposed to let him perish there, and keep Lúthien with them, and force Thingol to wed Lúthien to Curufin, and so build up their power and usurp Nargothrond and become the mightiest of the princes of the Gnomes. They did not think to go in search of the Silmarils, or suffer any others to do so, until they had all the power of the Elves beneath themselves and obedient to them. But their designs came to nought save estrangement and bitterness between the kingdoms of the Elves.

Huan was the name of the chief of the hounds of Celegorm. He was of immortal race from the hunting-lands of Oromë. Oromë gave him to Celegorm long before in Valinor, when Celegorm often rode in the train of the God and followed his horn. He came into the Great Lands with his master, and dart nor weapon, spell nor poison, could harm him, so that he went into battle with his lord and saved him many times from death. His fate had decreed that he should not meet death save at the hands of the mightiest wolf that should ever walk the world.

Huan was true of heart, and he loved Lúthien from the hour that he first found her in the woods and brought her to Celegorm. His heart was grieved by his master's treachery, and he set Lúthien free and went with her to the North.

There Thû slew his captives one by one, till only Felagund and Beren were left. When the hour for Beren's death came Felagund put forth all his power, and burst his bonds, and wrestled with the werewolf that came to slay Beren; and he killed the wolf, but was himself slain in the dark. There Beren mourned in despair, and waited for death. But Lúthien came and sang outside the dungeons. Thus she beguiled Thû to come forth, for the fame of the loveliness of Lúthien had gone through all lands and the wonder of her song. Even Morgoth desired her, and had promised the greatest reward to any who could capture her. Each wolf that Thû sent Huan slew silently, till Draugluin the greatest of his wolves came. Then there was fierce battle, and Thû knew that Lúthien was not alone. But he remembered the fate of Huan, and he made himself the greatest wolf that had yet walked the world, and came forth. But Huan overthrew him, and won from him the keys and the spells that held together his enchanted walls and towers. So the stronghold was broken and the towers thrown down and the dungeons opened. Many captives were released, but Thû flew in bat's form to Taur-na-Fuin. There Lúthien found Beren mourning beside Felagund. She healed his sorrow and the wasting of his imprisonment, but Felagund they buried on the top of his own island hill, and Thû came there no more.

Then Huan returned to his master, and less was the love between them after. Beren and Lúthien wandered careless in happiness until they came nigh to the borders of Doriath once more. There Beren remembered his vow, and bade Lúthien farewell, but she would not be sundered from him. In Nargothrond there was tumult. For Huan and many of the captives of Thû brought back the tidings of the deeds of Lúthien, and the death of Felagund, and the treachery of Celegorm and Curufin was laid bare. It is said they had sent a secret embassy to Thingol ere Lúthien escaped, but Thingol in wrath had sent their letters back by his own servants to Orodreth. Wherefore now the hearts of the people of Narog turned back to the house of Finrod, and they mourned their king Felagund whom they had forsaken, and they did the bidding of Orodreth.

But he would not suffer them to slay the sons of Fëanor as they wished. Instead he banished them from Nargothrond, and swore that little love should there be between Narog and any of the sons of Fëanor thereafter. And so it was.

Celegorm and Curufin were riding in haste and wrath through the woods to find their way to Himling when they came upon Beren and Lúthien, even as Beren sought to part from his love. They rode down on them, and recognizing them tried to trample Beren under their hooves.

But Curufin lifted Lúthien to his saddle. Then befell the leap of Beren, the greatest leap of mortal Men. For he sprang like a lion right upon the speeding horse of Curufin, and grasped him about the throat, and horse and rider fell in confusion upon the earth, but Lúthien was flung far off and lay dazed upon the ground. There Beren choked Curufin, but his death was very nigh from Celegorm, who rode back with his spear. In that hour Huan forsook the service of Celegorm, and sprang upon him so that his horse swerved aside, and no man for fear of the terror of the great hound dared go nigh. Lúthien forbade the death of Curufin, but Beren despoiled him of his horse and weapons, chief of which was his famous knife, made by the Dwarves. It would cut iron like wood. Then the brothers rode off, but shot back at Huan treacherously and at Lúthien. Huan they did not hurt, but Beren sprang before Lúthien and was wounded, and Men remembered that wound against the sons of Fëanor, when it became known.

Huan stayed with Lúthien, and hearing of their perplexity and the purpose Beren had still to go to Angband, he went and fetched them from the ruined halls of Thû a werewolf's coat and a bat's. Three times only did Huan speak with the tongue of Elves or Men. The first was when he came to Lúthien in Nargothrond. This was the second, when he devised the desperate counsel for their quest. So they rode North, till they could no longer go on horse in safety. Then they put on the garments as of wolf and bat, and Lúthien in guise of evil fay rode upon the werewolf.

In *The Lay of Leithian* is all told how they came to Angband's gate, and found it newly guarded, for rumour of he knew not what design abroad among the Elves had come to Morgoth. Wherefore he fashioned the mightiest of all wolves, Carcharas Knife-fang, to sit at the gates. But Lúthien set him in spells, and they won their way to the presence of Morgoth, and Beren slunk beneath his chair. Then Lúthien dared the most dreadful and most valiant deed that any of the Elves have ever dared; no less than the challenge of Fingolfin is it accounted, and may be greater, save that she was half-divine. She cast off her disguise and named her own name, and feigned that she was brought captive by the wolves of Thû. And she beguiled Morgoth, even as his heart plotted foul evil within him; and she danced before him, and cast all his court in sleep; and she sang to him, and she flung the magic robe she had woven in Doriath in his face, and she set a binding dream upon him – what song can sing the marvel of that deed, or the wrath and humiliation of Morgoth, for even the Orcs laugh in secret when they remember it, telling how Morgoth fell from his chair and his iron crown rolled upon the floor.

Then forth leaped Beren casting aside the wolvish robe, and drew out the knife of Curufin. With that he cut forth a Silmaril. But daring more he essayed to gain them all. Then the knife of the treacherous Dwarves snapped, and the ringing sound of it stirred the sleeping hosts and Morgoth groaned.

Terror seized the hearts of Beren and Lúthien, and they fled down the dark ways of Angband. The doors were barred by Carcharas, now aroused from the spell of Lúthien. Beren set himself before Lúthien, which proved ill; for ere she could touch the wolf with her robe or speak word of magic, he sprang upon Beren, who now had no weapon. With his right he smote at the eyes of Carcharas, but the wolf took the hand into his jaws and bit it off. Now that hand held the Silmaril. Then was the maw of Carcharas burned with a fire of anguish and torment, when the Silmaril touched his evil flesh; and he fled howling from before them, so that all the mountains shuddered, and the madness of the wolf of Angband was of all the horrors that ever came into the North the most dire and terrible. Hardly did Lúthien and Beren escape, ere all Angband was aroused.

Of their wanderings and despair, and of the healing of Beren, who ever since has been called Beren Ermabwed the One-handed, of their rescue by Huan, who had vanished suddenly from them ere they came to Angband, and of their coming to Doriath once more, here there is little to tell. But in Doriath many things had befallen. Ever things had gone ill there since Lúthien fled away. Grief had fallen on all the people and silence on their songs when their hunting found her not. Long was the search, and in searching Dairon the piper of Doriath was lost, who loved Lúthien before Beren came to Doriath. He was the greatest of the musicians of the Elves, save Maglor son of Fëanor, and Tinfang Warble. But he came never back to Doriath and strayed into the East of the world.

Assaults too there were on Doriath's borders, for rumours that Lúthien was astray had reached Angband. Boldog the captain of the Orcs was there slain in battle by Thingol, and his great warriors Beleg the Bowman and Mablung Heavyhand were with Thingol in that battle. Thus Thingol learned that Lúthien was yet free of Morgoth, but that he knew of her wandering; and Thingol was filled with fear. In the midst of his fear came the embassy of Celegorm in secret, and said that Beren was dead, and Felagund, and Lúthien was at Nargothrond. Then Thingol found it in his heart to regret the death of Beren, and his wrath was aroused at the hinted treachery of Celegorm to the house of Finrod, and because he kept Lúthien and did not send her home. Wherefore he sent spies into the land of Nargothrond and prepared for war. But he learned that Lúthien had fled and that Celegorm and his brother were gone to Aglon. So now he sent an embassy to Aglon, since his might was not great enough to fall upon all the seven brothers, nor was his quarrel with others than Celegorm and Curufin. But this embassy journeying in the woods met with the onslaught of Carcharas. That great wolf had run in madness through all the woods of the North, and death and devastation went with him. Mablung alone escaped to bear the news of his coming to Thingol. Of fate, or the magic of the Silmaril that he bore to his torment, he was not stayed by the spells of Melian, but burst into the inviolate woods of Doriath, and far and wide terror and destruction was spread.

Even as the sorrows of Doriath were at their worst came Lúthien and Beren and Huan back to Doriath. Then the heart of Thingol was lightened, but he looked not with love upon Beren in whom he saw the cause of all his woes. When he had learned how Beren had escaped from Thû he was amazed, but he said: 'Mortal, what of thy quest and of thy vow?' Then said Beren: 'Even now I have a Silmaril in my hand.' 'Show it to me,' said Thingol. 'That I cannot,' said Beren, 'for my hand is not here.' And all the tale he told, and made clear the cause of the madness of Carcharas, and Thingol's heart was softened by his brave words, and his forbearance, and the great love that he saw between his daughter and this most valiant Man.

Now therefore did they plan the wolf-hunt of Carcharas. In that hunt was Huan and Thingol and Mablung and Beleg and Beren and no more. And here the sad tale of it must be short, for it is elsewhere told more fully. Lúthien remained behind in foreboding, as they went forth; and well she might, for Carcharas was slain, but Huan died in the same hour, and he died to save Beren. Yet Beren was hurt to the death, but lived to place the Silmaril in the hands of Thingol, when Mablung had cut it from the belly of the wolf. Then he spoke not again, until they had borne him with Huan at his side back to the doors of Thingol's halls. There beneath the beech, wherein before she had been imprisoned, Lúthien met them, and kissed Beren ere his spirit departed to the halls of awaiting. So ended the long tale of Lúthien and Beren. But not yet was *The Lay of Leithian*, release from bondage, told in full. For it has long been said that Lúthien failed and faded swiftly and vanished from the earth, though some songs say that Melian summoned Thorondor, and he bore her living unto Valinor. And she came to the halls of Mandos, and she

sang to him a tale of moving love so fair that he was moved
to pity, as never has befallen since. Beren he summoned, and
thus, as Lúthien had sworn as she kissed him at the hour of
death, they met beyond the western sea. And Mandos suffered them to depart, but he said that Lúthien should become
mortal even as her lover, and should leave the earth once more
in the manner of mortal women, and her beauty become but
a memory of song. So it was, but it is said that in recompense
Mandos gave to Beren and to Lúthien thereafter a long span
of life and joy, and they wandered knowing thirst nor cold
in the fair land of Beleriand, and no mortal Man thereafter
spoke to Beren or his spouse.

THE NARRATIVE IN *THE LAY OF LEITHIAN* TO ITS TERMINATION

This substantial portion of the poem takes up from the last line of Canto VII in *The Lay of Leithian* ('But none would yield, and none would tell', p. 132), and the opening of Canto VIII corresponds to the very compressed account in the *Quenta* (p. 133) of the confinement of Lúthien in Nargothrond, imposed on her by Celegorm and Curufin and from which she was rescued by Huan, whose origin is told. A line of asterisks in the text of the *Lay* marks the start of a further Canto; Canto IX at line 329; Canto X at line 619; Canto XI at line 1009; Canto XII at line 1301; Canto XIII at line 1603; and Canto XIV, the last, at line 1939.

> Hounds there were in Valinor
> with silver collars. Hart and boar,
> the fox and hare and nimble roe
> there in the forests green did go.
> Oromë was the lord divine   5

of all those woods. The potent wine
went in his halls and hunting song.
The Gnomes anew have named him long
Tavros, the God whose horns did blow
over the mountains long ago;   10
who alone of Gods had loved the world
before the banners were unfurled
of Moon and Sun; and shod with gold
were his great horses. Hounds untold
baying in woods beyond the West   15
of race immortal he possessed:
grey and limber, black and strong
white with silken coats and long,
brown and brindled, swift and true
as arrow from a bow of yew;   20
their voices like the deeptoned bells
that ring in Valmar's citadels,
their eyes like living jewels, their teeth
like ruel-bone. As sword from sheath
they flashed and fled from leash to scent   25
for Tavros' joy and merriment.

    In Tavros' friths and pastures green
had Huan once a young whelp been.
He grew the swiftest of the swift
and Oromë gave him as a gift   30
to Celegorm, who loved to follow
the great god's horn o'er hill and hollow.
    Alone of hounds of the Land of Light,

when sons of Fëanor took to flight
and came into the North, he stayed   35
beside his master. Every raid
and every foray wild he shared,
and into mortal battle dared.
Often he saved his Gnomish lord
from Orc and wolf and leaping sword.   40
A wolf-hound, tireless, grey and fierce
he grew; his gleaming eyes would pierce
all shadows and all mist, the scent
moons old he found through fen and bent,
through rustling leaves and dusty sand;   45
all paths of wide Beleriand
he knew. But wolves, he loved them best;
he loved to find their throats and wrest
their snarling lives and evil breath.
The packs of Thû him feared as death.   50
     No wizardry, nor spell, nor dart,
no fang, nor venom devil's art
could brew had harmed him; for his weird
was woven. Yet he little feared
that fate decreed and known to all: 55
before the mightiest he should fall,
before the mightiest wolf alone
that ever was whelped in cave of stone.

     Hark! afar in Nargothrond,
far over Sirion and beyond,   60
there are dim cries and horns blowing,

and barking hounds through the trees going.
    The hunt is up, the woods are stirred.
Who rides to-day? Ye have not heard
that Celegorm and Curufin   65
have loosed their dogs? With merry din
they mounted ere the sun arose,
and took their spears and took their bows.
The wolves of Thû of late have dared
both far and wide. Their eyes have glared   70
by night across the roaring stream
of Narog. Doth their master dream,
perchance, of plots and counsels deep,
of secrets that the Elf-lords keep,
of movements in the Gnomish realm   75
and errands under beech and elm?

    Curufin spake: 'Good brother mine,
I like it not. What dark design
doth this portend? These evil things
we swift must end their wanderings!   80
And more, 'twould please my heart full well
to hunt a while and wolves to fell.'
And then he leaned and whispered low
that Orodreth was a dullard slow;
long time it was since the king had gone,   85
and rumour or tidings came there none.
    'At least thy profit it would be
to know whether dead he is or free;
to gather thy men and thy array.

"I go to hunt" then thou wilt say,   90
and men will think that Narog's good
ever thou heedest. But in the wood
things may be learned; and if by grace,
by some blind fortune he retrace
his footsteps mad, and if he bear   95
a Silmaril – I need declare
no more in words; but one by right
is thine (and ours), the jewel of light;
another may be won – a throne.
The eldest blood our house doth own.'   100

   Celegorm listened. Nought he said,
but forth a mighty host he led;
and Huan leaped at the glad sounds,
the chief and captain of his hounds.
   Three days they ride by holt and hill   105
the wolves of Thû to hunt and kill,
and many a head and fell of grey
they take, and many drive away,
till nigh to the borders in the West
of Doriath a while they rest.   110

   There were dim cries and horns blowing,
and barking dogs through the woods going.
The hunt was up. The woods were stirred,
and one there fled like a startled bird,
and fear was in her dancing feet.   115
She knew not who the woods did beat.

Far from her home, forwandered, pale,
she flitted ghostlike through the vale;
ever her heart bade her up and on
but her limbs were worn, her eyes were wan.   120
    The eyes of Huan saw a shade
wavering, darting down a glade
like a mist of evening snared by day
and hasting fearfully away.
He bayed, and sprang with sinewy limb   125
to chase the shy thing strange and dim.
On terror's wings, like a butterfly
pursued by a sweeping bird on high,
she fluttered hither, darted there,
now poised, now flying through the air –   130
in vain. At last against a tree
she leaned and panted. Up leaped he.
No word of magic gasped with woe,
no elvish mystery she did know
or had entwined in raiment dark   135
availed against that hunter stark,
whose old immortal race and kind
no spells could ever turn or bind.
Huan alone that she ever met
she never in enchantment set   140
nor bound with spells. But loveliness
and gentle voice and pale distress
and eyes like starlight dimmed with tears
tamed him that death nor monster fears.

Lightly he lifted her, light he bore   145
his trembling burden. Never before
had Celegorm beheld such prey:
'What hast thou brought, good Huan say!
Dark-elvish maid, or wraith, or fay?
Not such to hunt we came today.'   150

''Tis Lúthien of Doriath,'
the maiden spake. 'A wandering path
far from the Wood-elves' sunny glades
she sadly winds, where courage fades
and hope grows faint.' And as she spoke   155
down she let slip her shadowy cloak,
and there she stood in silver and white.
Her starry jewels twinkled bright
in the risen sun like morning dew;
the lilies gold on mantle blue   160
gleamed and glistened. Who could gaze
on that fair face without amaze?
Long did Curufin look and stare.
The perfume of her flower-twined hair
her lissom limbs, her elvish face,   165
smote to his heart, and in that place
enchained he stood. 'O maiden royal,
O lady fair, wherefore in toil
and lonely journey dost thou go?
What tidings dread of war and woe   170
in Doriath have betid? Come tell!
For fortune thee hath guided well;

friends thou hast found,' said Celegorm,
and gazed upon her elvish form.

In his heart him thought her tale unsaid   175
he knew in part, but nought she read
of guile upon his smiling face.
    'Who are ye then, the lordly chase
that follow in this perilous wood?'
she asked; and answer seeming-good   180
they gave. 'Thy servants, lady sweet,
lords of Nargothrond thee greet,
and beg that thou wouldst with them go
back to their hills, forgetting woe
a season, seeking hope and rest.   185
And now to hear thy tale were best.'

    So Lúthien tells of Beren's deeds
in northern lands, how fate him leads
to Doriath, of Thingol's ire,
the dreadful errand that her sire   190
decreed for Beren. Sign nor word
the brothers gave that aught they heard
that touched them near. Of her escape
and the marvellous mantle she did shape
she lightly tells, but words her fail   195
recalling sunlight in the vale,
moonlight, starlight in Doriath,
ere Beren took the perilous path.
    'Need, too, my lords, there is of haste!

No time in ease and rest to waste.   200
For days are gone now since the queen
Melian whose heart hath vision keen,
looking afar me said in fear
that Beren lived in bondage drear.
The Lord of Wolves hath prisons dark,   205
chains and enchantments cruel and stark,
and there entrapped and languishing
doth Beren lie – if direr thing
hath not brought death or wish for death':
then gasping woe bereft her breath.   210

   To Celegorm said Curufin
apart and low: 'Now news we win
of Felagund, and now we know
wherefore Thû's creatures prowling go',
and other whispered counsels spake,   215
and showed him what answer he should make.
  'Lady,' said Celegorm, 'thou seest
we go a-hunting roaming beast,
and though our host is great and bold,
'tis ill prepared the wizard's hold   220
and island fortress to assault.
Deem not our hearts and wills at fault.
Lo! here our chase we now forsake
and home our swiftest road we take,
counsel and aid there to devise   225
for Beren that in anguish lies.'

To Nargothrond they with them bore
Lúthien, whose heart misgave her sore.
Delay she feared; each moment pressed
upon her spirit, yet she guessed   230
they rode not as swiftly as they might.
Ahead leaped Huan day and night,
and ever looking back his thought
was troubled. What his master sought,
and why he rode not like the fire,   235
why Curufin looked with hot desire
on Lúthien, he pondered deep,
and felt some evil shadow creep
of ancient curse o'er Elfinesse.
His heart was torn for the distress   240
of Beren bold, and Lúthien dear,
and Felagund who knew no fear.

In Nargothrond the torches flared
and feast and music were prepared.
Lúthien feasted not but wept.   245
Her ways were trammelled; closely kept
she might not fly. Her magic cloak
was hidden, and no prayer she spoke
was heeded, nor did answer find
her eager questions. Out of mind,   250
it seemed, were those afar that pined
in anguish and in dungeons blind
in prison and in misery.
Too late she knew their treachery.

It was not hid in Nargothrond   255
that Fëanor's sons her held in bond,
who Beren heeded not, and who
had little cause to wrest from Thû
the king they loved not and whose quest
old vows of hatred in their breast   260
had roused from sleep. Orodreth knew
the purpose dark they would pursue:
King Felagund to leave to die,
and with King Thingol's blood ally
the house of Fëanor by force   265
or treaty. But to stay their course
he had no power, for all his folk
the brothers had yet beneath their yoke,
and all yet listened to their word.
Orodreth's counsel no man heard;   270
their shame they crushed, and would not heed
the tale of Felagund's dire need.

   At Lúthien's feet there day by day
and at night beside her couch would stay
Huan the hound of Nargothrond;   275
and words she spoke to him soft and fond:
'O Huan, Huan, swiftest hound
that ever ran on mortal ground,
what evil doth thy lords possess
to heed no tears nor my distress?   280
Once Barahir all men above
good hounds did cherish and did love;

once Beren in the friendless North,
when outlaw wild he wandered forth,
had friends unfailing among things   285
with fur and fell and feathered wings,
and among the spirits that in stone
in mountains old and wastes alone
still dwell. But now nor Elf nor Man,
none save the child of Melian,   290
remembers him who Morgoth fought
and never to thraldom base was brought.'

    Nought said Huan; but Curufin
thereafter never near might win
to Lúthien, nor touch that maid,   295
but shrank from Huan's fangs afraid.
    Then on a night when autumn damp
was swathed about the glimmering lamp
of the wan moon, and fitful stars
were flying seen between the bars   300
of racing cloud, when winter's horn
already wound in trees forlorn,
lo! Huan was gone. Then Lúthien lay,
fearing new wrong, till just ere day,
when all is dead and breathless still   305
and shapeless fears the sleepless fill,
a shadow came along the wall.
Then something let there softly fall
her magic cloak beside her couch.
Trembling she saw the great hound crouch   310

beside her, heard a deep voice swell
as from a tower a far slow bell.

Thus Huan spake, who never before
had uttered words, and but twice more
did speak in elven tongue again: 315
'Lady beloved, whom all Men,
whom Elfinesse, and whom all things
with fur and fell and feathered wings
should serve and love – arise! away!
Put on thy cloak! Before the day   320
comes over Nargothrond we fly
to Northern perils, thou and I.'
And ere he ceased he counsel wrought
for achievement of the thing they sought.
There Lúthien listened in amaze,   325
and softly on Huan did she gaze.
Her arms about his neck she cast –
in friendship that to death should last.

★ ★ ★ ★ ★

In Wizard's Isle still lay forgot
enmeshed and tortured in that grot   330
cold, evil, doorless, without light,
and blank-eyed stared at endless night
two comrades. Now alone they were.
The others lived no more, but bare

their broken bones would lie and tell   335
how ten had served their master well.

   To Felagund then Beren said:
''Twere little loss if I were dead,
and I am minded all to tell,
and thus, perchance, from this dark hell   340
thy life to loose. I set thee free
from thine old oath, for more for me
hast thou endured than e'er was earned.'

   'A! Beren, Beren hast not learned
that promises of Morgoth's folk   345
are frail as breath. From this dark yoke
of pain shall neither ever go,
whether he learn our names or no,
with Thû's consent. Nay more, I think
yet deeper of torment we should drink,   350
knew he that son of Barahir
and Felagund were captive here,
and even worse if he should know
the dreadful errand we did go.'

   A devil's laugh they ringing heard   355
within their pit. 'True, true the word
I hear you speak,' a voice then said.
''Twere little loss if he were dead,
the outlaw mortal. But the king,

the Elf undying, many a thing   360
no man could suffer may endure.
Perchance, when what these walls immure
of dreadful anguish thy folk learn,
their king to ransom they will yearn
with gold and gem and high hearts cowed;   365
or maybe Celegorm the proud
will deem a rival's prison cheap,
and crown and gold himself will keep.
Perchance, the errand I shall know,
ere all is done, that ye did go.   370
The wolf is hungry, the hour is nigh;
no more need Beren wait to die.'

    The slow time passed. Then in the gloom
two eyes there glowed. He saw his doom,
Beren, silent, as his bonds he strained   375
beyond his mortal might enchained.
Lo! sudden there was rending sound
of chains that parted and unwound,
of meshes broken. Forth there leaped
upon the wolvish thing that crept   380
in shadow faithful Felagund,
careless of fang or mortal wound.
There in the dark they wrestled slow,
remorseless, snarling, to and fro,
teeth in flesh, gripe on throat,   385
fingers locked in shaggy coat,
spurning Beren who there lying

heard the werewolf gasping, dying.
Then a voice he heard: 'Farewell!
On earth I need no longer dwell,   390
friend and comrade, Beren bold.
My heart is burst, my limbs are cold.
Here all my power I have spent
to break my bonds, and dreadful rent
of poisoned teeth is in my breast.   395
I now must go to my long rest
neath Timbrenting in timeless halls
where drink the Gods, where the light falls
upon the shining sea.' Thus died the king,
as elvish harpers yet do sing.   400

   There Beren lies. His grief no tear,
his despair no horror has nor fear,
waiting for footsteps, a voice, for doom.
Silences profounder than the tomb
of long-forgotten kings, neath years   405
and sands uncounted laid on biers
and buried everlasting-deep,
slow and unbroken round him creep.

   The silences were sudden shivered
to silver fragments. Faint there quivered   410
a voice in song that walls of rock,
enchanted hill, and bar and lock,
and powers of darkness pierced with light.
He felt about him the soft night

of many stars, and in the air   415
were rustlings and a perfume rare;
the nightingales were in the trees,
slim fingers flute and viol seize
beneath the moon, and one more fair
than all there be or ever were   420
upon a lonely knoll of stone
in shimmering raiment danced alone.

    Then in his dream it seemed he sang,
and loud and fierce his chanting rang,
old songs of battle in the North,   425
of breathless deeds, of marching forth
to dare uncounted odds and break
great powers, and towers, and strong walls shake;
and over all the silver fire
that once Men named the Burning Briar,   430
the Seven Stars that Varda set
about the North, were burning yet,
a light in darkness, hope in woe,
the emblem vast of Morgoth's foe.

    'Huan, Huan! I hear a song   435
far under welling, far but strong
a song that Beren bore aloft.
I hear his voice, I have heard it oft
in dream and wandering.' Whispering low
thus Lúthien spake. On the bridge of woe   440
in mantle wrapped at dead of night

she sat and sang, and to its height
and to its depth the Wizard's Isle,
rock upon rock and pile on pile,
trembling echoed. The werewolves howled,   445
and Huan hidden lay and growled
watchful listening in the dark,
waiting for battle cruel and stark.

    Thû heard that voice, and sudden stood
wrapped in his cloak and sable hood   450
in his high tower. He listened long,
and smiled, and knew that elvish song.
'A! little Lúthien! What brought
the foolish fly to web unsought?
Morgoth! a great and rich reward   455
to me thou wilt owe when to thy hoard
this jewel is added.' Down he went,
and forth his messengers he sent.

    Still Lúthien sang. A creeping shape
with bloodred tongue and jaws agape   460
stole on the bridge; but she sang on
with trembling limbs and wide eyes wan.
The creeping shape leaped to her side,
and gasped, and sudden fell and died.
    And still they came, still one by one,   465
and each was seized, and there were none
returned with padding feet to tell
that a shadow lurketh fierce and fell

at the bridge's end, and that below
the shuddering waters loathing flow   470
o'er the grey corpses Huan killed.
    A mightier shadow slowly filled
the narrow bridge, a slavering hate,
an awful werewolf fierce and great:
pale Draugluin, the old grey lord   475
of wolves and beasts of blood abhorred,
that fed on flesh of Man and Elf
beneath the chair of Thû himself.

    No more in silence did they fight.
Howling and baying smote the night,   480
till back by the chair where he had fed
to die the werewolf yammering fled.
'Huan is there' he gasped and died,
and Thû was filled with wrath and pride.
'Before the mightiest he shall fall,   485
before the mightiest wolf of all',
so thought he now, and thought he knew
how fate long spoken should come true.
    Now there came slowly forth and glared
into the night a shape long-haired,   490
dank with poison, with awful eyes
wolvish, ravenous; but there lies
a light therein more cruel and dread
than ever wolvish eyes had fed.
More huge were its limbs, its jaws more wide,   495
its fangs more gleaming-sharp, and dyed

with venom, torment, and with death.
The deadly vapour of its breath
swept on before it. Swooning dies
the song of Lúthien, and her eyes   500
are dimmed and darkened with a fear,
cold and poisonous and drear.

Thus came Thû, as wolf more great
than e'er was seen from Angband's gate
to the burning south, than ever lurked   505
in mortal lands or murder worked.
Sudden he sprang, and Huan leaped
aside in shadow. On he swept
to Lúthien lying swooning faint.
To her drowning senses came the taint   510
of his foul breathing, and she stirred;
dizzily she spake a whispered word,
her mantle brushed across his face.
He stumbled staggering in his pace.
Out leaped Huan. Back he sprang.   515
Beneath the stars there shuddering rang
the cry of hunting wolves at bay,
the tongue of hounds that fearless slay.
Backward and forth they leaped and ran
feinting to flee, and round they span,   520
and bit and grappled, and fell and rose.
    Then suddenly Huan holds and throws
his ghastly foe; his throat he rends,
choking his life. Not so it ends.

From shape to shape, from wolf to worm,   525
from monster to his own demon form,
Thû changes, but that desperate grip
he cannot shake, nor from it slip.
No wizardry, nor spell, nor dart,
no fang, nor venom, nor devil's art   530
could harm that hound that hart and boar
had hunted once in Valinor.

   Nigh the foul spirit Morgoth made
and bred of evil shuddering strayed
from its dark house, when Lúthien rose   535
and shivering looked upon his throes.

   'O demon dark, O phantom vile
of foulness wrought, of lies and guile,
here shalt thou die, thy spirit roam
quaking back to thy master's home   540
his scorn and fury to endure;
thee he will in the bowels immure
of groaning earth, and in a hole
everlastingly thy naked soul
shall wail and gibber – this shall be   545
unless the keys thou render me
of thy black fortress, and the spell
that bindeth stone to stone thou tell,
and speak the words of opening.'

With gasping breath and shuddering   550
he spake, and yielded as he must,
and vanquished betrayed his master's trust.

   Lo! by the bridge a gleam of light,
like stars descended from the night
to burn and tremble here below.   555
There wide her arms did Lúthien throw,
and called aloud with voice as clear
as still at whiles may mortal hear
long elvish trumpets o'er the hill
echo, when all the world is still.   560
   The dawn peered over mountains wan;
their grey heads silent looked thereon.
The hill trembled; the citadel
crumbled, and all its towers fell;
the rocks yawned and the bridge broke,   565
and Sirion spumed in sudden smoke.
   Like ghosts the owls were flying seen
hooting in the dawn, and bats unclean
went skimming dark through the cold airs
shrieking thinly to find new lairs   570
in Deadly Nightshade's branches dread.
The wolves whimpering and yammering fled
like dusky shadows. Out there creep
pale forms and ragged as from sleep.
crawling, and shielding blinded eyes: 575
the captives in fear and in surprise

from dolour long in clinging night
beyond all hope set free to light.

A vampire shape with pinions vast
screeching leaped from the ground, and passed,   580
its dark blood dripping on the trees;
and Huan neath him lifeless sees
a wolvish corpse – for Thû had flown
to Taur-na-Fuin, a new throne
and darker stronghold there to build.   585
    The captives came and wept and shrilled
their piteous cries of thanks and praise.
But Lúthien anxious-gazing stays.
Beren comes not. At length she said:
'Huan, Huan, among the dead   590
must we then find him whom we sought,
for love of whom we toiled and fought?'
    Then side by side from stone to stone
o'er Sirion they climbed. Alone
unmoving they him found, who mourned   595
by Felagund, and never turned
to see what feet drew halting nigh.

'A! Beren, Beren!' came her cry,
'almost too late have I thee found?
Alas! that here upon the ground   600
the noblest of the noble race
in vain thy anguish doth embrace!
Alas! in tears that we should meet

who once found meeting passing sweet!'
    Her voice such love and longing filled   605
he raised his eyes, his mourning stilled,
and felt his heart new-turned to flame
for her that through peril to him came.

    'O Lúthien, O Lúthien,
more fair than any child of Men,   610
O loveliest maid of Elfinesse,
what might of love did thee possess
to bring thee here to terror's lair!
O lissom limbs and shadowy hair,
O flower-entwinéd brows so white,   615
O slender hands in this new light!'

    She found his arms and swooned away
just at the rising of the day.

*****

Songs have recalled the Elves have sung
in old forgotten elven tongue   620
how Lúthien and Beren strayed
by the banks of Sirion. Many a glade
they filled with joy, and there their feet
passed by lightly, and days were sweet.
Though winter hunted through the wood   625
still flowers lingered where she stood.
Tinúviel! Tinúviel!

the birds are unafraid to dwell
and sing beneath the peaks of snow
where Beren and where Lúthien go.   630

The isle in Sirion they left behind;
but there on hill-top might one find
a green grave, and a stone set,
and there there lie the white bones yet
of Felagund, of Finrod's son –   635
unless that land is changed and gone,
or foundered in unfathomed seas,
while Felagund laughs beneath the trees
in Valinor, and comes no more
to this grey world of tears and war.   640

To Nargothrond no more he came;
but thither swiftly ran the fame,
of their king dead, of Thû o'erthrown,
of the breaking of the towers of stone.
For many now came home at last   645
who long ago to shadow passed;
and like a shadow had returned
Huan the hound, and scant had earned
or praise or thanks of master wroth;
yet loyal he was, though he was loath.   650
The halls of Narog clamours fill
that vainly Celegorm would still.
There men bewailed their fallen king,
crying that a maiden dared that thing

which sons of Fëanor would not do.   655
'Let us slay these faithless lords untrue!'
the fickle folk now loudly cried
with Felagund who would not ride.
Orodreth spake: 'The kingdom now
is mine alone. I will allow   660
no spilling of kindred blood by kin.
But bread nor rest shall find herein
these brothers who have set at nought
the house of Finrod.' They were brought.
Scornful, unbowed, and unashamed   665
stood Celegorm. In his eye there flamed
a light of menace. Curufin
smiled with his crafty mouth and thin.

   'Be gone for ever – ere the day
shall fall into the sea. Your way   670
shall never lead you hither more,
nor any son of Fëanor;
nor ever after shall be bond
of love twixt yours and Nargothrond.'

   'We will remember it,' they said,   675
and turned upon their heels, and sped,
and took their horses and such folk
as still them followed. Nought they spoke
but sounded horns, and rode like fire,
and went away in anger dire.   680

Towards Doriath the wanderers now
were drawing nigh. Though bare the bough,
though cold the wind, and grey the grasses
through which the hiss of winter passes,
they sang beneath the frosty sky   685
uplifted o'er them pale and high.
They came to Mindeb's narrow stream
that from the hills doth leap and gleam
by western borders where begin
the spells of Melian to fence in   690
King Thingol's land, and stranger steps
to wind bewildered in their webs.

There sudden sad grew Beren's heart:
'Alas, Tinúviel, here we part
and our brief song together ends,   695
and sundered ways each lonely wends!'

'Why part we here? What dost thou say,
just at the dawn of brighter day?'

'For safe thou'rt come to borderlands
o'er which in the keeping of the hands   700
of Melian thou wilt walk at ease
and find thy home and well-loved trees.'

'My heart is glad when the fair trees
far off uprising grey it sees
of Doriath inviolate.   705

Yet Doriath my heart did hate,
and Doriath my feet forsook,
my home, my kin. I would not look
on grass nor leaf there evermore
without thee by me. Dark the shore   710
of Esgalduin the deep and strong!
Why there alone forsaking song
by endless waters rolling past
must I then hopeless sit at last,
and gaze at waters pitiless   715
in heartache and in loneliness?'

'For never more to Doriath
can Beren find the winding path,
though Thingol willed it or allowed;
for to thy father there I vowed   720
to come not back save to fulfill
the quest of the shining Silmaril,
and win by valour my desire.
"Not rock nor steel nor Morgoth's fire
nor all the power of Elfinesse,   725
shall keep the gem I would possess":
thus swore I once of Lúthien
more fair than any child of Men.
My word, alas! I must achieve,
though sorrow pierce and parting grieve.'   730

'Then Lúthien will not go home,
but weeping in the woods will roam,

nor peril heed, nor laughter know.
And if she may not by thee go
against thy will thy desperate feet 735
she will pursue, until they meet,
Beren and Lúthien, love once more
on earth or on the shadowy shore.'

 'Nay, Lúthien, most brave of heart,
thou makest it more hard to part. 740
Thy love me drew from bondage drear,
but never to that outer fear,
that darkest mansion of all dread,
shall thy most blissful light be led.'

 'Never, never!' he shuddering said. 745
But even as in his arms she pled,
a sound came like a hurrying storm.
There Curufin and Celegorm
in sudden tumult like the wind
rode up. The hooves of horses dinned 750
loud on the earth. In rage and haste
madly northward they now raced
the path twixt Doriath to find
and the shadows dreadly dark entwined
of Taur-na-fuin. That was their road 755
most swift to where their kin abode
in the east, where Himling's watchful hill
o'er Aglon's gorge hung tall and still.

They saw the wanderers. With a shout
straight on them swung their hurrying rout   760
as if neath maddened hooves to rend
the lovers and their love to end.
But as they came their horses swerved
with nostrils wide and proud necks curved;
Curufin, stooping, to saddlebow   765
with mighty arm did Lúthien throw,
and laughed. Too soon; for there a spring
fiercer than tawny lion-king
maddened with arrows barbéd smart,
greater than any hornéd hart   770
that hounded to a gulf leaps o'er,
there Beren gave, and with a roar
leaped on Curufin; round his neck
his arms entwined, and all to wreck
both horse and rider fell to ground;   775
and there they fought without a sound.
Dazed in the grass did Lúthien lie
beneath bare branches and the sky;
the Gnome felt Beren's fingers grim
close on his throat and strangle him,   780
and out his eyes did start, and tongue
gasping from his mouth there hung.

    Up rode Celegorm with his spear,
and bitter death was Beren near.
With elvish steel he nigh was slain   785
whom Lúthien won from hopeless chain,
but baying Huan sudden sprang

before his master's face with fang
white-gleaming, and with bristling hair,
as if he on boar or wolf did stare.   790
    The horse in terror leaped aside,
and Celegorm in anger cried:
'Curse thee, thou baseborn dog, to dare
against thy master teeth to bare!'
But dog nor horse nor rider bold   795
would venture near the anger cold
of mighty Huan fierce at bay.
Red were his jaws. They shrank away,
and fearful eyed him from afar:
nor sword nor knife, nor scimitar,   800
no dart of bow, nor cast of spear,
master nor man did Huan fear.

    There Curufin had left his life,
had Lúthien not stayed that strife.
Waking she rose and softly cried   805
standing distressed at Beren's side:
'Forbear thy anger now, my lord!
nor do the work of Orcs abhorred;
for foes there be of Elfinesse,
unnumbered, and they grow not less,   810
while here we war by ancient curse
distraught, and all the world to worse
decays and crumbles. Make thy peace!'

    Then Beren did Curufin release;
but took his horse and coat of mail   815

and took his knife there gleaming pale,
hanging sheathless, wrought of steel.
No flesh could leeches ever heal
that point had pierced; for long ago
the dwarves had made it, singing slow   820
enchantments, where their hammers fell
in Nogrod ringing like a bell.
Iron as tender wood it cleft,
and sundered mail like woollen weft.
But other hands its haft now held;   825
its master lay by mortal felled.
Beren uplifting him, far him flung,
and cried 'Begone!', with stinging tongue;
'Begone! thou renegade and fool,
and let thy lust in exile cool!   830
Arise and go, and no more work
like Morgoth's slaves or curséd Orc;
and deal, proud son of Fëanor,
in deeds more proud than heretofore!'
Then Beren led Lúthien away,   835
while Huan still there stood at bay.

    'Farewell,' cried Celegorm the fair.
'Far get you gone! And better were
to die forhungered in the waste
than wrath of Fëanor's sons to taste,   840
that yet may reach o'er dale and hill.
No gem, nor maid, nor Silmaril
shall ever long in thy grasp lie!

We curse thee under cloud and sky,
we curse thee from rising unto sleep!   845
Farewell!' He swift from horse did leap,
his brother lifted from the ground;
then bow of yew with gold wire bound
he strung, and shaft he shooting sent,
as heedless hand in hand they went;   850
a dwarvish dart and cruelly hooked.
They never turned nor backward looked.
Loud bayed Huan, and leaping caught
the speeding arrow. Quick as thought
another followed deadly singing;   855
but Beren had turned, and sudden springing
defended Lúthien with his breast.
Deep sank the dart in flesh to rest.
He fell to earth. They rode away,
and laughing left him as he lay;   860
yet spurred like wind in fear and dread
of Huan's pursuing anger red.
Though Curufin with bruised mouth laughed,
yet later of that dastard shaft
was tale and rumour in the North,   865
and Men remembered at the Marching Forth,
and Morgoth's will its hatred helped.

    Thereafter never hound was whelped
would follow horn of Celegorm
or Curufin. Though in strife and storm,   870
though all their house in ruin red

went down, thereafter laid his head
Huan no more at that lord's feet,
but followed Lúthien, brave and fleet.
Now sank she weeping at the side   875
of Beren, and sought to stem the tide
of welling blood that flowed there fast.
The raiment from his breast she cast;
from shoulder plucked the arrow keen;
his wound with tears she washed it clean.   880
    Then Huan came and bore a leaf,
of all the herbs of healing chief,
that evergreen in woodland glade
there grew with broad and hoary blade.
The powers of all grasses Huan knew,   885
who wide did forest-paths pursue.
Therewith the smart he swift allayed,
while Lúthien murmuring in the shade
the staunching song that Elvish wives
long years had sung in those sad lives   890
of war and weapons, wove o'er him.

    The shadows fell from mountains grim.
Then sprang about the darkened North
the Sickle of the Gods, and forth
each star there stared in stony night   895
radiant, glistering cold and white.
But on the ground there is a glow,
a spark of red that leaps below:
under woven boughs beside a fire

175

of crackling wood and sputtering briar   900
there Beren lies in browsing deep,
walking and wandering in sleep.
Watchful bending o'er him wakes
a maiden fair; his thirst she slakes,
his brow caresses, and softly croons   905
a song more potent than in runes
or leeches' lore hath since been writ.
Slowly the nightly watches flit.
The misty morning crawleth grey
from dusk to the reluctant day.   910

　　Then Beren woke and opened eyes,
and rose and cried: 'Neath other skies,
in lands more awful and unknown,
I wandered long, methought, alone
to the deep shadow where the dead dwell;   915
but ever a voice that I knew well,
like bells, like viols, like harps, like birds,
like music moving without words,
called me, called me through the night,
enchanted drew me back to light!   920
Healed the wound, assuaged the pain!
Now are we come to morn again,
new journeys once more lead us on –
to perils whence may life be won,
hardly for Beren; and for thee   925
a waiting in the wood I see
beneath the trees of Doriath,

while ever follow down my path
the echoes of thine elvish song,
where hills are haggard and roads are long.'   930

       'Nay, now no more we have for foe
dark Morgoth only, but in woe,
in wars and feuds of Elfinesse
thy quest is bound; and death, no less,
for thee and me, for Huan bold   935
the end of weird of yore foretold,
all this I bode shall follow swift;
if thou go on. Thy hand shall lift
and lay on Thingol's lap the dire
and flaming jewel, Fëanor's fire,   940
never, never! A why then go?
Why turn we not from fear and woe
beneath the trees to walk and roam
roofless, with all the world as home,
over mountains, beside the seas,   945
 in the sunlight, in the breeze?'

       Thus long they spoke with heavy hearts;
and yet not all her elvish arts
nor lissom arms, nor shining eyes
as tremulous stars in rainy skies,   950
nor tender lips, enchanted voice,
his purpose bent or swayed his choice.
Never to Doriath would he fare
save guarded fast to leave her there;

never to Nargothrond would go   955
with her, lest there came war and woe;
and never would in the world untrod
to wander suffer her, worn, unshod
roofless and restless, whom he drew
with love from the hidden realms she knew.   960
'For Morgoth's power is now awake;
already hill and dale doth shake,
the hunt is up, the prey is wild:
a maiden lost, an elven child.
Now Orcs and phantoms prowl and peer   965
from tree to tree, and fill with fear
each shade and hollow. Thee they seek!
At thought thereof my hope grows weak,
my heart is chilled. I curse mine oath,
I curse the fate that joined us both   970
and snared thy feet in my sad doom
of flight and wandering in the gloom!
Now let us haste, and ere the day
be fallen, take our swiftest way,
till o'er the marches of thy land   975
beneath the beech and oak we stand,
in Doriath, fair Doriath
whither no evil finds the path,
powerless to pass the listening leaves
that droop upon those forest-eaves.'   980

Then to his will she seeming bent.
Swiftly to Doriath they went,
and crossed its borders. There they stayed

resting in deep and mossy glade;
there lay they sheltered from the wind   985
under mighty beeches silken-skinned,
and sang of love that still shall be,
though earth be foundered under sea,
and sundered here for evermore
shall meet upon the Western Shore.   990

  One morning as asleep she lay
upon the moss, as though the day
too bitter were for gentle flower
to open in a sunless hour,
Beren arose and kissed her hair,   995
and wept, and softly left her there.
  'Good Huan,' said he, 'guard her well!
In leafless field no asphodel,
in thorny thicket never a rose
forlorn, so frail and fragrant blows.   1000
Guard her from wind and frost, and hide
from hands that seize and cast aside;
keep her from wandering and woe,
for pride and fate now make me go.'

  The horse he took and rode away,   1005
nor dared to turn; but all that day
with heart as stone he hastened forth
and took the paths toward the North.

*****

Once wide and smooth a plain was spread,
where King Fingolfin proudly led   1010
his silver armies on the green,
his horses white, his lances keen;
his helmets tall of steel were hewn,
his shields were shining as the moon.

    There trumpets sang both long and loud,   1015
and challenge rang unto the cloud
that lay on Morgoth's northern tower,
while Morgoth waited for his hour.

    Rivers of fire at dead of night
in winter lying cold and white   1020
upon the plain burst forth, and high
the red was mirrored in the sky.
From Hithlum's walls they saw the fire,
the steam and smoke in spire on spire
leap up, till in confusion vast   1025
the stars were choked. And so it passed,
the mighty field, and turned to dust,
to drifting sand and yellow rust,
to thirsty dunes where many bones
lay broken among barren stones.   1030
    Dor-na-Fauglith, Land of Thirst,
they after named it, waste accurst,
the raven-haunted roofless grave
of many fair and many brave.
Thereon the stony slopes look forth   1035
from Deadly Nightshade falling north,

from sombre pines with pinions vast,
black-plumed and drear, as many a mast
of sable-shrouded ships of death
slow wafted on a ghostly breath.   1040

    Thence Beren grim now gazes out
across the dunes and shifting drought,
and sees afar the frowning towers
where thunderous Thangorodrim lowers.
    The hungry horse there drooping stood,   1045
proud Gnomish steed; it feared the wood;
upon the haunted ghastly plain
no horse would ever stride again.
'Good steed of master ill,' he said,
'farewell now here! Lift up thy head,   1050
and get thee gone to Sirion's vale
back as we came, past island pale
where Thû once reigned, to waters sweet
and grasses long about thy feet.
And if Curufin no more thou find,   1055
grieve not! but free with hart and hind
go wander, leaving work and war,
and dream thee back in Valinor,
whence came of old thy mighty race
from Tavros' mountain-fencéd chase.'   1060
    There still sat Beren, and he sang
and loud his lonely singing rang.
Though Orcs should hear, or wolf a-prowl,
or any of the creatures foul

within the shade that slunk and stared   1065
of Taur-na-Fuin, nought he cared
who now took leave of light and day,
grim-hearted, bitter, fierce and fey.

'Farewell now here, ye leaves of trees,
your music in the morning-breeze!   1070
Farewell now blade and bloom and grass
that see the changing seasons pass;
ye waters murmuring over stone,
and meres that silent stand alone!
Farewell now mountain, vale, and plain!   1075
Farewell now wind and frost and rain,
and mist and cloud, and heaven's air;
ye star and moon so blinding-fair
that still shall look down from the sky
on the wide earth, though Beren die –   1080
though Beren die not, and yet deep,
deep, whence comes of those that weep
no dreadful echo, lie and choke
in everlasting dark and smoke.
'Farewell sweet earth and northern sky,   1085
for ever blest, since here did lie,
and here with lissom limbs did run
beneath the moon, beneath the sun,
Lúthien Tinúviel
more fair than mortal tongue can tell.   1090
Though all to ruin fell the world,
and were dissolved and backward hurled

unmade into the old abyss,
yet were its making good, for this –
the dawn, the dusk, the earth, the sea –   1095
that Lúthien on a time should be!'

   His blade he lifted high in hand,
and challenging alone did stand
before the threat of Morgoth's power;
and dauntless cursed him, hall and tower,   1100
o'ershadowing hand and grinding foot,
beginning, end, and crown and root;
then turned to strike forth down the slope
abandoning fear, forsaking hope.

   'A, Beren, Beren!' came a sound,   1105
'almost too late have I thee found!
O proud and fearless hand and heart,
not yet farewell, not yet we part!
Not thus do those of elven race
forsake the love that they embrace.   1110
A love is mine, as great a power
as thine, to shake the gate and tower
of death with challenge weak and frail
that yet endures, and will not fail
nor yield, unvanquished were it hurled   1115
beneath the foundations of the world.
Beloved fool! escape to seek
from such pursuit; in might so weak
to trust not, thinking it well to save

from love thy loved, who welcomes grave   1120
and torment sooner than in guard
of kind intent to languish, barred,
wingless and helpless him to aid
for whose support her love was made!'

    Thus back to him came Lúthien: 1125
they met beyond the ways of Men;
upon the brink of terror stood
between the desert and the wood.
    He looked on her, her lifted face
beneath his lips in sweet embrace: 1130
'Thrice now mine oath I curse,' he said,
'that under shadow thee hath led!
But where is Huan, where the hound
to whom I trusted, whom I bound
by love of thee to keep thee well   1135
from deadly wandering into hell?'

    'I know not! But good Huan's heart
is wiser, kinder, than thou art,
grim lord, more open unto prayer!
Yet long and long I pleaded there,   1140
until he brought me, as I would,
upon thy trail – a palfrey good
would Huan make, of flowing pace:
thou wouldst have laughed to see us race,
as Orc on werewolf ride like fire   1145

night after night through fen and mire,
through waste and wood! But when I heard
thy singing clear – (yea, every word
of Lúthien one rashly cried,
and listening evil fierce defied) –,   1150
he set me down, and sped away;
but what he would I cannot say.'

    Ere long they knew, for Huan came,
his great breath panting, eyes like flame,
in fear lest her whom he forsook   1155
to aid some hunting evil took
ere he was nigh. Now there he laid
before their feet, as dark as shade,
two grisly shapes that he had won
from that tall isle in Sirion: 1160
a wolfhame huge – its savage fell
was long and matted, dark the spell
that drenched the dreadful coat and skin;
the werewolf cloak of Draugluin;
the other was a batlike garb   1165
with mighty fingered wings, a barb
like iron nail at each joint's end –
such wings as their dark cloud extend
against the moon, when in the sky
from Deadly Nightshade screeching fly   1170
Thû's messengers.
                        'What hast thou brought,

good Huan? What thy hidden thought?
Of trophy of prowess and strong deed,
when Thû thou vanquishedst, what need
here in the waste?' Thus Beren spoke,   1175
and once more words in Huan woke:
his voice was like the deeptoned bells
that ring in Valmar's citadels:

   'Of one fair gem thou must be thief,
Morgoth's or Thingol's, loath or lief;   1180
thou must here choose twixt love and oath!
If vow to break is still thee loath,
then Lúthien must either die
alone, or death with thee defie
beside thee, marching on your fate   1185
that hidden before you lies in wait.
Hopeless the quest, but not yet mad,
unless thou, Beren, run thus clad
in mortal raiment, mortal hue,
witless and redeless, death to woo.   1190
   'Lo! good was Felagund's device,
but may be bettered, if advice
of Huan ye will dare to take,
and swift a hideous change will make
to forms most curséd, foul and vile,   1195
of werewolf of the Wizard's Isle,
of monstrous bat's envermined fell
with ghostly clawlike wings of hell.
   'To such dark straits, alas! now brought

are ye I love, for whom I fought.   1200
Nor further with you can I go –
whoever did a great hound know
in friendship at a werewolf's side
to Angband's grinning portals stride?
Yet my heart tells that at the gate   1205
what there ye find, 'twill be my fate
myself to see, though to that door
my feet shall bear me nevermore.
Darkened is hope and dimmed my eyes,
I see not clear what further lies;   1210
yet maybe backwards leads your path
beyond all hope to Doriath,
and thither, perchance, we three shall wend,
and meet again before the end.'

    They stood and marvelled thus to hear   1215
his mighty tongue so deep and clear;
then sudden he vanished from their sight
even at the onset of the night.

    His dreadful counsel then they took,
and their own gracious forms forsook;   1220
in werewolf fell and batlike wing
prepared to robe them, shuddering.
    With elvish magic Lúthien wrought,
lest raiment foul with evil fraught
to dreadful madness drive their hearts;   1225
and there she wrought with elvish arts

a strong defence, a binding power,
singing until the midnight hour.

   Swift as the wolvish coat he wore,
Beren lay slavering on the floor,   1230
redtongued and hungry; but there lies
a pain and longing in his eyes,
a look of horror as he sees
a batlike form crawl to its knees
and drag its creased and creaking wings.   1235
Then howling under moon he springs
fourfooted, swift, from stone to stone
from hill to plain – but not alone:
a dark shape down the slope doth skim,
and wheeling flitters over him.   1240

   Ashes and dust and thirsty dune
withered and dry beneath the moon,
under the cold and shifting air
sifting and sighing, bleak and bare;
of blistered stones and gasping sand,   1245
of splintered bones was built that land,
o'er which now slinks with powdered fell
and hanging tongue a shape of hell.
   Many parching leagues lay still before
when sickly day crept back once more;   1250
many choking miles lay stretched ahead
when shivering night once more was spread
with doubtful shadow and ghostly sound

that hissed and passed o'er dune and mound.
    A second morning in cloud and reek   1255
struggled, when stumbling, blind and weak,
a wolvish shape came staggering forth
and reached the foothills of the North;
upon its back there folded lay
a crumpled thing that blinked at day.   1260

    The rocks were reared like bony teeth,
and claws that grasped from opened sheath,
on either side the mournful road
that onward led to that abode
far up within the Mountain dark   1265
with tunnels drear and portals stark.
    They crept within a scowling shade
and cowering darkly down them laid.
Long lurked they there beside the path,
and shivered, dreaming of Doriath,   1270
of laughter and music and clean air,
in fluttered leaves birds singing fair.
    They woke, and felt the trembling sound,
the beating echo far underground
shake beneath them, the rumour vast   1275
of Morgoth's forges; and aghast
they heard the stamp of stony feet
that shod with iron went down that street:
the Orcs went forth to rape and war,
and Balrog captains marched before.   1280

They stirred, and under cloud and shade
at eve stepped forth, and no more stayed;
as dark things on dark errand bent
up the long slopes in haste they went.
Ever the sheer cliffs rose beside,   1285
where birds of carrion sat and cried;
and chasms black and smoking yawned,
whence writhing serpent-shapes were spawned;
until at last in that huge gloom,
heavy as overhanging doom,   1290
that weighs on Thangorodrim's foot
like thunder at the mountain's root,
they came, as to a sombre court
walled with great towers, fort on fort
of cliffs embattled, to that last plain   1295
that opens, abysmal and inane
before he final topless wall
of Bauglir's immeasurable hall,
whereunder looming awful waits
the gigantic shadow of his gates.   1300

* * * * *

In that vast shadow once of yore
Fingolfin stood: his shield he bore
with field of heaven's blue and star
of crystal shining pale afar.
In overmastering wrath and hate   1305
desperate he smote upon that gate,

the Gnomish king, there standing lone,
while endless fortresses of stone
engulfed the thin clear ringing keen
of silver horn on baldric green.   1310
His hopeless challenge dauntless cried
Fingolfin there: 'Come, open wide,
dark king, your ghastly brazen doors!
Come forth, whom earth and heaven abhors!
Come forth, O monstrous craven lord   1315
and fight with thine own hand and sword,
thou wielder of hosts of banded thralls,
thou tyrant leaguered with strong walls,
thou foe of Gods and elvish race!
I wait thee here. Come! Show thy face!'   1320

   Then Morgoth came. For the last time
in those great wars he dared to climb
from subterranean throne profound,
the rumour of his feet a sound
of rumbling earthquake underground.   1325
Black-armoured, towering, iron-crowned
he issued forth; his mighty shield
a vast unblazoned sable field
with shadow like a thundercloud;
and o'er the gleaming king it bowed,   1330
as huge aloft like mace he hurled
that hammer of the underworld,
Grond. Clanging to ground it tumbled
down like a thunder-bolt, and crumbled

the rocks beneath it; smoke up-started,   1335
a pit yawned, and a fire darted.

    Fingolfin like a shooting light
beneath a cloud, a stab of white,
sprang then aside, and Ringil drew
like ice that gleameth cold and blue,   1340
his sword devised of elvish skill
to pierce the flesh with deadly chill.
With seven wounds it rent his foe,
and seven mighty cries of woe
rang in the mountains, and the earth quook,   1345
and Angband's trembling armies shook.
    Yet Orcs would after laughing tell
of the duel at the gates of hell;
though elvish song thereof was made
ere this but one – when sad was laid   1350
the mighty king in barrow high,
and Thorondor, Eagle of the sky,
the dreadful tidings brought and told
to mourning Elfinesse of old.
Thrice was Fingolfin with great blows   1355
to his knees beaten, thrice he rose
still leaping up beneath the cloud
aloft to hold star-shining, proud,
his stricken shield, his sundered helm,
that dark nor might could overwhelm   1360
till all the earth was burst and rent
in pits about him. He was spent.

His feet stumbled. He fell to wreck
upon the ground, and on his neck
a foot like rooted hills was set,   1365
and he was crushed – not conquered yet;
one last despairing stroke he gave:
the mighty foot pale Ringil clave
about the heel, and black the blood
gushed as from smoking fount in flood.   1370
    Halt goes for ever from that stroke
great Morgoth; but the king he broke,
and would have hewn and mangled thrown
to wolves devouring. Lo! from throne
that Manwë bade him build on high,   1375
on peak unscaled beneath the sky,
Morgoth to watch, now down there swooped
Thorondor the King of Eagles, stooped,
and rending beak of gold he smote
in Bauglir's face, then up did float   1380
on pinions thirty fathoms wide
bearing away, though loud they cried,
the mighty corse, the Elven-king;
and where the mountains make a ring
far to the south about that plain   1385
where after Gondolin did reign,
embattled city, at great height
upon a dizzy snowcap white
in mounded cairn the mighty dead
he laid upon the mountain's head.   1390
Never Orc nor demon after dared

BEREN AND LÚTHIEN

that pass to climb, o'er which there stared
Fingolfin's high and holy tomb,
till Gondolin's appointed doom.

    Thus Bauglir earned the furrowed scar   1395
that his dark countenance doth mar,
and thus his limping gait he gained;
but afterward profound he reigned
darkling upon his hidden throne;
and thunderous paced his halls of stone,   1400
slow building there his vast design
the world in thraldom to confine.
Wielder of armies, lord of woe,
no rest now gave he slave or foe;
his watch and ward he thrice increased,   1405
his spies were sent from West to East
and tidings brought from all the North,
who fought, who fell; who ventured forth,
who wrought in secret; who had hoard;
if maid were fair or proud were lord;   1410
well nigh all things he knew, all hearts
well nigh enmeshed in evil arts.
    Doriath only, beyond the veil
woven by Melian, no assail
could hurt or enter; only rumour dim   1415
of things there passing came to him.
 A rumour loud and tidings clear
of other movements far and near
among his foes, and threat of war

from the seven sons of Fëanor,   1420
from Nargothrond, from Fingon still
gathering his armies under hill
and under tree in Hithlum's shade,
these daily came. He grew afraid
amidst his power once more; renown   1425
of Beren vexed his ears, and down
the aisléd forests there was heard
great Huan baying.

                Then came word
most passing strange of Lúthien
wild-wandering by wood and glen,   1430
and Thingol's purpose long he weighed,
and wondered, thinking of that maid
so fair, so frail. A captain dire,
Boldog, he sent with sword and fire
to Doriath's march; but battle fell   1435
sudden upon him; news to tell
never one returned of Boldog's host,
and Thingol humbled Morgoth's boast.
Then his heart with doubt and wrath was burned:
new tidings of dismay he learned,   1440
how Thû was o'erthrown and his strong isle
broken and plundered, how with guile
his foes now guile beset; and spies
he feared, till each Orc to his eyes
was half suspect. Still ever down   1445
the aisléd forests came renown

of Huan baying, hound of war
that Gods unleashed in Valinor.

    Then Morgoth of Huan's fate bethought
long-rumoured, and in dark he wrought.   1450
Fierce hunger-haunted packs he had
that in wolvish form and flesh were clad,
but demon spirits dire did hold;
and ever wild their voices rolled
in cave and mountain where they housed   1455
and endless snarling echoes roused.
From these a whelp he chose and fed
with his own hand on bodies dead,
on fairest flesh of Elves and Men,
till huge he grew and in his den   1460
no more could creep, but by the chair
of Morgoth's self would lie and glare,
nor suffer Balrog, Orc, nor beast
to touch him. Many a ghastly feast
he held beneath that awful throne   1465
rending flesh and gnawing bone.
There deep enchantment on him fell,
the anguish and the power of hell;
more great and terrible he became
with fire-red eyes and jaws aflame,   1470
with breath like vapours of the grave,
than any beast of wood or cave,
than any beast of earth or hell
that ever in any time befell,

surpassing all his race and kin,   1475
the ghastly tribe of Draugluin.

    Him Carcharoth, the Red Maw, name
the songs of Elves. Not yet he came
disastrous, ravening, from the gates
of Angband. There he sleepless waits;   1480
where those great portals threatening loom
his red eyes smoulder in the gloom,
his teeth are bare, his jaws are wide;
and none may walk, nor creep, nor glide,
nor thrust with power his menace past   1485
to enter Morgoth's dungeon vast.

    Now, lo! before his watchful eyes
a slinking shape he far descries
that crawls into the frowning plain
and halts at gaze, then on again   1490
comes stalking near, a wolvish shape
haggard, wayworn, with jaws agape;
and o'er it batlike in wide rings
a reeling shadow slowly wings.
Such shapes there oft were seen to roam,   1495
this land their native haunt and home;
and yet his mood with strange unease
is filled, and boding thoughts him seize.

    'What grievous terror, what dread guard
hath Morgoth set to wait, and barred   1500

his doors against all entering feet?
Long ways we have come at last to meet
the very maw of death that opes
between us and our quest! Yet hopes
we never had. No turning back!'   1505
Thus Beren speaks, as in his track
he halts and sees with werewolf eyes
afar the horror that there lies.
Then onward desperate he passed,
skirting the black pits yawning vast,   1510
where King Fingolfin ruinous fell
alone before the gates of hell.

    Before those gates alone they stood,
while Carcharoth in doubtful mood
glowered upon them, and snarling spoke,   1515
and echoes in the arches woke:
'Hail! Draugluin, my kindred's lord!
'Tis very long since hitherward
thou camest. Yea, 'tis passing strange
to see thee now: a grievous change   1520
is on thee, lord, who once so dire
so dauntless, and as fleet as fire,
ran over wild and waste, but now
with weariness must bend and bow!
'Tis hard to find the struggling breath   1525
when Huan's teeth as sharp as death
have rent the throat? What fortune rare
brings thee back living here to fare –

if Draugluin thou art? come near!
I would know more, and see thee clear!'   1530

    'Who art thou, hungry upstart whelp,
to bar my ways whom thou shouldst help?
I fare with hasty tidings new
to Morgoth from forest-haunting Thû.
Aside! for I must in; or go   1535
and swift my coming tell below!'

    Then up that doorward slowly stood,
eyes shining grim with evil mood,
uneasy growling: 'Draugluin,
if such thou be, now enter in!   1540
But what is this that crawls beside
slinking as if 'twould neath thee hide?
Though wingéd creatures to and fro
unnumbered pass here, all I know.
I know not this. Stay, vampire, stay!   1545
I like not thy kin nor thee. Come, say
what sneaking errand thee doth bring,
thou wingéd vermin, to the king!
Small matter, I doubt not, if thou stay
or enter, or if in my play   1550
I crush thee like a fly on wall,
or bite thy wings and let thee crawl.'

    Huge-stalking, noisome, close he came.
In Beren's eyes there gleamed a flame;

the hair upon his neck uprose.   1555
Nought may the fragrance fair enclose,
the odour of immortal flowers
in everlasting spring neath showers
that glitter silver in the grass
in Valinor. Where'er did pass   1560
Tinúviel, such air there went.
From that foul devil-sharpened scent
its sudden sweetness no disguise
enchanted dark to cheat the eyes
could keep, if near those nostrils drew   1565
snuffling in doubt. This Beren knew
upon the brink of hell prepared
for battle and death. There threatening stared
those dreadful shapes, in hatred both,
false Draugluin and Carcharoth   1570
when, lo! a marvel to behold:
some power, descended from of old,
from race divine beyond the West,
sudden Tinúviel possessed
like inner fire. The vampire dark   1575
she flung aside, and like a lark
cleaving through night to dawn she sprang,
while sheer, heart-piercing silver, rang
her voice, as those long trumpets keen
thrilling, unbearable, unseen   1580
in the cold aisles of morn. Her cloak
by white hands woven, like a smoke,
like all-bewildering, all-enthralling,

all-enfolding evening, falling
from lifted arms, as forth she stepped   1585
across those awful eyes she swept,
a shadow and a mist of dreams
whereon entangled starlight gleams.

   'Sleep, O unhappy, tortured thrall!
Thou woebegotten, fail and fall   1590
down, down from anguish, hatred, pain,
from lust, from hunger, bond and chain,
to that oblivion, dark and deep,
the well, the lightless pit of sleep!
For one brief hour escape the net,   1595
the dreadful doom of life forget!'

   His eyes were quenched, his limbs were loosed;
he fell like running steer that noosed
and tripped grows crashing to the ground.
Deathlike, moveless, without a sound   1600
outstretched he lay, as lightning stroke
had felled a huge o'ershadowing oak.

* * * * *

Into the vast and echoing gloom,
more dread than many-tunnelled tomb
in labyrinthine pyramid   1605
where everlasting death is hid
down awful corridors that wind

down to a menace dark enshrined;
down to the mountain's roots profound,
devoured, tormented, bored and ground   1610
by seething vermin spawned of stone;
down to the depths they went alone.
    The arch behind of twilit shade
they saw recede and dwindling fade;
the thunderous forges' rumour grew,   1615
a burning wind there roaring blew
foul vapours up from gaping holes.
Huge shapes there stood like carven trolls
enormous hewn of blasted rock
to forms that mortal likeness mock;   1620
monstrous and menacing, entombed,
at every turn they silent loomed
in fitful glares that leaped and died.
There hammers clanged, and tongues there cried
with sound like smitten stone; there wailed   1625
faint from far under, called and failed
amid the iron clink of chain
voices of captives put to pain.

    Loud rose a din of laughter hoarse,
self-loathing yet without remorse;   1630
loud came a singing harsh and fierce
like swords of terror souls to pierce.
Red was the glare through open doors
of firelight mirrored on brazen floors,
and up the arches towering clomb   1635

to glooms unguessed, to vaulted dome
swathed in wavering smokes and steams
stabbed with flickering lightning-gleams.
To Morgoth's hall, where dreadful feast
he held, and drank the blood of beast   1640
and lives of Men, they stumbling came:
their eyes were dazed with smoke and flame.
The pillars, reared like monstrous shores
to bear earth's overwhelming floors,
were devil-carven, shaped with skill   1645
such as unholy dreams doth fill:
they towered like trees into the air,
whose trunks are rooted in despair,
whose shade is death, whose fruit is bane,
whose boughs like serpents writhe in pain.   1650
    Beneath them ranged with spear and sword
stood Morgoth's sable-armoured horde:
the fire on blade and boss of shield
was red as blood on stricken field.
Beneath a monstrous column loomed   1655
the throne of Morgoth, and the doomed
and dying gasped upon the floor:
his hideous footstool, rape of war.
About him sat his awful thanes,
the Balrog-lords with fiery manes,   1660
redhanded, mouthed with fangs of steel;
devouring wolves were crouched at heel.
And o'er the host of hell there shone
with a cold radiance, clear and wan,

the Silmarils, the gems of fate,   1665
emprisoned in the crown of hate.

    Lo! through the grinning portals dread
sudden a shadow swoopéd and fled;
and Beren gasped – he lay alone,
with crawling belly on the stone: 1670
a form bat-wingéd, silent, flew
where the huge pillared branches grew,
amid the smokes and mounting steams.
And as on the margin of dark dreams
a dim-felt shadow unseen grows   1675
to cloud of vast unease, and woes
foreboded, nameless, roll like doom
upon the soul, so in that gloom
the voices fell, and laughter died
slow to silence many-eyed.   1680
A nameless doubt, a shapeless fear,
had entered in their caverns drear
and grew, and towered above them cowed,
hearing in heart the trumpets loud
of gods forgotten. Morgoth spoke,   1685
and thunderous the silence broke:
'Shadow, descend! And do not think
to cheat mine eyes! In vain to shrink
from thy Lord's gaze, or seek to hide.
My will by none may be defied.   1690
Hope nor escape doth here await
those that unbidden pass my gate.

Descend! ere anger blast thy wing,
thou foolish, frail, bat-shapen thing,
and yet not bat within! Come down!'   1695

    Slow-wheeling o'er his iron crown,
reluctantly, shivering and small,
Beren there saw the shadow fall,
and droop before the hideous throne,
a weak and trembling thing, alone.   1700
And as thereon great Morgoth bent
his darkling gaze, he shuddering went,
belly to earth, the cold sweat dank
upon his fell, and crawling shrank
beneath the darkness of that seat,   1705
beneath the shadow of those feet.
    Tinúviel spake, a shrill, thin, sound
piercing those silences profound:
'A lawful errand here me brought;
from Thû's dark mansions have I sought,   1710
from Taur-na-Fuin's shade I fare
to stand before thy mighty chair!'

    'Thy name, thou shrieking waif, thy name!
Tidings enough from Thû there came
but short while since. What would he now?   1715
Why send such messenger as thou?'

    'Thuringwethil I am, who cast
a shadow o'er the face aghast

of the sallow moon in the doomed land
of shivering Beleriand!'   1720

'Liar art thou, who shalt not weave
deceit before mine eyes. Now leave
thy form and raiment false, and stand
revealed, and delivered to my hand!'

There came a slow and shuddering change: 1725
the batlike raiment dark and strange
was loosed, and slowly shrank and fell
quivering. She stood revealed in hell.
About her slender shoulders hung
her shadowy hair, and round her clung   1730
her garment dark, where glimmered pale
the starlight caught in magic veil.
Dim dreams and faint oblivious sleep
fell softly thence, in dungeons deep
an odour stole of elven-flowers   1735
from elven-dells where silver showers
drip softly through the evening air;
and round there crawled with greedy stare
dark shapes of snuffling hunger dread.
    With arms upraised and drooping head   1740
then softly she began to sing
a theme of sleep and slumbering,
wandering, woven with deeper spell
than songs wherewith in ancient dell

Melian did once the twilight fill,   1745
profound and fathomless, and still.

 The fires of Angband flared and died,
smouldered into darkness; through the wide
and hollow halls there rolled unfurled
the shadows of the underworld.   1750
All movement stayed, and all sound ceased,
save vaporous breath of Orc and beast.
One fire in darkness still abode:
the lidless eyes of Morgoth glowed;
one sound the breathing silence broke: 1755
the mirthless voice of Morgoth spoke.

 'So Lúthien, so Lúthien,
a liar like all Elves and Men!
Yet welcome, welcome, to my hall!
I have a use for every thrall.   1760
What news of Thingol in his hole
shy lurking like a timid vole?
What folly fresh is in his mind
who cannot keep his offspring blind
from straying thus? or can devise   1765
no better counsel for his spies?'

 She wavered, and she stayed her song.
'The road,' she said, 'was wild and long,
but Thingol sent me not, nor knows

what way his rebellious daughter goes.   1770
Yet every road and path will lead
Northward at last, and here of need
I trembling come with humble brow,
and here before thy throne I bow;
for Lúthien hath many arts   1775
for solace sweet of kingly hearts.'

   'And here of need thou shalt remain
now, Lúthien, in joy or pain –
or pain, the fitting doom for all,
for rebel, thief, and upstart thrall.   1780
Why should ye not in our fate share
of woe and travail? Or should I spare
to slender limb and body frail
breaking torment? Of what avail
here dost thou deem thy babbling song   1785
and foolish laughter? Minstrels strong
are at my call. Yet I will give
a respite brief, a while to live,
a little while, though purchased dear,
to Lúthien the fair and clear,   1790
a pretty toy for idle hour.
In slothful gardens many a flower
like thee the amorous gods are used
honey-sweet to kiss, and cast then bruised
their fragrance loosing, under feet.   1795
But here we seldom find such sweet
amid our labours long and hard,

from godlike idleness debarred.
And who would not taste the honey-sweet
lying to lips, or crush with feet   1800
the soft cool tissue of pale flowers,
easing like gods the dragging hours?
A! curse the Gods! O hunger dire,
O blinding thirst's unending fire!
One moment shall ye cease, and slake   1805
your sting with morsel I here take!'

   In his eyes the fire to flame was fanned,
and forth he stretched his brazen hand.
Lúthien as shadow shrank aside.
'Not thus, O king! Not thus!' she cried,   1810
'do great lords hark to humble boon!
For every minstrel hath his tune;
and some are strong and some are soft
and each would bear his song aloft,
and each a little while be heard,   1815
though rude the note, and light the word.
But Lúthien hath cunning arts
for solace sweet of kingly hearts.
Now hearken!' And her wings she caught
then deftly up, and swift as thought   1820
slipped from his grasp, and wheeling round,
fluttering before his eyes, she wound
a mazy-wingéd dance, and sped
about his iron-crownéd head.
Suddenly her song began anew;   1825

and soft came dropping like a dew
down from on high in that domed hall
her voice bewildering, magical,
and grew to silver-murmuring streams
pale falling in dark pools in dreams.   1830

   She let her flying raiment sweep,
enmeshed with woven spells of sleep,
as round the dark void she ranged and reeled.
From wall to wall she turned and wheeled
in dance such as never Elf nor fay   1835
before devised, nor since that day;
than swallow swifter, than flittermouse
in dying light round darkened house
more silken-soft, more strange and fair
than sylphine maidens of the Air   1840
whose wings in Varda's heavenly hall
in rhythmic movement beat and fall.
   Down crumpled Orc, and Balrog proud;
all eyes were quenched, all heads were bowed;
the fires of heart and maw were stilled,   1845
and ever like a bird she thrilled
above a lightless world forlorn
in ecstasy enchanted borne.
   All eyes were quenched, save those that glared
in Morgoth's lowering brows, and stared   1850
in slowly wandering wonder round,
and slow were in enchantment bound.

Their will wavered, and their fire failed,
and as beneath his brows they paled,
the Silmarils like stars were kindled   1855
that in the reek of Earth had dwindled
escaping upwards clear to shine,
glistening marvellous in heaven's mine.

Then flaring suddenly they fell,
down, down upon the floors of hell.   1860
The dark and mighty head was bowed;
like mountain-top beneath a cloud
the shoulders foundered, the vast form
crashed, as in overwhelming storm
huge cliffs in ruin slide and fall;   1865
and prone lay Morgoth in his hall.
His crown there rolled upon the ground,
a wheel of thunder; then all sound
died, and a silence grew as deep
as were the heart of Earth asleep.   .   1870

Beneath the vast and empty throne
the adders lay like twisted stone,
the wolves like corpses foul were strewn;
and there lay Beren deep in swoon:
no thought, no dream nor shadow blind   1875
moved in the darkness of his mind.
     'Come forth, come forth! The hour hath knelled,
and Angband's mighty lord is felled!

Awake, awake! For we two meet
alone before the awful seat.'   1880
This voice came down into the deep
where he lay drowned in wells of sleep;
a hand flower-soft and flower-cool
passed o'er his face, and the still pool
of slumber quivered. Up then leaped   1885
his mind to waking; forth he crept.
The wolvish fell he flung aside
and sprang unto his feet, and wide
staring amid the soundless gloom
he gasped as one living shut in tomb.   1890
There to his side he felt her shrink,
felt Lúthien now shivering sink,
her strength and magic dimmed and spent,
and swift his arms about her went.

    Before his feet he saw amazed   1895
the gems of Fëanor, that blazed
with white fire glistening in the crown
of Morgoth's might now fallen down.
To move that helm of iron vast
no strength he found, and thence aghast   1900
he strove with fingers mad to wrest
the guerdon of their hopeless quest,
till in his heart there fell the thought
of that cold morn whereon he fought
with Curufin; then from his belt   1905

the sheathless knife he drew, and knelt,
and tried its hard edge, bitter-cold,
o'er which in Nogrod songs had rolled
of dwarvish armourers singing slow
to hammer-music long ago.   1910
Iron as tender wood it clove
and mail as woof of loom it rove.
The claws of iron that held the gem,
it bit them through and sundered them;
a Silmaril he clasped and held,   1915
and the pure radiance slowly welled
red glowing through the clenching flesh.
Again he stooped and strove afresh
one more of the holy jewels three
that Fëanor wrought of yore to free.   1920
But round those fires was woven fate;
not yet should they leave the halls of hate.
The dwarvish steel of cunning blade
by treacherous smiths of Nogrod made
snapped; then ringing sharp and clear   1925
in twain it sprang, and like a spear
or errant shaft the brow it grazed
of Morgoth's sleeping head, and dazed
their hearts with fear. For Morgoth groaned
with voice entombed, like wind that moaned   1930
in hollow caverns penned and bound.
There came a breath; a gasping sound
moved through the halls, as Orc and beast

turned in their dreams of hideous feast;
in sleep uneasy Balrogs stirred,   1935
and far above was faintly heard
an echo that in tunnels rolled,
a wolvish howling long and cold.

* * * * *

Up through the dark and echoing gloom
as ghosts from many-tunnelled tomb,   1940
up from the mountains' roots profound
and the vast menace underground,
their limbs aquake with deadly fear,
terror in eyes, and dread in ear,
together fled they, by the beat   1945
affrighted of their flying feet.

    At last before them far away
they saw the glimmering wraith of day,
the mighty archway of the gate –
and there a horror new did wait.   1950
Upon the threshold, watchful, dire,
his eyes new-kindled with dull fire,
towered Carcharoth, a biding doom:
his jaws were gaping like a tomb,
his teeth were bare, his tongue aflame;   1955
aroused he watched that no one came,
no flitting shade nor hunted shape,
seeking from Angband to escape.

Now past that guard what guile or might
could thrust from death into the light? 1960

  He heard afar their hurrying feet,
he snuffed an odour strange and sweet;
he smelled their coming long before
they marked the waiting threat at door.
His limbs he stretched and shook off sleep, 1965
then stood at gaze. With sudden leap
upon them as they sped he sprang,
and his howling in the arches rang.
  Too swift for thought his onset came,
too swift for any spell to tame; 1970
and Beren desperate then aside
thrust Lúthien, and forth did stride
unarmed, defenceless to defend
Tinúviel until the end.
With left he caught at hairy throat, 1975
with right hand at the eyes he smote –
his right, from which the radiance welled
of the holy Silmaril he held.
As gleam of swords in fire there flashed
the fangs of Carcharoth, and crashed 1980
together like a trap, that tore
the hand about the wrist, and shore
through brittle bone and sinew nesh,
devouring the frail mortal flesh;
and in that cruel mouth unclean 1985
engulfed the jewel's holy sheen.

An isolated page gives five further lines in the process of composition:

> Against the wall then Beren reeled
> but still with his left he sought to shield
> fair Lúthien, who cried aloud
> to see his pain, and down she bowed
> in anguish sinking to the ground.

With the abandonment, towards the end of 1931, of *The Lay of Leithian* at this point in the tale of Beren and Lúthien my father had very largely reached the final form *in narrative structure* – as represented in the published *Silmarillion.* Although, after the completion of his work on *The Lord of the Rings*, he made some extensive revisions to *The Lay of Leithian* as it had lain since 1931 (see the Appendix, p. 257), it seems certain that he never extended the story any further in verse, save for this passage found on a separate sheet headed 'a piece from the end of the poem'.

> Where the forest-stream went through the wood,
> and silent all the stems there stood
> of tall trees, moveless, hanging dark
> with mottled shadows on their bark
> above the green and gleaming river,
> there came through leaves a sudden shiver,
> a windy whisper through the still
> cool silences; and down the hill,
> as faint as a deep sleeper's breath,

an echo came as cold as death:
'Long are the paths, of shadow made
where no foot's print is ever laid,
over the hills, across the seas!
Far, far away are the Lands of Ease,
but the Land of the Lost is further yet,
where the Dead wait, while ye forget.
No moon is there, no voice, no sound
of beating heart; a sigh profound
once in each age as each age dies
alone is heard. Far, far it lies,
the Land of Waiting where the Dead sit,
in their thought's shadow, by no moon lit.'

THE QUENTA SILMARILLION

In the years that followed, my father turned to a new prose version of the history of the Elder Days, and that is found in a manuscript bearing the title *Quenta Silmarillion*, which I will refer to as 'QS'. Of intermediate texts between this and its predecessor the *Quenta Noldorinwa* (p. 103) there is now no trace, though they must have existed; but from the point where the story of Beren and Lúthien enters the *Silmarillion* history there are several largely incomplete drafts, owing to my father's long hesitation between longer and shorter versions of the legend. A fuller version, which may be called for this purpose 'QS I', was abandoned, on account of its length, at the point where King Felagund in Nargothrond gave the crown to Orodreth his brother (p. 109, extract from the *Quenta Noldorinwa*).

This was followed by a very rough draft of the whole story; and that was the basis of a second, 'short' version, 'QS II', preserved in the same manuscript as QS I. It was very largely from these two versions that I derived the story of Beren and Lúthien as told in the published *Silmarillion*.

The making of QS II was a work still in progress in 1937; but in that year there entered considerations altogether aloof from the history of the Elder Days. On 21 September *The Hobbit* was published by Allen and Unwin, and was an immediate success; but it brought with it great pressure on my father to write a further book about hobbits. In October he said in a letter to Stanley Unwin, the chairman of Allen and Unwin, that he was 'a little perturbed. I cannot think of anything more to say about *hobbits*. Mr Baggins seems to have exhibited so fully both the Took and the Baggins side of their nature. But I have only too much to say, and much already written, about the world into which the hobbit intruded.' He said that he wanted an opinion on the value of these writings on the subject of 'the world into which the hobbit intruded'; and he put together a collection of manuscripts and sent them off to Stanley Unwin on 15 November 1937. Included in the collection was QS II, which had reached the moment when Beren took into his hand the Silmaril which he had cut from Morgoth's crown.

Long afterwards I learned that the list made out at Allen and Unwin of the manuscripts in my father's consignment contained, in addition to *Farmer Giles of Ham*, *Mr Bliss*, and *The Lost Road*, two elements referred to as *Long Poem* and *The Gnomes Material*, titles which carry a suggestion of despair. Obviously the unwelcome manuscripts landed on the desk at Allen and Unwin without adequate explanation.

I have told in detail the strange story of this consignment in an appendix to *The Lays of Beleriand* (1985), but to be brief, it is painfully clear that the *Quenta Silmarillion* (included in 'the Gnomes Material', together with whatever other texts may have been given this name) never reached the publishers' reader – save for a few pages that had been attached, independently (and in the circumstances very misleadingly) to *The Lay of Leithian*. He was utterly perplexed, and proposed a solution to the relationship between the Long Poem and this fragment (much approved) of the prose work (i.e. the *Quenta Silmarillion*) that was (very understandably) radically incorrect. He wrote a puzzled report conveying his opinion, across which a member of the staff wrote, also understandably, 'What are we to do?'

The outcome of a tissue of subsequent misunderstandings was that my father, wholly unaware that the *Quenta Silmarillion* had not in fact been read by anybody, told Stanley Unwin that he rejoiced that at least it had not been rejected 'with scorn', and that he now certainly hoped 'to be able, or to be able to afford, to publish the Silmarillion!'

While QS II was gone he continued the narrative in a further manuscript, which told of the death of Beren in *The Wolf-hunt of Carcharoth*, intending to copy the new writing into QS II when the texts were returned; but when they were, on 16 December 1937, he put *The Silmarillion* aside. He still asked, in a letter to Stanley Unwin of that date, 'And what more can hobbits do? They can be comic, but their comedy is suburban unless it is set against things more elemental.' But three days later, on 19 December 1937, he announced to

Allen and Unwin: 'I have written the first chapter of a new story about Hobbits – "A long expected party".'

It was at this point, as I wrote in the Appendix to *The Children of Húrin*, that the continuous and evolving tradition of *The Silmarillion* in the summarising, *Quenta* mode came to an end, brought down in full flight, at Túrin's departure from Doriath, becoming an outlaw. The further history from that point remained during the years that followed in the compressed and undeveloped form of the *Quenta* of 1930, frozen, as it were, while the great structures of the Second and Third Ages arose with the writing of *The Lord of the Rings*. But that further history was of cardinal importance in the ancient legends, for the concluding stories (deriving from the original *Book of Lost Tales*) told of the disastrous history of Húrin, father of Túrin, after Morgoth released him, and of the ruin of the Elvish kingdoms of Nargothrond, Doriath, and Gondolin of which Gimli chanted in the mines of Moria many thousands of years afterwards.

> *The world was fair, the mountains tall,*
> *in Elder Days before the fall*
> *of mighty kings in Nargothrond*
> *And Gondolin, who now beyond*
> *the Western Seas have passed away . . .*

And this was to be the crown and completion of the whole: the doom of the Noldorin Elves in their long struggle against the power of Morgoth, and the parts that Húrin and Túrin played in that history; ending with the *Tale of Eärendil*, who escaped from the burning ruin of Gondolin.

Many years later my father wrote in a letter (16 July 1964): 'I offered them the legends of the Elder Days, but their readers turned that down. They wanted a sequel. But I wanted heroic legends and high romance. The result was *The Lord of the Rings*.'

*

When *The Lay of Leithian* was abandoned there was no explicit account of what followed the moment when 'the fangs of Carcharoth crashed together like a trap' on Beren's hand in which he clutched the Silmaril; for this we must go back to the original *Tale of Tinúviel* (pp. 77–80), where there was a story of the desperate flight of Beren and Lúthien, of the hunt out of Angband pursuing them, and of Huan's finding them and guiding them back to Doriath. In the *Quenta Noldorinwa* (p. 138) my father said of this simply that 'there is little to tell'.

In the final story of the return of Beren and Lúthien to Doriath the chief (and radical) change to notice is the manner of their escape from the gates of Angband after the wounding of Beren by Carcharoth. This event, which *The Lay of Leithian* did not reach, is told in the words of *The Silmarillion*:

Thus the quest of the Silmaril was like to have ended in ruin and despair; but in that hour above the wall of the valley three mighty birds appeared, flying northward with wings swifter than the wind.

Among all birds and beasts the wandering and need of Beren had been noised, and Huan himself had bidden all things watch, that they might bring him aid. High above the realm of Morgoth Thorondor and his vassals soared, and seeing now the madness of the Wolf and Beren's fall came swiftly down, even as the powers of Angband were released from the toils of sleep. Then they lifted up Beren and Lúthien from the earth, and bore them aloft into the clouds. . . .

(As they passed high over the lands) Lúthien wept, for she thought that Beren would surely die; he spoke no word, nor opened his eyes, and knew thereafter nothing of his flight. And at the last the eagles set them down upon the borders of Doriath; and they were come to that same dell whence Beren had stolen in despair and left Lúthien asleep.

There the eagles laid her at Beren's side and returned to the peaks of Crissaegrim and their high eyries; but Huan came to her, and together they tended Beren, even as before when she healed him of the wound that Curufin gave to him. But this wound was fell and poisonous. Long Beren lay, and his spirit wandered upon the dark borders of death, knowing ever an anguish that pursued him from dream to dream. Then suddenly, when her hope was almost spent, he woke again, and looked up, seeing leaves against the sky; and he heard beneath the leaves singing soft and slow beside him LúthienTinúviel. And it was spring again.

Thereafter Beren was named Erchamion, which is the One-handed; and suffering was graven in his face. But at last he was drawn back to life by the love of Lúthien, and he rose, and together they walked in the woods once more.

*

The story of Beren and Lúthien has now been told as it evolved in prose and verse over twenty years from the original *Tale of Tinúviel*. After initial hesitation Beren, whose father was at first Egnor the Forester, of the Elvish people called the Noldoli, translated into English as 'Gnomes', has become the son of Barahir, a chieftain of Men, and the leader of a band of rebels in hiding against the hateful tyranny of Morgoth. The memorable story has emerged (in 1925, in *The Lay of Leithian*) of the treachery of Gorlim and the slaying of Barahir (pp. 94 ff.); and while Vëannë who told the 'lost tale' knew nothing of what had brought Beren to Artanor, and surmised that it was a simple love of wandering (p. 41), he has become after the death of his father a far-famed enemy of Morgoth forced to flee to the South, where he opens the story of Beren and Tinúviel as he peers in the twilight through the trees of Thingol's forest.

Very remarkable is the story, as it was told in *The Tale of Tinúviel*, of the captivity of Beren, on his journey to Angband in quest of a Silmaril, by Tevildo Prince of Cats; so too is the total subsequent transformation of that story. But if we say that the castle of the cats 'is' the tower of Sauron on Tol-in-Gaurhoth 'Isle of Werewolves' it can only be, as I have remarked elsewhere, in the sense that it occupies the same 'space' in the narrative. Beyond this there is no point in

seeking even shadowy resemblances between the two estab-
lishments. The monstrous gormandising cats, their kitchens
and their sunning terraces, and their engagingly Elvish-feline
names, *Miaugion*, *Miaulë*, *Meoita*, have all vanished without
trace. But beyond their hatred of dogs (and the importance
to the story of the mutual loathing of Huan and Tevildo) it is
evident that the inhabitants of the castle are no ordinary cats:
very notable is this passage from the *Tale* (p. 69) concerning
'the secret of the cats and the spell that Melko had entrusted
to [Tevildo]':

and those were words of magic whereby the stones of his evil
house were held together, and whereby he held all beasts of
the catfolk under his sway, filling them with an evil power
beyond their nature; for long has it been said that Tevildo was
an evil fay in beastlike shape.

It is also interesting to observe in this passage, as elsewhere, the manner in which aspects and incidents of the
original tale may reappear but in a wholly different guise,
arising from a wholly altered narrative conception. In the
old *Tale* Tevildo was forced by Huan to reveal the spell,
and when Tinúviel uttered it 'the house of Tevildo shook;
and there came therefrom a host of indwellers' (which was
a host of cats). In the *Quenta Noldorinwa* (p. 135) when
Huan overthrew the terrible werewolf-wizard Thû, the
Necromancer, in Tol-in-Gaurhoth he 'won from him the
keys and the spells that held together his enchanted walls
and towers. So the stronghold was broken and the towers

thrown down and the dungeons opened. Many captives were released . . .'

But here we move into the major shift in the story of Beren and Lúthien, when it was combined with the altogether distinct legend of Nargothrond. Through the oath of undying friendship and aid sworn to Barahir, the father of Beren, Felagund the founder of Nargothrond was drawn into Beren's quest of the Silmaril (p. 117, lines 157 ff.); and there entered the story of the Elves from Nargothrond who disguised as Orcs were taken by Thû and ended their days in the gruesome dungeons of Tol-in-Gaurhoth. The quest of the Silmaril involved also Celegorm and Curufin, sons of Fëanor and a powerful presence in Nargothrond, through the destructive oath sworn by the Fëanorians of vengeance against any 'who hold or take or keep a Silmaril against their will'. The captivity of Lúthien in Nargothrond, from which Huan rescued her, involved her in the plots and ambitions of Celegorm and Curufin: pp. 151–2, lines 247–72.

There remains the aspect of the story that is also the end of it, and of primary significance, as I believe, in the mind of its author. The earliest reference to the fates of Beren and Lúthien after Beren's death in the hunt of Carcharoth is in *The Tale of Tinúviel*; but at that time both Beren and Lúthien were Elves. There it was said (p. 87):

'Tinúviel crushed with sorrow and finding no comfort or light in all the world followed him swiftly down those dark ways that all must tread alone. Now her beauty and tender loveliness touched even the cold heart of Mandos, so that he suffered her to lead Beren forth once more into the world, nor has this ever been done since to Man or Elf . . .. Yet said Mandos to those twain: "Lo, O Elves, it is not to any life of perfect joy that I dismiss you, for such may no longer be found in all the world where sits Melko of the evil heart – and know that ye will become mortal even as Men, and when ye fare hither again it will be for ever . . .."'

> That Beren and Lúthien had a further history in Middle-earth is made plain in this passage ('their deeds afterward were very great, and many tales are told thereof'), but no more is said there than that they are *i-Cuilwarthon*, the Dead that Live Again, and 'they became mighty fairies in the lands about the north of Sirion.'
> In another of the *Lost Tales*, *The Coming of the Valar*, there is an account of those who came to Mandos (the name of his halls as well as that of the God, whose true name was Vê):

Thither in after days fared the Elves of all the clans who were by illhap slain with weapons or did die of grief for those who were slain – and only so might the Eldar die, and then it was only for a while. There Mandos spake their doom, and there they waited in the darkness, dreaming of their past deeds, until such time as he appointed when they might again be born into their children, and go forth to laugh and sing again.

With this may be compared the unplaced verses for *The Lay of Leithian* given on pp. 216–7, concerning 'the Land of the Lost . . . where the Dead wait, while ye forget':

> No moon is there, no voice, no sound
> of beating heart; a sigh profound
> once in each age as each age dies
> alone is heard. Far, far it lies,
> the Land of Waiting where the Dead sit,
> in their thought's shadow, by no moon lit.

The conception that the Elves died only from wounds of weapons, or from grief, endured, and appears in the published *Silmarillion*:

For the Elves die not till the world dies, unless they are slain or waste in grief (and to both these seeming deaths they are subject); neither does age subdue their strength, unless one grow weary of ten thousand centuries; and dying they are gathered to the halls of Mandos in Valinor, whence they may in time return. But the sons of Men die indeed, and leave the world; wherefore they are called the Guests, or the Strangers. Death is their fate, the gift of Ilúvatar, which as Time wears even the Powers shall envy.

It seems to me that the words of Mandos in *The Tale of Tinúviel* cited above, '*ye will become mortal even as Men*, and when ye fare hither again it will be for ever', imply that he was uprooting their destiny as Elves: having died as Elves could die, they would not be reborn, but be permitted – uniquely – to leave Mandos still in their own particular being. They would pay a price, nevertheless, for when they died a second time there would be no possibility of return, no 'seeming death', but the death that Men, of their nature, must suffer.

Later, in the *Quenta Noldorinwa* it is told (pp. 140–1) that 'Lúthien failed and faded swiftly and vanished from the earth . . . . And she came to the halls of Mandos, and she sang to him a tale of moving love so fair that he was moved to pity, as never has befallen since.'

Beren he summoned, and thus, as Lúthien had sworn as she kissed him at the hour of death, they met beyond the western sea. And Mandos suffered them to depart, but he said that Lúthien *should become mortal even as her lover*, and should leave the earth once more *in the manner of a mortal woman*, and her beauty become but a memory of song. So it was, but it is said that in recompense Mandos gave to Beren and to Lúthien thereafter a long span of life and joy, and they wandered knowing thirst nor cold in the fair land of Beleriand, and no mortal Man thereafter spoke to Beren or his spouse.

In the draft text of the story of Beren and Lúthien prepared for the *Quenta Silmarillion*, referred to on p. 218, there enters the idea of the 'choice of fate' proposed to Beren and Lúthien before Mandos:

And this was the choice that he decreed for Beren and Lúthien. They should dwell now in Valinor until the world's end in bliss, but in the end Beren and Lúthien must each go unto that appointed to their kind, when all things are changed: and of the mind of Ilúvatar concerning Men Manwë [Lord of the Valar] knows not. Or they might return unto Middle-earth without certitude of joy or life; then Lúthien should become mortal even as Beren, and subject to a second death, and in the end she should leave the earth for ever and her beauty become only a memory of song. And this doom they chose, that thus, whatsoever sorrow lay before them, their fates might be joined, and their paths lead together beyond the confines of the world. So it was that alone of the Eldalië Lúthien died and left the world long ago; yet by her have the Two Kindreds been joined, and she is the foremother of many.

This conception of the 'Choice of Fate' was retained, but in a different form, as seen in *The Silmarillion*: the choices were imposed on Lúthien alone, and they were changed. Lúthien may still leave Mandos and dwell until the end of the world in Valinor, because of her labours and her sorrow, and because she was the daughter of Melian; but thither Beren cannot come. Thus if she accepts the former, they must be separated now and for ever: because he cannot escape from his own destiny, cannot escape Death, which is the Gift of Ilúvatar and cannot be refused.

The second choice remained, and this she chose. Only so could Lúthien become united with Beren 'beyond the world': she herself must change the destiny of her being: she must become mortal, and die indeed.

As I have said, the story of Beren and Lúthien did not end with the judgement of Mandos, and some account of it, of its aftermath, and of the history of the Silmaril that Beren cut from the iron crown of Morgoth, must be given. There are difficulties in doing so in the form that I have chosen for this book, largely because the part played by Beren in his second life hinges on aspects of the history of the First Age that would cast the net too widely for the purpose of this book.

I have remarked (p. 103) of the *Quenta Noldorinwa* of 1930, which followed from and was much longer than the *Sketch of the Mythology*, that it remained 'a compression, a compendious account': it is said in the title of the work to be 'the brief history of the Noldoli or Gnomes, drawn from the *Book of Lost Tales*'. Of these 'summarising' texts I wrote in *The War of the Jewels* (1994): 'In these versions my father was drawing on (while also of course continually develop-ing and extending) long works that already existed in prose or verse, and in the *Quenta Silmarillion* he perfected that characteristic tone, melodious, grave, elegiac, burdened with a sense of loss and distance in time, which resides partly, as I believe, in the literary fact that he was drawing down into a brief compendious history what he could also see in far more detailed, immediate, and dramatic form. With the completion of the great 'intrusion' and departure of *The Lord of the Rings* it seems that he returned to the Elder Days with a desire to take up again the far more ample scale with which he had begun long before, in *The Book of Lost Tales*. The completion of the *Quenta Silmarillion* remained an aim; but the 'great tales', vastly developed from their original forms – from which its later chapters should be derived – were never achieved.'

We are here concerned with a story that goes back to the latest written of the *Lost Tales*, where it bore the title *The Tale of the Nauglafring*: that being the original name of the *Nauglamír*, the Necklace of the Dwarves. But we come here to the furthest point in my father's work on the Elder Days in the time following the completion of *The Lord of the Rings*: there is no new narrative. To cite my discussion in *The War of the Jewels* again, 'it is as if we come to the brink of a great cliff and look down from highlands raised in some later age onto an ancient plain far below. For the story of the Nauglamír and the destruction of Doriath . . . we must return through more than a quarter of a century to the *Quenta Noldorinwa* or beyond.' To the *Quenta Noldorinwa* (see p. 103) I will now turn, giving the relevant text in a very slightly shortened form.

The tale begins with the further history of the great treasure of Nargothrond that was taken by the evil dragon Glómund. After the death of Glómund, slain by Túrin Turambar, Húrin father of Túrin came with a few outlaws of the woods to Nargothrond, which as yet none, Orc, Elf, or Man, had dared to plunder, for dread of the spirit of Glómund and his very memory. But they found there one Mîm the Dwarf.

THE RETURN OF BEREN AND LÚTHIEN
ACCORDING TO THE QUENTA NOLDORINWA

Now Mîm had found the halls and treasure of Nargothrond unguarded; and he took possession of them, and sat there in joy fingering the gold and gems, and letting them run ever through his hands; and he bound them to himself with many spells. But the folk of Mîm were few, and the outlaws filled with the lust of the treasure slew them, though Húrin would have stayed them; and at his death Mîm cursed the gold.

[Húrin went to Thingol and sought his aid, and the folk of Thingol bore the treasure to the Thousand Caves; then Húrin departed.]

Then the enchantment of the accursed dragon gold began to fall even upon the king of Doriath, and long he sat and gazed upon it, and the seed of the love of gold that was in his heart was waked to growth. Wherefore he summoned the greatest of all craftsmen that now were in the western world, since Nargothrond was no more (and Gondolin was not known), the Dwarves of Nogrod and Belegost, that they might fashion the gold and silver and the gems (for much was as yet unwrought) into countless vessels and fair things; and a marvellous necklace of great beauty they should make, whereon to hang the Silmaril.*

But the Dwarves coming were stricken at once with the lust and desire of the treasure, and they plotted treachery. They said one to another: 'Is not this wealth as much the right of the Dwarves as of the Elvish king, and was it not wrested evilly from Mîm?' Yet also they lusted for the Silmaril. And Thingol, falling deeper into the thraldom of the spell, for his part scanted his promised reward for their labour; and bitter words grew between them, and there was battle in Thingol's halls. There many Elves and Dwarves were slain, and the howe wherein they were lain in Doriath was named Cûm-nan-Arasaith, the Mound of Avarice. But the remainder of the Dwarves were driven forth without reward or fee.

Therefore gathering new forces in Nogrod and in Belegost they returned at length, and aided by the treachery of certain Elves on whom the lust of the accursed treasure had fallen they passed into Doriath secretly.

There they surprised Thingol upon a hunt with but small

---

* A later version of the story concerning the Nauglamír told that it had been made by craftsmen of the Dwarves long before for Felagund, and that it was the sole treasure that Húrin brought from Nargothrond and gave to Thingol. The task that Thingol then set the Dwarves was to *remake* the Nauglamír and in it to set the Silmaril that was in his possession. This is the form of the story in the published *Silmarillion*.

company of arms; and Thingol was slain, and the fortress of the Thousand Caves taken at unawares and plundered; and so was brought well nigh to ruin the glory of Doriath and but one stronghold of the Elves [Gondolin] against Morgoth now remained, and their twilight was nigh at hand.

Queen Melian the Dwarves could not seize or harm, and she went forth to seek Beren and Lúthien. Now the Dwarf-road to Nogrod and Belegost in the Blue Mountains passed through East Beleriand and the woods about the River Gelion, where aforetime were the hunting grounds of Damrod and Díriel, sons of Fëanor. To the south of those lands between the river Gelion and the mountains lay the land of Ossiriand, and there lived and wandered still in peace and bliss Beren and Lúthien, in that time of respite which Lúthien had won, ere both should die; and their folk were the Green Elves of the South. But Beren went no more to war, and his land was filled with loveliness and a wealth of flowers, and Men called it oft Cuilwarthien, the Land of the Dead that Live.

To the north of that region is a ford across the river Ascar, and that ford is named Sarn Athrad, the Ford of Stones. This ford the Dwarves must pass ere they reached the mountain passes that led unto their homes; and there Beren fought his last fight, warned of their approach by Melian. In that battle the Green Elves took the Dwarves unawares as they were in the midst of their passage, laden with their plunder; and the Dwarvish chiefs were slain, and well nigh all their host. But Beren took the Nauglamír, the Necklace of the Dwarves, whereon was hung the Silmaril; and it is said and sung that Lúthien wearing that necklace and that immortal jewel on her white breast was the vision of greatest beauty and glory that has ever been seen outside the realms of Valinor, and that for a while the Land of the Dead that Live became like a vision of the land of the Gods, and no places have been since so fair, so fruitful, or so filled with light.

Yet Melian warned them ever of the curse that lay upon the treasure and upon the Silmaril. The treasure they had drowned indeed in the river Ascar, and named it anew Rathlorion, Goldenbed, yet the Silmaril they retained. And in time the brief hour of loveliness of the land of Rathlorion departed. For Lúthien faded as Mandos had spoken, even as the Elves of later days faded and she vanished from the world;* and Beren died, and none know where their meeting shall be again.'

Thereafter was Dior Thingol's heir, child of Beren and Lúthien, king in the woods: most fair of all the children of the world, for his race was threefold: of the fairest and goodliest of Men, and of the Elves, and of the spirits divine of Valinor; yet it shielded him not from the fate of the oath of the sons of Fëanor. For Dior went back to Doriath and for a time a part of its ancient glory was raised anew, though Melian no longer dwelt in that place, and she departed to the land of the Gods beyond the western sea, to muse on her sorrows in the gardens whence she came.

But Dior wore the Silmaril upon his breast and the fame

---

* The manner of Lúthien's death is marked for correction; subsequently my father wrote against it: 'Yet it hath been sung that Lúthien alone of Elves hath been numbered among our race, and goeth whither we go to a fate beyond the world.'

of that jewel went far and wide; and the deathless oath was waked once more from sleep.

For while Lúthien wore that peerless gem no Elf would dare assail her, and not even Maidros dared ponder such a thought. But now hearing of the renewal of Doriath and Dior's pride, the seven gathered again from wandering; and they sent unto Dior to claim their own. But he would not yield the jewel unto them, and they came upon him with all their host; and so befell the second slaying of Elf by Elf, and the most grievous. There fell Celegorm and Curufin and dark Cranthir, but Dior was slain, and Doriath was destroyed and never rose again.

Yet the sons of Fëanor gained not the Silmaril; for faithful servants fled before them and took with them Elwing the daughter of Dior, and she escaped, and they bore with them the Nauglafring, and came in time to the mouth of the river Sirion by the sea.

[In a text somewhat later than the *Quenta Noldorinwa*, the earliest form of *The Annals of Beleriand*, the story was changed, in that Dior returned to Doriath while Beren and Lúthien were still alive in Ossiriand; and what befell him there I will give in the words of *The Silmarillion*:

There came a night of autumn, and when it grew late, one came and smote upon the doors of Menegroth, demanding admittance to the King. He was a lord of the Green Elves hastening from Ossiriand, and the doorwards brought him to where Dior sat alone in his chamber; and there in silence he gave to the King a coffer, and took his leave. But in that coffer lay the Necklace of the Dwarves, wherein was set the Silmaril; and Dior looking upon it knew it for a sign that Beren Erchamion and Lúthien Tinúviel had died indeed, and gone where go the race of Men to a fate beyond the world.

Long did Dior gaze upon the Silmaril, which his father and mother had brought beyond hope out of the terror of Morgoth; and his grief was great that death had come upon them so soon.]

EXTRACT FROM THE LOST TALE
OF THE NAUGLAFRING

Here I will step back from the chronology of composition and turn to the *Lost Tale* of the Nauglafring. The reason for this is that the passage given here is a notable example of the expansive mode, observant of visual and often dramatic detail, adopted by my father in the early days of *The Silmarillion*; but the *Lost Tale* as a whole extends into ramifications unneeded in this book. A very brief summary of the battle at Sarn Athrad, the Stony Ford, appears therefore in the text of the *Quenta*, p. 235, while there follows here the much fuller account from the *Lost Tale*, with the duel between Beren and Naugladur, lord of the Dwarves of Nogrod in the Blue Mountains.

The passage begins with the approach of the Dwarves, led by Naugladur, to Sarn Athrad, on their return from the sack of the Thousand Caves.

Now came all that host [to the river Ascar], and their array was thus: first a number of unladen Dwarves most fully

armed, and amidmost the great company of those that bore
the treasury of Glómund, and many a fair thing beside that
they had haled from Tinwelint's halls; and behind these was
Naugladur, and he bestrode Tinwelint's horse, and a strange
figure did he seem, for the legs of the Dwarves are short and
crooked, but two Dwarves led that horse for it went not
willingly and it was laden with spoil. But behind these came
a mass of armed men but little laden; and in this array they
sought to cross Sarn Athrad on their day of doom.

Morn was it when they reached the hither bank, and high
noon saw them yet passing in long-strung lines and wading
slowly the shallow places of the swift-running stream. Here
doth it widen out and fare down narrow channels filled with
boulders atween long spits of shingle and stones less great.
Now did Naugladur slip from his burdened horse and prepare to get him over, for the armed host of the vanguard had
climbed already the further bank, and it was great and sheer
and thick with trees, and the bearers of the gold were some
already stepped thereon and some amidmost of the stream,
but the armed men of the rear were resting awhile.

Suddenly is all that place filled with the sound of elven
horns, and one [? brays] with a clearer blast above the rest,
and it is the horn of Beren, the huntsman of the woods. Then
is the air thick with the slender arrows of the Eldar that err
not neither doth the wind bear them aside, and lo, from every
tree and boulder do the brown Elves and the green spring
suddenly and loose unceasingly from full quivers. Then was
there a panic and a noise in the host of Naugladur, and those
that waded in the ford cast their golden burdens in the waters

and sought affrighted to either bank, but many were stricken with those pitiless darts and fell with their gold into the currents of the Aros, staining its clear waters with their dark blood.

Now were the warriors on the far bank [? wrapped] in battle and rallying sought to come at their foes, but these fled nimbly before them, while [? others] poured still the hail of arrows upon them, and thus got the Eldar few hurts and the Dwarf-folk fell dead unceasingly. Now was that great fight of the Stony Ford . . . nigh to Naugladur, for even though Naugladur and his captains led their bands stoutly never might they grip their foe, and death fell like rain upon their ranks until the most part broke and fled, and a noise of clear laughter echoed from the Elves thereat, and they forbore to shoot more, for the illshapen figures of the Dwarves as they fled, their white beards torn by the wind, filled them with mirth. But now stood Naugladur and few were about him, and he remembered the words of Gwendelin,* for behold, Beren came towards him and he cast aside his bow, and drew a bright sword; and Beren was of great stature among the Eldar, albeit not of the girth and breadth of Naugladur of the Dwarves.

Then said Beren: 'Ward thy life if thou canst, O crook-legged murderer, else will I take it,' and Naugladur bid him even

---

* Earlier in the tale, when Naugladur was preparing to leave Menegroth, he declared that Gwendelin the queen of Artanor (Melian) must go with him to Nogrod: to which she replied: 'Thief and murderer, child of Melko, yet art thou a fool, for thou canst not see what hangs over thine own head.'

the Nauglafring, the necklace of wonder, that he be suffered to go unharmed; but Beren said: 'Nay, that may I still take when thou art slain,' and thereat he made alone upon Naugladur and his companions, and having slain the foremost of these the others fled away amid elven laughter, and so Beren came upon Naugladur, slayer of Tinwelint. Then did that aged one defend himself doughtily, and 'twas a bitter fight, and many of the Elves that watched for love and fear of their captain fingered their bow-strings, but Beren called even as he fought that all should stay their hands.

Now little doth the tale tell of wounds and blows of that affray, save that Beren got many hurts therein, and many of his shrewdest blows did little harm to Naugladur by reason of the [? skill] and magic of his dwarfen mail; and it is said that three hours they fought and Beren's arms grew weary, but not those of Naugladur accustomed to wield his mighty hammer at the forge, and it is more than like that otherwise would the issue have been but for the curse of Mîm; for marking how Beren grew faint Naugladur pressed him ever more nearly, and the arrogance that was of that grievous spell came into his heart, and he thought: 'I will slay this Elf, and his folk will flee in fear before me,' and grasping his sword he dealt a mighty blow and cried: 'Take here thy bane, O stripling of the woods,' and in that moment his foot found a jagged stone and he stumbled forward, but Beren slipped aside from that blow and catching at his beard his hand found the carcanet of gold, and therewith he swung Naugladur suddenly off his feet upon his face: and Naugladur's sword was shaken from his grasp, but Beren seized it and slew him therewith, for he said: 'I will not sully my bright blade with thy dark blood, since there is no need.' But the body of Naugladur was cast into the Aros.

Then did he unloose the necklace, and he gazed in wonder at it – and beheld the Silmaril, even the jewel he won from Angband and gained undying glory by his deed; and he said: 'Never have mine eyes beheld thee O Lamp of Faëry burn one half so fair as now thou dost, set in gold and gems and the magic of the Dwarves'; and that necklace he caused to be washed of its stains, and he cast it not away, knowing nought of its power, but bore it with him back into the woods of Hithlum.

To this passage from the *Tale of the Nauglafring* there corresponds only the few words of the *Quenta* cited in the extract cited on p. 235:

In that battle [Sarn Athrad] the Green Elves took the Dwarves at unawares as they were in the midst of their passage, laden with their plunder; and the Dwarvish chiefs were slain, and well nigh all their host. But Beren took the Nauglamír, the Necklace of the Dwarves, whereon was hung the Silmaril . . .

This illustrates my observation on p. 231, that my father 'was drawing down into a brief compendious history what he could also see in a far more detailed, immediate, and dramatic form.'

I will conclude this short excursion into the *Lost Tale* of the Necklace of the Dwarves with a further quotation, origin of the story as told in the *Quenta* (pp. 236–7) of the deaths of Beren and Lúthien, and the slaying of Dior, their son. I take up this extract with words between Beren and Gwendelin (Melian) when Lúthien first wore the Nauglafring. Beren declared that never had she appeared so beautiful; but Gwendelin said: 'Yet the Silmaril abode in the Crown of Melko, and that is the work of baleful smiths indeed.'

Then said Tinúviel that she desired not things of worth or precious stones, but the elven gladness of the forest, and to pleasure Gwendelin she cast it from her neck; but Beren was little pleased and he would not suffer it to be flung away, but warded it in his [? treasury].

Thereafter did Gwendelin abide a while in the woods among them and was healed [of her overwhelming grief for Tinwelint]; and in the end she fared wistfully back to the land of Lórien and came never again into the tales of the dwellers of Earth; but upon Beren and Lúthien fell swiftly that doom of mortality that Mandos had spoken when he sped them from his halls – and in this perhaps did the curse of Mîm have [? potency] in that it came more soon upon them; nor this time did those twain fare the road together, but when yet was their child, Dior the Fair, a little one, did Tinúviel slowly fade, even as the Elves of later days have done throughout the world, and she vanished in the woods, and none have seen her dancing ever there again. But Beren searched all the lands of Hithlum and of Artanor ranging after her; and never has any of the Elves had more loneliness than his, or ever he too faded from life, and Dior his son was left ruler of the brown Elves and the green, and Lord of the Nauglafring.

Mayhap what all Elves say is true, that those twain hunt now in the forest of Oromë in Valinor, and Tinúviel dances on the green swards of Nessa and Vána daughters of the Gods for ever more; yet great was the grief of the Elves when the Guilwarthon went from among them, and being leaderless and lessened of magic their numbers minished; and many fared away to Gondolin, the rumour of whose growing power and glory ran in secret whispers among all the Elves.

Still did Dior when come to manhood rule a numerous folk, and he loved the woods even as Beren had done; and songs name him mostly Ausir the Wealthy for his possession of that wondrous gem set in the Necklace of the Dwarves. Now the tales of Beren and Tinúviel grew dim in his heart, and he took to wearing it about his neck and to love its loveliness most dearly; and the fame of that jewel spread like fire through all the regions of the North, and the Elves said one to another: 'A Silmaril burns in the woods of Hisilómë.'

The *Tale of the Nauglafring* told in greater detail of the assault on Dior and his death at the hands of the sons of Fëanor, and this last of the *Lost Tales* to receive consecutive form ends with the escape of Elwing:

She wandered in the woods, and of the brown Elves and the green a few gathered to her, and they departed for ever

from the glades of Hithlum and got them to the south towards
Sirion's deep waters, and the pleasant lands.

And thus did all the fates of the fairies weave then to one
strand, and that strand is the great tale of Eärendel; and to
that tale's true beginning are we now come.

*

There follow in the *Quenta Noldorinwa* passages concerned
with the history of Gondolin and its fall, and the history
of Tuor, who was wedded to Idril Celebrindal daughter of
Turgon king of Gondolin; their son was Eärendel, who with
them escaped from the destruction of the city and came
to the Mouths of Sirion. The *Quenta* continues, following
from the flight of Elwing daughter of Dior from Doriath to
the mouths of Sirion (pp. 236–7):

By Sirion there grew up an elven folk, the gleanings of
Doriath and Gondolin, and they took to the sea and the
making of fair ships, and they dwelt nigh unto its shores and
under the shadow of Ulmo's hand....

In those days Tuor felt old age creep upon him, and he
could not forbear the longing that possessed him for the sea;
wherefore he built a great ship Eärámë, Eagle's Pinion, and
with Idril he set sail into the sunset and the West, and came
no more into any tale. But Eärendel the shining became the
lord of the folk of Sirion and took to wife fair Elwing, the
daughter of Dior; and yet he could not rest. Two thoughts
were in his heart blended as one: the longing for the wide

sea; and he thought to sail thereon following after Tuor and Idril Celebrindal who returned not, and he thought to find perhaps the last shore and bring ere he died a message to the Gods and Elves of the West that should move their hearts to pity on the world and the sorrows of Mankind.

Wingelot he built, fairest of the ships of song, the Foam-flower; white were its timbers as the argent moon, golden were its oars, silver were its shrouds, its masts were crowned with jewels like stars. In *The Lay of Eärendel* is many a thing sung of his adventures in the deep and in lands untrod, and in many seas and many isles. . . But Elwing sat sorrowing at home.

Eärendel found not Tuor, nor came he ever on that journey to the shores of Valinor; and at last he was driven by the winds back East, and he came at a time of night to the havens of Sirion, unlooked for, unwelcomed, for they were desolate. . . .

The dwelling of Elwing at Sirion's mouth, where still she possessed the Nauglamír and the glorious Silmaril, became known to the sons of Fëanor; and they gathered together from their wandering hunting-paths.

But the folk of Sirion would not yield that jewel which Beren had won and Lúthien had worn, and for which fair Dior had been slain. And so befell the last and cruellest of the slaying of Elf by Elf, the third woe achieved by the accursed oath; for the sons of Fëanor came down upon the exiles of Gondolin and the remnant of Doriath, and though some of their folk stood aside and some few rebelled and were slain upon the other part aiding Elwing against their own lords, yet they won the day. Damrod was slain and Díriel, and Maidros and Maglor alone now remained of the Seven; but the last of the folk of Gondolin were destroyed or forced to depart and join them to the people of Maidros. And yet the sons of Fëanor gained not the Silmaril; for Elwing cast the Nauglamír into the sea, whence it shall not return until the End; and she leapt herself into the waves, and took the form of a white sea-bird, and flew away lamenting and seeking for Eärendel about all the shores of the world.

But Maidros took pity upon her child Elrond, and took him with him, and harboured and nurtured him, for his heart was sick and weary with the burden of the dreadful oath.

Learning these things Eärendel was overcome with sorrow; and he set sail once more in search of Elwing and of Valinor. And it is told in the Lay of Eärendel that he came at last unto the Magic Isles, and hardly escaped their enchantment, and found again the Lonely Isle, and the Shadowy Seas, and the Bay of Faërie on the borders of the world. There he landed on the immortal shore alone of living Men, and his feet climbed the marvellous hill of Kôr; and he walked in the deserted ways of Tûn, where the dust on his raiment and his shoes was a dust of diamonds and gems. But he ventured not into Valinor.

He built a tower in the Northern Seas to which all the sea-birds of the world might at times repair, and ever he grieved for fair Elwing, looking for her return to him. And Wingelot was lifted on their wings and sailed now even in the airs searching for Elwing; marvellous and magical was that ship, a starlit flower in the sky. But the Sun scorched it and the Moon hunted it in heaven, and long Eärendel wandered over Earth, glimmering as a fugitive star.

Here the tale of Eärendel and Elwing ends in the *Quenta Noldorinwa* as originally composed; but at a later time a rewriting of this last passage altered profoundly the idea that the Silmaril of Beren and Lúthien was lost for ever in the sea. As rewritten it reads:

And yet Maidros gained not the Silmaril, for Elwing seeing that all was lost and her children Elros and Elrond taken captive, eluded the host of Maidros, and with the Nauglamír upon her breast she cast herself into the sea, and perished, as folk thought. But Ulmo bore her up, and upon her breast there shone as a star the shining Silmaril, as she flew over the water to seek Eärendel her beloved. And on a time of night Eärendel at the helm saw her come towards him, as a white cloud under moon exceeding swift, as a star over the sea moving in strange course, a pale flame on wings of storm.

And it is sung that she fell from the air upon the timbers of Wingelot, in a swoon, nigh unto death for the urgency of her speed, and Eärendel took her into his bosom. And in the morn with marvelling eyes he beheld his wife in her own form beside him with her hair upon his face; and she slept.

From here onwards the tale told in the *Quenta Noldorinwa*, largely rewritten, reached in essentials that in *The Silmarillion*, and I will end the story in this book with citation of that work.

THE MORNING
AND EVENING STAR

Great was the sorrow of Eärendil and Elwing for the ruin of the havens of Sirion, and the captivity of their sons, and they feared that they would be slain; but it was not so. For Maglor took pity upon Elros and Elrond, and he cherished them, and love grew after between them, as little might be thought; but Maglor's heart was sick and weary with the burden of the dreadful oath.

Yet Eärendil saw now no hope left in the lands of Middle-earth, and he turned again in despair and came not home, but sought back once more to Valinor with Elwing at his side. He stood now most often at the prow of Vingilot, and the Silmaril was bound upon his brow; and ever its light grew greater as they drew into the West. . . .

Then Eärendil, first of living Men, landed on the immortal shores; and he spoke there to Elwing and to those that were with him, and they were three mariners who had sailed all the seas beside him: Falathar, Erellont, and Aerandir were their names. And Eärendil said to them: 'Here none but myself shall set foot, lest you fall under the wrath of the Valar. But that peril I will take on myself alone, for the sake of the Two Kindreds.'

But Elwing answered: 'Then would our paths be sundered for ever, but all thy perils I will take on myself also.' And she leaped into the white foam and ran towards him; but Eärendil was sorrowful, for he feared the anger of the Lords of the West upon any of Middle-earth that should dare to pass the leaguer of Aman. And there they bade farewell to the companions of their voyage, and were taken from them for ever.

Then Eärendil said to Elwing: 'Await me here; for one only may bring the message that it is my fate to bear.' And he went up alone into the land, and came into the Calacirya, and it seemed to him empty and silent; for even as Morgoth and Ungoliant came in ages past, so now Eärendil had come at a time of festival, and wellnigh all the Elvenfolk were gone to Valimar, or were gathered in the halls of Manwë upon Taniquetil, and few were left to keep watch upon the walls of Tirion.

But some there were who saw him from afar, and the great light that he bore; and they went in haste to Valimar. But Eärendil climbed the green hill of Túna and found it bare; and he entered into the streets of Tirion, and they were empty; and his heart was heavy, for he feared that some evil had come even to the Blessed Realm. He walked in the deserted ways of Tirion, and the dust upon his raiment and his shoes was a dust of diamonds, and he shone and glistened as he climbed the long white stairs. And he called aloud in many tongues, both of Elves and Men, but there were none to answer him. Therefore he turned back at last towards the sea; but even as he took the shoreward road one stood upon the hill and called to him in a great voice, crying:

'Hail Eärendil, of mariners most renowned, the looked for that cometh at unawares, the longed for that cometh beyond hope! Hail Eärendil, bearer of light before the Sun and Moon! Splendour of the Children of Earth, star in the darkness, jewel in the sunset, radiant in the morning!'

That voice was the voice of Eönwë, herald of Manwë, and he came from Valimar, and summoned Eärendil to come before the Powers of Arda. And Eärendil went into Valinor and to the halls of Valimar, and never again set foot upon the lands of Men. Then the Valar took counsel together, and they summoned Ulmo from the deeps of the sea; and Eärendil stood before their faces, and delivered the errand of the Two Kindreds. Pardon he asked for the Noldor and pity for their great sorrows, and mercy upon Men and Elves and succour in their need. And his prayer was granted.

It is told among the Elves that after Eärendil had departed, seeking Elwing his wife, Mandos spoke concerning his fate; and he said: 'Shall mortal man step living upon the undying lands, and yet live?' But Ulmo said: 'For this he was born into the world. And say unto me: whether is he Eärendil Tuor's son of the line of Hador, or the son of Idril, Turgon's daughter, of the Elven-house of Finwë?' And Mandos answered: 'Equally the Noldor, who went wilfully into exile, may not return hither.'

But when all was spoken, Manwë gave judgement, and he

said: 'In this matter the power of doom is given to me. The peril that he ventured for love of the Two Kindreds shall not fall upon Eärendil, nor shall it fall upon Elwing his wife, who entered into peril for love of him; but they shall not walk again ever among Elves or Men in the Outer Lands. And this is my decree concerning them: to Eärendil and Elwing, and to their sons, shall be given leave each to choose freely to which kindred their fates shall be joined, and under which kindred they shall be judged.'

[Now when Eärendil was long time gone Elwing became lonely and afraid; but as she wandered by the margin of the sea he found her.] Ere long they were summoned to Valimar; and there the decree of the Elder King was declared to them.

Then Eärendil said to Elwing: 'Choose thou, for now I am weary of the world.' And Elwing chose to be judged among the Firstborn Children of Ilúvatar, because of Lúthien; and for her sake Eärendil chose alike, though his heart was rather with the kindred of Men and the people of his father.

Then at the bidding of the Valar Eönwë went to the shore of Aman, where the companions of Eärendil still remained, awaiting tidings; and he took a boat, and the three mariners were set therein, and the Valar drove them away into the East with a great wind. But they took Vingilot, and hallowed it, and bore it away through Valinor to the uttermost rim of the world; and there it passed through the Door of Night and was lifted up even into the oceans of heaven.

Now fair and marvellous was that vessel made, and it was filled with a wavering flame, pure and bright; and Eärendil the Mariner sat at the helm, glistening with dust of elven-gems, and the Silmaril was bound upon his brow. Far he journeyed in that ship, even into the starless voids; but most often was he seen at morning or at evening, glimmering at sunrise or at sunset, as he came back to Valinor from voyages beyond the confines of the world.

On those journeys Elwing did not go, for she might not endure the cold and the pathless voids, and she loved rather the earth and the sweet winds that blow on sea and hill. Therefore there was built for her a white tower northward upon the borders of the Sundering Seas; and thither at times all the sea-birds of the earth repaired. And it is said that Elwing learned the tongues of birds, who herself had once worn their shape; and they taught her the craft of flight, and her wings were of white and of silver-grey. And at times, when Eärendil returning drew near again to Arda, she would fly to meet him, even as she had flown long ago, when she was rescued from the sea. Then the far-sighted among the Elves that dwelt in the Lonely Isle would see her like a white bird, shining, rose-stained in the sunset, as she soared in joy to greet the coming of Vingilot to haven.

Now when first Vingilot was set to sail in the seas of heaven it rose unlooked for, glittering and bright; and the people of Middle-earth beheld it from afar and wondered, and they took it for a sign, and called it Gil-Estel, the Star of High Hope. And when this new star was seen at evening, Maedhros spoke to Maglor his brother, and he said: 'Surely that is a Silmaril that shines now in the West?'

And of the final departure of Beren and Lúthien? In the words of the *Quenta Silmarillion*: None saw Beren and Lúthien leave the world or marked where at last their bodies lay.

APPENDIX

REVISIONS TO
THE LAY OF LEITHIAN

Among the first, perhaps even the very first, of the literary tasks that attracted my father after the completion of *The Lord of the Rings* was a return to *The Lay of Leithian*: not (needless to say) to continue the narrative from the point reached in 1931 (the attack on Beren by Carcharoth at the gates of Angband), but from the beginning of the poem. The textual history of the writing is very complex, and no more need be said of it here beyond remarking that whereas at first my father seems to have embarked on a radical rewriting of the *Lay* as a whole, the impulse soon died away, or was over-taken, and was reduced to short and scattered passages. I give here, however, as a substantial example of the new verse after the lapse of a quarter of a century, the passage of the *Lay* concerning the treachery of Gorlim the Unhappy that led to the slaying of Barahir, the father of Beren, and all his companions, save Beren alone. This is by far the longest of the new passages; and – conveniently – it may be compared

257

with the original text that has been given on pp. 94–102. It will be seen that Sauron (Thû), ridden here from 'Gaurhoth Isle', has replaced Morgoth; and that in the quality of the verse this is a new poem.

I begin the new text with a short passage entitled *Of Tarn Aeluin the Blessed* which has no counterpart in the original version: these verses are numbered 1–26.

> Such deeds of daring there they wrought
> that soon the hunters that them sought
> at rumour of their coming fled.
> Though price was set upon each head
> to match the weregild of a king, ·   5
> no soldier could to Morgoth bring
> news even of their hidden lair;
> for where the highland brown and bare
> above the darkling pines arose
> of steep Dorthonion to the snows   10
> and barren mountain-winds, there lay
> a tarn of water, blue by day,
> by night a mirror of dark glass
> for stars of Elbereth that pass
> above the world into the West.   15
> Once hallowed, still that place was blest:
> no shadow of Morgoth, and no evil thing
> yet thither came; a whispering ring
> of slender birches silver-grey
> stooped on its margin, round it lay   20
> a lonely moor, and the bare bones

of ancient Earth like standing stones
thrust through the heather and the whin;
and there by houseless Aeluin
the hunted lord and faithful men   25
under the grey stones made their den.

OF GORLIM UNHAPPY

Gorlim Unhappy, Angrim's son,
as the tale tells, of these was one,
most fierce and hopeless. He to wife,
while fair was the fortune of his life,   30
took the white maiden Eilinel:
dear love they had ere evil fell.
To war he rode; from war returned
to find his fields and homestead burned,
his house forsaken roofless stood,   35
empty amid the leafless wood;
and Eilinel, white Eilinel,
was taken whither none could tell,
to death or thraldom far away.
Black was the shadow of that day   40
for ever on his heart, and doubt
still gnawed him as he went about,
in wilderness wandring, or at night
oft sleepless, thinking that she might
ere evil came have timely fled   45
into the woods: she was not dead,

she lived, she would return again
to seek him, and would deem him slain.
Therefore at whiles he left the lair,
and secretly, alone, would peril dare,   50
and come to his old house at night,
broken and cold, without fire or light,
and naught but grief renewed would gain,
watching and waiting there in vain.

    In vain, or worse – for many spies   55
had Morgoth, many lurking eyes
well used to pierce the deepest dark;
and Gorlim's coming they would mark
and would report. There came a day
when once more Gorlim crept that way,   60
down the deserted weedy lane
at dusk of autumn sad with rain
and cold wind whining. Lo! a light
at window fluttering in the night
amazed he saw; and drawing near,   65
between faint hope and sudden fear,
he looked within. 'Twas Eilinel!
Though changed she was, he knew her well.
With grief and hunger she was worn,
her tresses tangled, raiment torn;   70
her gentle eyes with tears were dim,
as soft she wept: 'Gorlim, Gorlim!
Thou canst not have forsaken me.
Then slain, alas! thou slain must be!

And I must linger cold, alone,   75
and loveless as a barren stone!'

   One cry he gave – and then the light
blew out, and in the wind of night
wolves howled; and on his shoulder fell
suddenly the griping hands of hell.   80
There Morgoth's servants fast him caught
and he was cruelly bound, and brought
to Sauron captain of the host,
the lord of werewolf and of ghost,
most foul and fell of all who knelt   85
at Morgoth's throne. In might he dwelt
on Gaurhoth Isle; but now had ridden
with strength abroad, by Morgoth bidden
to find the rebel Barahir.
He sat in dark encampment near,   90
and thither his butchers dragged their prey.
There now in anguish Gorlim lay:
with bond on neck, on hand and foot,
to bitter torment he was put,
to break his will and him constrain   95
to buy with treason end of pain.
But naught to them would he reveal
of Barahir, nor break the seal
of faith that on his tongue was laid;
until at last a pause was made,   100
and one came softly to his stake,
a darkling form that stooped, and spake

to him of Eilinel his wife.

    'Wouldst thou,' he said, 'forsake thy life,
who with few words might win release   105
for her, and thee, and go in peace,
and dwell together far from war,
friends of the King? What wouldst thou more?'
And Gorlim, now long worn with pain,
yearning to see his wife again   110
(whom well he weened was also caught
in Sauron's net), allowed the thought
to grow, and faltered in his troth.
Then straight, half willing and half loath,
they brought him to the seat of stone   115
where Sauron sat. He stood alone
before that dark and dreadful face,
and Sauron said: 'Come, mortal base!
What do I hear? That thou wouldst dare
to barter with me? Well, speak fair!   120
What is thy price?' And Gorlim low
bowed down his head, and with great woe,
word on slow word, at last implored
that merciless and faithless lord
that he might free depart, and might   125
again find Eilinel the white,
and dwell with her, and cease from war
against the King. He craved no more.

    Then Sauron smiled, and said: 'Thou thrall!
The price thou askest is but small   130

for treachery and shame so great!
I grant it surely! Well, I wait:
Come! Speak now swiftly and speak true!'
Then Gorlim wavered, and he drew
half back; but Sauron's daunting eye   135
there held him, and he dared not lie:
as he began, so must he wend
from first false step to faithless end:
he all must answer as he could,
betray his lord and brotherhood,   140
and cease, and fall upon his face.

 Then Sauron laughed aloud. 'Thou base,
thou cringing worm! Stand up,
and hear me! And now drink the cup
that I have sweetly blent for thee!   145
Thou fool: a phantom thou didst see
that I, I Sauron, made to snare
thy lovesick wits. Naught else was there.
Cold 'tis with Sauron's wraiths to wed!
Thy Eilinel! She is long since dead,   150
dead, food of worms less low than thou.
And yet thy boon I grant thee now:
to Eilinel thou soon shalt go,
and lie in her bed, no more to know
of war – or manhood. Have thy pay!'   155

 And Gorlim then they dragged away,
and cruelly slew him; and at last

in the dank mould his body cast,
where Eilinel long since had lain
in the burned woods by butchers slain.   160
    Thus Gorlim died an evil death,
and cursed himself with dying breath,
and Barahir at last was caught
in Morgoth's snare; for set at naught
by treason was the ancient grace   165
that guarded long that lonely place,
Tarn Aeluin: now all laid bare
were secret paths and hidden lair.

OF BEREN SON OF BARAHIR & HIS ESCAPE

Dark from the North now blew the cloud;
the winds of autumn cold and loud   170
hissed in the heather; sad and grey
Aeluin's mournful water lay.
'Son Beren', then said Barahir,
'Thou knowst the rumour that we hear
of strength from the Gaurhoth that is sent   175
against us; and our food nigh spent.
On thee the lot falls by our law
to go forth now alone to draw
what help thou canst from the hidden few
that feed us still, and what is new   180
to learn. Good fortune go with thee!
In speed return, for grudgingly

we spare thee from our brotherhood
so small: and Gorlim in the wood
is long astray or dead. Farewell!'   185
As Beren went, still like a knell
resounded in his heart that word,
the last of his father that he heard.

    Through moor and fen, by tree and briar
he wandered far: he saw the fire   190
of Sauron's camp, he heard the howl
of hunting Orc and wolf a-prowl,
and turning back, for long the way,
benighted in the forest lay.
In weariness he then must sleep,   195
fain in a badger-hole to creep,
and yet he heard (or dreamed it so)
nearby a marching legion go
with clink of mail and clash of shields
up towards the stony mountain-fields.   200
He slipped then into darkness down,
until, as man that waters drown
strives upwards gasping, it seemed to him
he rose through slime beside the brim
of sullen pool beneath dead trees.   205
Their livid boughs in a cold breeze
trembled, and all their black leaves stirred:
each leaf a black and croaking bird,
whose neb a gout of blood let fall.
He shuddered, struggling thence to crawl   210

through winding weeds, when far away
he saw a shadow faint and grey
gliding across the dreary lake.
Slowly it came, and softly spake:
'Gorlim I was, but now a wraith   215
of will defeated, broken faith,
traitor betrayed. Go! Stay not here!
Awaken, son of Barahir,
and haste! For Morgoth's fingers close
upon thy father's throat; he knows   220
your trysts, your paths, your secret lair.'
    Then he revealed the devil's snare
in which he fell, and failed; and last
begging forgiveness, wept, and passed
out into darkness. Beren woke,   225
leapt up as one by sudden stroke
with fire of anger filled. His bow
and sword he seized, and like the roe
hotfoot o'er rock and heath he sped
before the dawn. Ere day was dead   230
to Aeluin at last he came,
as the red sun westward sank in flame;
but Aeluin was red with blood,
red were the stones and trampled mud.
Black in the birches sat a-row   235
the raven and the carrion crow;
wet were their nebs, and dark the meat
that dripped beneath their griping feet.
One croaked: 'Ha, ha, he comes too late!'

'Ha, ha!' they answered, 'ha! too late!'   240
   There Beren laid his father's bones
in haste beneath a cairn of stones;
no graven rune nor word he wrote
o'er Barahir, but thrice he smote
the topmost stone, and thrice aloud   245
he cried his name. 'Thy death', he vowed,
'I will avenge. Yea, though my fate
should lead at last to Angband's gate.'
And then he turned, and did not weep:
too dark his heart, the wound too deep.   250
Out into night, as cold as stone,
loveless, friendless, he strode alone.

   Of hunter's lore he had no need
the trail to find. With little heed
his ruthless foe, secure and proud,   255
marched north away with blowing loud
of brazen horns their lord to greet,
trampling the earth with grinding feet.
Behind them bold but wary went
now Beren, swift as hound on scent,   260
until beside a darkling well,
where Rivil rises from the fell
down into Serech's reeds to flow,
he found the slayers, found his foe.
From hiding on the hillside near   265
he marked them all: though less than fear
too many for his sword and bow

to slay alone. Then, crawling low
as snake in heath, he nearer crept.
There many weary with marching slept, 270
but captains, sprawling on the grass,
drank and from hand to hand let pass
their booty, grudging each small thing
raped from dead bodies. One a ring
held up, and laughed: 'Now, mates,' he cried, 275
'here's mine! And I'll not be denied,
though few be like it in the land.
For I 'twas wrenched it from the hand
of that same Barahir I slew,
the robber-knave. If tales be true, 280
he had it of some elvish lord,
for the rogue-service of his sword.
No help it gave him – he's dead.
They're parlous, elvish rings, 'tis said;
still for the gold I'll keep it, yea 285
and so eke out my niggard pay.
Old Sauron bade me bring it back,
and yet, methinks, he has no lack
of weightier treasures in his hoard:
the greater the greedier the lord! 290
So mark ye, mates, ye all shall swear
the hand of Barahir was bare!'
And as he spoke an arrow sped
from tree behind, and forward dead
choking he fell with barb in throat; 295
with leering face the earth he smote.

Forth then as wolfhound grim there leapt
Beren among them. Two he swept
aside with sword; caught up the ring;
slew one who grasped him; with a spring   300
back into shadow passed, and fled
before their yells of wrath and dread
of ambush in the valley rang.
Then after him like wolves they sprang,
howling and cursing, gnashing teeth,   305
hewing and bursting through the heath,
shooting wild arrows, sheaf on sheaf,
at trembling shade or shaken leaf.

In fateful hour was Beren born:
he laughed at dart and wailing horn;   310
fleetest of foot of living men,
tireless on fell and light on fen,
elf-wise in wood, he passed away,
defended by his hauberk grey,
of dwarvish craft in Nogrod made,   315
where hammers rang in cavern's shade.

As fearless Beren was renowned:
when men most hardy upon ground
were reckoned folk would speak his name,
foretelling that his after-name   320
would even golden Hador pass
or Barahir and Bregolas;
but sorrow now his heart had wrought
to fierce despair, no more he fought

in hope of life or joy or praise,   325
but seeking so to use his days
only that Morgoth deep should feel
the sting of his avenging steel,
ere death he found and end of pain:
his only fear was thraldom's chain.   330
Danger he sought and death pursued,
and thus escaped the doom he wooed,
and deeds of breathless daring wrought
alone, of which the rumour brought
new hope to many a broken man.   335
They whispered 'Beren', and began
in secret swords to whet, and soft
by shrouded hearths at evening oft
songs they would sing of Beren's bow,
of Dagmor his sword: how he would go   340
silent to camps and slay the chief,
or trapped in his hiding past belief
would slip away, and under night
by mist or moon, or by the light
of open day would come again.   345
Of hunters hunted, slayers slain
they sang, of Gorgol the Butcher hewn,
of ambush in Ladros, fire in Drûn,
of thirty in one battle dead,
of wolves that yelped like curs and fled,   350
yea, Sauron himself with wound in hand.
Thus one alone filled all that land

with fear and death for Morgoth's folk;
his comrades were the beech and oak
who failed him not, and wary things   355
with fur and fell and feathered wings
that silent wander, or dwell alone
in hill and wild and waste of stone
watched o'er his ways, his faithful friends.

    Yet seldom well an outlaw ends;   360
and Morgoth was a king more strong
than all the world has since in song
recorded: dark athwart the land
reached out the shadow of his hand,
at each recoil returned again;   365
two more were sent for one foe slain.
New hope was cowed, all rebels killed;
quenched were the fires, the songs were stilled,
tree felled, hearth burned, and through the waste
marched the black host of Orcs in haste.   370
    Almost they closed their ring of steel
round Beren; hard upon his heel
now trod their spies; within their hedge
of all aid shorn, upon the edge
of death at bay he stood aghast   375
and knew that he must die at last,
or flee the land of Barahir,
his land beloved. Beside the mere
beneath a heap of nameless stones

must crumble those once mighty bones,   380
forsaken by both son and kin,
bewailed by reeds of Aeluin.

   In winter's night the houseless North
he left behind, and stealing forth
the leaguer of his watchful foe   385
he passed – a shadow on the snow,
a swirl of wind, and he was gone,
the ruin of Dorthonion,
Tarn Aeluin and its water wan,
never again to look upon.   390
No more shall hidden bowstring sing,
no more his shaven arrows wing,
no more his hunted head shall lie
upon the heath beneath the sky.
The Northern stars, whose silver fire   395
of old Men named the Burning Briar,
were set behind his back, and shone
o'er land forsaken; he was gone.

   Southward he turned, and south away
his long and lonely journey lay,   400
while ever loomed before his path
the dreadful peaks of Gorgorath.
Never had foot of man most bold
yet trod those mountains steep and cold,
nor climbed upon their sudden brink,   405
whence, sickened, eyes must turn and shrink

to see their southward cliffs fall sheer
in rocky pinnacle and pier
down into shadows that were laid
before the sun and moon were made.   410
In valleys woven with deceit
and washed with waters bitter-sweet
dark magic lurked in gulf and glen;
but out away beyond the ken
of mortal sight the eagle's eye   415
from dizzy towers that pierced the sky
might grey and gleaming see afar,
as sheen on water under star,
Beleriand, Beleriand,
the borders of the Elven-land.   420

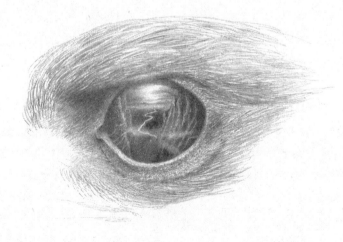

LIST OF NAMES IN THE
ORIGINAL TEXTS

I have made this *List of Names* (restricted to names that occur in the passages of my father's writing), which is obviously not an index, with two purposes in mind.

Neither of them is in any way essential to the book. In the first place, it is intended to assist a reader who cannot recall, among the mass of names (and forms of names), the reference of one that may be of significance in the narrative. In the second place, certain names, especially those that occur rarely or only once in the texts, are provided with a slightly fuller explanation. For example, while this is obviously of no significance in the tale, one may nonetheless want to know why the Eldar would not touch spiders 'because of Ungwelianté' (p. 41).

Aeluin   A lake in the northeast of Dorthonion where Barahir and his companions made their lair.
Aglon   A narrow pass between Taur-na-Fuin and the Hill of Himring, held by sons of Fëanor.
Ainur   (singular *Ainu*) 'The Holy Ones': the Valar and the Maiar.

[The name *Maiar* was a late introduction of an earlier conception: 'With the great ones came many lesser spirits, beings of their ownkind but of smaller might' (such as Melian).]

Aman The Land in the West beyond the Great Sea in which the Valar dwelt ('the Blessed Realm').

Anfauglith 'The Gasping Dust'. See *Dor-na-Fauglith, The Thirsty Plain*.

Angainu The great chain, made by the Vala Aulë, in which Morgoth was bound (later *Angainor*).

Angamandi (plural) 'The Hells of Iron'. See *Angband*.

Angband The great dungeon-fortress of Morgoth in the northwest of Middle-earth.

Angrim Father of Gorlim the Unhappy.

Angrod Son of Finrod (later Finarfin).

Arda The Earth.

Artanor 'The Land Beyond'; region subsequently named Doriath, the kingdom of Tinwelint (Thingol).

Aryador 'Land of Shadow', a name of Hisilómë (Dor-lómin) among Men. See *Hisilómë*.

Ascar River in Ossiriand, renamed *Rathlorion* 'Goldenbed' when the treasure of Doriath was sunk in it.

Aulë The great Vala known as Aulë the Smith; he is 'a master of all crafts', and 'his lordship is over all the substances of which Arda is made.'

Ausir A name of Dior.

Balrogs [In the *Lost Tales* the Balrogs are conceived as existing 'in hundreds'. They are called 'demons of power'; they wear iron armour, and they have claws of steel and whips of flame.]

Barahir A chieftain of Men, the father of Beren.

Bauglir 'The Constrainer', a name of Morgoth among the Noldor.

Beleg Elf of Doriath, a great archer, called *Cúthalion*, 'Strongbow'; close companion and friend of Túrin Turambar, by whom he was tragically slain.

Belegost One of the two great cities of the Dwarves in the Blue Mountains.

Beleriand (earlier name *Broseliand*) The great region of Middle-earth, largely drowned and destroyed at the end of the First Age, extending from the Blue Mountains in the East to the Mountains of Shadow in the North (see *Iron Mountains*) and the western coasts.

Bëor Leader of the first Men to enter Beleriand. See *Edain*.

Bitter Hills See *Iron Mountains*.

Blessed Realm See *Aman*.

Blue Mountains The great range forming the eastern bounds of Beleriand.

Boldog A captain of Orcs.

Bregolas Brother of Barahir.

Burning Briar The constellation of the Great Bear.

Calacirya A pass in the Mountains of Valinor in which was the city of the Elves.

Carcharoth See *Karkaras*.

Celegorm Son of Fëanor, called 'the Fair'.

Cranthir Son of Fëanor, called 'the Dark'.

i-Cuilwarthon 'The Dead that Live Again', Beren and Lúthien after their return from Mandos; *Cuilwarthien*: The land where they dwelt. (Later form *Guilwarthon*.)

Cuiviénen The Water of Awakening: the lake in Middle-earth where the Elves awoke.

Cûm-nan-Arasaith The Mound of Avarice, raised over the slain in Menegroth.

Curufin Son of Fëanor, called 'the Crafty'.

Dagmor Beren's sword.

Dairon A minstrel of Artanor, numbered among 'the three most magic players of the Elves'; originally the brother of Lúthien.

Damrod and Díriel The youngest sons of Fëanor. (Later names *Amrod* and *Amras*.)

Deadly Nightshade A translation of Taur-na-Fuin; see *Mountains of Night*.

Dior Son of Beren and Lúthien; father of Elwing, the mother of Elrond and Elros.

Doriath   The later name of Artanor, the great forested region ruled by Thingol (Tinwelint) and Melian (Gwendeling).

Dor-lómin   See *Hisilómë*.

Dor-na-Fauglith   The great grassy plain of Ard-galen north of the Mountains of Night (*Dorthonion*) that was transformed into a desert (see *Anfauglith*, *The Thirsty Plain*).

Dorthonion   'Land of Pines'; vast region of pinewoods on the northern borders of Beleriand; afterwards called *Taur-na-Fuin*, 'the Forest under Night'.

Drûn   A region to the north of Lake Aeluin; not named elsewhere.

Draugluin   Greatest of the werewolves of Thû (Sauron).

Eärámë   'Eagle's Pinion', Tuor's ship.

Eärendel   (later form *Eärendil*) Son of Tuor and Idril daughter of Turgon King of Gondolin; wedded Elwing.

Edain   'The Second People', Men, but used chiefly of the three Houses of the Elf-friends who came earliest to Beleriand.

Egnor bo-Rimion   'The huntsman of the Elves': the father of Beren, replaced by Barahir.

Egnor   Son of Finrod (later Finarfin).

Eilinel   Wife of Gorlim.

Elbereth   'Queen of the Stars'; see *Varda*.

Eldalië   (The people of the Elves), the Eldar.

Eldar   The Elves of the Great Journey from the place of their awakening; sometimes used in early texts to mean all Elves.

Elfinesse   An inclusive name for all the lands of the Elves.

Elrond of Rivendell   Son of Elwing and Eärendel.

Elros   Son of Elwing and Eärendel; first King of Númenor.

Elwing   Daughter of Dior, wedded Eärendel, mother of Elrond and Elros.

Eönwë   Herald of Manwë.

Erchamion   'One-handed', name given to Beren; other forms *Ermabwed*, *Elmavoitë*.

Esgalduin   River of Doriath, passing Menegroth (the halls of Thingol), and flowing into Sirion.

Fëanor   Eldest son of Finwë; maker of the Silmarils.

Felagund   Noldorin Elf, founder of Nargothrond and sworn friend of Barahir father of Beren. [On the relation of the names *Felagund* and *Finrod* see p. 104.]

Fingolfin   The second son of Finwë; slain in single combat with Morgoth.

Fingon   Eldest son of Fingolfin; king of the Noldor after the death of his father.

Finrod   The third son of Finwë. [Name replaced by *Finarfin*, when *Finrod* became the name of his son, *Finrod Felagund*.]

Finwë   Leader of the second host of the Elves, the Noldor (Noldoli), on the Great Journey.

Foamriders   The kindred of the Eldar named the *Solosimpi*, later the *Teleri*; the third and last host on the Great Journey.

Gaurhoth   The werewolves of Thû (Sauron); *Gaurhoth Isle*, see *Tol-in-Gaurhoth*.

Gelion   The great river of East Beleriand fed by rivers flowing from the Blue Mountains in the region of Ossiriand.

Gilim   A giant, named by Lúthien in her 'lengthening' spell sung over her hair (p. 55), unknown save for the corresponding passage in *The Lay of Leithian*, where he is called 'the giant of Eruman' [a region on the coast of Aman 'where the shadows were deepest and thickest in the world'].

Gimli   A very old and blind Noldorin Elf, long a captive slave in the stronghold of Tevildo, possessed of an extraordinary power of hearing. He plays no part in *The Tale of Tinúviel* or in any other tale, and never reappears.

Ginglith   River flowing into the Narog above Nargothrond.

Glómund, Glorund   Earlier names of Glaurung, 'Father of Dragons', the great dragon of Morgoth.

Gnomes   Early translation of *Noldoli, Noldor*: See pp. 32–3.

Gods   See *Valar*.

Gondolin   The hidden city founded by Turgon the second son of Fingolfin.

Gorgol   the Butcher An Orc slain by Beren.

Gorgorath (Also *Gorgoroth*) The Mountains of Terror; the precipices in which Dorthonion fell southwards.

Gorlim One of the companions of Barahir, the father of Beren; he revealed their hiding place to Morgoth (later Sauron). Called *Gorlim the Unhappy.*

Great Lands The lands east of the Great Sea: Middle-earth [a term never used in the *Lost Tales*].

Great Sea of the West Belegaer, extending from Middle-earth to Aman.

Green Elves The Elves of Ossiriand, called *Laiquendi.*

Grinding Ice Helkaraxë: the strait in the far North between Middle-earth and the Western Land.

Grond Weapon of Morgoth, a great club known as the Hammer of the Underworld.

Guarded Plain The great plain between the rivers Narog and Teiglin, north of Nargothrond.

Guilwarthon See *i-Cuilwarthon.*

Gwendeling Earlier name of Melian.

Hador A great chieftain of Men, called 'the Goldenhaired', grandfather of Húrin father of Túrin, and of Huor father of Tuor father of Eärendel.

Haven of the Swans See *Notes on the Elder Days*, p. 23.

Hills of the Hunters (also *The Hunters' Wold*) The highlands west of the river Narog.

Himling A great hill in the north of East Beleriand, a stronghold of the sons of Fëanor.

Hirilorn 'Queen of Trees', a great beech-tree near Menegroth (Thingol's halls); in its branches was the house in which Lúthien was imprisoned.

Hisilómë Hithlum. [In a list of names of the period of the *Lost Tales* it is said: '*Dor-lómin* or the "Land of Shadow" was that region named of the Eldar *Hisilómë* (and this means "shadowy twilights") . . . and it is so called by reason of the scanty sun which peeps over the Iron Mountains to the east and south of it.']

Hithlum   See *Hisilómë*.

Huan   The mighty wolfhound of Valinor, who became the friend and saviour of Beren and Lúthien.

Húrin   Father of Túrin Turambar and Niënor.

Idril   Called *Celebrindal* 'Silverfoot', daughter of Turgon King of Gondolin; wedded to Tuor, mother of Eärendel.

*Ilkorins, Ilkorind*i   Elves not of Kôr, city of the Elves in Aman (see *Kôr*).

Indravangs (also *Indrafangs*) 'Long Beards', the Dwarves of Belegost.

Ingwil   River flowing into the Narog at Nargothrond (later form *Ringwil*).

Iron Mountains   Also called the *Bitter Hills*. A great range corresponding to the later *Ered Wethrin, the Mountains of Shadow*, forming the southern and eastern borders of Hisilómë (Hithlum). See *Hisilómë*.

Ivárë   A renowned minstrel of the Elves, 'who plays beside the sea'.

Ivrin   The lake below the Mountains of Shadow where the Narog rose.

Karkaras   The huge wolf that guarded the gates of Angband (later *Carcharoth*), its tail named in Lúthien's 'lengthening spell'; translated 'Knife-fang'.

Kôr   City of the Elves in Aman, and the hill on which it was built; later the city became *Tûn* and the hill alone was *Kôr*. [Finally the city became *Tirion* and the hill *Túna*.]

Ladros   A region to the northeast of Dorthonion.

Lay of Leithian, The   See p. 88.

Lonely Isle   *Tol Eressëa*: a large island in the Great Sea near the coasts of Aman; the most easterly of the Undying Lands, where many Elves dwelt.

Lórien   The Valar Mandos and Lórien were called brothers, and named the *Fanturi*: Mandos was *Néfantur* and Lórien was *Olofantur*. In the words of the *Quenta* Lórien was the 'maker of visions and of dreams; and his gardens in the land of the Gods were the fairest of all places in the world and filled with many spirits of beauty and power.'

Mablung 'Heavy hand', Elf of Doriath, chief captain of Thingol; present at the death of Beren in the hunt of Karkaras.

Magic Isles Isles in the Great Sea.

Maglor The second son of Fëanor, a celebrated singer and minstrel.

Maiar See *Ainur*.

Maidros Eldest son of Fëanor, called 'the Tall' (later form *Maedhros*).

Mandos A Vala of great power. He is the Judge; and he is the keeper of the Houses of the Dead, and the summoner of the spirits of the slain [the *Quenta*]. See *Lórien*.

Manwë The chief and most mighty of the Valar, the spouse of Varda.

Melian The Queen of Artanor (Doriath), earlier name *Gwendeling*; a Maia, who came to Middle-earth from the realm of the Vala Lórien.

Melko The great evil Vala, Morgoth (later form *Melkor*).

Menegroth See *The Thousand Caves*.

Miaulë A cat, cook in the kitchen of Tevildo.

Mîm A dwarf, who settled in Nargothrond after the departure of the Dragon and laid a curse on the treasure.

Mindeb A river flowing into Sirion in the region of Doriath.

Mountains of Night The great heights (*Dorthonion*, 'Land of Pines') that came to be called *The Forest of Night* (*Taurfuin*, later *Taur-na-[-nu-]fuin*).

Mountains of Shadow, Shadowy Mountains See *Iron Mountains*.

Nan The only thing known of Nan seems to be the name of his sword, *Glend*, named in Lúthien's 'lengthening spell' (see *Gilim*).

Nan Dumgorthin 'The land of the dark idols' where Huan came upon Beren and Lúthien in their flight from Angband. In the alliterative poem the *Lay of the Children of Húrin* (see p. 78) occur these lines:

> in Nan Dungorthin   where nameless gods
> have shrouded shrines   in shadows secret,
> more old than Morgoth   or the ancient lords
> the golden Gods   of the guarded West.

Nargothrond   The great cavernous city and fortress founded by Felagund on the river Narog in West Beleriand.

Narog   River in West Beleriand; see *Nargothrond.* Often used in the sense 'realm', i.e. 'of Nargothrond'.

Naugladur   Lord of the Dwarves of Nogrod.

Nauglamír   The Necklace of the Dwarves, in which was set the Silmaril of Beren and Lúthien.

Nessa   The sister of Oromë and spouse of Tulkas. See *Valier.*

Nogrod   One of the two great cities of the Dwarves in the Blue Mountains.

Noldoli, later *Noldor*   The second host of the Eldar on the Great Journey, led by Finwë.

Oikeroi   A fierce warrior-cat in the service of Tevildo, slain by Huan.

Orodreth   Brother of Felagund; King of Nargothrond after the death of Felagund.

Oromë   The Vala called the Hunter; led on his horse the hosts of the Eldar on the Great Journey.

Ossiriand   'The Land of Seven Rivers', Gelion and its tributaries from the Blue Mountains.

Outer Lands   Middle-earth.

Palisor   The region of the Great Lands where the Elves awoke.

Rathlorion   River in Ossiriand. See *Ascar.*

Ringil   The sword of Fingolfin.

Rivil   River rising in the west of Dorthonion and flowing into Sirion at the fens of Serech, north of Tol Sirion.

Sarn Athrad   The Ford of Stones, where the river Ascar in Ossiriand was crossed by the road to the cities of the Dwarves in the Blue Mountains.

Serech   Great fens where the Rivil flowed into the Sirion; see *Rivil.*

Shadowy Mountains, Mountains of Shadow   See *Iron Mountains.*

Shadowy Seas   A region of the Great Sea of the West.

Sickle of the Gods   The constellation of the Great Bear [which Varda set above the North as a threat to Morgoth and an omen of his fall.]

Silmarils   The three great jewels filled with the light of the Two Trees of Valinor, made by Fëanor. See pp. 36–7.

Silpion   The White Tree of Valinor, from whose flowers there fell a dew of silver light; also called *Telperion.*

Sirion   The great river of Beleriand, rising in the Mountains of Shadow and flowing southward, dividing East from West Beleriand.

Taniquetil   The highest Mountain of Aman, the abode of Manwë and Varda.

Taurfuin, Taur-na-fuin, (later *-nu-*)   The Forest of Night; see *Mountains of Night.*

Tavros   Gnomish name of the Vala Oromë: 'Lord of Forests'; later form *Tauros.*

Tevildo   The Prince of Cats, mightiest of all cats, 'possessed of an evil spirit' (see pp. 49, 69); a close companion of Morgoth.

Thangorodrim   The mountains above Angband.

Thingol   King of Artanor (Doriath); earlier name *Tinwelint.* [His name was *Elwë*: he was a leader of the third host of the Eldar, the Teleri, on the Great Journey, but in Beleriand he was known as 'Greycloak' (the meaning of *Thingol*).]

Thirsty Plain   See *Dor-na-Fauglith.*

Thorondor   King of Eagles.

Thousand Caves   Menegroth: The hidden halls of Tinwelint (Thingol) on the river Esgalduin in Artanor.

Thû   The Necromancer, greatest of the servants of Morgoth, dwelling in the Elvish watchtower on Tol Sirion; later name *Sauron.*

Thuringwethil   Name taken by Lúthien in bat-form before Morgoth.

Timbrenting   Old English name of Taniquetil.

Tinfang Warble   A famous minstrel [*Tinfang* = Quenya *timpinen* 'fluter'.]

Tinúviel   'Daughter of Twilight', nightingale: name given to Lúthien by Beren.

Tinwelint   King of Artanor; see *Thingol*, the later name.

Tirion   City of the Elves in Aman; see *Kôr*.

Tol-in-Gaurhoth   Isle of Werewolves, the name of Tol Sirion after its capture by Morgoth.

Tol Sirion   The island in the river Sirion on which there was an Elvish fortress; see *Tol-in-Gaurhoth*.

Tulkas   The Vala described in the *Quenta* as 'the strongest of all the Gods in limb and greatest in all feats of valour and prowess'.

Tuor   Cousin of Túrin and father of Eärendil.

Túrin   Son of Húrin and Morwen; named *Turambar* 'Master of Doom'.

Uinen   A Maia (see *Ainur*). 'The Lady of the Seas', 'whose hair lies spread through all the waters under sky'; named in Lúthien's 'lengthening spell'.

Ulmo   'Lord of Waters', the great Vala of the Seas.

Umboth-Muilin   The *Twilight Meres*, where Aros, the southern river of Doriath, flowed into Sirion.

Umuiyan   An old cat, the doorkeeper of Tevildo.

Ungweliantë   The monstrous spider, dwelling in Eruman (see *Gilim*), who with Morgoth destroyed the Two Trees of Valinor; (later form *Ungoliant*).

Valar   (singular Vala) 'The Powers'; in early texts referred to as the *Gods*. They are the great beings who entered the World at the beginning of Time. [In the *Lost Tale of the Music of the Ainur* Eriol said: 'I would fain know who be these Valar; are they the Gods?' He received this reply: 'So be they, though concerning them Men tell many strange and garbled tales that are far from the truth, and many strange names they call them that you will not hear here.']

Valier   (singular *Valië*) The 'Queens of the Valar'; in this book are named only Varda, Vána and Nessa.

Valinor   The land of the Valar in Aman.

Valmar, Valimar   City of the Valar in Valinor.

Vána   The spouse of Oromë. See *Valier*.

Varda   Greatest of the Valier; the spouse of Manwë; maker of the stars [hence her name *Elbereth*, 'Queen of the Stars'].

Vëannë   The teller of *The Tale of Tinúviel*.

Wingelot   'Foamflower', Eärendel's ship.

Wizard's Isle   Tol Sirion.

Wood-elves   Elves of Artanor.

GLOSSARY

This glossary contains words (including forms and meanings of words differing from modern usage) that seemed to me liable to give difficulty. The content of such a list as this cannot of course be systematic, deriving from some external standard.

an   if, 45, 52, 80, 82, etc.
bent   open place covered with grass, 144
bid   offered, 241
chase   hunting ground, 181
clomb   old past tense of *climb*, 202
corse   corpse, 193
croft   small plot of land, 122
drouth   dryness, 125
entreat   treat, 60, 65; [modern sense] 61, 83
envermined   full of noxious creatures, 186. This word seems not
   to be otherwise recorded.
fell   hide, 72, 101, 146, 153–4, 185–8, etc.
flittermouse   bat, 210

forhungered   starved, 173
frith   wood, woodland, 143
frore   very cold, 113
glamoury   magic, enchantment, 125
haggard   (of hills) wild, 177
haply   perhaps, 45, 96, 118
hem and hedge   enclose and fence off, 101
howe   burial mound, barrow, 234
inane   empty, 190
lave   wash, 55
leeches   physicians, 173, 176
let   hinder, 124: *their going let* 'hinder their passing'
like   please, 88 (in *doth it like thee?*)
limber   supple, 143
march   borderland, 178, 195
neb   beak, bill, 97, 265–6
nesh   soft, tender, 215
opes   opens, 198
parlous   dangerous, 268
pled   old past tense of *plead*, 170
quook   old past tense of *quake*, 192
rede   counsel, 48, 59
rove   past tense of *rive* 'rend, tear apart, cleave', 213
ruel-bone   ivory, 143
runagate   deserter, renegade, 48
scullion   kitchen drudge, 51
shores   supports, 203
sigaldry   sorcery, 125
slot   track of an animal, 83–4
spoor   the same as *slot*, 84
sprite   spirit, 49
sylphine   of the nature of a sylph (a spirit inhabiting the air), 210.
    This adjective is not recorded.
swath   (space left after passage of a mower) track, trace, 127
tarn   a small mountain lake, 258

thews bodily strength, 76

thrall a slave, one who is in bondage (thraldom), 20, 47–9, 59, 69, 73, etc.

trammelled hampered, impeded, 151

unkempt uncombed, 51

viol a stringed instrument played with a bow, 158, 176

weft woven fabric, 173

weird fate, 144, 177

weregild (Old English) the price set upon a man in accordance with his rank, 258

whin gorse, 259

wolfhame wolfskin, 185

woof woven fabric, 213

would wished, 184–5, 205